From the
EDITOR-IN-CHIEF

Dear Reader,

What do Raymond Chandler, Somerset Maugham, Dorothy Sayers, and John Grisham have in common? They are all authors who had careers doing "something else" before their lives as novelists took off. *(See below for what they did.)*

The authors in this volume have also had past lives—lives that paid the bills and taught them a lot but that maybe weren't as gratifying as being a full-time writer.

For instance, **Lee Child** had a long career as a television producer. That is, until he came back from a vacation to find his position gone. But his TV job had showed him how to shape a good story, and he proved a natural as a novelist.

Karen Harter knew she was good at selling mortgages. But she always had a feeling that she would be even better at selling her own stories. One of her happiest days was when she quit the real estate business to concentrate full-time on writing.

When she was a young widow with five children, **Mary Higgins Clark** made a living by writing and producing for radio. Each morning, though, she found the time to craft her hit book, *Where Are the Children?,* and she has never looked back.

And lastly, **Alan Titchmarsh** had carved out a very successful career as England's gardening guru before he wrote his first novel. *Rosie* is his fifth foray into fiction, and he calls making up stories "a supreme luxury."

Very truly yours,

Laura E. Kelly

Chandler: public relations exec;
Maugham: doctor; Sayers: advertising
copywriter; Grisham: (surprise!) lawyer.

EDITORIAL

Global Editor-in-Chief: Laura E. Kelly

Deputy Editor: James J. Menick

Managing Editor: Joseph P. McGrath

Senior Editors: Barbara K. Clark, Thomas S. Clemmons, Amy M. Reilly

Editorial Administrator: Ann Marie Belluscio

EDITORIAL OPERATIONS

Senior Production Manager: Dianne Robinson

Art Director: Robin Arzt
Assistant Art Director: Gretchen Schuler-Dandridge

Production Editor: Lorraine Burton
Production Assistant: Joanna Luppino

RIGHTS AND PERMISSIONS

Director: Lisa Garrett Smith
Manager: Carol Weiss Staudter
Rights Associate: Arlene Pasciolla

INTERNATIONAL EDITIONS

Executive Editor: Gary Q. Arpin
Senior Editor: Bonnie Grande

VOLUME 5 2006

SELECT EDITIONS

Selected and Edited by Reader's Digest

THE READER'S DIGEST ASSOCIATION, INC.

PLEASANTVILLE, NEW YORK • MONTREAL

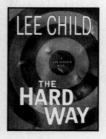
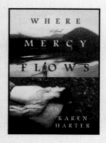

TWO LITTLE GIRLS IN BLUE
Mary Higgins Clark

Who has kidnapped those poor little girls? And why? Get ready for nonstop suspense from one of America's most popular storytellers.

AFTERWORDS: *The family secret of Mary Higgins Clark, plus some mysterious twin talk.*

page 296

ROSIE
Alan Titchmarsh

At the age of 87, Rosie believes that life should be lived to the fullest, and she is going to make sure that her grandson Nick starts believing it, too.

AFTERWORDS: *The many interests of Alan Titchmarsh, and England's best-kept secret.*

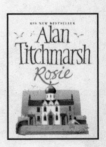

page 444

LEE CHILD

NEW YORK TIMES BESTSELLING AUTHOR OF *ONE SHOT*

A
JACK REACHER
NOVEL

THE
HARD
WAY

JACK Reacher ordered espresso, double, no peel, no cube, foam cup, and before it arrived at his table, he saw a man's life change forever. Not that the waiter was slow. Just that the move was slick. So slick, Reacher had no idea what he was watching. It was just an urban scene, repeated everywhere in the world a billion times a day: a guy unlocked a car and got in and drove away. That was all.

But that was enough.

THE espresso had been close to perfect, so Reacher went back to the same café exactly twenty-four hours later. Two nights in the same place was unusual for Reacher, but he figured great coffee was worth a change in his routine. The café was on the west side of Sixth Avenue in New York City, in the middle of the block between Bleecker and Houston. It occupied the ground floor of an undistinguished four-story building. The café itself had low light and a dented chrome machine as hot and long as a locomotive, and a counter. Outside there was a single line of metal tables behind a low canvas screen. Reacher took the same end table he had used the night before and chose the same seat. He stretched out and got comfortable. His back was against the café's outside wall, and he was looking east, across the sidewalk and the width of the avenue. He liked to sit outside, in New York City. Especially at night. He liked the electric darkness and the hot dirty air and the blasts of noise and traffic and the crush of people. It helped a lonely man feel connected and isolated at the same time.

He was served by the same waiter as the night before and ordered the same drink, double espresso in a foam cup, no sugar, no spoon. He paid for it as soon as it arrived and left his change on the table. That way he could leave exactly when he wanted to without insulting the waiter. Reacher always arranged the smallest details in his life so he could move on at a split second's notice. He owned nothing and carried nothing. Physically he was a big man, but he cast a small shadow and left very little in his wake.

He drank his coffee slowly. He watched cars and people. Watched taxis flow north. Saw knots of young people heading for clubs. Saw a blue German sedan park on the block. Watched a compact man in a gray suit get out and walk north. Watched him thread between two sidewalk tables and head inside to where the café staff was clustered. Watched him ask them questions.

The guy was medium height, not young, not old, too solid to be called wiry, too slight to be called heavy. His hair was gray at the temples and cut short and neat. He kept himself balanced on the balls of his feet. His mouth didn't move much as he talked. But his eyes flicked left and right tirelessly. The guy was about forty, Reacher guessed, and furthermore Reacher guessed he had gotten to be about forty by staying relentlessly aware of everything that was happening around him.

Then Reacher's waiter turned and pointed straight at him. The compact man in the gray suit stared over. Reacher stared back. The man in the suit mouthed *thank you* to the waiter. He stepped back out through the door and threaded his way down to Reacher's table. Reacher let him stand there while he made up his mind. Then Reacher said "Yes" to him, like an answer, not a question.

"Yes, what?" the guy said back.

"Yes, whatever," Reacher said. "Yes, I'm having a pleasant evening; yes, you can join me; yes, you can ask me whatever it is you want to ask me."

The guy sat down. "Actually I do have a question," he said.

"I know," Reacher said. "About last night."

"How did you know that?" The guy's voice was low, and his accent was flat and clipped and British.

"The waiter pointed me out," Reacher said. "And the only thing that distinguishes me from his other customers is that I was here last night and they weren't."

"You're certain about that?"

"Turn your head away," Reacher said. "Watch the traffic."

The guy turned his head away. Watched the traffic.

"Now tell me what I'm wearing," Reacher said.

"Green shirt," the British guy said. "Cotton, baggy, cheap, over a green T-shirt, also cheap, untucked over flat-front khaki chinos, no socks, English shoes, pebbled leather, brown, expensive. Frayed laces, like you pull on them too hard when you tie them."

"Okay," Reacher said. "You notice things. And I notice things. We're two of a kind. I'm the only customer here now who was also here last night. I'm certain of that. And that's what you asked the staff. That's the only reason the waiter would have pointed me out."

The guy turned back. "Did you see a car last night?" he asked.

"I saw plenty of cars last night," Reacher said.

"A Mercedes Benz. Parked over there." The guy pointed at a length of curb by a fire hydrant on the other side of the street.

Reacher said, "Silver, four-door sedan, an S-420, New York vanity plates starting *OSC*. Dirty paint, scrapes on both bumpers."

"You saw it," the guy said.

"It was right there," Reacher said. "Obviously I saw it."

"Did you see it leave?"

Reacher nodded. "Just before eleven forty-five a guy got in and drove it away."

"You're not wearing a watch."

"I always know what time it is."

"It must have been closer to midnight."

"Maybe," Reacher said. "Whatever."

"Did you get a look at the driver?"

"I told you, I saw him get in and drive away."

The guy stood up. "I need you to come with me," he said.

"Where?"

"To see my boss. A man called Lane."

"You're not a cop," Reacher said. "That's my guess. Based on your accent, you're British. The NYPD isn't that desperate."

"Most of us are Americans," the British guy said. "But you're right, we're not cops. We're private citizens."

"What kind?"

"The kind that will make it worth your while if you give them a description of the individual who drove that car away."

"Worth my while how?"

"Financially," the guy said. "Is there any other way?"

"Lots of other ways," Reacher said. "I think I'll stay here."

"This is very serious."

"How?"

The guy sat down again. "I can't tell you," he said. "Mr. Lane made it mission-critical that nobody knows. For good reasons."

"You got a name?" Reacher asked.

The guy stuck a thumb into the breast pocket of his suit coat and slid out a single card. He passed it across the table. At the top it said: *Operational Security Consultants.*

"OSC," Reacher said. "Like the license plate." He smiled. "You're security consultants, and you got your car stolen?"

The guy said, "It's not the car we're worried about."

Lower down on the business card was a name: *John Gregory.* Under the name was a subscript: *British Army, Retired.* Then a job title: *Executive Vice President.*

"How long have you been out?" Reacher asked.

"Of the British army?" Gregory said. "Seven years."

"Unit?"

"SAS."

"You've still got the look."

"You too," Gregory said. "How long have you been out?"

"Seven years," Reacher said.

"Unit?"

"U.S. Army CID, mostly."

Gregory looked up. Interested. "Investigator?"

"Mostly."

"Rank?"

"Major," Reacher said. "That's as far as I got."

"Career problems?"

"I had my share."

"You got a name?"

"Reacher."

"You need work?"

"No," Reacher said. "I don't."

"I was a sergeant," Gregory said.

Reacher nodded. "I figured. SAS guys usually are."

"So will you come with me and talk to Mr. Lane?"

"Seems like a lot of fuss over a stolen car."

"This is not about the car."

"So what is it about?"

"Life and death," Gregory said. "Right now more likely death than life."

Reacher checked his cup. There was an eighth-inch left, thick and scummy with espresso mud. That was all. He put the cup down.

"Okay," he said. "So let's go."

THE blue German sedan turned out to be a new BMW 7 Series with OSC vanity plates. Gregory unlocked it with a remote, and Reacher got in the front passenger seat. Gregory pulled out a small silver cell phone and dialed a number.

"Incoming with a witness," he said, clipped and British. Then he closed the phone and fired up the engine and moved into traffic.

Gregory drove north on Sixth Avenue through midtown to Fifty-seventh Street and then two blocks west. He turned north on Eighth Avenue, onto Central Park West, and onto Seventy-second Street. He stopped outside the Dakota apartment building.

"Nice digs," Reacher said.

They got out together, and another compact man stepped out of the shadows and into the car and drove it away. Gregory led Reacher into the building and up in the elevator.

They got out on five, and an apartment door opened. The lobby staff must have called ahead. The door was heavy oak the color of honey, and the warm light that spilled out into the corridor was the color of honey, too. There was a small square foyer open to a big square living room. The living room had yellow walls and comfortable chairs and sofas. It was full of six men. They were all standing up, silent. Three wore gray suits similar to Gregory's, and three were in black jeans and black nylon warm-up jackets. Reacher knew immediately they were all ex-military. They all had the look. The apartment itself had the desperate quiet feel of a command bunker far from some distant point where a battle was going to hell.

All six men turned and glanced at Reacher. Then five men glanced at the sixth, which Reacher guessed identified him as Mr. Lane. The boss. He was half a generation older than his men. He was in a gray suit. He had gray hair, buzzed close to his scalp. He was maybe an inch above average height, and slender. His face was full of worry. He was standing absolutely straight, racked with tension, with his fingertips touching the top of a table that held a telephone and a framed photograph.

"This is the witness," Gregory said. "He saw the driver."

The man at the table moved toward Reacher, assessing him. He stopped a yard away and offered his hand.

"Edward Lane," he said. "I'm very pleased to meet you, sir." His accent was American. Reacher said his own name and shook Lane's hand. It was dry, not warm, not cold.

"Tell me what you saw," Lane said.

"I saw a guy get in a car," Reacher said. "He drove it away."

"I need detail," Lane said.

"Reacher is ex–U.S. Army CID," Gregory said. "He described the Benz to perfection."

"Where were you?" asked Lane.

"In a café. The car was a little north and east, across Sixth Avenue. A twenty degree angle, maybe ninety feet away."

"Why were you looking at it?"

"It was badly parked. I guessed it was on a fireplug."

"It was," Lane said. "Then what?"

"Then a guy crossed the street toward it. Through gaps in the traffic, at an angle. So most of what I saw was his back."

"Then what?"

"He stuck the key in the door and got inside. Took off."

"Going north, this being Sixth Avenue. Did he turn?"

"Not that I saw."

"Can you describe him?"

"Blue jeans, blue shirt, blue baseball cap, white sneakers. The clothing was old and comfortable. The guy was average height, average weight."

"Age?"

"I didn't see his face. But he didn't move like a kid. He was at least in his thirties. Maybe forty."

"How exactly did he move?"

"He was focused. And the way he held his shoulder, I think he might have had the key out in front of him, horizontally. Focused, and urgent. That's how he moved."

"Where did he come from?"

"From behind my shoulder, more or less."

"Would you recognize him again?"

"Only by his clothes and his walk and his posture."

"If he crossed through the traffic, he must have glanced south to see what was coming at him. So you should have seen the right side of his face. Then when he was behind the wheel, you should have seen the left side."

"He was white," Reacher said. "No facial hair."

"It's not good enough," Lane said.

"Didn't you have insurance?" Reacher asked.

"This is not about the car," Lane said.

"It was empty," Reacher said.

"It wasn't empty," Lane said.

"So what was in it?"

"Thank you, Mr. Reacher," Lane said. "You've been helpful."

He turned and walked back to the table with the phone and the photograph. He stood beside it and spread his fingers again and laid the tips lightly on the polished wood, next to the telephone, like his touch might detect an incoming call before the electronic pulse started the bell.

"You need help," Reacher said. "Don't you?"

"I've got help," Lane said. He gestured around the room. "Navy SEALS, Delta Force, Recon Marines, Green Berets, SAS from Britain. The best in the world."

"You need a different kind of help. The guy who took your car, these folks can start a war against him, that's for sure. But first you need to find him."

No reply.

"What was in the car?" Reacher asked.

"Tell me about your career," Lane said.

"It's been over a long time. That's its main feature."

"Army CID?"

"Thirteen years."

"Investigator?"

"Basically."

"A good one?"

"Good enough."

"One hundred and tenth Special Unit?"

"Some of the time. You?"

"Rangers and Delta. Started in Vietnam, ended in the Gulf the first time around. Finished a full colonel."

"What was in the car?"

Lane looked away. Then he looked back.

"You need to give me your word about something," he said.

"Like what?"

"No cops."

Reacher shrugged. "Okay," he said.

"Say it."

"No cops."

"No FBI, no nobody," Lane said. "We handle this. Understand? You break your word, I'll have you blinded."

"My word is good," Reacher said.

"Say you understand what I'll do if you break it."

Reacher looked around the room. Took it all in. A desperate atmosphere and six Special Forces veterans, all as hard as nails, all looking right back at him, all full of unit loyalty and hostile suspicion of the outsider.

"You'll have me blinded," Reacher said.

Lane picked up the framed photograph. He held it flat against his chest, so that Reacher felt he had two people staring back at him. Above, Lane's worried features. Below, under glass, a woman of breathtaking classical beauty. Dark hair, green eyes, high cheekbones, a bud of a mouth, photographed with passion and expertise and printed by a master.

"This is my wife," Lane said.

Reacher nodded. Said nothing.

"Her name is Kate," Lane said. "Kate disappeared late yesterday morning. I got a call in the afternoon. From her kidnappers. They wanted money. That's what was in the car. You watched one of my wife's kidnappers collect their ransom."

Silence.

"They promised to release her," Lane said. "And it's been twenty-four hours. And they haven't called back."

EDWARD Lane held the framed photograph like an offering, and Reacher stepped forward to take it. He tilted it to the light. Kate Lane was beautiful. She was hypnotic. She was younger than her husband by maybe twenty years, which put her in her early thirties. In the picture she was gazing at something just beyond the edge of the print. Her eyes blazed with love. Her mouth seemed ready to burst into a wide smile. The details were immaculate.

"My Mona Lisa," Lane said. "That's how I think of that picture."

Reacher passed it back. "Is it recent?"

Lane propped it upright again. "Less than a year old."

"Why no cops? They usually do a good job."

"You can do what they do," Lane said.

"I can't," Reacher said. "I don't have their resources."

"You can make a start."

"How much money did they want?" Reacher asked.

"One million dollars in cash," Lane answered.

"And that was in the car? A million bucks?"

"In the trunk. In a leather bag."

"Okay," Reacher said. "They're going to call back. Let's all sit down. Start at the beginning. Tell me about yesterday."

So Lane sat down and started to talk about the previous day. Reacher sat at one end of a sofa. Gregory sat next to him. The other five guys distributed themselves around the room.

"Kate went out at ten o'clock in the morning," Lane said. "She was heading for Bloomingdale's, I think."

"You think?"

"I allow her some freedom of action."

"Was she alone?"

"Her daughter was with her."

"*Her* daughter?"

"She has an eight-year-old by her first marriage. Jade."

"She lives with you here?"

Lane nodded.

"So where is Jade now?"

"Missing, obviously," Lane said.

"So this is a *double* kidnapping?" Reacher said.

Lane nodded again. "Triple, in a way. Their driver didn't come back either."

"You didn't think to mention this before?"

"Does it make a difference? One person or three?"

"Who was the driver?"

"A guy called Taylor. British, ex-SAS. A good man. One of us."

"What happened to the car?"

"It's missing."

"Does Kate go to Bloomingdale's often?"

Lane shook his head. "Only occasionally. And never on a pre-dictable pattern. We do nothing regular or predictable. I vary her drivers, vary her routes."

"Because? You got a lot of enemies?"

"My fair share. My line of work attracts enemies."

"You're going to have to explain your line of work to me. You're going to have to tell me who your enemies are."

"Why are you sure they're going to call?"

"I'll get to that," Reacher said. "Tell me about the first conversation. Word for word."

"They called at four o'clock in the afternoon. It went pretty much how you would expect. You know, we have your wife, we have your daughter."

"Voice?"

"Altered. One of those electronic squawk boxes. I asked them what they wanted. They said a million bucks. I asked them to put

18 | Lee Child

Kate on the line. They did, after a short pause." Lane closed his eyes. "She said, Help me." He opened his eyes. "Then the guy with the squawk box came back on, and I agreed to the money. The guy said he would call back in an hour with instructions."

"And did he?"

Lane nodded. "I was told to wait six hours and put the money in the trunk of the Mercedes you saw and have it driven down to the Village and parked in that spot at eleven forty exactly. The driver was to lock it up and walk away and put the keys through a mail slot in the front door of a certain building on the southwest corner of Spring Street and West Broadway. Then he was to walk south on West Broadway. Someone would collect the keys. If my driver stopped or even looked back, Kate would die. Likewise if there was a tracking device on the car."

"Who drove the car down?" Reacher asked.

"Gregory," Lane said.

"I followed the instructions," Gregory said. "To the letter."

"What was the building with the mail slot?" Reacher asked.

"Abandoned," Gregory said. "It was empty, anyway."

"How good was this guy Taylor? Did you know him in Britain?"

Gregory nodded. "Taylor was very good indeed."

"Okay," Reacher said. "There are some obvious early conclusions. The first is that Taylor is already dead. These guys clearly know you, and therefore we should assume they knew who Taylor was. They wouldn't keep him alive. Too dangerous."

Lane asked, "Why do you think they know me?"

"They asked for a specific car," Reacher said. "And they suspected you might have a million dollars in cash lying around. They asked for it after the banks were closed and told you to deliver it before the banks reopened. Not everyone could comply with those conditions."

Nobody spoke.

"And there are three of them," Reacher said. "One to guard Kate and Jade. One to watch Gregory's back while he walked south on West Broadway, on a cell phone to a third, who was waiting to move in and pick up the keys."

Nobody spoke.

"And they're based a minimum two hundred miles upstate," Reacher said. "Let's assume the initial action went down before about eleven o'clock yesterday morning. But they didn't call for more than five hours. Because they were driving. Then they issued instructions at five o'clock for a ransom drop more than six hours later. Because two of them had to drive all the way back. Five, six hours, that's two hundred miles."

"Why upstate?" Lane said. "They could be anywhere."

"Not south or west," Reacher said. "Or they would have asked for the ransom car south of Canal, so they could head for the Holland Tunnel. Not east on Long Island, or they would have wanted to be near the Midtown Tunnel. No, north on Sixth was what they wanted. That implies the George Washington Bridge, or the Henry Hudson and the Saw Mill, or the Triborough and the Major Deegan. Eventually they hit the Thruway, probably. They could be in the Catskills. A farm. Somewhere with a big garage or a barn."

"Why?"

"They just inherited your Mercedes Benz. Right after hijacking whatever Taylor drove to Bloomingdale's yesterday. They need a place to hide them."

"Taylor was driving a Jaguar."

"There you go. Must look like a luxury car lot by now."

"Why are you so sure they're going to call back?"

"Because of human nature. Right now they're kicking themselves. They asked for a million dollars in cash, and you bagged it up without a moment's hesitation. You should have stalled. Because now they're saying, Damn it, we should have asked for more. So they're going to hit you up for another chunk."

"Why wait so long?"

"Because it's a significant change in strategy," Reacher said. "Therefore they're arguing about it. That's human nature, too. Three guys always argue, pro and con, play it safe or take the risk."

Nobody spoke.

"Five million," Reacher said. "That's what they'll ask for."

"Is Kate safe?" Lane asked.

"Right now, she's safe," Reacher said. "She's their meal ticket. And you did the right thing, asking to hear her voice the first time. That set up a good pattern. The problem will come after they've had the last payment. That's the toughest part of any kidnap."

"Good conclusions," Lane said to nobody in particular. "Three guys, far away. Upstate. On a farm."

2

THE phone rang at exactly one o'clock in the morning. Lane snatched it out of the cradle and said, "Yes?" Reacher heard a faint voice from the earpiece, distorted. Lane said, "Put Kate on the phone." There was a pause, and then there was a woman's voice, panicked, breathy. It said just one word, and then it exploded in a scream. Lane screwed his eyes shut, and the electronic robot voice barked six short syllables. Lane said, "Okay, okay," and Reacher heard the line go dead.

Lane sat in silence, his breathing ragged. Then his eyes opened and moved from face to face and stopped on Reacher's.

"Five million dollars," he said. "How did you know?"

"It was the obvious next step," Reacher said. "One, five, ten, twenty. That's how people think."

"You've got a crystal ball. I'm putting you on the payroll. Twenty-five grand a month, like all these guys."

"This isn't going to last a month," Reacher said. "It can't."

"I couldn't stall," Lane said. "They were hurting her."

Reacher nodded. Said nothing.

Gregory asked, "Instructions later?"

"In an hour," Lane said.

All around the room men settled back imperceptibly. Lane stared off into space.

"We need to talk," Reacher said quietly.

"About what?"

"Background. We should try to figure out who these guys are."

"Okay," Lane said vaguely. "We'll go to the office."

He led Reacher out of the living room and through a kitchen to a maid's room in back. It had been fixed up as an office. Desk, computer, fax machine, phones, file cabinets, shelves.

"Tell me about Operational Security Consultants," Reacher said.

Lane sat down in the desk chair. "Not much to tell," he said. "We're just a bunch of ex-military trying to keep busy. Bodyguarding, mostly. Corporate security. Like that."

There were two framed photographs on the desk. One was a smaller reprint of Kate's stunning picture from the living room. The other was of another woman, about the same age, blond where Kate was dark, blue eyes instead of green. But just as beautiful.

"You're not convincing me, Mr. Lane. Bodyguards don't make twenty-five grand a month."

"My business is confidential," Lane said.

"Not if you want your wife and daughter back."

No reply.

"A Jaguar, a Mercedes, and a BMW," Reacher said. "Plus a co-op in the Dakota. Plus lots of cash lying around. Plus half a dozen guys on twenty-five grand a month."

"All legal."

"Except you don't want the cops involved."

Involuntarily, Lane glanced at the photograph of the blond woman. "That's not the reason."

Reacher followed Lane's gaze. "Who is she?" he asked.

"Anne," Lane said. "She was my first wife."

"And?"

"You see, I've been through this before," Lane said. "Five years ago. Anne was taken from me. In just the same way. But back then I called the cops, even though the men on the phone had been very clear that I shouldn't. The cops called the FBI."

"And what happened?"

"The FBI screwed up somehow," Lane said. "They must have

been spotted at the ransom drop. Anne died. They found her body a month later in New Jersey."

Reacher said nothing.

"That's why there's no cops this time," Lane said.

Reacher and Lane sat in silence for a long time. Then Reacher said, "Fifty-five minutes. You should be ready for the next call."

"You're not wearing a watch," Lane said.

"I always know what time it is."

Reacher followed him back to the living room.

THE phone rang right on time, at two o'clock in the morning. Lane picked it up. Reacher heard faint robot squawks. Lane said, "Put Kate on," but his request must have been refused, because then he said, "Please don't hurt her." He listened for a minute and said, "Okay." Then he hung up.

"Seven o'clock in the morning," he said. "Same place, same routine. The blue BMW. One person only."

"I'll do it," Gregory said.

"We should all be there," one of the others said. He was a small dark American, whose eyes were as flat and dead as a hammerhead shark's. "Ten minutes later we would know where she is."

"One man," Lane said. "That was the instruction."

"This is New York City," the guy with the shark's eyes said. "They can't be expecting deserted streets."

"Apparently they know us," Lane said. "They'd recognize you."

"I could go," Reacher said. "They wouldn't recognize me."

"You came in with Gregory. They might be watching the door."

"Conceivable," Reacher said. "But unlikely."

Lane said nothing.

"Your call," Reacher said.

"I'll think about it," Lane said. "Decision in one hour." He headed back toward the office. Gone to count out the money, Reacher thought. He wondered briefly what five million dollars looked like. The same as one million, he guessed. But with hundreds instead of twenties.

"How much money has he got?" Reacher asked.

"A lot," Gregory said.

The guy with the shark's eyes smiled.

"We'll get it back," he said. "As soon as Kate's home safe, we'll make our move. They'll be sorry they were ever born."

Reacher glanced into the guy's empty eyes and believed every word he said. Then the guy stuck out his hand, abruptly. "I'm Carter Groom," he said.

The four other men introduced themselves with a quiet cascade of names and handshakes. Reacher tried to tie the names to faces. Gregory he already knew. A guy with a big scar over his eye was called Addison. The shortest guy was a Latino called Perez. The tallest was called Kowalski. There was a black guy called Burke.

"Lane told me you do bodyguarding and corporate security," Reacher said.

Sudden silence. No reply.

"My guess is you guys were all operational noncoms. Fighting men. So I think your Mr. Lane is into something else entirely."

"Like what?" Gregory asked.

"I think he's pimping mercenaries," Reacher said.

"We're a private military corporation," Groom said. "We're legal. We work for the Pentagon, just like we always did, and just like you did, back in the day."

"How many guys have you got?" Reacher asked.

"We're the A-team," Groom said. "Then there's a Rolodex full of B-team squad members. We took a hundred guys to Iraq."

"Is that where you've been? Iraq?"

"And Colombia and Panama and Afghanistan. We go anywhere Uncle Sam needs us."

"My guess is the Pentagon pays by check," Reacher said. "But there seems to be an awful lot of cash around here. Africa?"

No response.

"Whatever," Reacher said. "Not my business. All I need to know is where Mrs. Lane has been. For the last couple of weeks."

"What difference does that make?" Kowalski asked.

"There was some surveillance," Reacher said. "Don't you think? I don't suppose the bad guys were just hanging out at Blooming-dale's every day on the off chance."

"Mrs. Lane was in the Hamptons," Gregory said. "With Jade, most of the summer. They came back three days ago."

"Anything happen out in the Hamptons? Anything unusual?"

"A woman showed up at the door one day," Gregory said.

"What kind of a woman?"

"Just a woman. Fat. Kind of heavyset. About forty. Long hair, center part. Mrs. Lane took her walking on the beach. Then the woman left. I figured it was a friend on a visit."

"Ever saw her before?"

Gregory shook his head.

"What did Mrs. Lane do after she got back to the city?"

"I don't think she did anything."

"No, she went out once," Groom said. "I drove her. To Staples."

"The office supply store? What did she buy?"

"Nothing," Groom said. "I waited twenty minutes on the curb, and she didn't bring anything out."

"Did she take something in?" Gregory asked. "Maybe she was returning something."

"She had her tote," Groom said. "It's possible." Then he looked up. Edward Lane was back in the room, struggling with a large leather duffel. Five million dollars, Reacher thought. So that's what it looks like. Lane dropped the bag on the floor.

"I need to see a picture of Jade," Reacher said.

"Bedroom," Lane said.

So Reacher followed him to a bedroom. It was painted a chalky off-white. There was a cherrywood king-size bed. Matching tables at each side. A matching armoire. A matching desk, with a framed photograph sitting on it. It was a portrait of two people. On the right was Kate Lane. It was the same shot as in the living room print. But the living room print had been cropped to exclude the object of her affection, which was her daughter. They were about to look at each other, love in their eyes, smiles about to break out on their faces. In the picture Jade was maybe seven years old. She had long dark hair, slightly wavy, as fine as silk. She had green eyes and porcelain skin.

"May I?" Reacher asked.

Lane nodded. Reacher picked the picture up and looked closer. The photographer had caught the bond between mother and child perfectly and completely. It was a great picture. Although the print quality wasn't quite as good as the living room copy.

"Very nice," Reacher said. He put the photograph back on the desk, quietly. The room was totally silent.

"Okay?" Lane said. "Seen enough?"

"You mind if I check the desk?" Reacher asked.

Lane shrugged, and Reacher started with the bottom drawers. The left-hand drawer held boxes of stationery. The right-hand drawer was fitted with file hangers, and the contents related exclusively to Jade's education. She was enrolled at a private school. The checks were all drawn on Kate Lane's personal account. The upper drawers held pens and pencils, envelopes, stamps, a checkbook. And credit card receipts. But nothing significant. Nothing recent. Nothing from Staples, for instance.

The center drawer at the top held nothing but two American passports, one for Kate and one for Jade.

"Who is Jade's father?" Reacher asked.

"He's dead," Lane said. "He died when Jade was three."

"Who was he?"

"He owned a jewelry store. Kate ran it for a year, afterward. She had been a model. But that's where I met her. In the store. I was buying a watch."

"Any other relatives?"

"Nobody that I ever met."

Reacher closed the center drawer. "Closet?" he said.

Lane pointed at one of a pair of narrow white doors.

"What was she wearing when she went out?" Reacher asked.

"I'm not sure," Lane said. "We all left before her. I don't think anyone was still here. Except Taylor."

Reacher closed the closet door and stepped to the armoire. It had double doors at the top and drawers below. One of the drawers held jewelry. One was full of miscellaneous junk like buttons. One was full of lacy underwear.

"May I see Jade's room?" Reacher asked.

Jade's room was all pale pastels and kid stuff. Furry bears, china dolls, toys, games. A low bed. A low desk covered in drawings done with wax crayons on butcher paper. A small chair.

Nothing that meant anything to a military cop.

"I'm done," Reacher said. "I'm very sorry to intrude."

He followed Lane back to the living room. Gregory and the five other soldiers were still in their places.

"Decision time," Lane said. "I think Reacher should be on the street at seven o'clock."

There was no objection. Reacher nodded.

"I'll watch the front of the Spring Street building," he said. "That way I'll see one of them at least."

"Surveillance only. Absolutely no intervention."

"Don't worry."

"They'll be there early," Lane said.

"Don't worry," Reacher said again. "I'll leave right now."

"Don't you want to know which building you're supposed to be watching?"

"I don't need to know," Reacher said. "I'll see Gregory leave the keys." Then he let himself out of the apartment and rode down in the elevator and walked out to the street. Headed for the subway at Seventy-second and Broadway.

THE woman who was watching the building saw him go. She had seen him arrive with Gregory, and now he was leaving alone. She checked her watch and made a note of the time. She craned her neck and tracked his progress west. Then she lost sight of him and moved back deep in the shadows.

REACHER rode eleven stops south to Houston Street. Then he walked south on Varick. It was past three o'clock in the morning, so he was about three hours and forty minutes ahead of schedule. He walked with the leisurely gait of a man with a place to go but in no hurry to get there. As he ambled past Spring Street he had a good view of the southwest corner. There was a narrow iron-fronted building with a dull red door set high. Three steps up to it. The upper-story windows were filthy and backed with some kind of a dark fabric. On the ground floor there was a single window, pasted over with faded building permits. There was a mail slot in the door.

That's the one, Reacher thought. Got to be.

He completed a circuit around the block. Walked south on West Broadway and found a doorway on the east sidewalk. He lay down on his back, his head canted sideways like a somnolent drunk, and focused on the dull red door seventy feet away.

THE clock in Reacher's head crept around to six in the morning. Down in the brick and iron canyons of SoHo it was still dark, but the sky above was already brightening. So far he had seen no activity at the dull red door. The early people were already out and about. But nobody was looking at him. He was just a guy in a doorway.

He figured whoever was coming would be in position soon. They clearly weren't fools. They would check rooftops and windows and parked cars for watching cops.

Cops, he thought. The word snagged in his mind the way a twig on a current catches on a riverbank. It hung up just briefly before spinning clear and floating away.

REACHER had no watch, but he figured when he saw Gregory it must have been between eight and nine minutes after seven o'clock. Eight or nine minutes was about right for the walk down from the fireplug on Sixth. So Gregory was right on time. He stopped outside the dull red door and walked up the three short steps, light and easy. Then Reacher saw Gregory lift the mail slot's flap and shovel the keys through. Saw him walk away. He didn't look back, he just played his part, trying to keep Kate Lane alive.

Reacher kept his eyes on the red door. Waited. Three minutes, he figured. Five million bucks was a lot of money. As soon as the one guy confirmed that Gregory was safely distant, the other guy would be in through the door.

One minute. Two minutes.

Three minutes. Nothing happened.

Reacher kept his eyes half closed but stared at the door so hard that its details etched themselves in his mind.

Six minutes. Eight. Nine. Nothing happened.

Reacher asked himself: Did they see me? He answered himself: Of course they did. Guys good enough to take down an SAS veteran were going to check the street pretty carefully. But were they worried? Answered himself: No, they weren't. People in doorways were like trash cans or mailboxes. Street furniture. And he was alone. Cops or FBI would have come in a group.

So they saw me, but they didn't scare.

So what was happening?

Nineteen minutes.

Reacher gave it up after twenty. Hustled all the way north to the curb with the fireplug. It was empty. No BMW.

REACHER headed south again, back to Spring Street. He found Gregory outside the dull red door.

"Well?" Gregory said.

"Nothing," Reacher said. "Nobody showed up. The car is gone."

"How is that possible?"

"There's a back door," Reacher said. "That's my best guess."

"We should check it out."

They found an alley entrance two buildings west. It was gated and chained. Above the gates was a single iron screen extending twenty feet in the air.

No way in.

The target building's right-hand neighbor was a chocolate shop. There was a light on in back of the store. Reacher cupped his hands against the glass. Saw a small shadowy figure moving about. He banged on the door. The small figure turned around. It was a

woman. Short, dark, young, tired. She turned numerous compli-
cated locks and opened the door against a thick steel chain.

"Department of Health," Reacher said.

"You don't look like it," the woman said. And she was right.
Reacher had looked convincing as a bum. He didn't look convincing as a bureaucrat. So he nodded at Gregory, in his neat gray suit.

"He's with the city," he said. "I'm with him."

"I was just inspected," the woman said.

"This is about the building next door," Reacher said.

"What about it?"

"Rats," Reacher said. "I'm the exterminator."

"You got a key for the alley gate?" Gregory asked her.

The woman nodded. "But you can use my back door."

She led them inside through air intense with the smell of cocoa.
The front of the store was dressed up for retail, and there was a
working kitchen in back. Ovens, just now warming up. Vats of
melting chocolate. Steel work surfaces. A rear door, at the end of a
short tiled hallway. The woman let them out through it, and
Reacher and Gregory found themselves in a brick alley. The alley
ran east to west across the block with a single gated exit on Thompson Street at one end and a right-angle dogleg to the gate they had
seen on Spring at the other. The target building looked just as bad
from the back as it had from the front. Or maybe even worse.

One ground floor window. And a back door. It had a good solid
deadbolt. Reacher grabbed it and pushed. The door gave an eighth-
inch and then stopped dead against the lock's steel tongue.

No way in.

Reacher turned back and headed for the kitchen.

"You ever seen anyone next door?" he asked.

"Nobody," the chocolatier said. "It's a vacant building."

"Are you here every day?"

"From seven thirty in the morning. I fire up the ovens first thing,
and I turn them off at ten in the evening. I'm out of here by eleven
thirty. I'm regular as clockwork."

"Seven days a week?"

"Small business. We never rest."

Reacher nodded. "Who's the owner next door?"

"I've got no idea," the woman said. "Check the building permits on the front window."

"Thanks," Reacher said.

"Want a chocolate?"

"Not on duty," he said.

He followed Gregory out the front of the store, and they checked the target building's front window. There were a dozen permits pasted to the glass. All of them were long expired. But they still had phone numbers handwritten with a black marker pen. Gregory took out his small silver cell phone and took a picture with it.

He and Reacher walked back into the Dakota's lobby at eight thirty exactly.

THE bad news put Edward Lane on a knife-edge. Reacher watched him struggling for control.

"I'm revising my conclusions," Reacher said. "Maybe there aren't three guys. Maybe there are only two. One stays with Kate and Jade, the other comes down to the city alone. He doesn't need to watch Gregory walk away, because he's planning on using the back door anyway. He's already in the alley, out of sight."

"Risky. Safer to be loose on the street."

Reacher shook his head. "They did their homework. The neighbor is in her building from seven thirty in the morning until eleven thirty at night. Which explains the times they chose. Seven o'clock this morning, before she arrived. Eleven forty the first night, after she left. Eleven forty is a weirdly precise choice of time, don't you think? There had to be some reason for it."

Edward Lane said nothing.

Reacher said, "Or maybe there's only one guy. If Kate and Jade are secured upstate, he could have come down alone. Maybe he was actually inside the building, waiting and ready."

Lane paced. It was like he had been hit with a new consideration. Reacher had been expecting it. Here it comes, he thought.

"Maybe it's four guys," Lane said. "And maybe you're the fourth guy. Maybe that's why you were in that coffee shop the first night. You were watching your buddy's back. Making sure he got away."

Reacher said nothing.

"It was you who elected to watch the front door this morning," Lane said. "Because you knew nothing would happen there. You should have watched the car. You should have been on Sixth Avenue, not Spring Street. And you knew they were going to ask for five million more. You're one of them, aren't you?"

"Two questions," Reacher said. "Why would I have gone back to the coffee shop the second night? Nothing was happening the second night. And if I was a bad guy, why would I have told Gregory I had seen anything at all?"

"Because you wanted to worm your way inside, where you could steer us wrong."

Reacher looked down at Kate Lane's photograph.

"Pity," he said. "Your wife is a beautiful woman, Mr. Lane. And your daughter is a lovely kid. And if you want to get them back, then I'm all you've got. Because like I said, these guys here aren't investigators. They can't find what you're looking for."

Nobody spoke.

"You know where I live?" Reacher asked.

"I could find out," Lane said.

"You couldn't," Reacher said. "Because I don't really live anywhere. I move around. Here, there, and everywhere. So if I choose to walk out of here today, you'll never see me again. Or Kate."

Nobody spoke.

"I'm not here to steer you wrong," Reacher said. "If I wanted to steer you wrong, I'd have given you descriptions of two fantasy guys this morning. I'd have had you chasing shadows all over the place. But I didn't. I came back here and told you I'm sorry that I'm not steering you anyplace yet. Because I am sorry about that."

The room stayed quiet. Then Lane exhaled. "I apologize," he said. "Please forgive me. It's the stress."

Reacher said, "No offense taken."

Lane said, "One million dollars to find my wife."

"For me?" Reacher said. "That's some raise."

"Will you accept?" Lane asked.

"We'll talk about a fee afterward," Reacher said. "If I succeed."

"If?"

"I'm way behind the curve here. Success depends on how much longer we can keep this thing going."

"Will they call back again?"

"Yes, I think they will."

LANE went to his office, and five men went out for breakfast. Reacher stayed in the living room. Gregory stayed with him.

"Can you get her back?" Gregory asked.

"I don't know," Reacher said. "Usually this kind of a thing doesn't end happily. Kidnapping is a brutal business."

"You think they were in the building when I dropped the keys?"

"It's possible."

"Okay," Gregory said. "So how about this: that's their base. That's where they *are*. Not upstate."

"It would be one hell of a double-bluff," Reacher said. "They led us right there. Gave us the exact address."

"But it's conceivable."

Reacher shrugged. "Not very. But stranger things have happened. So call those numbers. Aim to have someone meet us with a key. But on the corner of Thompson. Out of sight. Just in case."

"When?"

"Now. We need to be back before the next ransom demand."

REACHER left Gregory working his cell phone and wandered back to Lane's office. Lane was at his desk, staring at the photographs in front of him. His two wives. One lost. Maybe both lost.

"Did the FBI find the guys?" Reacher asked. "With Anne?"

Lane shook his head.

"But you found out later who they were."

"It became a threshold question," Lane said. "Who would do such a thing?"

"You surprise me. You move in a world where hostage-taking and abduction aren't exactly unknown."

"But this was domestic," Lane said. "This was right here in New York City. And it was my wife, not me or one of my men."

"But you did find the guys."

"Did I?"

Reacher nodded. "You're not asking me if I think it could be the same people all over again. It's like you know for sure it isn't."

Lane said nothing.

"How did you find them?" Reacher asked.

"Someone who knew someone heard some talk."

"What happened to the guys?"

"Let's just say I'm completely confident that this isn't the same people doing it again."

"Do you have a rival in this business?"

"No. And even if I did, they wouldn't do something like this. It would be suicide."

Reacher didn't reply.

"Will they call again?" Lane asked.

"I think they will."

"What will they ask for?"

"Ten," Reacher said. "That's the next step."

"That's two bags," Lane said.

Reacher thought: This guy is right now looking at a running total of seventeen million dollars, and he hasn't even blinked.

"When will they call?" Lane asked.

"Drive time plus argument time," Reacher said. "Late afternoon, early evening. Not before."

There was a quiet knock at the door, and Gregory stuck his head in the room.

"I got what we need," he said, to Reacher, not to Lane. "The building on Spring Street? The owner is a bankrupt developer. One

of his lawyer's people is meeting us there in an hour. I said we were
interested in buying the place."

"Good work," Reacher said. "Let's go."

THEY were met at the curb by another new BMW 7 Series sedan.
This one was black. The driver stayed behind the wheel, and Gregory and Reacher climbed in the back. The woman who was watching the building saw them go and noted the time.

3

THE guy from the bankrupt developer's lawyer's office was a reedy
paralegal of about thirty. Gregory gave him an OSC business card
and introduced Reacher as a contractor whose opinion he valued.

"Is the building habitable?" Gregory asked. "As of right now?"

"You worried about squatters?" the reedy guy asked.

"Or tenants," Gregory said. "Or anybody."

"There's nobody in there," the guy said. "No water, no power,
capped sewer. Also, there's another feature that makes it unlikely.
I'll show you."

He unlocked the Thompson Street alley gate. The three men
walked to the target building's rear door. He shoved the key in the
lock and pushed it open. Then he raised his arm to stop Gregory
and Reacher from crowding in behind him. Because the feature that
made habitation of the building unlikely was that it had no floors.

The back door was hanging open over a yawning ten-foot pit. At
the bottom of the pit was the original basement floor. It was knee-
deep in trash. Above it was nothing at all. Just fifty feet of dark
void, all the way up to the underside of the roof slab.

"See?" the lawyer's guy said. "Not exactly habitable, is it?"

There was a ladder set next to the rear door. A nimble person
could grasp the door frame and swing sideways and get on it and

climb down. Then that person could pick his way forward to the front of the building and root through the garbage and collect anything that had fallen the thirteen feet from the letter slot above.

Or, a nimble person could be already waiting down there and could catch whatever came through the slot.

"Who else has keys to this place?" Reacher asked.

"Everyone, probably," the guy said. "It's been vacant nearly twenty years. The first thing you'll need to do is change the locks."

"We don't want it," Gregory said. "We were looking for something ready to move into."

"We could be flexible on price," the guy said.

"A dollar," Gregory said. "That's all I'd pay for this dump."

"You're wasting my time," the guy said.

He pulled the door closed. Then he relocked it and walked back up the alley without another word. Reacher and Gregory followed him out to Thompson Street. The guy relocked the gate and walked away south. Reacher and Gregory stayed on the sidewalk.

"Not their base, then," Gregory said. "Just a drop for the car keys. They must be up and down that ladder like trained monkeys."

"I guess they must."

"So next time we should watch the alley."

"I guess we should."

Thirty-six minutes later the two men were back in the Dakota, and the woman who was watching the building had made another entry in her log.

REACHER dozed for a while. He woke up and found himself all alone in the living room except for Carter Groom. The guy with the shark's eyes. He was sitting in an armchair, doing nothing.

"You pulled guard duty?" Reacher asked.

"You're not exactly a prisoner," Groom said. "You're in line to get a million bucks."

"Does that bother you?"

"Not really. You find her, you'll have earned it."

"Did you drive her often?"

"My fair share."

"When Jade was with her, how did they ride?"

"Mrs. Lane always rode in the front. The kid in the back."

"What were you, back in the day?"

"Recon Marine," Groom said. "First Sergeant."

"How would you have done the takedown at Bloomingdale's?"

"Only one way to do it clean," Groom said. "You'd have to keep all the action inside the car, before they even got out. Bloomie's is on the east side of Lexington Avenue. Lex runs downtown. So Taylor would pull over on the left and stop opposite the main entrance. Whereupon our guy would grab the rear door and slide in next to the kid. Our guy puts a gun straight to the kid's head. That's game over right there. Nobody on the street is worried. And Taylor would do what he's told from that point on. And what can he do anyway?"

"And then what?"

"Then our guy makes Taylor drive somewhere quiet. Then he shoots him, spine shot through the seat. He makes Mrs. Lane dump him out. Then he makes her drive the rest of the way. He wants to stay in the back with the kid."

Reacher nodded. "That's how I see it."

"They haven't found his body yet," Groom said.

"You optimistic?"

Groom shook his head. "It's not somewhere populated, that's all it means."

"How long was he with you?"

"Three years."

"Was he good?"

"He was good," Groom said. "SAS is a good outfit."

"What was he like as a person?"

"Off duty he was gentle. He was good with the kid. Mrs. Lane seemed to like him. Taylor was inner circle. I'm outer circle. I'm nothing, away from the action."

"Were you here five years ago?"

"For Anne? No, I came just after."

AROUND A QUARTER TO FIVE in the afternoon Lane came back into the room, and people started drifting in after him. The vigil around the telephone started up again.

In her apartment across the street the woman who had been watching the building picked up her phone and dialed.

THE woman across the street was called Patricia Joseph, Patti to her few friends, and she was dialing an NYPD detective named Brewer. He answered on the second ring.

"There's a new character on the scene," Patti said.

Brewer didn't ask who his caller was. He didn't need to.

"Who?"

"I don't have a name for him yet."

"Description?"

"Very tall, heavily built. Late thirties or early forties. Short fair hair, blue eyes. Green shirt, chinos. He showed up late last night."

"One of them?" Brewer asked.

"He doesn't dress like them. And he's much bigger than the rest. But he acts like them. The way he walks. The way he moves."

"Okay," Brewer said. "Good work. Anything else?"

"One thing," Patti Joseph said. "I haven't seen the wife or the daughter in a couple of days."

INSIDE the Dakota living room the phone rang at what Reacher figured was five o'clock exactly. Lane snatched the receiver out of the cradle and clamped it to his ear. Reacher heard the squawk of the electronic machine, faint and muffled. Lane said, "Put Kate on," and there was a long pause. Then the electronic squawk came back. Lane listened, his face working. Then the call ended.

Lane put the receiver back in the cradle. His face was half filled with hope, half filled with despair.

"They want more money," he said. "Instructions in an hour."

"Maybe I should get down there now," Reacher said.

But Lane was already shaking his head. "They said they're changing the procedure. It's not going to be the same as before."

"Is Mrs. Lane okay?" Gregory asked.

Lane said, "There was a lot of fear in her voice."

"What about the guy's voice?" Reacher asked. "Word choice, word order, cadence. Is it an American or a foreigner?"

"It's an American," Lane said. "I think." He closed his eyes and concentrated. "Yes, American. Certainly a native speaker. No stumbles. Never any weird or unusual words. Just normal."

"How much money?" Reacher asked. "Ten?"

"Four and a half," Lane said. "That's what they want."

REACHER spent the remaining fifty-five minutes puzzling over the choice of amount. It was a bizarre figure. A bizarre progression. One, five, four and a half. Altogether ten and a half million dollars. It made no kind of sense at all. Or did it?

"They know you," he said to Lane. "But maybe not that well. As it happens you could afford more, but maybe they don't know that. Was there a time when ten and a half million was all you had?"

Lane said, "No. I've had less, and I've had more."

"But you've never had exactly ten and a half?"

"No," Lane said. "There's absolutely no reason for anyone to believe that they're cleaning me out at ten and a half."

So Reacher gave it up and just waited for the phone to ring.

IT RANG right on time, at six in the evening. Lane picked it up and listened. He didn't speak. He didn't ask for Kate. The call lasted less than two minutes.

"This is the final installment," Lane said. "After this, it's over. They promise I get her back."

Reacher thought, Ain't going to happen.

"One hour from now," Lane said. "One man leaves here alone with the money in the black BMW and cruises. He'll be carrying my cell phone, and he'll get a call anywhere between one and twenty minutes into the ride. He'll be given a destination. He's to keep the line open from that point on so they know he's not conversing with anyone else in the car or on any kind of a radio net. He'll drive to the destination. He'll find the Jaguar parked on the street there. The car that Taylor drove Kate in. He's to put the money on the back-seat and drive away. Any tricks, and Kate dies."

"I'll do it," Burke said. The black guy.

Lane nodded. "Thank you."

"Then what?" Reacher asked. "How do we get her back?"

Lane said, "After they've counted the money, there'll be another call. It will take time. Counting large sums is an arduous process."

Reacher nodded. If the money was in hundreds, that would give them forty-five thousand bills. If they could count to a hundred every sixty seconds, that would take them four hundred and fifty minutes, or seven and a half hours. A long night ahead, he thought.

"Office," Lane said. "Burke and Reacher."

In the office Lane took a small silver Samsung phone out of a charging cradle and handed it to Burke. Then he disappeared, to his bedroom, maybe.

"Gone to get the money," Burke said.

Reacher nodded. Gazed at the portraits on the desk. Anne Lane had long straight hair parted in the middle. She had clear guileless eyes and an innocent smile.

Lane came back awkwardly with a bulging leather bag. He dropped the bag on the floor and sat down at his desk.

"How long?" he asked.

"Forty minutes," Reacher said.

"Go wait in the other room," Lane said. "Leave me alone."

Burke went for the bag, but Reacher picked it up for him. He carried it to the foyer and dropped it near the door. Reacher took a seat. Burke paced. Carter Groom drummed his fingers on the arm of a chair. Next to him Gregory sat quiet. Next to him was Perez, the Latino, tiny. Next to him was Addison, with the scarred face. Then Kowalski, taller than the others.

Reacher glanced at Kate Lane's picture next to the phone and went a little cold. She was closer to dead now than at any point in the last three days, and he knew it. He guessed they all knew it.

"Time," Burke said. "I'm going."

"I'll carry the bag for you," Reacher said.

They rode down in the elevator. The black BMW was waiting at the curb. Burke opened the rear door.

"Stick the bag on the backseat," he said. "Easier for me that way, for a seat-to-seat transfer."

"I'm coming with you," Reacher said.

"That's stupid, man."

"I'll be on the floor in back. It'll be safe enough."

"What's the point?"

"You know as well as I do there's not going to be any cute little Checkpoint Charlie scene in this story. She's not going to come toward us through the mist, smiling bravely, with Jade holding her hand. So we're going to have to get proactive."

"What are you planning to do?"

"After you've switched the bag, I'll get out around the next corner. I'll double back and see what I can see."

"Lane will kill me."

"He doesn't have to know about it. I'll say I went for a walk."

"Lane will kill you if you screw it up."

"I'll kill myself if I screw it up."

Burke paused. "Get in," he said.

Burke stuck Lane's cell phone in a cradle on the BMW's dash, and Reacher crawled into the rear foot well on his hands and knees.

Burke started up and waited for a hole in the traffic and then U-turned and headed south on Central Park West. Reacher squirmed around until the transmission tunnel was wedged above his hips and below his ribs. "Don't hit any big bumps," he said.

"We're not supposed to talk," Burke said. "You see this?"

Reacher struggled upright and saw Burke pointing at a small black bud on the driver's-side window molding, up near the visor.

"Microphone," Burke said. "For the cell. Real sensitive."

"Will I hear them? On a speaker?"

"On ten speakers," Burke said. "The phone is wired through the audio system."

Reacher lay down, and Burke drove on, slowly. Then he made a tight right turn.

"Where are we now?" Reacher asked.

"Fifty-seventh Street," Burke said. "Traffic is murder. I'm going to get on the West Side Highway and head south. My guess is they'll want us downtown somewhere. Street parking for the Jaguar would be impossible anyplace else now."

Reacher felt the car stop and start, stop and start. Above him the money bag rolled one way and then the other.

"What were you?" Reacher asked. "Back in the day?"

"Delta," Burke said.

"How would you have done the thing outside Bloomingdale's?"

"Quick and dirty inside the car. As soon as Taylor stopped."

"That's what Groom said."

"Groom's a smart guy, for a jarhead. You disagree?"

"No. But why would you have been at Bloomingdale's at all?"

"It's Mrs. Lane's favorite store. She gets all her stuff there."

"But who would have known that?"

Burke was quiet. "That's a very good question," he said.

Then the phone rang.

"Shut up now," Burke said and hit a button on the cell.

"Hello?" he said.

"Good evening," a voice said back.

The voice was so heavily processed that there would be no chance of recognizing it again without the electronic machine. Over the BMW's ten speakers it sounded huge and alien. Gigantic. Like a direct connection to a nightmare.

"Who am I speaking with?" it asked. "I want your name."

Burke said, "My name is Burke."

The voice asked, "Who's that in the car with you?"

"There's nobody in the car with me," Burke said.

After a second the voice calmly asked, "Where are you now?"

"Fifty-seventh Street," Burke said. "I'm heading west. I'm about to get on the West Side Highway."

"Take the highway. Go south."

"Give me time," Burke said. "Traffic is real bad."

"Stay on the line," the voice said.

The sound of distorted breathing filled the car. It was slow and deep. Unworried, Reacher thought. He felt the car sprint and hook left. Onto the highway through a yellow light, he thought. Take care, Burke. A traffic stop could be real awkward tonight.

"I'm at Forty-second Street now," Burke said.

"Keep going," the voice said. "Just keep on driving."

American, Reacher thought. For sure.

"I'm at the Javits Center now," Burke said.

"Just keep going," the voice said back.

Young, Reacher thought. Or at least not old. Not a big guy. There was a lightness.

"Coming up on Twenty-fourth Street," Burke said.

"Keep going."

Reacher thought, We're going back to Greenwich Village.

The voice asked, "Where are you now?"

"Perry Street," Burke said.

"Keep going. But stand by now."

Reacher thought, Stand by now? That's a military term.

"Morton Street," Burke said.

"Left turn in three blocks," the voice said.

Reacher felt the car slow. It stopped. It waited and inched forward. Then it sprinted to catch the light. Reacher rolled heavily against the rear seat.

"Sixth Avenue next," Burke said.

The voice said, "Take it."

Burke turned left.

The voice said, "Get in the right-hand lane. Now."

The car jumped right. And slowed.

The voice said, "You'll see your target on the right. The green Jaguar. From the first morning. Halfway up the block."

Reacher thought: The same place? It's on the same fireplug?

The voice said, "Stop and make the transfer."

Reacher felt the transmission slam into park, and he heard the click of the hazard lights start up. Then Burke's door opened. Ten seconds later the door next to Reacher's head opened. Burke leaned in and grabbed the bag. Then the door shut. Reacher heard the Jaguar's door open. Then he heard it shut again. He heard a faint hydraulic thunk from somewhere outside. Ten seconds after that Burke was back in his seat.

"The transfer is done," he said. "The money is in the Jaguar."

The nightmare voice said, "Good-bye." The phone clicked off.

"Go now," Reacher said. "Turn right on Bleecker."

Burke took off. Accelerated for twenty yards and then jammed on the brakes hard. Reacher found the door handle and scrambled out. Then he hustled back to the corner.

REACHER stopped while he was still on Bleecker and jammed his hands in his pockets and then restarted at a more appropriate pace. He turned left onto Sixth like a man walking home. Just blending in, which he was surprisingly good at, given that he was always a head taller than anyone else. He looked straight ahead and put the green Jaguar firmly in his peripheral vision. Checked left. Nothing. Checked right, over the Jaguar's roof.

And saw a guy six feet from the driver's door.

It was the same guy he had seen the very first night. Same stature, same movements, same clothes. White, a little sunburned, lean, chiseled, clean-shaven, jaw clamped, not smiling, maybe forty years old. Calm, focused, intent. Fluid, economical movements. The guy pulled the door and slid into the seat and started the engine and took a glance over his shoulder at the traffic. Then he pulled out neatly and took off north. The guy flashed past, out of sight.

Reacher glanced south. There were no cabs coming. So he turned again and jogged back to the corner of Bleecker to see if Burke had waited for him. But Burke hadn't. So Reacher set out walking. He was too frustrated to take the subway. He needed to walk it off.

Twenty minutes and twenty blocks later he saw a Staples store on the opposite sidewalk. Windows full of office supply bargains. He crossed over. He didn't know which branch Carter Groom had taken Kate Lane to, but he figured chains carried the same stuff everywhere. He went inside and passed a corral where shopping carts were racked together. Beyond that on the left were the check-out registers. On the right was a print shop full of industrial-strength photocopiers. In front of him were about twenty narrow aisles with shelves that reached the ceiling. They were piled high with an intimidating array of stuff. He had absolutely no idea at all what Kate Lane might have been looking for.

He stood in a daze and watched a photocopier at work. Then he pushed past a line of people at the checkout counter and headed for the street.

Another twenty minutes and twenty blocks later he was at Bryant Park, eating a hot dog from a street vendor. Twenty minutes and twenty blocks after that he was in Central Park, drinking a bottle of water from another vendor. Twelve more blocks north he was still in the park, directly opposite the Dakota, under a tree, stopped dead, face-to-face with Anne Lane, Edward Lane's first wife.

THE first thing Anne Lane did was tell Reacher he was wrong.

"You saw Lane's photograph of her," she said.

He nodded.

"We were very alike," she said.

He nodded again.

"Anne was my sister," she said.

"I'm sorry," Reacher said. "I'm sorry for staring. And I'm sorry for your loss."

"Thank you," the woman said.

"Were you twins?"

"I'm six years younger. Which means right now I'm the same age as Anne was, in that photograph."

"You look exactly like her."

"I try to," the woman said. "It feels like I'm keeping her alive. Because I couldn't, back when it mattered."

"How could you have kept her alive?"

"We should talk," the woman said. "My name is Patti Joseph."

"Jack Reacher."

"Come with me," the woman said. "We have to double back. We can't go too near the Dakota."

She led him south through the park, to Sixty-sixth Street. Across to the far sidewalk. Then north again, and finally into the lobby of a building at 115 Central Park West.

"Welcome to the Majestic," Patti Joseph said.

The apartment was on the seventh floor. Its living room window looked out over Seventy-second Street, directly at the Dakota's entrance. There was a dining chair placed in front of the sill. On the sill was a notebook. And a pen. And a Nikon camera with a long lens, and a pair of Leica 10x42 binoculars.

"Do you work for Lane?" Patti asked.

"No, I don't."

"Did you know Lane in the service?"

"No, I didn't."

Patti Joseph smiled.

"I thought not," she said. "Otherwise you wouldn't be there. I told Brewer, you're not one of them."

"Who is Brewer?"

"NYPD." She pointed at the notebook. "I do all this for him."

"You're watching Lane and his guys? For the cops?"

"For myself, mostly. But I check in."

"Why?"

"Because hope springs eternal."

"Hope of what?"

"That he'll slip up, and I'll get something on him."

Reacher glanced at the notebook. The last entry read: *2014 hrs. Burke returns alone, no bag, in black BMW OSC 23.*

"You know Burke by name?"

"Burke was around when Anne was there."

"Why are you showing me all this?" Reacher asked.

"A recent decision," she said. "I decided to watch for new guys and waylay them and warn them. About what Lane did."

"What did he do?"

"I'll make coffee," Patti said.

She ducked into a small kitchen and started fiddling with a machine. Pretty soon Reacher could smell coffee. He figured he could stay for a cup.

Patti called out, "No cream, no sugar, right?"

"I need you to get to the point," Reacher said.

"Okay," Patti Joseph said. "Anne wasn't kidnapped five years ago. That was just a cover story. Lane murdered her."

Patti Joseph brought Reacher black coffee in a huge white Wedgwood mug and sat on the chair at the window.

"Edward Lane is a cold man," she said. "He demands loyalty and respect and obedience. He *needs* those things, like a junkie needs a fix. That's what this whole mercenary venture is about, really. He needs to give orders and have them obeyed. Like you or I need to breathe. He's borderline mentally ill, I think. Psychotic."

"And?" Reacher said.

"He ignores his stepdaughter. Have you noticed that?"

Reacher said nothing. He didn't mention Jade had been taken until later, he thought. He had her cropped out of the picture in the living room.

"My sister Anne wasn't very obedient," Patti said. "Nothing unreasonable. But Edward Lane ran the marriage like a military operation. Anne couldn't handle it. And the more she chafed, the more Lane demanded discipline. It became his fetish."

"What was she before?"

"A model. Just like the next one."

"What happened?"

"Between them they drove the marriage on the rocks. One day she told me she wanted a divorce. I was all in favor of that. But she tried to do the whole thing. Alimony, division of assets. I told her just to get out. But she had brought money to the relationship. Lane had used it for part of his initial stake. Lane couldn't handle his wife wanting out of the marriage. To be made to give her money as well was out of the question. And it would have been a public humiliation, because he would have had to go out and find another investor. So he faked a kidnapping and had her killed."

"The police were involved," Reacher said. "The FBI, too."

Patti smiled, sadly. "He made it seem very real."

"How?"

"His men. He employs a bunch of killers. They're all used to obeying orders. And they aren't virgins. Probably every single one of them has killed before, up close and personal."

Reacher nodded. No question about it. Every one of them has. Many times.

"You got any particular suspects in mind?" he asked.

Patti said, "Nobody who's still in the A-team. But I don't think he would have used B-teamers."

"So who?"

"A-team guys who aren't around anymore. There were two. A guy called Hobart and a guy called Knight. Shortly after Anne died there was an operation overseas. Those two men didn't come back."

"That would be a coincidence," Reacher said.

"I think Lane made sure they didn't come back."

Reacher said nothing.

"I know," Patti said. "The little sister is crazy, right?"

Reacher gazed at her. She didn't look crazy. She had long blond hair, straight, just the same as Anne in the photograph. Big blue eyes, a button nose, a dusting of freckles, pale skin.

"How do you think it went down?" he asked.

"Knight drove Anne that day," Patti said. "He took her shopping. Waited. But she never came out of the store. Next thing anyone knew was a phone call four hours later. The usual. No cops, a ransom demand."

"How much was the ransom?"

"A hundred grand."

"But Lane did call the cops."

Patti nodded. "It was like he wanted independent witnesses. Very important to retain his credibility with the other guys that weren't in on the scheme."

"Then what?"

"The FBI tapped the phones and moved in on the ransom drop. Lane's story is that they were seen. But the whole thing was phony. Nobody showed up. It was all a performance. Lane acted it all out and came home and gave the word that the cops had bought the story, that the FBI was convinced, and then Anne was killed."

"Where was the other guy during all of this? Hobart?"

"He was off duty. He said he was in Philadelphia. But obviously he had been in the store, waiting for Anne to show."

"Did you go to the cops at the time?"

"They ignored me," Patti said. "This was not long after the Twin Towers. Everyone was preoccupied."

"What about this cop Brewer? Now?"

"He tolerates me. I'm a taxpayer."

"You got any evidence against Lane at all?"

"No," Patti said. "None at all. All I've got is context and intuition. That's all I can share."

"Context?"

"Do you know what a private military corporation is really for?"

"Fundamentally its purpose is to allow the Pentagon to escape congressional oversight."

"Exactly," Patti said. "They're there to break the rules. Nobody can call them on it. The government is insulated."

"Does Lane know you're here?"

She shook her head. "I'm very careful."

"What do you want me to do?"

"I want you to just walk away from him. For your own sake. Don't dirty your hands with his business."

Silence for a moment.

"I'll be careful," Reacher said. "I always am. But I'll walk away on my own schedule."

Patti Joseph said nothing.

"I'd like to meet with this guy Brewer," Reacher said. "Because he'll have checked with the original detectives and the FBI agents. He might have a clearer picture."

"He usually comes over after I phone in a report. He drops by, at the end of his shift."

"When does his shift end?" Reacher asked.

"Midnight. I'm not involved with him or anything," Patti said. "He's lonely. I'm lonely. That's all."

Reacher said nothing.

"Check my window." Patti said. "If Brewer's here, the light will be on. If he isn't, it won't be."

4

REACHER let himself out. He walked clockwise around her block for caution's sake and came up on the Dakota from the west. It was a quarter to ten in the evening. A perfect late-summer night.

Reacher stepped inside the building. The lobby staff called up and let him go to the elevator. He found Gregory waiting for him.

"We thought you'd quit on us," Gregory said.

"Went for a walk," Reacher said. "Any news?"

"Too early."

Reacher followed him into the apartment. Edward Lane was in the armchair next to the phone. At the end of a sofa was an empty place. A dented cushion. Recently occupied by Gregory, Reacher guessed. Then came Burke. And Addison, and Perez, and Kowalski. Groom was leaning on the wall, facing the door.

"When will they call?" Lane asked.

Good question, Reacher thought. Or will you call them? And give them the okay to pull the triggers?

But he said: "They won't call before eight in the morning."

Lane glanced at his watch. "Ten hours from now."

"Yes," Reacher said.

"I did everything they asked," Lane said.

Nobody replied.

HALFWAY THROUGH THE second hour Lane looked at Reacher and said, "There's food in the kitchen, if you want some."

Reacher didn't want food. But he wanted to get out of the living room. "Thanks," he said.

He walked into the kitchen. There were dirty plates and open containers of Chinese food on the countertop. He glanced to his right at the open office door.

He listened. Nobody coming. He stepped inside the office. Desk, computer, fax, phones, file cabinets, shelves.

He started with the shelves.

There were phone books and manuals for firearms and a one-volume history of Argentina and mugs full of pens and pencils and an atlas of the world. There was a Rolodex full of five hundred index cards with names and phone numbers and MOS codes on them. *Military Occupational Specialties.* Reacher flipped to G and looked for Carter Groom. Not there. Then B for Burke. Not there either. So clearly this was the B-team candidate pool. Some names had KIA or MIA notations. *Killed in Action*, *Missing in Action*.

Reacher touched the computer mouse. The dialog box on the screen asked for a password. Reacher glanced at the open door and tried Kate. Access was denied. He tried *O5LaneE* for Colonel Edward Lane. Access denied. He gave it up.

He moved on to the file cabinets.

There were four of them. Two drawers in each. Unlabeled. Unlocked. He stood still and listened and then slid the first drawer open. It had twin hanging rails with six file dividers made of thin yellow cardboard slung between them. All six were full of paperwork. Financial records. He closed the drawer.

He opened the bottom drawer on the left. Same yellow dividers. But they were bulky with the kind of big plastic wallets that come in the glove boxes of new cars. Instruction books, warranty certificates, service records. BMW, Mercedes Benz, Jaguar, Land Rover. Some had valet keys. Some had spare keys and remote fobs. There were E-ZPass toll records. Receipts from gas stations.

Reacher closed the drawer. Glanced back at the door. Saw Burke standing there, silent, just watching him.

Burke didn't speak for a long moment. Then he said, "I'm going for a walk."

"Okay," Reacher said. "You want company?"

Burke just shrugged. Reacher followed him out through the kitchen. Through the foyer. Lane glanced at them from the living room, briefly, preoccupied with his thoughts. Reacher followed Burke out to the corridor. They rode down in the elevator in silence. Stepped out to the street and turned toward Central Park. Reacher looked up at Patti Joseph's window. It was dark. Therefore she was alone.

"That question you asked," Burke said.

"What question?" Reacher said.

"Who knew Mrs. Lane loved Bloomingdale's?"

"What about it?"

"I think there's inside involvement," Burke said. "Somebody tipped somebody off."

"Was it you?"

"No."

Reacher stopped at the crosswalk on Central Park West. Burke stopped beside him. He was as black as coal, a small man, about the size and shape of an old-fashioned major league second baseman.

The light changed. Reacher stepped off the curb.

"What happened after Anne?" he asked.

"With the guys who took her? No comment."

"Did they admit it?"

"No," Burke said.

The park loomed ahead of them, dark and empty.

"Where are we going?" Reacher asked.

"Doesn't matter," Burke said. "I just wanted to talk."

"Who do you think it was?" Reacher asked.

"I have no idea," Burke said, turning south.

"But who got tipped off?" Reacher asked. "Not who did the tipping. That would be the more important answer. And I think that's what you want to tell me."

Burke walked on in silence.

"You going to make me play Twenty Questions?"

"That might be the best way to do it," Burke said.

"You think this is about the money?"

"No," Burke said. "Half the equation at best."

"The other half of the equation being punishment?"

"You got it."

"There's someone out there with a grudge against Lane?"

"Yes. More than one person."

"Two?"

"Yes."

"What kind of a grudge?"

"What's the worst thing one man can do to another?"

"Depends who you are," Reacher said.

"Exactly," Burke said. "So who are we?"

Reacher thought. "Special Forces soldiers," he said.

"Exactly," Burke said again. "So what don't we do?"

"You don't leave bodies behind on the battlefield."

Burke said nothing.

"But Lane did. He left two bodies behind."

Burke stopped on the north curve of Columbus Circle.

"So what are you saying?" Reacher asked. "Someone's come out of the woodwork looking for revenge? On their behalf?"

Burke didn't answer. Reacher stared at him.

"You left two guys behind alive?"

"Not me," Burke said. "Not us. It was Lane."

"Hobart and Knight," Reacher said.

"You know their names. How? There's nothing about them in those file cabinets. Or in the computer. It's like they never existed."

"What happened with them?"

"They were wounded. According to Lane. We never saw them. He said we couldn't bring them in. He flat ordered us to pull out."

"And what do you suppose happened to them?"

"We assumed they'd be taken prisoner. In which case we assumed their life expectancy would be about a minute and a half."

"Where was this?" Reacher asked.

"I can't tell you," Burke said. "I'd go to jail."

"Why did you stick around afterward? All this time?"

"I obey orders. And I let officers decide things. That's how it always was, and that's how it always will be. That's a code."

"Does he know they're back? Lane?"

"You're not listening," Burke said. "Nobody *knows* they're back. Nobody even knows if they're alive. I'm just guessing, is all."

"Who would be talking to them? From the inside?"

"I don't know."

"What were they?"

"Jarheads."

"Like Carter Groom."

"Yes," Burke said. "Like Carter Groom."

Reacher said nothing.

"Marines hate that," Burke said. "Leaving guys behind."

"So why does he stick around?"

"Same reason I do. Ours is not to reason why."

"Maybe in the service," Reacher said. "Not necessarily in some half-assed private company."

"Watch your mouth, pal. I'm earning you a million bucks. You find Hobart and Knight, you find Kate and Jade, too."

"I don't need to watch my mouth," Reacher said. "If you've still got a code, then I'm still an officer. I can say what I like, and you can stand there and take it and salute."

Burke turned and headed back north. Reacher caught up and fell in beside him. Nothing more was said. Ten minutes later they turned into Seventy-second Street. Reacher glanced up. Patti Joseph's window was blazing with light.

REACHER said, "You go on ahead. I'm going to walk."

"Why?" Burke asked.

"No point looking for Hobart and Knight inside the apartment."

"That's for sure. They were erased."

"One more thing," Reacher said. "Do Lane and Kate get along?"

"They're still married," Burke said.

"What does that mean?"

"It means they get along."

"As well as Lane and Anne got along?"

Burke nodded. "About the same."

"I'll see you later," Reacher said.

Reacher watched Burke disappear inside the Dakota.

He doesn't trust me, Reacher thought.

A Delta noncom doesn't trust an MP.

Well, there's a big surprise.

THE doorman at the Majestic called upstairs. Three minutes later Reacher was shaking hands with Brewer, the cop. Patti Joseph said, "I'll leave you guys to talk. I'll go for a walk. Nighttime is about the only time it's safe for me to be out."

Then she left, with a nervous glance back, as if her future was at stake. Reacher watched the door close behind her and turned and took a better look at Brewer. He was everything anyone would expect a New York City detective to be, except magnified a little. A little taller, a little heavier, longer hair, more unkempt, more energetic. He was about fifty. Or forty-something and prematurely gray.

"What's your interest here?" he asked.

"Lane wants to hire me," Reacher said. "And I heard Patti's story. So I want to know what I'm getting into. That's all."

"What's your line of work?"

"I was in the army," Reacher said.

"It's a free country," Brewer said. "You can work for whoever you want." Then he sat on Patti Joseph's sofa like he owned it.

Reacher leaned on the wall. "I was a cop once myself," he said. "Military police."

"Is that supposed to impress me?"

"Plenty of your guys came from the same place as me."

Brewer shrugged. "I guess I can give you five minutes," he said.

"Bottom line," Reacher said. "What happened five years ago?"

"I can't tell you that. Nobody in the NYPD can tell you," Brewer said. "If it was a kidnap, that's FBI business, because kidnapping is a federal crime. If it was a straightforward homicide, then that's New Jersey business, because the body was found on the other side of the George Washington Bridge. Therefore it was never our case."

"So why are you here?"

"Community relations. The kid is hurting, and she needs an ear. Plus she's cute, and she makes good coffee."

"Your people must have gotten copied in on the paperwork."

Brewer nodded. "There's a file," he said. "The only thing anyone knows for sure is that Anne Lane died five years ago in New Jersey. She was a month decomposed when they found her. But there was a definitive dental identification. It was her."

"Cause of death?"

"Fatal gunshot wound to the back of her head. Large-caliber handgun, probably a nine, probably jacketed."

"Anything else at the scene?"

"There was a playing card. The three of clubs. Shoved down the neck of her shirt, from the back. Nobody knew what it meant."

"So what do you think?" Reacher said. "Kidnap or murder?"

Brewer yawned. "You hear hoofbeats, you look for horses, not zebras. A guy calls in that his wife has been kidnapped, you assume it's true. And there were real phone calls, there was real money."

"But?"

Brewer went quiet for a moment. Took a long pull on his coffee.

"Patti kinds of sucks you in," he said. "Sooner or later you have to admit it's just as plausible the other way around."

"Gut feeling?"

"I just don't know," Brewer said. "Which is a weird feeling for me. I mean, sometimes I'm wrong, but I always know."

"So what are you doing about it?"

"Nothing," Brewer said. "It's an ice-cold case outside of our jurisdiction."

Silence for a moment.

"One thing Patti told me," Brewer said. "She hasn't seen the new Mrs. Lane for a couple of days. Or the kid."

Reacher said nothing.

Brewer said, "Maybe she's missing, and you're looking for parallels in the past."

Reacher stayed quiet.

Brewer said, "You were a cop, not a combat soldier. So I'm wondering what Lane would want to hire you for."

More silence. A long hard look, cop to cop.

"So what do you do with the stuff she calls in?"

"I pass it on," Brewer said. "To someone with an interest."

"Who?"

"A private detective. A woman. She's cute, too. Older."

"NYPD is working with private detectives now?"

"She's retired FBI. The lead agent on the Anne Lane case."

"What's this woman's name?"

"I thought you'd never ask," Brewer said.

REACHER left Patti Joseph's apartment with two business cards. One was Brewer's and the other was an elegant item with *Lauren Pauling* engraved at the top and *Private Investigator* under the name. Then: *Ex-Special Agent, Federal Bureau of Investigation*. At the bottom was a downtown address, with phone numbers for landline and cell, and e-mail. It was a busy card.

Reacher tossed Brewer's card in a trash can and put Lauren Pauling's in his shoe. Then he took a circuitous route back toward the Dakota. It was close to one o'clock in the morning. He saw a cop car on Columbus Avenue. Cops, he thought. The word hung up in his mind as it had in SoHo. But it spun away again. He turned into the Dakota's lobby. The night doorman called upstairs. On five Gregory was out in the corridor. Reacher followed him inside, and Gregory said, "Nothing yet. But we've got seven more hours."

Everyone was still in the living room. The lights were low and yellow, and the drapes were drawn, and the air was hot.

"Wait with us," Lane said.

"I need to sleep," Reacher said. "Three or four hours."

"Use Jade's room," Lane said.

Reacher nodded and headed off to Jade's room. The bed was way too small for a guy Reacher's size.

He took the pillow and the sheet and the comforter off the bed and made himself a bivouac on the floor. He cleared bears and dolls out of his way. The bears were all plush and new, and the dolls looked untouched. He moved the desk to make room, and all the papers fell off it. Drawings, in crayon on cheap paper. Trees, like bright green lollipops on brown sticks, with a big gray building beyond. The Dakota, maybe. There was another of three stick figures, one much smaller than the others. The family, maybe. Mother, daughter, stepfather. Mother and daughter were smiling, but Lane was drawn with black holes in his mouth like someone had punched half his teeth out. There was a picture of an airplane low in the sky. The plane's fuselage had three portholes with faces in them. The last picture was of the family again, but twice over. Two Lanes, two Kates, two Jades.

Reacher restacked the papers neatly. He set the alarm in his head for five a.m. He closed his eyes, breathed once, and fell asleep.

REACHER woke as planned at five o'clock, still tired. He found Carter Groom in the kitchen, next to a big Krups drip machine.

"Three hours to go," Groom said.

Then Burke came in. He didn't say anything. He acted like the previous evening had never existed. Groom filled three mugs with coffee. Took one, and left the room. Burke took one and followed him. Reacher drank his sitting on the counter.

Time for ex–Special Agent Lauren Pauling's wake-up call.

He stopped in the living room on his way out. Lane was still in the same chair. Real or phony, it was one hell of a display of endurance. Gregory and Perez and Kowalski were asleep on sofas. Addison was awake. Groom and Burke were drinking their coffee.

"I'm going out," Reacher said. "Breakfast."

Reacher turned right on Seventy-second and headed for Broadway. Nobody came after him. He found a pay phone and dialed Pauling's cell.

She answered on the third ring. "Hello?" she said.

Rusty voice, not sleepy, just not yet used today.

Reacher asked, "You heard the name Reacher recently?"

"Should I have?" Pauling asked back.

"It will save us a lot of time if you just say yes. From Anne Lane's sister Patti, through a cop called Brewer."

"Yes," Pauling said. "Late yesterday."

"I need an early appointment," Reacher said.

"You're Reacher?"

"Yes, I am. Half an hour, at your office?"

"You know where it is?"

"Brewer gave me your card."

"Half an hour," Pauling said.

And so half an hour later Reacher was standing on West Fourth Street, with a cup of coffee in one hand and a doughnut in the other, watching Lauren Pauling walk toward him.

PAULING was an elegant woman of about fifty. Brewer had said she was cute, and he had been right. She was about an inch taller than average, dressed in a black pencil skirt. Black stockings, black shoes with heels. An emerald green blouse that could have been silk. A rope of big fake pearls at her neck. Hair frosted gold and blond. It fell in big waves to her shoulders. Green eyes that smiled.

"Jack Reacher, I presume," she said.

Reacher shoved his doughnut between his teeth and wiped his fingers on his chinos and shook her hand. Then he waited as she unlocked her street door. Watched as she deactivated an alarm with a keypad in the lobby. The keypad was a standard three-by-three cluster with the zero alone at the bottom. She was right-handed. She used her middle finger, index finger, ring finger, index finger, without moving her hand much. Probably 8461, Reacher thought.

Reacher followed her up to the second floor. He finished his doughnut on the way. She unlocked the door to a two-room suite. Waiting room first, and then a back room for her desk and two visitor chairs. Very compact, but the décor was good.

"I spoke to Brewer," she said. "I called him at home after you called me. He's curious about your motives."

Lauren Pauling's voice was low and husky. Reacher could have sat and listened to it all day.

Reacher sat down. She squeezed around the end of her desk. She was slender, and she moved well. She sat down.

"Brewer said you were a military cop."

"Once upon a time."

"Then you know you shouldn't be talking to me," she said.

"Why not?"

"Because I'm not a reliable witness. I'm hopelessly biased."

"Why?"

"Think about it," she said. "If Edward Lane didn't kill his wife, who did? Well, I did, that's who. Through my own carelessness."

Reacher said, "Nobody scores a hundred percent. Not in the real world. So get over it."

"That's your response?" Pauling said.

"I probably got more people killed than you ever met. I don't beat myself up over them."

Pauling nodded. "It's the sister. She's up there in that weird little aerie all the time. She's like my conscience."

"Tell me about the three of clubs," Reacher said.

Pauling paused, like a gear change.

"We concluded it was meaningless," she said. "There had been a book or a movie or something where assassins left calling cards. So we tended to get a lot of that at the time. But there was nothing in the databases about threes. Not much about clubs, either. We had people with brains the size of planets working on it. Nothing. So the three of clubs was designed to make us chase our tails."

"Did you look at Lane back then?"

Pauling nodded. "We looked at him carefully, and all his guys. Like, who knew he had money? Who even knew he had a wife?"

"And?"

"He's not a very pleasant man. He's borderline mentally ill. He has a psychotic need to command."

"Patti Joseph says the same things."

"She's right."

"His men are a couple of sandwiches short of a picnic, too," Reacher said. "They've got a psychotic need to be commanded."

"They're a weird bunch. All Special Forces and black ops, so naturally the Pentagon wasn't very forthcoming. But we noticed that there were far fewer medals among them than you would expect. And most of them got general discharges. Not honorable discharges. Including Lane himself."

Reacher nodded. "It kind of explains why they're sticking with Lane. Where else are they going to get twenty-five grand a month with their records?"

"Is that what they get? Is that what Lane offered you?"

Reacher said nothing.

"What's on your mind?"

Reacher shrugged. "Brewer said something to me. He said he just didn't know, which was weird for him, he said, because whereas he was sometimes wrong, he always knew. And I'm exactly the same. I always know. Except this time I don't know. So what's on my mind right now is that I have nothing on my mind."

"I think it was a genuine kidnap," Pauling said. "I think I blew it. God knows I *want* Lane to have done it. And maybe he did. But I have to acknowledge that's mostly wishful thinking, to excuse myself. And usually the simple option is the right option anyway. So it was a simple kidnap, not an elaborate charade. And I blew it."

"How did you blow it?"

"I don't know."

"So maybe it was an elaborate charade."

"What's on your mind, Reacher?"

He looked at her. "Whatever it was, it's happening again."

Lauren Pauling sat forward in her chair and said, "Tell me." So Reacher told her everything, from the first double espresso in its foam cup to the nightmare electronic voice guiding the black BMW back to the exact same fireplug.

"If that's a charade it's unbelievably elaborate," Pauling said.

"My feeling exactly," Reacher said.

"Were they getting along? Man and wife?"

"Nobody says otherwise."

"So it's real."

Reacher nodded. "There's an internal consistency to it. The initial takedown must have depended on an inside tip, as to where Kate and Jade were going to be, and when. And they know exactly what cars he's got."

"And what else?"

"Something about cops. I asked Lane to repeat what was said during the first phone call. And he did. And the bad guys never said no cops. Which suggests these people knew the story from five years ago. They knew Lane wouldn't go to the cops anyway."

"That would suggest that five years ago was for real."

"Not necessarily. It might only reflect what Lane put out there for public consumption. But there's one thing I can't make fit under any scenario. Which is the initial takedown itself. The only viable method would have been quick and dirty inside the car, as soon as it stopped. Everyone agrees on that. And the problem is, Bloomingdale's is a whole block long. How could anyone have predicted exactly what yard of Lexington Avenue Taylor's Jaguar was going to stop on? And if they didn't predict it exactly right, then the whole thing would have fallen apart immediately."

"So what are you saying?"

"I'm saying there's something wrong with this whole thing. I can't get a handle on what happened. I can't get traction. I'm saying for the first time in my life I just don't know."

"So what are you going to do?"

"I'm going to have to do it the hard way," Reacher said.

"What way is that?"

"It's what we called it in the service when we didn't catch a break. When we actually had to work for a living. You know, start at square one, re-examine everything, sweat the details, work the clues."

"Can I help?"

"I need to know about two guys called Hobart and Knight."

Pauling nodded. "Knight was the driver the day Anne was taken, and Hobart was in Philadelphia. They died overseas."

"Maybe they didn't die. They were abandoned wounded but alive. I need to know what's likely to have happened to them."

"You think they're alive? You think they're back?"

"I don't know what to think. But at least one of Lane's guys wasn't sleeping too well last night."

"I met Hobart and Knight, you know. Five years ago."

"Did either of them look like the guy I saw?"

"Medium-sized and ordinary-looking? Both of them, exactly."

"That helps."

"What are you going to do now?"

"I'm going back to the Dakota. Maybe we'll get a call and this whole thing will be over. But more likely we won't."

"Give me three hours," Pauling said. "Then call my cell."

5

BY THE time Reacher got back to the Dakota it was seven o'clock, and dawn had given way to full morning. The sky was a pale hard blue. Inside the apartment Reacher didn't need to ask whether the phone had rung. Clearly it hadn't. The tableau was the same as it had been nine hours earlier. Lane upright in his chair. Then Gregory, Groom, Burke, Perez, Addison, Kowalski, all silent.

Lane turned his head slowly and looked straight at Reacher and asked, "Where have you been?"

"Breakfast," Reacher said.

"I pay you to work. I don't pay you to be out stuffing your face."

"You don't pay me at all," Reacher said.

"Is *that* your problem?" Lane asked. "Money?" He kept his body facing forward and his head turned ninety degrees to the side. Like a querulous sea bird. His eyes were dark and wet and glittering.

Reacher said nothing.

"That's easily solved," Lane said. He levered himself upright, with an effort, like it was the first time he had moved in nine hours.

"Come," he said. Reacher followed him to the master bedroom. Lane opened his closet. Inside was a another door. To the left of the door was a security keypad. It was the same type of three-by-three-plus-zero matrix as Lauren Pauling had used at her office. Lane used his left hand. Index finger. Ring finger. Middle finger. Middle finger. Probably 3785, Reacher thought. The keypad beeped and Lane opened the inner door. Reached inside and pulled a chain. A light came on and showed a chamber maybe six feet by three. It was stacked with cube-shaped bales wrapped tight in heavy plastic.

The printing was French, and it said *Banque Centrale*. Central Bank. Money.

U.S. dollars, bricked and banded and wrapped. Some cubes were neat and intact. One was torn open and spilling bricks.

Lane dragged the open bale out into the bedroom. Two slim bricks of cash fell out.

"Pick it up," Lane said. "It's yours."

Reacher stood still.

Lane picked up a spilled brick. "Take it."

Reacher said, "We'll talk about a fee if I get a result."

"*Take it!*" Lane screamed. Then he hurled the brick straight at Reacher's chest. It bounced off and hit the floor. Then he bent down and plunged his hands into the plastic. He threw bricks wildly. They hit Reacher in the legs, in the stomach, in the chest, in the head. Wild random salvos, ten thousand dollars at a time. There were tears streaming down Lane's face, and he was screaming uncontrollably: "*Take it! Take it!*" Then: "*Get her back!*" Then: "*Please! Please!*" There was rage and pain and hurt and fear and anger and loss in every desperate yelp.

Reacher stood there, hundreds of thousands of dollars at his feet, and he thought: Nobody's that good of an actor. This time it's real.

REACHER waited in the inner hallway and listened to Lane calm down. He heard the quiet crackle of plastic as the bale of cash was reassembled. He heard Lane drag the bale back into the inner closet. He heard the door close, and he heard the keypad beep to confirm it was locked. Then he walked back to the living room. Lane followed a minute later and sat down in his chair, like nothing at all had happened, and stared at the silent phone.

It rang just before seven forty-five. Lane snatched it out of the cradle and said "Yes?" Then his face went blank. Wrong caller. He listened for ten seconds more and hung up.

"Who was it?" Gregory asked.

"Just a friend," Lane said. "Cops found a body in the Hudson River this morning. A floater. At the Seventy-ninth Street boat basin. Unidentified white male, maybe forty years old. Shot once."

"Taylor?"

"Has to be," Lane said.

Gregory asked: "So what do we do?"

"Now?" Lane said. "Nothing. We wait for the right phone call."

It never came. By a quarter to ten in the morning all the resolve had leaked out of Lane's body. He sank into the chair cushion and laid his head back and stared up at the ceiling.

"It's over," he said. "She's gone. Isn't she?"

Nobody answered. The room was totally silent.

At ten o'clock Lane raised his head off the back of the chair and said, "Okay." Then he said, "Now we move on. We seek and destroy. Justice will be done. Our kind of justice."

Nobody spoke.

"For Kate," Lane said. "And for Taylor."

Then he sat forward, newly energized. He turned to face Reacher directly. "Almost the first thing you ever said in this room was that these guys of mine could start a war against them, but first we had to find them. Do you remember that?"

Reacher nodded.

"So find them," Lane said.

REACHER detoured via the master bedroom and picked up the framed photograph from the desk. The inferior print. The one with Jade in it. He held it carefully. Looked at it, long and hard. For you, he thought. For both of you. Not for him. Then he put the photograph back and walked quietly out of the apartment.

He started at the same pay phone he had used before. Took the card out of his shoe and dialed Lauren Pauling's cell. Said, "It's real this time, and they're not coming back."

She said, "Can you be at the United Nations in half an hour?"

REACHER saw Lauren Pauling waiting for him on the First Avenue sidewalk. She had a printed scarf around her shoulders. She looked good. He started toward her, and they met in the middle.

"I called in a favor," she said. "We're meeting with an army officer who liaises with one of the UN committees."

"On what subject?"

"Mercenaries," Pauling said. "We're supposed to be against them. We signed all kinds of treaties."

"The Pentagon loves mercenaries."

"But it likes them to go where it sends them. It doesn't like them to fill their down time with unauthorized sideshows."

"Is that where they lost Knight and Hobart? A sideshow?"

"Somewhere in Africa," Pauling said.

"Does this guy have the details?"

"Some of them. He's reasonably senior, but he's new. He's not going to tell you his name."

"Okay."

Her cell phone chimed. She listened and looked around.

"We have to go to a coffee shop on Second Avenue," she said. "He'll follow."

The coffee shop was one of those mostly brown places that survive on equal parts counter trade, booth trade, and to-go coffee in cardboard cups. Pauling led Reacher to a booth in back and sat so she could watch the door. Reacher slid in next to her. He never sat any other way than with his back to a wall. Long habit, even in a place with plenty of mirrors, which the coffee shop had. Pauling waved to the waitress and mouthed *coffee* and held up three fingers. The waitress came over and dumped three heavy brown mugs on the table and filled them from a Bunn flask.

Reacher took a sip. Hot, strong, and generic.

He made the Pentagon guy before he was even in through the door. Dull. Not old, not young, corn-colored buzz cut, cheap blue wool suit, white button-down shirt, striped tie, shoes polished to a mirror shine. A different kind of uniform.

The guy paused inside the door and looked around. Not looking for us, Reacher thought. Looking for anyone else who knows him. If he sees somebody, he'll fake a phone call and leave.

But the guy evidently saw nothing to worry about. He walked on back and slid in opposite Pauling and Reacher, and after a brief glance at each of their faces he centered his gaze between their heads and kept his eyes on the mirror. Up close, Reacher saw that he was wearing a black subdued-order crossed-pistols lapel pin.

"I don't have much for you," the guy said. "Private-enterprise Americans fighting overseas are rightly considered to be very bad news, especially in Africa. So this stuff is very need-to-know, and it was before my time, so I don't know very much about it."

"Where was it?" Reacher asked.

"I'm not even sure of that. Burkina Faso or Mali. It was the usual deal. Civil war. A scared government, a bunch of rebels ready to come out of the jungle. An unreliable military. So the government buys what protection it can on the international market."

"Does one of those countries speak French?"

"As their official language? Both of them. Why?"

"I saw some of the money. In plastic wrap printed in French. Banque Centrale.

"U.S. dollars?"

Reacher nodded. "Lots of them."

The guy said, "The story that did the rounds was that Edward Lane took the money and ran. They were hopelessly outnumbered and strategically weak."

"But not everyone got out."

The guy nodded. "It seemed that way. But getting information out of those places is like trying to get a radio signal from the dark side of the moon. So usually we rely on the Red Cross or Doctors Without Borders. And eventually we got a solid report that two Americans had been captured. A year later we got names. It was Knight and Hobart."

"It surprises me that they stayed alive."

"The rebels won. Anyone who had worked for the old regime was suddenly in big trouble. And a couple of Americans were like trophies. So they were kept alive. But they suffered very cruelly. The Doctors Without Borders report was horrific."

"Anything about what happened in the end?"

"It's sketchy. One died in captivity, but the other one got out, according to the Red Cross. Some humanitarian gesture that they pushed for. End of story. But if you jump to the INS, you find a lone individual entering the U.S. from Africa shortly afterward on Red Cross documentation. And then if you jump to the Veterans Administration, there's a report of someone just back from Africa getting the kind of remedial outpatient care consistent with tropical diseases and some of the mutilations that Doctors Without Borders reported on."

Reacher asked, "Which one got out?"

"I don't know," the guy said.

"I need his name," Reacher said. "And his address, from the VA."

"That's a tall order," the guy said. "I would have to go way beyond my remit. And I would need a very good reason to do that."

"Look at me," Reacher said.

The guy took his eyes off the mirror and glanced at Reacher.

Reacher said, "Ten-sixty-two."

No reaction.

Reacher said, "So pony up, okay?"

The guy looked at the mirror again. Nothing in his face.

"I'll call Ms. Pauling's cell," the guy said. "When, I don't know. But I'll get what I can as soon as I can."

Then he slid out of the booth and walked straight to the door. Opened it and made a right turn and was lost to sight.

"What was that ten-sixty-two thing?" Pauling asked.

"He was wearing a military police lapel pin. MP is his day job. Ten-sixty-two is MP radio code for *fellow officer in trouble, requests urgent assistance.* So he'll help. He has to."

"Then maybe you won't have to do it all the hard way."

"Maybe. He seemed a little timid. Me, I'd have busted straight into somebody's file cabinet."

"Maybe that's why he's getting promoted and you didn't."

"A timid guy like that won't get promoted."

"He's already a brigadier general," Pauling said. "Actually."

"That guy?" Reacher stared at the door, as if it might have retained an afterimage. "He was kind of young, wasn't he?"

"No, you're kind of old," Pauling said. "But putting a general on it shows how seriously the U.S. is taking this mercenary stuff."

"Sure does."

Silence for a moment. The waitress came over and offered refills. Pauling declined, Reacher accepted. Said, "NYPD found a body in the river this morning. White male, about forty. Lane got a call."

"Taylor?"

"Almost certainly."

"So what next?"

"We work with what we've got," Reacher said. "We adopt the theory that Knight or Hobart came home with a grudge."

"How do we proceed?"

"With hard work," Reacher said. "I'm not going to hold my breath on getting anything from the Pentagon."

"Talk it through. Think out loud. What doesn't fit? What's out of place?"

"The initial takedown. That doesn't work at all."

"What else?"

"Everything."

"That's too big," Pauling said. "Start small. Name one thing that surprised you."

Reacher sipped his coffee and said, "I got out of the black BMW after Burke had switched the bag into the Jaguar, and I was surprised how fast the guy was in the driver's seat."

"So what does that mean?"

"That he was waiting right there on the street."

"But he wouldn't risk that. If he was Knight or Hobart, Burke would have recognized him in a heartbeat."

"Maybe he was in a doorway," Reacher said.

"Three times running? He used that same fireplug on three separate occasions. It would be hard to find appropriate cover each time."

Reacher thought: Appropriate cover.

Remembered thinking: It's right there on the same fireplug?

He put his coffee cup down, and then picked up Pauling's hand. Kissed it tenderly. Her fingers were cool and slim and fragrant.

"Thank you," he said. "Thank you very much."

"For what?"

"He used the same fireplug three times running. Why? What makes a person like one fireplug more than another?"

"What?"

"Nothing," Reacher said. "What this guy had was a vantage point that he liked. The vantage point came first, and the fireplug was merely the nearest one to it. He needed cover that was reliable and unobtrusive, late night, early morning, and rush hour. So wherever this guy was waiting, he was comfortable doing it."

"But does this help us?"

"You bet it does. It's the first link in the chain. It was a fixed, identifiable location. We need to get down to Sixth Avenue and figure out where it was. Someone might have seen him."

REACHER and Pauling caught a cab to Sixth Avenue and Houston Street. They got out on the southeast corner and turned north together into a warm breeze full of trash and grit.

"So show me the famous fireplug," Pauling said.

They walked until they came to it, right there in the middle of the block. Fat, short, squat. Pauling stood near the hydrant.

"Where would a military mind want to be?" she asked.

Reacher recited, "A soldier knows that a satisfactory observation point provides an unobstructed view to the front and adequate security to the flanks and the rear. He knows it provides protection from the elements and concealment of the observers. He knows it offers a reasonable likelihood of undisturbed occupation for the full duration of the operation."

"What would the duration be?"

"Say an hour maximum, each time."

"How did it work, the first two times?"

"He watched Gregory park, and then he followed him down to Spring Street."

"So he wasn't waiting inside the derelict building?"

"Not if he was working alone."

"But he still used the back door."

"On the second occasion, at least."

"Have we definitely decided he was working alone?"

"Only one of them came back alive."

"So where was his observation point?"

"West of here," Reacher said. "He wanted a full-on view."

"Across the street?"

Reacher nodded. "Middle of the block, or not too far north or south of it. Nothing too oblique."

"So set some limits."

"A maximum forty-five-degree arc. That's twenty-some degrees north to twenty-some degrees south. Maximum radius, about a hundred feet."

Pauling turned to face the curb. She spread her arms out straight and forty-five degrees apart and held her hands flat and upright like mimed karate chops. Scoped out the view. A total of five establishments to consider. The center three were possibilities. The one to the north and the one to the south were marginal. Reacher stood directly behind her and looked over her head. Her left hand was pointing at a flower store. Then came his new favorite café. Then came a picture framer. Then a wine store. Her right hand was pointing at a vitamin shop.

"A flower store would be no good," she said. "It wouldn't be open at eleven forty at night."

Reacher said nothing.

"The wine store was probably open," she said. "But it wouldn't have been at seven in the morning."

Reacher said, "Can't hang around in a flower store or a wine store for an hour at a time."

"Same with all of them," she said. "Except the café."

"The café would have been pretty risky. Three lengthy spells, someone would have remembered him."

"So maybe he was just out on the street."

"No protection from the elements and no concealment. Three times in a row. This part of town, he would have been afraid of getting busted for being a drug dealer. Or a terrorist."

"So where was he?"

Reacher looked left, looked right. Then he looked up.

"Patti Joseph's place," he said. "You called it an aerie."

"So?"

"Patti's place is reasonably high up. Seven prewar floors, that's above treetop height. An unobstructed view. A Recon Marine wants an unobstructed view. And he can't guarantee that at street level."

Lauren Pauling turned back to face the curb and spread her arms again, this time raised at an angle. They bracketed the upper floors of the same five buildings.

"Where did he come from, the first time?" she asked.

"From south of me," Reacher said. "But he was coming from Spring Street then. No way of knowing where he had started out."

"And the second time?"

"Actually it was very similar to the first time," he said. "North and east through the traffic. From the south of where I was sitting."

Pauling brought her right hand south. That cut the view to half of the building with the flower store in it, and most of the building with the café in it. Above the flower store were three stories of windows with blinds and printers and stacks of paper on their sills.

"Office suites," Pauling said.

Above the café were three stories of windows filled variously with faded drapes, or suspended discs of stained glass. One had nothing at all. One was papered over with newsprint.

"Apartments," Pauling said.

Between the flower store and the café was a blue recessed door. To its left was a silver box, with buttons and nameplates. Reacher said, "A person who came out that door heading for the fireplug would have to cross north and east through the traffic, right?"

Pauling said, "We found him."

THE silver box to the left of the blue door had six black call buttons in a vertical array. The top nameplate had Kublinski written very neatly in faded ink. The bottom had *Super* scrawled with a black marker pen. The middle four were blank.

"Low rent," Pauling said. "Short leases. Transients. Except for Mr. or Ms. Kublinski. Shall we try the super?"

"Use one of your business cards. Put your finger over the *Ex* part. Make out like you're still with the Bureau."

Pauling put an elegant nail on the super's call button and pressed. She was answered by a distorted burst of sound from the speaker.

"Federal agents," Pauling called. Which was remotely true. Both she and Reacher had once worked for Uncle Sam. There was another burst of noise from the speaker.

"He's coming," Reacher said.

The blue door opened inward and revealed a tall gaunt man in a stained T-shirt. He had a black knit cap on his head and a flat Slavic face like a length of two-by-four.

"Yes?" he said. Strong Russian accent.

Pauling waved her card long enough for some of the words to register. "Tell us about your most recent tenant," she said.

"Number five," the guy said. "One week ago. He responded to an advertisement."

"We need to see his apartment," Pauling said.

"I'm not sure I should let you," the guy said. "There are rules in America."

"Homeland Security," Reacher said. "The Patriot Act. There are no rules in America anymore."

The guy shrugged. Headed for the stairs. Reacher and Pauling followed him. Number five was on the third floor, looking east across the street. Pauling glanced at Reacher, and Reacher nodded.

"Is the guy in?" he asked.

The super shook his head. "I only ever saw him twice. He's out now for sure. I was just all over the building fixing pipes." He used a master key from a ring on his belt and unlocked the door.

The apartment was completely empty.

Except for a single upright dining chair. It was not old, but it was well used. It was the kind of thing you see for sale on Bowery sidewalks, where the bankrupt restaurant dealers hawk seized inventory. It was set in front of the window and turned slightly north and east.

Reacher stepped over and sat on the chair. The way his body settled put the fireplug across Sixth directly in front of him. He stood up again and turned a full circle. Saw a door that locked. Saw three solid walls. A soldier knows that a satisfactory observation point provides an unobstructed view to the front and adequate security to the flanks and the rear, provides protection from the elements and concealment of the observers, and offers a reasonable likelihood of undisturbed occupation for the full duration of the operation.

Reacher turned to the super and said, "Tell us about this guy."

"He can't talk," the super said.

"What, like he's a mute? Like something struck him dumb?"

"Not emotional," the super said. "Physical. He communicated by writing on a pad. He wrote that he had been injured in the service. And he kept his mouth tight shut. Like he was embarrassed about me seeing something. It reminded me very strongly of something I saw more than twenty years ago."

"Which was?"

"I am Russian. For my sins I served with the Red Army in

Afghanistan. Once we had a prisoner returned to us by the tribesmen as a warning. His tongue had been cut out."

The super took Reacher and Pauling down to his own apartment. He found the current lease papers for apartment five. They had been signed exactly a week previously by a guy calling himself Leroy Clarkson. Which, as expected, was a blatantly phony name. Clarkson and Leroy were the first two streets coming off the West Side Highway north of Houston, just a few blocks away.

"You don't see ID?" Pauling asked.

"Not unless they want to pay by check," the super said. "This guy paid cash."

The signature was illegible.

The super gave a decent physical description, but it did nothing more than match what Reacher himself had seen. Late thirties, maybe forty, white, medium height and weight, no facial hair. Blue jeans, blue shirt, ball cap, sneakers, all worn and comfortable.

"How long did he pay for?"

"A month. It's the minimum. Renewable."

"This guy's not coming back," Reacher said. "Go ahead and run your ad again."

Reacher and Pauling came out the blue door and took three paces north and stopped in for espresso.

Pauling said, "So he wasn't working alone. Because he couldn't have made the phone calls."

Reacher didn't reply.

Pauling said, "Tell me about the voice you heard."

"American," Reacher said. "Intelligent, in control, not worried. Familiar with the geography of New York City. Possibly military. He wanted to know Burke's name, which suggests he's familiar with Lane's crew. The distortion was huge. But I felt he wasn't old. There was a lightness there."

"Unworried and in command makes him sound like the prime mover here. Not like a sidekick."

Reacher nodded. "Good point."

"So who is he?"

"If your Pentagon guy hadn't told us different, I'd say it was both Hobart and Knight, working together."

"But it isn't," Pauling said. "My guy wouldn't get that wrong."

"So whichever one came back picked up a new partner."

"One that he trusts," Pauling said. "And he did it fast."

Reacher gazed over at the hydrant.

"Would a remote clicker work at this distance?" he asked.

"For a car?" Pauling said. "Maybe. Why?"

"After Burke switched the bag, I heard a sound like car doors locking. I guess the guy did it from up there in his room. He was watching. He didn't want to leave the money in an unlocked car for a second longer than he had to."

"Sensible."

"But you know what isn't sensible? Why was he up there and not the other guy? Why would the guy who can't talk rent the apartment? Anyone who comes into contact with him isn't going to forget him. And what's an observation point for? It's for command and control. But this guy couldn't even get on a cell phone."

"You can send written words by cell phone."

"Okay," Reacher said. "But I still don't see why they sent the guy who couldn't talk to meet with the building super."

"Neither do I," Pauling said.

Silence for a moment.

"What next?" Pauling asked.

"Hard work," Reacher said. "You up for it?"

"Are you hiring me?"

"No, you're volunteering. Because if we do this right, you'll find out what happened to Anne Lane. No more sleepless nights."

"Unless I find out five years ago was for real. Then I might never sleep again."

"Life's a gamble," Reacher said. "It wouldn't be fun otherwise."

"Okay," she said. "I'm volunteering."

Reacher said, "Go hassle our Soviet pal again. Get the chair. We'll walk it over to the Bowery and find out where it came from. Maybe the new buddy picked it out. Maybe someone will remember him."

REACHER CARRIED THE CHAIR, and he and Pauling walked east. South of Houston the Bowery had organized itself into a sequence of distinct retail areas. There were electrical supplies and used office gear and industrial kitchen equipment and restaurant-fixture outlets. Reacher liked the Bowery. It was his kind of street.

They started with the northernmost of six separate chaotic establishments. Less than a hundred yards of real estate, but if someone buys a used dining chair in Manhattan, chances are he buys it somewhere in that hundred yards.

In the first three stores they found no visual matches, and nobody admitted selling the chair that Reacher was carrying.

The fourth store was where they found what they wanted.

It was a double-wide place that had chrome diner furniture in front and a bunch of Chinese owners in back. Behind the gaudy padded stools in front were sets of chairs stacked six high. Behind the stacks were two chairs hung high on a wall that were exact matches for the specimen in Reacher's hand.

"We shoot, we score," Pauling said.

Reacher carried the chair to the back of the store, where a Chinese guy was sitting behind a table. The guy was old and impassive.

"You sold this chair." Reacher held it up and nodded toward the wall where its siblings hung. "About a week ago."

"Five dollars," the old guy said.

"I don't want to buy it," Reacher said. "And it isn't yours to sell. You already sold it once. I want to know who you sold it to."

"Five dollars," the guy said again. "You want information, and information has a price. In this case, the price is five dollars."

"Who bought it, a week ago?"

"Five dollars."

"Two-fifty plus the chair."

"You'll leave the chair anyway. You're sick of carrying it."

"I could leave it next door."

For the first time the old guy's eyes moved.

"Four bucks and the chair," he said.

"Guys, please," Pauling said. She opened her purse. Took out a wallet and snapped off a crisp ten from a wad as thick as a book.

"Ten dollars," she said. "And the chair. So make it good."

The old Chinese man nodded. "Women," he said. "Always ready to focus."

"Tell us who bought the chair," Pauling said.

"He couldn't talk," the old man said. "He just kept his mouth closed and gulped like a fish. I concluded that he had a deformity."

"Description?" Reacher asked.

The old guy launched into the same rundown that the Sixth Avenue super had given. A white man, late thirties, maybe forty, medium height and weight, clean and neat, no beard, no mustache.

The old man asked, "Was my information helpful?"

"Maybe," Pauling said. "But it didn't add anything."

"I'm sorry," the old man said. "You may keep the chair."

"I'm sick of carrying it around," Reacher said.

The old man inclined his head. "As I thought. In which case, feel free to leave it here."

Pauling led Reacher out to the Bowery sidewalk.

"The hard way," Pauling said.

"Makes no sense," Reacher said. "Why are they sending the guy that can't speak to meet with everyone?"

"There must be something more distinctive about the other one."

"I hate to think what that might be."

"Lane abandoned those two guys. Why are you helping him?"

"I'm not helping him. This is for Kate and the kid now."

"They're dead."

"Then they need a story. An explanation. The who, the where, the why. Someone needs to stand up for them."

"And that's you?"

"They need to be avenged, Pauling. Because it wasn't their fight. If Hobart or Knight had come after Lane directly, maybe I'd have been on the sidelines cheering him on. But he didn't. He came after Kate and Jade. And two wrongs don't make a right."

"Neither do three wrongs."

"In this case they do," Reacher said.

"I wouldn't want you mad at me," Pauling said.

"No," Reacher said back. "You wouldn't."

Pauling's cell phone must have vibrated, because she pulled it out of her pocket before Reacher heard it ring.

She said her name and then listened for a minute. Said thanks and snapped the phone shut.

"My Pentagon buddy," she said. "He has a location. It was Burkina Faso. It used to be called Upper Volta. It's a former French colony. Population thirteen million, with a GDP about a quarter of what Bill Gates is worth."

"But with enough spare cash to hire Lane's crew."

"Not according to my guy," Pauling said. "It's where Knight and Hobart were captured, but there's no record of their government contracting with Lane."

"Would your guy expect there to be a record?"

"He says there's always a record somewhere. He's working on it."

"But not fast enough. We need to try something on our own," Reacher said.

"Like what?"

"Our guy called himself Leroy Clarkson. Maybe it was because he lives over there."

"Near Clarkson or Leroy?"

"Maybe on Hudson or Greenwich."

Pauling nodded. "We should stop by my office. Start with the phone book."

THERE were a few Hobarts and half a page of Knights in the Manhattan white pages, but none of them were in the part of the West Village that would have made Leroy Clarkson an obvious pseudonym. Pauling had other databases, but no unexplained Knights or Hobarts cropped up.

"He's been away five years," Pauling said. "He'll have dropped out of sight, won't he? Disconnected phone, unpaid utilities?"

"Probably," Reacher said. "But not necessarily. These guys are used to sudden travel. They usually set up automatic payments."

"His bank account would have emptied out."

Reacher nodded.

"So what do we do?"

"I guess we wait," Reacher said. "For your bureaucratic buddy. Unless we grow old and die first."

But a minute later Pauling's phone went off again. She answered it and listened for a minute. Then she closed it slowly.

"Hobart," she said. "It was Hobart who came back alive."

6

REACHER asked, "First name?"

Pauling said, "Clay. Clay James Hobart."

Reacher asked, "Address?"

Pauling said, "We're waiting on an answer from the VA."

"So what did he have for us?"

"Lane is on an official Pentagon blacklist."

"Why?"

"You know what Operation Just Cause was?"

"Panama," Reacher said. "Against Manuel Noriega. More than fifteen years ago. I was there, briefly."

"Lane was there, too. He did very well there. That's where he made full colonel. Then he went to the Gulf the first time around, and then he quit under a bit of a cloud. But not enough of a cloud to stop the Pentagon hiring him on as a private contractor. They sent him to Colombia. He took the beginnings of his present crew with him to fight one of the cocaine cartels. He took our government's money to do it, but when he got there, he also took the target cartel's money to go wipe out one of their rival cartels instead. The Pentagon never hired him again."

"His guys said they'd been to Iraq and Afghanistan."

Pauling nodded. "But only as subcontractors. The Pentagon hired someone they trusted, and that someone laid off the work to Lane."

"Was Lane subcontracting in Burkina Faso, too?" Reacher asked.

"He must have been," Pauling said. "Otherwise why isn't he in the records as a principal?"

"Was our government involved there?"

"It's possible. My official friend seems a little tense."

Reacher nodded. "That's why he's helping, isn't it? This is not one MP to another. This is a bureaucracy trying to control the situation, so we don't go making a lot of noise in public."

Pauling said nothing. Then her phone went off again. She listened and wrote a dollar sign, and then two numbers, and then six zeros on a yellow pad. She clicked off the phone.

"Twenty-one million dollars," she said. "In cash. That's how rich Lane got in Africa."

"Okay," Reacher said. "What's half of twenty-one?"

"Ten and a half."

"Exactly. Kate's ransom was exactly half of the Burkina Faso payment. Now it makes some kind of sense. Lane probably skimmed fifty percent as his profit. So Hobart got home and figured he was entitled to Lane's share for his suffering."

"Reasonable," Pauling said.

"I would have wanted all of it," Reacher said.

Pauling's cell buzzed again. This time she wrote just three lines. Then she closed her phone.

"We have his address," she said. "Hobart moved in with his widowed sister. To a building on Hudson Street that I'm betting is on the block between Clarkson and Leroy."

The widowed sister was called Dee Marie Graziano, and she was in the phone book at an address on Hudson. Pauling looked up a city tax database on her computer and confirmed her domicile.

"Rent-stabilized," she said. "Been there ten years." She copied Dee Marie's social security number and typed it into a different database. "Thirty-eight years old. Marginal income. Her late husband was a Marine, too. He died three years ago."

Then the screen rolled down.

"Well, look at this," Pauling said. "She sued the government. State and the DOD."

"For what?"

"For news about her brother."

Pauling hit the PRINT button and fed Reacher the pages. Dee Marie Graziano had waged a five-year campaign to find out what had happened to her brother, Clay James Hobart. It had been a long, hard, bitter campaign.

At the outset, Hobart's employer, Edward Lane of Operational Security Consultants, had signed an affidavit swearing that Hobart had been a subcontractor for the U.S. government at the relevant time. So Dee Marie had petitioned her congressman and both her senators. She had called the chairmen of the Armed Services Committees in both the House and the Senate. She had written to newspapers and talked to journalists. She had hired an investigator, briefly. Finally, she filed a string of Freedom of Information Act petitions. More than half of them had already been denied, and the others were still choked in red tape.

"She was really going at it," Pauling said. "Wasn't she?"

"Like Patti Joseph," Reacher said. "This is a tale of two sisters."

"The Pentagon knew Hobart was alive after twelve months. And they knew where he was. But they kept quiet for four years. They let this poor woman suffer."

"What was she going to do anyway? Lock and load and go to Africa and rescue him single-handed? Bring him back to stand trial for Anne Lane's homicide?"

"There was never any evidence against him."

Pauling went quiet.

"What?" Reacher said.

"We agree that Hobart picked up a new partner, right?" she said. "As soon as he got back? One that he trusts, and real fast? Could it be the sister? Is it possible that the voice you heard on the car phone was a woman?"

"It's possible," Reacher said. "Those machines could make Minnie Mouse sound like Darth Vader."

"You said there was a lightness to the voice."

Reacher nodded. "Yes, I did."

"Therefore like a woman."

"Maybe," Reacher said. "Gregory told me a woman showed up in the Hamptons. A fat woman. She and Kate talked."

"Maybe it was Dee Marie. Maybe she was asking for money. Maybe Kate blew her off, and that was the last straw."

"This is about more than money."

"But that doesn't mean it isn't partly about money," Pauling said. "Dee Marie's share would be more than five million dollars. She might think of it as compensation. For five years of stonewalling."

"Maybe," Reacher said again.

Pauling pulled a city directory off her shelf and checked the Hudson Street address.

"They're south of Houston," she said. "Between Vandam and Charlton. Not between Clarkson and Leroy. But they're only fifteen minutes from here."

"They've got blood on their hands and money in their pockets, Pauling. They'll be in the Caymans by now. Or Bermuda."

"So what do we do?"

"We head over to Hudson Street, and we hope like crazy that the trail is still a little bit warm."

REACHER and Pauling were coming from a position of weakness, in that neither of them was armed and Hobart had met Pauling twice before. She had interviewed Lane's crew at length after Anne Lane's disappearance. Balancing those weaknesses was Reacher's conviction that the Hudson Street apartment would be empty.

There was no doorman. It was a boxy five-story tenement faced with dull red brick. It had a black door with an aluminum squawk box chiseled into the frame. Ten black buttons. *Graziano* was written neatly against *4L*.

"Walk-up," Pauling said. "Four L will be on the fourth floor, on the left."

Reacher hit every button except 4L's and said in a loud slurred voice, "Can't find my key." The door buzzed twice, and Pauling pushed it open.

Inside was a dim center hallway with a staircase on the right.

"Now we wait," Reacher said. "At least two people are going to be sticking their heads out looking for whoever lost their key."

Way above them in the gloom a door opened. Then closed again. Then another door opened. Thirty seconds later it slammed shut.

"Okay," Reacher said. "Now we're good to go."

He put his weight on the bottom tread of the staircase, and it creaked loudly. Pauling started up behind him.

When they got to the third floor hallway, they glanced up into the fourth-floor gloom. Reacher took the stairs two at a time to cut the number of creaks by half. Pauling put her feet near the edges of the treads, where any staircase is quieter. They made it to the top.

Four L's door had been painted a dull green. There was a clouded spy lens about level with Reacher's chest.

Reacher bent forward and put his ear on the crack where the door met the jamb. Listened.

"There's someone in there," he whispered. "A woman, talking." Then he straightened up and stepped back.

Pauling asked, "Who's she talking to?"

Reacher whispered, "I don't know."

He took another step back. Pointed at 4R's door.

"Wait there," he said. "If you hear shooting, call an ambulance. If you don't, follow me in six feet behind."

"You're just going to knock?"

"No," Reacher said. "Not exactly."

He took another step back. He was six feet five inches tall and weighed about two hundred and fifty pounds. His shoes were bench-made in England. Size twelve. The soles were heavy composite items. The heels were an inch and a quarter thick.

Each shoe weighed more than two pounds.

"Stand by now," Reacher whispered.

He put his weight on his back foot and stared at the door and bounced like a high jumper. Then he launched. One pace, two. He smashed his right heel into the door just above the knob, and wood splintered, and dust filled the air, and the door smashed open, and he continued running. Two paces put him in the living room. He stopped dead there. Lauren Pauling crowded in behind him.

In front of Reacher lay a dilapidated kitchen, with a twelve-foot living room on the left. There was a worn-out sofa and a dim window. The air was hot and still and foul. In the kitchen doorway stood a heavyset woman in a shapeless cotton shift. She had long brown hair parted in the center. In one hand she held an open can of soup and in the other she held a wooden spoon. Her eyes and her mouth were open wide in surprise.

In the living room, horizontal on the worn-out sofa, was a man.

Not a man Reacher had ever seen before.

This man was sick. Emaciated. He had no teeth. His skin glittered with fever. He had no hands. He had no feet.

Pauling said, "Hobart?"

There was nothing left that could surprise the man on the sofa. Not anymore. With a lot of effort he just moved his head and said, "Special Agent Pauling. It's a pleasure to see you again."

He had a tongue. He could talk just fine.

Pauling looked at the woman and said, "Dee Marie Graziano?"

"Yes," the woman said.

Pauling turned back to Hobart. "What happened to you?"

"Africa," Hobart said. "Africa happened to me."

He was wearing stiff new denims, dark blue. Jeans, and a shirt. The sleeves and legs were rolled to clear the stumps of his wrists and his shins, which were all smeared with a clear salve of some kind. The amputations were crude and brutal.

"What happened?" Pauling asked again.

"Why? The FBI is here to help me now?"

"I'm not FBI," Pauling said. "Not anymore."

"So what are you now?"

"A private investigator."

Hobart's eyes moved to Reacher's face. "And you?"

"The same," Reacher said. "More or less. I used to be an MP."

Nobody spoke for a minute.

"I was making soup," Dee Marie Graziano said.

Pauling said, "Go ahead. Please."

Reacher stepped back through the hallway and pushed the shattered door as far shut as it would go. When he got back to the living room, Dee Marie was in the kitchen. Pauling was still staring at the man on the sofa.

"What happened to you?" she asked him for the third time.

"First he eats," Dee Marie called.

HIS sister sat on the sofa next to him and cradled Hobart's head and fed him the soup slowly and carefully. From time to time Hobart started to raise one of his missing hands to wipe a dribble off his chin. Each time it happened, his sister would wait patiently for his handless wrist to return to his lap, and then she would wipe his chin with a cloth, tenderly, lovingly, as if he were her child. By the time the bowl was empty, the cloth was badly stained.

"Edward Lane," Pauling said finally. "When was the last time you saw him?"

"Five years ago," Hobart said. "In Africa."

"What happened there?"

"I was taken alive. Not smart."

"And Knight, too?"

Hobart nodded. "Knight, too," he said.

"How?" Reacher asked.

"You ever been to Burkina Faso?"

"I've never been anywhere in Africa."

Hobart paused for a long moment.

"There was a civil war," he said. "There usually is. We had a city to defend. This time it was the capital. It's called Ouagadougou. We called it O-Town."

"What happened there?" Pauling asked.

"All the action was to the northeast. The tree line was about a mile outside the city limit. Two roads in, like spokes in a wheel. We called them the One O'clock Road and the Two O'clock Road. Like the face of a wristwatch. The One O'clock Road was the one the rebels were going to be using. Except they would be flanking it in the jungle. We wouldn't see them until they passed the tree line and came out in the open. They had a mile of open ground to cross, and we had heavy machine guns."

"So where was the problem?"

"We figured they'd be tracking the One O'clock Road with half their force on the right shoulder and the other half on the left shoulder. We figured about two miles out the half that was on the right would wheel ninety degrees to its left and attempt an outflanking maneuver. But that meant that maybe five thousand guys would have to cross the Two O'clock Road. We'd see them."

"So what happened?" Pauling asked.

"Knight and I had been Recon Marines. So we volunteered to set up forward observation posts. We crawled out about three hundred yards and found a couple of good depressions. Old shell holes, from back in the day. Knight set up with a good view of the One O'clock Road, and I set up with a good view of the Two O'clock Road. Plan was if they didn't attempt to outflank us, we'd take them head-on, and if we were making good progress with that, our main force would join us. If their attack was heavy, Knight and I would fall back to the city limit and set up a secondary line of defense there. And if I saw the outflanking maneuver in progress, we'd fall back immediately and reorganize on two fronts."

Reacher asked, "So where did it all go wrong?"

"I made two mistakes," Hobart said. Four words, but the effort of getting them out seemed to exhaust him. He started wheezing.

"He has malaria and tuberculosis," his sister said.

"Is he getting care?" Pauling asked.

"We have no benefits. The VA does a little. Apart from that I take him to the St. Vincent's ER."

"How? How do you get him up and down the stairs?"

"I carry him," Dee Marie said. "On my back."

Reacher asked Hobart, "What two mistakes?"

"There was an early feint," Hobart said. "About ten point men came out of the trees a mile ahead of Knight. They were going for death or glory, running and firing unaimed. Knight let them run, and then he dropped them all with his rifle. I couldn't see him. I crawled over to check he was okay."

"And was he?"

"He was fine. When I got to Knight's position, I realized I could see the Two O'clock Road even better from his hole. Plus, when the shooting starts, it's always better to be paired up. So that was my first mistake. I put myself in the same foxhole as Knight."

"And the second mistake?"

"I believed what Edward Lane told me."

Reacher asked, "What did Edward Lane tell you?"

But Hobart couldn't answer for a minute. He was consumed with another bout of coughing. His caved chest heaved. Blood and thick yellow mucus rimed his lips. He coughed twice more and then stopped as the fluid settled lower in his lungs.

Then he said, "About thirty minutes after that first feint, Lane showed up in Knight's foxhole. He seemed surprised to see me there, too. He told me he had new intelligence that we were going to see men crossing the Two O'clock Road but that they would be government troops coming in to reinforce us. Lane told me the higher the number the better, because they were all on our side."

"And you saw them?"

"Thousands and thousands of them."

"And then?"

"We sat tight. All day, into the night. Then all hell broke loose. About five thousand guys stepped out of the trees. They were the same guys I had counted earlier. They weren't government troops. They were rebels. Lane's intelligence had been wrong. At least that's what I thought at first. Later I realized he had lied to me."

"What happened?" Pauling said.

"At first the rebels started firing from way too far away. At that point Knight and I were kind of relaxed. We expected some suppressing fire from behind us to allow us to fall back. But it never came. I turned around, staring at the city behind me. It was just three hundred yards away. But it was all dark and silent. Then I turned back and saw these ten thousand guys coming at me. Suddenly I had the feeling Knight and I were the only two Westerners left in-country. Turns out I was probably right. The way I pieced it together afterward, Lane and all the other crews had pulled out twelve hours before. He must have gotten back from his visit with us and just hopped straight into his jeep and headed to the airport."

Reacher said, "What we need to know is why he did that."

"That's easy," Hobart said. "Lane abandoned us because he wanted Knight dead. I just happened to be in the wrong foxhole, that's all. I was collateral damage."

"Why did Lane want Knight dead?"

"Because Knight killed Lane's wife."

Pauling asked, "Did Knight confess that to you?"

Hobart said, "He confessed to about a thousand different things." Then he smiled ruefully. "You had to be there. Knight was raving for four years. Me, too, probably."

"So how was it?" Pauling asked. "Tell us."

Dee Marie Graziano said, "I don't want to hear this again. I can't hear this again. I'm going out."

Pauling opened her purse and took out her wallet. Handed a sheaf of bills to Dee Marie. "Get stuff," she said. "Food, medicine."

"I don't like charity."

"Then get over it," Reacher said. "Your brother needs everything he can get."

"Take it, Dee," Hobart said. "Get something for yourself."

Dee Marie shrugged, then took the money. Collected her keys and walked out. Reacher heard the front door open. The hinges squealed where he had damaged them.

"We should call a carpenter," Pauling said.

"Call that Soviet super from Sixth Avenue," Reacher said. "He looked competent, and I'm sure he moonlights."

Pauling nodded.

Reacher said to Hobart, "You're lucky to have a sister like that."

"But it's hard on her," he said.

"Tell us about Knight."

Hobart's ruined body settled and quieted.

"At first we didn't do anything. Then we just looked at each other, and I guess we just took an unspoken decision to go down fighting. They just kept on coming, and we just kept putting them down. We started to have equipment problems. When they sensed it, they all charged. Okay, I thought, bring it on."

"But?" Reacher said.

"They got to the lip of the hole and stopped. Some kind of an officer walked through the crowd. He looked down at us and smiled. Black face, white teeth, in the moonlight. We'd just killed hundreds of their guys, and we were about to be captured."

"How did it go down?"

"The first few days were chaos. We were chained all the time. They had no jail facilities. They had nothing, really. But they fed us. Then after a week it was clear the coup had succeeded, so they all moved into O-Town proper and put us in a separate wing in the city prison. We figured they were negotiating with Washington. They fed us and left us alone. So altogether the first month was a day at the beach compared to what came later."

"What came later?"

"Evidently they gave up on Washington, because they tossed us in with the others. And that was bad. Incredible overcrowding, filth, disease, no clean water, almost no food. We were skeletons inside a month. There were worms. At night the place crawled with them. People were dying from starvation. Then they put us on trial."

"You had a trial?"

"I guess it was a trial. I had no idea what they were saying. Then they found us guilty. I figured I was about as low as I could go. But I was wrong. I had a birthday."

"What happened on your birthday?"

"They hauled out about a dozen guys. I guess we all shared the same birthday. They took us to a courtyard. First thing I noticed was a big bucket of tar on a propane burner. It was bubbling away.

Then I saw next to the bucket was a big stone block. Then some big guard grabbed a machete and started screaming at the first guy in line. The guy next to me spoke a little English and translated for me. He said we had a choice. Three choices, actually. To celebrate our birthdays we were going to lose a foot. First choice, left or right. Second choice, short pants or long pants. It meant we could be cut above the knee or below. Third choice, we could use the bucket or not. The boiling tar seals the arteries and cauterizes the wound. Choose not to, and you bleed out and die. Our choice."

Nobody spoke.

Hobart said, "I chose left, long pants, and yes to the bucket. Twelve months later, on my next birthday, I chose right, long pants, and yes to the bucket."

Reacher said, "They did this to Knight, too?"

Hobart nodded. "We thought we had been close before. But some things really bring you together."

Pauling was white as a sheet.

"The things you remember," Hobart said. "The third birthday I spent in there, they took me back to the courtyard. The second choice was phrased slightly different. Long sleeves or short? Nobody ever chose short sleeves."

Silence in the room.

"Knight told you about Anne Lane?" Pauling said.

"He told me about a lot of things. But remember, we were sick and starving. We had infections. We had malaria and dysentery. We were out of our heads for weeks at a time with fevers."

"What did he tell you?"

"He told me he shot Anne Lane in New Jersey."

"Did he tell you why?"

"He gave me a whole bunch of different reasons. Sometimes it was that he had been having an affair with her, and she broke it off. Other times it was that Lane was mad at her and asked him to do it. Other times he said he was working for the CIA."

"Did he kidnap her?"

Hobart nodded, slowly, painfully. "Drove her to the store, but didn't stop there. Just pulled a gun and kept on going, all the way to New Jersey. Killed her there."

"Immediately?" Pauling asked.

Hobart said, "Yes, immediately. She was dead a day before you ever heard of her. There was nothing wrong with your procedures."

"Were you really in Philadelphia?" Reacher asked.

"Yes, I really was," Hobart said.

"Who faked Anne's voice on the phone?" Pauling asked. "Who set up the ransom drop?"

"Sometimes Knight would say it was a couple of his buddies. Sometimes he would say Lane took care of all of that."

Pauling said, "What was the truth?"

Hobart smiled, sadly.

"The truth?" he said. "I thought about that a lot. Because basically it was responsible for what was happening to me."

Another silence.

"They weren't having an affair. Knight was timid around women. And Anne Lane was way out of his league. She wouldn't have responded. Not in a million years. And Knight wouldn't have offered anyway, because Anne was the CO's wife. That's the biggest no-no of all time for an American fighting man."

"You sure?"

"I knew him very well. And he didn't have the kind of buddies that could have faked the voices. Certainly not a woman's voice. That's when I knew he was lying. There was nobody he knew where he could just walk up to them and say, Hey, help me out with this phony kidnap thing, why don't you?"

"So why did he even try lying to you?"

"Because he understood better than me that reality was over for us. There was no difference between truth and fantasy for us at that point. He was just amusing himself. The only story I believed was that Lane set the whole thing up because Anne wanted a divorce and alimony, and Lane's ego couldn't take it. So he had her killed."

"Why would Lane want Knight dead if all he had done was act on Lane's own orders?"

"Lane was covering himself. And he was avoiding being in someone else's debt. That was the main thing. A guy like Lane, his ego couldn't take that, either. Being grateful to someone."

"What happened to Knight in the end?" Reacher asked.

"His fourth birthday," Hobart said. "He didn't go for the bucket. He didn't want to go on. He just quit on me. Some jarhead he was."

TEN minutes later the squawk box in the hallway sounded and Dee Marie asked for help carrying packages. Reacher went down and hauled four grocery bags back to the kitchen.

Reacher said to her, "We heard that Kate Lane had a visitor in the Hamptons. Was it you?"

"I went to the Dakota first," she said. "But the doorman told me they were away. I went to the Hamptons two days later."

"You went there to warn Anne Lane's successor."

"We thought she should be told what her husband was capable of doing," Dee Marie said.

"How did she react?"

"She listened. We walked on the sand, and she listened."

"How definite were you?"

"I said we had no proof. Equally, I said we had no doubt. She took it all in."

"Did you tell her about your brother?"

"It's a part of the story. She listened to it."

"What happened to your husband?"

"Vinnie? Iraq happened to Vinnie. A roadside booby trap. They told me he was killed instantly. But they always say that."

Reacher left Dee Marie in the kitchen and stepped back into the living room.

"What would the three of clubs mean to you?" he asked Hobart.

"Knight. Three was his lucky number. Club was his nickname in the corps. Because of how he liked to party, and because of the pun on his name. Knight Club, nightclub, like that."

"He left a playing card on Anne Lane's body. The three of clubs."

"He did? He told me that. I didn't believe him."

Dee Marie came back to the living room.

Reacher said, "I need to know what you've been doing for the last four days."

Dee Marie answered. No hesitation. Just a slightly incoherent and therefore completely convincing pieced-together narrative account. The four days had started with Hobart in St. Vincent's hospital with a severe malaria relapse. The ER doctor had admitted him for forty-eight hours of IV medication. Dee Marie had stayed with him most of the time. Then she had brought him home in a taxi. They had been alone in the apartment since then, eating what was in the kitchen cupboards, doing nothing, seeing nobody, until their door had smashed open and Reacher had ended up in their living room.

"Why are you asking?" Hobart said.

"The new Mrs. Lane was kidnapped. And her kid."

"You thought I did it?"

"For a spell. We got a basic report on you and Knight. We heard about mutilations. No details. Then we heard about a guy with no tongue. We thought it was you."

"No tongue?" Hobart said. "I'd take that deal."

"We apologize," Pauling said.

"No harm, no foul," Hobart said.

"We'll have the door fixed. And we'll help you if we can."

"See to the woman and the child first."

"We think we're already too late."

"Don't say that. Where there's hope, there's life. Hope kept me going, five hard years."

REACHER and Pauling left Hobart and Dee Marie together on their battered sofa. They walked down four flights to the street and stepped out into the afternoon shadows of a fabulous late-summer day. Traffic ground past on the street, slow and angry. Horns blared and sirens barked. Fast pedestrians swerved by on the sidewalk.

Reacher said, "Eight million stories in the naked city."

Pauling said, "We're nowhere."

7

"**What** now?" Pauling said.

"Back to the hard way. My fault. I was stupid."

"How?"

"Did you see how Hobart was dressed?"

"Cheap new denims."

"The guy I saw driving the cars away was wearing old denims. No way was the guy just back from Africa. It takes ages to get jeans and a shirt looking like that. The guy I saw has been safe at home for five years doing his laundry."

Pauling said nothing.

"You can split now," Reacher said. "You got what you wanted. Anne Lane wasn't your fault. You can sleep at night."

"But not well. Because I can't touch Edward Lane. Hobart's testimony is meaningless. He freely admits that both he and Knight were as good as insane most of the time."

"So you can settle for half a loaf. Patti Joseph, too. I'll drop by and tell her."

"Would you be happy with half a loaf?"

"Not me. I'm not quitting yet. My agenda is getting longer and longer by the minute."

"I'll stick with it, too."

"Your choice."

"I know. You want me to?"

Reacher looked at her. Answered honestly. "Yes, I do."

"Then I will."

"I'll meet you at Patti Joseph's," Reacher said. "Two hours from now. We should travel separately."

"Why?"

"I'm going to try to get killed."

Pauling said she would be in the Majestic's lobby in two hours and headed for the subway. Reacher started walking north on Hudson, not fast, not slow.

REACHER found Pauling waiting in an armchair in the Majestic's lobby. She had freshened up. She looked good.

"I stopped by and asked that Russian super," she said. "He'll go over later tonight to fix the door."

"Good," Reacher said.

"You didn't get killed," she said.

He sat down. "Something else I got wrong," he said. "I've been assuming there was inside help from one of Lane's crew. But now I don't think so. Yesterday morning Lane offered me a million bucks. Anyone watching from the inside would have to assume I was pretty well motivated. And I've shown them that I'm at least partially competent. But nobody has tried to stop me. And they would try, wouldn't they? Any kind of an inside ally would be expected to. But I just spent two hours strolling through Manhattan. I gave whoever it might be a dozen chances to take me out. Nobody tried."

"How could they have done this thing without inside help?"

"I have absolutely no idea."

They checked in at the desk and rode up to seven. Patti Joseph was out in the corridor. There was a little awkwardness. Patti had spent five years thinking Pauling had failed her sister. So there was ice to break. But the implied promise of news helped Patti thaw.

"Coffee?" Patti said.

"I thought you'd never ask," Reacher said.

Patti went to the kitchen to set up the machine, and Pauling walked straight to the window. Looked at the stuff on the sill, and then checked the view. Raised her eyebrows in Reacher's direction and gave a small shrug that said: *Weird, but I've seen weirder.*

"So what's up?" Patti called.

Reacher said, "Let's wait until we're all sitting down." And ten minutes later they all were, with Patti Joseph in tears. Tears of grief, tears of relief, tears of closure. Tears of anger.

"Where is Knight now?" she asked.

"Knight died," Reacher said. "And he died hard."

"Good. I'm glad. What are we going to do about Lane?"

"That remains to be seen."

"I should call Brewer."

"Brewer can't do anything. There's no evidence."

"You should tell the other guys about Hobart. Tell them what Lane did to their buddy. Send them to see for themselves."

"We can't risk it. Not unless we know ahead of time what their reactions would be. Because Lane will see Hobart as a loose end now. And a threat. Therefore, Lane will want Hobart dead now. And his sister would get caught in the crossfire."

"Why are you here?"

"To give you the news."

"Not *here*. In New York, in and out of the Dakota?"

Reacher said nothing.

"I'm not a fool," Patti said. "And I know that the day after I stop seeing Kate Lane and Jade anymore, you show up, and people put bags in cars, and you interrogate Brewer about the last time one of Edward Lane's wives disappeared. I think he's done it again."

Reacher looked at Pauling, and Pauling shrugged like maybe she agreed Patti deserved to hear the story. So Reacher told her everything he knew. When he finished, Patti stood up and stepped over to an armoire drawer and pulled out a packet of photographs. Tossed the packet into Reacher's lap. Close to the end of the stack he saw Dee Marie Graziano, coming out of the Dakota's lobby.

"That's Hobart's sister, am I right?" Patti said. "That's when the Dakota doorman told her the family was in the Hamptons. Then she went out there."

"So?"

"Isn't it obvious? Kate Lane takes this weird woman walking on the beach, and she hears a fantastical story, but there's something about it that stops her from just dismissing it. Maybe enough to make her ask her husband for an explanation. In which case all hell would break loose. Suddenly Kate's as bad as Anne was.

And suddenly she's a loose end, too. Maybe even a serious threat."

"Lane would have gone after Hobart and Dee Marie, too."

"If he could find them."

"Two questions," Reacher said. "If this is Anne all over again, why is Lane pushing me to help?"

"He's putting on a show for his men," Patti said.

"Second question," Reacher said. "Who could be playing Knight's part this time around?"

Patti paused. Looked away. "It's an inconvenient detail," she said. "Because there's nobody missing." Then she said, "Okay, I apologize. Maybe you're right. Just because it was fake for Anne doesn't mean it's fake for Kate."

REACHER and Pauling rode down to the Majestic's lobby in silence. They stepped out to the sidewalk. Early evening. Lovers in the park. Dogs on leashes.

Pauling asked, "Where now?"

"Take the night off," Reacher said. "I'm going back to the lions' den."

Pauling headed for the subway, and Reacher headed for the Dakota. The doorman sent him up without making a call.

There was nobody waiting for him in the corridor on five. Lane's door was closed. Reacher knocked, and Kowalski opened up. He seemed to be alone. Reacher stepped inside.

"Where is everybody?" Reacher asked.

"Out shaking the trees," Kowalski said.

"What trees?"

"Burke thinks we're being visited by ghosts from the past."

"Knight and Hobart," Reacher said. "Waste of time. They died in Africa."

"Not true," Kowalski said. "A friend of a friend of a friend called a VA clerk. Only one of them died in Africa."

"Which one?"

"We don't know yet. But we'll find out. Everyone has a price. And a VA clerk's is pretty low."

They moved to the deserted living room.

"Did you know them?" Reacher asked. "Knight and Hobart?"

"Sure," Kowalski said.

"So whose side are you on? Theirs or Lane's?"

"Lane pays me. They don't."

Reacher headed for the master bedroom. Kowalski kept close behind him.

"You going to follow me everywhere?" Reacher asked.

"Probably," Kowalski said. "Where are you going anyway?"

"To count the money."

"Is that okay with Lane?"

"He wouldn't have given me the combination if it wasn't."

Left hand. Index finger, curled. Ring finger, straight. Middle finger, straight. Middle finger, curled. Three seven eight five. I hope.

Reacher pulled the closet door and entered 3785 on the security keypad. There was an agonizing second's wait, and then it beeped and the inner door's latch clicked.

Reacher opened it and stepped inside. A narrow space on the left, money on the right. Bales of it. All of them intact except for one that was half empty. Reacher dragged it out. Carried it to the bed and dumped it down. Kowalski stayed at his shoulder.

"You know how to count?" Reacher asked Kowalski.

"Funny man," Kowalski said.

Reacher stepped back to the closet. Hefted an intact plastic bale off the top of the pile. On one face under the legend *Banque Centrale* there was smaller print that said *Government National, Ouagadougou, Burkina Faso*. Under that was printed: *USD 1,000,000.* Reacher saw Ben Franklin's face. Hundred-dollar bills. Ten thousand of them in the bale. A million bucks.

Altogether there were ten intact bales. And ten empty wrappers.

"Fifty packets," Kowalski called from the bed. "Ten thousand dollars each."

That's five hundred grand, Reacher thought. Total of ten and a half million still here, total of ten and a half million gone.

Original grand total, twenty-one million dollars.

Kowalski appeared in the closet doorway with the torn wrapper. He had repacked the remaining money neatly. Reacher heaved the open bale onto the top of the stack. Pulled the chain and killed the light and closed the door. The electronic lock clicked and beeped.

He led Kowalski back to the living room and then detoured to the kitchen and glanced in at the office. At the file drawers. Something about them nagged at him. Then a new thought struck him. Like an ice cube dropped down the back of his neck.

"What trees are they shaking?" he asked.

"Hospitals," Kowalski said. "We figure whoever is back has got to be sick."

Silence for a moment.

"I'm going out again," Reacher said. "You stay here."

Three minutes later he was at the pay phone, dialing Pauling's cell. She answered on the second ring.

Reacher said, "Jump in a cab and get over to Dee Marie's place. Lane and his guys are out scouting hospitals. It's only a matter of time before they hit St. Vincent's and buy Hobart's address. So I'll meet you. We're going to have to move them."

Then he hung up and flagged a cab.

UP ON the fourth floor the apartment door still hung open. Beyond it were voices in the living room. Dee Marie's and Pauling's. Reacher stepped inside. Pauling was wearing jeans and a T-shirt. She looked good. Hobart was propped up on the sofa. He looked bad. But his eyes were blazing.

"Lane's coming here?" he asked.

"Maybe," Reacher said. "Can't discount the possibility."

"So what are we going to do?"

"We're going to make sure he finds an empty apartment."

Hobart nodded, a little reluctantly.

"Where should you be?" Reacher asked him. "Medically?"

Dee Marie said, "Birmingham, Alabama, or Nashville, Tennessee. One of the big university hospitals down there. I got brochures. They're good."

"We can't get him to Birmingham or Nashville tonight."

"We can't get him there ever. The surgery alone could be over two hundred thousand dollars. The prosthetics could be even more than that." She picked up two brochures from the table and handed them over. There were glossy photographs on the fronts. Blue skies, green lawns, warm brick buildings. Inside were details of surgical programs and prosthetics designers. The captions were full of optimism.

"Looks good," Reacher said. He put them on the table.

"A motel tonight," Pauling said. "Somewhere close."

"I can't afford it," Dee Marie said.

The room went quiet, and Reacher stepped to the window. He glanced north. He glanced south. And saw a black Range Rover pulling in to the curb.

License plate: OSC 19.

Reacher spun around. "They're here," he said. "Now."

"What do we do?" Dee Marie said.

"Bathroom," Reacher said. "All of you."

He stepped over to the sofa and grabbed the front of Hobart's shirt and lifted him in the air. Carried him to the bathroom and laid him gently in the tub. Dee Marie and Pauling crowded in after him.

"Lock the door," Reacher said. "Sit tight and keep quiet."

He stood in the hallway, and a second later the intercom buzzed. He hit the button and said, "Yes?" Heard a voice. "VA visiting nurse service."

Reacher smiled. Nice. He hit the button again.

Then he walked back to the living room and sat on the sofa.

He heard loud creaking from the staircase. Three people, he guessed. He heard them stop at the head of the stairs, surprised by the broken door. Then he heard the door open, and after that there was nothing but the sound of footsteps in the foyer.

First into the living room was Perez, the tiny Spanish guy.

Then Addison, with the knife scar above his eye.

Then Edward Lane himself.

"The hell are you doing here?" he asked.

"I beat you to it," Reacher said.

"It was you who broke down the door?"

"I didn't have a key."

"Where is Hobart?"

"In the hospital."

"Bull. We just checked."

"Not here. In Alabama, or Tennessee."

"How do you figure that?"

"He needs specialized care. St. Vincent's recommended one of those big university hospitals down south."

Reacher pointed at the small table, and Edward Lane picked up the shiny brochures. "Which one?"

Reacher said, "It doesn't matter. Hobart didn't kidnap Kate."

"You think?"

"No, I know. You should have asked why he was at St. Vincent's in the first place."

"We did. They said malaria."

"He's a quadruple amputee," Reacher said. "Can't walk, can't drive, can't hold a gun or dial a telephone."

Nobody spoke.

"It happened in prison," Reacher said. "Back in Burkina Faso. The new regime had a little fun."

Nobody spoke.

"After you all ran away and left him behind," Reacher said.

"You don't know how it was," Lane said.

"But I know how it is now," Reacher said.

"I still want to find him," Lane said.

"Why?"

No answer. *Checkmate.* Lane couldn't say why without admitting what he had asked Knight to do for him five years previously.

"I'm close," Reacher said. "I'll give you the guy."

"When?"

"When you give me the money."

"What money?"

"You offered me a million bucks."

"To find my wife. It's too late now."

"Okay," Reacher said. "So I won't give you the guy."

"I could have it beaten out of you."

"You couldn't," Reacher said. He hadn't moved at all. He was sitting back on the sofa, relaxed, sprawled, arms resting easy along the back cushions, legs spread, six-five, two-fifty, a picture of supreme physical self-confidence.

"Okay," Lane said.

"Okay what?" Reacher said.

"Okay, a million bucks. When do I get the name?"

"Tomorrow," Reacher said.

Lane nodded. Said to his men, "Let's go."

Addison said, "I need the bathroom."

Reacher stood up, slowly. Said, "Go home and use yours."

"What?"

"You're not fit to use the same bowl as him. You left him behind."

"You weren't there."

"For which you can thank your lucky stars."

Edward Lane took a step forward.

"Get these runts out of here," Reacher said.

Silence. Shrewd judgment in Lane's eyes.

"The name," Lane said. "Tomorrow."

"I'll be there," Reacher said.

Lane nodded to his men, and they trooped out. Reacher waited for the street door to bang, and then he stepped back to the window. Watched them climb into the Range Rover and take off north. He walked back to the bathroom.

"They're gone," he said.

Reacher carried Hobart back to the sofa. Pauling said, "We heard everything."

Hobart said, "You were minutes away from getting hurt bad. Lane doesn't hire nice people."

"He hired you."

"I'm not a nice person," Hobart said. "I fit right in."

Reacher asked, "Suppose it had been Perez and Addison in those forward OPs in Africa? Would you have left them there?"

Hobart stared into space. "No way."

Pauling said, "We should move you."

"No need now," Dee Marie said. "They won't come back."

Then the buzzer sounded, and they heard a Russian accent on the intercom. The super from Sixth Avenue, come to fix the broken door. Reacher met him in the hallway. He was carrying a bag of tools and a length of spare lumber.

"Now we're definitely okay," Dee Marie said.

So Pauling just paid the Russian, and she and Reacher walked down the stairs to the street.

Pauling was quiet and faintly hostile as they walked.

"What?" Reacher asked.

"You signed on with Lane. You sold out."

"I wanted to test him," Reacher said. "I still need proof it's for real this time. If it wasn't, he'd have backed off. He wants the guy. Therefore there is a guy."

"I don't believe you. Lane's putting on a show for his men and gambling that he's smarter than you are."

"But he had just found out that he's not smarter than I am. I found Hobart before he did."

"Whatever, this is about the money, isn't it?"

"Yes," Reacher said. "It is."

"What are you going to do with a million dollars? Buy a house? A car? A new shirt? I thought you were better than this."

He said, "Pauling, give me a break."

"Why would I?"

"Because first I'm going to pay you for your time and your services and your expenses, and then I'm going to send Hobart down to Birmingham or Nashville and get him fixed up right. I'm going to rent him a place to live, and I'm going to give him some walking-around money. And then if there's anything left, then sure, I'll buy myself a new shirt."

"Seriously?"

"Of course. I need a new shirt."

Pauling stopped walking. "I'm sorry," she said.

"Then make it up to me."

"How?"

"Work with me. We've got a lot to do."

"You told Lane you'd give him a name tomorrow."

"I had to get him out of there."

"Can we do it by tomorrow?"

"I don't see why not."

"Where are we going to start?"

"I have absolutely no idea."

THEY started in Lauren Pauling's apartment. She lived in a small co-op on Barrow Street, near West Fourth. Her apartment was painted mostly yellow and felt warm and friendly. There was an alcove bedroom and a bathroom, and a kitchen, and a room with a sofa and a chair and a television set and a lot of books. There were small framed photographs of children, but Reacher knew without asking that they were nephews and nieces.

He sat on the sofa and rested his head on the cushion. The clock in his head crawled around to nine thirty. The sky outside the window turned from blue to black, and the city lights burned bright.

"Do that thing again," Reacher said. "The brainstorming thing."

"Okay," Pauling said. "Start at the beginning. What was the very first false note? The first red flag?"

Reacher closed his eyes and recalled the beginning: the granular feel of the foam espresso cup in his hand. He recalled Gregory's walk in from the curb. His direct approach to the sidewalk table.

He said, "Gregory asked me about the car I had seen the night before, and I told him it drove away before eleven forty-five, and he said no, it must have been closer to midnight."

Pauling said, "You don't wear a watch."

"I'm usually pretty sure what time it is."

"What was the next thing?"

Reacher said, "Something about getting into Gregory's car. The blue BMW. Something rang a bell. In retrospect."

"You don't know what?"

"No. Then we arrived at the Dakota, and it was off to the races."
After that, Reacher thought, everything was about the photograph.

Pauling said, "We need to take a break. I've got white wine."

"I'm being selfish. You didn't blow it five years ago. We should take a minute to celebrate that."

Pauling took a bottle out of the refrigerator and opened it. Filled two glasses.

She moved back to the sofa with the wine. Reacher asked, "Did you quit because of Anne Lane?"

She said, "Not directly. Not right away. But ultimately, yes."

He said nothing.

She took a sip of wine and pulled her legs up under her and turned a little sideways so she could see him better. He turned a little too, until they were facing each other from a foot away.

"Why did you quit?" she asked him.

He said, "Because they told me I could."

"You were looking to get out?"

"No, I was looking to stay in. But as soon as they said that leaving was an option, it kind of broke the spell. Made me realize I wasn't personally essential to their plans."

"You need to be needed?"

"Not really. It just broke the spell, is all. I can't really explain it."

Reacher stopped talking and watched her. She looked great. Liquid eyes, soft skin. Reacher liked women as much as any guy, but he was always ready to find something wrong with them. The shape of an ear, the thickness of an ankle, height, size, weight. Any random thing could ruin it for him. But there was nothing wrong with Lauren Pauling. Nothing at all.

"Anyway, congratulations," he said. "Sleep well tonight."

"Maybe I won't get the chance." she said.

He could smell her fragrance. Subtle perfume, soap, clean skin. Her hair fell to her collarbones.

She said, "Maybe we'll be working all night."

He said, "All work and no play makes Jack a dull boy."

"You're not a dull boy," she said.

"Thank you," he said, and leaned forward and kissed her, just lightly, on the lips. Pulled her closer and kissed her harder.

"I don't usually do this," she said, her mouth against his. "Not to people I work with."

"We're not working," he said. "We're taking a break."

"We're celebrating. We're celebrating the fact that we're not Hobart, aren't we? Or Kate Lane."

"I'm celebrating the fact that you're you." He smiled and kissed her neck below her ear.

Afterward they showered together and drank their wine and went back to bed. Reacher just floated, warm, spent, happy.

MUCH later Reacher woke up to find Pauling's hands over his eyes. She asked him in a whisper, "What time is it?"

"Eighteen minutes to seven," he said. "In the morning."

"You're unbelievable."

"It's not a very useful talent."

"What would it mean if Gregory was wrong about the time and you were right?"

He opened his mouth to say I don't know.

But then he stopped.

Because suddenly he saw what it would mean.

"You got a flashlight?" he asked.

"There's a small Maglite in my purse."

"Put it in your pocket," he said. "Leave the purse home. And wear pants."

8

THEY walked, because it was a beautiful city morning. They took it slow, to time it right. They turned east on Spring Street at seven thirty exactly.

Reacher stopped outside the chocolate shop. Peered in. There was a light in the kitchen. He could see the owner moving about.

He knocked on the glass, loud, and the owner turned. Then she walked to the front. Undid the locks and opened the door.

He asked, "Can we come through to the alley again?"

The owner asked, "Are you really exterminators?"

"Investigators," Pauling said.

"What are you investigating?"

"A woman disappeared," Reacher said. "And her child."

The owner asked, "You think they're next door?"

"No," Reacher said. "This is just routine."

Pauling and Reacher stepped inside. Pauling followed Reacher through the kitchen and out through the back door to the alley.

The rear of the abandoned building was exactly as Reacher had last seen it. The dull red door, the corroded black knob, the filthy ground floor window. He bent down. Took off his shoe and used the heel to break the window glass. He put his shoe back on. Put his arm through the hole in the glass and groped until he found the inside door handle. He unlocked it and withdrew his arm carefully. Then he opened the door to let Pauling get a good look.

"You up for a trip down the ladder?" he said.

Pauling craned in and took a look. "I did worse at Quantico," she said. "But that was a long time ago."

Reacher said, "It's only ten feet if you fall."

"Thanks." She turned and backed up to the void. Reacher took her right hand, and she swung her left foot and left hand onto the ladder. Let Reacher's hand go and climbed down into the dark.

He saw her flashlight beam stab the gloom. She called, "Where am I going?"

"The front of the building. Directly underneath the door."

The flashlight beam leveled out and jerked forward. Pauling reached the front wall. Lined herself up directly beneath the door.

"Look down now," Reacher called. "What do you see?"

The beam stabbed downward. "I see trash," Pauling called.

Reacher called, "Look closer."

The flashlight beam traced a small random circle. Then a wider one. Then it stopped dead and held steady.

"Okay," Pauling called. "Now I see. But how did you know?"

Reacher said nothing. Pauling bent down. Stood up again. In her right hand was the flashlight. In her left hand were two sets of car keys, one for a Mercedes Benz and one for a BMW.

PAULING waded through the garbage back to the ladder and tossed the keys up to Reacher. Both sets were on chrome split rings and both had black leather fobs decorated with enamel car badges. Both had a single large car key and a remote clicker. He put them in his pocket. Then he caught Pauling's arm and hauled her off the ladder to the safety of the alley.

"We're one for one," he said.

He closed the door and put his arm back through the hole in the glass and clicked the lock from the inside.

"This whole thing with the mail slot was a pure decoy," he said. "The guy already had keys from the file cabinet in Lane's office."

"So you were right about the time."

Reacher nodded. "The guy was in the apartment above the café. He watched Gregory park at eleven forty and just came out and crossed Sixth Avenue and used the valet key from his pocket. Immediately, much closer to eleven forty than midnight."

"Same thing with the blue BMW the second morning."

"Exactly the same thing," Reacher said.

"And that's why he specified the cars so exactly. He needed to match them with the stolen keys."

"And that's why it bugged me when Gregory let me into his car that first night. Gregory used the remote thing from ten feet away, like anyone would. But the night before the other guy didn't do that with the Mercedes. Because he didn't have the remote. All he had was the valet key. Which also explains why he used the Jaguar for the final installment. He wanted to lock it from the other side of the street, as soon as Burke put the money in it. The only remote he had was for the Jaguar. He inherited it at the initial takedown."

Pauling was quiet for a second. "You're back to saying there was inside help. Aren't you?"

"The guy with no tongue. He's the key."

PAULING and Reacher were back in Pauling's office before nine.

"We need Brewer now," Reacher said. "And Patti Joseph."

"Brewer's still asleep," Pauling said. "He works late."

"Today he's going to work early. Because we need a definitive ID on that body from the Hudson River."

"Taylor?"

"We need to know for certain it's Taylor. I'm sure Patti has got a photograph of him. If she gave a good shot to Brewer, he could make the ID for us."

So Pauling called Patti Joseph. Patti confirmed that she had a file of photographs of all Lane's men. She agreed to pick out the best full-frontal and put it aside for Brewer to collect. Then Pauling called Brewer and woke him up. He was bad-tempered about it, but he agreed to pick up the picture.

"Now what?" Pauling asked. "Lane is expecting a name today."

"Today lasts until midnight. There's something I want to check."

"What?" Pauling asked.

"The phone book," he said. "*T* for Taylor."

She hauled the white pages off the shelf and opened it on the desk. She asked, "Initial?"

"No idea," he said. "Work off the street addresses. Look for private individuals in the West Village."

Pauling ended up with seven possibilities. West Eighth Street, Bank, Perry, Sullivan, West Twelfth, Hudson, and Waverly Place.

Reacher said, "Start with Hudson Street. Check the city directory, and find out what block that address is on."

"It's exactly halfway between Clarkson and Leroy," she said. "What's going on here?"

"Your best guess?"

"The guy with no tongue knew Taylor? Lived with him? Was working with him? Killed him?"

Reacher said nothing.

"Wait," Pauling said. "Taylor was the inside man, wasn't he? He stole the valet keys. He stopped the car outside Bloomingdale's exactly where the other guy wanted him to. That's the only way it could have worked."

Reacher said nothing.

"What exactly is going on here?"

"We're sweating the details, and we're working the clues. We're doing it the hard way. Next step, we go visit the Taylor residence."

Pauling took a sheet of paper and copied G. *Taylor* and the address from the phone book.

They walked. Panel trucks and taxis jammed the streets. Second-story air conditioners dripped condensation like fat raindrops. Vendors hawked fake watches and umbrellas. The city, in full tumult. Reacher liked New York more than most places. He liked the indifference of it all and the frantic hustle and the total anonymity.

Hudson Street between Clarkson and Leroy had buildings on the west side and a park on the east. Taylor's number matched a brick cube sixteen stories high. It had a plain entrance but a decent lobby. Reacher could see one lone guy behind a long desk.

"Approach?" Pauling asked.

"The easy way," Reacher said. "The direct approach."

They pulled the street door and stepped inside. Reacher walked straight to the desk, and the guy behind it looked up, and Reacher pointed to Pauling.

"Here's the deal," he said. "This lady will give you four hundred bucks if you let us into Mr. G. Taylor's apartment."

Concierges are human. And it was a well-chosen sum. It was big enough to feel like serious cash. And in Reacher's experience it created an irresistible temptation to bargain upward toward five hundred. And in Reacher's experience once that temptation had taken hold, the battle was won.

The desk guy glanced left, glanced right. Saw nobody.

"Alone?" he asked.

"I don't care," Reacher said. "Come with us. Send a handyman."

The guy paused. Said, "Okay, I'll send a handyman."

But you'll keep the cash for yourself, Reacher thought.

"Five hundred," the guy said.

Reacher said, "Deal."

Pauling opened her wallet and counted off five hundred-dollar bills and slipped them across the desk.

"Twelfth floor," the concierge said. "Turn left, go to the door at the end on the right. The handyman will meet you there." Reacher and Pauling stepped over to the elevator and pressed the up arrow. A door slid open.

"You owe me a lot of money," Pauling said.

"I'm good for it," Reacher said. "I'll be rich tonight."

The elevator car stopped on twelve, and the door slid back. They turned left and found the end door on the right.

Reacher asked, "What is he paying for a place like this?"

"Rental?" Pauling said. She glanced at the distance between doors to judge the size of the apartments and said, "Small two-bedroom, maybe four grand a month. Maybe four and a quarter."

"That's a lot."

"Not when you make twenty-five."

To their right the elevator bell dinged, and a man in a green uniform stepped off. The handyman. He walked up and unlocked Taylor's door.

Reacher went in first. The air inside was hot and still. There was a foyer and then a stainless steel kitchen on the left and a coat closet on the right. Living room dead ahead, two bedrooms side by side away to the left. The kitchen and the living room were spotlessly clean. The décor was mid-century modern, restrained, tasteful, masculine. Not cheap. Classic pieces. There were lots of books, shelved alphabetically. A small television set. Lots of CDs.

"Very elegant," Pauling said.

The bigger bedroom was spare, almost monastic. White walls, a king-size bed, gray linens. The closet was full of suits and jackets and shirts and pants grouped precisely by season and color. Each garment was clean and pressed. Each hanger was exactly one inch from the next. The shoes were black and brown, shined like mirrors.

"This is amazing," Pauling said. "I want to marry this guy."

Reacher moved on to the second bedroom. It was a small plain undecorated space. There was no light bulb in the ceiling fixture. The room held nothing but two narrow iron beds. There were used sheets on them. Dented pillows. The window was covered with a width of black fabric.

Reacher said, "This is where Kate and Jade were hidden."

"By who? The man who can't talk?"

"Yes," Reacher said. "The man who can't talk hid them here."

Pauling examined the pillows. "Long dark hairs," she said.

Reacher walked back to the living room and checked the desk. The handyman watched him from the doorway. Some personal papers, some financial papers. Taylor's first name was Graham. He was a UK citizen and a resident alien. There was a console telephone on the desk. It had ten speed-dial buttons; under plastic next to them were paper strips marked with initials. At the top was *L.* For Lane, Reacher guessed. He hit the corresponding button, and a 212 number lit up in a gray LCD window. He hit the other nine buttons one after the other. The gray window showed three 212 numbers, three 917 numbers, two 718s, and a long number with 01144 at the beginning. The 212s would all be Manhattan. Buddies, probably. The 917s would be cell phones. Maybe for the same set of guys. The 718s would be for the outer boroughs. The long 01144 number would be for Great Britain. Family, maybe. The corresponding initial was *S.*

Reacher kept pressing buttons on the phone for a while. "Are doormen here twenty-four hours?" Reacher asked.

"I doubt it," Pauling said. "Not this far downtown. They're probably part-time here. Maybe until eight."

"Then that might explain the delays. He couldn't bring them in past a doorman. The first day, he would have had to wait hours. Then he kept the intervals going for consistency."

"And to create an impression of distance."

"That was Gregory's guess."

Pauling asked, "What next?"

"I'd like to talk with the Pentagon guy again. Make him an offer."

"What can we offer him?"

"Tell him we'll take Lane's crew off the board if he helps us out with one small piece of information. He'll take that deal. One whole band of real live mercenaries out of action forever."

"Can we deliver that?"

"Sooner or later it's going to be them or us."

So Pauling called around the UN building looking for her friend. He agreed to meet in the same coffee shop, at three o'clock in the afternoon.

"Time is moving on," Pauling said.

"It always does. Try Brewer again."

But Brewer wasn't at his desk, and his cell was off.

THEY were in the Second Avenue coffee shop forty minutes early. Pauling tried Brewer again. Still no answer.

"You've got a theory," Pauling said to Reacher. "Haven't you? Like a physicist. A unified theory of everything."

"No," Reacher said. "Not everything. Not even close. I'm missing a big component. But I've got a name for Lane."

"What name?"

"Let's wait for Brewer," Reacher said. He waved to the waitress and ordered coffee. Same brown mugs. Same strong, generic taste.

Pauling's phone buzzed with thirty minutes to go before the Pentagon guy was due to show. She listened for a spell, and then she gave their location. Then she hung up.

"Brewer," she said. "Finally. He's meeting us here."

"He's going to arrive at the same time as your guy."

"My guy's not going to like that."

"If I see him balking, I'll talk to him outside."

But Pauling's Pentagon friend showed up a little early. He walked quickly through the room and slid into the booth. He was wearing the same blue suit.

"I'm concerned about your offer," he said. "I can't condone illegality."

Reacher thought, Be grateful for once in your miserable life. But he said, "I understand your concern, sir. And you have my word that no cop or prosecutor anywhere in America will think twice about anything that I do. I guarantee it."

"You can do that, realistically?"

"I can do that absolutely."

The guy paused. "So what do you want me to do?"

"I need you to check a passenger name against flight manifests out of this area during the last forty-eight hours."

"Military?"

"No, commercial."

"That's a Homeland Security issue."

Reacher nodded. "Which is why I need you to do it for me. I don't know who to call. Not anymore. But I'm guessing you do."

"Which airport? What flight?"

"I'd start with JFK. British Airways, United, or American to London. I'd start with late evening the day before yesterday. Failing that, try Newark. No hits, try JFK again yesterday morning."

"Okay," the guy said. Then he asked, "Who am I looking for? One of Edward Lane's crew?"

Reacher nodded. "A recent ex-member."

"Name?"

Reacher said, "Taylor. Graham Taylor. He's a UK citizen."

The Pentagon guy left with a promise to liaise via Pauling's cell phone. Pauling said, "You didn't find Taylor's passport in his apartment. So either he's alive or someone's impersonating him."

Reacher said nothing.

Pauling said, "Let's say Taylor was working with the guy with no tongue. Let's say they fell out over something. One of them killed the other and ran, on Taylor's passport, with all the money."

"If it's the guy with no tongue, why would he use Taylor's passport?"

"Maybe he doesn't have one of his own. Maybe he couldn't get through an airport with his own name."

"Passports have photographs."

"Do you look like your passport photograph?"

"A little."

Pauling said, "A little is sometimes all you need. Going out, they don't care as much as when you're coming in."

Reacher looked up and saw Brewer. He hurried through the room and slid into the spot the Pentagon guy had just vacated.

He said, "The body in the river was not the guy in Patti's photograph."

"You sure?" Reacher asked.

"As sure as I've ever been about anything. Patti's guy is about five-nine and athletic, and the floater was six-three and wasted."

Pauling asked, "Did he have a tongue?"

"A what?" Brewer said.

"We're looking for a guy who had his tongue cut out."

Brewer looked straight at her. "Then the floater ain't yours. He's got everything except a heartbeat."

Reacher asked, "Did you get an ID?"

Brewer nodded. "From his fingerprints. He was an NYPD snitch. Relatively valuable. Methamphetamine out of Long Island. He was due to testify."

"Then we don't know anything about him," Reacher said. "He's completely unrelated."

Brewer gave him a long hard look, then shrugged. "Okay."

Reacher said, "You still got Patti's photograph?"

"Photographs," Brewer said. "She gave me two."

They were in a standard white letter-size envelope. Brewer laid it on the table. Then he left. Just stood up and walked back out to the street with the same kind of speed and energy and hustle he had used on the way in.

Reacher looked at the envelope but left it unopened.

"What have we got?" he asked.

"We've got Taylor and the guy who can't talk."

Reacher shook his head. "Taylor *is* the guy who can't talk."

Pauling said, "That's absurd. Lane wouldn't employ anyone who can't talk. Why would he?"

"Two words," Reacher said. "Two words, and the whole thing makes perfect sense."

"What two words?"

"We've been saying the guy can't talk. Truth is, he can't *afford to* talk."

Pauling paused. Then she said: "Because of his accent."

Reacher nodded. "Exactly. We've been saying nobody was missing, but by definition Taylor was missing from the start. And Taylor was behind this whole thing. He rented the apartment, and he bought the chair. And he couldn't risk opening his mouth. Because he's English. He knew he had to be leaving a trail. And if whoever was tracking him heard all about an average-looking forty-year-old man with an English accent, they would have made him in a second. Because he was the last one to see Kate and Jade alive."

"He did the same thing as Knight, five years ago."

"Exactly," Reacher said again. "It's the only way to explain it. Possibly he drove them to Bloomingdale's, but certainly he didn't stop there. He just pulled a gun and kept on going. Maybe threatened to shoot Kate in front of the kid. That would have kept her quiet. Then he just dropped off the radar and started relying on a kind of double alibi he had created for himself. First, he was presumed dead. And second, all anyone would ever remember of him was a guy who couldn't speak. A guy with no tongue. It was a perfect piece of misdirection."

"Open the envelope," Pauling said. "Confirm it."

So Reacher slid the two photographs out, facedown. Then he flipped the top picture over.

It was the guy he had seen twice before. Taylor.

"No doubt about it," Reacher said. "That's the guy I saw getting into the Mercedes and the Jaguar."

He turned the second picture over. It was a closer shot. This time the guy's mouth was open. He had terrible teeth. Some were missing. The rest were gappy and uneven.

"There you go," Reacher said. "He was concealing two pieces of evidence. His English accent, and his British dentistry."

"Where is he now? England?"

"That's my guess. He flew home, where he feels safe."

"With the money?"

"Checked luggage. Three bags."

"Could he do that? With all the X-rays?"

"I don't see why not. I once had a lesson about paper money from an expert. It's mostly linen and cotton fibers. I think it would show up like clothing on an X-ray."

Pauling slid the photographs in front of her.

"It's a shame," Reacher said. "I liked him when I thought he was dead. Everyone spoke well of him."

"Well, you've got the name to give to Lane," she said.

Reacher didn't reply.

"A unified theory of everything," Pauling said. "Like a physicist. I don't see why you say it's only partial. Taylor did it all."

"He didn't," Reacher said. "He didn't make the phone calls. An American made the calls. That's why it's only a partial theory."

"Lane won't settle for half a loaf. He's not going to pay."

"He'll pay part. We'll get the rest later. When we tell him who the partner was."

"How do we find out who the partner was?"

"The only sure way is to find Taylor and make him tell us."

"In England?"

"If that's where your Pentagon buddy says he went. He could check for us who Taylor was sitting next to on the flight. There's a slim chance they flew together."

So Pauling left a voice-mail message for the UN guy.

"What now?" she said.

"Wait for your guy to get back to you," Reacher said. "Then book us a car to the airport and flights to London, if that's where Taylor went. I'm betting Lane will ask me to go there to do the advance work. Then he'll bring his crew over for the kill. And we'll deal with them there."

Pauling looked up. "That's why you promised no cop or prosecutor in America is going to think twice."

Reacher nodded. "But their opposite numbers in England are going to get pretty uptight. That's for sure."

He put Patti Joseph's photographs back in their envelope and jammed it in the front pocket of his shirt. Kissed Pauling on the sidewalk and headed for the subway. He was outside the Dakota before five in the afternoon.

EDWARD Lane fanned the two photographs of Taylor between his finger and his thumb and asked one simple question: "Why?"

"Greed," Reacher said. "Or malice, or jealousy."

"Where is he now?"

"My guess is England. I'll know soon."

Lane said, "He must have had a partner. Who was it?"

"You'll have to ask Taylor that."

"I want you to find him for me."

"I want my money."

"Ten percent now. The rest when I'm face-to-face with Taylor."

"Twenty percent now."

Lane said, "Fifteen percent now."

"Twenty. Or I'm out of here."

Lane said, "Okay, twenty percent now. But you'll leave now, tonight. Then we'll follow you twenty-four hours later. The seven of us. We'll be at the Park Lane Hilton."

"With the rest of the money?"

"I'll show it to you at the hotel, and you tell us where Taylor is. I'll give it to you when I've got visual contact with him."

"Deal," Reacher said. And ten minutes later he was back in the subway, with two hundred thousand U.S. dollars in a shopping bag.

Reacher met Pauling at her apartment and gave her the bag and said, "Take out what I owe you and hide the rest. It's enough to get Hobart started at least."

Pauling opened the bag and peeled off some bills and put them on the kitchen counter. Then she put the bag in the oven.

"I don't have a safe here," she said.

Then she took four bills from the stack on the counter and handed them to Reacher.

"For new clothes," she said. "We leave for England tonight."

"Your guy got back to you?"

She nodded. "Taylor was on British Airways to London less than four hours after Burke put the money in the Jaguar."

"Alone?"

"Apparently. He was seated next to some British woman. Checked three bags."

Reacher said, "I don't need four hundred dollars for clothes."

Pauling said, "You do if you're traveling with me."

Thirty minutes later Reacher was doing something he had never done in his life. He was buying clothes in a department store. He was in Macy's, in the men's department, in front of a cash register, holding a pair of gray pants, a gray jacket, a black T-shirt, a black V-neck sweater, a pair of black socks, and a pair of white boxer shorts. He shuffled to the head of the line and paid. He showered and dressed back at Pauling's apartment and took his battered passport and Patti Joseph's photographs out of his old pants and shoved them in his new pants. Took his folding toothbrush out of his old shirt pocket and put it in his new jacket pocket. Carried his old clothes down the corridor to the compactor room and dropped them in the garbage chute. Then he waited with Pauling in the lobby until the car service showed up to take them to the airport.

9

PAULING had booked them business class on the same flight that Taylor had taken forty-eight hours previously. Reacher's window seat faced aft, and next to him Pauling faced forward.

"What's the strategy?" Pauling asked.

"We'll find Taylor, Lane will take care of him, and then I'll take care of Lane."

"What about the others?"

"If I think the crew will fall apart with Lane gone, then I'll leave the rest alone and let it. But if one of them wants to step up to take over, I'll do him, too."

"Taylor won't be easy to find," she said.

"We'll get by."

"How?"

"You know any British private investigators?"

"I've got some numbers. But we could have done that by phone."

"We didn't have time."

Pauling took a blanket from a stewardess and reclined her seat. Reacher lay down with his knees up. The cabin lighting was soft and blue, and the hiss of the engines was restful. Reacher liked flying. Going to sleep in New York and waking up in London was a fantasy that could have been designed expressly for him.

THE stewardess woke him to give him breakfast. Mugs of hot coffee and bacon rolls. He drank six and ate six. Pauling watched him, fascinated.

"What time is it?" she asked.

"Five to five," he said. "In the morning. Which is five to ten in the morning in this time zone."

Then all kinds of signs went on to announce the start of their approach into Heathrow Airport.

Reacher put his forehead against the window and stared down. Saw the Thames, glittering in the sun like polished lead. Saw Tower Bridge, white stone, recently cleaned. He craned his neck and looked for St. Paul's Cathedral. Saw the big dome, crowded by ancient winding streets.

He asked Pauling, "You know any hotels?"

"Do you?"

"Only the sort where you wear your shoes in bed."

"We can't stay anywhere close to Lane and his guys. We can't be associated with him. Not if we're going to do something to him."

"That's for sure. We need to stay low-profile. We need the kind of place where they don't look at your passport and they let you pay cash. Bayswater, maybe."

Reacher turned to the window again and saw a wide east-west highway with slow traffic driving on the left. Then the airport fence. The plane landed hard and roared and braked, and then suddenly it was quiet again, rolling toward the terminal. The flight attendant welcomed the passengers to London over the public address system.

They filled in landing cards and had their passports stamped by an official. Pauling changed a wad of the O-Town dollars, and they found the fast train to Paddington station. Convenient for the Bayswater hotels. They came out to the street in central London just before twelve noon. The city was bright and fresh and cold.

Reacher carried Pauling's bag, and they walked toward Sussex Gardens. From previous trips he recalled groups of row houses joined together into cheap hotels. Pauling rejected the first two places he found before understanding that there wasn't going to be anything better around the next corner. So she gave up and agreed to the third. The desk guy was happy to take cash. There was no register. The bed was a queen with a green nylon bedspread.

"We won't be here long," Reacher said.

"It's fine," Pauling said.

She didn't unpack. Reacher kept his toothbrush in his pocket. He sat on the bed while Pauling washed up. Then she came out of the bathroom and moved to the window.

"Nearly ninety-five thousand square miles," she said. "Where do we start?"

"Let's call on the PI's," Reacher said.

So Pauling fetched her purse and took out a small device. A Palm Pilot. She found a name and an address.

"Gray's Inn Road," she said. "Is that near here?"

"I don't think so," Reacher said. "We can get there on the subway, I guess."

She dialed the phone on the night table. Reacher listened to Pauling's end of the conversation. She explained who she was and asked for an appointment. Then she asked, "How does six o'clock sound?" and then said, "Thank you, six o'clock it is," and hung up.

Reacher said, "I hope Edward Lane doesn't have a Palm Pilot full of London numbers."

THEY walked down to the tube stop at Lancaster Gate. It was a crowded six-stop ride. They came up out of the Chancery Lane station and walked north on Gray's Inn Road. There were old buildings, modernized on the ground floors, ancient above. A sign said that the house where Charles Dickens had lived was ahead.

Pauling was checking buildings for numbers. She spotted the one she wanted. It had a narrow maroon door with a glass fanlight. Reacher pushed it open, and they walked up two flights until they found a brass plate that said INVESTIGATIVE SERVICES PLC. The office was nothing more than a small room with a desk. The occupant was a small man with thin hair. He was maybe fifty years old.

"You must be the Americans," he said. "I stayed open especially for you. I didn't have any other appointments."

Pauling said, "Sorry to hold you up."

"Not a problem," the guy said. "Always happy to help a fellow professional."

"We're looking for someone," Pauling said. "He arrived from New York two days ago. He's English, and his name is Taylor."

"Twice in one day," the guy said. "Mr. Taylor is popular."

"What do you mean?"

"A man telephoned directly from New York with the same inquiry. Wouldn't give his name. I imagined he was trying all the London agencies."

Pauling turned to Reacher and mouthed *Lane*.

She turned back to the desk. "What did you tell him?"

"That there are sixty million people in Great Britain and that several hundred thousand of them are called Taylor. That without better information I couldn't help him."

"Can you help us?"

"That depends on what extra information you have."

"We have photographs."

"They might help eventually. But not at the outset."

Reacher said, "I've got a phone number for his closest relative. We searched Taylor's apartment in New York, and we found a desk phone that had ten speed dials programmed. The only British number was labeled with the letter *S*."

"What was the number?" the guy asked.

Reacher closed his eyes and recited the 01144 number he had memorized back on Hudson Street. The guy wrote it down.

"Okay," he said. "We delete the international prefix, and we add a zero in its place. Then we fire up the old computer, and we look in the reverse directory. This will give us the address only, you understand. We'll have to go elsewhere to discover the identity of the person who lives there." He hit several buttons, and the screen came up with an address.

"Grange Farm," he said. "In Bishops Pargeter. Not far from Norwich, judging by the postcode."

"Bishops Pargeter is the name of a town?"

The guy nodded. "It'll be a small village, probably. In the county of Norfolk. Farming country, very flat, windy. North and east of here, about a hundred and twenty miles away."

"Find the name."

"Hang on, hang on, I'm getting there." The guy opened up a different database. "The electoral register," he said. "Here we are. Two voters at that address. Mr. Anthony Jackson, and let's see, yes, Mrs. Susan Jackson. So there's your *S. S* for Susan."

"A sister," Pauling said. "Married. This is like Hobart."

"Now then," the guy said. "Let's do a little something else. Not quite legal this time, but I'm among colleagues." He opened a new database. "The Department of Work and Pensions." He entered Jackson's name and address and then added a complex keyboard command. "Anthony Jackson is thirty-nine years old, and his wife, Susan, is thirty-eight. Her maiden name was indeed Taylor. They have one child, a daughter, age eight, by the name of Melody."

The guy scrolled up the screen. "Melody seems to have been born in London." He opened another site. "The Land Registry," he said. He entered the address. Hit another SUBMIT command. "They bought the place in Bishops Pargeter just over a year ago. Which would suggest they're city folk heading back to the land."

"Thank you," Reacher said. "We appreciate your help. Maybe you could forget about this if the guy from New York calls again."

"First come, first served," the guy said. "My lips are sealed."

"Thank you," Reacher said again. "What do we owe you?"

"Oh, nothing at all," the guy said. "It was my pleasure entirely."

Back on the street Pauling said, "All Lane has to do is check Taylor's apartment and find the phone, and he's level with us."

"He won't find the phone," Reacher said. "And if he did, he wouldn't make the connection. Different skill set."

"Are you sure?"

"Not entirely. So I took the precaution of erasing the number."

"So what next?"

"We're going to have to go up there."

REACHER and Pauling walked down to Marble Arch to find a car rental office. Reacher had neither a driver's license nor a credit card, so he left Pauling to fill in the forms and went down Oxford Street to look for a bookstore. He found one that had a whole shelf of road atlases of Britain. The first three he checked didn't show Bishops Pargeter at all. Too small, he figured. Then he saw a cache of Ordnance Survey maps. He pulled all the Norfolk maps off the shelf and tried them one by one. He found Bishops Pargeter on the fourth attempt. It was a crossroads hamlet about thirty miles south and west of the Norwich outskirts.

He bought the map for detail and the cheapest road atlas for basic orientation. Then he hiked back to the rental office and found Pauling waiting with the key to a Mini Cooper.

He said, "I think Taylor might be there. With his sister."

"Why?"

"His instinct would be to go hide somewhere isolated. And he was a soldier, so he'd want somewhere defensible. It's flat as a pool table there. I just read the map. He'd see someone coming from five miles away. If he's got a rifle, he's impregnable. And if he's got four-wheel-drive, he's got a three-sixty escape route."

"It's possible," Pauling said. "So what's our play?"

"Taylor was with Lane three years," Reacher said. "So he never met you, and he never met me. He's not going to shoot every stranger who comes to the house. He can't really afford to."

"We're going right to the house?"

Reacher nodded. "At least close enough to scope it out. If Taylor's there, we back off and wait for Lane. If he isn't, we go all the way in and talk to Susan."

The rental guy brought the Mini Cooper out from a garage, and Reacher slid inside. Pauling got in the driver's seat and started the engine. She said, "We need to exit the city from the east."

"Northeast," Reacher said. "On a highway called the M11."

They made halting progress until they found the M25, which was a kind of beltway. They hit it clockwise, and two exits later they were on the M11, heading north and east. Nine o'clock in the evening, and getting dark.

Pauling asked, "What's Grange Farm going to be like?"

"I don't know," Reacher said. "Technically, in Old English a grange was a large barn for grain storage. Then later it became a word for the main building on a gentleman's arable farm. So I guess we're going to see a big house and a bunch of small outbuildings."

"You know a lot."

"I know that I don't like anything about this situation. It feels wrong. I can't get past the feeling that I'm making a bad mistake."

Much later they blew through a town called Fenchurch St. Mary. Then they saw a sign that said NORWICH 40 MILES. So Reacher started hunting for the turn to Bishops Pargeter. The road signs were clear and helpful. But the longer names were abbreviated. Reacher saw a sign to B'SH'PS P'TER, and they were two hundred yards past it before he figured out what it meant. So Pauling U-turned and went back, then turned onto a much smaller road. It was narrow and winding.

"How far?" Pauling asked.

"Nine miles," Reacher said. Then he looked out the window.

"This is pointless," he said. "It's too dark. We're not even going to see the house, let alone who's living in it." The map showed buildings about four miles ahead. One was labeled PH. He checked the legend in the corner of the sheet.

"Public house," he said. "A pub. Maybe an inn. We should get a room. Go out again at first light."

Pauling said, "Suits me, boss."

Eight minutes later they saw a glow in the distance that turned out to be the pub's spotlit sign. THE BISHOP'S ARMS. The windows looked warm and inviting.

Pauling turned in at the entrance of the parking lot and slotted the tiny car between a dirty Land Rover and a battered sedan. Turned the motor off. Reacher carried Pauling's bag to the pub's door. Dead ahead was a hotel reception counter made from dark old wood varnished to an amazing shine. It was unattended. To the left was a doorway marked SALOON BAR. It led to a room that seemed to be empty. To the right beyond the stairs was a doorway marked PUBLIC BAR. Through it Reacher could see a bartender and the backs of four drinkers hunched on stools. In the far corner he could see the back of a man sitting alone at a table.

Reacher dinged the bell. A long moment later the bartender came in. He was about sixty, large and florid.

"We need a room," Reacher said to him.

"It'll cost you forty pound. But that's with breakfast."

"Sounds like a bargain."

"You want one with a bath?"

Pauling said, "Yes, a bath. That would be nice."

She gave him four ten-pound notes, and he gave her a brass key. Then he handed Reacher a pen and squared a register in front of him. Reacher wrote "J. & L. Bayswater" on the NAME line. Then he checked a box for PLACE OF BUSINESS and wrote Yankee Stadium's street address on the next line. "East 161st Street, Bronx, New

York, USA." In a space labeled MAKE OF VEHICLE he scrawled "Rolls-Royce." Then he asked the bartender, "Can we get a meal?"

"You're a little too late for a meal, I'm afraid," the bartender said. "But you could have sandwiches, if you like."

"That would be fine," Reacher said.

"Go on and have a drink. Your sandwiches will be ready soon."

Reacher left Pauling's bag at the foot of the stairs and stepped through to the public bar. Five heads turned. The four guys at the bar looked like farmers. Red weathered faces, thick hands.

The guy alone at the table in the corner was Taylor.

LIKE the good soldier he was, Taylor kept his eyes on Reacher long enough to assess the threat level. Pauling's arrival behind Reacher's shoulder seemed to reassure him. *A well-dressed man, a refined woman, a couple, tourists.* He looked away. Turned back to his beer. Beginning to end he had stared only a fraction of a second longer than any man would in a barroom situation.

Reacher led Pauling to a table on the other side of the room from Taylor and sat with his back to the wall and watched the farmers turn back to the bar. A moment later the bartender reappeared.

Reacher said, "We should act normally. We should buy a drink."

Pauling said, "I guess I'll try the local beer."

So Reacher got up and stepped over to the bar. He said, "A pint of best, please, and a half for the lady." He turned to the four farmers and added: "And will you gentlemen join us?" Then he glanced at the bartender and said: "And can I get yours?" Taylor looked up from his table, and Reacher mimed a drinking action and called, "What can I get you?"

Taylor looked back at him and said, "Thanks, but I've got to go." A flat British accent. Calculation in his eyes. But no suspicion. A guileless half-smile. Then he got up and headed for the door.

The bartender pulled six and a half pints of best bitter and lined them up. Reacher paid. Then he picked his own up and carried Pauling's glass over to her, and the four farmers and the bartender all turned toward their table and toasted them. Reacher thought: Instant social acceptance for less than thirty bucks. But he said, "I hope I didn't offend that other fellow somehow."

"Don't know him," one of the farmers said.

"He's at Grange Farm," another farmer said. "Must be, because he was in Grange Farm's Land Rover."

"Is he a farmer?" Reacher asked.

"He don't look like one," the first farmer said. "I never saw him before."

"Where's Grange Farm?"

"Down the road apiece. There's a family there now."

"Ask Dave Kemp," the third farmer said. "He'll tell you."

Reacher said, "Who's Dave Kemp?"

"Dave Kemp in the shop," the third farmer said. "In Bishops Pargeter. Dave knows everything, on account of the post office. Nosy bugger."

"Is there a pub there?"

"This is the only pub for miles, lad. Why else do you think it's so crowded?"

Reacher didn't answer that.

"They're offcomers at Grange Farm," the first farmer said, completing his earlier thought. "From London. Organic, they are."

And that information seemed to conclude what the farmers felt they owed in exchange for a pint of beer, because they fell to talking among themselves about the advantages and disadvantages of organic farming. It felt like a well-worn argument.

"You were right," Pauling said. "Taylor's at the farm."

"But will he stay there now?" Reacher said.

"I don't see why not. Your big dumb generous American act was pretty convincing. Maybe he thought we're just tourists."

Their sandwiches were good. Fresh crusty homemade bread, butter, rare roast beef, creamy horseradish sauce, farmhouse cheese on the side. They ate them and finished their beers. Then they headed upstairs to their room. Reacher set the alarm in his head for six in the morning.

THE view out the window at six the next morning was one of infinite misty flatness. The land was level and gray-green all the way to the far horizon. The trees had long thin supple trunks and round compact crowns to withstand the winds.

Outside it was cold, and the car was misted with dew. They climbed inside without saying much. Pauling backed out of the parking space and joined the road, due east toward the morning sky. Five miles to Bishops Pargeter. Five miles to Grange Farm.

They found the farm before they found the village. It was bounded by ditches, not fences. Then came flat fields, neatly plowed, dusted pale green with late crops recently planted. Closer to the center were small stands of trees. Then a large gray stone house. Larger than Reacher had imagined. In the distance to the north and the east of the house were five outbuildings. Barns, long, low, and tidy. Three of them made a three-sided square around some kind of a yard. Two stood alone.

The road they were driving on was flanked by the ditch that formed the farm's southern boundary. The driveway crossed the boundary ditch on a small flat bridge and then ran north into the distance. The house itself was end-on to the road, a half-mile in. The Land Rover was parked between the back of the house and one of the stand-alone barns.

"He's still there," Reacher said.

Pauling slowed. There was no sign of activity around the house. She coasted to a halt and buzzed her window down. Reacher did the same thing, and cold damp air blew through the car.

Then the silence was shattered by a shotgun. Reacher and Pauling both ducked instinctively. Then they scanned the horizon.

"Hunters?" Pauling asked.

Reacher listened hard. Heard nothing more.

"I think it was a bird scarer," he said. "They just planted a winter crop. They don't want the crows to eat the seeds. I think they have machines that fire blanks all day at random."

"I hope that's all it was."

"We'll come back," Reacher said. "Let's go find Dave Kemp."

Pauling took off again. Reacher twisted in his seat and watched the eastern half of the farm go by. Trees near the house, then wide flat fields, then a ditch on the boundary. Then came the Bishops Pargeter crossroad. Then the hamlet itself, which was little more than an ancient stone church standing alone and a fifty-yard string of buildings along the road opposite. One of them was a multi-purpose store. It was a newspaper shop and a grocery and a post office. It was already open.

"The direct approach?" Pauling asked.

"A variant," Reacher said.

They got out of the car into a stiff wind. The village store felt warm and snug by comparison. There was a shuttered post office window and a central section that sold food and a newspaper counter at the far end. There was an old guy behind the counter.

"Are you Dave Kemp?" Reacher asked.

"That's my name," the old guy said.

"We're here to buy farms."

"You're Americans, aren't you?"

"We represent a large agricultural corporation in the United States, yes. And we can offer very generous finders' fees. Generally we want good places that were recently bought up by amateurs. But we want them before they're ruined."

"Grange Farm," Kemp said. "They're bloody amateurs. They've gone organic. It should be top of your list. They've bitten off more than they can chew there. And that's when they're both at home."

"Grange Farm sounds like a good prospect," Reacher said. "But we heard that someone else is snooping around there, too. He's been seen recently."

"Really?" Kemp said, excited, conflict in the offing. Then his face fell. "No, that's the woman's brother."

"Are you sure about that?"

Kemp nodded. "The chap came in here and introduced himself. Said his wandering days were over. He was posting a packet to America. We had quite a nice chat."

Pauling asked, "What did he post to America?"

"He didn't tell me what it was. It was going to a hotel in New York. Addressed to a room, not a person."

Reacher asked, "Did you guess what it was?"

"It felt like a thin book," Kemp said. "Not many pages. A rubber band around it. Not that I squeezed it or anything."

"Didn't he fill out a customs declaration?"

"We put it down as printed papers. Don't need a form."

"Thanks, Mr. Kemp," Reacher said.

"What about the fee?"

"If we buy the farm, you'll get it," Reacher said.

If we buy the farm, he thought. Unfortunate turn of phrase.

THEY went back to the farmhouse. The place was still quiet.

"You were very plausible," said Pauling. "It fit in with last night. Assuming Kemp spreads the word, Taylor's going to put you down as a con man looking to make a fast buck."

"I can lie with the best of them," Reacher said. "Sadly."

Then he shut up fast, because the farmhouse door was opening. He made out four figures emerging. Two big, one slightly smaller, one very small. Probably two men, a woman, and a little child.

Pauling said, "Four people. It's the Jacksons and Taylor, right?"

"Must be."

They all had things on their shoulders. Long poles.

"What are they doing?" Pauling asked.

"Those are hoes," Reacher said. "They're going to the fields."

The tiny figures moved north, away from the road, just faint remote blurs in the mist.

"He's staying," Pauling said. "Isn't he? You don't go out to hoe weeds for your sister if you're thinking about running."

Reacher nodded. "We've seen enough. The job is done. Let's get back to London and wait for Lane."

THEY hit commuter traffic on the road to London. Lots of it. It moved slowly, circulating like water around a bathtub drain before yielding to the pull of the city.

The stick shift was hard work in the congestion. Two hours into the ride they pulled off and got gas, and Reacher changed places with Pauling, even though he wasn't on the paperwork.

They came in through St. John's Wood, past Regent's Park, through Marble Arch, and onto Park Lane. The Hilton hotel was at the south end. They parked in a commercial garage at a quarter to eleven in the morning.

"Want lunch?" Pauling said.

"Can't eat," Reacher said. "I feel like I'm delivering Taylor to an executioner."

"He deserves to die."

"I'd rather do it myself."

"So make the offer."

"Lane wants the partner's name. I'm not up for torturing it out of the guy personally."

"So walk away."

"I can't. I want retribution for Kate and Jade, and I want the money for Hobart. And we have a deal with your Pentagon buddy. But all things considered I think I'll skip lunch."

Pauling asked, "Where do you want me?"

"In the lobby. Watching. Then go get a room somewhere else. Leave me a note at the Hilton's desk. Use the name Bayswater. I'll take Lane to Norfolk, Lane will deal with Taylor, I'll deal with Lane. Then I'll come back and get you. Then we'll try to get clean again."

They went up a flight of steps to the Hilton. Pauling detoured to a distant group of armchairs, and Reacher walked to the desk. He stood in line. Above a Xerox machine was a plaque that said BY

STATUTE SOME DOCUMENTS MAY NOT BE PHOTOCOPIED. Like bank-notes, Reacher thought. Then he moved to the head of the line.

"Edward Lane's party," he said. "Have they checked in yet?"

The clerk tapped his keyboard. "Not yet, sir."

"When they get here, tell them I'm across the lobby."

"Your name, sir?"

"Taylor," Reacher said. He walked away and found a quiet spot. He was going to be counting eight hundred thousand dollars in cash, and he didn't want an audience. He dumped himself down in one of a group of four armchairs. A nearby family was watching him warily. Two kids and a mother. The mother had unpacked half their stuff, trying to keep them amused. Coloring books, battered teddy bears, a doll missing an arm, video games. He could hear the mother's halfhearted suggestions: Why don't you do this? Why don't you do that? Why don't you draw a picture of something you're going to see?

He turned away and watched the door.

He saw Perez walk in. Then Kowalski. Then Edward Lane himself. Then Gregory and Groom and Addison and Burke. Roll-on bags, duffels. A little creased and crumpled. But awake and alert and aware. They looked exactly like what they were: a group of Special Forces soldiers trying to travel incognito.

He watched them check in. Watched the clerk give Lane the message. Saw Lane turn around. Lane's gaze moved over the lobby. Onto Reacher's face. Lane nodded. All seven men hoisted their luggage again and eased their way through the crowds and stopped in a group outside the ring of armchairs. Lane dropped one bag and kept hold of another and sat down opposite Reacher.

"Show me the money," Reacher said.

"Do you know where Taylor is?"

Reacher nodded. "I know where he is. I made visual contact twice. Last night, and then again this morning."

"So tell me where he is."

"Show me the money first."

Lane said nothing.

Reacher said, "You called a bunch of London private eyes. Behind my back. You tried to get ahead of me."

Lane said, "A man's entitled to save an unnecessary expense."

"Did you get ahead of me?"

"No."

"Therefore the expense is necessary. So show me the money."

"Okay," Lane said. He placed the duffel on the floor and unzipped it. Reacher leaned down. The duffel was full of money.

Reacher put a fingernail under one of the paper bands. It was tight. Therefore full. There were four stacks of twenty bricks each. Total of eighty bricks. A hundred hundreds in each brick. Eighty times a hundred times a hundred was eight hundred thousand.

He lifted the edge of a bill and rubbed it between his finger and thumb. They were real. He could feel the engraving. He could smell the paper and the ink. Unmistakable.

"Okay," he said, and sat back.

Lane zipped the duffel. "So where is he?"

Reacher said, "There are civilians there. Noncombatants."

"We won't be shooting," Lane said. "A bullet is too good for Taylor. We'll go in, and we'll get him, and we'll bring him out without harming a hair on his or anyone else's head. He'll tell us about his partner, and then he'll die, slow and hard. So a gunfight is no good to me. Not because I care about noncombatants. But because I don't want any accidents with Taylor."

"Okay," Reacher said.

"So where is he?"

Reacher paused. Thought about Hobart, and Birmingham, Alabama, and Nashville, Tennessee.

"He's in Norfolk," he said. "It's a county, north and east of here. About a hundred and twenty miles."

"Where in Norfolk?"

"A place called Grange Farm."

"Nearest big city?"

"It's about thirty miles south and west of Norwich."

"Nearest town?"

Reacher didn't reply.

"Nearest town?" Lane asked again.

Reacher glanced at the reception desk. By statute some documents may not be photocopied. He watched a Xerox machine at work, a ghostly stripe of green light cycling horizontally back and forth beneath a lid. He heard the harassed mother's voice in his head: *Why don't you draw a picture of something you're going to see?* He looked at the kid's doll, missing an arm. Heard Dave Kemp's voice, in the country store: *It felt like a thin book.*

Lane said, "Reacher?"

Reacher heard Lauren Pauling's voice in his mind: *A little is sometimes all you need. Going out, they don't care as much as when you're coming in.*

Lane said, "Reacher? Hello? What's the nearest town?"

Reacher dragged his focus back, and he looked directly into Lane's eyes. He said, "The nearest town is called Fenchurch St. Mary. Be ready to leave in one hour. I'll come back for you."

Then he stood up and concentrated hard on walking slowly across the lobby floor. He caught Pauling's eye. Walked out the door onto the sidewalk.

Then he ran for the parking garage.

REACHER had parked the car, so he still had the keys. He blipped the door and wrenched it open and threw himself inside. Hurled the tiny car out of the parking space. He threw a ten-pound note at the barrier guy. He blasted up the ramp and shot straight across two lanes of traffic and jammed to a stop because he saw Pauling hurrying toward him. She slid inside, and he took off again.

"North," he said. "Which way is north?"

"North is behind us," she said. "What the hell is going on?"

"Just get me out of town. Use the atlas. There's a city plan."

Pauling turned pages, frantically. "Go straight. Make a right onto St. John's Wood Road. That will take us back to Regent's Park. Then make a left, and go out the same way we came in. And please tell me exactly what is going on."

"I made a mistake," Reacher said. "Remember I told you I couldn't shake the feeling I was making a bad mistake? Well, I was wrong. It wasn't a bad mistake. It was a catastrophic mistake."

"What mistake?"

"Tell me about the photographs in your apartment. Nieces and nephews, right?"

"Lots of them," Pauling said.

"Tell me about their favorite toys. Their old favorites. What would they run into a fire to save?"

"I guess a teddy bear or a doll. Something they'd had since they were tiny."

"Exactly," Reacher said. "Something they love. The kind of thing they would want to take on a journey. Like the family next to me in the lobby just now."

"So?"

"What do those things look like?"

"They look like crap."

Reacher nodded at the wheel. "The bears all worn, with the stuffing out? The dolls all chipped, with the arms off?"

"Yes, like that. All kids have toys like that."

"Jade didn't. That's what was missing from her room."

"What are you saying?"

"I'm saying that if Jade had been kidnapped on the way to Bloomingdale's, I would have found all her favorite old toys still in her room afterward. But I didn't."

"But what does that mean?"

"It means Jade knew she was leaving. She packed."

REACHER figured he was about two hours ahead of Edward Lane. It would take an hour for Lane to realize he had been ditched, and then it would take at least another hour for him to organize pursuit.

Pauling said, "Jade packed?"

"Kate packed, too," Reacher said. "Her most precious thing. The photograph with her daughter. From the bedroom."

"But you saw it," Pauling said. "She didn't take it."

Reacher shook his head. "I saw a photocopy. From Staples. It was very good, but not quite good enough."

"But who packs for a kidnap?"

"They weren't kidnapped," Reacher said. "That's the thing. They were set free. They're alive somewhere. Alive and well and happy."

They drove on through the northern reaches of London, through Finchley and Swiss Cottage, toward Hendon.

"Kate believed Dee Marie," Reacher said. "That's what happened. Out there in the Hamptons. Dee Marie told her about Anne and warned her, and Kate believed her. Like Patti Joseph said, there was something about the story and something about her husband that made Kate believe. Maybe she was already feeling the same kinds of things that Anne had felt five years before. Maybe she was already planning to go down the same road."

Pauling said, "You know what this means?"

"Of course I do."

"Taylor helped them. He rescued them, and he hid them, and he risked his life for them. He's the good guy."

Reacher nodded. "And I just told Lane where he is."

They negotiated their last London traffic circle and joined the highway at its southern tip. Reacher forced the Mini up to ninety-five miles an hour.

Pauling said, "What about the money?"

"Alimony," Reacher said. "We thought it was half of the Burkina Faso payment, but in Kate's eyes it was also half of their community property. She probably put money in, way back. That's what Lane seems to want his wives for. Apart from their trophy status."

"Hell of a plan," Pauling said. "But they made mistakes."

"They sure did. If you really want to disappear, you take nothing with you. Absolutely nothing at all. It's fatal."

"Who helped Taylor? He had an American partner. On the phone."

"You were half right, days ago. It was a woman using that machine. It was Kate herself. She did all the talking, because Taylor couldn't. Not easy for her. Every time Lane wanted to hear her voice for a proof of life she had to pull the machine off the mouth-piece and then put it back on again."

"Did you really tell Lane where Taylor is?"

"As good as. He'll be able to work it with the right map."

Pauling was quiet for a second. "He's two hours behind us right now. But he won't always be. We have to try to warn them. There's the sister to think about. And Melody."

"Susan and Melody are perfectly safe."

"How can you say that?"

"Ask yourself where Kate and Jade are."

"I have no idea where they are."

"You do," Reacher said. "You know exactly where they are. You saw them this morning."

THEY turned off the highway at Newmarket and set out toward Norwich. The road was familiar, but that didn't make it any faster.

Reacher said, "Think about the dynamic here. Why would Kate ask Taylor for help? How could she ask any of them for help? They're all insanely loyal to Lane."

Pauling said, "They already had a thing going."

"That's the only way to explain it. And there were signs. Groom said that Kate liked Taylor and Taylor got on well with the kid."

"Dee Marie showing up must have acted like a tipping point."

Reacher nodded again. "Kate and Taylor made a plan and put it in action. But first they explained it to Jade."

"Big secret for a kid to keep."

"She didn't exactly keep it," Reacher said. "She was worried about it. She straightened it out in her head by drawing it. Mothers always say, Draw a picture of something you're going to see."

"What picture?"

"There were four in her room. Kate didn't sanitize well enough. There was a big gray building with trees in front. I thought it was the Dakota. Now I think it was the Grange Farm farmhouse. They must have shown her photographs. She got the trees just right. Like green lollipops on brown sticks. And then there was a picture of a family group. I thought the guy was Lane. But there was something weird about his mouth. Like half his teeth had been punched out. So it was Taylor. She drew her new family. Taylor, Kate, and her."

"And you think Taylor brought them here to England?"

"They needed a safe haven. Jade did a picture of three people in an airplane. Then she did one of two families together. Like double vision. I had no idea what it meant. But now my guess is that was Jackson and Taylor, and Susan and Kate, and Melody and herself. Her new extended family."

"But their passports were still in the drawer," Pauling said.

"That was crude," Reacher said. "Leaving them on show like that was a message. Hey, we're still in the country. Which meant actually they weren't."

"How do you get out without a passport?"

"You don't. But you once said they don't look as closely on the way out."

Pauling paused a beat. "Someone else's passport?"

"Who do we know that fits the bill? A woman in her thirties and an eight-year-old girl?"

Pauling said, "Susan and Melody."

"Susan and Melody had flown to the States. They got all the correct entry stamps. Then they gave their passports to Kate and Jade. Then Taylor booked on British Airways. He was sitting next to a British woman on the plane. A buck gets ten she's on the passenger manifest as Susan Jackson. And another buck gets ten that next to her was Melody Jackson. But they were really Kate and Jade Lane."

"But that leaves Susan and Melody stuck in the States."

"Temporarily," Reacher said. "What did Taylor mail back?"

"A thin book. Not many pages."

"Two passports, bundled together. Mailed to Susan's New York City hotel room."

"But when they leave, they'll be exiting without having entered."

Reacher nodded. "It's an irregularity. But what are the people at JFK going to do about it? Deport them? That's what they want. So they'll get home okay."

"Sisters," Pauling said. "This whole thing has been about the loyalty of sisters."

JOHN Gregory was hitting the gas, too. He was at the wheel of a rented dark green seven-seat Toyota Land Cruiser SUV. Edward Lane was next to him. Kowalski and Addison and Groom were on the rear bench. Burke and Perez were on the jump seats. They were joining the highway at its southern tip, having blasted through central London to the northeast corner of the inner city.

THIS time Reacher saw the sign to B'SH'PS P'TER and slowed well in advance. It was close to two o'clock in the afternoon. The sun was high. A perfect English late-summer day. Almost.

Pauling said, "What are you going to tell them?"

"That I'm sorry," Reacher said.

"Then what?"

"Then I'll probably say it again."

"Don't beat yourself up. They faked a kidnap. Don't blame yourself for taking it seriously."

"I should have seen it," Reacher said.

They passed the Bishop's Arms. The pub. They passed the ditch that marked Grange Farm's western boundary.

Reacher slowed the car well before the small flat bridge. Turned in wide. Small vehicle, low speed. Unthreatening. He hoped.

The driveway was long, and it looped through two curves. The earth was muddy and less even than it had looked from a distance. Reacher opened his window and heard nothing at all except the noise of his engine and the slow crunch of his tires on gravel.

"Where is everybody?" Pauling said.

The driveway split thirty yards in front of the house. West, the formal approach to the front door. East, a shabbier track toward the barns. Reacher went east. The Land Rover wasn't there. The barn doors were closed. The whole place was quiet.

Reacher backed up. Took the wider path west. He stopped ten feet from the front door.

"What now?" Pauling asked.

"We knock," Reacher said.

Then they walked to the front door. It was a large slab of ancient oak, as black as coal. There was a twisted ring hinged in the mouth of a lion and positioned to strike down on a nail head as big as an apple. Reacher used it, twice. It resonated like a bass drum.

Reacher called, "Taylor? Graham Taylor?"

No response. No sound at all.

Except for the shuffle of a tiny foot, thirty feet away. Reacher glanced to his left. Saw a small bare knee pull back around the far corner of the house.

"I saw you," Reacher called. "Come on out now. It's okay."

No response.

A long moment later Reacher saw a small dark head peer out from around the corner. A small face, pale skin, big green eyes. A little girl, about eight years old.

"Hello," Pauling called. "What's your name?"

"Melody Jackson," Jade Lane said.

THE kid was instantly recognizable from the imperfect Xerox Reacher had seen on the desk in the Dakota bedroom. It had been a striking photograph, but the reality was way better. Jade Lane was a truly beautiful child.

"My name is Lauren," Pauling said. "This man is Reacher."

Jade nodded her head. She was wearing a summer dress, sleeveless, green seersucker stripes. She had white socks on, and thin summer sandals.

Pauling said, "We're here to talk to the grown-ups. Do you know where they are?"

A voice said, "One of them is right here," and Kate Lane stepped out from around the other corner of the house. She was pretty much unchanged from her photograph, too. Extremely, impossibly beautiful. She was maybe five feet nine inches tall, slim and willowy. She was wearing a man's flannel shirt. She looked great in it.

"I'm Susan Jackson," she said.

Reacher shook his head. "You're not, but I'm very glad to meet you anyway. And Jade, too. You'll never know how glad I am."

"Who are you?"

"My name is Reacher. Where's Taylor?"

"Who?"

Reacher took a step toward Kate. "Can we talk? I don't want to upset your daughter."

"She knows what's going on."

"Okay," Reacher said. "We're here to warn you. Edward Lane is an hour behind us. Maybe less."

"Edward is here?" Kate said. For the first time, real fear in her face. "Edward is here in England? Already?"

Reacher nodded. "Heading this way. He paid me to find Taylor."

"So why warn us?"

"Because I just figured out it wasn't for real."

Kate said nothing.

"Where's Taylor?" Reacher asked again.

"He's out," Kate said. "With Tony."

"Anthony Jackson? The brother-in-law?"

Kate nodded. "Norwich. For a part for the backhoe."

"When did they leave?"

"About two hours ago."

About a two-hour trip. "Let's all go inside," Reacher said.

Kate seemed reassured by the presence of another woman. She opened the front door. Led them all in. The farmhouse had low beamed ceilings. Thick walls and flowered wallpaper and small leaded windows. The kitchen was a large rectangular room. There were bright copper pans hanging from hooks, and sofas and chairs and a fireplace big enough to live in and a huge old-fashioned range. There was a massive oak dining table with twelve chairs around it and a separate desk with a phone and stacks of papers.

Reacher said, "I think you should get out, Kate. Right now. You and Jade. Until we see what happens."

"How?" Kate asked. "The truck isn't here."

"Take our car." Pauling said. "Or I'll drive you."

"Where to?"

"Anywhere you want to go. Until we see what happens."

"Does he know?"

"That it was all a sham? Not yet."

"Okay," Kate said. "Take us somewhere. Now. Please."

She grabbed Jade's hand. No purse, no coat. She was ready to go, right there and then. Reacher tossed Pauling the Mini's keys and followed them all outside again.

"Wait," Reacher said.

On the road a mile to the west he could see a dark green shape moving fast. Clean and shiny, not filthy like the farm truck.

A mile away. Ninety seconds. No time.

"Everybody back in the house," he said. "Right now."

Kate and Jade and Pauling ran upstairs, and Reacher headed for the southeast corner of the house and crept around to where he could get a look at the bridge over the ditch. He got there just in time to see a dark green truck turn in. Two guys in it. One of them was Tony Jackson. The other was Taylor. The truck was the Grange Farm Land Rover, newly cleaned and polished. Unrecognizable from the night before. Clearly the Norwich itinerary had included a stop at the car wash as well as the backhoe dealership.

Reacher shouted an all clear up the stairs. Then he went back outside. The Land Rover skidded to a halt between the back of the house and the barns. The doors opened, and Jackson and Taylor climbed out. Jackson walked up to Reacher and said, "Dave Kemp told me what you want. And the answer is no. I'm not selling."

"I'm not buying," Reacher said.

"So why are you here?"

Jackson was a compact guy, not unlike Taylor. Same kind of generic English features. Better teeth.

Reacher said, "I'm here to see Taylor."

Taylor stepped up and said, "What for?"

"To apologize to you," Reacher said. "And to warn you."

Taylor paused a beat. Then his eyes flicked left, flicked right, full of intelligence and calculation.

"Lane?" he asked.

"He's less than an hour away."

"Okay," Taylor said. He sounded calm. Not surprised. But surprise was for amateurs. And Taylor was a professional.

"I saw you on Sixth Avenue," Taylor said. "When I was getting in the Jaguar. Didn't think much of it, but I saw you again last night. In the pub. So then I knew. I thought you'd be heading up to your room to call Lane. But he mobilized himself faster than I thought."

"He was already en route."

"Does he have this precise location?"

"I said Grange Farm. I stopped myself saying Bishops Pargeter. I said Fenchurch St. Mary instead."

"He'll find us in the phone book."

"I'm sorry," Reacher said.

"When did you figure it all out?"

"Just a little bit too late."

"What tipped you off?"

"Toys. Jade packed her best toys."

Taylor smiled. "What are you, a private cop?"

"I was a U.S. Army MP."

"What's your name?"

"Reacher."

"You're good. But it was always only a matter of time. The longer nobody found my body, the more people would get to thinking. But I thought I might have a couple of weeks."

"You've got about sixty minutes."

They gathered in the farmhouse kitchen for a council of war. Jade sat at the table and drew. First thing Taylor said was, "Let's light the fire again. It's cold in here. And let's have a cup of tea."

Pauling asked, "Do we have time for that?"

"The British army," Reacher said. "They always have time for a cup of tea."

Jackson didn't seem very worried. Just calm and competent.

"What were you, back in the day?" Reacher asked him.

"First Para," Jackson replied.

The First Parachute Regiment. The British equivalent of the U.S. Army Rangers. Airmobile tough guys.

"Lane's got six guys with him," Reacher said.

"The A-team?" Taylor asked. "Used to be seven guys. Before I resigned."

"Used to be nine guys," Reacher said.

"Hobart and Knight," Taylor said. "Kate heard that story. From Hobart's sister."

"Was that the trigger?"

"Partly. And partly something else. Hobart isn't the only one. He's the worst, maybe, but Lane got a lot of people killed and wounded over the years."

"Is that why you wanted the money?"

"The money is Kate's alimony. She's entitled to it. But I'm sure she'll do the right thing."

Tony Jackson poured the tea, hot and sweet and strong, into five chipped and unmatched mugs.

"Do we have time for this?" Pauling asked again.

"Reacher?" Taylor said. "Do we have time for this?"

"That depends," Reacher said. "On what exactly your aim is."

"My aim is to live happily ever after."

"Okay," Reacher said. "If it was Kansas, Dave Kemp's store would be selling rifles and ammunition. But this isn't Kansas. And no way did Lane bring anything in on the plane. So if he shows up now, he's unarmed."

"But there have to be weapons somewhere," Pauling said.

Taylor nodded. "All over. But it takes time to find them."

"How much time?"

"Twelve hours minimum, I would guess. So, if Lane wants to lock and load first, he can't show up until at least tomorrow. Plus, he likes dawn raids."

"Are you armed here?" Reacher asked.

"This is a farm," Jackson answered. "Farmers are always prepared for vermin control."

Something in his voice. Some kind of lethal determination.

Reacher got up and walked over and took a look at the phone. It was an old-fashioned black instrument. No memory. No speed dial.

He turned to Taylor. "You wanted this," he said. "You used the name Leroy Clarkson. To point the way to your apartment."

Taylor said nothing.

"You could have stopped Jade from bringing her toys. You could have told Kate to leave the photograph behind. Your sister Susan could have brought Tony's passport over for you. Then there would have been three Jacksons on the airplane manifest, not two Jacksons and a Taylor. Without your real name you couldn't have been followed back to England."

Taylor said nothing.

"The phone in your apartment was new," Reacher said. "You bought it so that you could leave Susan's number in it."

Taylor said nothing.

"You talked to Dave Kemp," Reacher said. "And he's the biggest gossip in the county. Then you hung out in the pub with a bunch of nosy farmers. Because you wanted to lay a clear trail. Because you wanted to bring Lane here for a showdown."

Silence in the room.

Reacher said, "You wanted to be on your home turf. And you figured this is an easy place to defend."

Taylor nodded. "He was a little faster than we expected. But yes, we wanted him to come. We wanted closure."

"Why now?"

Kate Lane looked up from her chair by the fire.

"I'm pregnant," she said.

IN THE soft light of the flames from the hearth, Kate's simple and vulnerable beauty was emphasized to the point of heartbreak. She said, "When Edward and I first started fighting, he accused me of being unfaithful. Which wasn't actually true then. He said if he ever caught me sleeping around he would show me how much it hurt him by doing something to Jade that would hurt me even more. I persuaded myself not to take it seriously. But after hearing about

Anne and Knight and Hobart I knew I had to take it seriously. By which time I really did have something to hide. So we ran."

"With Lane right behind you." Reacher turned to Jackson. "You're not fixing the backhoe to dredge ditches, are you? You're fixing the backhoe to dig graves."

Taylor said, "You got a problem with that?"

"No," Reacher answered. "I don't have a problem with that."

Taylor said, "Ms. Pauling? What about you?"

Pauling said, "I ought to have a huge problem. Once upon a time I swore an oath to uphold the law."

"But?"

"I can't get to Lane any other way."

"So we're in business," Taylor said. "Welcome to the party."

After they finished their tea, Jackson took Reacher into a small mudroom off the kitchen and opened a wall cupboard. In it were racked four Heckler & Koch G36 automatic rifles. The G36 was a modern design that had shown up in service just before Reacher's military career had ended. Like most German weapons, it looked very expensive and beautifully engineered.

Reacher asked, "Where did you get these?"

"I bought them. From a bent quartermaster in Holland."

"Got ammunition?"

Jackson opened another cupboard. Reacher could see the glint of black metal. A lot of it.

"We can't use more than three or four rounds. Too noisy."

"How close are the cops?"

"Not very. Norwich. But people here have phones."

"The bird scarer is new, too?"

Jackson nodded. "Part of the planning. Set to start firing at dawn. That's when we expect Lane to come."

"If I had a sister and a brother-in-law, I'd want them to be like you and Susan."

"I go way back with Taylor."

"You okay with all of this? You've got roots here, literally."

"We'll be okay."

Jackson locked both cupboards. Reacher stepped back into the kitchen and sat down next to Taylor.

"Tell me about Gregory," he said.

"What about him?"

"Is he going to stand by Lane? Or you?"

"Lane, I think. Gregory always wanted an officer's commission, but he never got it. And then Lane made him a kind of unofficial lieutenant. Plus he'll be offended that I didn't share my secret."

"What about the others? Will any of them turn?"

"The best we can hope for is neutrality from Groom and Burke. And I wouldn't bet the farm on that."

"How good are they? All of them, as a whole?"

"They're about as good as me. They used to be outstanding, and now they're well on the way to average. Plenty of experience and ability, but they don't train anymore."

"Why did you join them?"

"The money," Taylor said. "Then I stayed because of Kate."

They drew lots for the first round of lookout duty. Jackson and Pauling pulled the short straws. Jackson sat in the Land Rover at the back of the house, and Pauling sat in the Mini at the front. That way each of them could cover a little more than one hundred and eighty degrees. Across the flat land they could see a mile or more. Ninety seconds' warning if Lane came in by road, a little more if he came in across the fields, which would be a slower approach.

Reasonable security. As long as the daylight lasted.

11

THE daylight lasted until a little after eight o'clock. By then, Reacher was in the Land Rover and Kate Lane was in the Mini. Twilight rolled in fast, and with it came an evening mist that cut visibility to less than a hundred yards.

Taylor and Jackson were in one of the barns, working on the backhoe. Pauling was in the kitchen, opening cans for dinner. Jade was at the table, drawing.

By eight thirty visibility was so marginal that Reacher headed for the kitchen. Taylor appeared out of the gloom.

"Ten hours to go," he said. "We're safe until dawn."

"You sure?" Reacher said. "We could take Kate and Jade someplace else."

"Better if they stay," Taylor said. "I don't want my focus split."

Privately Reacher agreed with Taylor. Split focus was a bad thing. And Lane's guys might already have covert surveillance going. If so, they would have the roads covered. If they were given the chance to see Kate and Jade Lane, then the whole game would change.

They planned as they ate dinner. Agreed to set up two two-person watches, sequential, five hours each. That would take them through until dawn. Each would be armed with a loaded G36. The first watch would be Taylor and Jackson, and at half past one Reacher and Pauling would take over. Kate Lane would sit it out. The possibility that a hostile nighttime reconnaissance probe might identify her was too much of a risk.

Reacher washed the dishes, and Taylor and Jackson went outside with their G36s. Kate went upstairs to put Jade to bed. Pauling put logs on the fire.

A half-hour later Kate Lane came downstairs again.

"Jade's asleep," she said.

Reacher asked, "Is she doing okay?"

Kate said, "She's not sleeping great. The jet lag has screwed her up. And she's a little nervous. She doesn't understand why there are no animals here. She doesn't understand arable farming. She thinks we're hiding a bunch of cute little creatures from her."

Reacher said, "Tell me how the whole thing went down."

"It was pretty easy, really. We did stuff in advance. Bought the voice machine, rented the room, got the chair, took the car keys."

"Taylor did most of that?"

"But I had to buy the voice machine. Too weird if a guy who couldn't talk wanted one."

"I guess."

"Then I copied the photograph at Staples. That was tough. I had to let Groom drive me. It would have been too suspicious to insist on Graham all the time. But after that it was easy. We left for Bloomingdale's that morning and went straight to Graham's apartment instead. Just holed up there and waited. Then later we started the phone calls. Right from the apartment."

"You forgot to say no cops."

"I know. I thought I'd blown it. But Edward didn't seem to notice. Then it got much easier later. With practice."

"Why did you split the demands into three parts?"

"Because to ask for it all at once would have been too much of a clue. We thought we better let the stress build up. Then maybe Edward would miss the connection."

"I don't think he missed it. But I think he misinterpreted it. He started thinking about Hobart and the Africa connection."

"How bad is Hobart, really?"

"About as bad as it gets."

"That's unforgivable."

"No argument from me."

"Do you think I'm cold-blooded?"

"If I did it wouldn't be a criticism."

"Edward wanted to own me. Like a chattel. And he said if I was ever unfaithful he would hurt Jade. He said he would tie me up and make me watch him do it. They say you should never get between a lioness and her cub. I never understood that before. Now I do."

The flames in the fireplace flickered and danced.

Reacher asked, "Are you planning on staying here forever?"

"I hope to," Kate said. "Organic farming is going to be a big thing. Better for people, better for the land."

"Hard to picture you as a farmer."

"I think I'm going to enjoy it."

"Even when Lane is out of the picture permanently?"

"In that case I guess we would go back to New York occasionally. But downtown only. I won't go back to the Dakota."

"Anne's sister lives directly opposite the Dakota. She's been watching Lane every day for four years."

Kate said, "I'd like to meet her. And I'd like to see Hobart's sister again."

"Like a survivors' club," Pauling said.

Reacher walked to the window. Saw nothing but blackness.

"First we have to survive," he said.

THEY kept the fire going and dozed quietly in the armchairs. When the clock in Reacher's head hit one-thirty in the morning, he tapped Pauling on the knee. They headed outside together into the dead-of-night dark and cold. Called softly and met Taylor and Jackson in a huddle outside the front door. Reacher took Taylor's weapon and headed for the south end of the house.

He settled in and waited. After a minute his eyesight had adjusted, and he saw that there was a little moonlight behind heavy cloud. Nobody would see him from a distance.

He stepped forward two paces and stood still. Turned his head slowly and scoped out a two hundred degree arc all around him.

At first he heard nothing. Just an absolute absence of sound. Then as he relaxed and concentrated, he started to pick up tiny imperceptible sounds drifting in across the flat land. The thrill of faint breezes in distant trees. The hum of power lines a mile away. The soak of water turning earth to mud in ditches. He knew that any human approach might as well be accompanied by a marching band. He would hear it clearly a hundred yards away.

Reacher, alone in the dark. Armed and dangerous. Invincible.

He stood in the same spot for five straight hours. Nobody came. By six thirty in the morning there was a bright horizontal band of pink in the sky. Gray visibility was spreading westward slowly, like an incoming tide.

Taylor and Jackson came out of the house carrying the third and fourth rifles. Reacher took up a new station against the rear façade of the house, facing south. Taylor mirrored his position against the front wall. Reacher knew that sixty feet behind them Jackson and Pauling were doing the same thing. Reasonable security.

For as long as they could bear to stay in position.

THEY stayed in position all day long and well into the evening. Fourteen straight hours.

Lane didn't come.

One at a time they took short meal breaks and shorter bathroom breaks. Their eight-pound rifles started to feel like eight tons in their hands.

Kate and Jade stayed in the house, out of sight. They made food and poured drinks. The sun burned through the mist, and the day grew warm, and then it grew cold again in the late afternoon.

Lane didn't come.

Jade drew pictures. She drew the red Mini Cooper, she drew Pauling with her gun. She drew Reacher, taller than the house. Then she drew farm animals in the barns, even though she had been told that the Jacksons didn't have any.

Lane didn't come.

Jade took to asking everyone in turn if she could come outside and explore. Everyone in turn said no. On the third go-round Reacher heard her modify her request and ask Taylor if she could come out after dark, and he heard Taylor say maybe, like worn-down parents everywhere.

At eight thirty in the evening they all met in a loose huddle by the front door, shaky with fatigue.

Taylor said, "He's waiting us out."

"Therefore he's going to win," Jackson said. "We can't keep this up much longer."

Pauling said, "We have to assume he's armed by now."

"He'll come tomorrow at dawn," Taylor said.

"You sure?" Reacher asked.

"Not really. How would you do it?"

"Three guys walk in from the north. The other four come up the driveway, maybe two in a car, lights off, high speed, with the other two flanking it on foot. Seven guys, their choice of seven windows, we couldn't stop at least three of them getting inside."

"We'd get them before they got near the house."

"Only if all four of us can stay alert for the next eight hours. Or the next thirty-two hours. Or the next fifty-six. He's in no hurry."

Taylor said, "This place is a stronghold."

"But time is on Lane's side, not ours. We're going to run out of food, and sooner or later all four of us are going to be asleep at the same time." Reacher shook his head. "It's time to get aggressive."

"How?"

"I'm going to go find them. They won't be expecting that."

"Alone?" Pauling said. "That's insane."

"I have to anyway," Reacher said. "I didn't get Hobart's money yet. There's eight hundred grand out there."

REACHER fetched the big Ordnance Survey map from the Mini's glove compartment. Then he went over it with Jackson. The map clarified most of the terrain issues. Grange Farm and Bishops Pargeter were roughly in the center of a wide triangle of empty space bounded to the east by the road that ran south from Norwich to Ipswich and to the west by the Thetford road that Reacher and Pauling had driven three times already. Elsewhere in the triangle some of the larger buildings were shown. The only one within any reasonable distance from Bishops Pargeter was the Bishop's Arms.

"Are they there, do you think?" Reacher asked.

Jackson said, "If they stopped in Fenchurch St. Mary first and then aimed for Bishops Pargeter, then that's the only place they could have passed. But nearer Norwich there are a lot of places."

"I think they stayed close," Reacher said.

"Then the Bishop's Arms could be it," Jackson said.

Five miles, Reacher thought. On foot, that's a three-hour round trip. Back by midnight.

"I'm going to check it out," he said.

He detoured via the mudroom and collected two spare magazines for his G36. Found Pauling's purse and borrowed her little Maglite. Folded the map and put it in his pocket. Then he huddled with the others and agreed on a password. He didn't want to get shot when he arrived back. Jackson suggested *Canaries*, which was the Norwich soccer team's nickname, for its yellow uniforms.

"Are they any good?" Reacher asked.

"They used to be," Jackson said. "Twenty-some years ago, they were great."

Them and me both, Reacher thought.

He started by walking north behind the house. Then he turned west, staying parallel to the road. There was a little leftover twilight in the sky. Ragged clouds with pale stars beyond. The dirt was soft and heavy underfoot. He carried his G36 by its handle, left-handed, ready to swing it up into position when needed.

Reacher, alone in the dark.

The Grange Farm boundary was a trench ten feet across with a muddy bottom six feet down. Drainage, for the flat land. Reacher had to slide down the near bank, struggle through the mud, and then climb up the far bank again.

Two miles into the trip he was very tired. And slow. He changed course and moved closer to the road. Found a tractor route through the next farmer's fields. Huge tires had beaten the earth into hard ruts. He speeded up a little. He followed the tire tracks until they turned abruptly north. Then he struck off through the fields again.

After four miles the clock in his head told him that it was ten thirty at night. The clouds had cleared, and the moon was bright.

Five minutes before eleven o'clock he spotted the glow from the pub's sign. He could smell wood smoke from a chimney. He looped around toward the light and the smell, staying well to the north of the road. He kept to the fields until he was facing the back of the building from four hundred yards away. He saw small squares of harsh white fluorescent light. Windows. Kitchens and bathrooms, he guessed. Therefore frosted or pebbled glass. No view out.

He headed south, straight for the squares of light.

REACHER CIRCLED THE BUILDING away from the windows. Around the corner in the front wall east of the entrance there were three windows into the public bar. From a distance Reacher peered in and saw the same four farmers he had seen two nights previously. And the same bartender. None of the tables was occupied.

Reacher moved on.

The parking lot had four cars in it. None of the cars was new. None of them was the kind of thing a Park Lane rental company could have produced in a hurry. They were all dirty and battered.

Reacher moved on.

West of the entrance were three more windows, into the saloon bar. Two nights previously the saloon bar had been empty. It wasn't empty anymore. Now a single table was occupied. By three men: Groom, Burke, and Kowalski.

On the table in front of them Reacher could see the remains of a meal and three half-full glasses. Kowalski and Burke were on one side, and Groom was opposite them. Kowalski was talking, and Burke was listening to him. Groom had his chair tipped back and was staring into space. There was a log fire burning in a soot-stained grate beyond him. The room was warm and bright and inviting.

Reacher moved on.

Around the next corner there was a single window in the end wall, and through it Reacher got a different version of the same view.

Reacher backtracked four short steps and then headed for the front corner of the building. Invisible from any window. He touched the wall and dropped to his knees. He kept his right palm on the brick and stretched out his left arm and very carefully laid his rifle on the ground directly under the west-facing window. Then he shuffled back and stood up again and checked. Nobody would find the rifle, unless they tripped over it.

He backed away and looped through the parking lot. Headed for the front door. Opened it up and stepped into the foyer. The low beams, the patterned carpet. The shiny reception desk. The register.

He stepped to the desk. To his right he could hear the bartender, working quietly in the bar. To his left he could hear Kowalski's voice, muffled by the closed door.

He turned the register a hundred and eighty degrees. He opened it up. Two nights previously, J. & L. Bayswater. The following night three guests had registered: C. Groom, A. Burke, L. Kowalski. MAKE OF VEHICLE had been given as Toyota Land Cruiser.

No Toyota Land Cruiser in the lot.

Where were Lane, Gregory, Perez, and Addison?

He leafed backward and saw that the Bishop's Arms had a maximum of three rooms to let. So assuming that Groom and Burke and Kowalski had been given a room each, there had been no room at the inn for the others. They had driven somewhere else.

Reacher went into the public bar. The bartender looked up at him, and the four farmers nodded guarded greetings and turned back to their pint glasses. The bartender stayed poised and polite, ready for fast service.

Reacher asked, "Where did you send the other four?"

The bartender said, "Who?"

"Seven guys showed up yesterday. Three of them are here. Where did you send the other four?"

"I sent them down to Maston Manor."

"Where's that?"

"The other side of Bishops Pargeter. About six mile beyond."

One of the farmers half turned and said, "It's a bed and breakfast hotel. Very nice. Classier than this place."

"Thanks," Reacher said. He headed back to the foyer. Closed the door behind him. Stopped in front of the saloon bar's door. He put his hand on the knob. Paused and then pushed the door open.

Carter Groom was facing the door. He looked up. Kowalski and Burke spun around and stared. Reacher stepped into the room and closed the door gently behind him. Stood completely still.

"You've got some nerve," Groom said.

Reacher moved toward the fireplace. Tapped the toes of his shoes against the hearth to shed some mud. Took a heavy iron poker from a hook and used the end to scrape dirt off his heels. Then he hung the poker back up. The three guys were just sitting there, waiting.

"The situation has changed," Reacher said. He moved toward the west-facing window. He pulled out a chair from the table nearest to it and sat down, six feet away from the three guys, four feet and one pane of glass away from his rifle.

"Changed how?" Burke said.

"There was no kidnap," Reacher said. "It was faked. Kate and Taylor fell in love, they eloped. And they took Jade with them."

"Kate's alive?" Groom said. "Where?"

"Somewhere in the States, I guess."

"So why is Taylor here?"

"He wants a showdown with Lane on his own turf."

"He's going to get one."

Reacher shook his head. "That's a bad idea. He's on a farm, and it's surrounded by ditches too deep to drive through. So you'd be going in on foot. And he's got eight of his old SAS buddies with him, and his brother-in-law was a kind of Green Beret for the Brits, and he's brought in six of his guys, too. They've got Claymores on a hundred-yard perimeter and heavy machine guns in every window. They've got night vision and grenade launchers."

"They can't possibly use them. Not here. This is England."

"He's prepared to use them. But actually he won't have to. Because four of the SAS guys are snipers. They'll drop you all three hundred yards out. Game over."

The room went quiet. Kowalski picked up his drink and sipped. Then Burke did, and then Groom. Kowalski was left-handed. Burke and Groom were right-handed. Reacher said, "So your best play is to just forget it and go home now. Lane is going to die."

Burke said, "We can't just walk away."

"You walked away in Africa," Reacher said. "You left Hobart and Knight behind, to save the unit. So now you should leave Lane behind, to save yourselves."

Groom asked, "Are you with Taylor?"

Reacher nodded. "And I'm good with a rifle."

"They stole all that money," Burke said.

"Alimony. Easier than asking for it straight up. Asking for alimony is what got Anne Lane killed. Kate found that out."

"That *was* a kidnap."

Reacher shook his head. "Knight offed her. For Lane, because Anne wanted out. That's why you all abandoned Knight in Africa. Lane was covering himself. He sacrificed Hobart, too, because he was in the same OP."

"That's bull."

"I found Hobart. Knight told him all about it. While they were busy getting their hands and feet cut off."

Silence.

Burke looked at Groom. Groom looked at Burke. They both looked at Kowalski. There was a long pause.

"Okay," Burke said. "I guess we could sit this one out."

"Smart decision," Reacher said. He moved toward the door. Stopped at the hearth. Asked, "Where are Lane and the others?"

Quiet. Then Groom said, "There was no room here. They went up to Norwich. Some hotel up there."

Reacher nodded. "And when is he locking and loading?"

Another pause. "Dawn the day after tomorrow."

"What did he buy?"

"Submachine guns. MP5Ks, one each plus two spares. Ammunition, night vision, flashlights, various bits and pieces."

"Are you going to call him? As soon as I'm gone?"

"No," Burke said. "He's not the kind of guy you call with this kind of news."

"Okay," Reacher said. Then he stepped fast to his left and lifted the poker off its hook. Spun around and swung it hard and caught Carter Groom across the upper right arm. Groom's humerus bone shattered like a piece of dropped china. Groom opened his mouth, but before any kind of a scream got out, Reacher had broken Kowalski's left arm with a vicious backhanded blow. Kowalski was left-handed. Burke and Groom were right-handed. Reacher knocked Kowalski out of his way with his hip, and smashed Burke across the right wrist with a line drive. Then he turned away and stepped to the fireplace and put the poker back on its hook.

"Just making sure," he said. "You didn't convince me with your answers. Especially the one about Lane's hotel."

Then he walked out of the saloon bar and closed the door quietly behind him. It was exactly eleven thirty-one in the evening, according to the clock in his head.

AT EXACTLY eleven thirty-two Edward Lane closed the Toyota's rear door on nine Heckler & Koch MP5K submachine guns, sixty thirty-round magazines of 9 mm Parabellums, seven sets of night vision goggles, ten flashlights, six rolls of duct tape, and two long coils of rope. Then Gregory started the engine. Behind him on the rear bench were Perez and Addison. Lane climbed into the front passenger seat, and Gregory took off west. Standard Special Forces doctrine called for dawn assaults, but it also called for the insertion of a small advance force for a period of surveillance.

AT EXACTLY eleven thirty-three by the clock on her night table Jade woke up. She sat up in bed. Then she swung her feet to the floor. Crossed the room and pulled back her curtain. It was dark out. And she could go outside in the dark. Taylor had said so. She could visit the barns, and find the animals she knew had to be there.

REACHER retrieved his G36 at eleven thirty-four and set out to walk back on the road, which he figured would make the return trip faster, about seventy-five minutes total. He was tired, but content. Three trigger fingers out of action.

He walked on. Alone in the dark. Invincible.

THAT feeling ended just after he walked the length of the Grange Farm driveway and saw the dark and silent bulk of the house looming in front of him. He had called the password at least half a dozen times. At first quietly, and then louder.

He had gotten no response at all.

REACHER raised his rifle to the ready position. He stood absolutely still. Listened hard. Heard nothing.

Lane, he thought.

He wasn't surprised. Surprise was strictly for amateurs, and Reacher was a professional. He just walked backward and to his left, away from the house. Making himself smaller as a target and improving his angle of view. The windows were all dark. Just a faint red glow from the kitchen. The remains of the fire. The front door was closed. Near it was the faint shape of the Mini Cooper. Canted down at the front, like it was kneeling.

He walked toward it, near the front fender, and felt for the tire. There were torn shreds of rubber and a vicious curled length of bead wire. He shuffled quietly to the other side. Same situation.

He listened hard. Heard nothing. Headed for the front door. It was unlocked. He turned the handle. Pushed the door open. Raised the rifle. The house was dark. It felt empty. He checked the kitchen. It was warm. Dull red embers in the hearth. Jade's drawings were on the chair. The room looked exactly like he had left it, except there were no people in it.

He switched on the flashlight and clamped it in his left palm under the rifle's barrel. Used it to check all the other ground floor rooms. All empty.

He crept up the stairs. The first room he came to was clearly Jade's. The battered old toys that had been missing from the Dakota were all arrayed in a line along the bed. A one-eyed bear with the fur worn down to its backing. A doll, one eye open and one eye closed. The bed had been slept in. No sign of the child herself.

The next room belonged to the Jacksons. There was a vanity table cluttered with British cosmetic brands. There were framed photographs of a girl that wasn't Jade. Melody, Reacher guessed.

The next room was Kate's and Taylor's. An old queen bed, an oak night table. Undecorated, like a guest room. The photograph was propped on a dresser. Kate and Jade, together. The original print.

He moved on. Then he stopped halfway along the hallway.

Because there was blood on the floor.

It was a small thin stain, like flung paint. Suggestive of rapid movement. Reacher sniffed. There was a faint smell of gunpowder. He sighted down the hallway and saw an open bathroom door at the far end. A smashed tile on the back wall, at chest height. A neat burst, contained by a single ceramic square. A running target, a raised gun, three shots, a flesh wound, probably to an upper arm.

Reacher eased down the stairs and back out into the night.

He circled the house, clockwise. The barns were distant and dark and quiet. The old Land Rover was collapsed on its rims. Four blown tires. He walked past it and stopped. Turned the Maglite off and stared into the darkness.

How had it happened?

He trusted Pauling because he knew her, and he trusted Taylor and Jackson even without knowing them. Three professionals. Tired, but functioning. A long perilous approach from the intruders' point of view. He should have been looking at four riddled bodies and a wrecked rental car. Right about then Jackson should have been firing up the backhoe. Pauling should have been cracking cans of beer, and Kate should have been making toast and heating beans.

So why weren't they?

Distraction, he figured. As ever, the answer was in Jade's pictures. The animals in the barns. She's not sleeping great, Kate had said. Reacher pictured the child waking, running out of the house into the imagined safety of the darkness, four adults scrambling after her, panic, a search, unseen watchers moving in. Lane blasting up the driveway in the rented SUV. Taylor and Jackson and Pauling holding their fire in case they hit each other or Kate or Jade.

Lane, headlights on now, recognizing his own stepdaughter.

His own wife.

Reacher shivered once, a violent uncontrollable spasm. He clicked the Maglite on to light his way and walked on down the driveway. Then he started to run. Toward the road.

PEREZ flipped his night vision goggles into the up position on his forehead and said, "Okay, Reacher's gone."

Edward Lane nodded. He turned to Perez and said, "Find a telephone. Call the Bishop's Arms. Tell the others to get here now."

"We've got the truck," Perez said.

"Tell them to walk," Lane said.

Jackson said, "Reacher will come back, you know." He was the only one without tape on his mouth.

Lane said, "I know he'll come back. Worst case for us he'll walk six miles east and find nothing and walk back here again. It will take him four hours. You'll be dead by then. He can watch the child die, and then Ms. Pauling, and then I'll kill him. Slowly."

"You're insane," Jackson said.

"I'm angry," Lane said. "And I think I have a right to be." Perez left.

REACHER ran through a curve in the driveway. Then he slowed a little. Then he stopped dead. He killed the flashlight beam. Stood still and concentrated on the afterimage of what he had just seen.

All the way through the curve the track was soft and damp. Muddy, even though it hadn't rained for days.

And the mud showed tire tracks. Three sets.

First, Tony Jackson's old Land Rover. Second, the Mini Cooper.

The third set was a single large vehicle, open treads, new and crisp. The kind of tires a rented Toyota Land Cruiser would wear.

One set only. One way.

Lane was still on the property.

LANE hit Jackson with a flashlight, hard. The lens smashed and Jackson went down.

"I need a new flashlight," Lane said. "This one seems broken."

Addison smiled and took a new one out of a box. Lauren Pauling stared at the door. Her mouth was taped, and her hands were bound behind her. The door was going to open any minute. Through it would come either Perez or Reacher. Bad news or good.

Let it be Reacher, she thought. *Please.*

Lane took the new flashlight from Addison and stepped up close to Kate. Eye to eye. He lit up the flashlight beam and held it just under her chin, shining it directly upward, turning her exquisite face into a ghastly Halloween mask.

"Till death us do part," he said. "That's a vow I take seriously."

Kate turned her head away.

"Forsaking all others," he said. "I took that part seriously, too. I'm so sorry that you didn't."

Kate closed her eyes.

REACHER kept on walking to the end of the driveway, over the bridge, east on the road, away from the farm, his flashlight on. He figured he needed to let them see him go. To see a small spectral night-vision figure strolling south, and then east, sets up an irresistible temptation to believe that it's going to go east forever. And then you forget all about it, and you don't see it coming back.

He walked east for two hundred yards and clicked off the Maglite. Then he turned ninety degrees and hiked north across the shoulder and slid down the boundary ditch's nearside slope. Clawed his way up the far side with his rifle held one-handed high in the air. Then he ran, fast, straight north.

Two minutes later he was a quarter mile in, level with the cluster of barns, three hundred yards behind them to the east, and out of breath. He paused to recover. Thumbed his fire selector to single shots. Then he put the stock against his shoulder and walked forward. Toward the barns.

Reacher, alone in the dark. Armed and dangerous. Coming back.

EDWARD Lane was still face to face with Kate. He said, "I'm assuming you've been sleeping with him for years."

Kate said nothing.

"You could catch a disease from a guy like that."

Then he smiled. A new thought. A joke, to him.

"Or you could get pregnant," he said.

Something in her terrified eyes.

He paused. "What?" he said. "What are you telling me?"

She shook her head.

"You're pregnant," he said. He put the flat of his hand on her belly. She pulled away, hard against the pole she was tied to. He shuffled forward half a step. "Oh man, this is unbelievable. You're going to die with another man's child inside you."

Then he spun away. Stopped, and turned back.

"Can't allow that," he said. "We'll have to abort it first."

Kate closed her eyes.

"You're going to die anyway," Lane said, like the most reasonable man in the world.

REACHER knew they were in a barn. Where else could they hide their truck? He knew there were five barns in total. He had seen them in the daylight, vaguely, in the distance. But now, in the dark, the dirt wouldn't show tire marks. No point in risking a flash of the Maglite beam.

So which barn?

He started with the nearest, hoping to get lucky. But he didn't get lucky. Reacher put his eye on a crack between two boards and saw nothing. Just darkness.

He moved on to the second barn, hoping to get lucky. But the second barn was just as dark and quiet as the first. He moved on through the blackness, toward the three barns grouped around the yard. Then he stopped dead.

Because in the corner of his eye, he saw light and movement, in the house. The kitchen window.

LANE turned to Gregory and said, "We need an operating table. Find something flat."

Gregory found an old door—rustic, made from lapped boards and Z-braced on the back—in a stack of discarded lumber. He pulled it out and stood it upright.

"That's perfect," Lane called to him. "And turn the truck's lights on. I need to be able to see what I'm doing."

REACHER moved fast and quiet to the back door of the house. Waited. He could hear a voice through the door. A slight Hispanic accent. Perez, on the phone. Reacher reversed his rifle in his hands. Gripped the forestock in front of the carrying handle.

Then he waited.

Perez stepped out into the night and turned to close the door behind him, and Reacher swung. The sight block of the G36 caught Perez in the temple. He was dead before he hit the ground.

LANE turned to Addison and said, "Go find out what Perez is up to. He should have been back by now."

"Reacher's out there," Jackson said. "That's why Perez isn't back."

Lane smiled. "So what should I do? Go out and search? With my two men? Leaving you all alone in here to organize a pathetic escape attempt behind my back? Not going to happen. Because right now Reacher is walking past the Bishops Pargeter church."

REACHER was crouching outside the kitchen door, sorting through all the things that Perez had dropped. An MP5K with a thirty-round magazine. A flashlight, now broken. A black-handled kitchen knife.

Reacher tucked the knife in his shoe. Picked up the MP5 submachine gun and slung it over his left shoulder. Kicked the broken flashlight into the shadows.

Then he headed back north and east toward the barns.

Reacher, alone in the dark. Doing it the hard way.

REACHER stepped into the beaten-earth yard. It was a little more than a hundred feet square, with barns barely visible in the dark on the north side, the east, and the south. All three barns had sliding doors and tile roofs and wood wall planks, dull gray in the starlight.

He crossed the yard, slow and silent. He made it to the near left-hand corner of the north barn. Circled it, clockwise.

He came around to the right-hand front corner and paused. There was no way in except for the main front doors. They were made from four-inch timbers banded together and hung from sliders at the top. Wheels the size of the Mini Cooper's were bolted to the doors. They would slide apart like theater curtains.

He crept along the front wall and put his ear on the space between the door and the wall. Heard nothing. Saw no chink of light.

Wrong one, he thought.

He turned and glanced east. Has to be, he thought. He set off toward it. He was twenty feet away when the door rolled back. A yard-wide bar of bright blue light spilled out. The Toyota SUV, parked inside, its headlights on. Addison stepped out. His MP5 was slung over his shoulder. He turned to roll the door shut again. He got it to within six inches of closed and left it like that. Still open a crack. He clicked on a flashlight and set off toward the house.

Reacher took a deep breath and fell in behind Addison, twenty feet back, fast and silent. Then he was fifteen feet back. Then ten.

Then the two figures merged in the dark. They stopped. The flashlight hit the dirt. Addison stumbled and went down, his throat ripped by the knife from Reacher's shoe.

Reacher was on his way even before Addison had stopped twitching. With an automatic rifle, two submachine guns, and a knife. But he didn't head back to the barns. He walked on down to the house instead. Made his first port of call upstairs in the master bedroom. Then he stopped in the kitchen, at the hearth, and at the desk. Then he came back out and walked toward the barns.

He stopped beside the eastern barn and considered his ordnance. Rejected the G36. It was possible that the barrel was bent. He had hit Perez hard enough to do some damage. So he dropped the magazine out of Perez's MP5. Nine rounds left. Perez had been the designated trigger man. Which meant that Addison's magazine should still be full. Which it was. He put Addison's magazine in Perez's gun. A magazine he knew to be full, in a gun he knew to be working. A sensible step for a man who planned to live through the next five minutes.

Showtime.

He sat on the ground with his back against the partly open door. Assembled the things he had brought from the house. A kindling stick, from the basket on the hearth. Three rubber bands, from a jar on the desk. A hand mirror from Susan Jackson's vanity table.

The stick was a straight seventeen-inch length of an ash bough, as thick as a child's wrist, cut to fit the kitchen grate. He fixed the mirror handle to the ash bough with the rubber bands. Then he lay down flat and inched the bough forward. Toward the six-inch gap where the barn door stood open. Left-handed. He tilted the stick until he could see a perfect reflection of the view inside.

THE mirror showed that the barn had vertical poles inside that held up the roof ridge and reinforced the timber-peg rafters. There were twelve. Five of them had people tied to them. From left to right in the mirror Reacher could see Taylor, then Jackson, then Pauling, then Kate, then Jade. Their arms were pulled behind them, and their wrists were tied behind the poles. Their ankles were tied together. They had duct tape across their mouths. All except Jackson. But his mouth was a bloody mess. He had slumped down into a semiconscious crouch at the base of his pole.

It was Taylor who had been wounded. His shirt was torn and soaked with blood, upper right arm. Pauling looked okay. Kate was as white as a sheet, and her eyes were closed. Jade had slid down her pole and was sitting on her heels, head down.

The Toyota had been backed in and turned so that it was hard up against the end wall on the left. Its headlights were turned full on.

Gregory was wrestling with some kind of a large flat panel. An old door, maybe. He was walking it across the floor of the barn.

Lane was standing in the middle of the floor, his right fist around his MP5's pistol grip and his left fist around the fore grip. His finger was on the trigger. He was facing the door. Borderline mentally ill, people had said. Crossed that border long ago, Reacher thought.

Gregory got the big flat panel front and center, and Reacher heard him say, "Where do you want this?"

Lane answered, "We need sawhorses." Lane kicked Jackson in the ribs and asked him, "Do you have sawhorses here?" and Jackson said, "In the other barn," and Lane said, "I'll send Perez and Addison for them when they get back."

"Reacher's out there, and he's got them." Jackson said.

"You're annoying me," Lane said. But Reacher saw him glance toward the door. And he saw what Jackson was trying to do. He was trying to focus Lane's attention outside the barn. Away from the prisoners. He was trying to buy time.

Then Reacher saw Lane's reflection grow large in the mirror. He pulled the ash bough back, slowly. Aimed his MP5 at a spot an inch outside the door. *Put your head out,* he thought. *Please.*

But no such luck. Reacher heard Lane stop just inside the door and scream, "Reacher? You out there?"

Reacher waited.

Lane screamed, "Reacher? You there? Ten seconds from now, I'm going to shoot Jackson. In the thighs. He'll bleed out through his femoral arteries."

Reacher waited.

"Ten," Lane screamed. "Nine. Eight." His voice faded as he stalked back to the center of the barn. Reacher slid the mirror back into place. Saw Lane stop near Jackson and heard him say, "He isn't out there." Then Lane turned again and yelled, "Seven. Six. Five." Gregory was standing with the panel held in front of him.

"Four," Lane screamed.

Reacher considered taking the risk of sacrificing Jackson. One KIA out of five hostages wasn't excessive.

"Three," Lane screamed.

But Reacher liked Jackson, and there were Susan and Melody to consider. And there was Kate Lane's dream to think about, the new extended family farming together.

"Two," Lane screamed.

Reacher dropped the mirror and extended his right arm like a swimmer and hooked his fingers around the edge of the door. Crawled backward, fast, hauling the door with him. Opening it wide, staying out of sight.

Silence inside the barn. He knew Lane's eyes were on the black void outside. The oldest of all atavistic human fears: *There's something out there.*

Reacher heard a thump as Gregory dropped the panel. Then it was a foot race. From Lane's perspective the door had opened right to left, driven by some unseen agency. Therefore that agency was now outside and to the left. Reacher stood up and ran counterclockwise around the barn. Now he was outside and to the right.

Silence inside the barn. Reacher planted his feet and leaned his left shoulder on the wall, his elbow tucked in, his wrist turned, his hand on the MP5's front grip, lightly. His right index finger had already moved the trigger through its first eighth-inch of slack. His left eye was closed, and his right eye had lined up both iron sights. He waited. Heard a soft footfall on the barn's concrete floor. Saw a shadow in the spill of light. Saw the back of Lane's head, just a narrow arc like a crescent moon, craning out, peering left into the darkness. Reacher wanted to fire parallel with the barn, not into it. Moving his gun would put hostages in the line of fire. He had to be patient. He had to let Lane come to him.

Reacher concentrated exclusively on the MP5's sights. Lane inched into them. First, the right-hand edge of his skull. Then a larger sliver. Then more. Then more. Then the front sight was on the bony ridge at the back of his head. Dead-on centered.

For half a second he thought about calling Lane's name. Making him turn around. Listing his many transgressions. Like the equivalent of a legal process.

Then he thought about Hobart, and he pulled the trigger.

A strange blurred purr, like a sewing machine or a distant motorcycle at a light. The empty thump of flesh and bone hitting concrete was clearly audible, muffled only by cotton clothing.

Then Reacher stepped into the doorway. Gregory was looking left, but the shots that had killed Lane had come from the right.

"Shoot him," Jackson said.

Reacher didn't move.

"Shoot him," Jackson said again. "Don't make me tell you what that table was for."

Reacher risked a glance at Taylor. Taylor nodded. Reacher glanced at Pauling. She nodded, too. So Reacher put three in the center of Gregory's chest.

CLEANUP took the rest of the night and most of the next day. They didn't try to sleep. Except for Jade. Kate put her to bed and sat with her while she slept. The child had fainted early and had missed most of what had gone on and seemed not to have understood the rest.

Kate herself looked like she had been to hell and back. She had stared down at Lane's body for a long moment. Understood for sure that there was going to be no Hollywood moment where he reared up again, back to life. That kind of certainty helps a person.

Taylor's right tricep was all torn up. Reacher field-dressed the wound as best he could with a first-aid kit in the upstairs bathroom. But Taylor was going to need attention. He volunteered to delay it by a couple of days. It seemed smart to distance an ER visit from mayhem in the night.

Jackson was okay apart from cut eyebrows and some facial bruising and a split lip and a couple of loose teeth.

Pauling was fine. She seemed to have had total confidence that Reacher would show up and work something out. He wasn't sure if she was telling the truth or flattering him. Either way he didn't mention how close he had come to walking away on a phantom pursuit. Didn't mention how lucky it was that a stray glance at the driveway's surface had fired some random synapse in his brain.

Reacher searched the Toyota and found Lane's leather duffel. The eight hundred thousand dollars. It was all there. Untouched. He gave it to Pauling for safekeeping. Then he sat on the floor. He was calm. Just another night of business as usual. He was used to it. And where some men might have agonized over justification, he spent his energy figuring out where best to hide the bodies.

They hid them in a ten-acre field near the northwest corner of the farm. Fallow land, hidden by trees. Jackson fired up the backhoe. Started work immediately on a massive pit. A ninety-yard excavation, because they had decided to bury the cars as well.

Reacher asked Pauling, "Did you check the box marked 'extra insurance'?"

She nodded.

He said, "Call them tomorrow. Tell them it was stolen."

Taylor was walking wounded, so he scoured the whole area for every piece of physical evidence he could find. He came up with all that anyone could think of, including all twenty-seven shell casings from Perez's MP5. Pauling scrubbed his blood off the upstairs hallway floor and replaced the shattered bathroom tile. Reacher piled the bodies inside the Toyota Land Cruiser.

The sun had been up for hours before the pit was finished. Jackson had left a neat graded slope at one end, and Reacher drove the Toyota down it. Jackson drove the backhoe to the house and maneuvered the Mini all the way to the pit and rolled it down the grade. Taylor threw the other items in the hole. Then Jackson started to fill it. Reacher sat and watched. The sky was pale blue, and the sun was watery. There were thin high clouds and a mild breeze. He watched Jackson work until the dirt hid the top of the cars, and then he walked away, slowly, back to the house.

EXACTLY twelve months later to the hour the ten-acre field was dusted pale green with a brand new winter crop. Tony and Susan Jackson and Graham and Kate Taylor were working the field next to it. Back at the house the nine-year-old cousins and best friends Melody Jackson and Jade Taylor were watching Jade's baby brother, a healthy five-month-old boy named Jack.

Three thousand miles west of Grange Farm Lauren Pauling was in her Barrow Street apartment, drinking coffee and reading *The*

New York Times. She had missed a piece inside the main section that reported the deaths of three newly arrived private military contractors in Iraq. Their names were Burke, Groom, and Kowalski, and they had died two days previously when a land mine exploded under their vehicle. But she caught a piece in the Metro section in which it was reported that the cooperative board at the Dakota building had foreclosed on an apartment after twelve consecutive months of unpaid monthly maintenance. On entering the apartment they had found more than nine million dollars in a locked closet.

Six thousand miles west of Grange Farm Patti Joseph was fast asleep in a waterfront condominium in Seattle, Washington. She was ten months into a new job as a magazine copy editor. Her perseverance and her relentless eye for detail made her good at it. She was seeing a local journalist from time to time. She was happy.

Far from Seattle, far from New York City, far from Bishops Pargeter, down in Birmingham, Alabama, Dee Marie Graziano was up early, in a hospital gymnasium, watching her brother grasp his new metal canes and walk across the floor.

Nobody knew where Jack Reacher was. He had left Grange Farm two hours after the backhoe had shut down, and there had been no news of him since.

The Writing Life of
Lee Child

FOR Lee Child, all books fall into one category: suspense. "It's where the humanity is," he says. "In evolution we developed story-telling, and that must have been for a serious purpose. Right from caveman days, we had stories that involved danger and peril, and eventually safety and resolution. Why do we turn the page if we're not in suspense about what's going to happen next?"

Child, who was born in Coventry, England, in 1954, began his career as a writer in an unusual way: he was fired from his job as a presentation director at Granada Television. Child had been at the job, which he likens to "an air traffic controller of the network airwaves," for eighteen years, working on award-winning mini-series like *Brideshead Revisited* and *The Jewel in the Crown*. Then, returning home from a European

Vital Stats

WHAT HE DRIVES: A supercharged Jaguar
WHAT HE WEARS: Shoes that last at least fifteen years
WHAT HE READS: Books by Alafair Burke, Harlan Coben, Joseph Kanon, and Michael Connelly
WHAT HE DISLIKES: Returned and remaindered books
WEBSITE: www.leechild.com

vacation in 1995, he discovered a phone message telling him there had been a restructuring and his severance check was in the mail.

At the time, Child's wife, Jane, was an archaeologist writing a historical novel about Queen Emma of Normandy. The process of helping her with rewrites made him realize that he liked writing.

In addition, he says, "I didn't want to leave entertainment. It's the only thing I've ever done. So I figured the novel is the purest form

A Tale of Two Buildings

The Dakota . . .

The world-famous New York City apartment building called the Dakota is home to *The Hard Way*'s Edward Lane. Many real-life celebrities have also called the building home, including Judy Garland and Lauren Bacall. It's also famous for providing the setting for the 1968 film *Rosemary's Baby*, and many recall the day  that John Lennon was shot outside its main entrance in 1980.

Standing at 1 West 72 Street, on the northwest corner of Central Park West, the Dakota was designed by architect Henry Hardenbergh, who also designed New York's Plaza Hotel, and was completed in 1884. At the time, it was said to be so far north that it might as well have been in the Dakota Territory, hence its name.

. . . and the Majestic

Directly across Seventy-second Street from the Dakota, on the southwest corner of Central Park West, stands another historic New York apartment building: the Majestic, where *The Hard Way*'s Patti  Joseph has an apartment. She uses her convenient view of the Dakota to spy on Edward Lane. Whether any real-life residents spy on each other is anyone's guess.

The twin-towered, art deco–style Majestic was designed by architect Jacques Delmarre and was completed in 1931. Its famous early tenants include columnist Walter Winchell and gangster Frank Costello. Bruno Richard Hauptmann, the convicted kidnapper of Charles Lindbergh's baby, worked on the building as a carpenter.

of entertainment. It's certainly the closest I'd ever get to an audience." Two years later, in 1997, he published his first novel, *The Killing Floor*. Soon after, he and his family moved to New York.

Now, with ten Jack Reacher novels under his belt, Child's writ-

> ## "I just start somewhere and let the story work itself out."

ing habits are fairly regular. He writes from around noon until 6 or 7 p.m. in his home office, and it takes about six months for him to complete a novel. He figures out the "trick or the surprise or the pivotal fact" before he starts writing. Then, without an outline, he says, "I just start somewhere and let the story work itself out."

Dialogue has always been one of Child's strengths, and the author confesses to an unusual source of inspiration for his style: his former physics teacher. Child recalls, "He made us write in the most brief and concise way. He was an absolute tyrant." Now, the author realizes, "by careful word choice and construction you can make speech seem very natural."

Child is also careful about his first pages. He says, "Most bookstore browsers check out the first page, and that's where you've got to hook them. There are always plenty of other books in the store." And he never saves an idea for later. "I'm not one of these guys who have boxes of index cards with plot ideas stretching into the future," he explains. "I just trust that by the time I start the next book, I'll have an idea."

In interviews, Child often refers to maxims he lives by. Some are familiar to writers, like "Don't get it right, get it written." Another of his favorites concerns police procedurals: "Don't show the detective working on the case, show the case working on the detective." Ultimately, though, Child doesn't write with a formula in mind. To quote yet another saying he likes, "If you can see a bandwagon, then it's already too late to jump aboard."

Child maintains a Zen-like belief that a book is created as much by the reader as by the writer. He posits that "a book is a transaction. It needs to be written, then read; then it exists." Knowing his books are read by millions, he considers himself fortunate indeed. "It's a great life," he says. "There's really nothing more I want." ∎

WHERE

A Novel

MERCY

FLOWS

KAREN HARTER

CHAPTER ONE

THE Judge always had the final say. Right or wrong, he was God. His truth was a hard, unbending line that never wavered. Not even for me.

When I was young, I called him Daddy.

Of course, I also lay in the cool grass of summer and imagined that clouds were dinosaurs and that just as the sky had no beginning or no end, life held limitless possibilities for me.

My world was twelve acres framed by a wadable

178 | Karen Harter

creek in a gully to the east, the Stillaguamish River to the south, a stand of poplars lining our long driveway on the west, and Hartles Road to the north. Our river came like a train from far away. It slowed as it rounded the bend to pass our house on its way to somewhere—the ocean, I guessed—and I believed, as children do, that my life, like the river, was destined to flow as easily around each bend.

I knew little of death, except that Great-grandpa Dodd had died while plowing the back quarter of his sixty acres. The job accomplished, he promptly had a heart attack and drove the old John Deere straight down the hill into the churning river. No one seemed to mind much, because he was very old and they thought it fitting that he and his rusty tractor had gone down together.

There were no lamenting dirges at the graveside and only a few quiet tears. Most of the friends and relatives gathered in the dewy grass sang hymns. My father stood silently, gripping my hand firmly so I couldn't stare down into the hole where they put Great-grandpa. My sister held a tissue in her white gloves and sang all the songs by heart. Auntie Pearl smiled at me afterward and said Grandpa had gone home to be with Jesus.

That seemed right to me. The way it was supposed to be. My life and the lives of the ones I loved would follow a similar course, meandering yet purposeful, ending only upon reaching old age.

My father, the only son of the fourth generation of Norwegian-American Dodds, had been expected to churn and plant the rich valley soil as his fathers before him. Instead, he enrolled in the University of Washington to study law. His father, Lee Dodd, raised his children within twenty square miles of farms and woodlands in northwest Washington. I suppose the way my father turned out was largely due to this narrow upbringing.

The sound of windshield wipers squeaking across dry glass broke my musings. I switched them off, wondering when the rain had stopped and how I had driven so far with no memory of the passing scenes. As I continued north, the sky burned a path from the Olympic Mountain Range on the west to the Cascades on the east.

I was going home. After seven hard years, home to my river valley, Mom—and the Judge. The thought alternately warmed, then chilled me to the bone.

"TJ." I ran one hand through my son's dark hair as I steered onto the freeway off ramp. He raised himself to peer out the window.

"Are we there?"

"Not yet. We're getting close. Look how green it is."

He glanced at a field of cows and craned his neck in all directions before reaching for the map on the dashboard. His fingers traced the lines leading to the X that represented his grandma and grandpa's house, as he had done a dozen times in the past two days.

"Don't turn on this line, Mom. This is a river."

"That's the river that runs behind their backyard. And don't you ever go down there alone. You hear me?"

He nodded. I made a mental note to mention it again.

"Does my grandma make cookies?"

"Probably."

For the next twenty miles TJ asked questions while I became increasingly apprehensive. The heaviness in my chest was noticeable again. I took several deep breaths and tried not to think about it.

I slowed the Jeep as we pulled into the parking lot of a small store with gas pumps out front. The Carter Store. The sign had big letters that lit up now and a new roof that hadn't been there before.

"You want a pop or something?"

TJ's head bobbed enthusiastically. He jumped out and rushed toward the store. "Come on, Mama!" His brows rose imploringly above his dark eyes, and I marveled for the thousandth time at how beautiful he was and that he could possibly be mine.

"Give me a minute." I climbed out and stretched my stiff legs before following him into the store.

When I was a young girl, the Carter Store was smaller. Just the essentials crowded the board shelves, in no logical order. Dish soap and tinfoil were lined up next to motor oil. Best of all was the array of candy in a glass case by the cash register.

TJ knew his way around convenience stores, even this little

ma-and-pa shack. He headed straight for the glass doors of the cooler and pulled out an orange soda. "You wanna soda, Mama?"

"I'll have whatever you're having." He passed me a bottle and followed me to the cash register, where a tall young man stooped with his elbows on the counter, talking to the middle-aged cashier.

"Oh, sorry." He waved me up to the counter. "I'm not buying anything. Just yackin'." He stepped aside, pulling a fly-fishing magazine from the worn wooden counter. I nodded a half smile and paid the heavy-jowled man behind the cash register.

"Did that fish come out my grandpa's river?" I turned to see TJ pointing up to the cover of the guy's magazine.

"I don't know. Which river is your grandpa's?"

TJ looked to me for help. "The Stilly," I said, which was the local abbreviation for the Stillaguamish River.

"Oh, no." He pointed to the red print beneath the photo of a brown trout. "Says here this guy came out of the Yellowstone in Montana. You ever caught a fish like that?"

TJ shook his head. "I never caught a fish yet. But I'm going fishing with my grandpa. He doesn't know I'm coming. We drove a long time, 'cause we're going to surprise him."

"And what's your grandpa's name?"

He giggled. "I just told you. Grandpa."

"Judge Dodd," I volunteered.

The guy shook his head. The name meant nothing to him. I surmised he was new to the area or just passing through.

"The worm man." This came from the proprietor as he passed me my change. The man was obviously confused.

"My father is Judge Blake Dodd. He lives about three miles downstream." I passed TJ his soda and turned toward the door.

"Did you say Blake?" The tall guy rolled his eyes toward the man behind the counter with a *how-could-I-be-so-stupid* look. "I know Blake. Met him fishing under the bridge. He gave me one of his flies. Tied it himself. I didn't know he was a judge, though."

"Anyway, see you around." I took TJ's hand to leave.

"Hey, wait a minute!" The proprietor sounded mildly annoyed.

"Tell him I need more baby crawlers. A couple dozen cartons."

"What?" In my confusion I glanced back at TJ's new friend, who flashed an amused grin.

"So," he pushed his hands into his back pockets. "I take it you and your father are not real close."

He had unknowingly trodden on forbidden ground. "First of all," I snapped, "my relationship with my father is none of your business! And second, you guys have him mixed up with someone else. My father is a justice of the State Supreme Court. If you've read the papers at all, you've probably heard of him."

My tone must have been condescending. The tall guy adopted a moronic expression and cocked his head toward the storekeeper. "Well, we got one o' them city newspapers out here once, but none of us could read them big words." The old guy thought that was pretty funny. A laugh gurgled up from his belly like a big belch.

"Come on, TJ." I grabbed his arm and pushed him through the door, while he called weakly over his shoulder, "Bye, guys."

The town of Carter consisted of the store, Fraser's Tavern, and a Methodist church. The nearest schools were a twenty-mile bus ride down the highway in Darlington, where one could also find a single movie theater and a good slab of meatloaf at the Halfway Café.

My childhood surrounded me as we drove. Maple trees shone in the afternoon sun, and the air smelled as sweet as it had each spring of my first seventeen years. Where the road forked, I caught glimpses of my river between the trees. "There's the river, Teej!" The trees parted to reveal a long stretch rushing around a great chunk of rock. Then, teasingly, the trees closed our window.

The Duncans' Appaloosa Ranch appeared on my right, and with a pang I wondered whatever became of Donnie Duncan, my childhood friend. Finally the stretch of rail fence on my left ended at the familiar gravel drive. To my surprise, stuck in the ground was a cockeyed sign with WORMS $1.00 hand painted in red.

I nosed the Jeep into the long driveway. TJ began to chatter with delight. "Are we here, Mama? Why are you going so slow?"

I wanted a cigarette. Out of habit my hand crawled toward the purse beside me but returned empty when I remembered that I had thrown them away for good. To seal the deal, I had actually told TJ, who believed in me with the unshakable faith of a child. How or why he still believed in me after all the broken promises was a mystery to me. So to light up in his presence was unthinkable.

Too late to turn back. I took a deep breath. What had happened here in the past seven years? What could possibly have driven the Judge to selling worms? What would they do when they saw us? This is for you, TJ, I thought, but I knew there was more to it than I had been willing to admit, even to myself.

The left side of the driveway was fenced pasture, now overgrown and going to hay. The barn still stood beneath an ancient broadleaf maple. Directly in front of us was the house, a sprawling log rambler with a deep covered wraparound porch. The garage was attached to the house by a covered walkway.

I stopped the car, and TJ jumped out, his footsteps making loud crunching sounds in the gravel. I imagined my parents peering through the blinds, asking themselves who these strangers were who had just arrived. Even if they hadn't heard the tires on the noisy gravel, our presence was certainly announced now by TJ's excited babbling. He charged up the front steps and knocked on the door.

When no one answered, I got brave. I stepped out and joined TJ on the long shaded porch. We peeked through the window into the spacious living room with its vaulted ceiling and log beams. I didn't recognize the leather furniture or the Oriental rug, and fleetingly I worried that my parents had moved. But there above the stone fireplace hung the familiar painting of a trout bursting from the water.

TJ sighed. "You should have told them we were coming, Mom." He stomped around the corner to the side of the house. I followed. At the kitchen window I lifted him to see for himself that Grandma was not there. Everything was spotless and in its place. TJ jumped off the steps and headed for the river without looking back.

"Hey! Where do you think you're going?"

"I'm not going *to* the river," he said. "I'm going *by* the river."

"Oh." I sat on a wood step leading down to the lawn. TJ stared at me for a moment, then came back and put his hands on my knees. "Do you don't feel good again, Mom?"

I kissed his forehead. "No, I don't feel very good."

"Do you want me to wait for you?"

I smiled and shook my head. "Do you see that picnic table there?" He nodded. "See how long it is? That's how far you need to stay from the river." I made him pace it out, and then he was gone.

I watched him hurl rocks toward the swirling water for some time before dropping my head to my knees. It had been a long, tiring day. The miles of Oregon and Washington freeway replayed in my mind. When I lifted my head, TJ was not in sight. My heart fluttered, and I pushed myself up from the step.

I called to him, but the river drowned my voice. A dirt trail, muddy enough to capture his footprints, followed the river, in some places veering dangerously close to the bank. I flogged myself as I stumbled along the bumpy terrain. How could a five-year-old be expected to carry around the mental measurement of a picnic table?

I came around a cedar stump and saw TJ on a spit of sand and smooth rocks, and a fly fisherman just beyond him standing knee deep in a quiet stretch of water. TJ seemed planted where he was, watching with obvious wonder the graceful movements of a dry fly on the end of a tapered line. My heart suddenly burst into flight.

It was that perfect stance, arm moving just so. That slight tip of his head. Despite the unfamiliar cap, I knew. TJ stepped closer. Upon hearing the crunch of the boy's shoes in the river rocks, the Judge turned to face him. I gasped and ducked behind the stump.

My first impulse was to retreat up the trail. Then I remembered that I was a grown-up now. I dug my fingernails into the ragged cedar and watched. The Judge glanced upstream and down. His voice was rumbly like the river, so I could only guess that he was questioning the little stranger as to the whereabouts of his parents.

A childish voice pierced the air. "Up there!" I heard the slosh of my father wading to shore. I peered around the stump. The Judge placed his hand on TJ's shoulder and pointed toward the trail. They hiked toward my asylum in silence. What was it about this man, I wondered, that caused even TJ to obey without question?

When they were almost upon me, I stepped onto the trail.

The Judge stopped short, incredulous. TJ ran to me. "Mama!"

I pulled him in front of me like a shield. "Hi." I tried to make my voice sound strong. "Remember me?"

"Samantha." He breathed my name as if I had been dead and buried these seven years.

Thank God for TJ. Oblivious to the chasm between my father and me, he became a sort of bridge. "This is my son, TJ."

The Judge's eyes stayed fixed on mine for several long seconds before he dropped to one knee before my son. "Hello, TJ." He held out his massive hand. "I'm . . . your grandpa."

TJ returned the handshake and said, "You don't look old like a grandpa." It was true. I felt like I had aged a decade beyond my twenty-four years, but my father looked the same. TJ's awe turned to unbridled excitement. "Grandpa"—one pudgy hand patted the Judge's thigh—"I came to see you! I came to go fishing with you!"

At that the Judge melted. He scooped my son up and waltzed around that muddy trail like TJ was his long-lost lamb. The two of them laughed and chattered, while I led them back to the house. Their banter relieved the tension. My son did the talking, and I only had to fill in the details, like *Wednesday* and *Reno*. Still, I felt the Judge's eyes on me and his unspoken questions.

My mother saw us from the porch. She swooped down the steps, a dove in her gray silk skirt. I felt her cool damp cheek against mine, and when she eventually pulled away, there were tears in her eyes.

"Samantha Jean. Where have you been?" She pushed the bangs off my face and studied me.

"Reno."

Mom's face took on a concerned frown. I expected her to point out how sallow I looked. "Red hair is nice on you," she finally said.

"It's auburn." The box had clearly said *auburn*.

Her gaze turned to TJ as the Judge slid him to the ground. "Sam"—she looked from his face to mine as if searching for some resemblance—"is this my grandson?" I had never mentioned in my sparse letters that TJ had the pecan-colored skin and black eyes of his Mexican sire. Mom gently cupped his face between her hands.

For that moment I was happy. If my parents were shocked at the color of TJ's skin, they hid it well. In fact, they seemed to embrace him and their role as grandparents instantly.

I had not craved my mother's presence during nine hours of grueling labor in a Nevada hospital. I hadn't needed handholding. But when I first held my son, I wanted my mother desperately. He was the most beautiful thing I had ever seen. He was the best thing I had ever done. Now my mother knew—I saw it in her eyes—that something good could come from me.

No one asked why we had come or how long we would stay. I guess it was evident by the amount of stuff that we unloaded from the Jeep that it might be more than an overnight visit. Mom seemed to sense my fatigue. She warmed some chowder while the Judge found a cot for TJ in the garage. It felt good to be mothered again.

That night, I slept in my old bedroom. With the window open, the sweet scent of cottonwoods floated in like it had on hundreds of childhood nights. I could hear the river rushing past. The sound of it used to stir longings in me that I couldn't understand.

Maybe it was the river's fault that I had wandered so far, for so long. Then again, it was possibly the very thing that called me back. Tomorrow I will explore it again, I told myself, and in my dreams I was twelve again, running as fast as the river.

THE Judge and TJ tromped past my bedroom window at some ungodly hour of the morning. After that I couldn't sleep. I followed the scent of coffee down the hall. The kitchen was empty, so I poured myself a cup and took it back to my room.

My hand smoothed the bright new quilt at the foot of the bed. I was seventeen the last time I slept here. I wondered whatever happened to the collection of animal skulls that had graced my shelf.

My son's voice snapped me back to adulthood. I opened the window and called to him.

"Mama!" He bounded toward me through field grass half his height. "Me and Grandpa went to the river!"

The Judge waved to me. "Come out here. I want to show you something!"

What could it hurt? I stuffed my nightshirt into my jeans and slid out the window until the dewy grass surprised my toes.

"Hey!" The Judge sounded stern. "What have I told you about using the door?"

"Sorry," I called back, "just habit."

"Bring the garbage bucket by the back porch!" he called, and he and TJ headed off toward the barn.

By the time I caught up, there were coffee grounds and something orange on my leg. "What are you doing? Raising pigs?"

The Judge just smiled proudly and guided us through the open barn door. My pupils adjusted to the dim light as he led us between two wood-framed troughs filled with dirt. "Look here." He thrust his arm into the soil and pulled up a writhing fistful of worms.

"Worms!" TJ was impressed. "Can I hold them?"

My father placed them tenderly on TJ's little palm.

"What do they eat, Grandpa?"

The Judge reached for the bucket at my feet. "See that oatmeal you didn't finish?" TJ peered into the mess of scraps, then nodded. "That's their favorite." He set TJ on a turned-over washtub and passed him the pail. "Okay, dump it on in there."

I sat on a stool observing the man I used to know as my father. Actually, I can't say that I ever knew him. The Judge's mind had always been mysterious to me. His opinions were as solid as boulders, and as a teenager, I was crushed by them. In the courtroom the Judge's words had been known to bring hardened attorneys to the brink of tears. Anyone who spent time in his presence left either loving him or hating him. There was no in-between.

What went on in court was never discussed at our dinner table. But my ninth-grade teacher had us dissect the *State v. Ronald Enrich* case because it was a current event, and one that raised a buzz since both the accused and the judge (my father) lived in Carter. Ronald

Enrich was only seventeen when he smashed his mother's head repeatedly on the stone fireplace mantle in their home.

Once the wave of horror at the killing spread through town, people began probing for a reason. Ron was such a handsome boy. Sure he was involved in a few scuffles with opposing football teams, but that aggressive tenacity got Darlington High into the state playoffs.

The Judge had Ronald tried as an adult, and he was sentenced to life in the state penitentiary. The outcry was heard beyond Carter. I saw my father's picture in the *Seattle Times* and the headline above it that read THE JUDGEMENT OF ALMIGHTY DODD.

The class chewed and swallowed the facts, then barfed up the verdict. Seventy percent thought Ronald ought to have been given leniency. Most of my classmates thought my father was a merciless tyrant, and the rest were undecided. I was in the seventy percent.

As a child, I remember the Judge going to the courthouse every morning, returning faithfully every night. After dinner he would retire to his study. The Judge was intense when he was deciding a case. If my sister Lindsey and I weren't noisy, he might keep his door open a crack. Once in a while his murmurings drew us to the hall to spy. He would lean back in his chair and talk to the ceiling, and then he might be quiet for a long time. Finally, he would proclaim, "That's it!" startling his little spies.

That's the way I remember him. And now the powerful hand that raised the gavel was elbow deep in a trough of horse dung.

"So what's the plan? Are you going to retire from the bench and sell worms?"

The Judge looked up, obviously amused. "No, I don't think so."

"Then why are you doing this?"

"Well, I enjoy it." He raised one eyebrow. "When I'm not here, the locals know to just dish up their own. Donnie Duncan comes by once in a while. He asks about you."

"He's still here?" I was shocked. Donnie was the one who couldn't wait to get out of this nowhere town. The Judge looked at me, his eyebrows curving down like lazy question marks. He was always frugal with his words. I knew that somehow a connection had been made to the past simply by the mention of my old friend's name. Not yet. I wasn't ready for questions. I turned back toward the open barn door. "I think I'll go see what Mom is doing."

Over my shoulder I saw him staring after me.

CHAPTER TWO

I HAD no valid reason for parking my Jeep against the curb beneath the spreading branches of a Japanese cherry. The house across the street was painted green now. The laurel hedge had grown thick and tall. There was no tire swing hanging from the maple tree, no red Chevy truck with a lanky young man reaching beneath its hood.

Sometimes revisiting the past is a mistake. Some things are better left in your mind the way they were.

Every time a breeze blew, pale pink blossoms wafted across my windshield. It was a warm day, and the air was saturated with the sweet scents of new green grass and flowers. Like the spring when I fell in love with Tim. But he didn't live here anymore. He and I left town in his shiny red Chevy seven years ago. I thought maybe his mother had moved on also. The house was just too different. There was no sign of life in the house, no vehicles in the drive. It was a hauntingly lonely sight.

I don't know what I would have done if Mrs. Weatherbee had poked her head out the door and waved. Not that she would. If she recognized me, she would be more likely to turn away and close the drapes. But then, she would have heard only Tim's side of the story. I would have liked the chance to explain.

I drove around Darlington for a while, past my alma mater, Darlington High. A cluster of students sprawled on the lawn. They looked so young. Was I really that young when I left?

My stubbornness had been my downfall more than once. It was one of the things I got from my father. But in our final contest my tenacity had won over his, or lost, depending on how you looked at it. I packed what I could carry in a duffel bag and walked right past the Judge. He didn't stop me. My mother followed, trying to reason with me, but he reached out his hand and held her. Before I was all the way off the steps, the porch light went off. My father would no longer be a lamp unto my feet and a light unto my path. He made that clear. I could find my own way through the dark.

It wasn't until after TJ was born that I started admitting how much I missed them. Mom especially. I always wondered what she would do about this and that. How do you soothe a colicky baby? Is this diaper rash or the plague? I reached for the phone sometimes but always stopped myself. I did send short notes on occasion, but I feared that once I heard my mother's voice, I might spill my carefully guarded secrets and never be able to clean up the mess.

Coming home to the river had been TJ's idea originally. All those nights, as we cuddled in our big chair back in our dreary Reno apartment, I told him stories. The characters were my sister, our friend Donnie from down the road, and me in any one of our true adventures by the river. In TJ's mind the river valley of my childhood was more magical than any elfin kingdom.

And then there was fishing. Fishing was the thing that intrigued TJ the most. Maybe because I could not speak of it without a wistful longing, nor could I separate the Judge, his grandfather, from this inherited passion for the pursuit of fish.

My son often interrupted our story time with questions that, as he grew older, became harder to answer. "Why don't we ever go there?" he would ask.

"Because it's too far."

"We could take a airplane."

"Plane tickets cost money."

"Or we could drive our Jeep. How long will it take if we drive?"

I explained that driving costs money too. I said I couldn't get off work for that long and changed the subject as skillfully as I could.

The truth was a horse pill, too big for a five-year-old to swallow. I had estranged my family and my husband and I had no real friends. My pain was the closest thing I had to a friend. It was constant and dependable.

It was physical pain that eventually caused me to consider TJ's plan. Both TJ and I had caught a flu bug that winter. In a few days TJ was back to normal. My initial symptoms, including a fever of 104 degrees, lingered a few days longer than his. I had a cough for weeks and very little energy. I did go back to work waiting tables at the Starlight Room but found it hard to work a full eight-hour shift. There was a heaviness in my chest that just wouldn't go away. My boss was patient for a long time. But one day, when I had to ask if I could leave early, he said to go home and don't bother coming back.

I didn't have medical insurance. After paying the rent that month, I had exactly $172.58. My roommate was in about the same financial condition, only she still had her job.

Hard times were not new to me. When things got tough, I just had to get tougher. But this time I didn't have the strength. I worried myself into a dither. What was wrong with me? I couldn't get any answers from my doctor until I paid my overdue bill. If I paid the bill, I would have nothing left. How would I feed my son?

TJ found me crying in my room one night. "What happened, Mommy? Did you get hurt?" He had never seen me like this before.

"No, I'm not hurt, baby." I managed a sheepish smile. "I just felt like crying tonight. I feel better now."

"But why?"

"I don't know. I guess grown-ups cry sometimes for the same reasons kids cry. Remember the first time I left you at the new day care?" He nodded. "That was a brand-new situation for you. You weren't comfortable with it and it made you cry."

"I wanted you to come back." He climbed onto the bed, and I put my arms around him. "Maybe you want *your* mommy."

I turned my head to look at him, astonished. One whack and he had driven the nail home. He was so right. I needed someone to take care of me. I desperately wanted to find healing.

"Let's go home, Teej," I finally said. "You've got a grandma and grandpa to meet."

Eight days later and here we were, back in the home of my childhood. I didn't mention my illness to Mom or the Judge. I was as dependent as a toddler again, only not so naïve. I could never crawl up on my father's lap again as I once did, believing that he was my daddy and I was his own flesh and blood and that his love was as constant as the law of gravity. Love, it seemed, had its limits.

Oh, he tolerated me. What else could he do? Besides, I had brought my angel-faced son, his grandson, an offering that seemed to please him. If nothing else, TJ had bought me some time.

Just after lunch that first day back at the river, the Judge and TJ had headed for the creek with worms and spinning rods. I had declined their invitation to come along, my unstated reason that I was not sure I could make it down the ravine in my weakened state.

It was late afternoon when I went into the kitchen and saw TJ standing on a chair pulled up to the counter watching the Judge gut a trout in the sink. Déjà vu. It used to be me watching wide-eyed.

"Mom, look! We caught two fish!"

They were small cutthroats, barely legal keepers. The big trout were mostly in the river, but TJ was not old enough to fish beyond the creek yet.

"Wow! They're beautiful."

The Judge looked over at me. "Want to see what they're eating?"

I nodded. I was still curious even after all those years. He separated the stomach and ran the blade down its length. "Periwinkles."

The phone rang. The Judge held up his bloody hands helplessly, and I reached for the portable phone. "Hello. Dodd residence."

The caller didn't speak, but I sensed that someone was there. I shrugged my shoulders and held the phone away from my ear.

Immediately the Judge snatched the receiver away, bloody hands and all. "Hello?"

I heard a male voice; then my father spun away down the hall to his study. Curious, I followed, pausing outside the door. I heard nothing until the receiver slammed on the desk. He let out a sigh.

"Who was that?" I asked.

He looked startled to see me there. "Nobody. Just a prank call."

We returned to the kitchen in time to see TJ *cleaning* his fish with soap and a sponge. I laughed, but the humor seemed to be lost on the Judge. He rinsed his hands and left the room without speaking.

THOUGH it was not quite May, Mom had prepared a Thanksgiving feast. The family congregated in the dining room, along with Matthew, my father's comrade since they had roomed together in college. Matthew was a doctor with a family practice in Seattle. I sat facing the window where the river winked at me through the trees.

My sister, Lindsey, scooted next to her new husband, who looked like she cut him out of an Eddie Bauer catalog. His dark, wavy hair seemed to be polished with something, and a supposedly wayward strand was carefully positioned on his forehead. I wondered if he ironed the crease in his khaki pants himself.

The last time I saw Lindsey, we were both seventeen and she wore a ponytail. Now her hair was bobbed and she had graduated from cheerleader skirts to a silk dress and pearls. She tossed a blond wisp behind her ear with a manicured hand. "So, Samantha," she smiled too hard, "we have so much catching up to do."

"You first," I said.

Mom placed the turkey platter near the Judge, and everyone grew quiet until he bowed his head. "Father, we are grateful for all you provide and for bringing Samantha and TJ home. Amen."

"Amen," we repeated in unison.

Lindsey continued where we had left off. "Okay," she tipped her head adoringly toward her husband. "Well, as you know, David and I were married about two years ago. David passed his bar exam last June and had a position waiting for him at Wiley and Murdock. They're already talking about making him a partner."

"That's good," I said as sincerely as I could. "Where do you work, Lindsey?"

"Oh"—the question caught her off guard—"well, I don't, really."

"You work, honey," my mother pitched in. "You just don't get paid for it." Then she turned to me. "Your sister does volunteer work at the hospital in Darlington. She uses puppets to entertain children in extended care, runs errands, and even decorates the wards. Sometimes the nurses call her in to sit with a worried mom."

Lindsey smiled humbly. "I've made a lot of friends."

I tried to concentrate on cutting my son's turkey. Lindsey was still perfect. The Judge's eyes ignited at her smile. She had married the perfect man, the son that our father never had, educated and respectable and a law enthusiast to boot.

Matthew spoke next. "Samantha, last time I saw you, you were on your hands and knees in the creek groping under logs for crawdads. You must have been about fifteen." Matt's wiry hair had crept away from his dark forehead and had gone prematurely gray. I loved to pat his head when I was young.

Lindsey giggled. "She was always like that! She would stay down at the creek all by herself until after dark."

"But you ended up in Nevada." Matthew shook his head. "Quite a contrast. Any decent fishing there?"

I shrugged. "I don't know. I was working all the time."

"What kind of work did you do?"

"I waited tables. Before that I worked on a ranch near Reno."

"And she was a dancer," TJ volunteered proudly.

"Who told you that?" My face was instantly hot.

"Mindy." We had shared an apartment with Mindy and her son. "She said you were a dancer just like her."

I couldn't think of a thing to say. Mom mercifully began to offer second helpings. When I raised my eyes, they met Lindsey's, but hers flitted nervously away. My father became broodingly silent. His eyes took on a distant glare.

David and my mother started comparing their stocks and mutual funds. Mom said Microsoft stock was down due to recent legal battles and she was going to pick up a few more shares tomorrow.

"What does she mean by a few?" Matthew looked to my father with amusement in an attempt to lighten him up. Matt was one of a handful of men who was not intimidated by the Judge. He had been like a beloved uncle to us as far back as I could remember.

The Judge leaned back and sighed deeply before letting his eyes sparkle at Mom, with a hint of a smile. "She knows what she's doing. If she can just cut down on new shoes, I can retire soon."

"Are you serious?" I blurted. "About retiring, I mean."

"Why not?"

"How old are you, anyway?" I remembered an article in the local paper that said that our father was the youngest man ever appointed to the bench in our state.

"Forty-nine."

I studied him for a moment. "You look good for an old guy."

"Old!" He acted insulted. "I'm in my prime . . . right, Doc?" Matthew nodded. "I challenge you to a game of tennis, young lady. Then we'll see who's old."

Matthew had succeeded. The smoke had cleared, and everyone seemed more comfortable. "You play tennis now?" I asked.

"I had to take it up. Your mother made me."

"We play poker, don't we, Mom?" Good old TJ. "You wanna know how much money I have now, Grandma?" He held up six fingers. "I have seven dollars." He giggled along with everyone else at the table. "One time my Mom won all my quarters and then I had to give her my shoes." He was as delighted with the telling of it as he had been during the game.

"That's terrible!" Lindsey feigned shock. "Then what did she do with them?"

He shrugged. "I don't know."

"Well, I'm going back to cash only with you," I said, shaking my head. "Those shoes of yours pinched my toes. And they light up in the dark when I'm trying to sneak around."

When the hill beyond the river turned to blue green, the Judge pushed back his chair. "It'll be dark soon."

Matthew nodded and excused himself. "Can you still handle a fly rod, Sam?"

"I've done it in my sleep,"

"Come on," my father said. "I'll rig you up."

Lindsey helped Mom clear the table, and David followed us out to the garage. We equipped ourselves with rods and reels, but David didn't come to the river, as he didn't have the proper shoes. TJ begged to come, but his grandma bribed him back into the house with a piece of pie.

The Judge's rod tip pointed the way through the trees along the riverbank, a route he could surely navigate blind. Before we spread out on the river, he offered me his open fly box like a box of cigars. I chose a parachute Adams and waded into the shocking coolness until I was wet to the thighs. The Judge and Matthew had positioned themselves downstream and were already casting as I fumbled with rod and line. My casts were a little awkward at first but got worse as I imagined my father's watchful eye.

It was on my twelfth birthday that my father gave me my first fly rod. He had first coached me on the front lawn. "Forward, pause, back, pause." His hand was wrapped around mine on the handle of the rod. "Watch the path of your line. Now let it load behind you."

From my perch in my favorite cottonwood tree, I had observed him many times, hypnotized by the graceful dance of arm and rod and line. I always liked my father best when he was knee-deep in the river. He wore soft flannel shirts instead of the stiff white ones that he wore to the courthouse. And he rarely frowned. That first day of lessons, though, I had tried his patience. Not once had my fly landed near the target. He gestured to a spot about ten yards upstream. "See that white rock? Plop your fly on the middle of it."

It was too far away. I made a sloppy attempt just to humor him. "I can't! It's too far!"

"Do it anyway," he had said.

I tried again twice and failed. "I can't do it!"

"Samantha Dodd!" His tone had been sharp. "Don't ever say *I can't!*" He waded out to me and wrapped his hand around mine on the rod handle. His other hand reached around me to the loose line hanging from the reel. Together we cast the line, dropping the dry fly to the exact middle of the rock. "Anything you believe, you can achieve," he had said. "If you want to be successful, see what you want, not what you don't want. Then speak it until you believe it. That's called faith. Faith has the power to move mountains."

Standing in the river, I wondered what my father thought of me now. Everything he taught me about life and success and fly fishing had stagnated through seven long, dry Nevada years. TJ was all I had to show for them. I had expected questions, but there had been none from him and no reference to what happened between us.

I shuddered. My bones were cold, and I found myself exhausted. It was almost dark. I found a rock at the river's edge and sat hugging my knees for what seemed like a long time, until the two men finally joined me and started up the path toward home. They took long, quick strides, and I couldn't keep up. My chest hurt, worse than ever before. I had to slow down and concentrate on breathing.

I followed them up the trail all the way to the edge of the backyard before stopping by a tree, suddenly becoming desperate for breath. My chest heaved, and I couldn't get enough air.

The Judge and Matthew were talking. They couldn't hear the strange sounds that grated past my throat as I clung to the scabby tree trunk. My knees buckled, and I dropped to the moist grass.

I heard Matthew's alarmed cry and the thuds of hip boots on the lawn as the men ran back to me. I was on my hands and knees now, fighting for air, desperate for relief from the pressure in my chest.

"Samantha, what is it?" My father's hand was on my back.

"Get her inside and get her warm!" Matt barked as he ran off.

I couldn't answer. I just shook my head. The Judge scooped me up and bolted for the house.

"TJ," I finally managed to whisper. "Don't let TJ see me."

But it was too late. Matthew's 911 call had alarmed the whole household. They hovered anxiously above me as my father laid me on the leather sofa, muddy feet and all. Mom stripped me of wet socks, shoes, and jeans and tucked a comforter around me. The pain soon subsided, and I found myself breathing normally again. "I'm okay now," I said, but no one would call off the emergency-aid car.

Matthew the fisherman metamorphosed back into a doctor. He sat calmly on the edge of the sofa taking my pulse and gently asking questions, while TJ hugged my feet.

"Yes," I said, "it's happened a few times, but never like this. At first I thought it was some lingering symptom from a flu I had."

"Did you see a doctor?"

"No." Actually, I had tried to make an appointment at the clinic where I took TJ whenever he had an ear infection, but I was informed that I would have to pay the outstanding balance on my delinquent account before a doctor would see me.

Matthew listened to my chest and then without comment nodded reassuringly at my parents. I felt relieved. Finally I was not alone. Whatever it was that had been plaguing me would be discovered now. Matt would probably prescribe some antibiotics or something, and soon I would be my wild old self again. A siren wailed from somewhere in the darkness.

I swore and slunk into the couch. "Do they have to do that?" TJ shook his head at me, and I apologized for the bad word.

Within minutes a pickup truck with a strobing cherry on top stormed down the long driveway. A huge man barged through the door, dropped a metal supply case on the floor, and began hooking me up to things and asking questions. Matt and my father did much of the talking. The woman who accompanied the big man repeated my vital signs into a radio transmitter.

They were there a long time. Mom served coffee while the men exchanged top-secret fishing-hole locations. Lindsey was busy mothering me and asking the woman what we should do next. The general consensus was that I should rest at home through the night but see a specialist first thing in the morning.

Which I did. Matthew said not to worry but that he heard something irregular when he listened to my heart. He sent me to a Dr. Talbot, who took blood, urine, and half my day. My mother came in to wait with me between tests. I read her the quiz from *Glamour* magazine, *How Daring Is Your Sex Life?* but she was pretty uncooperative. Finally Dr. Talbot came back in. "Okay, Samantha. One more test." He slid an ultrasound wand between my breasts. The room was quiet as we studied the image on a nearby monitor. My mother rose slowly to her feet, clutching a tissue to her chest.

I found myself staring at a gray, sluggish shape. Some wounded animal in a cage of ribs. The revelation came to me slowly. I was looking at the very organ that I felt laboring even now and on which my life depended. Biology was not my best subject, but I knew the basic shape and structure of a heart. Something was wrong.

Dr. Talbot called it viral myocarditis. He pointed to the swollen mass and said that the muscle had become inflamed and was not working as it should. "That's why you've been having chest pains and shortness of breath. Your heart has to work harder, especially when you exert yourself, to pump the blood your body needs." He sighed. "Tell me more about this flu you had. Did your symptoms begin immediately after that?"

I thought they had.

He asked more questions and scribbled more notes.

"What caused this?" I asked.

He shook his head. "My guess is it's the work of that virus."

Mom lifted her chin and acted confident and collected now, for my sake. "How do we fix it, Doctor?"

"I'm going to refer Samantha to another specialist." He passed her a card. "Dr. Sovold is a cardiologist at the University Medical Center in Seattle. Let him take a look, and we'll go from there. In the meantime, Samantha, I'm going to put you on a drug known as an ACE inhibitor." He wrote out the prescription and passed me the paper. "I'm not going to lie to you, Samantha. Your heart has suffered severe damage. Hopefully this drug treatment will succeed. If not, sometimes surgical treatment of the problem is possible."

I asked him what I could and couldn't do, and he basically ruled out anything fun. No exertion, no overeating, no drinking, no smoking. "Listen to your body," he said, "and call me immediately if any of your symptoms become more severe."

Mom and I walked down the steps of the doctor's office into a light rain. We didn't say much. Mom was always good about giving me my space.

We ate lunch in a house turned restaurant with window boxes that burgeoned geraniums and blue lobelia. Mom was still being very brave and in control. It was one of the things I loved about her.

She glanced at the menu and recommended I try the chicken Caesar. "They make a good one here."

I could have eaten dog food. I didn't taste a thing.

"Is this why you came home, Sammy?" she finally asked.

I nodded, rearranging the food on my plate. Yes, it was the heart thing. But it was more. When I looked up at her, my eyes were watery. "I knew something was wrong. I just didn't know what. I didn't know what to do. I was waitressing, but I couldn't keep up anymore. Then I started calling in sick, and they said sayonara, and there I sat. No money. No medical insurance. I owe TJ's day care three hundred bucks; I owe Mindy, my roommate—"

"Shhh, it's okay, Sam. You did the right thing. You came home. We'll work out the details. You need to work on getting better." ·

Good old Mom. It *was* the right thing. I felt it in my gut. "I like how you are with TJ," I said. "He's been needing a grandma."

Mom laughed. "I didn't know how much I needed him until I saw him face to face. I guess I couldn't let myself think about him too much. I knew so little about him. I wish you had written more. You could have at least sent me a picture!"

"Then you would have seen that he's a Mexiwegian and I'd have to explain, and I didn't want to explain."

"Sammy"—she smiled and put her hand on my arm—"you tell me all about it when you're ready, okay?"

I didn't look up, and a tear fell on the table. "Okay."

MY FATHER took the news of my diagnosis calmly. "Well," he said, "we'll know more after you see the other cardiologist. Hopefully they can correct this without surgery. Do you have medical insurance, Samantha?"

I shook my head.

"I told her we would take care of the finances," Mom said. They exchanged a glance, which I couldn't read. I had never heard my parents fight, but I wondered if there might be heated words exchanged behind closed doors that night. In my mind I could still hear his tirades over lights left on or long-distance phone calls. I had seen the Judge pick up a penny from a parking lot and drop it into his pocket. I wondered what open-heart surgery might cost.

"Yes. Good," he said without expression. "Let's just do what it takes to get you well."

I imagined he must be thinking how convenient it was for me to just show up when I happened to need a roof over our heads, food to eat—oh, and someone to pay a pending heap of medical expenses besides. Good old Samantha. Independent as one of those aloof cats until it's hungry enough to come rubbing against your leg as if it really liked you all along.

I did like my father once.

Back then he smelled of damp earth and the spicy cottonwood buds that found their way into his pockets from the trees along the riverbank. His eyes sometimes glimmered like sun-dappled ripples, though they could quickly take on the hard gray of winter. Like the river, I loved and feared him.

I remember the peace that came through the door with him every evening and the way our world revolved around his presence. When our father sat in his big chair, we huddled near him telling about the adventures of our day. He would smile as we chattered.

Like the river, he was a boundary around my small world. The problems came when I grew older and realized that there was a realm to be explored beyond his rigid control. But the raging current of his will was a dangerous thing to cross.

Maybe that was why I did the things I did. Any prisoner longs for freedom. I found mine by crawling out my bedroom window for clandestine meetings with stupid boys. I took up drinking. I was the life of every party—the one who could be counted on to do the crazy things that we could all laugh about back at school.

But these were not the things that caused the Judge to send me packing when I was only seventeen. I finally committed that unforgivable sin—the one that still lurked behind me like a shadow. I resented him for that. It was his standard—not mine—that sent me away. But he was the Judge. Guilty! His verdict clung to my back like a clawed thing that I had not been able to shake even after all those years.

TJ came over and straddled the Judge's lap, facing him and patting his hands on his grandpa's cheeks as if he had known him from birth instead of for just a few days. "Do you wanna go feed the worms when we wake up, Grandpa?"

"Tell you what, son. Let's do it when I get home tomorrow night. You'll probably still be asleep when I go to work." He tousled TJ's hair. "What I need you to do is catch some bugs—as many as you can. Grandma will give you something to put them in."

TJ nodded in earnest. "Okay."

Mom and I exchanged amused glances. My son—my treasure, my trophy—then went over to kiss his grandma, and when he eventually wandered off toward his new bedroom, we were all smiling.

"So what are the bugs for?" I asked.

The Judge shrugged. "To keep him busy. A man need's a mission. Besides, you need a lot of rest." He looked at his watch. "In fact, it's after ten. Why don't you go on to bed now? Your mom and I have some things to talk about."

I nodded, gathering up the shoes I had kicked off, though I had not considered retiring that early. Just like old times. I had been dismissed. I paused by my mother's chair, thinking of bending down to kiss her as I used to do, but it would be awkward. I walked to the doorway. "Good night," I said.

"Good night."

"Sleep well."

But I tossed and turned until dawn.

CHAPTER THREE

I FOUND myself at home in the semidarkness at a table in the rear, like a coyote finally back in her den. Not that I'd ever been inside this particular establishment, though I had pedaled my bike across the gravel parking lot of Fraser's Tavern at least a hundred times.

I hadn't planned to end up there. I just knew I needed to get out of the house for a while. I needed to think. The image of my enlarged heart seemed to appear on my eyelids every time I blinked, and with it came an overwhelming sadness.

I leaned back, propping my boots on a vacant chair. The night was young, and many tables were empty. A few men straddled stools at the old bar, loudly offering advice to the baseball players on an overhead TV screen. Two women played darts in the corner.

"You lied." A voice startled me. "You said you'd never grow up."

I turned to gaze into the strangely familiar face of a young man carrying two bottles and a glass mug. I squinted up at him, suppressing any sign of recognition. "Are you the waiter? It's about time."

He grinned and pulled the chair out from under my feet. "How ya' doin', Sam? I heard you were back." He sat down, poured cold beer into the mug, and pushed it toward me. "You're lookin' good."

"Hello, Donnie."

"It's Don now. Just plain Don, if you don't mind."

I smiled mischievously. "You'll always be little Donnie Duncan to me." My eyes fell on the crop of hair protruding from his open shirt and the bronze forearms resting on the table, like two legs of mutton, and I was well aware that Donnie Duncan had grown up.

"And I'll always remember you as the kid who hung by her knees from cottonwood branches with her shirt falling over her head."

I laughed. "Those were the days, weren't they? Remember the rope swing by the river?"

He took a swig. "How about the night we swung out double and you fell off. Your sister and I heard the splash, but it was so stinkin' dark we couldn't see a thing. We called and called, but you didn't answer. Then Lindsey went blatso on me."

"I lived to freak out Lindsey. It was my major life purpose."

For a moment we surveyed one another. Donnie's coarse blond hair was cropped short, and his eyes were bluer than I remembered. "Last time I saw you," I said, "you had hair down to here and you were singing *Stairway to Heaven* at the school prom." I emptied my mug, and Donnie signaled the waitress to bring us a pitcher.

"And *you* danced with Tim Weatherbee all night. Next thing anybody knew, you dropped out of school and ran off with him."

"But I'm back."

He raised his brows. "No Tim?"

I shook my head. "No Tim."

Don seemed to be waiting for an explanation. I paused before changing the subject. "Looks like you're still bucking hay." I nodded toward his burly shoulders.

He shrugged. "That's right. You didn't believe me when I said I was going to be an attorney, did you?"

I studied his face. He was acting too casual. "Yes, I believed it. And so did you. What happened? You know you're smart enough. I heard you one time when you were on the debate team."

"You did?"

I nodded. "I was just walking by the door of the classroom, and I heard your voice. I stopped and listened for a long time. You were good. You kind of reminded me of the Judge."

"Thank you."

"What makes you think that was a compliment?"

He sighed. "You still have that burr in your boot? I like your dad. I buy worms from him. We hang out in the barn talking."

"Good for you," I said. "Tell me, has he measured you up yet? Has he taken out his invisible tape and run it from your toes to the top of your head and left you feeling like a midget?" My words tasted bitter, and I knew my eyes were getting squinty and mean-looking. I deliberately pulled up the corners of my mouth. "So. Come here often?"

He shook his head. "I saw a pretty girl speed by the ranch in a dirty old Jeep. Followed her here."

"I was thinking about calling you. I've only been here a week."

"I heard you've been in Nevada. What brought you back?"

I brightened. "Donnie, I have a son." I reached for my wallet and placed a snapshot on the table. "His name is TJ. He's five."

"Good-lookin' kid. Your dad told me you had a son. I've always asked about you, you know." He studied the picture some more. "So does Tim have some Indian blood in him?"

204 | Karen Harter

"Subtle," I said. "Hey, if you want to know who I've been sleeping with, just ask. I've never kept secrets from you."

His mouth spread slowly into a grin, and his blue eyes danced. "Dang, I've missed you. You're still just the same. And you haven't answered my question. Why did you come home? The truth."

I wanted to tell him everything. Who knew me better than my childhood playmate? We had been best friends up until puberty. Then things got confusing. Donnie started playing basketball and hanging out with some guys from school. He didn't want to fish much anymore. Once, when I went over to the Appaloosa Ranch to help him with his chores, he pressed me up against a stall door and kissed me. I kicked like a branded mare and wiped the kiss from my mouth in disgust. He never tried that again.

After that I avoided him for a while, and he didn't seem to have much interest in me. Sometimes he helped me do my homework on the morning school bus, though. Donnie was smart for a rancher.

I couldn't tell him I came home because I was sick or that I couldn't keep a job. Tim was long gone. I had been feeding my son Top Ramen three nights a week. "The truth is," I finally said, "I needed to smell the cottonwoods again." That was not a lie. "Also for TJ. A kid needs a family. He needed to meet his grandma and grandpa. He's a wonderful person. I want you to meet him."

"Are you going to tell me about his daddy?"

I drained my beer. "TJ has no daddy." Donnie refilled my glass. I made a mental note that this would be my last one. "I'll tell you the gory details after you tell me why you're still here in Carter."

He held up his glass and stared into the golden liquid. "I don't know. Seems like there's always a barn to rebuild or a lame tractor or a fence down. There are a lot of things Dad can't do anymore."

"Is he sick?"

He glared. "You really have been out of touch. Four years ago a hay fork came out of the loft and nearly nailed him to the barn floor."

My jaw dropped. "A hay fork *came* out of the loft? How?"

"I threw it."

I stared at him and waited.

"I didn't mean to hit him. We were up in the hayloft rigging up a pulley. You know how he can be. He expects everything, appreciates nothing. I put off law school for two years because he needed me at the ranch. I was all set to go to the U.W. that fall and he tells me it's a waste of money. He reminded me for the thousandth time that I was just a country hick and I could never hold my own against those slick city boys. 'Your place is here, boy,' he says, and he goes down the ladder. I thought he had left the barn. I grabbed the pitchfork and hurled it into space like a javelin. Then I heard him scream." He paused. "It got his thigh and severed a tendon in his knee. He walks with a limp now. Has to use a cane on bad days."

I whispered a curse. "I'm sorry. Sorry for you, mostly."

"Why?"

"Because he's got you now, right where he wants you."

Don pushed away from the table. "Let's get out of here." He threw some bills on the table and took my arm.

"Let me go to the bathroom first." I stopped at the restroom, and when I came out, there was the cigarette machine looking right at me. What the heck, I thought. I'll be good starting tomorrow. Donnie was already outside. I popped my money in, and a pack of Kool Filters slid out. As I tapped one out of the package, someone flicked a lighter in my face and it startled me. The man's face was too close to mine. He lit my cigarette. "Those things'll kill ya, you know."

"Yeah," I mumbled. "Thanks." When I stepped toward the door, he blocked my path, staring at me with an evil smile that made me feel sick. I pushed him aside and stormed out the door.

"You okay?" Donnie asked. He frowned at my cigarette.

I held up my hand. "Don't say it." I gestured toward the man watching me through the tavern window. "Who is that guy?"

"Him? That's Dwight Enrich. Was he giving you a hard time?"

I nodded.

"He's just a bitter old drunk. Remember Ron Enrich? The kid that bashed his mother's head in? That's his dad. Fraser's is his home away from home. Ignore him." We hopped in his shiny Ford truck, leaving my Jeep behind in the parking lot in a cloud of dust.

The moon was a half disk of white neon. Scents of alfalfa and honeysuckle rode through the open windows, and Ray Charles sang on the radio. We sang along and laughed all the way to Dixon, where we stopped for a bag of chips, huge navel oranges, and some beer. After that we pulled off at a rest stop by the river.

"How do things turn out the way they do, Sam?" Donnie leaned against his door with his feet on the dash, while I ravenously attacked the bag of chips. "You're the one who said you'd build a cabin on the river and live off the land. Remember that? And I said I'd hit the road the day I turned eighteen and never look back."

I bit off a corner of my tortilla chip. Was I supposed to have an answer to that question? It was not like I left the valley on purpose; I was more or less shot out of my father's cannon and landed in Reno with powder burns that still hadn't healed.

"And what about you and me," he continued. "Why didn't we ever date or anything?"

I looked at him like he was nuts. "Correct me if I'm wrong, but as I recall, you never asked me out."

He laughed. "I kissed you once. What do ya want?"

"A little warning would have been nice, for starters. You scared the snot out of me. You never acted like that before."

"You never looked like that before. At least, it was the first time I really noticed. Guess I should have checked in a little sooner. Tim slid in there ahead of me. So what happened between you two?"

"We're still married."

"Oh, I didn't know. You're not wearing a ring or anything."

"After I didn't see or hear from him for a few years, I took it off."

"That jerk! He walked out on you? Takes you away from your family and friends to some God-forsaken desert and then dumps you there?" He twisted the cap off a beer and passed it to me.

I took a swig and leaned back. "It wasn't like that, exactly." It wasn't fair to blame Tim. Tim loved me. I never doubted that. Not even when we were fighting. I was such a shrew that summer of my third trimester—my belly protruding, ankles swollen, still trying to earn my keep on the ranch. The pregnancy was unplanned, but after what happened the first time—well, I couldn't consider that alternative again. Tim told me if it was a girl, we'd get her a pony. But I knew he really wanted a boy. "My son's gonna know how to rebuild his own truck from headlight to tailpipe," he'd say.

Donnie was respectfully silent.

Finally I said, "Tim was not the bad guy. It was me."

"You left *him*?"

"No. The last time I saw Tim was in the hospital after TJ was born. They laid the baby on my belly, and I knew the minute I laid eyes on him that he wasn't Tim's. He was as brown as milk chocolate, with a head full of coal-black hair."

"Seems like there's a big chunk of this story you've left out."

"Tijuana. That's what everyone called the guy who gave me TJ. That's how I came up with his name."

"So where's this Tijuana now?"

I shrugged. "Siberia, for all I care." I felt myself relaxing into the truck's upholstery. "Maybe we should take a little nap."

Donnie had other ideas. He slid an orange into each of my jacket pockets and stashed the bag containing the six-pack under his arm. "Come on." He opened his door and pulled me out on his side.

"Where are we going?" It was unlike me to ask. Usually, I was up for any adventure. We walked down a dirt trail through some alder trees to where the railroad track paralleled the river. The cool night air revived me, but I took the tracks in slow double steps. Even in my slightly inebriated state I remembered that I had to be careful.

The moonlight touched the edges of the metal rails. The tracks veered off to our left up ahead and then spanned the river on a huge suspension trestle whose framework was hazily silhouetted on the sky. I knew then where we were headed.

The span of the railroad bridge seemed longer than it was when we were kids. We finally reached the middle and sat on the edge, our legs dangling above the current. Long spirals of orange peel dropped into the darkness and disappeared without a sound.

"So . . ." I broke the silence. "You never got married?"

"Nope."

"What's the holdup?"

"Pretty slim pickin's around here."

"Well, you're not getting any younger. You might want to consider shopping out of town."

He looked at me funny for a moment. "Yeah. Good idea."

We drank beer in silence for a while. In the distance we heard the first muted thunder of the train. "Here she comes." We listened to the rumble fade in and out as it rounded hilly bends. Ten minutes later the whistle blew, heralding the train's slow clatter through Dixon, and then the thunder mounted as the engine picked up speed outside the little town. By the time it neared the trestle, I was trembling from both the vibration and a rush of adrenaline.

Don pulled me to my feet. "Okay, it's showtime!" He climbed onto the metal gridwork above the bridge and held an arm down to me. "You coming?"

I shook my head. "No. I want to be right next to it!" The train erupted onto the bridge, racing straight for us, engine lights blazing. Feet planted on a railroad tie, I leaned against a girder for support. In seconds the train was upon us. Donnie hollered something, but his voice was strangled by the explosion of diesel power and the crashing and clanking of each passing freight car.

This was the part where we used to hoot with laughter, defying the monster and leaning as close as we dared. The strange thing was that I was not having fun. My heart ached. I felt it trying too hard. My eyes closed, and I tottered dizzily before grabbing the girder. I wanted the train to pass, but boxcar after boxcar, it torpedoed on. My mind swirled in the darkness like the river below. When I looked down, everything became a blur. I felt myself falling.

The next few seconds were recorded in slow motion in my mind. The clanking of the train, my body slamming against something, the top of my torso hanging precariously over a sharp edge. I threw up.

"Sam! Don't move!"

My body stopped vibrating as the last freight car left the bridge. Donnie pulled me from the low metal railing, laying my body alongside the warm track. "Sam, are you okay?"

"I think so. Let's just rest for a while."

Donnie hoisted me to my feet. "Come on, you little lush." He wrapped my arm around his shoulders and started walking down the railroad tracks. My legs were surprisingly weak.

"I'm not drunk."

"Yeah. You just puked your guts out for the fun of it. Dang it, Sam! If I'd known, I never would have left you alone down there."

Donnie got me back to the truck, and we drove in silence. Long, peaceful silence. I think I dozed off. The crunch of gravel under the truck tires roused me, and I knew I was home.

"Stop here, Donnie." We were only halfway down the long drive-way. "I'm just going to get out here, okay?"

"Why?"

"I'm not in the mood to talk to anybody."

He shook his head and started to put the truck back into gear.

"I *am* a little drunk," I finally admitted. "I don't want TJ to see me like this. If you let me off here, I can sneak in the back door without anyone hearing me."

I slid out on my side and crossed over to his open window. We stared at each other for a moment. "Thanks, Donnie."

His face broke into a grin. He winked and shoved the truck into reverse. I climbed between the fence rails and headed across the field toward the barn.

The grass in my parents' field was long and cool. I saw my mother's shape cross the living room to turn off a lamp. Hopefully they would turn in soon and so could I. Mom had been fine with watching TJ when I told her I needed to get out for a while, but it had not occurred to me when I slipped into Fraser's Tavern that I would be gone so long. I felt a twinge of guilt for not phoning.

The nausea had passed with the freight train, but the ever present laboring in my chest still nagged ominously. I had tried to ignore it all day. Lindsey had come by that morning with frozen raspberries from last year's garden. She made a happy face with them on TJ's cereal, and then she and I took our coffee onto the deck. Mom had gone into town with the Judge and wouldn't be back until afternoon. Maybe that was why Lindsey was there. I felt watched ever since the night of the 911 call.

I remembered the cigarettes in my pocket. Just one smoke before bed. Tomorrow I'd throw them away. I wandered to the barn where I heard the flapping of wings in the rafters—a barn owl, no doubt. The back door slammed on the house, probably Mom setting out a bucket of kitchen scraps for the worms. Just inside the barn door on one side was a pile of loose hay surrounded by bales. It was TJ's new fort. I made myself comfortable on one of the ramparts.

Suddenly I heard a sound to my right, and at the same instant the barn was shocked with light. Like a guilty twelve-year-old, I whipped the cigarette behind my back.

The Judge didn't see me at first. He started off toward the worm troughs with his pail of scraps.

"Hey," I said.

He spun around. "Samantha! Why are you sitting out here in the dark?"

I shrugged. "I was getting ready to come in. What are you doing out here so late? Giving your wormies a midnight snack?"

He scrutinized me. "We didn't know where you were. Your mother and I have been waiting for you to get home."

"Wow, I'm having déjà vu. I'm twenty-four now. You don't need to wait up for me. Don't you think I can take care of myself?"

"Well, I would," he said as he casually picked up the bucket of scraps he had dropped, "but you have a serious heart condition, you're drunk, and you're on fire."

He was halfway to the worm troughs before I noticed the smoke. I jumped up and started stomping on the little blaze behind me. Dry stubble ignited instantly around it.

My father calmly dumped his pail of goodies into the worm beds and raked the soil.

"Hello!" I shouted. "Are you going to help me here? Your barn is about to burn down!"

He glanced at me over his shoulder. "It's just a barn."

This was not funny. "Water! Do you have any water in here?"

He set his bucket down and gestured with his head. "Right over there. There's a hose. Do you want me to get it?" He sauntered over toward the corner and returned with the hose. First he sprayed the loose hay; then he kicked the burning bales toward the center of the barn floor and sprayed them until they were sopping.

"What the . . ." I felt a wounded bird flailing in my chest. "What was that all about?" I demanded.

Suddenly the Judge yanked an antique lantern off its nail and swung it like a bat against the wall. Glass shattered and metal crumpled. The fire blazed now in his eyes.

I took a step backward and stared at him in shock.

"Does that bother you?" he shouted. "You can destroy things different ways, Samantha. You can do it deliberately, or you can do it by just not doing the right things in time. When are you going to start taking care of yourself? What were you thinking tonight? Drinking, smoking, staying out late. Your condition is serious. Life-or-death serious. This is not just about you. You have a son to think of. For God's sake, Sam. Do the right thing this time!"

"Or what? Are you going to kick me out again?"

"I never kicked you out."

"I was barely seventeen years old and you kicked me out on my fanny!" I was furious now, and hot tears stung my eyes.

"I didn't want you to go. I wanted you to make the right choice."

"Yeah. *Your* choice. *Your* way. Did you ever think about me? About how I felt? Do you have any idea what it's like to face raising a kid for the rest of your life when you haven't even lived yet?"

"We weren't dealing with a disagreement over summer school or whether or not you got braces. You wanted to kill your baby, Sam. That's the truth. You can whitewash it and call it your *choice,* your *right.* The fact is, you can't have an abortion without killing a baby. This is not my opinion, Sam. It's straight out of the Word of God."

I didn't need to hear this from him. Not again.

"You could have at least let someone else raise the child. It was wrong. You wouldn't murder TJ, would you? No matter how inconvenient he may be sometimes."

"Shut up!" I put my hands to my ears and staggered toward the door. "That's enough!"

I tripped. He reached to help me to my feet. "Look, Sam, that's all over now. Let's put it behind us."

I pushed him away and headed for the house.

What he didn't know was that it was always behind me. Like a wolf lurking just out of sight.

IT WAS November the night I had awoke to squeals of laughter. I remember, because I had just turned eight. My mother and her old friend Minnie, from Redwood City, were having midnight cups of coffee. I crept from my bed and peered into the living room, where they sat by the fire. The wilted balloons from my party still hung from the dining-room chandelier. I heard their voices take on a serious tone, and my mother shook her head sadly. "If Blake hadn't done something—well, I can't even think about that."

"Tell me from the beginning, Lucy." Minnie's satin pajamas shimmered in the firelight. "I remember you and Blake tried for so long to have a baby, and the next thing I know, you've got two. We sure got sloppy about writing to one another after our babies came."

Mom stretched her feet toward the fire. "This woman was an attorney at the firm where Blake started out. Kathleen Mayes," she said with a frown. "What a loud, obnoxious . . ." She caught herself and smiled sheepishly. "Well, I guess you've got to have some voltage to be as dramatic—and I must say, effective—in the courtroom as she was. She had such wild hair; it was red at the time, but in reality probably brown like Samantha's. I know Sam inherited the wildness. It takes forever to get a comb through her hair."

I lay silently on the floor of the hallway. What were they talking about? What did this wild-haired woman have to do with me?

"The first time I saw her was at a Christmas party at the home of one of the partners. Everyone was dressed up—tuxedos and floor-length gowns. Anyway, Kathleen shows up in tight red satin pants and some weird spangly halter-top contraption. Of course, everyone was shocked, and Kathleen loved every minute of it.

"A few months later Kathleen is standing by the coffeepot at the office and announces to everyone that she is pregnant. Blake didn't mention it to me at first. Here we were trying so hard to get pregnant, and this single woman who doesn't even want a baby . . ."

"Who was the father?"

"Supposedly, a former client. A married man. When Blake found out she had scheduled an abortion, he tried to talk her out of it. He came home that night still brooding and told me all about it. That's when I thought of it. If she didn't want the baby, why couldn't she just give her to us? That would solve the problem for all of us."

Minnie leaned forward. "Go on."

"So we drew up a proposal. We pay all her expenses; she gives us the baby. Of course, it was more elaborate than that." She shrugged impishly. "But I was happy. I painted a mural on the nursery wall, refinished an antique crib, shopped. I was so busy and so happy that I hardly noticed my own symptoms."

"So when you found out you were pregnant, didn't you try to get out of your contract with Kathleen?" Minnie asked.

It got quiet. I held my breath.

"Yes. I was overwhelmed with the thought of having two infants at once. When I realized that I, myself, was carrying a child—Blake's and mine—well, it changed everything. I suddenly wanted all of our attention on the little miracle happening in my body."

"Of course you did." Minnie touched my mother's arm reassuringly. "That's perfectly normal."

I couldn't see my mother's face. "Blake said it wasn't the written contract that bound us to our agreement. It was his word."

"But honey, sometimes circumstances change. Everybody has to go back on their word sometimes."

Mother shook her head. "Not Blake." She looked Minnie square in the eyes. "Not ever."

I crept back to my bed. People always seemed confused when Lindsey and I were introduced as sisters. They would inevitably ask our ages, which eight months out of the year were the same. "One is natural, the other chosen," my father would say. No explanation.

Immediately he would turn the conversation to something else, which I realized now was his way of saying none of your business. I knew that I was adopted, but until that night, I had no concept of what that really meant. It had never seemed important somehow.

The next morning, I poured cereal in a bowl and sat by the kitchen window. My mother stumbled in and began making coffee while Minnie used the shower. Lindsey popped bread in the toaster. My father's newspaper and empty coffee mug were abandoned in their usual place, and I knew he had left for the courthouse. Everything seemed the same. Everyone seemed normal, except for me.

CHAPTER FOUR

MY TROUBLES were temporarily forgotten on the Fourth of July. I basked in the smell of the sweet corn boiling and the hickory smoke from the barbecue, the hot sun on my hair, and TJ's squeals of delight at catching a young cutthroat in the creek. The fish was too small but ended up on the barbecue anyway because it had swallowed the hook so deep—and because TJ was not much for the silly rule that said a keeper trout had to be at least six inches.

Dr. Matt brought his sons. They used to play with Lindsey and me sometimes, though they were younger. We didn't see them often, because they lived with their mother in Tacoma. Sweet little Kevin turned out to be a bruiser. He played linebacker for the Huskies. His older brother, Jess, showed up wearing slacks and a pressed shirt, looking out of place among the rest of us in our shorts and T-shirts, until Lindsey's husband, David, showed up.

Donnie brought his parents and a load of manure for the worms from the Appaloosa Ranch. Old Chester, Donnie's father, had insisted that as long as they were coming over, they might as well make the trip count. Donnie backed the truck up behind the barn, and while the Judge passed out shovels, David ducked into the kitchen.

I followed him inside. "Hey, David, Dad wants you," I lied. "He wondered if you could help get that pile of poo off the truck."

"He does?" David walked tentatively onto the deck and peered around the corner where he could see Donnie and Chester leaning against the pickup talking to the Judge, who had a shovel in his hand. I watched David saunter across the field, slowly as if hoping the other men might get the whole stinking pile unloaded before his arrival. I was laughing when Lindsey came up behind me.

"What's so funny?"

"Oh, just your husband."

She peered toward the barn. "Is he . . . He's not going to . . ."

"Yup. There he goes. Dockers and all. What a trouper. What a great guy." I couldn't stop grinning.

Lindsey shook her head in disbelief. "That's so unlike him."

"I think it's a male bonding thing."

As it turned out, that's exactly what it was. After unloading the truck and hosing out its bed, the men attempted to spray the gourmet worm food off each other's feet. The hose got away from someone, and it turned into a water fight. By the time they joined the rest of us on the deck, laughing and tossing insults, we were all wishing we had shoveled manure. Even David seemed undaunted by his dripping clothes and scrambled hair. I had done my good deed. One less stuffy person in the world, at least for today.

The Judge and Matthew manned the barbecues, producing platters mounded with juicy steaks and chicken. A table was set up on the lawn, and we piled our plates. Some of David and Lindsey's friends arrived with a little boy about TJ's age. TJ ran up to him. Minutes later the two new friends scampered off to see the worms.

After the meal the only adults who didn't join the rowdy volleyball game were Donnie's mother, Gladys, and me. I hated sitting there watching like an old lady. When I told Donnie I had a bad knee, my mother gave me a sideways look. I shot a look back that said, *I'll tell him when I'm ready—which isn't now.*

When the sky turned to steel, we loaded every available chair onto pickup trucks and set up theater seating in the big field by the barn. A cool breeze came off the river. Mom sent out blankets and quilts to bundle in while we sat around the bonfire waiting for the sky to become the perfect backdrop of black felt. Donnie pulled his chair up next to mine. I had hoped he would, but when he reached for my hand, I pulled it away pretending I hadn't noticed his attempt. Better not start something I couldn't finish.

Matt and my father laid a sheet of plywood out in the field as a launching pad. Fireworks were unloaded from several car trunks. At this point, every grown man regressed to adolescence. A mass missile attack was staged by arranging bottle rockets all along one edge of the platform. The darkness was instantly pierced with screaming projectiles that burst into fountains of colored light punctuated with loud bangs. The crowd clapped and cheered.

This was all new to TJ. He snuggled with me inside a quilt cocoon, his dark eyes wide with wonder. But before the grand finale, he was gone. He hardly stirred when Donnie carried him across the field and into the house where we tucked him into his bed. I think it aroused some kind of paternal instinct in Donnie. He touched TJ's hair and smiled down at him and then looked up at me like we were in some Norman Rockwell painting. What was I supposed to do? Clasp my hands at my chest and smile lovingly back?

After Donnie and the other guests had gone, Lindsey popped her head in my bedroom doorway. "Got room for one more in that big bed? I sent David home. I'm staying over so I can help with cleanup in the morning."

"Oh. Are you a thrasher?"

"No. I lay perfectly still. And I don't snore."

"That's what they all say."

The Judge came by on his way to bed. "Okay, girls." He tried to sound stern. "Lights out, and no giggling."

Lindsey tossed a pillow at him when he turned to leave. She sprawled across the foot of the bed. "Donnie turned out nice, didn't he? I thought he would have gone off to law school by now."

I told her about how old Chester caught a pitchfork in the leg and had been using it to his advantage ever since. "It's too bad," I said. "Donnie has a brilliant mind. He could be a great trial lawyer. If I were him, I'd just take off. Chester would survive."

"So what's going on between you two?"

I shrugged. "Same as usual. We're friends."

"Well, you better tell him that. He wants more. You do see the signals, don't you?"

I sighed.

"He's a hunk, Sam. You could do worse. He's funny and—"

"Lindsey," I interrupted, "do you know I'm married?"

She seemed taken aback. "You and Tim never got a divorce?"

"Nope. We're not even legally separated. He's just gone."

"Have you tried to find him?"

I fell back on my pillow in exasperation.

"Sam, talk to me. It's me, your almost twin. I'm on your side."

I sat up with a sigh. "Okay. You want it from the top?"

She nodded. "From the top."

"Tim is not TJ's daddy."

She rolled her eyes. "I figured that part out all by myself."

"Well, you know the part about Tim and me working at the ranch. I wrote to Mom about that, right?"

"Sam, you've got to tell me everything. We've had less than a dozen notes from you in seven years."

"Sorry. Anyway, when I ran away from home, I went to a clinic in Seattle for the . . . well, you know, abortion. Then we drove down to Elko because Tim's uncle Rich told him if he ever needed a job, just show up and he'd put him to work as a mechanic. We found Uncle Rich drunk on his butt outside a ratty single-wide trailer. He didn't even own a garage. We found work at the Wilders' Ranch. Tim was in charge of maintaining all the vehicles, and he did odd jobs like fixing fences and building cabins for the tourists to stay in. It was a functioning horse ranch with a dude ranch on the side."

"What did you do?"

"Housekeeping for Mrs. Wilder. Babysitting. In the summer I was like a maid for the dude cabins. They gave us our own little cabin to live in. The Wilders were good people."

"What happened between you and Tim?"

I fiddled with my toes and took a deep breath. "Well, we had a fight. It was no big deal, really. We were both tired from working all day. I loved our little cabin, but sometimes it was too small. No place to get away and think, you know? Anyway, I got mad and stormed out—took one of the horses and rode off into the sunset. Not for good. I didn't even take a toothbrush."

When I got to that part, I had to think for a minute. Despite my bent for shocking my sister, I felt uncomfortable. Was there a version of this story that was suitable for Pollyanna? "It was dry and barren out there. After a while I got cold and hungry and wanted to go home, but it was too soon. My exit had been so dramatic; I couldn't just stroll in an hour later and stick my head in the fridge. So I rode around until I saw a campfire in this dry creek bed."

I remembered the first time I saw Tijuana out in the corral breaking a chestnut stallion. He was shirtless and as brown and sinewy as the horse. The stack of clean bedding I was delivering to a cabin ended up on the rusty tailgate of a pickup truck while I observed from the rail fence. The horse was beautiful, wild and defiant, but it was the man who captured my attention.

No one at the ranch knew much about him. He walked out of the desert one day with a bedroll on his back and approached Mr. Wilder for a job. Hank Wilder didn't speak Spanish and became frustrated when he couldn't get answers to his questions. He finally shook his head, said, "No job here," and walked away. When he glanced back over his shoulder, Tijuana (the nickname the ranch hands gave him) stood silently in the corral staring down a wild horse that had been brought in that morning. The horse's head was down, nostrils flared. In an instant he wheeled. His powerful flank swept within inches of the man. When the dust cleared, Tijuana stood in the same position, as cool as an ice statue. Hank and a couple of hands sauntered over to the rail. After an hour-long performance the men watched in awe as the Mexican walked up to the subdued stallion, ran his hand along the sweat streaked neck, and slid a rope over its head.

Hank showed the stranger the bunkhouse and that was that.

When the Wilder family, their employees, and their guests gathered in the large informal dining room off the kitchen of the main house, the Mexican spoke little. I usually sat by Tim, the only love of my life. So it was unsettling to feel myself blush when the dark-eyed caballero looked my way. Once, when our eyes met, they lingered too long. The corners of his lips spread into a smile, and I looked away.

The Mexican never stayed in the bunkhouse. In the evenings after supper he could be seen walking out on the range, a bedroll and pack on his back, until he disappeared beyond the low hills.

I have wondered since that fateful night—the night I stumbled upon him in a dry gully a mile outside the ranch—if it was in the back of my mind all along. Hadn't I thought I might run into him out there? The moment he saw me, he dropped his blanket and stood forebodingly as my horse and I descended the sandy slope.

When my face came into the fire's glow, he flashed that grin, almost like I was expected. Almost as if I were as predictable as one of his wild horses. What happened next was a blaze of passion that swept over us like flames on a dry plain. Hard, almost painful kisses led to groping and clothes frantically discarded. His skin was hot and smelled of soap. The fire was beyond my control, and even a river could not quench it. But it did eventually burn out, leaving a charred wake that would haunt me for years to come.

I later realized that he never spoke my name. I lay awake staring at the stars until his breath was shallow, then crept around gathering clothes by firelight. Tim. Kind, strong, tender Tim. I suddenly yearned for him and yet dreaded looking into his clear blue eyes.

I couldn't tell Lindsey everything. I couldn't tell her about the lust or that I didn't even know his real name. I told her it was a terrible accident, which it was. She asked me why I never told Tim. "When you were pregnant, didn't you ever wonder if the baby might be from this . . . Tijuana?"

"Of course I wondered. But it seemed to me the odds were in Tim's favor." I shook my head. "Got that one wrong." Lindsey smiled sympathetically. "Anyway," I continued, "when we found out I was pregnant, Tim was so happy. The first time, you know, he sort of wanted me to keep the baby, but the timing was all off. We didn't have jobs, we weren't married. I'm the one that insisted on the abortion. But this time he was sure about being a dad. He talked about the baby more than I did. He told everybody at the ranch, and I guess he got me believing . . ." I felt like an idiot.

Lindsey nodded. "So when TJ was born . . ."

"He came out looking like a little Milk Dud. Tim knew right away, but it took a while to sink in. At first he went along with everything—cutting the umbilical cord and holding the baby—but he looked like he was in shock. He went out for a while. He came back about forty-five minutes later and just stood in the doorway of my room."

At this part I felt myself choking up. I had to take a deep breath before continuing. "He said, 'That's not my son, is it?' I couldn't look at him. I just looked down at the little brown baby, and when I looked back up, Tim was gone. I never saw him again."

Lindsey was respectfully silent. She brought me a tissue, and I blew my nose.

"Mrs. Wilder, the ranch owner, had to come pick me up from the hospital the next day. She said Tim packed up his things and left that morning and asked her to bring me and TJ home. He never said where he was going or anything. I thought he might have gone to his uncle Rich's, but the phone number there was disconnected."

"What about Tijuana? Does he know about TJ?"

"He was long gone before I was even showing. Maybe he heard that I was pregnant; I don't know. One payday he got his check and wandered into the desert, never to return. That was fine with me. He had been a reminder of my shame every time our paths crossed."

"Sam," Lindsey hesitated. "You were very young when you left home. You made some mistakes. My biggest decisions back then were what outfit to wear with which shoes, and fortunately, those weren't life-changing choices."

I was tired. We crawled under the yellow quilt and turned out the lamp. My sister prayed out loud, thanking God for the wonderful day we just had. When she got to the part about forgiving us for our sins, she added, "And help Samantha forgive herself."

I didn't say a word.
"Good night, Sam."
"Good night."

THE morning's series of tests had left me tired. More mining for blood from my almost invisible veins. Another echocardiogram. The last time I was here, Dr. Sovold, my cardiologist, mentioned surgery. Open-heart surgery. I'd been having nightmares about them sawing through the bones in my chest and opening me like some gory book.

Finally there was a light knock on the door and Dr. Sovold entered the exam room. He was tall, with long strands of hair carefully plastered across his bald spot. He looked straight at me without even attempting a smile. "I've been reviewing your test results, Samantha." His eyes dropped to the papers in his hand.

"I want my mother," I said. "She's out in the waiting room."

"Yes. Good idea."

After Mom slipped into the chair next to mine with a reassuring smile, the doctor continued. "Well, Samantha, as you know, your heart pumps oxygen and nutrient-rich blood to every cell and organ in your body. When you work or play hard, your body's need for oxygen increases and your heart pumps harder and faster. Your heart has been struggling just to keep you supplied with adequate oxygen while you're at rest." He pulled out a picture of my floppy heart and pointed out the deformities. "We are convinced that this damage was caused by a virus."

I had heard all this before. "Do I have to have surgery?"

He took a deep breath and nodded. My stomach rolled.

"Since reviewing your previous test results, I've consulted with the other cardiologists on staff here at the hospital as to whether your heart walls can be repaired surgically. The consensus is that the damage is too widespread. What I would like to do, Samantha, is get you lined up for a heart transplant."

My mother gasped. I just stared at him.

"This is not something I recommend lightly. It is our last resort.

It can be a long, drawn-out process and will require a commitment from you, Samantha"—then he looked at Mom—"and your family and friends. You are going to need a strong network of support."

"What other options do I have?"

He shook his head. "None that I can see."

"So what are you saying? If I don't get a heart transplant, I die?"

"Well . . . we can't really predict a time line on these things." He leaned toward Mom. "What we do know is that current treatments have not proved successful, and the quality of life for someone—"

"Dr. Sovold," I interrupted. "Cut the canned doctor talk. I want to know the facts. I need to know. If I don't get this heart transplant, will I see my five-year-old son enter first grade?"

Doctor Sovold paused. "No, Samantha, you probably won't."

I held my stomach as if I'd been punched. He placed his fingers gently on my wrist for a pulse. "Put your head between your knees if you need to." I did. He spoke, but I barely heard. I was glad my mother was there to process all the details. At last I sat up straight and watched the doctor's lips move. Concentrate.

". . . and once you're registered with this network, you'll be placed on the waiting list for a donor organ. When a donor heart becomes available, the organ procurement organization enters all vital information in their computer. That information is used to match up a donated organ with a recipient." He passed me a stack of pamphlets and a reading list. "There are a number of determining factors, including blood type, body size, geography . . . and the severity of a potential recipient's condition. A seriously ill patient may be given priority for an organ at a nearby transplant center. On the other hand, if a patient becomes too ill to withstand major surgery, they could be ruled out. The truth is that the number of patients on the waiting list outweighs the number of acceptable donors."

The avalanche of information came too fast. I couldn't outrun it. There was no place to go. Here I was, suspended in a cold, lonely place between life and death, with a decision to make.

"God, help me," I said.

CHAPTER FIVE

IT WAS not until late afternoon that Lindsey mentioned it. We had been together all morning cutting and stringing garlands of construction-paper leaves to adorn the cafeteria at Darlington Hospital where she volunteered. Then, as casually as if she were commenting on the hint of autumn in the air, she lit the fuse. The news exploded inside me. Paper leaves fell in a flurry to the kitchen floor.

"What? How do you know Tim is in town? Why are you just getting around to telling me this now?"

"I didn't know if I should . . . I mean, you shouldn't get upset."

"This is what gets me upset!" I stood, and my hand involuntarily reached for my chest.

"Okay. I'm sorry. I wanted to tell you. I ran into Tim's sister at the hospital. Their mom is in chemo. Breast cancer." Lindsey shook her head sympathetically. "Sarah was there waiting for her mom. We were both in the line in the cafeteria, and she called out my name. So we sat and had coffee until her mom came back down."

"What did you say? Did you say anything about me?"

"I said you were home."

"What else?"

Lindsey fidgeted. "I told her about TJ. I hope that was okay."

I nodded. Surely Tim's family must know about the grandson/nephew they almost had.

"Sarah's getting married. I guess Tim has been living in Oregon driving a log truck. He's here for her wedding, and he might stay on if he can get a job up here. He wants to be there for his mom, you know. Since their dad died, he's the only man in the family."

Tim's father had taken two years to die. All through Tim's sophomore and junior years in high school his dad suffered from some rare liver disease. It broke Tim's heart. I watched manhood overtake him while other guys hung out drinking beer. Tim worked as a mechanic in town. He drove his sisters to piano lessons. He repaired the roof, changed the oil in his mother's car, and, finally, bore a corner of a sleek casket and laid his father in the ground.

Tim said I was the light at the end of his tunnel. I made him laugh. Sometimes he complained that I was unpredictable. He said I flirted with danger and that I shouldn't be so quick to make decisions, but he didn't try to change me. "At least we'll never be bored," he quipped.

"Come on," I said to Lindsey. "There's more, isn't there?"

She punched holes in a stack of orange and yellow leaves. "Well, she invited me to her wedding."

I pondered for a moment. "Is Tim in it?"

She glanced up. "Yes. He's one of the groomsmen."

"I'll go with you."

"Oh, no, Sam. I don't think . . ."

"You got an invitation, didn't you? Did it by any chance say to Lindsey Matthews and Guest?"

"Yes, but . . . you and Tim need to get together and talk. I just don't think the wedding is going to be the right atmosphere."

I got up and poured a cup of coffee while I considered what she said. "Maybe I don't want to talk to him. I just want to see him from afar. Maybe he's bald now and missing teeth."

Lindsey gave me that long motherly look. "I think it wouldn't make any difference to you. I think you still love him."

I swirled the coffee around in my mug. I would love him until the day I died. But the truth was that if he wanted to, he could have found me. I had left a trail more obvious than a slug's. For five years I had looked behind me, hoping. I thought I glimpsed him driving by or sitting in the shadows at the Starlight Room, where I waited tables. I guess I always thought Tim would eventually show up at my door. He would forgive me and embrace TJ as his own.

"I don't know him anymore, and he doesn't know me," I said, and began cleaning up our paper debris.

A minute later Mom came through the kitchen door with an

armload of packages. TJ burst in behind her. "But why, Grandma?"

"Because it will spoil your dinner. We'll have our treats after we eat our pork roast and Brussels sprouts."

I pulled TJ into my arms. "Ooh. Is Grandma making you eat Brussels sprouts? What did you do? Shoplift or something?"

"I didn't do anything bad."

Lindsey reached for him. "Give Auntie some sugar." He obliged her with a kiss, but his mind was obviously on other things. He pushed away as politely as he knew how.

"Mom, can you take me to see Mikey?" he said.

I knew TJ was referring to the new foal at the Duncan's place, which he named after the buddy he left behind in Reno.

"Not today, baby. Mommy's going to take a nap."

TJ wilted dramatically. "You always take naps," he whined. Suddenly he sprang back to life. "Donnie could come get me."

I ran my fingertips through his dark hair. TJ adored Donnie. Maybe too much. "No. It will be dinnertime soon. You want to be here when Grandpa comes home, don't you?" TJ finally obliged.

Lindsey packed up her project. "I suppose I should get home before David and do the Suzy Homemaker thing."

I helped carry Lindsey's things to her car. She patted my face before slipping onto the leather seat. "Get some rest." I didn't argue. She had backed her SUV partway down the drive when she rolled her window down and called to me. "Hey, Sammy!"

I stopped and looked back.

"About that wedding. Let's do it! It might be fun!"

LINDSEY'S house was like her. Elegant. Tasteful. Perfect. It could have been on a postcard, the way it stood up there on a knoll with the manicured lawn, a huge maple hovering protectively over it. With some financial help from David's parents, they had purchased the five-acre parcel just outside of Darlington—about a fifteen-minute drive from the Judge and Mom's place on the river—and had built their dream home.

"Samantha, are you coming?" I followed my sister through the living room into the master suite and sprawled across the bed. Something like gauze was draped from corner to corner over the framework of the four posters. The walls were papered in a fancy flower print. An awful lot of fu-fu if you asked me.

Wedding photos lined the top of the cherry dresser. Set apart from the others, in a gold frame, was a close-up of Lindsey and our father, dancing. They grinned for the camera, cheeks touching. I had seen the same shot proudly displayed on the Judge's dresser back home. There were no photos on my father's dresser of me.

"What about this one?" Lindsey held up a peach-colored dress.

I shook my head. "I don't think so." She frowned and returned to the closet, emerging again with a two-piece knit. "Definitely not!" I said. "That looks like something Mom would wear."

"Are you kidding? I just bought this! Sam, this would look good on you. You've got the body for it."

I didn't bite. She sighed and went in again. "You can't put on your clunky boots and a string of pearls and clomp into a wedding at the country club. Hey, how about a simple skirt and blouse?" She produced a black tapered skirt and white blouse.

"Okay. I'll try it. It looks a little small, don't you think?" I stripped down to bra and panties and maneuvered myself into the ensemble. "It's too tight."

"Are you sure?" Lindsey stepped back. "Oh, Sam. Go look at yourself."

I stood in front of the full-length mirror in the master bath and stared. Lindsey smiled smugly over my left shoulder.

"I have the perfect shoes!" She ran out and returned holding them over her head like trophies. Lindsey always loved playing dress-up.

The delicate shoes had heels and straps. Because of the skirt, I couldn't bend far enough to get them on, so I sat on the bed and Lindsey bowed at my feet to clasp the tiny buckles. She spent more time dressing me than she did herself. Then we applied makeup and fussed with our hair. I thought I was done until Lindsey screwed up her face and cocked her head to one side. "Let me try something. Have you ever put your hair up like this?" She teased and pinned and sprayed, then let me select earrings from her jewelry box until I picked the right ones.

David was sprawled across the sofa in the family room watching a preseason Seahawks game. When he saw us, he sat up with his jaw hanging open. "Wow. Sam, you look great. I had no idea . . ."

I looked down at myself. "Yeah. I clean up pretty good, don't I?" Lindsey smiled like she was da Vinci and I was the Mona Lisa.

Suddenly her brows drew together. "Sam, you look a little pale. Are you sure you want to do this? We'll be out late."

"It won't hurt me. Stop mothering me, just for tonight, okay?"

It seemed like a good idea to rest for a while. I settled into a big chair. Lindsey and David crammed themselves into one corner of the long leather sofa. His arm rested around her shoulders as they talked, and I remembered the joy of being with the one person in the world that could make me feel complete. I was happy for my sister. David was a good guy. Lindsey deserved a good man.

I stared at the TV, trying to quiet the voice that kept saying, *This is a bad idea*. What would Tim do when he saw me? What would I do? What would I say? I watched while football players scrambled across the screen, piling up into tangles of butts and elbows.

My insides were on their third down with nine yards to go.

THE Port Lawson Country Club parking lot was full. I was surprised at the number of motorcycles lined up against the front of the building. We parked along the street, and I tried to walk the curb like it was a balance beam. I had coached Lindsey on what to say and what not to say. Bottom line, under no circumstances was anyone to know I was sick. I held my head high, took a long breath, and walked in the door like the queen of the country club.

A few minglers chatted in the lobby. For the millionth time I thought I saw the back of Tim. He stood like a marine, dressed in a black tuxedo, with his arm on the bare back of a woman in a long blue dress. Only this time it really was him! My heart squished violently. Lindsey saw him too. We watched him guide the woman through the doors at the far end of the lobby. Lindsey got me to the doors nearest us, where an usher led us to the second row from the back on the right-hand side. I fought for control. Something told me this was not a good time to stick my head between my knees.

When I dared look toward the left side of the auditorium, I saw Tim again. This time he showed an elderly couple to their seat. I chided myself. Of course, stupid. He's an usher.

I felt safely hidden among what I assumed to be the groom's friends and family, as I didn't recognize a single one. All the bikers were on our side. They stood out from the traditionally dressed wedding-goers because of their leather vests and jackets.

Tim went away, and I didn't see him again until a girl with a guitar started singing and he appeared at the front with two other tuxedoed men that I didn't recognize. His hair was shorter and a little darker. He looked better than ever. Lindsey thought so too. I could feel her watching me.

I recognized Tim's mother, Lila. She was a nice lady. I was glad the chemo had not made her hair fall out, at least not yet. One November day seven years ago she cut figures of Santa and his reindeer out of plywood to decorate their front lawn, and I helped her paint them out in their garage. I was just Tim's girlfriend then. We didn't know that I was pregnant, or that my father would find out, or that within weeks we would be fleeing to Reno in Tim's red pickup. I didn't know then that my childhood was officially over.

The couple sitting on the opposite aisle from Mrs. Weatherbee must have been the groom's parents. She was a large woman wearing a peasant-style skirt and blouse. The man's tux was a poor disguise. I figured him to be the King of the Bikers. He had a face as pocked as the grill of a semitruck after a cross-country run, and his mustache hung Yosemite Sam–style below his chin.

The music changed, and the groom showed up at the front, along with his best man. From the safe camouflage of the crowd, my eyes fixed on Tim, even as the bridesmaids stepped down the carpeted aisle. They all wore the same powder-blue dress, tightly fitted at the bodice and spraying out from the waist. The last one to park her fluffy little tail on the platform steps cast a flirtatious glance directly at Tim. She looked like Glinda, the Good Witch of the North. He returned her smile, and I summoned my telepathic powers, hoping to knock her flat on her face.

Sarah shone with joy; you could see it even through her veil. We all stood when she strolled down the pathway to marital bliss, all of us probably wondering the same thing: Will this one last? Her husband-to-be looked at her the way Tim used to look at me. They spoke their vows with the same confidence TJ had when he assured me that he would never grow up and leave me.

The reception was held upstairs in a huge hall with a balcony overlooking Port Lawson Bay. Along one wall the wedding party had lined up to greet the long chain of guests waiting to express their congratulations. We skipped the lineup and found seats at a round table scattered with blue glitter stars. I purposely sat with my back to the reception line. Lindsey knew quite a few people, both from high school and just from living and volunteering in the area for so long. They stopped by to greet her, and when she introduced me, some seemed surprised that she had a sister.

When we were somewhat alone, Lindsey leaned toward me and whispered, "So what's the plan? Are you going to go talk to him?"

"What's he doing now?"

She glanced casually in his direction. "The line is broken up. Uh-oh. Some girl is dragging him to the dance floor."

I stole a look. "It's Glinda, Good Witch of the North."

Lindsey giggled. "You're right! She looks just like her."

"Would you get me a glass of champagne please?"

"No. You don't drink alcohol anymore, remember? Why don't you go get yourself some punch?"

"Because I don't want to walk by the dance floor. Not yet. Can you get me some punch?"

She decided to oblige me. She left the table, and I gathered up handfuls of glitter stars and dumped them into the contents of her purse. I knew she would find them stuck to things for months. After a few songs the best man took the microphone from the band and summoned all the single ladies up front. The bride was about to throw her bouquet. What was taking Lindsey so long? I finally spied her off in a corner laughing with a bunch of friends.

I scanned the room. Tim was nowhere to be seen. With the current distraction on the dance floor, I decided to meander to the beverage bar. A black-vested waiter made small talk as he poured the bubbly pink liquid. I was nice and got a glass for Lindsey too.

A crowd had gathered to watch the bouquet toss, blocking the way to my seat. I detoured across a corner of the dance floor. Suddenly my right heel caught the strap of my left shoe. I felt myself lurch forward. In a split second of horror the glasses shot from my hands. I dove toward the bevy of wannabe brides. The bouquet slapped me in the chest, and I was down. Flat on my face. Derriere in the air. Skirt split from north to south like a dinner bun.

When I lifted my head, I saw shoes. Lots of pointy shoes pointing right at me. Someone had the decency to throw a jacket over my exposed behind. The crowd was impressed. They whistled and cheered. "Nice catch!" "Hey, we need her on our team!" More laughter and applause. A biker helped me to my feet.

I was too stunned to speak. My heart flapped like a bird. Lindsey was still in the corner chattering with her friends. The biker asked if I was okay. He had a tattoo of Jesus on his biceps. "I just need some air," I said, tying the jacket around my waist. "Thank you." I headed for the balcony door, almost running into Glinda.

She tossed her frizzy blond hair over her shoulder and sneered. "Well, I guess you wanted it worse than I did." She looked down at the mangled bunch of roses that I was surprised to see still in my hand.

"Oh, go to Kansas," I said, and stepped out into the salty air.

I slouched in a deck chair with my shoeless feet propped up on the rail, trying to calm my breathing. With a shiver I pulled the tuxedo jacket up over my shoulders. It smelled of men's cologne.

My heart hurt. I wanted to go home. My life was a series of blunders as long as a freight train. One mistake after another.

A door opened. I slid lower in the big deck chair and feigned an intense interest in something off to my right.

"I thought you hated weddings."

My head snapped in the direction of the voice.

"You always said they were boring." Tim's arms rested casually on the railing. "This one was until a little while ago."

I swore under my breath. He saw me! "Somebody had to liven things up. I did what I could."

His eyes still crinkled at the corners when he almost smiled. "What's new, Sam?"

I breathed deeply to still the trembling. "What's new since when? Since last time I saw you?"

He shrugged, and squinted out over the bay. I wished I hadn't said that. The last time I saw Tim he stood in the doorway of my hospital room, his eyes burning with pain and anger. I held another man's son in my arms and watched my destiny walk away. After all the conversations I had imagined over the past five years, not one remnant came to mind. I stood and leaned on the rail within five feet of him. "I'm staying at my parents' place for awhile. TJ and I. That's my son. He's five now." His lack of response made me nervous. "Sarah looks happy. Where did she meet this guy?"

Tim pulled a shelled peanut from his pocket. "At her church. It's kind of a biker church. Ross is the preacher's kid. Pretty cool guy. He plays the drums on Sunday mornings. Sarah plays bass guitar."

"Oh." There was a long, awkward pause. "My sister said you've been in Oregon."

He nodded. "I have a place at Grants Pass. Just a cabin, really. But I've got it fixed up the way I like it. I drove a log truck for the past few years. Also did a stint as a river guide on the Deschutes."

"Really? That sounds fun."

He got quiet on me and flicked at some peeling paint on the rail. "Yeah, it was lots of fun—until a lady popped out of my raft in white water and we found her body three hours later wrapped around a submerged tree. The river never looked the same to me after that." He turned to glare at me. "Funny how one little incident can change your whole perspective."

I returned his gaze. "Tim, I've wanted to tell you . . . I know I screwed up big-time, and I want you to know I'm sorry. I never—"

With a scowl he said, "Save it, Sam. I don't want to hear it."

"You've got to hear it! Just let me get it off my chest, okay?" I took advantage of his silence. "I've waited over five years for a chance to explain. I should have told you what happened with Tijuana." His jaw clenched. "It happened one time. *One time.* And I regretted it from that moment on. I thought the baby was yours. In fact, I still think of him as yours. I always have."

"Well, you have twisted thinking. You always have."

A door opened, and Glinda, of all people, stepped out. "Oh, there you are." She smiled sweetly, swished her powder-blue taffeta fanny up to the rail next to Tim, and took his arm possessively.

"Luanne, this is Samantha." Tim was at least civil.

"Nice to meet you. That was quite a catch you made in there. You didn't get hurt, did you?"

"I twisted my ankle, bruised both knees, and scraped my wrist"—I held the mutilated bouquet up triumphantly, and a clump of rosebuds fell out—"but it was worth it. I really needed one of these."

She must have detected some cynicism in my voice. Her lips spread into one of those straight smiles you give someone just before you insult them. "Looks like your skirt was too tight, too."

"Not anymore." I bent over and flashed my leopard panties her way. "See?" I straightened and smiled a smile as syrupy as hers.

She gasped and cast a horrified look toward Tim. I thought I detected an amused smirk on his face before he turned away.

"See ya later, Sam."

She escorted him back to the door and then stopped. "Isn't that your tux jacket, Tim?"

"Oh, yeah." His eyes met mine. "That's okay. Just leave it on a chair or something when you go."

ALL that next week the clouds hung low. Raindrops fell consistently by my window like someone turned on the sprinkler and left for vacation. The rain suited my mood.

I had made a fool of myself in front of Tim, not to mention his mother and everyone else close to him. But I had seen him. Face to face. He was no longer the elusive ghost I had glimpsed in every crowd. He was real, and he was here in Darlington. There was a glimmer of hope now. If only he could forgive me and love me again, the void inside me would be filled. Then, of course, my only little challenge would be to survive.

I awoke from a nap to find the house quiet except for subdued male voices behind the door of my father's study. I was happy to see Matt's car in the driveway. He hadn't been up to the river for over a month.

Matt had always been an uncle to me, though we weren't related. The thing I liked best about him was that he seemed to favor me over Lindsey, which was rare. He's the one I confided in after I found out I was unnecessarily adopted. I told him that by the time my parents found out they didn't need me, it was too late. They already had me, and then along came Lindsey. Their own flesh and blood and cute as a blue-eyed kitten. Matt told me I was special in my own way, which I didn't take as a compliment at first. After a while, though, I understood what he meant.

I thought I heard Matt and the Judge arguing. That was unusual. I rose from my bed and listened from my bedroom door. Their voices hushed and were drowned by the sounds of rain on the roof.

Mom and TJ must have gone shopping. I walked to the kitchen and opened a can of soup. As I stood by the stove watching the rain, I had the sensation of being trapped in a submarine. Claustrophobic. My Jeep hadn't been out of the garage for weeks. Everyone else came and went while I sat here hoping for the phone to ring. Waiting for someone to die. Waiting to live.

I shuddered. Somebody was going to die. There would be pain and grief, and it would ripple outward in ever increasing circles. Would it be me and mine? My weary heart seemed to droop lower in my chest. Any way you looked at it, it was not a happy thought.

The voices from the study grew louder. I edged closer to the kitchen door to listen. Matt and my father were the best of friends.

I had never heard them argue. Now I heard only a hushed murmur. My curiosity drew me toward the study door. Matt's voice elevated again, both in volume and pitch. "Because it's asinine, that's why! Not to mention illegal. You could never pull it off. And even if you could, there are no guarantees that all the pieces would line up. You're a judge, for God's sake! Judge yourself!"

I couldn't move. My father—a criminal? I couldn't comprehend it. What kind of trouble could my father possibly be in? I remembered the strange phone call—the one he answered with bloody hands. He had snatched the receiver from me so suddenly—as if he knew who it was. As if he had something to hide. By now my ear was plastered to the study door. "Matt, I'm sorry to put you in this position, but I need your help. If there was any other way—"

"There *is* another way! Don't you get it?"

"I've got to have a plan B. Just think about it. Please."

A chair screeched against the floor. I scurried quietly back to the kitchen, working to steady my breath. The study door opened, and Matt stormed into the kitchen. He stopped short upon seeing me standing there by the stove. "Sammy! Where did you come from?"

"Hi, Matthew." I yawned. "I was just taking a nap. Do you want some soup?"

He shook his head and walked by me like someone who just found out his best friend wasn't who he thought he was. He grabbed his raincoat off a kitchen chair and stomped out the door.

CHAPTER SIX

TJ SAT between Donnie and me on the seat of Donnie's truck, straining to see out the side windows. Our valley in October was paradise, with maples fluttering in shades of red, orange, and yellow against a backdrop of cool evergreens. I was as happy as TJ to be getting out on such a beautiful afternoon.

Donnie wore faded jeans and a gray sweatshirt with cutoff sleeves. His burly arms were no longer as brown as they had been during summer. He whistled "Zip-A-Dee-Doo-Dah" as he drove.

TJ puckered his lips too, but no sound came out. "How do you do that?"

"What? Whistle? It's easy." Donnie demonstrated. "Make a tiny hole for the air to get out. Purse your lips so tight, all you could get in there is a blade of grass. Take a deep breath and let it out real easy." We finally heard a peep as small as a baby bird's.

TJ's eyes widened, and he peeped again. *Peep. Peep. Peeeeeep.* And then he was off, whistling like a tea kettle.

Of course, I later regretted this new talent, but at the time, I was so proud. Not just of TJ for persevering, but of Donnie. He was patient with my son. I found myself gazing at him in awe sometimes, and not just because he was handsome. He had this quiet confidence, like he knew exactly who he was and he was okay with that. I knew Donnie was not living his dream. His dream had been to become a trial attorney. And yet, he was not a bitter man.

A woman could get real comfortable with having a man like Donnie around. Don't think I never thought about that, because I did. Sometimes when I saw his truck coming down the drive for an unexpected visit, my heart felt like it just went over a bump. And when he got too close to me, I found myself wanting to touch. But I had gotten myself into trouble that way before.

I had a husband to think about. For five years I regretted the mistake I made. Tim should have been TJ's daddy. And now he was so close. I still hoped for the chance to make things right with him.

The truck turned down a dirt lane between two cornfields. Locals had always called the riverside park Stilly Field, though there were no signs. You just had to know it was back there—a dirt parking lot, access to the river, and a sports field. As the parking lot came into view, TJ exclaimed, "Wow, look at all the motorcycles!"

There were as many Harleys as cars and trucks combined. I looked at Donnie. "Who did you say is playing who?"

"I don't think I did. Van's Tavern against the Set Free Church.

They're bikers mostly. I mean, the church team. I'm on the Tavern team, sort of. Actually, a temporary recruit."

"Oh." I knew they were the same crowd as the guests at Sarah's wedding. How many biker churches could there be?

"It's a long walk over to the field," Donnie said. "Want a piggy-back ride?" Since hearing about my heart condition, Donnie had never doted on me. In fact, he rarely mentioned it. It wasn't that he didn't care. I knew that he did. I figured he was either in denial or simply confident that everything was going to turn out all right.

"No. I'm fine. You go on ahead; it's time for the game to start. I'll just take my time. TJ, you wait for me at the bleachers okay?"

TJ skipped off with Donnie as I pulled out a bottle of water and locked the truck. I knew it was silly to get an adrenaline rush just because some people connected with Tim's sister happened to be there at the same time as me. I sauntered toward the field, a skill I had mastered, gazing at the trees and sky as if I were just in a day-dream. Yes, I told myself, to look at me one would think I was as healthy as anyone, just a bit distracted or, at worst, lazy.

I joined TJ at the weathered wood bleachers that were scattered with onlookers. I quickly scanned the crowd, not recognizing any-one. We sat on the bottom row with our feet on the ground.

The players organizing themselves for the flag football game were in high spirits. I knew the faces of some players from both teams, ei-ther from high school or due to small-town crossing of paths. I even saw my husky biker friend with the Jesus tattoo—the one that helped me back to my feet at the wedding. Sarah and her new hus-band were not there. Neither was Tim.

The tavern team stripped off their shirts, and players began to line up for the kickoff. Donnie bent forward at the waist, his hands on his thighs. His broad shoulders and back glowed in the after-noon sun as he mentally prepared for battle.

"There he is!" someone yelled. "Weatherbee! Get over here!" I followed their gaze, and there was Tim, running toward the crowd.

"Sorry!" Tim ran past the bleachers and onto the field. Adrena-line surged through my body. He hadn't noticed me, but I saw his face up close. There was my missing part. My only hope for wholeness. He slapped some guy's back and took his position in the line across from Donnie. And then, to my surprise, Donnie turned his head and glanced at me.

A whistle blew, the ball was kicked, and bodies scattered. TJ climbed onto my lap. I wrapped my arms around him, resting my chin in his hair. "Where's Donnie?" he asked.

"Right there. See, he's running backward. Yes! He caught it!" We watched as Donnie let out a whoop in midair and lit on the ground like a spring, immediately dodging an opposing player trying to capture his flag. He found a hole and charged through it as the fans behind us went wild. "Go!" I shouted. Donnie ran full throttle toward the goal line, like a speed boat with a wake of bodies at his heels. "Touchdown!" someone shouted.

In the end, the Set Free team won with a final score of twenty-four to eighteen. The men on the field dispersed slowly, still chiding and challenging one another. TJ ran onto the field toward Donnie, who was caught up in a conversation with one of the players. I could see Tim joking with some guy. Finally Tim sauntered my way, still grinning—until he saw me. He almost stopped dead in his tracks, but then recovered. "Hello, Sam."

"Hi." I smiled. "Good game. You looked really good out there."

"Thanks." He glanced around. "You here alone?"

"No. I came with a friend." I didn't mention TJ. Things were awkward enough as it was. "I can't tell you how good it is to see you again. I've missed you."

His eyes grew soft and familiar. "Yeah." His head dropped momentarily. "Me too." A silence fell between us. I wanted to touch him, but I couldn't move. "You were quite a hit at the wedding," he said eventually. "They're still talking about it."

I smiled impishly. "I think your friend really wanted that bouquet," I said. "She didn't like me one bit."

"Luanne? No. She liked you even less when she found out you were my ex-wife."

"Ex?"

"Well, you know what I mean." There was a lot going on in the space between us—a flurry of positive and negative ions, it seemed, that made it hard to talk except with our eyes. "So what are you doing now?" he asked. "Working somewhere?"

I shook my head. "I haven't found anything yet. Actually, it feels pretty good to have a break from working. I get to spend more time with TJ." I immediately saw the glimmer in his eyes disconnect. "That's my son."

"Yeah," he nodded. "I know."

As if on cue, TJ appeared at my side. "Let's go, Mom."

Tim began to back up. "Well, see you around, Sam." He turned just as Donnie approached. "Hey, Don. Good game."

Donnie still had his shirt off, and used it like a towel to dry his chest. He grabbed the water bottle from my hand and squirted the remaining liquid down his throat. "Yeah, it felt good." Donnie put his arm around my shoulder and began to guide me away as if he was a dog marking his territory. "We should do it again sometime."

I was so angry with Donnie I hardly spoke on the way home. I resented him showing up when he did and even more so that he drank from my water bottle—like we were intimate enough to share one another's saliva. He'd made a blatant and intentional statement. My mind replayed the conversation with Tim. He had missed me. That much he had said. Did he still love me? Could he forgive me?

When we pulled up in front of my parents' log house, TJ scrambled over me and jumped out, but Donnie reached for my arm and pulled me back onto the seat. "Shut the door. We need to talk."

"What is there to talk about?"

"You're mad at me; that's as plain as stripes on a skunk."

"You deliberately ran him off."

"What did you want me to do? Invite him home for dinner?"

"How about just letting us finish our conversation in private?"

"TJ was there. How private could that be? I figured you were done. So what did he say?"

"Nothing, really. There wasn't enough time."

"Does he want to get back together?"

"I don't know."

"Is that what *you* want?"

Something in his voice made me turn to look at him. His eyes were fixed straight ahead at the trees beyond the house.

Tears came to my eyes, and my voice softened. "Donnie, it's all I've thought about for five years. And now it seems like maybe it's meant to happen. We're both back here in the valley. I keep thinking maybe we could start over if he can forgive me for what I did."

"What if he can't forgive you?"

I shook my head. "I don't know." I couldn't bear to think about that. All I knew was that for one brief moment I saw a familiar softness in my husband's eyes. Then he blinked and it was gone.

WITH each day that went by, my hopes of Tim showing up at the front door diminished. I busied myself with the things I could do— reading, peeling potatoes for dinner, working the crossword puzzle from the newspaper—but my restless soul was not easily stilled.

My mind had too much free time, and it kept replaying the desperation I had heard in my father's voice the previous week when he argued with Matt. Whatever my father proposed had infuriated his friend. I wondered if he was in financial trouble of some sort. Whatever it was, Matthew seemed shocked at the Judge's plea to help him do something illegal, and I must admit, I was as well. But I was left in the dark, with my imagination still racing in circles.

I asked my mother about it one day as she was painting. The walls of her studio out in the garage were adorned with her works of art. She liked to do cows, which were flat, lifeless shapes on muddy backgrounds. The landscapes were a little better, but not much. Her forehead drew together, and she pondered for a moment. "No, honey. I can't think of any trouble your father could possibly be in. He would tell me if there was something wrong. Are you sure you heard them clearly?"

"I heard the parts with yelling. Matt said it was illegal to do whatever Dad was talking about."

Mom put her brush down and wiped paint from her hands. She

went to the window and stood silently looking out at the fine, almost invisible rain. Frosted-blond strands had escaped from her French roll, dangling at her cheeks. She turned to look at me. "Whatever it is, your father will make the right decision," she said. Her eyes were like the smooth gray pebbles at the edge of the stream. I couldn't read them clearly. I thought I saw faith there. She trusted my father. And yet another ripple passed and there was fear, or maybe sorrow. Did she know something about this or not?

That evening, the Judge popped his head into my room and announced that he and Mom were going for a little drive. He acted jovial, but I felt it was just that. An act. He put his fishing cap on TJ and told him to "man the fort" while Mom stood by the doorway. "Got your pager on, Sam?" Usually it was Mom who asked that.

I tipped my head toward the bedside table. "It's right there."

"Please clip it on. If you go out to the kitchen, you won't be able to hear it. I'll have my cell phone on if you need us for anything." Within minutes the Mercedes crunched down the gravel drive and out of sight. TJ went back to watching his cartoon video on the TV in my room. I went out to the living room to read.

I turned on a lamp and settled into my usual chair to immerse myself in my novel. The wind had been picking up all evening. I heard it thrashing the bushes at the side of the house while I read. Right at the part where the heroine crawled stealthily into the dark old house through the cellar door, something crashed onto our front porch. The book dropped to my knees. I always felt things first in the chest. A little startle was a boxer's jab with ensuing ripples that ran down my arms. I stood and strained to see the old maple tree through the window. Its limbs flailed wildly against the night sky.

A branch must have been torn loose and hurled against the house. I opened the front door a crack. Just a branch, I assured myself, then locked the door. I went in to check on TJ. The TV screen was fuzzy, and he was sound asleep. This was not good. In my condition I couldn't carry him to his room, which meant we would be sharing the double bed, and TJ slept as wildly as he played.

I tried to read again. Mom and the Judge had been gone for al-

most two hours. I figured they were talking about something important and private. What was going on? I found myself reading the
same page over again. I plopped the book down and rested my
head on the back of the chair.

The ring of the phone startled me awake. Darkness covered my
eyes. In my confusion I felt the objects around me and realized I
was still in the living room. The telephone rang loudly again from
across the room. Who had turned off all the lights? And who would
call at this hour? Suddenly I knew. My heart. They found me a
heart! I scrambled across the black room and picked up the receiver on the fourth ring. "Hello?"

There was only silence.

"Hello," I repeated. Someone was there. I could hear breathing.

"Who is this?" It was a male voice, hoarse like an older man or a
heavy smoker.

"This is Samantha Weatherbee, but this is the Dodd residence."

"Samantha." There was a long pause. "Samantha. Formerly
Samantha Dodd, by any chance?"

"Yes, I'm . . . visiting. Who is calling, please?"

"Hey, Samantha. Is it dark there?"

My heart did a sluggish flip-flop. For the first time, I noticed that
the darkness was total, inside and out. The floodlight on the garage
turned on automatically every night. The lawn should have been
bathed in its light.

"Who is this? What do you want?"

A chuckle rose up from his raspy throat. "What do I want? I
want your daddy, girl. I want to see him squirm. Just like those
worms he's got out in that barn." There was another long pause.
"He ought not have done what he done. I'm going to see him pay.
You tell him that for me. You tell him I'm going to see him hang."

I dropped the receiver as if it had turned into a snake, and I stared
into the darkness. Terror radiated from my chest. I felt my way into
the bedroom and touched TJ's body beneath the quilt. His breath
was slow and steady. The light switches were worthless. I called the
Judge's cell phone. Two rings, then a canned voice. "I'm sorry. The

cellular customer you have dialed is not available at this time. . . ."

I swore. The wind grew wilder. Rain pelted the window as I picked up the receiver again. Donnie's phone rang and rang. It was Saturday night. Wherever he went, he didn't invite me. I wasn't much fun anymore. I thought of calling Lindsey and David but remembered they had gone to Seattle for a Seahawks game and were spending the night in a hotel. Weakness overwhelmed me. I huddled in the big living-room chair and felt the familiar painful heaviness of my heart. My father really was in trouble. What had he done? Why had they been gone so long?

"Oh, God," I finally whispered, hugging my knees. "God . . . I'm afraid." I knew I sounded like a little girl; there was a pathetic whine in my voice. "Please keep us safe. Please be real."

A peaceful feeling settled over me then. When the wind began to howl again, it was not so scary. Eventually I drifted off on a gentle cloud of sleep.

THE next morning, Sheriff Byron leaned against the kitchen counter sipping a cup of coffee, a revolver hanging against his hip.

It turned out that the lights were off for miles around last night, not just our house. The wind had thrown a tree onto a major power line serving greater Darlington, Carter, and Dixon. That's why the sheriff asked the Judge so many questions about his relationship with local folks. The caller had known the power was out. But the Judge just shook his head. "The oldest James boy from across the ravine—Cameron—I sent him up to the state pen for a couple of years on his third felony charge. He's made no secret about how he feels about me, but the voice doesn't match. I can't think of anyone else around here that would have reason to threaten me."

Mom's forehead was pinched, and her eyes had the look of crying. I couldn't help but suspect that she knew something. Before the sheriff came, I had asked her what she and the Judge talked about last night. She shook her head and said, "Oh, nothing in particular." But I didn't believe her. Secrets buzzed like hornets around us, and I was the only one acknowledging their presence.

My father tried to brush off the phone threat. "It was probably just someone's idea of a joke."

For some reason he didn't mention the call he received the day that he and TJ were cleaning the fish. He had said it was nothing—just a prank call. I almost brought it up but thought better of it, remembering Matt's fiery words: *You're a judge, for God's sake. Judge yourself!* If my father was involved in something illegal, I would not be the one to implicate him. "It was a grown man," I said in a subdued voice, "and he wasn't joking."

Sheriff Byron folded the written statement and pushed it into his shirt pocket. "I'm just going to look around outside."

The Judge stood at the kitchen window and watched the sheriff stride through the wet field toward the barn. I sat at the table with my coffee as Mom rinsed dishes and placed them in the dishwasher.

My father's jaw did not flinch; his countenance was expressionless. He seemed deep in thought, as if he had forgotten that Mom and I were there. If he had broken his own law, then more than the law would be broken. There would be a shattering of hearts all around him.

I realized then that I loved him. I needed him to be the towering rock we all thought he was. And worse than anything, like a child, I still needed him to love *me*.

The sheriff eventually stomped up the back steps and poked his head through the kitchen doorway. "There are a lot of prints out there, but it's a mess with all the debris from the storm. Keep an eye out, though, when you go out there. If you see any prints you don't recognize, give me a call."

"So where did you two go last night?" I asked after the sheriff had gone.

"All the way to Bellingham." The Judge was overly cheerful for a man whose life was being threatened by a crazy guy. "We had a nice long dinner. The kind your mother likes. Four courses, with plenty of time to linger in between." He winked at her.

Mom forced a weak smile and dropped her eyes before turning to leave the room.

CHAPTER SEVEN

NOVEMBER crawled by like a garden slug. I watched the leaves go from gold to orange to brown. They swirled in the wind and stuck to the wet ground. The old maple tree finally stood naked out by the barn, its arthritic bones reaching plaintively into the sky.

Donnie took me down to the river a few times. At first we walked slowly, and on the way back up the trail, I leaned heavily on his arm. When I could no longer make the whole trek, he carried me part of the way, but only after I had tried very hard to make it by myself.

I drank herb teas with my stockinged feet propped on the living-room windowsill. The doctor said I did not have a cold. This annoying cough was some kind of reflex in response to my huge heart putting pressure on my lungs. Mornings were especially long and quiet because TJ was gone—I had signed him up for preschool.

Lately I had visions of this busy household buzzing along without me. There wouldn't be much difference. Just that shape over there in the reclining chair would be gone. TJ would miss me for a while, but I knew he would be okay. He was loved. Lindsey and David had agreed to raise him if I died, which was somewhat of a relief. I tried not to think about Tim anymore. Living beyond the new year was about all I could hope for.

Thanksgiving came and went. The following day was the holiday known as the Biggest Shopping Day of the Year. Mom and Lindsey left just after dawn and planned to stay overnight in a Seattle hotel. I could tell they felt guilty about leaving me home, but at this point there was no discussing it. Lindsey asked me to write down some Christmas gift ideas for TJ and me. For TJ it was easy. Anything to do with bugs, worms, fish, or frogs. Anything *I* wanted was either too expensive to mention or not for sale in any store.

TJ and I watched cartoons in our pajamas until almost eleven a.m. The Judge never liked having the TV on in the daytime. He used to say watching TV was for people who didn't have a life of their own. I finally told TJ to turn it off and get dressed. He pulled on his jeans and skipped out to the garage to join his grandpa.

I stood in the shower until the water turned cold. The mirror on the bathroom door was steamed up, but I wiped it off and turned to see how big my behind was getting from waiting for my pager to go off. My breasts hadn't changed, but they would. I traced the line where they would saw through my breastbone and shuddered.

The phone rang. This could be the one. I called from the bathroom door. "Is anybody out there?" No answer. I swore under my breath, pinching a towel around me and walking down the hall.

"Hello."

"Samantha?"

I froze. "Yes, this is Samantha."

"This is Tim."

"I know."

There was a slight pause. "Um . . . are you going to be there for a while? I need to talk to you—in private."

"I'm not going anywhere."

"Okay." He cleared his throat. "Well, I'll see you soon, then."

I held back my cough until the receiver was down. "Well, it's about time," I said out loud, running my fingers through my wet hair. My hair! I dropped the hair dryer twice in my hurry to get the job done. Luckily, Mom had washed my best blue jeans—the ones that fit just right. I pulled on a white scooped-neck T-shirt. A blue velvet box on the dresser held a delicate chain with a silver charm. My fingers struggled with the clasp. A little lipstick, a little blush. I had just slipped on my shoes when he drove down the drive.

At that moment, the back door burst open. "Mom!" TJ ran from the kitchen, almost knocking me down. "It's Christmas! We got all the decorations. Lots of 'em! We're going to surprise Grandma."

The Judge trudged in carrying a cardboard box. I could tell by his raised eyebrow that he was just getting warmed up to the idea. He put the box on the floor. "You're looking well today, Samantha."

I grabbed his arm. "Tim is here." He stared at me blankly and then glanced around the room. "He just drove up. He wants to talk to me. Alone."

There was a knock on the door. TJ ran to open it. My father touched my hand. I looked up at him, and I swear a sadness fell across his face and then just as quickly washed away. He winked. "Come here, boy," he said, but TJ had already flung the door open.

Tim stood there awkwardly. I came up behind my son, placing my hands on his shoulders. "Hi. Tim, I don't think you two have officially been introduced. This is TJ. TJ, this is Tim Weatherbee."

"Hey." TJ looked up at me. "He has the same name as us."

Tim nodded politely, glanced down at the porch, up to me, then nervously over his shoulder toward his truck. My father came to the door and greeted Tim with a handshake. "Nice to see you again, Tim. It's been a long time."

Tim stood a little taller. "It's nice to see you too, sir."

"TJ and I are just on our way out to find the Christmas lights." He ushered TJ toward the back door.

Tim sat on the leather sofa across from me, elbows on spread knees. He looked good. "How's your mom?" I asked.

"She's all done with the chemo. You know she has cancer, right?" I nodded. "I think she's going to be okay."

"Are you going back to your place at Grants Pass, then?"

He shook his head. "I've got it rented out to a friend. I decided to stay here for a while. This thing with Mom . . . I didn't know how it was going to turn out. There are still no guarantees." He stared out the window at the dark clouds. "They say it might snow."

I coughed. My hand went habitually to my chest.

"Are you okay?" Tim studied my face. "You don't look so good. You got that flu that's going around?"

I shook my head. "Just getting over it. I'm fine." I pulled my feet up and crossed my legs.

"You're still wearing that necklace I got you," Tim said.

My hand went to the silver mizpah, half of a heart with jagged edges. "Do you still have yours?"

He laughed. "No, I don't think so. What did it say when both pieces were together?"

"The Lord watch between me and thee while we are absent from one another."

"Oh, yeah." He looked out the window again. Finally he sat back and sighed. "Hey, I'm getting married."

My chest constricted. The cough overtook me again, this time bringing tears to my eyes. When I could, I straightened and took a deep breath. "You're already married."

"Yeah. Well, that's why I'm here. Our marriage was over a long time ago." He reached inside his jacket and pulled out some folded papers. "You and I both know that, Sam. It's time to get on with life. We just need to take care of the paperwork."

AT FIRST it snowed wads of cotton that disappeared as soon as they hit the wet ground. By nightfall the flakes poured from the windless sky, until the grass and driveway were uniformly white. It covered the tracks left by Tim's truck when he turned around.

I didn't sign his papers. He left them on the coffee table, still folded, saying something about it all being pretty self-explanatory but if I had any questions, just give him a call. He got the forms from the stationery store in town. We didn't need an attorney, he said, because there were no custody or property issues involved.

I watched the snow all day with a grief so heavy that I could not cry. TJ came in from time to time, rosy-cheeked and wide-eyed with excitement. "Mom, I made a snowman! Can I have a carrot for his nose?" I made an early dinner of tomato soup and grilled cheese sandwiches. The Judge came in from hanging Christmas lights and sat at the kitchen table with us. I guess I wasn't saying much. TJ stopped chattering for a moment and patted my hand thoughtfully. "Too bad you can't come out and play in the snow, Mommy."

There was so much I wanted to do with him, for him, but I had nothing to give. "I wish I could, baby." He gave me the look. I was not supposed to call him that.

He brought his dishes to the sink, then ran out to play. I started to clear the table, but my father touched my arm. "Sit. I'll do that."

"It doesn't bother me. I've got to do something."

"Talk to me."

I hesitated and then sat back down. "Okay."

"Tim wasn't here very long, was he?"

I shook my head. "He just came by to bring divorce papers."

The Judge was silent for a moment. "Where are they?"

"Out there on the coffee table."

He rose from the table and returned with the documents, which he shook open and skimmed through briefly, like an attorney. " 'Irreconcilable differences, hmpf. There's no such thing." He removed his reading glasses. "Just people who aren't willing to work things out. Whatever happened between you two, Samantha?"

I didn't know what to say. Too much just couldn't be told.

"Do you still love Tim?"

I looked my father straight in his eyes. "Yes. Yes, I do."

"Well, I can only imagine that there was some sort of love triangle. TJ tells me he doesn't have a daddy. But you and Tim and I know differently. Somewhere out there is a dark-eyed ghost that's going to haunt all three of you for the rest of your lives if you don't deal with him. Am I getting warm, Samantha?"

I nodded. "But I don't know where he is, and I don't care. I haven't seen him or talked to him in almost six years."

"So he doesn't know about TJ?"

"Right. And TJ doesn't know about him. But TJ sure was happy to find out he had a grandma and grandpa. Once I told him that, he just couldn't get it out of his head."

"Is that why you came home?"

I nodded. "That was a big part of it. Oh. And I was sick and jobless and broke."

He laughed. "I wish you had come home a long time ago. We've missed a lot." I knew he meant TJ. He glanced out the window. Darkness was falling, and snow swirled in the light of the porch lamp. We heard TJ laugh out loud, and both of us rose to watch him. He was throwing snowballs at his snowman. The Judge chuckled.

"He reminds me of you. There's never a dull moment in his life."

"I've had a few lately."

"This will pass, Samantha."

"Or I will." He raised his eyebrows disapprovingly. "Well, let's face it. I'm not getting any better. I feel weaker every day, and now this cough. I've been waiting for months, and not even one possible heart donor has surfaced." I was so sorry for myself I almost cried.

"You are going to be fine," he said with his annoying optimism.

The phone rang, and as usual, I lurched. My father grabbed the receiver off the wall. "Hello." A smile spread across his face. "There you are. Are you still in Nordstrom? . . . Oh. What's the matter, did they run out of shoes?"

His eyes always lit up when he talked to Lindsey. "I love you too, baby. Let me talk to your mom."

He told her they should stay down there a few days to finish up their Christmas shopping if they wanted to. "We'll be fine," he said. "This is the perfect time for you to get away. I don't have to be back in court until Tuesday."

I knew what he meant by that. Someone had to be here at all times to babysit me. To be ready to drive me to the hospital at a moments notice. Mom and Lindsey needed the break.

Having a sister like Lindsey was a blessing and a curse. She would do anything for me. She called me almost every day or just happened to drop by with a little something to cheer me up. She had agreed to raise my son for me after I was gone. What more could I ask—other than an occasional failure or shortcoming? Nothing Lindsey touched ever went bad. Her husband adored her. She never had a bad hair day, her Lexus didn't break down, and if she lost a tennis match, it was to avoid pulverizing the ego of her opponent. Next to her I was one of my father's worms. A pathetic squiggle peeking out of the manure of my life.

I hoped that I would live and that someday I would make something good of my life. Maybe I could make my father proud of me.

Getting TJ to bed that night was easy. He crawled under the covers without being asked and fell asleep during story time.

I went to my own room and read until my eyes burned, then turned out the light. The phone rang. The red numbers on my clock read ten-thirty. I sat up and heard the Judge answer from his study. "Hello." I couldn't hear much, but something made me slip into the hallway. "Who is this?" A sudden chill raced through me. From the study doorway I saw my father sink slowly into his chair. "Why are you threatening me? Do I know you?" He listened intently, then placed the phone back in its cradle with a sigh.

"Was it him?" I asked.

He nodded, still shaken. "I know that voice."

"Who is it?"

"I wish I knew. It will come to me."

"You should call the sheriff. Maybe he can trace it somehow."

"Yes. He asked me to call if it happened again." He punched in the numbers and got Sheriff Byron on the phone. "Yes, I'm sure it was the same one that spoke to Samantha. Coarse voice. The first thing he said was something about watching my blood melt the snow." He looked over at me uncomfortably. I didn't budge. He turned his back to me and lowered his voice, but I still heard him clearly. "He said he would nail me up; they'd put me in the ground, and if I was really God, I would rise again. That's what he said."

He and the sheriff discussed the Judge's recent cases. Nobody seemed to fit. The sheriff said he would check out some possibilities. When my father hung up, he turned to me. "This is nothing to concern yourself about. Just some crackpot. If the guy was really going to kill me, he'd be on my back porch. Not the telephone."

The thought of him lurking on the back porch made me shudder. I locked all the doors. Once the adrenaline drained from my system, I realized I was exhausted. I crawled into bed and pulled the covers up to my chin. My father tapped his knuckles on the door and poked his head in. "We didn't finish our talk about you and Tim." His silhouette filled the doorway.

"There's nothing you can do. It's over." My words shocked me. It had never been over. Not when he walked away from me at the hospital, not three years later when I pulled the wedding ring from my finger and placed it in a drawer. Up until this moment, I had hoped. "He's going to marry someone else." The words that came from my throat seemed to release the tears that I had kept all day. I rolled over to face the wall before my father could see them.

"Oh, Sam, I'm sorry." I felt him touch my shoulder.

"I'm very tired." I couldn't hold back the sobs much longer.

"Good night, Sammy."

I wanted to cry like his little girl again. I needed him to rock me in his arms, to make this hurt go away. But something held me back.

"Good night," I said.

THE snow fell for days. From my bedroom I heard the back door open and close, TJ's joyful exclamations, the crinkle of grocery bags, my parents' voices, footsteps in the hall. The divorce papers lay under my bed. I wrestled with the idea of calling Tim. In fact, the thought consumed me. Could he really love that Glinda woman?

Finally I brought the phone into my room and closed the door. I dialed his mother's number and held my breath.

"Hello," Tim answered.

"Hey. It's Samantha. Got a minute?"

"Sure."

I held my chest to keep it from exploding. "I have a problem with these papers," I said. "I don't want to sign them. Tim, what happened in Reno, I'm so sorry." I felt myself trembling. "I never had a chance to explain. You just disappeared. For years I tried to find you. I've been miserable. The least you can do is hear me out."

"*You've* been miserable? You poor little thing. And you think I owe you something for all your suffering?"

"Tim, I screwed up. Don't you think I know that? I'm asking you to forgive me. Can you . . . Will you forgive me?"

I heard a sigh, then silence. "Samantha," he finally breathed, "I've spent the past five years trying—for my own sake. When I saw you again . . . well, I thought maybe I could. You don't know how many times I thought of calling you, of maybe giving it a try. But then I realized it could never work."

"But why?"

"Because I could never love that boy of yours."

I felt like he spat on me. I couldn't speak.

"I've finally found someone I can trust. I think I can love again. Don't screw this up for me, Sam. Just sign the papers. Please."

I hung up the phone and sobbed until there was nothing left. The hope that had trickled through me all those years dried up like a creek in a drought. Later that night, I signed his loathsome papers.

Lindsey and David came for dinner the next night. "Room service," she announced, pushing through my bedroom door and passing me a china plate of crackers and cheese. "Samantha, you've been in here for days. Why don't you come out and join us? I'll make a bed for you on the sofa."

"No, thanks." I slunk down on my bed, but it made me cough violently. "Nobody wants to hear that over and over. I haven't even showered today."

"We don't care. It's just family. Or hop in the shower if it will make you feel better. You know, I'll be taking you to the doctor in the morning, and we should get an early start because of the snow."

"I'm not going to the doctor. I'm too tired. I'm just flat out too tired to live." Lindsey cocked her head and gave me one of her motherly looks. "I'm getting worse by the day. I don't need to drive all the way into Seattle to have Dr. Sovold tell me that. Not that he would. He'll just give me another pep talk. *Hang in there, trouper, Any day now.* Do you know how many times I've heard that?"

"Samantha, this is about Tim and those divorce papers, isn't it? You're just depressed, that's all."

"I'm not going. I've made up my mind. I need to talk to you about something else. We need to talk about TJ." I pushed myself higher against the pillows behind me. "I don't want him to be overprotected. I want him safe, of course, but he should be able to run free in the woods and fish until dark if he wants. Not now, of course. I'm talking about later."

Lindsey smiled sadly, patiently. "Is there anything else?"

I sighed. This was not coming out right. What was I really trying to say? "You know how TJ is? Happy, innocent. So full of life. He just assumes that everybody likes him because he likes them. Can you help TJ to not lose himself in the process of growing up?"

Lindsey walked to my bedroom window. The snow had stopped. "I know what you're saying, Sam. I can't promise that TJ won't lose that sweet naïveté of his. I wish I could. If you die . . . well, that will be his first slap of reality. He's already meeting kids that won't share. It's just a matter of time before some redneck local points out to him that the only Mexicans around here are seasonal farm-workers. The fact is, people can't be trusted. Even the people who love TJ are going to let him down. We're not perfect."

She walked to my bedside table. "Where's that Bible I gave you?" Finding it on the lower tier, she sat next to me on the bed. "God is the only one that can be trusted like a child trusts a loving father. I'll teach him that. TJ will lose his innocence—we all lose ours. But when we ask God to forgive us, it's like our screwups never happened. He doesn't even remember them anymore."

I found myself wanting to believe her. God loomed threateningly in my subconscious mind, glaring down with displeasure from his mighty throne. That's the way I still felt with my father, even though he had shown nothing but kindness to me and TJ. There was always this thing between us that I didn't know how to fix. A stink all over me that wouldn't wash away. And when you know you stink, you keep your distance.

Tim couldn't get past it either.

Innocence. If only I could start all over as a little child.

"COME on, lazy. Get up."

I rolled over and pulled the blanket off my face. When my eyes focused, I saw Donnie leaning over me. "Who let you in here?"

"It's not exactly the White House. You don't even have a mean dog."

"Where is everybody?"

He shrugged and walked to my closet. Hangers scraped back and forth on the rod until he pulled out a black skirt Lindsey had

254 | Karen Harter

bought me on one of our trips to Seattle for my doctor's appointment. He tossed it onto the bed.

"I'm not wearing that." I stretched across the crumpled sheets.

"Come on, Samantha. Get ready. Let's go."

"I'm *not* going to the doctor. It takes all day to go to Seattle, and he never tells me anything I don't already know. I know my heart is failing. I'm dying, and there's not a thing anybody can do about it."

"Doctor? I'm not taking you to the doctor. Go brush your teeth and do whatever you gotta do in the bathroom."

"How dare you come in here and—?" A cough interrupted me. "Leave me alone, Donnie." I coughed again. "I can't go anywhere!"

For an instant I thought he would go. He looked me over like maybe I wasn't worth the effort after all. Instead, he went out to the bathroom, returning with my hairbrush. He sat me up and began brushing my hair. "Ouch!" I yanked the brush from his hand. "Just where is it you think we are going?"

"To a funeral. A close friend of mine. I'd really like it if you could be there."

"Believe me, Donnie. You do not want to take me out in public."

"It's okay. Trust me. I'll carry you if you want me to."

"Oh, yeah. That would be good. That would be real good."

THE outside air surprised my face. I inhaled deeply, which caused me to hack. Donnie helped me into the truck, and I settled against the seat. The black skirt draped just above my ankles, and I wore a nice sweater but rebelliously insisted on my brown logger boots.

"So why won't you tell me who died?"

"I don't think you're ready yet."

I quit asking. One thing I hated about Donnie was that he could be just as stubborn as I could. It was already early afternoon. I wasn't sure what day it was. Probably a weekday, because TJ was gone. Mom must have gone to pick him up from preschool. When we got to the Carter Store, Donnie turned the truck toward Dixon. "I should have left a note," I muttered.

"I did. I left them my cell phone number on the kitchen

counter." He reached into his pocket and tossed something into my lap. I stared down at my pager. He must have grabbed it from my lamp table. That was the first time I'd forgotten it. In a flash I remembered all the times I had run to it, thinking I heard the signal. My hand closed around the device, but it lay there, mutely taunting me. I rolled down the window and hurled it into a pile of snow.

Donnie skidded to a stop on the shoulder. "Why'd you do that?"

"It doesn't work." His glare made me recoil. "Well, it doesn't. I might as well be carrying a potato everywhere I go."

I thought he would go look for it. He should have found it and clipped it to my jacket and made me promise not to do it again. Instead, he checked his side mirror and pulled back onto the road with a shrug. "Yeah. I don't blame you. I want you to know I admire you. I don't know if I could have held on this long."

I felt good for about a minute. What did he mean by that?

We drove in silence until we reached the rest stop by the river where we had parked that summer night to climb on the train trestle. I was surprised when Donnie pulled in. "What's going on?"

"We're here," he said.

"You liar. This is not a funeral." Donnie came around and opened my door. "I can't walk out on those tracks, if that's what you're thinking. I'm not supposed to overexert myself."

He pulled a knapsack from under the seat. "We'll go slow."

"It's too far."

"Get on my back."

Curiosity momentarily empowered me. I stood on the running board, hiked up the skirt, and wrapped my arms and legs around him. He linked his arms around my legs and strolled down the path through the trees that led to the trestle. I heard the river and closed my eyes. One hand inadvertently slipped inside his jacket and the open collar of his shirt, but I didn't move it. His skin was warm and smelled faintly spicy.

We reached the middle of the bridge where the metal gridwork arched above us. He put me down next to a vertical support. I linked my forearm inside its crisscrossing metal and looked down.

It was not the carefree river of summer. The water was swollen with the melting snow. Heavy clouds dragged slowly across the foothills, leaving cottony combings among the treetops.

Donnie respected my reverie. I had not been this close to the river for a while. We sat and dangled our feet like that night in June. He opened his knapsack and pulled out a bottle of Irish whiskey. "I would like to propose a toast."

I laughed and slapped his shoulder. "I can't drink that!"

"Why not? You're dying anyway."

I was shocked and offended. "You jerk! I can't believe you said that. What kind of a friend—?"

"The kind who calls it as he sees it. You've got lots of people telling you to hang in there. One more day. Tomorrow, tomorrow. And how long has that been going on? You've told me yourself, Sam, your blood type is the hardest to match. What are your chances of getting a heart in time? A person knows when they're dying. When I heard that you refused to go to the doctor, I knew that you know. After all, they drop you from the transplant program for stuff like that. But I'm not telling you anything you haven't already given a lot of thought."

"So this is *my* funeral."

He nodded. "I thought you might like to really be here for it. It's a shame to give a person all that attention after they're dead."

"Then what? Are you going to push me in front of the train?"

He shook his head. "Nah. I'd have too much explaining to do."

"Okay." I reached for the glass in his hand. "Pour."

He obliged and then raised his glass. "Here's to the only girl I ever knew who would feel around in the mud for crawdads." We clinked glasses. He pulled a tightly folded piece of paper from his pocket but didn't open it. "You were always a good guy to have on my side during a war. You could throw a pinecone grenade almost as far as I could." He swirled the liquor in his glass. "Then we went to junior high and got too cool to crawl in the dirt. We were still neighbors, rode the same school bus, but I didn't really see you anymore. You didn't see me. We just took each other for granted. Then one day I saw you again. You were holding hands with Tim Weatherbee. It was strange how I felt. It caught me off guard."

"You were jealous?"

He grinned. "Yeah. I snoozed, I losed. Anyway, that doesn't matter anymore. The important thing is that we got a chance to be friends again before"—he took a swig—"as adults, I mean." He unfolded the paper he had pulled from his pocket. "Okay. I wrote this eulogy. It might sound dumb today. I tipped the bottle a little last night. That's when I got this idea, for the funeral and all."

He cleared his throat. "Samantha Dodd Weatherbee will be missed by all who knew her. She died at the tender age of twenty five and is survived by her son, TJ; her father, Judge Blake Dodd; her mother, Lucy Dodd; and her sister, Lindsey Matthews. She was a skilled fly-fisher and could exactly mimic the call of a loon. Her dream was to live in a house overlooking the Stillaguamish River.

"Those of us who knew her will not miss her frank observation of our faults or her stubborn pride. We *will* miss her passion for the people and things she loved. She loved to hear the wind in the cottonwoods. Sometimes she made anyone nearby stop to listen."

These were things about myself I had forgotten. I watched Donnie's jaw muscle flinch as he read. His blue-green eyes were shaded beneath his wiry brow and were hard to read.

"She was devoted to her son, TJ, who will miss her most of all. He will miss the way she let his tree frogs crawl on her face. He'll remember the way she tucked him into bed at night and taught him how to cheat at cards. Every birthday, every Christmas she will be the one gift he wanted but didn't get. When he dunks the winning shot at his high school game, he will miss her face in the crowd."

I didn't usually cry at funerals, and I wasn't about to start. "I want to go home now." I listened intently for distant rumblings or the woeful whistle of a train. "You know, if a train comes, I can't—"

"I'm almost done." Donnie turned the paper over. "We will grieve for a while, but life must go on. TJ will be loved by those who remain. Samantha's parents will pause by her photo from time to time with sad smiles, then go on about their day. I will probably move away. I'll marry a tall beauty that looks great on my arm and she'll always say the right thing. But sometimes I will long for a friend that knows me, who will call bull on my self-deception, who is never boring, and I will think of Sam. I'll close my eyes and see the mischief in her green eyes, her wry smile, and I'll reach for the phone and then remember that she is no longer in my world."

Donnie poured us each another shot. "So I tell you now"—his hand reached out and brushed my face—"while I can still touch you. I have loved you, Samantha. I'll miss you more than you know."

He held his glass to mine, and I returned his gaze before we tipped them back. The liquid ran like lava down my throat.

WHEN Donnie brought me home from my funeral, the sky was already dark, though it was not yet five o'clock. Multicolored Christmas lights outlined the eaves of our covered porch. Mom invited Donnie to stay for dinner, which annoyed me because I was exhausted and wanted to be alone. He stuck his head in the oven and smelled lasagna, and the next thing I knew, he was cutting garlic bread and arranging the slices in a basket for the table.

Neither Donnie nor I mentioned my funeral. He just said we drove down to Dixon and sat by the river for a while. TJ was indignant that we didn't bring him along, but Donnie promised to take him next time. "Just us guys," he said. "We'll launch driftwood boats, then go up on the bridge and bomb them." Donnie crinkled his nose and shook his head. "No girls, though. They might make us eat the crust on our sandwiches and be quiet."

TJ liked that idea. His eyes stayed fixed on Donnie all through the meal. When Donnie laughed, TJ laughed. He even ate his green beans after Donnie piled a second helping on his own plate.

After dinner I crawled into TJ's bed and read a story while the Judge and Donnie played chess. I figured that by now the Judge would have Donnie's queen running for her life, but I also knew that winning was not as important to Donnie as the privilege of being in His Honor's presence. He still addressed my father as sir.

Later Donnie tapped my bedroom door open. "Hey, I saw your light on." My father walked past him down the hall, and Donnie looked over his shoulder. "Good night, sir."

"Good night, Don. I'm open to a rematch anytime. Good night, Sam."

"Good night."

Donnie waited until the Judge closed his bedroom door before coming in and sitting on the edge of my bed. "How do you feel? I hope I didn't get you too tired today."

I put my book down and shook my head. Tired? What else was there? "It was good to get my funeral out of the way." Why did I always say things I didn't mean?

"Yeah. Well, they'll probably have another one down at the Community Church." Donnie's eyes wandered around my room until they settled on the framed photo of TJ and me eating watermelon on the Fourth of July. We beamed at each other, our cheeks bulging. That was before I considered death an option. Now it was just a question of when. "Then all the women will go into a cooking frenzy. Mom will bring over shepherd's pie and crescent rolls."

I pictured everyone I knew gathering to grieve over Hungarian goulash and green bean casserole. "Ask your mother to bring lobster and caviar instead. I might even come back from the grave for that." I made light of it, though it now seemed to loom as an inevitable event. I screamed inside, but to Donnie I must have looked as calm as a lake on a windless morning.

I yawned. "Are you coming over tomorrow?"

"No." He stood deliberately and walked toward the door. His muscular chest and shoulders showed through his white T-shirt. "I'm not coming by tomorrow or the next day or the day after that. I'm not going to watch you die, Sam. Today was my good-bye."

There was this long look between us. I wanted him to hold me in his arms, to be close enough to smell the cottonwood of his skin. I wanted to cry against his chest and then feel him kiss the tears from my eyes. But he didn't move. "Thank you," I finally said.

"For what?"

"For being my friend."

He nodded. "Good-bye, Sammy."

The door closed behind him. It latched quietly, like I imagined the lid would close on a coffin. Quietly, reverently, permanently.

CHAPTER EIGHT

I'M EMBARRASSED to say that I was not one of those people who die graciously like that sweet southern Melanie in *Gone With the Wind.*

The reality of my pending death was more than I could bear. I wallowed in sorrow in a darkened room. When TJ came to see me, I clung to him, breaking down and weeping twice in his presence, which I had vowed I would not do. Upsetting my son was the last thing I wanted; it's just that to me it was like TJ was dying. He would be lost to me forever, whether it was him or me.

Donnie had not been kidding when he said good-bye. He didn't visit; he didn't call. I tried to phone him a few times, but he wasn't home, and after that I talked myself out of it. He had obviously meant what he said, and really, I didn't want him to see me in this morose state. I didn't do a thing with my hair or face. I just sat there most of each day staring at the TV the Judge had moved into my room. It was better that Donnie remember me laughing, fishing with him and TJ, singing the oldies while he worked on his truck.

But I missed him. He was the one person I felt knew me to the core—and he liked me anyway. And I knew *him* I was sure, better than anyone despite the seven-year interruption in our relationship.

My mother bought me a new green chenille robe. Sometimes she played cheery music and insisted on opening my curtains. Lindsey offered pep talks and manicures. But it all seemed so pointless.

The Judge finally couldn't stand it. He stormed into my room one morning, tossed me the robe, and insisted I get out of bed.

"Why? What's going on?" I asked.

"Life. Life is going on." He gestured for me to follow him. "Come on now or you're going to miss it."

Curiosity got the better of me. I stepped tentatively from the bed, wrapped the robe around me, and followed my father out of the room. Weak and slightly dizzy, I skimmed my hand along the wall for support. Mom was in her bathrobe too, propping TJ on the sill of the big picture window in the dining room. He was giggling.

"I wanna play with them, Grandma."

The Judge guided me up to the window. "Mama Bear wouldn't like that, son. Besides, those guys have sharp claws."

They were black bears. Two big cubs, tumbling together at the edge of the back lawn. "Where's the mother?" I asked.

My father pointed. "Over there by the tree. Do you see her?"

The sow was rolling a rotted log with her paw. "How do you know that's the mother? She's not much bigger than they are."

"I saw her with these guys last spring when they were the size of a twenty-pound bag of flour. She'll keep them with her through next summer, until they're old enough to go out on their own."

The big cubs suddenly turned and scrambled toward the sow bear. Their rich brown fur flowed loosely in waves along their bodies as they ran. "Shouldn't they be hibernating now?" I asked.

The Judge shook his head. "Bears don't shut down completely. They can wake up from time to time during the winter. It looks like Mama got hungry." The cubs were now snacking along with their mother on something inside the log. Probably grubs.

Eventually the bear family headed downstream, and Mom announced that she was going back to making waffles.

"Eat out here with us, Sam," my father said.

"Oh, I don't think so. I feel gross."

"Go take a shower. We'll wait." He wasn't asking.

I didn't feel like showering, but I obeyed my father.

The water washed over me in rivulets. I realized my body was almost as sleek as it was at seventeen. I should have been in my prime. My eyes closed, and I pretended I was a child again, letting the little waterfall on the creek wash over me. Remembering my river. How as a child I thought it flowed forever. The water spiraled at my feet and disappeared down the drain.

At breakfast I was quiet—not on purpose, but because I felt my very soul had washed down that drain. It had gone on before me, awaiting my physical body in some dark place. TJ covered my silence with questions about bears, which my father—the talking encyclopedia—answered in vivid detail. After poking at my food for some time, I excused myself and returned to my room.

Later the Judge knocked on my door. "Samantha?"

I pulled the front of my robe together. "Yes. Come in."

He immediately walked to my window and pulled the curtains aside. "It's gloomy in here. Why don't you let the light in?"

I shrugged. "I don't know. It glares on the TV sometimes."

"While you sit here in the dark, you're missing things that go on in the light. Like the bears. That was a nice surprise, wasn't it?"

I nodded. "Life is full of surprises." The irony of what I just said hit me. I looked up at him sheepishly.

"You need to get back to the doctor, Samantha." He pulled a chair close to the bed and sat down. "I know you think it's point-less, but it *is* necessary. If for no other reason, just to show you're still in the program. Donor hearts are too scarce to chance on some-one that's not willing to fight."

I sighed deeply and coughed. "I can't." As soon as I said it, I knew I had made a mistake.

The Judge shot to his feet, and his chair fell backward with a crash. "That's a lie! You *can* fight, Samantha! Forget your body for a minute. This battle is in your mind." He was pacing now, his eyes ablaze. "You give up in your mind and your body's naturally going to follow. But if you have faith and hope, you can do anything."

In my weakness I didn't argue. My eyes filled with tears.

The Judge's anger eddied. He pulled the chair upright and sat down, remaining quiet for some time. When he spoke again, his voice was soft. "If you really want to die, Samantha, then dwell on how sick you are. Think about it day and night. Imagine never see-ing TJ again. But if you want to live, do the opposite. Pray for a new heart. Believe that it's on its way and speak accordingly. Speak of the future. Choose life, Samantha. *Decide* to live."

I ACTUALLY got up and dressed myself that afternoon. I sat by the dining-room window with a cup of tea. TJ played with his cars and trucks at my feet. I practiced what my father said. I thought of taking my son to kindergarten next fall. Not Lindsey, but *me* walking him to the door of his classroom.

That night I dreamed. I dove into the warm sea and swam right to the bottom with the strength of a porpoise and stayed there for a long time with my eyes wide open and never craving air. I burst up through the surface into the sky, soaring like a swallow. I was aware only of infinite freedom, dazzling light, and energy that radiated from some invisible source.

I awoke the next morning to the smell of coffee brewing in the kitchen. I closed my eyes and tried to soar like a swallow again. If only I could retrieve the dream. Where did my mind conceive it? I gradually understood. Love. That's what it was. I was surrounded by it, swimming in it, flying through it. Fear did not exist.

I know now that the dream was a gift. I felt the love I had been so starved for—but didn't believe in. It was the love I always wished my father could have for me.

It would take a lot of love for me to break down the dam that was stopping up my life. Hope rose up in me and, with it, a surge of strength. I could do it. I would love my son enough to fight for my life. And Donnie. I knew now that he was the man I wanted. I would be strong for him and my parents. I'd make them all proud.

Choose Life. Little by little the dam was coming down.

SINCE I had *misplaced* my pager, the Judge stopped by RadioShack on his way back from the city for a replacement.

I called my social worker, Irma Krueger, from the privacy of my room. She had been out to the house back in July after my cardiologist determined that conventional treatments were not working on my damaged heart. I knew that Irma had come to evaluate whether

I had the grit to stay committed to the heart transplant program.

Irma answered her phone on the second ring. "Hello."

"Hi, Irma. This is Samantha."

"Well, well. I thought you didn't want to talk to me anymore." Her voice was tinged with a German accent and a smile.

"Sorry. I was having a bad day last time you called." I closed my eyes and remembered the dream. I pictured myself soaring like a barn swallow with the sun on my back, full of joy, and I drew on that strength. "Irma, I don't want to die. I want to live."

"That's good. That's good, Samantha. Now we can get back on track. Christopher said you missed your last appointment. Do you want me to reschedule?" I said yes.

"You have to be willing to fight," she added. "Are you ready?"

I didn't give it a moment of thought. "Yes, I'm ready."

CHRISTOPHER was the nurse assigned to me by the hospital. His dark hair was woven into a single braid that fell down his back. He was about thirty, going on thirteen. He always made irreverent jokes about the hospital staff, including my transplant surgeon, Dr. Wilhelm. Christopher told me not to get beeped between five and seven because that's when Dr. Wilhelm goes to happy hour.

"I don't want to know this," I said, still chuckling.

Christopher grew quiet momentarily as he checked my pulse. He scrawled something on his clipboard, then motioned for me to lie back on the padded table.

"The doctor will be right in." He winked as he left the room.

The trip to Seattle had tired me. I lay back and closed my eyes. As usual, my palm rested on my heart. *Squish-squish*.

Dr. Sovold's entrance startled me. He swung into the room, plopping onto a wheeled stool and sliding toward me in one motion. He wore a plaid shirt today instead of the usual white coat.

"Good morning, Samantha. I hope I didn't wake you. You looked like Sleeping Beauty lying there."

I raised myself up on one elbow and studied him. "You look like a long, tall Texan on a Shetland pony."

"I always wanted to be a cowboy," he grinned. "But I found out I was allergic to horses and became a cardiologist instead."

He stood and began the echocardiogram, sliding the cold wand over my chest, studying the pulsing image on the screen. Finally he wiped the gel from my skin. "Okay." He sighed. "Wrap yourself up."

I sat up, relieved that it was over.

"Well, Samantha, we're seeing increased weakness in the walls of the left ventricle. You've probably been feeling it." I nodded. "Your heart's cavity has enlarged, and it's really working overtime trying to pump blood around your body. It's tired. You're tired."

I couldn't argue with that. I stared back at him, waiting.

"I want to check you into the hospital. You need the rest."

"But it's Christmastime."

His eyes softened. "I know. But I think it's necessary, Sam."

I had planned to call Donnie that night when I got home. I missed him so badly, and now that I had decided to live, he might change his mind about not seeing me anymore. "I can rest at home. I have my mother and my sister . . ."

"I need to have you close to me right now. Once every few weeks is not enough. I need to check on you every day. If"—he corrected himself—"*when* a compatible donor heart becomes available, you've got to be strong enough to go through surgery."

"I have to go home first. My son . . . and all my things . . ."

"Your parents will bring them. They'll bring your boy too. I've already talked to them."

So it had been decided. My life had veered off course again.

My father had promised that everything would be all right. He often spoke of the future, and I was always in it. He said I should check into Cub Scouts for TJ when he reaches second grade. He brought books home for me on career choices and pamphlets from Northwest Junior College in Darlington.

I remembered Irma's lilting German voice when it hardened. *You have to be willing to fight.* I closed my eyes and saw myself in the dream. Strong. Alive. Fearless. I would fight this battle. But apparently I would fight it lying down.

That evening, alone in my hospital room, I dialed Donnie's number. He would be glad to hear that I was fighting for my life now. I was not the pathetic weakling he had toasted at my premature funeral. How had I been so blind? He said he had loved me. What kind of love did he mean?

"Hey." A breathless Donnie finally answered the phone. "Sorry, I know I'm late, but I just got in from the barn. I'll be there in a half hour. You're probably wearing one of your great dresses, right?"

I was confused and didn't speak.

"Rachel?"

My hand clenched the receiver like a climber's last lifeline, then slowly lowered it back to its cradle.

FOR the first couple of days, I had no roommate. My mother sprawled across the vacant bed with the *Seattle Times*. When TJ came, he snuggled into bed with me, but only for a few minutes at a time. There was so much to see and do. Christopher brought empty syringes, teaching TJ how to suck water from my drinking glass and then squirt innocent pedestrians on the sidewalk below my window.

On day three I got Lulu. Her real name, she said, was Luella, but all her friends just called her Lulu, which was exactly what she was. A real one. She wore a pink satin bed jacket, like Doris Day.

"So what are you in for?" Lulu promptly removed her swirly strawberry-blond hair, placing it on a white foam head on her bedside table and giving it a little fluff. "Don't tell me it's the C word."

I was a little distracted by the hair thing. Her own thin gray down was cut close to the head.

"Huh? Oh, you mean cancer? No, it's not that. My heart. I have dilated cardiomyopathy."

"Oh." She shook her head sympathetically. "You poor little thing. And you're so young. I've got the heart thing going on too. Come to think of it, I guess we all do in this ward. I'm here to get a heart transplant." She turned to me with a smile. "I've done a lot of livin'. Had two good husbands. A one-legged one that could dance 'til sunup and a two-legged one that wouldn't dance if he stepped in a nest of fire ants. He was a shy one." She let her head fall back on her pillow. "How 'bout you? You got a husband?"

Lulu made me smile. "I used to. He was a good one."

Christopher sauntered in wearing his blue scrubs and checked my heart monitor. Lulu reached for her glasses. Christopher must have felt her scrutiny. He looked up and grinned disarmingly.

"Well, if I'd a known we were having a gentleman caller, I would have put on my hairdo." She ran her painted fingernails through her silver fuzz. "Aren't you special!" she exclaimed to me. "I get Nurse Marshmallow Butt and you get Fabio. What does a girl gotta do around here to get such special attention?"

Christopher leaned toward her and whispered, "She's flying first class."

"Well, sign me up, honey. I don't care what it costs."

"This is first class? Then how do you explain this?" I held out a plate of half-eaten meatloaf that had stiffened as it cooled.

"You should see what they got back there in the tail section." Christopher smiled and scribbled my vital signs onto my chart.

I was asleep that evening when the Judge came. When my eyes opened, his were closed and he was slouched in a chair by my bed. "Hey," I said.

His eyes opened, and he smiled. "How ya doin' in here?"

"Okay, I guess." I glanced over at Lulu, who was also napping. "I got a roommate."

"I saw that."

"I didn't think you were coming today. Didn't you have court?"

He nodded. "I adjourned early." He reached out and touched the tape on my arm that held my IV in place. "Does it hurt?"

"No. It's just annoying. They make me walk around the hall, and I have to drag this thing with me." I motioned toward the IV pole on wheels, which also supported my heart monitor.

He glanced at the equipment; then his eyes roamed the room. "We got a Christmas tree," he said. "TJ picked it out. He found it down by the creek." He chuckled. "I think he felt sorry for it. We'll have to put the naked side against the wall."

"I wish I could be there." I didn't realize how much until I almost choked on the end of my sentence.

"Donnie asks about you."

Donnie. At the mere mention of his name my throat tightened. It didn't take him long to find Rachel, whoever that was. It was a good bet that she didn't wear clunky logger boots like me, though. I cried quietly sometimes after the lights were out, remembering his tender ways with TJ and the times he looked longingly into my eyes, but I had turned away. "Tell him I'll be home soon. I hope."

The Judge tousled my hair. "That's the spirit. That's my girl talking."

His comment surprised me. I always thought of Lindsey as *his girl.* I noticed I got more respect lying with a hose stuck in my arm. The same mother who used to vacuum around me at home brought flowers and chocolates to the hospital. And she drove three hours to do it. I must say it felt good. I had been a fool to stay away from my family for so long.

It was dark outside my window. Lulu snored softly. We watched a documentary on penguins. My father laughed at their antics as they dove down icy banks on their chests into the frigid water.

When we turned off the TV, Lulu's breathing grew more labored, but she did not wake up. My father rose and went to her bedside. He watched the lines on her monitor until he was sure she was all right. I wondered what he was thinking as he stood there looking down at her. I know what I was thinking, and I'm not proud of it: Lulu is too old. I, on the other hand, had a son who would be in kindergarten next year. Lulu's kids were grown. She had seen them board the school bus hundreds of times. She had been the Tooth Fairy, den mother, chaperone. She danced at their weddings.

I hoped Lulu didn't get a heart before me. Even though I liked her. Even though she had waited longer. She told me she had been on the transplant recipient list for over a year. She was in the hospital before but was allowed to go home when she seemed strong enough. That was a month ago, but now she was back. When we padded through the halls, our IV poles lending awkward support, we passed other pole people, as we called ourselves. Lulu knew most of them. She asked about Roy. A thin man in a plaid robe shook his head sadly. "Roy didn't make it, Lu." They exchanged a long gaze before Lulu reached out and touched the man's arm.

"And Curtis?"

"Oh, didn't you hear? He got a heart three weeks ago. He's out among the living now. Went to his kids' soccer game already." The man nodded and shuffled his way slowly down the hall.

Lulu watched him turn the corner toward his room. "Hank's been passed up four times. The last time a match came in, they got him all prepped for surgery, but the heart was too small. Right blood type, wrong size." She shook her head. "It just ain't fair."

"Why do they make us walk around like this?"

Lulu chuckled. "Because we're vultures and that's what we do. We circle and wait for someone to die."

"That's sick," I had said.

"Oh, lighten up, honey. You gotta have a sense of humor in here or you won't survive."

I watched her tired old face twitch while she slept. With or without a sense of humor, some of us wouldn't make it.

The Judge finally yawned and stretched. "I'd better hit the road."

"Tuck in TJ for me. Tell him I'll call him in the morning."

"I forgot to tell you. He's staying at Lindsey's for a few days."

"She never told me that!" I jerked forward. "I talked to her this morning. Why wouldn't she tell me TJ was there?" My chest grew instantly heavy. "I'm not even dead yet and I'm being replaced."

The Judge leaned over me. "Don't ever say that again! Not unless that's what you want. Is that what you want, Samantha?"

"Of course not! But what am I supposed to think? Last time I checked, I was still TJ's mother. I think I have a right to have some say in where he goes and what he does. Why wouldn't she tell me that?"

The Judge scooted the chair up and sat by the edge of my bed. "I'm sorry, Sammy. You're right. We should have told you." He sighed, and his red-rimmed eyes fastened on mine. "I didn't want to upset you. It's just a precaution." He hesitated. "I've seen some footprints around the place. A man's boot print, and it's not mine."

"Has Donnie been over there? Or Matt or anybody?"

He shook his head. "Sheriff Byron is working on it. Most of the prints are around the barn—coming from the woods. It could be someone just needed a place to get in out of the rain."

"Or it could be the guy that wants you dead."

He shrugged and shook his head unconvincingly. I instantly understood the reason for his bloodshot eyes.

"So you shipped TJ off to Lindsey's." My voice was calmer now, but my insides were unsettled. "What about you and Mom?"

"Well, I've asked your mother to stay at Lindsey's too. Just for now." He kissed my forehead and stood to reach for his coat. He was almost to the door before I thought to ask. "Wait a minute. Where are you going now?"

"Well, home."

"Why aren't *you* staying at David and Lindsey's?"

He pulled his leather gloves out of his coat pocket. "Don't you worry about that. I'm not. You just take care of yourself." He winked and walked out the door.

CHAPTER NINE

LULU had frog slippers with eyes that bugged out like headlights. They were a gift from one of her friends in the Wacky Widows club, of which Lulu was president. She spoke often with the other three members on the phone, as they were planning a car trip to Monterey in June. Not once, in any of her dialogues, did Lulu mention the possibility that she might not be well enough to go.

So I was naturally concerned the morning that she refused to join the march of the pole people, which we undertook right after breakfast. I finally pushed my IV pole out into the corridor to make my rounds. "Don't take the corners too fast!" she called after me.

It felt good to be out of that bed. I walked slowly around the block, and I was considering a second lap when I saw Donnie exit the elevator just ahead of me. He seemed surprised to see me.

"Hey," I said with a casual smile, as if I had seen him just yesterday. My insides were immediately in turmoil.

"Hey, you." He waited for me to catch up to him. "How ya doin'?" He looked at me like I was an accident victim lying on the side of the road. I hated that.

"Good. I'm doing great, actually. I didn't think I'd see you again. After all, you did say good-bye."

Donnie grinned. "I've come to bust you out of here."

"Hah!"

"I'm serious. Where's your room?"

I led him back to 417. Lulu smiled when we entered, but she did not reach for her strawberry-blond hair. "Lulu, this is Donnie."

"Oh, very handsome. My goodness, girl. You been holdin' out on me." She feebly reached out her hand, and Donnie took it in his.

"Hello, Lulu."

I caught my reflection in the mirror, and my hand combed through my bedraggled hair. "What's this talk about breaking out?"

"TJ wants his mom home for Christmas."

I pushed my pole to the edge of the bed and sat down. Tears came to my eyes. "But the doctor said . . ."

"We'll bring you back after Christmas. Your dad arranged everything with the doctor. They're sending your meds and some kind of portable gizmo with you."

"Okay."

I pushed the button to summon my nurse. "My clothes are in that little closet." Donnie passed them to me, along with my cosmetic bag, and waited outside while Christopher unplugged me and helped me dress. He rigged me up with an IV pump that I could carry with me in a fanny pack. I could walk around like a normal person again. The truth of it finally settled in. "Woohoo!" I yelped, and then sang, "There's no place like home for the holidays. . . ."

Lulu stretched out her hand toward me as they wheeled me by her bed. Our fingers touched. "Merry Christmas, Lulu. I'll be back in a few days," I said.

"I'll leave the light on for ya."

THE December sky spread out in a canopy of smoke-colored clouds. Donnie said it felt like snow. He lifted me into his truck and tucked a plaid blanket around me. We drove through the University District, where shoppers crowded the sidewalks and lights twinkled from shopwindows. Christmas was going on as usual.

Donnie whistled a tune as he steered with one hand, his other elbow resting on the driver's side door. He asked a lot of questions about my treatment and seemed sincerely interested. I explained the waiting process and why the next person in line did not automatically get the next available donor organ. I did not remind Donnie that my type AB blood was the hardest to match or that my chances for survival were about as good as winning the lottery.

When the heater kicked in, I pulled the blanket off my knees, not because I was warm enough, but to avoid looking like an ailing grandma. I sat cross-legged, wondering what Donnie thought of me now. My hair had grown longer, and out of sheer boredom I had painted my nails with Lulu's Tangerine Sunset enamel.

Donnie whistled quietly for a while. He looked good to me. Good enough to touch. I wanted to scoot up next to him, close enough to smell his skin, to feel his shoulder next to mine. I wondered what he would do if I did. My mind filled again with conjured images of Rachel, the woman he thought I was when I tried to call. Whoever she was, she was probably a healthy specimen with an active future.

"Why did you come for me?" I asked.

"Your father asked me to bring you home. He's in court this week. Trying to wrap this case up before Christmas. It was important to him to have the whole family together for Christmas." He looked uncomfortable for a second. "I guess you know about the threats he's had—and the prowler." I nodded. "Well, your mom and TJ have been staying over at your sister's. They're coming home today too. Your dad asked me to stay over at your place, just as a precaution. I hope you don't mind."

I smiled. "The more the merrier." As much as the Judge liked Lindsey's husband, David, I found it amusing that he apparently didn't consider him a worthy ally in the face of danger.

"Hey, look up there."

I followed his gaze toward the mountains, which were shrouded by clouds. The foothills were already dusted with white. "Snow."

"And it's coming our way. We'll have snow before morning."

Fifteen minutes after Donnie's prediction a blinding flurry of dry crystals hurled themselves at the windshield. He drove slowly, and I was glad he knew the road so well, as it was difficult to see.

My relief when we pulled into the driveway at home turned to disappointment. The house was dark. TJ did not come out and rush into my arms, as I had imagined. Instead, Donnie helped me up the front steps and unlocked the door in silence. He led me to the couch with my blanket and proceeded to turn on lights and start a fire.

"I have to go to the bathroom." I pushed myself up from the sofa. Donnie looked worried. "Are you . . . Do you need any help?"

I laughed. "No, but thanks for offering."

Donnie didn't hear me when I came back down the hall. His back was to me, and he had the hall closet door open. I saw the handgun just as he tucked it under a hat on the top shelf.

"Is it loaded?" I asked.

He flinched. "Sam. You weren't supposed to see that."

"What's going on, Donnie? Do you think this guy is for real?"

He shook his head. "No, I think your dad is right. Whoever he is, he just wants to make your dad sweat. If he was going to do anything, he would have done it by now. The gun is only a precaution."

Donnie headed for the kitchen and stuck his nose in the fridge. "You want some leftover spaghetti?"

"Yes, I'm starved." He microwaved the pasta while I buttered soft French bread. "What does this remind you of?" I asked as he plopped his plate down on the kitchen table and pulled in his chair.

He looked at his plate and then at me. "I give up."

"Bologna sandwiches."

He twirled a forkful of pasta and shoved it into his mouth. Now his mouth was too full for a response.

"Remember? My mom always made us bologna sandwiches with sweet pickles. You always sat right in that chair and I sat here."

He shook his head. "I don't remember bologna. I remember those tuna things with cheese melted over the top. Those were worth coming in out of the rain for. Pass me some more bread, would ya?"

I shoved the plate toward him and watched him eat. His eulogy to me ended *I have loved you, Samantha.* What did he mean by that? We were friends since childhood. Was that what he meant?

"So," I finally broke the silence, "what was that funeral all about? You put me in the ground and then you go dig me up again. At least one of us is confused."

He smirked and took a long drink of milk. "It's you. It's always you that's confused. I had the funeral because you had given up. You kept talking about dying and making plans for TJ after you were gone. Being around dead people is a drag."

"It was psychological warfare. You did it to snap me out of it."

He shrugged. "Maybe. Did it work?"

I smiled and lifted the bottom of my sweater, revealing the pager on my belt. "I'm doing everything they tell me to do. And I haven't said anything negative all day, have I?"

He thought about it momentarily. "No, I guess not." He grinned and tweaked my nose like I was twelve. "Good girl. Keep it up."

BY SIX o'clock that night, two days before Christmas, the family had congregated in the house of my childhood. That is, everyone but the Judge. TJ burst through the front door, stumbling into my arms. He pulled me to the Christmas tree to show off the ornaments he had made, while the others carried armloads of packages in from David's car. At our father's request, Lindsey and David were to stay with us at the river all weekend and would sleep in Lindsey's old room. TJ was delighted to share his room with Donnie.

My mother made me sit in the big yellow chair. She brought a tray with mugs of hot spiced cider and played Christmas carols on the stereo while the blaze in the fireplace danced and snapped.

By the time we heard the Judge on the front porch stomping the snow from his shoes, TJ was asleep under the Christmas tree. Mom greeted him at the door, took his coat, and shook it before hanging it in the closet. His face looked drawn and tired. He smiled at me and bent to kiss my head.

Lindsey threw her arms around him. "Daddy, we were worried. What took you so long?"

"I wanted to wrap up this case." He sighed in relief. "It's done. Now, let's have Christmas. I just want to be with my family." He turned and stood over TJ, where he slept among the packages. When he stooped to pick him up, Donnie protested. "I can do that, sir." But my father shook his head. He slid his big hands beneath TJ and drew him to his chest. TJ's hand went to his grandpa's face, and I saw my father kiss it as he passed by on his way to the bedroom.

"Mama, is he okay?" I asked when the Judge was out of the room. "He doesn't look right."

"He's just tired. He's been obsessed with getting caught up on his work and hasn't been home before nine in over two weeks."

"What about the bad guy? Does Sheriff Byron have any leads?"

Mom shook her head. "Nothing. They couldn't trace the calls, and there haven't been any more since they put a tracer on the phone. We found footprints out next to the garage." She shivered. "He may have been watching us through the kitchen window."

"I don't want to hear another word about this!" The Judge stood in the doorway. "He can't steal our peace unless we let him. For the next two days we will speak only of what is good and right with the world—life and truth and love. Do you understand?"

We nodded, though at the time no one really understood.

The next morning, the mountains held the snow clouds back for a few hours while the sun chased every dark thought away. Donnie took TJ with him to the ranch to do some chores. Mom diced celery and onions for stuffing, while Lindsey and I rolled out our traditional Norwegian potato lefse. That night, for Christmas Eve dinner, the thin pancakes would be buttered and sprinkled with brown sugar, then rolled and cut into finger-length logs.

The Judge caught our mother beneath the mistletoe that Lindsey had hung over the entry to the dining room. I watched him kiss her. She laughed, embarrassed by this show of passion "in front of the children." He never passed my chair without touching me. He brought me tea. He insisted that Donnie sit in his big leather chair because it was more comfortable for a guy as big as he.

That evening, the snow fell again. We ate Cornish game hens with stuffing. There were stories and laughter and even an outbreak of song when Donnie found out that TJ didn't know the words to "Rudolph the Red-Nosed Reindeer." My son's face glowed.

Donnie and David brought in wood and stoked the fire in the living-room fireplace. Fresh cedar branches lined the mantle where old-fashioned kerosene lanterns glowed. The Judge read the story of Jesus's birth from the Gospel of Luke, just as he had done every Christmas Eve throughout my childhood. TJ lay on the floor near his grandpa's feet as he listened.

The Judge closed his Bible reverently and looked at each face around the room. "Let's pray." He prayed a blessing on each one by name, even Donnie. He talked to God about us, like it was just him and God and we weren't even there listening. I peeked at Donnie. His head was bowed, and he wiped his eyes. My own eyes misted.

The room remained hushed after the Amen, until TJ sprung to his feet. "Now can we open a present, Grandpa? Just one!"

My father grinned. "Okay, son. Pick one."

TJ zoomed right in on the package from Donnie, which he had shaken all day. He tore off the paper, and we all oohed and aahed as TJ took aim and snapped his first slingshot.

My son hung his stocking on the hook beneath the fireplace mantle where I used to hang mine. Then Donnie carried him off to bed and I followed a few minutes later to tuck him in. I was weak by the time I reached the end of the hall. The bedroom door was open, and I rested against the wall, smiling as I listened to their dialogue.

"Hey, Don?"

"Yeah, buddy."

"Maybe we can go shoot my slingshot tomorrow."

"Sure. You come over to the ranch with me."

"And let's don't bring that lady this time."

"Who, Rachel? You don't like Rachel?"

My heart began its slow sink.

"Mm. She's okay. I just like it better when it's just you and me. So we can pee in the snow if we want to."

"No girls next time," Donnie said. "Now let's get some sleep. Santa's probably up there waiting."

I returned to the living room to find Mom starting a movie. "Come on, Sam. It's time for *It's a Wonderful Life*."

"I'll pass," I said.

Mom came over and brushed the hair off my forehead. "You've overdone it, haven't you, honey? Why don't you go on to bed now."

"I think I will. Good night, Mom." I kissed her cheek.

If Santa were up there waiting for me to fall asleep, he would be circling all night. Who on God's green earth was this Rachel person? I had become used to sleeping in an upright position against a bank of pillows, as it relieved the pressure my oversized heart put on my lungs. But that night, nothing worked.

Finally I pushed myself up and pulled the curtains away from the window. There was no moon, but I could see snow falling in the soft yellow light off the back porch. I pulled the quilt from my bed and slipped my boots on without tying the laces. The house was dark except for the nightlight in the hall and the colored lights on the tree. I tiptoed to the kitchen and slipped out the back door.

Under the eaves of the porch was the old Adirondack chair that Matthew had made for my mother. It squeaked as I settled into it, wrapping the quilt around myself. Matt would be coming tomorrow for Christmas dinner, and I was happy about that. But at the moment, my Christmas joy was smothered by a dark cloud named Rachel. Donnie should be TJ's daddy. He was meant to be a part of us. Of me. It was a pity that it took the threat of another woman to make me finally realize what Donnie meant to me.

I stifled the cough that tore from my chest. The cold had seeped inside my blanket. I stood to go inside just as I heard a muffled sound. I had thought nothing of the light escaping through the doorway in the barn until now. Didn't the Judge usually turn the lights out after he tended to the worms? Was he still out there?

I was off the steps before I knew it, headed for the barn, terrified by what I might find. I trudged in the footprints my father must have made hours ago, now half filled with new snow. Snow stung my face. I paused to catch my breath, then pressed on to where the yellow light from the barn door fell on the rumpled snow.

I gripped the edge of the door, which was open slightly. My father's sobs rang out clearly.

"Oh, God, my God. Let there be some other way!"

I was shocked to find my father alone. His back was to me, and he knelt by a bale of hay. His shoulders shook, and he wept audibly.

My throat grew tight. In a moment I found myself at his side, my own eyes welling up with tears. "What's wrong?"

He spun to look at me. "Samantha!" His face was wet.

I knelt, and my arms went around his neck. "What happened?"

"Oh, Sammy." He pulled me to his chest in a fierce embrace.

I felt his arms close around me. He rocked me back and forth, and I was eight years old again. He smelled the same. Old Spice and sweat. A warm tear fell on my neck. I held him tight.

Moments later he straightened. "What are you doing out here?" He brushed the melting snow from my hair and studied my face. I lifted my chin, trying to ignore the pain that radiated from my chest.

"I heard you," I gasped. "I thought you were in trouble."

He smiled sadly. "I was just praying." He sat up on the hay bale and pulled me onto his lap, wrapping the blanket that was still on my shoulders tightly around me. "Tell me something, Sammy. What do you see yourself doing when you're thirty? Where will you live? What will you do for fun?"

"I'm sorry. I don't know how to play this game."

"It's no game; it's dreaming. A very important part of life. You can have anything you want; you can be anything you want; you can be with anyone you want."

"Okay. I'd be with TJ, of course. He would be—what?—eleven by then, fifth grade. We would live in a little house on the river."

My father was pleased with this. He closed his eyes and leaned his head back ever so slightly.

"I'm not really good at anything, so I don't know what I'd do for a living. But in my spare time I'd like to fish. I would teach TJ to fly-fish. I'll probably volunteer at his school a lot too."

"Will you get married?"

This one threw me. "I guess I would marry Donnie. If he . . ."

"If he what?"

"Well, I'm not the spunkiest trout in the pond, you know. I think he has other options."

"Oh. Well, maybe you're going to have to fight for him."

"Like I said, I don't have the spunk or the splash or the succotash that I used to. I'm too tired to fight right now."

"That will be over soon. After your surgery you'll feel great."

I nodded. "That's what they say. Am I getting too heavy?"

"Yes. But I don't want to put you down. It's been so long since you would do this."

"Probably because I'm a grown-up now."

"No. It started long before that."

I slid off his lap but stayed close to him. "You didn't love me like you love Lindsey. I always knew that. But it's probably because I was adopted and she . . . well, she's your own."

His eyes looked pained, like I had calmly slid a knife into his belly. "Is that what you thought? By God, Samantha. I never loved one of you more than the other. Your mom and I loved you before we ever laid eyes on you. You were our first, you know—you were the first to take a step, the first to say my name. Your sister was always four months behind you. And the two of you together, well, let's just say I felt like a blessed man. But you were different. I had to treat you differently. Lindsey was happy to stay by your mother's side, learning to cook, having tea parties and the like. You, on the other hand, were an adventurer. Always doing the unexpected. I had to discipline you more, but that was because I loved you."

I felt myself melting into him, both from weakness and a strange, overwhelming need. "I was a pain in the butt, wasn't I? I'm a screwup. I always have been." This gush of honesty was a surprise to me, but I let it go. "I guess I turned out to be everything you hate."

His eyes narrowed. "You know what I hate? I hate the choices you've made that are destructive. But I love you. I always have. I abhor the lies that you've believed. You say you're nothing. I say you're destined for greatness. You can do anything!"

He sighed, raking his fingers through his hair. "I know how I am when I get angry. Like a swarm of Kansas twisters. But you have to understand, Sammy, you're my daughter. I hate anything that might destroy you, whether it's a diseased heart or some lie that you've chosen to embrace. I can't just sit back and see what happens."

A single bulb lit our corner of the barn. My father's shadow covered mine so that I could see only his shape on the dusty floor. "There is a line between right and wrong, Sam. Truth and lies. That's all there is. There is no neutral ground." He paused thoughtfully. "And only the truth will set you free."

I didn't understand the words, but I felt his passion. Something stirred in my spirit.

"The truth is," I said humbly, "if I don't get a new heart very soon, I'm going to die."

My father held my face so I had to look him straight in the eye. "You will have your heart," he said, his eyes ablaze, his deep voice booming with authority. I envied his unwavering optimism. It may have been childish, but I believed him with all my soul.

It felt good to cry. It felt good to lean into my father while he spoke of the future. *My* future. I had forgotten how to dream.

One thing bothered me. "Dad"—it seemed right to call him that, and he looked pleased—"is something wrong? You never told me what you were praying about. Are you in some kind of trouble?"

He shook his head thoughtfully. "No trouble. It's nothing you need to concern yourself with."

I squinted my eyes at him, unconvinced.

It was after midnight when my father helped me to my feet and led me toward the door. He turned off the light over the worm bed, but as he headed for the switch near the barn door, he stopped short. The shadowy figure of a man leaned against the doorframe.

"I saw your light on." The raspy voice was instantly familiar.

"Enrich." My father pushed me gently toward the barn door, away from where the man stood. "I wasn't expecting you tonight."

"But you *were* expecting me." The man swayed slightly.

I looked back at my father, and he waved me toward the house, but as I slid past the opening, the man grabbed my arm. I jerked away reflexively. My father lurched toward him. "Don't touch her!"

"Why?" the man jeered. I saw the gun in his hand. I fell to my knees, and when I looked up, the barrel was pointed at my head. My father pulled back, but like a cobra poised to strike. "Why, Dodd? You got a problem with seeing your kid's blood in the snow?"

My chest was unbearably heavy, and I fought to stay conscious.

The man's eyes were red-rimmed. "That's the way it was with my Ronnie. It looked like him, but there wasn't nobody home. He just laid there like a slab of smoked salmon," he slurred. "He couldn't hear a word I said. And he never will."

"I'm sorry about your son, Enrich. I heard he hung himself in his cell, and I'm sorry about that. I really am. He would have been up for parole in a few more years."

The man swung the gun toward the Judge. "A few?" he cried. "He was in that hole for nine years! The prime of his life. He was the best quarterback this county ever saw. *You* put him there."

My father's fingers moved slightly. I knew he was signaling me to run, but the anvil in my chest anchored me to the spot.

"Your son committed murder. He killed your wife, Enrich. Doesn't that mean anything to you?"

"She had it comin'. She thought she could control everything and everybody. Couldn't even divorce her. She said she would get Ronnie if I did. Said she would convince the court that I was an unfit crazy drunk. I always thought I'd kill her myself, put an end to her abuse. I told Ronnie she would destroy him in the end. I was right about that." He tottered slightly. "I don't know why he did it," he whined. "I told him I would take care of it."

"You had murder in your heart, Enrich, and you still do. You programmed it right into your boy. Ronald was so full of hatred that he was a time bomb ready to go off. *You* destroyed your family. The truth is, *you* killed them. Both of them."

"Shut up!" he sobbed, raising the gun toward my father's face. I heard the hammer click back. Suddenly the gun swung toward me. I was on my hands and knees in the snow.

"No!" My father screamed just as the shot rang out into the night. The sound of it tore through my body. I fell face-first into the snow, plunging like Alice through a bottomless tunnel, helpless and very cold.

CHAPTER TEN

I REMEMBER, as if in a dream, the shouts of strangers, the slamming of vehicle doors, and flashing red-and-blue lights. Once, when I opened my eyes, my mother's distraught face was just above mine. When I looked again, she was gone. I felt myself moving. The man with me held my arms down gently when I tried to push something off my face. I tried to ask him about my father. And Mom. He said, "They're on their way to the hospital. Now you keep breathing. That's it. Good girl. Hang in there." I must have slept for a long time. The siren sounded as though it were the wail of a train, miles away.

In the gray light of morning, I awoke to find myself between fresh sheets in my old hospital room. Tubes ran from hanging IV bags into needles stuck to my arm. The familiar electronic blipping noise of my heart monitor was comforting. I felt no pain other than the usual nagging ache in my chest. Had it all been a dream?

The bed next to mine was empty.

"Welcome home." Christopher leaned through the open door.

Normally I would have said, "If this is home, where is hell?" or something of the sort. Instead, I weakly implored, "Am I shot?"

Christopher shook his head. "No. You're okay."

"Chris, I remember. Some lunatic tried to shoot me."

"So I heard. Lucky for you he missed." He touched my forehead. "You need to rest now. You have to do whatever it takes to get your strength back." He checked the IV needles.

"Where's my family? Is my father okay?"

"They'll be here. I guess there's quite a blizzard going on up north. Now get some sleep while you can."

"Where did Lulu go?"

He patted my shoulder and turned toward the door.

"You know something, Chris. Now tell me!"

Christopher paused with a grin. "I think the old Sam's back." He slipped out the door, then poked his head back in. "I heard your boyfriend blew the lunatic's kneecap off. That ought to teach him." He was gone, leaving me with more questions than I had before.

In spite of it, sleep overcame me again. I awoke to find Dr. Sovold next to me studying my chart. "How do you feel?" he asked.

"Okay."

"Do you think you can get up and walk?" He helped me sit up.

"Where did you put Lulu?"

Dr. Sovold stepped backward and sunk into the chair by my bed. He studied my face for too long, and I knew.

"She passed away in her sleep."

I stared at him for several moments before I could speak. "But I was only gone for two days." She was supposed to drive to Monterey with the Wacky Widows in June. She just wanted to dine on enchiladas and watch the sea lions. How could she be dead?

The doctor watched me intently. "She was tired. I think she knew she wouldn't have the strength to go through the operation even if she did get a donor heart. She called her son earlier that day and spoke for some time. Her daughter too. Lulu seemed ready. At peace, you know? Are you okay?"

I nodded.

Dr. Sovold helped me out of bed. "I'd like you to take a walk down the hall. Can you do that for me?"

I felt a little shaky. "Did you guys put something in my IV?"

The doctor smiled. "Something to help you sleep. It should be just about out of your system now. Give me a walk around the hall, and when you get back, your nurse is going to take some blood."

When I returned from my journey, I was hungry. Christopher took blood from my arm. I had seen food trays going into other rooms, but Chris said I would have to eat later. We had to do some more tests. He ran me through the procedures, which seemed to go faster than usual, and then wheeled me back to my room.

Dr. Sovold met us there. "You're looking more awake now. Are you feeling good?"

"Good?" I shrugged. "I wouldn't go that far, but I'm better. Except I missed lunch." I shot Christopher an accusing glare.

Dr. Sovold leaned toward me. "You need to have an empty stomach to go into surgery."

"What surgery?"

"We may have a donor, Samantha." I sat up straight. "There is an accident victim with type AB blood that may be a match. That's why we had to run the tests on you again. I think you're strong enough to undergo the surgery. What do you think?"

This was it. Maybe my only chance for survival. "I'm ready."

"Your family has been informed. They're having a hard time getting here because of the snow. We may have to go before they can get here, Samantha. Can you handle that?"

Tears came to my eyes. I nodded. "But I need to talk to TJ first."

"Let me see what I can do," Christopher said, and left the room.

"What happened? Is it a woman or . . ."

The doctor shook his head. "You know we can't tell you that. The donor heart is in another city. The transplant team is flying there now. Once the heart is harvested, we'll know if it's a match. Then we'll have a matter of a few hours to transport it and get it up and running inside you." Dr. Sovold smiled reassuringly.

"Is it still snowing?" I asked.

"It's clearing up. The pilot is good. He's flown in worse weather than this. Now rest for a little bit. I'll be back."

I settled onto the bed, my mind whirling. It was happening. "Oh, dear God. Let it be a match." Immediately I felt guilty. "I'm sorry about those other people whose . . . person died." I pictured them wailing over their loved one's body. "Help them. Help me."

The ringing of the telephone by my bed startled me. "Hello."

"Sammy."

"Mom!" I began to cry. "Where are you? I'm getting a heart. I'm about to go into surgery."

"I know, we heard. We're coming, honey."

"I'm all by myself here. What happened to you guys?"

"I'll tell you all about it when I get there." I thought she was crying too. "We're coming as soon as we can. You be strong, Samantha Jean. I'm praying for you." Now she sobbed openly. "I'm not crying because I'm afraid. Do you understand? I just want to be there with you. This is what we've been waiting for, Sammy."

"I love you, Mom."

She didn't answer. I thought I heard Lindsey's voice in the background. "Mom?"

"Sam, this is David. We're about to lose you. This is a bad cell zone. We're on our . . . sorry about—" The phone went dead.

Christopher returned to my bedside. "Okay, here's the phone number where your son is staying." I recognized the number immediately. I had dialed it almost every day when Donnie and I used to play together. Christopher punched in the number. "Hello. This is Samantha Dodd's nurse. Is TJ there?" I reached for the phone.

"Teej?"

"Mommy!"

"What are you doing, baby? Is Donnie with you?"

"No, just his mother. Why did you go back to the hospital? We were s'pose to have Christmas. But when I waked up, I was here."

"I'm sorry, Teej. I didn't mean to get sick again. But I have good news. I think they found me a heart! I'll probably be better soon."

"Oh." His voice was tiny, and I heard sniffles. "Mommy, I want to go home. Please. Just you and me and Grandpa and Grandma. I have a present for you under the Christmas tree. I made it."

"Ooh, I wish I could have it right now." Christopher passed me a tissue. "TJ, we'll have Christmas—just a little late, that's all."

"When is Donnie coming back? I don't have my slingshot here."

"I don't know. I want to ask you something, Teej. Do you know your aunt Lindsey loves you? And David too. You have a big family now. It's not just you and me anymore. You have Grandpa and Grandma—lots of people to love you. Do you know that?"

"Uh-huh."

"Do you love them?"

"Yeah."

Dr. Sovold was back, along with two other doctors. A nurse wheeled in a tray with syringes and pills on it.

"I have to go, sweetie." I longed to touch his perfect skin. "I'm going to have an operation now. I love you, TJ. I love you."

I rolled my face into the pillow and had a good cry. Christopher rubbed my back gently. "Are you okay now?" he asked after a respectful silence. I wiped my face on the sheet and nodded.

Dr. Wilhelm, the transplant surgeon, smiled patiently down at me. "It looks like we've got a match, Samantha."

I managed a smile. "That's great. Okay, let's get this over with."

I took a pill to discourage my T cells from attacking the foreign tissue, while Dr. Wilhelm described the horrible things they were about to do to me. The donor heart was flying here by chopper in a cooler. They would have my chest sawed open before the cooler hit the elevator. My old heart would be cut out while a machine took over, pumping blood and breathing for me, and the new heart would be inserted and attached one blood vessel at a time.

"This is going to help you relax," Dr. Sovold said as he slid a needle into the IV receptor they had attached to the back of my hand. "Let's let that kick in; then we'll wheel you on down to the OR."

My own family should have been gathering around a ham and

sweet potatoes right then instead of fighting their way out of a blizzard to be by my side. How could my thinking have become so twisted that I thought I didn't need them? I longed to see their faces now, every one of them—Mom, Dad, Lindsey, even David.

All too soon the doctor said it was time to go.

"Can we wait just a little longer for my family to get here?"

"We've got a healthy heart on the way, Samantha. Good tissue match, good size. We need to have that pumping in you within a few hours. Dr. Tyler's going to hook you up to his magic formula, you'll shut your eyes, and when you open them again, you'll see your family. It'll be like blinking. Poof! And there they are."

"Poof!" I liked the sound of that. "Poof!"

"It's working already," I heard someone say.

They were wheeling me out when Donnie came. He shouted from the elevator. "Wait!"

I rolled my face to the side and smiled. "Hi, Donnie."

He ran to my side. "Sam, I tried to get here sooner. Are you . . . I guess you're going into . . . Hey, buddy, can you slow down?"

"Ooh, Donnie's cranky."

He glanced at Christopher, who grinned. "She's feeling happy."

"Sammy, I'll be here when you wake up," Donnie said. "You're going to be fine."

"Maybe." I yawned. "If not, you've got a backup."

"Backup? What do you mean?"

"You know. Rachel. Plan B. Or maybe she's Plan A and I'm Plan B. Which is it, pray tell?"

We arrived at the doors to the OR. Donnie leaned into my face. "Do you really care, Sam? Tell me. Do you love me, Sam?"

"I'm sorry," Christopher interjected. "I hate to interrupt, but you can't come in here and we've got to keep moving." Donnie stepped aside, and the doors parted. The gurney pushed through.

I couldn't see him anymore. "Donnie!" I tried to shout. "Yes. I do. I love you!" The doors closed. "Isn't that amazing, Christopher?" I yawned. "I think he loves me too."

The blue people with white masks laughed and cheered.

IN AND OUT OF CONSCIOUSNESS, in and out of the light. Voices were real, and then they were a dream. Finally my eyes opened. A tube had been shoved down my throat; hoses ran from my nose, my arm. I moved one hand slowly toward my chest. A nurse beckoned to someone behind her. Dr. Sovold appeared and grinned.

"Well?" I tried to say. It came out as a moan. I rolled my head to one side. Machines, wires, and tubes all around me. There was a dull pain in my chest, and the thing in my throat made me want to gag.

"How are you feeling, Sam?" Dr. Sovold asked.

I could only blink. In Morse code it was not a nice answer.

The nurse left, returning momentarily with Dr. Wilhelm, my transplant surgeon. He glanced at the monitors and smiled at me. "It went real well, Samantha." Above his surgical mask his blood-shot eyes looked kind and sincere. "You've got a beautiful, healthy heart. We were in surgery for less than five hours. We hooked that baby up and she started running like she never missed a beat." He winked. "How about that?" A blink was all I could do. "I know you're feeling uncomfortable. This tube in your throat is a ventilator. Try to let it do the breathing for you. It's only for a few days. . . ."

A beautiful, healthy heart. I didn't hear much after that. It pumped inside me now. I listened. Closing my eyes, I imagined my-self strong—running, laughing, chasing TJ. Like highlights from a movie preview, the images played before me, and in each scene I beamed with joy. I splashed through the creek, skipped like a schoolchild. I twirled, arms outstretched, spinning beneath the sun.

My mother cried when she saw me. I knew she felt terrible about not being with me before I went into the OR, and now here I lay with tubes everywhere, bandaged like a mummy, unable to speak. David supported her by the arm and led her out of the room. "I'm sorry," she said, and then I heard her sobbing in the hall.

My sister came in and stood beside me, gently touching the fin-gers that protruded below my IV splint. "She's exhausted," Lindsey explained. "We all are. None of us have slept." She smiled at me, but I could tell by her swollen eyes that she had cried too. "We're so happy for you, Sam. You're going to be fine now."

I tried to ask about my father and Donnie and TJ, but Lindsey couldn't understand me. She started fussing with my pillows and covering up my toes. "Do you want me to get the nurse?" I closed my eyes and pretended to be tired.

I cradled my new heart, embraced it with body and soul. With every pulse I sensed my donor. Sometimes I cried for her, or him. Most of the time I found myself silently saying *thank you,* and our heart seemed to answer in an unspoken language. One body lay on my bed, and yet I was not alone. I would never be the same.

On the third day the doctors removed the tube from my throat. I sat up from my bed, raised my arms, and laughed. "I have risen!"

Christopher chuckled. He helped me take a short walk and then checked all my vitals. "You are a new woman! You'll be on the treadmill in a few days. Time to get back in shape."

"Bring it on. I can handle anything. I'm ready to see TJ now. I don't look so scary anymore. Will you tell my mother, Chris? And where is my father? He hasn't been here at all."

"Are you sure? You've been sleeping a lot." He tossed my cosmetic kit onto the bed. "You might want to do something with your hair."

I looked in the mirror and smiled. "Did you notice, Chris? Look at the color in my cheeks. That's not makeup."

He took the comb from my hand. "Let's see what a French braid looks like on you." He pulled my hair back gently.

"What's the matter, Chris?"

"What do you mean?"

"You seem preoccupied . . . or sad."

He kept braiding silently for a moment. "I guess I'm just concerned about you," he said.

"There's nothing to worry about, Chris. Trust me; my body won't reject this heart. I'm going to do all the right things. I've changed. I feel it, Chris. I can do anything now. I can get a job—and a house! A house by the river so TJ can have the kind of childhood I did."

He grinned and hugged me.

There was a light tap on the door. Dr. Sovold peered in, then motioned and was followed by Mom and Matthew.

"Hey, Matt! Hey, Mom." They all pulled up chairs next to my bed. "What's up? Where's Dad?"

I called him Dad again, which still seemed new to me, but no one seemed to notice. Mom was smiling. "You look wonderful." She touched my cheeks, and I knew she was seeing me healthy for the first time since I left home as a teenager. Matt leaned forward, resting his arms on his knees. Dr. Sovold's chair was pushed back a little, like he was just there as an observer or something. Christopher nervously excused himself and left the room.

"Is something up?" Mom's eyes darted toward Matt as he cleared his throat. I sat up a little straighter and took a deep breath.

Matt sighed, then let his eyes meet mine. His lower lids immediately filled with tears. He shook his head with a weak laugh. "I wasn't going to do that." Mom reached over and placed her hand on his arm. "You know I love you, Sammy," he began. "I'm so happy for you. You look like you've come back to life again." He placed his hand over Mom's. "This is a happy day, Sammy." He sighed. "But we got ourselves some sadness too."

"Where's Dad?" I stifled a sob. "Where's my father, Matthew?"

He broke down and cried. "I'm sorry. I'm sorry."

My body fell against the pillows propped behind me.

Mom took a deep breath and squared her shoulders. "Sammy, we're going to tell you the truth now. The doctor says you're strong enough. I don't know what you were doing out in the barn that night." She shook her head. "I thought you were asleep in your bed. Dwight Enrich is the one who's been prowling around, harassing us. Do you remember, honey? Do you remember that night?"

I nodded. It was all coming back to me. It seemed so unreal. I had been whisked into surgery so fast afterward that it seemed like a bad dream. "I was on my knees. His gun was pointed at me."

Matt wiped his face. "Your father took the bullet, Sammy. We found him on top of you." He began to stroke my hand.

It was supposed to be me. Enrich wanted to kill me. "I asked Christopher that next morning. He said Dad was alive!"

Matt shook his head. "The bullet went through here"—he pointed to his jaw—"and lodged in his head. He was unconscious. An ambulance took him to Darlington. Another one took you here. The surgeons were trying to get the bullet out . . . but Sammy, they couldn't save him."

My eyes were fixed on my mother. She sat there, regal and strong, with moist eyes. My father was the only man she had ever loved.

"Mom," I croaked, "I'm so sorry." It was a while before any of us spoke. I used my sheet as a tissue. "Where is he now?"

Mom smiled. Matthew reached out and took my hand, gently placing it on my chest. "He's here, Sammy. He's right here."

CHAPTER ELEVEN

MAY came again. Purple lilacs bloomed on the bush outside my mother's bedroom window, and their scent, combined with the spicy fragrance of the new cottonwood buds, was almost more than I could bear. I swear there has never been a spring so perfect.

Donnie climbed the grand old cottonwood that stood near the intersection of our creek and the river and tied one end of a rope to a thick limb; the other end he triple-knotted around an old tire. He held the tire in the crook of his elbow as he climbed the nearby slope and then, with a running start and a Tarzan yell, swung out over the creek. He and TJ went double next, laughing like two little boys. They wanted to go again, but I wrestled the tire away from them and ran up the hill. I pushed off and swung wide over the creek and back again. The tire began to spin as I lay back, holding onto the knot, admiring the sky above me.

When I was a child, I hung by my knees from the lower branches of that very tree. Sometimes I sprawled on the heavy limbs and watched my father fish. He would turn his head from time to time and look at me there among the leaves that flapped in the breeze.

I never went to his grave, and I never will. He is not there.

The Judge's memorial service was held at the Darlington Community Church. The place was packed. Friends and relatives gave glowing tributes, including Matt, who broke down and cried twice, as we all did, right along with him.

It was a terrible thing that happened, the father of a convicted killer taking his revenge on the judge who sentenced his son. But Enrich's rage had turned on me. What better way to repay the Judge? An eye for an eye, a daughter for a son. The news media loved it. My father saved me twice. Once by taking my bullet and then by giving me his heart. It was a great story, but the media really didn't get it. How could they? They didn't know what I knew—what Matt told me while I was still in the hospital—which I couldn't comprehend for some time. In fact, there are still days when I am so overtaken by the truth that I fall to my knees and cry.

After the service a lot of people came to our house with food. They milled about, reminiscing and chatting. People said a lot of nice things to me about my father. They said they were happy for me and that I must be proud to have his heart beating inside me. After the hundredth person asked me how it felt to have my father's heart, I ducked down the hall to the refuge of the Judge's study.

The room had not changed. I settled into my father's leather throne and pulled my feet up. My mother had dusted the worn leather Bible on the Judge's desk, an antique brass fishing reel, a glass display case of tied flies. Everything was left in its place, like she expected him to return any day.

My father knew that he had type AB blood, just like mine. I was not his daughter by blood, but somehow we ended up with the same blood type. Matthew said the Judge called him one day last fall and asked him to come up; he had something serious to discuss. The Judge confided in his trusted friend his knowledge of our blood match and pumped the doctor with questions about other factors necessary for a good match. He asked Matthew to run tests on his heart. My father wanted to know if his heart was strong.

I was still in the hospital when Matt told me these things. "I'll be honest with you, Samantha," Matt had said. "I told him he was crazy. I told him it's not like giving blood. You've only got one heart, and when it's gone, so are you. He understood all that and yet he kept probing. He wouldn't let it die. Wouldn't let *you* die."

"What on earth did he have in mind? How could he have planned what happened? He couldn't—could he, Matt?"

Matt shook his head. "He didn't really have a plan. He wanted me to help him come up with one. I just couldn't, Sam. I'm a doctor. To him it was a necessary sacrifice; to me it was suicide. I told him I would have no part in helping him arrange his own death."

I remembered that day in early November when Matt stormed out of this very study, leaving the Judge to brood alone. My father must have seen me differently than I saw myself. How else could he even consider giving up his own life for mine?

I closed my eyes and snuggled into the leather chair, pretending that its arms were the arms of my father, holding me like he did that December night in the barn. My father had not been shocked to see Dwight Enrich. Not really. He must have figured out who was making threats on his life. I wondered how long he had known.

My heart beat strongly now. My father's heart, I mean. I placed my hand on my chest, and with every beat I heard his message to me. *I love you . . . love you . . . love you.* He knew just what I was, and yet he loved me all along. I let my body slide to the floor, turning to kneel at the foot of his leather throne, my face on my hands.

I finally understood.

"Oh, Daddy," I wept, "I love you too."

The Newfound Career of
Karen Harter

Vital Stats

RESIDENCE: Mt. Vernon, WA
FAMILY: Husband Jeff, three children
FORMER CAREER: Real estate
FAVORITE AUTHORS: Barbara Kingsolver, Harper Lee, John Steinbeck, Mark Twain
HOBBIES: Boating, kayaking, fishing
WEBSITE: www.karenharter.com

ALTHOUGH she always harbored dreams of writing, it wasn't until she was married, had raised three children, and was deep into a business career that Karen Harter published *Where Mercy Flows,* her first novel.

Like her protagonist, Samantha Dodd, Harter grew up in Washington State, where she and her three siblings spent their youth camping, fishing, and enjoying the outdoors. In high school, an English teacher encouraged Harter's poetry-writing talents and ignited the writing bug in the young student.

For the next several years, Harter continued to write poetry and faithfully kept a journal. Although she was a business major in college, she took several literature courses and read a great deal. But upon graduation, she knew that writing poetry wouldn't pay the rent, so she got a job as a loan officer for a real estate and mortgage company.

Home ownership, marriage, and children quickly followed, and Harter found herself sucked into the world of making money to pay the bills, with no time to pursue her writing dream. "My houses owned me and demanded that I work harder and harder in the mortgage business," she said. "The day after our first child was born, I wrote one joyful sentence in my journal, got interrupted, and didn't make another entry for several years."

But one day many years later, Harter was sitting in church and suddenly felt that she was meant to write a book. Family and friends humored her "revelation," but Harter began attending writers conferences and plugging away at what would eventually become her first novel. In addition, she began freelancing and selling nonfiction articles, including true-life humor stories that were very well received.

In 2003, Harter retired from her real estate career and buckled down to complete *Where Mercy Flows*. Finally, after rewrites and input from her writers conference friends, she finished the manuscript, crossed her fingers, and

Heart Matters

In *Where Mercy Flows*, Samantha Dodd learns she needs a heart transplant to survive. In the United States, a heart transplant is the fourth most common transplant operation, with more than 2,200 cases each year. Thousands more people need transplants every year, but there are not enough donor hearts to go around.

If a patient is lucky enough to find a donor, a new heart doesn't come cheap. Heart transplants cost anywhere from $50,000 to $287,000, with the average being about $148,000.

How successful are heart transplants? The one-year survival rate is about 85 percent, and the five-year survival rate is about 70 percent. The main problem with transplants is graft rejection. Thus, patients must take antirejection drugs for the rest of their now extended lives.

sent it off to agents and publishers. The emotional first novel was quickly scooped up by a major publisher, and Harter's newfound career was truly launched. ∎

MARY HIGGINS CLARK

Two Little Girls in Blue

A NOVEL

1

"HOLD on a minute, Rob. I think one of the twins is crying. Let me call you back."

Nineteen-year-old Trish Logan put down her cell phone, got up from the couch, and hurried across the living room. It was her first time baby-sitting for the Frawleys, the nice people who had moved into town a few months earlier. Trish had liked them immediately. Mrs. Frawley had told her that when she was a little girl, her family often visited friends who lived in Connecticut, and she liked it so much, she always wanted to live there, too. "Last year when we started looking for a house and happened to drive through Ridgefield, I knew it was where I wanted to be," she told Trish.

The Frawleys had bought the old Cunningham farmhouse, a fixer-upper. Today, Thursday, March 24, was the third birthday of their identical twin girls, and Trish had been hired to help first with the party, then to stay for the evening while the parents attended a black-tie dinner in New York.

After the excitement of the party, I'd have sworn the kids were dead to the world, Trish thought as she started up the stairs, heading to the twins' room. The Frawleys had ripped out the worn carpet that had been in the house, and the nineteenth-century steps creaked under her feet.

Near the top step, she paused. The light she had left on in the hall was off. Probably another fuse had blown, she reasoned. The wiring in the old house was a mess. That had happened in the kitchen once this afternoon.

The twins' room was at the end of the hall. There was no sound coming from it now. Probably one of the twins had cried out in her sleep, Trish thought as she inched her way through the darkness. Suddenly she stopped. It's not just the hall light. I left the door open so I could hear them if they woke up. The night-light in the room should be showing. The door's closed. But I couldn't have heard one of them crying if it was closed a minute ago.

Suddenly frightened, she listened intently. What was that sound? In an instant of sickening awareness, she identified soft footsteps. A hint of soft breathing. The acrid smell of perspiration. *Someone was behind her.*

Trish tried to run, but her legs would not move. She felt a hand grab her hair and yank her head back. The last thing she remembered was a feeling of pressure on her neck.

The intruder released his grip on Trish and let her sink to the floor. He turned on his flashlight, tied her up, and blindfolded and gagged her. Then, directing the beam onto the floor, he stepped around her, swiftly covered the length of the hall, and opened the door to the twins' bedroom.

Three-year-olds Kathy and Kelly were lying in the double bed they shared, their eyes both sleepy and terrified. Kathy's right hand and Kelly's left hand were entwined. With their other hands they were trying to pull off the cloths that covered their mouths.

The man who had planned the details of the kidnapping was standing beside the bed. "You're sure she didn't see you, *Harry?*"

"I'm sure. I mean, I'm sure, *Bert,*" the other responded. They carefully used the names they had assumed for this job: Bert and Harry, after the cartoon characters in a '60s beer commercial.

Bert picked up Kathy. "Get the other one. Wrap a blanket around her. It's cold out."

The two men raced down the back stairs, rushed through the kitchen and out to the driveway, not bothering to close the door behind them. Once in the van, Harry sat on the floor of the backseat, the twins wrapped in his beefy arms. Bert drove the van as it moved forward from the shadows of the porch.

TWENTY minutes later they arrived at the cottage where Angie Ames was waiting. "They're adorable," she cooed as the men carried the children in and laid them in the hospital-style crib that had been prepared for them. With a quick, deft movement of her hands she released the gags that had kept the little girls silent.

The children grabbed for each other and began to wail. "Mommy . . . Mommy!" they screamed in unison.

"Sshhhh, sshhhh, don't be scared," Angie said soothingly as she pulled up the side of the crib. She then slipped her arms through the rails and began to pat the girls's dark blond ringlets. "It's all right," she singsonged. "Go to sleep. Kathy, Kelly, go back to sleep. Mona will take care of you. Mona loves you."

Mona was the name she'd been ordered to use around the twins.

"Quiet them down," Bert snapped. "They're making too much noise."

"Relax, Bert. No one can hear them," Harry reassured him.

He's right, thought Lucas Wohl, the one called Bert. One of the reasons he had invited Clint Downes—"Harry"—to join him on the job was because Clint lived as caretaker in a cottage on the grounds of the Danbury Country Club. From Labor Day to May 31 the club was closed and the gates locked. The cottage was barely visible from the service road. It was an ideal spot to hide the twins, and the fact that Clint's girlfriend, Angie, often worked as a babysitter completed the picture.

"They'll stop crying," Angie said. "I know babies. They'll go back to sleep." She began to rub their backs and sing, *Two little girls in blue, lad, two little girls in blue . . ."*

Lucas cursed under his breath, made his way through the narrow space between the crib and the double bed, and walked out of the bedroom, through the living room, and into the kitchen. Only then did he and Clint pull off their hooded jackets and gloves. They had left out a full bottle of Scotch as a reward for success in their mission.

The men sat at opposite ends of the kitchen table, silently eyeing each other. Lucas was reminded once more that they could not have been more different in appearance and temperament. Unsentimental about his appearance, he sometimes played eyewitness and described himself to himself: about fifty years old, scrawny build, average height, receding hairline, narrow face. A self-employed limousine driver, he knew he had perfected the outward appearance of a servile and anxious-to-please employee, a persona he inhabited whenever he dressed in his black chauffeur's uniform.

He had met Clint when they were in prison together and had worked with him on a series of burglaries over the years. They had never been caught, because Lucas was careful. They had never committed a crime in Connecticut, because Lucas did not believe in soiling his own nest. This job had been too big to pass up, and he had broken that rule.

Now he watched as Clint opened the Scotch and filled two glasses to the brim. "To next week on a boat in St. Kitts with our pockets bulging," he said with a hopeful smile, his eyes searching Lucas's face.

Lucas stared back once again, assessing his partner in crime. In his early forties, Clint was desperately out of shape. Fifty extra pounds on his already short frame made him perspire easily, even on a cool March night like this. His barrel chest and thick arms looked incongruous with his cherubic face and long ponytail, which he had grown because Angie, his longtime girlfriend, had one.

Angie. Skinny as a twig, Lucas thought contemptuously. Terrible complexion. Like Clint, she always looked slovenly, dressed in a tired T-shirt and ragged jeans. Her only virtue in Lucas's eyes was that she was an experienced babysitter. Nothing must happen to either one of those kids before the ransom was paid and they could be dropped off. Now Lucas reminded himself that Angie had something else going for her. She's greedy. She wants the money. She wants to live on a boat in the Caribbean.

Lucas lifted the glass to his lips. The Chivas Regal felt smooth on his tongue, and warm and soothing down his throat. "So far, so good," he said flatly. "I'm going home. You got the cell phone I gave you handy?"

"Yeah."

"If you hear from the boss, tell him I have a five a.m. pickup. I'm turning off my cell phone. I need some sleep."

"When do I get to meet him, Lucas?"

"You don't." Lucas downed the rest of the Scotch in his glass and pushed back his chair. From the bedroom they could hear Angie continue to sing.

"They were sisters, we were brothers, and learned to love the two . . ."

THE screeching of brakes on the road in front of the house told Ridgefield Police captain Robert "Marty" Martinson that the parents of the missing twins had arrived home.

They had phoned the police station only minutes after the 911 call came in. "I'm Margaret Frawley," the woman had said, her voice shaking with fear. "We live at Ten Old Woods Road. We can't reach our babysitter. She doesn't answer the house phone or her cell phone. She's minding our three-year-old twins. Something may be wrong. We're on our way home from the city."

"We'll get right over there and check," Marty had promised. Because the parents were on the highway, he'd seen little use in telling them that he already knew something was terribly wrong. The babysitter's father had just phoned from 10 Old Woods Road: "My daughter is tied up and gagged. The twins she was minding are gone. There's a ransom note in their bedroom."

Now, an hour later, the property around the house had already been taped off, awaiting the arrival of the forensic team. Marty would have liked to keep the media from getting wind of the kidnapping, but he knew that was hopeless. The babysitter's parents had told everyone in the hospital emergency room where Trish Logan was being treated that the twins were missing. Reporters would be showing up anytime. The FBI had been notified, and agents were on the way.

Marty braced himself as the kitchen door opened and the parents rushed in. In their early thirties, he thought, as Margaret and Steve Frawley moved hurriedly toward him. A handsome couple in evening clothes. The mother's brown hair hung loose around her shoulders. She was slender, and her intense eyes were a shade of dark blue that seemed almost black as they stared at him.

Steve Frawley, the father, was tall, about six foot three, with dark blond hair and light blue eyes. His broad shoulders and powerful arms caused his too-small tuxedo jacket to strain at the seams. "Has anything happened to our daughters?" he demanded, putting his hands on his wife's arms as though to brace her against possibly devastating news.

There was no gentle way to tell parents that their children had been kidnapped and a ransom note demanding eight million dollars left on their bed. Absolute incredulity showed on their faces.

"Eight *million* dollars! Why not *eighty* million?" Steve Frawley demanded, his face ashen. "We brought every dime we had to the closing on this house. We've got about fifteen hundred dollars in the checking account right now, and that's it."

"Are there any wealthy relatives in either of your families?"

The Frawleys began to laugh, the high-pitched laugh of hysteria. Then Steve spun his wife around, and they hugged each other. The laughter broke, and the harsh sound of his dry sobs mingled with her wail. "I want my babies. I want my babies."

AT ELEVEN o'clock the special cell phone rang. Clint picked it up. "Hello, sir," he said.

"The Pied Piper here."

This guy, whoever he is, is trying to disguise his voice, Clint thought as he moved across the small living room to get away from the sound of Angie's crooning. For God's sake, the kids are asleep, he thought irritably. Shut up.

"I can't reach Bert," the Pied Piper said.

"He told me to tell you he has a five a.m. pickup, so he turned off his phone. I hope that—"

"Harry, turn on the television," the Pied Piper interrupted. "There's a breaking story about a kidnapping. I'll get back to you in the morning."

Clint grabbed the remote and snapped on the TV, then watched as the house on Old Woods Road came into view, the porch light revealing its peeling paint and sagging shutters. The yellow crime-scene tape used to keep the press and onlookers back extended to the road.

"The new owners, Stephen and Margaret Frawley, moved in only a few months ago," the reporter was saying. "Neighbors expected the house to be torn down, but the Frawleys intend to gradually renovate the existing structure. This afternoon some of the neighbors' children attended a birthday party for the missing twins."

The screen was suddenly filled with the faces of the identical twins, their eyes wide in excitement as they looked at their birthday cake. Three candles were on each side of the festive confection. In the center was one larger candle. "The neighbor tells us that the center candle is the one to grow on. The twins are so identical in every way that their mother joked it would be a waste to put a second candle to grow on there."

Clint switched channels. A different picture of the twins in their blue velvet party dresses was being shown. They were holding hands.

"Clint, look how sweet they are. They're just beautiful," Angie said, startling him. "Even asleep they're still holding hands. Isn't that precious?"

He had not heard her come up behind him. Now she put her arms around his neck. "I always wanted to have a baby, but I was told I couldn't," she said as she nuzzled his cheek.

"I know, Angie, honey," he said patiently. This was a story he had heard before.

"Then for a long time I wasn't with you."

"You had to be in that special hospital, honey. You hurt someone real bad."

"But now we're going to have a lot of money, and we'll live on a boat in the Caribbean."

"Very soon. We've always talked about that."

"I've got a good idea. Let's bring the little girls with us."

Clint snapped off the television and grabbed her wrists. "Angie, why do we have those children?"

She swallowed nervously. "We kidnapped them."

"Why?"

"So we'd have lots of money and could live on a boat."

"What happens to us if the police catch us?"

"We go to prison for a long, long time."

"What did you promise to do?"

"Take care of the kids, play with them, feed them."

"And in a couple of days we'll give them back and get our money."

"Clint, maybe we could . . ." Angie stopped. She knew he would be angry if she suggested they keep one of the twins. But we *will,* she promised herself slyly. I know how to make it happen. Lucas thinks he's so smart. But he's not as smart as I am.

MARGARET Frawley folded her hands around the steaming cup of tea. She shivered with cold. Steve had pulled an afghan from the couch in the living room and wrapped it around her, but it did nothing to stop the trembling that shook her entire body.

The twins were missing. Kathy and Kelly were missing. Someone had taken them and left a ransom note. It didn't make sense. Like a litany, the words beat a cadence in her head: *The twins are missing.*

The police had not allowed them to go into the girls' bedroom. "Our job is to get them back," Captain Martinson told them. "We can't risk losing fingerprints or DNA samples by contaminating the area."

The restricted area also included the hall upstairs, where someone had attacked the babysitter. Trish was going to be all right. She was in the hospital. She had told the police everything she remembered. She said she'd been on her cell phone talking to her boyfriend when she thought she heard one of the twins crying. She'd gone up the stairs and realized someone was behind her. She remembered nothing after that.

Had there been someone else, Margaret wondered, someone in the room with the girls? Kelly's the lighter sleeper, but Kathy might have been restless. She may be getting a cold.

If one of the girls started to cry, did someone make her stop?

Margaret dropped the cup she was holding and winced as hot tea splattered the blouse and skirt she had worn for tonight's company dinner. I have to go upstairs, she thought. Maybe the twins are hiding in the closet. They did that once. I pretended to look for them. I could hear them giggling when I called their names.

They must have been terrified when somebody grabbed them, she thought. Somebody is hiding them now.

This isn't happening. It's a nightmare, and I'm going to wake up. *I want my babies.* Margaret closed her eyes.

"Mrs. Frawley."

She looked up. A man had come into the room.

"Mrs. Frawley, I'm FBI agent Walter Carlson. I have three kids, and I know how you must be feeling. I'm here to help you get your children back, but we need your help. Can you answer some questions?"

Walter Carlson's eyes were kind. He didn't look to be more than his mid-forties, so his children were probably not much older than teenagers. "Why would someone take my babies?" Margaret asked.

"That's what we're going to find out, Mrs. Frawley."

Carlson moved swiftly to catch Margaret as she began to slide from the chair.

2

FRANKLIN Bailey, the chief financial officer of a family-owned grocery chain, was Lucas's five a.m. pickup. A frequent overnight traveler up and down the East Coast, Bailey was a regular customer. Some days, like today, Lucas would drive him into Manhattan for a meeting, then wait for him and drive him home.

Bailey lived in Ridgefield, on High Ridge, two blocks from Old Woods. Lucas pulled into his driveway at five minutes to five and kept the car idling to be sure it stayed nice and warm for the bigshot accountant.

The front door of the handsome Tudor-style home opened. Lucas sprang out of the car and opened the rear door.

Bailey, a silver-haired man in his late sixties, murmured a greeting, his tone distracted. But when the car began to move, he said, "Lucas, turn onto Old Woods Road. I want to see if the cops are still there."

Lucas felt his throat tighten. What would make Bailey decide to go by there? he wondered uneasily. He wasn't a gawker. He had to have a reason. Of course, Bailey was a big shot in town. He'd been mayor at one time. The fact that he showed up there wouldn't draw attention to the limo he was in.

"Anything you say, Mr. Bailey. But why would there be cops on Old Woods Road?"

"Obviously you haven't been watching the news, Lucas. The

three-year-old twins of the couple in the old Cunningham house were kidnapped last night."

"Kidnapped! You've got to be kidding, sir."

"I wish I were," Franklin Bailey said grimly. "Nothing like this has ever happened before in Ridgefield. I've met the Frawleys a number of times and am very fond of them."

Of course the cops have no reason to give me a second look, Lucas assured himself. I've been picking up people in and around this town for twenty years, and I've always kept below the radar screen. He knew that his neighbors in nearby Danbury, where he lived, looked at him as a quiet, steady guy.

Lucas drove two blocks, then turned the car onto Old Woods Road. Police barricades were in front of the house where eight hours earlier he had broken in and grabbed the kids. There were media trucks across the street and two policemen in front of the barricades, carrying notebooks.

Franklin Bailey opened the back window and was recognized immediately by the sergeant in charge, who began to apologize that he could not allow him to park.

Bailey cut him short. "Ned, I don't intend to park. But maybe I can be of service. I've got a meeting in New York and will be back by eleven. Who's inside? Marty Martinson?"

"Yes, sir. And the FBI."

"Give Marty my card. I've been listening to the reports half the night. The Frawleys are new in town and don't seem to have close relatives to rely on. Tell Marty that if I can be any help as contact person for the kidnappers, I'm available. Tell him I remember that during the Lindbergh kidnapping, a professor who offered to be a contact person was the one who heard from the kidnappers."

"I'll tell him, sir." Sergeant Ned Barker took the card, then with a somewhat apologetic tone said, "I have to identify anyone who drives past, sir."

"Of course."

Barker then looked at Lucas. "May I see your license, sir?"

Lucas used his eager, anxious-to-please smile. "Of course, officer, of course."

The sergeant examined the driver's license. His eyes flickered over Lucas. Without comment he returned it and wrote something in his notebook.

Franklin Bailey closed the window and leaned back. "All right, Lucas. Let's step on it. That was probably a wasted gesture, but somehow I felt I had to do it."

CLINT was pulled from a heavy Chivas Regal–assisted sleep by the persistent voices of two children calling "Mommy." Having gotten no response, they had begun to try to climb over the high sides of the crib.

Angie lay next to him, snoring. He wondered how much she had had to drink after he went to bed. Angie loved to sit up half the night and watch old movies, a bottle of wine next to her.

He dug an elbow into her side. "Get up."

She burrowed deeper into the pillow.

He shook her shoulder. "I said, 'Get up,' " he snarled.

Reluctantly she lifted her head and looked over at the crib. "Lie down! Get back to sleep, you two!" she snapped.

Kathy and Kelly saw the anger on her face and began to cry. "Mommy . . . Daddy."

"Shut up, I said! Shut up!"

Whimpering, the twins lay down, clinging to each other. The soft sound of their muted sobs escaped from the crib.

"I said, 'Shut up!' "

Angie poked Clint. "At nine o'clock Mona will start to love them. Not one minute sooner."

MARGARET and Steve sat up all night with Marty Martinson and Agent Carlson. After her fainting spell, Margaret had adamantly refused to go to the hospital. "You said yourself that you need my help," she insisted.

Together she and Steve answered Carlson's questions. Once again they emphatically denied they had access to any meaningful sum of money, let alone millions of dollars.

"My father died when I was fifteen," Margaret told Carlson. "My mother's a secretary in a doctor's office. I'll be paying off college and law school loans for another ten years."

"My father is a retired New York City fire captain," Steve said. "He and my mother live in a condo in North Carolina. They bought it before prices went crazy."

When they were questioned about other relatives, Steve admitted that he was on bad terms with his half brother, Richie. "He's thirty-six, five years older than I am. My mother was a young widow when she met my father. Richie always had a kind of wild streak in him. We were never close."

"Where is Richie now?" Carlson asked Steve.

"He's a baggage handler at Newark Airport. He's been divorced twice. He dropped out of college and resents me for getting a law degree." He hesitated. "I might as well tell you. He had a juvenile record and spent five years in prison for his part in a money-laundering scam. But he'd never do anything like this."

"Maybe not, but we'll check him out," Carlson said. "Now let's go over anyone else who might have a grudge against you or who might have come in contact with the twins and decided to kidnap them. Have you had any workmen in the house since you moved in?"

"No. My dad could fix anything, and he was a good teacher," Steve explained. "I've been spending nights and weekends doing basic repairs."

"What about the people you work with?"

"I've been with my company only three months. C.F.G. and Y., a global investment firm."

Carlson seized on the fact that until the twins were born, Margaret had worked as a public defender in Manhattan. "Mrs. Frawley, is it possible that one of the people you defended might hold a grudge against you?"

"I don't think so." Then she hesitated. "There was one guy who ended up with a life sentence. I begged him to accept a plea bargain, but he refused, and when he was found guilty, the judge threw the book at him. His family was screaming obscenities at me when they took him away."

It's odd, she thought as she watched Carlson write something in his notebook. Right now I just feel numb. Nothing else, just numb.

At seven o'clock, as light began to show through the drawn shades, Carlson stood up. "I urge you two to get some sleep. I promise we'll let you know the minute the kidnappers make contact. You can go up to your own room, but do *not* go near the girls' bedroom. The forensic team is still going over it."

Steve and Margaret nodded mutely. Their bodies sagged with fatigue as they got up and walked through the living room, heading to the staircase.

"They're on the level," Carlson said flatly to Martinson. "I'd stake my life on it. They don't have any money. Which makes me wonder if this ransom demand isn't a hoax. Somebody who just wanted the kids may be trying to throw us off."

"I've been thinking that. Isn't it a fact that most ransom notes would warn the parents not to call the police?"

"Exactly. I only pray to God that those kids aren't on a plane to South America right now."

ON FRIDAY morning the kidnapping of the Frawley twins was headline news all along the East Coast, and by early afternoon it had become a national media event. The birthday picture of the beautiful three-year-olds, with their angelic faces and long, blond hair, and dressed in their blue velvet party dresses, was shown on television news and printed in newspapers all over the country.

A command center was set up in the dining room of 10 Old Woods Road. At five o'clock in the afternoon Steve and Margaret appeared on television in front of their home, begging the captors to return the girls unharmed. "We don't have money," Margaret said imploringly. "But our friends have been calling all day. They're taking up a collection. It's up to nearly two hundred thousand dollars. Please, you must have mistaken us for people who could raise eight million dollars. We can't. But please don't hurt our girls. Give them back. I can promise you we will have two hundred thousand dollars in cash."

Steve, his arm around Margaret, said, "Please get in touch with us. We need to know that our girls are alive."

Captain Martinson followed them in the interview. "We are posting the phone and fax number of Franklin Bailey, who at one time was mayor of this town. If you are afraid to contact the Frawleys directly, please contact him."

But Friday evening, Saturday, and Sunday all passed without word from the kidnappers.

Then on Monday morning Katie Couric was interrupted on the *Today* show as she was interviewing a retired FBI agent about the Frawley kidnapping. She suddenly paused in the middle of asking a question, pressed her hand against her earphone, and said, "This may be a hoax, but someone claiming to be the kidnapper is on the phone. At his request our engineers are putting the call on the air."

A husky, obviously disguised voice said, "Tell the Frawleys time is running out. We said eight million, and we mean eight million. Listen to the kids."

Young voices said in unison, "Mommy, I love you. Daddy, I love you." Then one of the girls cried, "We want to go home."

AN INCREASINGLY nervous Lucas stopped in at the cottage on Saturday and Sunday evenings. The last thing he wanted was to spend any time around the twins, so he timed his arrival for nine o'clock, when he thought they would be asleep.

On Saturday evening he tried to feel reassured by Clint's boast that Angie was great with the kids. "They ate real good. She played games with them, put them down for naps. She really loves them. But I tell you, it's almost spooky to watch them. It's like they're two parts of the same person."

"Did you get them on tape?" Lucas snapped.

"Oh, sure. They sound real good. Then one of them started yelling, 'We want to go home,' and Angie raised her hand like she was going to hit her, and they both started crying. We got all of that on the tape, too."

Lucas pocketed the tape. By prearrangement with the boss, he drove to Clancy's Pub on Route 7, arriving there at ten thirty. As instructed, he left the limo in the crowded parking lot with the door unlocked and the tape on the seat and then went in for a beer. When he returned, the tape was gone.

That was Saturday night. On Sunday night it had been clear that Angie's patience was wearing thin. "Damn dryer is broken, and of course we can't call anyone to fix it. You don't think 'Harry' knows how, do you?" As she spat out the words, she was taking two sets of identical shirts and overalls from the washing machine and draping them on wire hangers. "You said it would be a couple of days. How long am I supposed to keep this up?"

"The Pied Piper will tell us when and where to drop the kids off," Lucas reminded her, biting back the desire to tell her to go to hell.

You got to hand it to the boss, Lucas thought the next morning as he watched the show and witnessed the dramatic response to the Pied Piper's phone call. The whole world will be wanting to send money to get those kids back.

But we're the ones taking all the risk, he thought hours later, after listening to the commentators on every station jabbering about the kidnapping. We grabbed the kids. We're hiding them. We're the ones who will pick up the money when they raise it. I know who the boss is, but there's nothing to tie him to me. If we get caught, he could say I was nuts if I say he's behind it.

Lucas had no jobs scheduled until the next morning, Tuesday, and at two o'clock decided there was no way he could sit in his apartment and stew. The Pied Piper had told him to be sure to watch the *CBS Evening News.*

He decided he had time to go for a plane ride. He drove to Danbury Airport, where he was a member of a flying club. There he rented one of the single-engine prop planes and went for a spin. His favorite trip was to fly up the Connecticut coast to Rhode Island, then go out over the Atlantic for a while. Flying two thousand feet above the earth gave him a sense of control he badly needed.

It was a cold day with only a slight breeze and some clouds to the west: fine flying weather. But as he tried to relax in the cockpit and enjoy the freedom of being airborne, Lucas could not shake off a persistent worry that was plaguing him.

He felt certain he had missed something, but figuring out just what—that was the problem. Grabbing the kids had been easy, Lucas thought as he flew over Newport. And, according to news reports, the babysitter only remembered that whoever had come up behind her smelled of perspiration. She got that one right, Lucas thought with a brief grin. Angie should stick Clint's shirts in that washing machine of hers every time he peels one off.

That was it! *Those clothes she was washing.* Two sets of identical shirts and overalls. Where did she get them? The kids had been wearing pajamas when they grabbed them. Had that stupid airhead gone shopping for twin outfits that would fit three-year-olds?

She had. He was sure of it.

THERE was no way to put a good face on delivering the latest communication from the kidnapper. On Monday evening Walter Carlson received a phone call and went into the living room, where Margaret and Steve Frawley were sitting side by side on the couch. "Fifteen minutes ago the kidnapper called the network during the *CBS Evening News,*" he said grimly. "They're replaying that segment now. It has the same tape of the twins' voices they played this morning on Katie Couric, with an addition."

It's like watching people being thrown into a cauldron of boiling oil, he thought as he saw the agony on the couple's faces at the sound of a childish voice protesting, "We want to go home . . ."

"Kelly," Margaret whispered.

A pause.

Then the wailing of the twins began.

Margaret buried her face in her hands. "I cannot . . . cannot—"

Then a harsh, obviously disguised voice snarled, "I said *eight million.* I want it now. This is your last chance."

"Margaret," Walter Carlson interrupted, his tone urgent, "there *is* a bright spot here. The kidnapper is communicating with us. You have proof that the girls are alive. We are going to find them."

"And are you going to come up with an eight-million-dollar ransom?" Steve asked bitterly.

Carlson did not know whether to raise their hopes yet. Agent Dom Picella, heading a team of agents, had spent the day at C.F.G.&Y., interviewing Steve's coworkers to learn if any of them knew of someone who resented Steve, who perhaps had wanted his job. The firm had recently suffered bad publicity because of insider trading accusations, and Picella had learned that a board of directors meeting had been hastily scheduled with conference-call links to directors all over the world. The rumor was that the company might offer to put up the ransom money.

"One of the secretaries is a world-class gossip," Picella had told Carlson late that afternoon. "She says the firm just paid a whopping five-hundred-million-dollar fine imposed by the Securities and Exchange Commission. Her guess is that paying the eight-million ransom gives C.F.G. and Y. better publicity than if they hired a slew of PR agencies to whitewash their image. The board meeting is scheduled for eight o'clock tonight."

Carlson studied the Frawleys, who in the four days since the twins went missing seemed to have aged ten years. Both were pale, their eyes heavy with fatigue, their shoulders slumping. He knew that neither one of them had touched a morsel of food all day. He knew from experience it was a time when relatives rallied around, but he'd overheard Margaret begging her mother to stay in Florida. "Mom, you can do me more good by praying round the clock," she had said. "If you were here crying with me, I don't think I could handle it."

Steve's mother had recently had knee replacements and could neither travel nor be left alone. Friends had flooded the house with calls, but they had been asked to get off the line quickly in case the kidnapper called the Frawleys directly.

Carlson hesitated, then spoke. "I don't want to raise hopes only to have them dashed, but, Steve, your CEO has called an emergency board of directors meeting. I understand there's a chance they'll vote to pay the ransom."

Don't let it go the other way, he prayed as he saw hope come alive in their faces. "Now I don't know about you two," he said, "but I'm hungry. Your next-door neighbor has dinner cooked for you and will send it over anytime you want."

KATHY and Kelly looked up from the couch. They had been watching Barney tapes, but Mona abruptly switched to a television station and listened to the news.

They were both scared of Mona. A little while ago Harry was mad after he got a phone call. Mona had yelled back, "Of *course* I bought some clothes for them, and some toys, and some Barney tapes. And now shut up and go out and get some hamburgers for all of us. I'm sick of cooking. Got it?"

Then, just when Harry came back with the hamburgers, they heard the man on television say, "We may be receiving a call from the kidnapper of the Frawley twins."

As they listened, they could hear Kelly's voice, saying, "We want to go home."

Kathy then squeezed back tears and whispered, "I *do* want to go home. I want Mommy. I feel sick."

"I can't understand a word the kid is saying," Harry complained.

"Sometimes when they talk to each other, I can't understand it, either," Mona said. "They have twin talk. I read about it." She dismissed the subject. "Why didn't the Pied Piper tell them where to leave the money? What's he waiting for? Why did he just say, 'You'll hear from me again'?"

"Bert says it's his way of wearing them down. He's going to make another contact tomorrow." Harry was still holding the McDonald's bag. "Let's eat these while they're hot. Come to the table, kids."

Kelly jumped up from the couch, but Kathy lay down and curled up into a ball.

Mona hurried over and felt her forehead. "This kid is getting a fever." She looked at Harry. "Finish that hamburger fast and go get some baby aspirin. That's all we need is for one of them to get pneumonia."

She bent over Kathy. "Oh, sweetie, don't cry. Mona will take good care of you. Mona loves you best, Kathy. You're Mona's little girl, aren't you?"

3

IN THE Park Avenue boardroom of C.F.G.&Y., Robinson Alan Geisler, the chairman and chief executive officer, waited impatiently while the out-of-town directors confirmed their presence at the eight-o'clock meeting. His job already in jeopardy as a result of the fallout from the SEC fine, Geisler knew that the position he was going to take in the agonizing Frawley situation might be a fatal mistake.

The question was simple: If C.F.G.&Y. offered to pay the eight-million-dollar ransom, would it be a superb public relations gesture or, as he knew some of the directors believed, an invitation for other kidnappers to have a field day?

Gregg Stanford, the chief financial officer, took the latter position. "It's a tragedy, but if we pay to get the Frawley kids back, what do we do when another employee's wife or child is taken? We're a global company, and a dozen of the places where we have offices are potential hot spots for this kind of thing."

Geisler knew that at least a third of the fifteen directors shared that same viewpoint. On the other hand, he told himself, how would it look for a company that had just paid a five-hundred-million-dollar fine to refuse to pay a fraction of that amount to save the lives of two little girls?

At age fifty-six, Rob Geisler had finally achieved the job he wanted. A small, thin man, he had to overcome the inevitable prejudice the business world held against people of short stature. He had made it to the top, but on the way up he had made enemies, and at least three of them were sitting at the table with him now.

The final off-site director reported in, and all eyes turned to Geisler. "We all know why we're here," he said brusquely, "and I'm very much aware of the feeling some of you hold that we're caving in to kidnappers if we pay the ransom."

"That's *exactly* the way some of us feel, Rob," Gregg Stanford said quietly. "This company has already had enough bad publicity. Cooperating with criminals shouldn't even be a consideration."

Geisler looked disdainfully at his colleague, not bothering to hide his intense dislike for the man. In appearance, Stanford was the television version of a corporate executive. He was forty-six years old, six feet four inches in height, uncommonly handsome, with sun-streaked sandy hair. Stanford was always impeccably dressed, his manner unfailingly charming even when he was stabbing a friend in the back. He had married his way into the corporate world—his third and current wife was an heiress whose family owned ten percent of the shares of the company.

Geisler knew that Stanford coveted his job and that if he prevailed in his "no ransom" position, Geisler would be the one the media would turn on when the company publicly declined to offer the money. He nodded to the secretary who was taking minutes of the meeting, and she got up and turned on the television. "I want all of you to watch this," he snapped. "Then put yourself in the Frawleys' position."

At his order the media department had put together a videotape sequencing the events of the kidnapping: the exterior of the Frawley house, the desperate pleas of the parents on TV, the call to Katie Couric, and the later call to CBS. The tape ended with a small voice saying, "We want to go home," then the terrified crying of the twins, followed by the ominous demands of the kidnappers.

"Most of you at this table are parents," he said. "We can at least try to save those children. We may not succeed. We may recover the money, or we may not. But I don't see how any one of you could sit here and refuse to vote to pay the ransom."

He watched heads turn to get Gregg Stanford's reaction. "I say we should not cooperate with criminals," Stanford said.

Norman Bond was the next director to offer an opinion. "I was responsible for hiring Steve Frawley, and I made a very good choice. I vote for offering to put up the money, and I urge that it be a unanimous vote. These children are in jeopardy, and the faster we move to save them, the better the chances that the kidnappers won't harm them."

Bond had hired Frawley when three others in the company had been panting for the job. For the right man it was a shortcut to upper management. "Thank you, Norman," Geisler said. "I suggest we watch the tape one more time and then take a vote."

At eight forty-five the vote was fourteen to one to pay the ransom. Geisler turned to Stanford. "I want a unanimous vote," he said, his tone icy. "Then, as usual, you can feel free to have an anonymous source let the media know that you felt the payment might jeopardize the children. But as long as I sit in this chair and you don't, I want a unanimous vote."

MARGARET managed to swallow a few bites of the roast chicken dinner that neighbor Rena Chapman had sent over. Then, while Steve waited with FBI agent Carlson to learn the outcome of the C.F.G.&Y. meeting, she slipped upstairs to the twins' bedroom.

It was the one room they had fully decorated before they moved in. Steve had painted the walls pale blue and tacked down a remnant of white carpet over the shabby floorboards. Then they had splurged on an antique white four-poster double bed and a matching dresser. We knew it was silly to buy two single beds, Margaret thought as she sat on the slipper chair that had been in her own bedroom as a child. They would have ended up in the same bed anyhow.

The FBI agents had taken the sheets, blanket, quilt, and pillowcases to test for DNA evidence. They had dusted for fingerprints and taken clothing the twins had worn after the party to be sniffed by the dogs that for the past four days had been led by Connecticut state police handlers through the nearby parks. Margaret knew what that kind of search meant. But I don't believe that, she told herself. *They are not dead; I would know it if they were dead.*

On Saturday, after the forensic team was finished and she and Steve made their plea to the media, it had been an emotional outlet to come upstairs and clean their room and remake the bed with Cinderella sheets. *They'll be tired and frightened when they come home,* Margaret had reasoned. *After they come back, I'll lie down with them until they're settled.*

She shivered. *I can't get warm,* she thought. *Even with a sweater under a running suit, I still can't get warm. I want my babies back.*

Margaret got up and walked across the room to the window seat. She bent down and picked up the shabby teddy bears that were the twins' favorite stuffed animals, hugging them against her. She looked out the window and was surprised to see rain. It had been sunny all day—cold, but sunny. *Kathy had been starting a cold.* Margaret could feel sobs beginning to choke her throat. She forced them back and reminded herself of what Carlson had told her.

There are FBI agents searching for the twins—dozens of them. *Others are going through the files at FBI headquarters and investigating anyone who has any record for extortion or child abuse. Captain Martinson is sending policemen to every house in town to ask if anyone saw anybody suspicious. They've even talked to the Realtor who sold us the house to find out who would be familiar with the layout. They say there will be a break. Somebody must have seen something. They're putting the girls' pictures on flyers, on the Internet, on the front pages of newspapers.*

Holding the teddy bears, Margaret walked over to the closet and opened it. She ran her hand over the velvet dresses the twins had worn on their birthday. *The twins had been wearing their pajamas when they were kidnapped. Were they still wearing them?*

The bedroom door opened. Margaret turned, looked at Steve's face, and knew from the vast relief she saw in his eyes that his company had volunteered to pay the ransom money.

"They're making the announcement immediately," he said.

AT NINE FIFTEEN ON MONDAY night, sitting in his apartment over a hardware store in Danbury, Lucas was watching television when a news bulletin interrupted the programming. C.F.G.&Y. had agreed to pay the ransom for the Frawley twins. An instant later his special cell phone rang. Lucas turned on the recording device he had purchased on his way home from the airport.

"It's beginning to happen," the hoarse voice whispered.

Deep Throat, Lucas thought sarcastically. The police have sophisticated voice-imaging stuff. Just in case anything goes wrong, I have something that will help cut a deal with them. I deliver you.

"I was watching for the announcement," he said.

"I called Harry an hour ago," the Pied Piper told him. "I could hear one of the kids crying. Have you checked on them?"

"I saw them last night. I'd say they were okay."

"Mona is taking good care of them? I don't want any slipups."

It was too much for Lucas. "That dumb broad is taking such good care that she's buying matching outfits for them."

This time the voice was not disguised. "Where?"

"I don't know."

"Does she plan to have them all dressed up when we dump them? Does she plan to have the cops tracing the clothes?"

Lucas liked the way the Pied Piper was getting agitated. It took some of the fear off him. "I told Harry not to let her out of the house again."

"In forty-eight hours this will be over. Tomorrow I give instructions about the money. Wednesday you pick up the cash. Wednesday night you leave the kids, wearing exactly what they were wearing when you grabbed them."

The connection ended.

Lucas pushed the stop button on the recording device. Seven million for you; half a million each for me and Clint, he thought. I don't think so, Mr. Pied Piper.

THE time for Robinson Geisler to stand with Margaret and Steve Frawley and address the media was set for ten a.m. on Tuesday morning. Shortly before ten Margaret and Steve walked down the stairs of their farmhouse. In the foyer she approached Robinson Geisler. "I am so grateful to you and your company," she said.

Steve opened the front door and took her hand as cameras began to flash. Joined by Geisler, they walked to the table and chairs that had been set up for the interview. She was glad to see that Franklin Bailey, who had offered to be the intermediary, was also present.

The overnight rain had stopped. The late March morning hinted of spring. Margaret looked blankly at the gathered media, at the police officers holding back the onlookers, at the row of media trucks along the road. She listened to Geisler offer to pay the ransom and to Franklin Bailey as he offered his services as contact person.

"Mrs. Frawley, now that you know the kidnapper's demands are being met, what is your greatest fear?" someone asked.

A stupid question, Margaret thought. "Of course my greatest fear is that something will go wrong between the payment of the ransom and the return of our children. I believe Kathy was beginning to get a cold. She goes into bronchitis easily. We almost lost her when she was an infant." She stared into the camera. "Please, I beg of you, if she is sick, get some medicine. The girls were just wearing pajamas when you took them."

I didn't know I was going to say that, she thought. Why did I say that? There was a reason, but she couldn't remember it. It was something about the pajamas.

Mr. Geisler, Steve, and Franklin Bailey were answering questions. So many questions. Suppose the girls were watching them. I must talk to them, Margaret thought. Interrupting a reporter, she said abruptly, "I love you, Kelly. I love you, Kathy. We'll find a way to bring you home very soon."

AT FIVE o'clock that afternoon Franklin Bailey's neighbor, retired judge Benedict Sylvan, pounded on his door. When Bailey yanked it open, a breathless Sylvan blurted out, "Franklin, I just received a phone call. I think it's from the kidnapper. He's going to call you at my house in three minutes."

The two men rushed across the wide lawns that separated their houses. They had barely reached the judge's open door when the phone rang in his study. The judge raced ahead to grab the phone. Gasping for breath, he managed to say, "Franklin Bailey is with me," and handed the phone to Bailey.

The caller identified himself as the "Pied Piper." His instructions were brief and explicit: By ten tomorrow morning, when he would call again, C.F.G.&Y. was to be prepared to wire seven million dollars to an overseas account. The remaining million dollars—divided evenly into two suitcases—was to be ready for delivery. Used fifty- and twenty-dollar bills, and their serial numbers must be nonsequential. "When the wire transfer goes through, further instructions will be issued for delivery of the cash."

Bailey had been scribbling on a pad on the judge's desk. "We must have proof that the girls are alive," he said.

"Hang up now. In one minute you will hear the voices of the two little girls in blue."

Franklin Bailey and Judge Sylvan stared at each other as Bailey returned the phone to the cradle. Moments later it rang. When he picked it up, a childish voice said, "Hello, Mr. Bailey. We saw you on television with Mommy and Daddy."

A second voice whispered, "Hello, Mr.—" But a deep, racking cough interrupted her words as the line went dead.

As the Pied Piper was giving instructions to Franklin Bailey, Angie was pushing a cart through the aisles of the local CVS drugstore, shopping for anything she thought might keep Kathy from getting any sicker. She'd already tossed baby aspirin, nose drops, rubbing alcohol, and a vaporizer into the cart.

Grandma used to put Vicks in the vaporizer when I was a kid, she thought. I wonder if you're still supposed to do that. Maybe I'd better ask Julio. He's a good pharmacist. She knew that Lucas would have a fit if he thought she was buying any baby products. But what does he want me to do, let the kid die?

She pushed the cart into the pharmacy section, then felt her mouth go dry. A life-size picture of the twins was displayed next to the counter. In bold letters the headline read MISSING. REWARD FOR INFORMATION.

There was no one waiting, and Julio beckoned to her. "Hi, Angie," he said, then pointed to the picture. "Pretty awful, that kidnapping. You have to wonder who could do anything like that."

"Yeah, it's awful," Angie agreed.

He shook his head. "Angie, what can I do for you?"

Aware of the nervous perspiration gathering on her forehead, Angie made a show of fishing through her pocketbook. "Can't do much. I guess I forgot my prescription." Even to her ears, the explanation sounded lame.

"I can call your doctor."

"Oh thanks, but he's in New York. I know he won't be there now. I'll come back later."

She thought back to the time she'd gotten liniment for Clint's shoulder. She had talked with Julio for a couple of minutes and had happened to mention that she lived with Clint in the caretaker cottage of the country club. That had been at least six months ago, yet Julio had remembered her name. Would he remember where she lived as well? Sure he would!

She watched as his gaze flickered over the contents of her cart. Will he get to wondering why I was buying stuff for a sick kid? Angie pushed back the frightening possibility. She was there on a mission. I'll buy a jar of Vicks and stick some of it in the vaporizer, she decided. It worked good enough when I was a kid.

She hurried back to aisle 3, grabbed the jar of Vicks, and rushed to the checkout. One register was closed; the other one had six people on line.

Hurry up, Angie thought, giving her cart an impatient push.

The guy in front of her, a heavyset man with a loaded shopping cart, turned around. His look of annoyance changed to a broad grin. "Hi, Angie. What are you trying to do, cut my feet off?"

"Hi, Gus," Angie said, attempting a smile. Gus Svenson was a pesky guy they sometimes ran into when she and Clint ate at the

Danbury Pub, the kind of jerk who was always trying to start a conversation with other people at the bar. A plumber with his own business, he did work at the golf club during the season. So the fact that she and Clint lived in the caretaker cottage made Gus act as if they had something big in common. Blood brothers because they did grub work for people with money, she thought with contempt.

"How's my boy Clint?" Gus asked.

Gus was born with a loudspeaker on his vocal cords, Angie thought as people turned to look at them. "Never better, Gus."

Gus peered in Angie's basket. "Baby aspirin. Baby nose drops. Hey, you two got news for me?"

Angie's worry about the pharmacist now deepened into outright fear. Lucas was right, she thought. I shouldn't be shopping for anything for the kids, or at least I shouldn't be shopping where they know me. "Don't be silly, Gus," she snapped. "I'm babysitting for a friend, and the kid's getting a cold."

"Listen, if you're stuck babysitting, maybe Clint would like to meet me for a few beers. I'll pick him up. That way you don't have to worry if he ties one on. I quit when I've had enough. I'll give him a call."

Before she could respond, he had turned back to unload his purchases on the counter. Angie looked at the vaporizer in her cart. She'd had to use the credit card to pay for the outfits for the twins, and she had to use it now.

It'll be over soon, she promised herself. According to Lucas, tomorrow the Pied Piper would get the wire transfer. Tomorrow evening they'd get the million dollars cash. After they were sure it was all there, early Thursday morning they'd drop the kids somewhere and tip the parents off where to find them.

According to Lucas, Angie thought. But not according to me.

4

ON WEDNESDAY morning the unpredictable March weather had once again turned bitterly cold. A biting wind rattled the windows of the dining room where Steve and Margaret sat with Walter Carlson and his colleague, Agent Tony Realto. A second pot of coffee sat untouched on the table.

Carlson had not thought it his right to soft-pedal what Franklin Bailey had said, that one of the twins had a deep bronchial-sounding cough. "Steve and Margaret, I know it's frightening to think that Kathy is sick," he told them.

Across the table, Margaret Frawley's skin was paper white. Her dark blue eyes were heavily circled. "I wonder if whoever has them is giving Kathy anything to keep her from going into pneumonia," she said, her voice breaking.

"My guess is that whoever has the children wants to return them safely."

It was a quarter to ten. The Pied Piper had said he would be in touch at ten o'clock. The three fell into silence. They could only wait.

At ten o'clock Rena Chapman, the Frawleys' neighbor, raced over from her house. "Somebody on my phone says he has important information about the twins for the FBI," she said breathlessly to the police officer on guard outside the house.

Seconds later Realto and Carlson were running to the Chapman home, Steve and Margaret at their heels. Once inside, Carlson grabbed the phone and identified himself.

"Have you got pen and paper?" the caller asked.

Carlson pulled his notebook and pen from his breast pocket.

"I want seven million dollars transferred to account 507964 in the Nemidonam Bank in Hong Kong. You have three minutes. When I know the transfer is completed, I'll call back."

"It will be completed immediately," Carlson snapped. He heard the click of the phone.

"Is it the kidnapper?" Margaret demanded. "Were the girls with him?"

"It was the kidnapper. He didn't refer to the girls. It was only about the ransom." Carlson dialed Robinson Geisler's private number at the executive office of C.F.G.&Y.

Geisler had promised to be waiting there for instructions about the money transfer. In his precise, clipped voice, he repeated the name of the bank in Hong Kong and the account number. "The transfer will be made within sixty seconds, and we have the suitcases with the cash waiting to be delivered," he assured the agent.

Margaret listened as Carlson next barked instructions to the FBI communications unit to try to triangulate the Chapmans' phone line in the hope that they might pinpoint the Pied Piper's location when he called back.

He's too smart for that, Margaret thought. Now he has the seven million dollars. Will we hear from him again?

Carlson had explained to her and Steve that, for a commission, some overseas banks will accept wire transfers, then allow them to be moved again immediately. Suppose that satisfies him, she agonized. Suppose we never hear from him again.

"Mr. Carlson. Another call. Three houses down." A Ridgefield policeman on duty outside the Frawley house had rushed to Rena Chapman's kitchen door and opened it without knocking.

The wind blew Margaret's hair into her eyes as she and Steve, their hands joined, ran behind Carlson and Realto to a house where a neighbor she had never met was frantically waving them in.

The Pied Piper had disconnected, but he called back less than a minute later. "You have been very wise," he told Carlson. "Thank you for the wire transfer. Now get this straight. Your helpful friend, Franklin Bailey, must be standing in Manhattan in front of the Time Warner building at Columbus Circle at eight o'clock tonight. Tell him to wear a blue tie and to have a red tie in his pocket. He must have the suitcases with the money and be carrying a cell phone. What is the number of your cell phone, Mr. FBI Agent?"

"It's 917-555-3291," Carlson said.

"Give your cell phone to Franklin Bailey. Remember, we will be watching him. Any attempt to follow him or to apprehend the messenger who accepts the suitcases will mean that the twins disappear forever. The alternative is that once we have validated the cash, sometime after midnight someone will receive a phone call telling you where to pick up the twins. They're very homesick, and one of them has a fever. I suggest you make sure there are no slipups."

WALKING back from their neighbor's house, clutching Steve's arm, Margaret tried to believe that within twenty-four hours the twins really would be home. I *have* to believe it, she told herself. Kathy, I love you. Kelly, I love you.

In her rush to get first to Rena Chapman's house, then to the second call, she had not even been conscious of the media vans parked on the street. But now the reporters were clamoring for a statement.

"Have the kidnappers contacted you?"

"Has the ransom been paid?"

"Have you got confirmation that the twins are alive?"

"There will be no statement at this time," Carlson said.

Margaret and Steve darted up the walk. Captain Martinson was waiting for them on the porch. Yesterday people in town had pledged a ten-thousand-dollar reward for any information that would lead to the safe return of the twins. Could someone have responded to that? she wondered.

Martinson waited until they were in the living room before he spoke. "We've got a problem," he said. "Franklin Bailey had a fainting spell early this morning and was rushed to the hospital. His cardiogram was okay. His doctor thinks he had an anxiety attack brought on by stress."

"We've just been told by the kidnapper that Bailey is to be in front of the Time Warner building at eight o'clock tonight," Carlson said. "If he doesn't show up, whoever has the children will suspect a double cross."

"But he's *got* to be there!" Margaret heard the hint of hysteria in her voice. "He's *got* to be there."

"He's planning to be there," Martinson said. "He wouldn't stay at the hospital." He and the agents looked at each other.

But it was Steve who voiced what they all were thinking: "Suppose he has another weak spell and becomes confused or passes out while he's getting the instructions on delivering the cash. What happens then? If Bailey doesn't make contact, the Pied Piper said we'd never see our children again."

Agent Realto did not reveal the concern that had been growing in his mind to a virtual certainty. We never should have let Bailey get involved, he thought. And why did he insist on helping?

AT TWENTY minutes past ten on Wednesday morning, Lucas was staring out the front window of his apartment, puffing nervously on his fifth cigarette of the day. Suppose the Pied Piper gets the seven-million-dollar wire transfer and decides to dump us? I have the voice recording of him, but maybe that isn't enough, he thought. If he pulls out, what do we do with the kids?

Even if the Pied Piper plays it straight and arranges delivery of the million in cash, he thought, it will take both me and Clint to try to make the pickup and get away without being caught.

His special cell phone rang. Lucas turned on his recorder.

"Things are going smoothly, Bert," the Pied Piper said. "The wire transfer went through. It's very clear to me that the FBI won't jeopardize the children by following you too closely."

He was using the phony growl that he thought passed for a disguised voice. Lucas ground out the rest of his cigarette on the window sill. Keep talking pal, he thought.

"It's your ball game now," the Pied Piper continued. "If you want to be counting money tonight, listen carefully. As you know, you will need a stolen vehicle."

"Yeah. It's the one thing Harry's good at."

"We will begin making contact with Franklin Bailey at eight o'clock this evening in Manhattan. Here is the way we're going to work it."

As Lucas listened, he grudgingly admitted that the plan had a good chance of succeeding. After the connection was broken, he thought, Okay, I know what we're doing. As he lit a fresh cigarette, his own cell phone rang.

It was on the dresser in his bedroom, and he hurried to answer it. "Lucas," a weak and strained voice began, "this is Franklin Bailey. I need you this evening. If you are already engaged, please use your replacement driver for that engagement. I have a most important errand and must be in Manhattan at eight o'clock."

Lucas's brain raced. "I do have a booking, but maybe we can work it out. How long do you expect to be, Mr. Bailey?"

"I don't know."

Lucas thought of the funny way the cop had eyed him on Friday when Bailey had him drive over to the Frawleys' house to offer to be the go-between. If the Feds found out Lucas was unavailable, they might start asking what was so important that he couldn't accommodate a longtime client. "I'll get someone for my other job. What time do you want me, sir?"

"At six o'clock. We'll probably be quite early, but I cannot take any chance of being late."

"Six on the button, sir."

Lucas threw his cell phone on the bed, went back to his dingy living room, and picked up the special cell phone. When the Pied Piper answered, he told him what had happened. "I couldn't refuse, so we can't go ahead with the plan."

Even though the Pied Piper was still trying to disguise his voice, the note of amusement in it crept through. "You're both right and wrong, Bert. You couldn't refuse, but we are going ahead with our plan. In fact, this little development may work beautifully for us. You're going for a plane ride, aren't you?"

"Yeah. After I get the stuff from Harry."

"Make sure that the typewriter used for the ransom note goes with you, as well as the clothing bought for the children. There should be no trace of children having been in Harry's cottage."

"I know. I know." They'd already gone over this.

"Have Harry phone me when he has secured the car. You phone me as soon as you drop off Bailey. I'll tell you what to do next."

AT TEN thirty Angie was at the breakfast table with the twins, on her third cup of black coffee. She'd had a lousy night's sleep. She looked at Kathy. She could tell the vaporizer and aspirin had done some good. Though the bedroom reeked of Vicks, at least the steam had loosened her cough a bit. She was still a pretty sick kid, though, and had been awake a lot during the night, crying for her mother. I'm tired, Angie thought, really tired. At least the other one slept pretty well, even though sometimes when Kathy was coughing hard, Kelly would start coughing, too.

"Is she getting sick, too?" Clint had asked a half-dozen times.

"No, she isn't. Get back to sleep," Angie had ordered. "I don't want you to be half dead tomorrow night."

Now she looked at Kelly, who stared back at her. It was all she could do not to slap that fresh kid. "We want to go home," she kept saying every other minute.

I can't *wait* for you to go home, Angie thought.

It was obvious that Clint was a nervous wreck. He'd taken his coffee over to the sofa in front of the television set and kept drumming his fingers on the piece of junk that passed for a coffee table. Kelly had eaten some cereal, and Kathy had had at least a few bites.

Angie pushed back her chair. "Okay, kids. Time for a nap."

They had gotten used to being shoved back into the crib after breakfast. Kathy even raised her arms to be picked up. She knows I love her, Angie thought, then cursed under her breath as Kathy's elbow hit the bowl of cereal, which then spilled down the front of her pajamas.

Kathy began to cry, a sick wail that ended in a cough.

"It's okay. It's okay," Angie snapped. Now what do I do? she wondered. That jerk Lucas is getting here soon, and I was told to leave the kids in their pajamas all day. Maybe if I just pin a towel under the wet part, it'll dry. "Shush," she said impatiently as she picked up Kathy and carried her into the bedroom. Kelly got down from the chair and walked beside them, reaching up to pat her sister's foot.

Angie put Kathy in the crib and grabbed a towel from the top of the dresser. By the time she pinned it under the pajama top, Kathy had folded herself into a ball and was sucking her thumb. That was something new, Angie thought as she dropped Kelly into the crib.

Kelly struggled to her feet and put her hands around the railing. "We want to go home now," she said.

"You're going home tonight," Angie said. "So shut up." She went back to the kitchen, slamming the door as a warning. Last night when Kelly had started to rock the crib, a good pinch on her arm had taught her it wasn't a good idea.

Clint was still watching television. Angie began to clear the table. "Pick up those Barney tapes," she ordered him as she dumped dishes in the sink. "Put them in the box with the typewriter." The Pied Piper, whoever he was, had ordered Lucas to dump in the ocean anything they had that could be connected to the kidnapping.

"Angie, this box is too big," Clint protested. "It'll be hard for Lucas to dump it."

"It's not too big," she snapped. "I'm putting the vaporizer in it. Okay? Okay?"

"Too bad we can't put the crib in it."

"When we drop off the kids, you can come back here and take it apart. Tomorrow you get rid of it."

Two hours later she was prepared for Lucas's explosive reaction when he caught sight of the box. "Couldn't you have found a smaller one?" he barked.

"This one was in the cellar. It will do the job, okay?" She said.

"Angie, we have smaller boxes downstairs," Clint volunteered.

"I sealed and tied this box," Angie shouted. "This is it."

A minute later she watched with intense satisfaction as Lucas carried the bulky box to his car.

LILA Jackson, a salesclerk at Abby's Quality Discount on Route 7, had become something of a celebrity to her family and friends. She had been the one to sell the twins' blue velvet dresses to Margaret

Frawley two days before the kidnapping. Thirty-four years old, small of stature, and bustling with energy, Lila had recently quit her well-paid secretarial job in Manhattan, moved in with her widowed mother, and taken the job at Abby's. She loved selling clothes. The day the news of the kidnapping broke, she recognized Margaret and the twins' dresses in the picture she saw on television.

"She was the nicest person," Lila breathlessly told a widening group of people who were fascinated that only a couple of days before the twins were stolen, she had been in contact with their mother. "Mrs. Frawley is real class, in a quiet, nice way. And she really knows quality. I told her that the same dresses cost four hundred dollars each in Bergdorf's and that at forty-two dollars they were a steal. She kind of laughed and said she only hoped she'd get a good picture of her twins in them before something got spilled.

"We had a nice chat," Lila reminisced. "I told Mrs. Frawley that another lady had just been in, buying matching outfits for twins. They couldn't have been hers, though, because she wasn't sure what size to get. She said they were average-size three-year-olds."

Lila caught the news on Wednesday morning as she was getting ready for work. She stared in sympathy at the video of Margaret and Steve Frawley racing to a neighbor's home down the street.

"Although neither the family nor the FBI will confirm it, it is believed that this morning the Pied Piper, as the kidnapper calls himself, has communicated his ransom demands by calling the Frawleys' neighbors," the CBS anchorman was saying.

Lila watched as a close-up showed Margaret Frawley's anguished expression and the deep circles under her eyes.

"Robinson Geisler, chairman of C.F.G. and Y., is not available to answer questions as to whether a transfer of funds is in process," the reporter continued, "but if that is the case, the next twenty-four hours will be crucial. It is the sixth day since Kathy and Kelly were taken from their bedroom. The kidnapping took place around nine p.m. last Thursday night."

They must have been in their pajamas, Lila thought as she reached for her car key. It was a thought that teased her as she drove to work and then stayed with her as she hung up her coat. She pinned on her WELCOME TO ABBY'S—I'M LILA badge and went straight to the cubicle where the accounting was handled.

"I just want to check my sales from last Tuesday, Jean," she explained to the accountant. I don't remember that woman's name, she thought, but she bought two sets of matching overalls and polo shirts, underwear, and socks.

In five minutes Lila found what she wanted. The receipt had been signed by Mrs. Clint Downes, using a Visa credit card. Lila asked Jean to phone Visa to try to get the woman's address.

"Sure, Lila. If they give me any grief, I'll say that the woman may have left a package here."

"Thanks, Jean."

At Visa, Mrs. Clint Downes was recorded as living at 100 Orchard Avenue in Danbury.

Uncertain now of what to do, Lila remembered that Jim Gilbert, a retired Danbury cop, was having dinner with her mother that night. She'd ask him about it.

When she arrived home, her mother and Jim were having a cocktail in the study. Lila poured a glass of wine for herself and sat on the raised hearth, her back to the fire. "Jim," she said, "I guess Mother told you I sold those blue dresses to Margaret Frawley."

"I heard." Jim's amiable expression hardened. "Mark my words. They're not going to get those kids back, alive *or* dead. My guess is they're out of the country by now, and all this talk of ransom was just meant to be a diversion."

"Jim, a short while before I sold the dresses, I waited on a woman buying matching outfits for three-year-olds, who didn't even seem to know the right size to buy."

"So?"

Lila took the plunge. "I mean, wouldn't it be extraordinary if that woman was connected to the kidnapping? The Frawley twins were wearing pajamas when they were taken. Kids that age can't be in the same outfit six days."

"Lila, you're letting your imagination run away with you,"

Gilbert said indulgently. "Do you know how many tips like that the Ridgefield cops and the FBI have been getting?"

"The woman's name is Mrs. Clint Downes, and she lives right here in Danbury," Lila persisted.

"Lila, I know Clint Downes. He's the caretaker who lives in the cottage at the club. Was the woman skinny with kind of a sloppy ponytail?"

"Yes."

"That's Clint's girlfriend, Angie. She may be signing herself as Mrs. Downes, but she's *not* Mrs. Downes. She does a fair amount of babysitting. Cross both of them off your list of suspects, Lila. In a million years neither one of those two is bright enough to pull off a kidnapping like this."

LUCAS knew that Charley Fox, a new mechanic at the airport, was watching him as he climbed into the plane, the bulky box in his arms. He's going to figure out that I'm going to dump it, Lucas told himself. Then he's going to decide that it must be something I want to get rid of real bad or maybe that I'm ferrying drugs somewhere.

Still, it was a good idea to clear the house of anything that could connect the twins to the cottage, he admitted as he plopped the box down on the copilot's seat in the cockpit. Tonight, after we drop the kids, I'll help Clint take the crib apart, and then we'll lose the parts somewhere. The kids' DNA would be all over the mattress.

The wind was still brisk. It wasn't the best day to go flying in a light plane. As he performed his checkout before taking off, Lucas permitted himself a sour smile. He'd read somewhere that identical twins had the same DNA. So they could only prove we had *one* of them, he thought. Swell!

It was a short flight, just long enough to get out over the ocean a few miles, hold the yoke firm with his knees, reduce his speed, position the box on his lap, carefully open the door, and give the box a shove. He watched its descent. The ocean was gray and choppy. The box disappeared into the waves, sending a spray of foam cascading through the air. Lucas pulled the door closed and put his hand on the yoke. Now for the real job, he thought.

When he landed at the airport, he did not see Charley Fox, which was fine with him. That way he won't know whether I brought the box back with me or not, he thought.

It was almost four o'clock. The wind was starting to die down, but the clouds overhead were threatening. Would rain be good for them or a problem? Lucas walked over to the parking lot and got into his car. Only time will tell, he decided. For now, he should get the limo out of the garage and run it over to the car wash.

Two hours later, freshly showered and shaved, neatly dressed in his chauffeur's uniform, Lucas drove his clean and polished limousine into the driveway of Franklin Bailey's home.

IT's getting dark, Margaret thought. It's seven o'clock. In another hour Franklin Bailey will be waiting outside the Time Warner building. If he delivers the money, I may have my babies tonight.

An hour ago Steve insisted that I take a sedative. I don't like the feeling it gives me.

"Margaret, listen," Steve urged.

Margaret could hear the sound of the kettle beginning to whistle. Rena Chapman had come over carrying a casserole of baked macaroni and cheese and slices of freshly baked Virginia ham. We have such good neighbors, she thought. When we get the twins back, I'll invite all of them in to thank them.

"Margaret, I want you to look at the files of some of the people you defended," Carlson was saying. "We've narrowed it down to three or four who, after their convictions, blamed you for the fact they lost their cases."

Margaret forced herself to focus on the names. "I gave them the best defense I could. The evidence against them was very strong," she said. "I'd worked out good plea bargains, but they wouldn't accept them. Then, when they were found guilty at trial and got longer sentences than if they'd accepted the plea, it became my fault. That happens a lot to public defenders."

"After his conviction Donny Mars hanged himself in his cell,"

Carlson persisted. "At his funeral his mother screamed, 'Wait till Frawley finds out what it is to lose a child.'"

"That was four years ago, long before the girls were born. She was hysterical."

"She may have been hysterical, but she's dropped out of sight completely, and so has her other son."

"Donny was bipolar. I begged the judge to send him to a hospital. His brother wrote a note apologizing to me. His mother didn't mean it." Margaret closed her eyes, then opened them slowly. "That's the other thing I've been trying to remember," she said.

Carlson and Steve stared at her. The sedative was beginning to make her sleepy. The timbre of her voice was softening, and they had to lean forward to hear what she was saying. "I should call Dr. Harris," Margaret whispered. "Kathy is sick. When we get her and Kelly back, I want Dr. Harris to be the one to take care of Kathy."

Carlson looked at Steve. "Is Dr. Harris a pediatrician?"

"Yes. She's at New York–Presbyterian in Manhattan and has written extensively about twins. She's been taking care of the girls."

"When we know where to find the girls, they'll be taken immediately to a nearby hospital for a checkup," Carlson told them. "Maybe Dr. Harris could meet us there."

As rain began slapping at the windows, Carlson concentrated on something Margaret had just said. "That's the *other* thing I've been trying to remember." Margaret, he thought, what else?

5

THE trip from Ridgefield to Manhattan took an hour and fifteen minutes. At a quarter past seven Lucas parked on Central Park South, half a block from the Time Warner building.

The rain had started falling in earnest. On the drive into the city, Bailey had explained the reason he had almost insisted Lucas be available for him. "The kidnappers will suspect that an agent is driving me. If somehow they were able to watch us at home, by my arriving with the driver and limousine I always use, the kidnappers may understand all we want is to get the children back safely."

"I can understand that, Mr. Bailey," Lucas said.

"I know there are agents swarming around the Time Warner building and driving cabs by it, all ready to follow me when I get instructions," Bailey said, his voice a nervous quiver.

Lucas glanced in the rearview mirror. He looks as shaky as I feel, he thought bitterly. This is all a trap for me and Clint. The FBI is just waiting to spring it. For all I know, they're putting cuffs on Angie right now.

"Lucas, you have your cell phone?" Bailey asked.

"Yes, sir, I do."

"When the transfer of money is completed, I'll call you immediately. You'll be parked around here?"

"Yes, sir, and ready to pick you up wherever you are." Lucas felt his hands grow clammy, and he rubbed them together. Enough of this waiting, he thought.

At two minutes to eight he pulled the car in front of the Time Warner building. He pushed the trunk button, sprang out of the limo, and opened the door for Bailey. His gaze lingered on the two suitcases and luggage cart in the trunk.

With hands that itched to grab the suitcases and run, Lucas stacked them on the cart and secured them to the handle.

The rain was a steady downpour now, and Bailey turned up the collar of his coat. He had put on a cap but not soon enough to prevent strands of damp white hair from falling onto his forehead. From his pocket he pulled out Carlson's phone.

"I'd better go, Mr. Bailey," Lucas said. "Good luck, sir. I'll be waiting to hear from you."

"Thank you, Lucas."

Lucas got into the limo and took a quick look around. Bailey was at the curb. Traffic was moving slowly around Columbus Circle. Lucas pulled out and drove slowly back along Central Park South.

THE TWINS HAD BEEN ASLEEP for most of the afternoon. When they woke up, Angie noticed that Kathy was looking flushed, and sure enough, she was getting another fever. I shouldn't have left her in those wet pajamas, she chided herself, feeling them. They're still damp. Still, she waited until Clint left at five o'clock to change Kathy into the overalls and polo shirt she hadn't thrown away.

At seven o'clock Clint phoned to say that he had purchased a new car, a black Toyota, in New Jersey, meaning he'd stolen a car and it now had Jersey plates. He ended the call by saying, "Don't worry, Angie. We'll be celebrating tonight."

You *bet* we will, Angie told herself.

At eight o'clock she put the twins back in the crib. Kathy's breathing was heavy, and she was still warm. Angie gave her another aspirin, then watched as she curled up into a bundle, her thumb in her mouth. Right now Clint and Lucas are hooking up with whoever has the money, she thought, her nerves tingling.

Kelly was sitting up, her arm around her sister. Her blue teddy-bear pajamas were wrinkled. Kathy's overalls were dark blue, the polo shirt a blue-and-white check.

"Two little girls in blue, lad," Angie began singing. *"Two little girls in blue . . ."*

Kelly looked up at her, her eyes solemn as Angie repeated the last line of the refrain: *"But we have drifted apart."*

Angie turned out the light, closed the bedroom door, and went into the living room. Apple-pie order, she thought. Better than it's looked in a long time. I should have kept the vaporizer though. Getting rid of it was Lucas's fault.

SIXTY-THREE years old, with compassionate hazel eyes and finger-waved gray hair, Dr. Sylvia Harris was the director of pediatric services at the Children's Hospital of New York–Presbyterian. When the news of the kidnapping first broke, she had tried to get through to the Frawleys but had only been able to leave a message. Frustrated, she had phoned Steve's office and asked his secretary to tell him that she had everyone she knew praying for the safe return of the twins.

Like a videotape being constantly replayed, Dr. Harris remembered the late autumn day three and a half years ago when Margaret Frawley had called to make an appointment with her. Even before the twins arrived, her relationship with the couple had evolved into warm friendship. She had given them a stack of books to read about the special bond between twins, with examples of identical twins experiencing each other's physical pain and receiving telepathic messages from each other, even when they were continents apart.

Now, as she locked her desk and prepared to leave her office, Sylvia's telephone rang. For a moment she was tempted to let the service pick it up, but on impulse she reached for the receiver. It was Margaret, a Margaret whose voice was almost catatonic.

"Dr. Sylvia. The ransom is being paid right now, and we believe we are going to get the girls back soon. Could you possibly come up and be with us? I know it's asking a lot, but we don't know what may have happened to them. I do know Kathy has a heavy cough."

"I'm on my way," Sylvia Harris said. "Put someone on to give me directions to your house."

THE cell phone Franklin Bailey was holding began to ring. His fingers trembling, he snapped it open and pressed it to his ear. "Franklin Bailey," he said as his mouth went dry.

"Mr. Bailey, you are admirably prompt. My congratulations." The voice was a husky whisper. "You must immediately walk down Eighth Avenue, turn right on Fifty-seventh Street, and walk west to Ninth Avenue. Wait on the northwest corner. You are being watched every step of the way. I will call you back in five minutes."

FBI agent Angus Sommers, dressed in the tattered clothes of a homeless man, was curled on the sidewalk, leaning against the architectural curiosity that had once been the Huntington Hartford Museum. Beside him stood a shabby cart filled with newspapers. Like a score of other agents, his cell phone had been programmed to pick up the call from the Pied Piper. Now he watched Bailey drag the luggage cart across the street in the rain.

With narrowed eyes Sommers scanned the circumference of Columbus Circle. Was the kidnapper somewhere in the crowd of people scurrying under umbrellas? Or was he sending Bailey on a wild-goose chase all over New York to shake off anyone following him?

As Bailey moved out of sight, Sommers got up, pushed his shopping cart to the corner, and waited for the light. He knew cameras at the Time Warner building were filming every inch of the scene. He crossed Fifty-eighth Street and turned left. There a junior agent, also dressed in shabby garb, took over his cart. Sommers then got into a waiting FBI car, and two minutes later, changed into a Burberry raincoat and matching hat, was dropped off at the Holiday Inn on Fifty-seventh Street, half a block from Ninth Avenue.

"BERT, this is the Pied Piper. State your location."

"I'm parked at Fifty-fifth between Eighth and Ninth. I'm in front of a hydrant. I can't stay long. According to Bailey, this place is swarming with FBI."

"I would expect no less of them. Drive to Tenth Avenue, then turn east on Fifty-sixth. Pull over to the curb and wait. I'll be giving Harry the same instructions."

FRANKLIN Bailey waited on the northwest corner of Ninth Avenue and Fifty-seventh Street, soaked to the skin and out of breath. Even though he was certain FBI agents had tracked his every step, his hand shook so much when the cell phone rang again that he dropped it. Praying that it was still functioning, he snapped it open and said, "I'm here."

"I can see that. You are now to walk to Fifty-ninth Street and Tenth Avenue. Go into the Duane Reade store on the northwest corner. Purchase a cell phone with prepaid hours and a box of trash bags. I will call in ten minutes."

HE'S going to make him get rid of our phone, Agent Sommers thought as he stood in the driveway of the Holiday Inn and listened to the call. If he's able to observe Bailey's every move, he may be in one of those apartment buildings around here. He watched as a taxi pulled up across the street and a couple got out. He knew that a dozen agents were driving cabs with other agents in the backseat. The plan was to drop the supposed passengers off near where Bailey was waiting so that if he were told to hail a cab, it would not seem unusual that one became immediately available. But now the Pied Piper was trying to make sure that anyone following Bailey would become obvious.

Four more blocks in this rain, dragging those suitcases, Sommers worried as he watched Bailey turn north, following the Pied Piper's instructions. I just hope he doesn't collapse before he gets to hand over the money.

A car with Taxi and Limousine Commission license plates pulled up at the curb. Sommers raced to get it. "We'll go around Columbus Circle," he said to the agent who was driving, "and park on Tenth around Sixtieth Street."

WHEN Bailey came out of the Duane Reade store, he was holding a small package and a phone in his left hand, but Sommers could no longer hear what the Pied Piper was telling him. As Sommers watched, Bailey got into a car and was driven away.

EXCEL driver Angel Rosario pulled up to the corner of Fifty-ninth Street and Tenth Avenue and double-parked. The old guy dragging a luggage cart and looking at the cars at the curb had to be his passenger. Angel jumped out. "Mr. Bailey?"

"Yes. Yes."

Angel reached for the cart. "I'll open the trunk, sir."

"No. I must get something out of the bags. Put them in the backseat."

"They're wet," Angel objected.

"Then put them on the floor," Bailey snapped. "Do it. Do it."

"Okay. Okay." In his twenty years of driving for Excel, Angel had had his share of kooky passengers, but this old guy looked like he was about to have a heart attack, and Angel didn't intend to contribute to it by arguing. Besides, there might be a good tip if he was helpful. Even though Bailey's clothes were soaked, Angel could tell they were expensive.

Angel opened the rear door of the car, but Bailey wouldn't get in until the suitcases had been hoisted onto the floor. Angel tossed the cart into the front passenger seat and got in. "The Brooklyn Museum, right, sir?"

"That's what you've been told."

"Yeah. We're going to pick up your friend and bring him back with you to the Pierre Hotel. I warn you. It's gonna take a long time. With the rain, the driving is lousy."

"I understand."

As the car started, Franklin Bailey's new cell phone began to ring. "Transfer the money into two trash bags. Secure the bags with the blue tie you are wearing and the red tie you were instructed to carry. I will call you again shortly."

It was twenty minutes to nine.

AT NINE fifteen the phone in the cottage rang, a loud jangle that made Angie almost jump out of her skin. Hastily she pulled the bedroom door closed and picked up the receiver. "Hello."

"Angie, I'm insulted, ree-al-ly insulted. I thought my old buddy Clint was going to call me about having a beer last night."

Oh, no, Angie thought. It was that stupid dope Gus, and from the sounds in the background, he was in the Danbury Pub. So much for you knowing how much suds to drink, Angie thought, noting his slurred voice. Suddenly careful, she remembered that one time Gus had shown up uninvited at the door, looking for company.

"Hi, Gus," she said, trying to sound friendly. "Didn't Clint phone you? I told him to. He felt lousy last night and went to bed early."

From inside the bedroom she heard Kathy begin to cry, a loud, distressed wail, and she realized she had not closed the door completely. She tried to cover the mouthpiece, but it was too late.

"Is that the kid you're minding? I can hear the crying."

"That's the one, and I got to go check on the kid right now. Clint went to look at a car some guy is selling in Yonkers. I'll tell him to meet you tomorrow night for sure, Gus. Okay?"

Angie hung up, but before the receiver was in its cradle a now-awakened Kelly began to scream, "Mommy, Mommy!"

Would Gus realize that he was hearing two kids, or was he too drunk to know the difference? Angie wondered. It would be just like him to call back. She went into the bedroom. Now both twins stood grasping the crib rails and hollering for their mother. Well, I can fix one of you, Angie thought as she yanked a sock out of the dresser and began to tie it around Kelly's mouth.

AGENT Angus Sommers held his cell phone to his ear. With Agent Ben Taglione at the wheel, Sommers kept his eyes riveted to the sedan containing Franklin Bailey. Immediately upon seeing the Excel Driving Service logo, Sommers had contacted the dispatcher at the company. Car 142's destination was the Brooklyn Museum for a passenger pickup and from there the Pierre Hotel on Sixty-first Street and Fifth Avenue. It's too pat, Sommers thought, a feeling shared by the rest of the team. Even so, a dozen FBI agents were already on their way to the museum, and several were also staked out at the Pierre.

Five other vehicles with agents were following Bailey's car. On the West Side Drive the traffic was almost at a standstill. Whoever was waiting to meet Bailey might easily get nervous. Sommers worried silently. Were they to panic, there was no predicting what the kidnappers might do to the twins.

At what had been the exit to the World Trade Center, the cause of the delay became apparent. A fender bender had tied up two lanes. When they finally inched around the battered vehicles, the traffic began to move faster. Sommers leaned forward, squinting to be sure that the Excel sedan, one of many dark vehicles that looked alike in the rain, did not get away from them.

Keeping three cars between them and the sedan, they followed it down around the tip of Manhattan. It turned north on the FDR Drive, the Brooklyn Bridge lights dim in the windswept rain. Then at South Street the Excel made an abrupt left turn and disappeared onto the exit. Agent Taglione tried to shift to the left lane, but it was impossible to do without colliding with the SUV parallel to them.

As Sommers clenched his hands into fists, his cell phone rang. "We're still behind them," Agent Buddy Winters told him. "He's heading north again."

It was nine thirty p.m.

DR. SYLVIA Harris wrapped her arms around a sobbing Margaret Frawley. Words are not just inadequate at a time like this, she thought. They are useless. Over Margaret's shoulder Steve met her gaze. Gaunt and pale, he looked vulnerable and younger than his thirty-one years. She could see that he was fighting his own tears.

"They've *got* to come back tonight," Margaret whispered. "They're *going* to come back. I *know* they are!"

"We need you, Dr. Sylvia." Steve's voice choked with emotion. Then, with an obvious effort, he said, "Even if whoever has the girls has treated them decently, we know they're bound to be upset and frightened. And Kathy has a heavy cough."

"Margaret told me that when she called," Sylvia said quietly.

Walter Carlson saw the concern on her face and felt that he could read her mind. If Dr. Harris had already treated Kathy for pneumonia, she had to be thinking that an untreated heavy cough was particularly dangerous for her little patient.

"I made a fire in the study," Steve said. "Let's go in there."

Carlson did not follow them into the study and went back to the dining room, where the monitored phone was on the table. Something in his gut told him that the Pied Piper might still decide to make direct contact with the Frawleys.

It was nine forty-five, almost two hours since Franklin Bailey had begun to follow the Pied Piper's orders to initiate the ransom drop.

"BERT, in the next two minutes you will receive a call from Franklin Bailey instructing you to wait for him on Fifty-sixth Street, at the passageway that runs between Fifty-sixth and Fifty-seventh streets just east of Sixth Avenue," the Pied Piper told Lucas. "Harry will already be parked there. When I have confirmed that you are in place, I will direct Bailey to drop the trash bags with the money onto the curb in front of Cohen Fashion Optical on Fifty-seventh Street. He will place them on top of the trash bags already there, waiting for the sanitation department to pick up. They will each be fastened with a necktie. You and Harry will run up the passageway, grab the bags, run them back through the passageway, and place them in the trunk of Harry's car. Harry should be gone before the agents are able to connect with him."

"You mean we have to run the length of a block, carrying the trash bags? That doesn't make sense," Lucas protested.

"It makes a great deal of sense. Even if the FBI has managed to continue to follow Bailey's car, they will be far enough behind to give you the opportunity to grab the bags and for Harry to drive away. You will stay there, and when Bailey and the FBI show up, you will truthfully state that you were directed by Mr. Bailey to pick him up where you are waiting. No agents would dare follow you too closely down the passageway, where you might spot them. When they do arrive, you will be their witness and say that you saw two men drop bags into a car parked near you. Then you will provide a misleading description of that car."

IT WAS six minutes to ten.

It had been necessary for Franklin Bailey to tell Angel Rosario why they were changing directions. From his rearview mirror Angel had been able to see that cash was being transferred from the suitcases to the trash bags and had threatened to drive to the nearest police station. Frantically, Bailey had explained that the money was ransom for the Frawley twins and begged his cooperation.

"I've got two kids myself," Angel had said.

After veering off the South Street exit, they had been instructed to drive up First Avenue, turn west on Fifty-fifth Street, and find a place to stand near Tenth Avenue. Fifteen minutes passed before the Pied Piper called again.

"Mr. Bailey, we are at the final phase of our association. You are to phone your personal driver and instruct him to wait for you on West Fifty-sixth Street, at the passageway that connects Fifty-seventh to Fifty-sixth. Tell him it is just a quarter of a block east of Sixth Avenue. I will be back in touch."

Ten minutes later the Pied Piper phoned again. "Have you reached your driver?"

"Yes. He was in the vicinity. He'll be there momentarily."

"It is a rainy night, Mr. Bailey. I want to be considerate of you. Proceed to Fifty-seventh, turn right, and drive east, slowing down and keeping near the curb after you cross over Sixth Avenue. You will see a pile of trash bags in front of Cohen Fashion Optical. Place the trash bags with the money on top of the other trash bags, making sure your neckties are clearly visible. Then continue driving east. I will call you back."

It was six minutes after ten.

"Bert, this is the Pied Piper. Proceed immediately through the passageway. The trash bags are being dropped now."

Lucas had taken off his chauffeur's cap and pulled on a hooded rain slicker and dark glasses. He leaped out of the car, opened his large umbrella, and followed Clint, who was similarly dressed and also carrying an umbrella. The rain was so heavy that Lucas was certain the few people in the corridor were oblivious to them.

From the protection of the umbrella shielding his face, he saw Franklin Bailey climbing into a car. He held back as Clint grabbed the trash bags with the ties and ran back across the sidewalk to the corridor. Lucas waited until Bailey's car pulled away before joining Clint and grabbing one of the bags.

In seconds they were back on Fifty-sixth Street. Clint pushed the trunk button of the stolen Toyota, but it would not open. Swearing under his breath, he yanked at the back door nearest the curb, but it, too, was locked.

Lucas knew they had only seconds to spare. He flipped open the trunk of the limo. "Throw them in there," he snarled.

Seconds later he was back behind the wheel, the slicker rolled under the front seat, his uniform cap on. Men he was sure must be FBI agents came running through the corridor and from both ends of the block. His nerves racing but his demeanor calm, Lucas responded to the sharp rap on his window. "Is something wrong?" he asked as the window rolled down.

"Did you see a man dragging trash bags come out of this passageway a minute ago?" Agent Sommers demanded.

"Yes. They were parked right here." Lucas pointed to the spot Clint had just vacated.

"They? You mean there were two of them?"

"Yes. One was stocky, the other a tall, thin guy."

Sommers had been too far back to see the drop because their car got boxed in at the light on Sixth Avenue. They arrived in time to glimpse the Excel car pulling away from the curb in front of the optical store. Seeing no sign of the suitcases, they had continued to follow the car to Fifth Avenue.

Alerted by a call from another agent, they parked and ran back. A pedestrian who had stopped to answer his cell phone told them he had seen a stocky man drag two just-abandoned trash bags into the corridor.

"Describe the car you saw," Sommers ordered Lucas.

"Dark blue or black, sir. Late model, four-door Lexus."

His hands clammy, Lucas managed to answer in the obsequious voice he used when he addressed Franklin Bailey. They'll probably have every cop in New York looking for a Lexus, he thought. The car Clint stole was an older black Toyota.

A few minutes passed, and the Excel car carrying Franklin Bailey pulled up behind him. Bailey, now on the verge of collapse, was helped into the limo. Accompanied by two agents and followed by others, Lucas drove back to Ridgefield, listening as they queried Bailey on the instructions he had received from the Pied Piper. He was gratified to hear Bailey say, "I had asked Lucas to remain in the vicinity of Columbus Circle. At about ten o'clock I was instructed to tell Lucas to wait for me at that spot on Fifty-sixth Street. My final order was to drive to that place. The Pied Piper said he didn't want me to get wet."

At quarter past twelve Lucas pulled up in front of Bailey's home. The agents assisted Bailey inside. With the ransom money still in the trunk, Lucas drove to his garage, switched the money to his car, and drove to the cottage, where a jubilant Clint and a strangely quiet Angie were waiting for him.

THE ransom drop had been completed, but the agents had lost the people who picked up the money. Now they could only wait. Steve and Margaret and Dr. Harris sat quietly, silently praying that the phone would ring, that someone, maybe another neighbor, would say, "I just had a phone call telling me where the twins are." But there was only silence.

Where would they leave them? Margaret agonized. They couldn't walk into a public place without being noticed. Everyone looks at the twins when I'm out with them. My two little girls in blue. That's what the papers call them.

Suppose we don't hear from the kidnappers?

"THE king was in the counting house, counting up his money," Clint chortled. "I can't believe you drove the money home with the FBI guys in the car."

The piles of bills were on the floor of the living room in the cottage, mostly fifties, the remainder in twenties. As directed, the bills were not new. A random check showed they were not in sequence.

"Believe it," Lucas snapped. "Start throwing your half in one of the bags. I'll take mine in the other." Even though he was sitting here with the money in front of him, Lucas was certain that something would go wrong. That airhead, Clint, had been too dumb to test the trunk of the car he'd stolen, Lucas thought. If I hadn't been there with the limo, he'd have been caught red-handed. Lucas felt as though his guts were twisted into knots.

Why hadn't the Pied Piper called?

At five minutes after three in the morning the sharp crack of the cottage phone made them all jump. Angie scrambled up from the floor to answer it. "Put Bert on," the Pied Piper ordered.

Lucas got up, crossed the room, and took the receiver. "I was wondering when you'd get around to us," he snarled.

"You don't sound like a man who's staring at a million dollars. Listen carefully. You are to drive in the borrowed car to La Cantina, a restaurant on the northbound Saw Mill River Parkway in Elms- ford. It has been closed for many years."

"I know where it is."

"Then you must also know that the parking lot is behind the building and out of sight of the parkway. Harry and Mona are to follow you in Harry's van, bringing the twins. They must transfer their charges to the borrowed car and lock them in it. The three of you will return to the cottage in the van. I will call by five a.m. to confirm you have followed instructions. I will then take the final step. After that, none of you will hear from me again."

At three fifteen they began the trip. From behind the wheel of the stolen car, Lucas watched as Angie and Clint carried out the sleeping twins. If they get a flat tire in that old rattletrap, if we come across a road check, if some drunk slams into one of us . . . The pos- sibilities for disaster leaped into his head as he started the engine and then drove through Danbury, heading west in light rain.

A short time later he was turning onto the Saw Mill River Park- way. Another ten minutes and he'd be there. There was not much traffic. His blood froze when he spotted a state trooper's car com- ing up behind him. He glanced at the speedometer—he was okay.

The trooper turned off at the next exit. So far, so good, Lucas thought. He wet his lips with the tip of his tongue. Less than five minutes. Four minutes. Two minutes.

The aging structure that had been La Cantina Restaurant was

coming up on the right. With a quick flip of the switch, Lucas turned off the headlights, turned right onto the road that passed the restaurant, and drove to the parking lot behind it. There he turned off the ignition and waited until the sound of an approaching car told him that the final phase of the plan was about to be completed.

"IT TAKES a long time to count one million dollars by hand," Walter Carlson said, hoping he sounded reassuring.

"The money was transferred at a little after ten," Steve replied. "That was five hours ago." He glanced down, but Margaret did not open her eyes. She was curled on the couch, her head in his lap. Dr. Harris was sitting in the wing chair beside the couch.

Despite trying to sound encouraging, Carlson knew that every passing minute suggested that they would not hear from the kidnappers. The Pied Piper told me we'd get a call after midnight. Steve's right, he thought. They've had the money for hours. For all we know, the twins are already dead.

As the hours wore on, a hunch had been taking shape in Carlson's mind, a kind of gut-level hunch to check out Lucas Wohl, the ubiquitous chauffeur who so conveniently happened to be parked exactly where he could observe the kidnappers carrying the money and then give a description of the car they were supposedly driving.

Angus Sommers, the FBI agent in charge of the New York group, had driven up with Bailey and was convinced he and the chauffeur were on the level. Even so, Carlson decided, he was going to put in a call to Connor Ryan, special agent in charge in New Haven, and Carlson's immediate boss. Ryan was in his office now with his guys, ready to jump if word came that the twins had been left in northern Connecticut. He could start a rundown on Lucas immediately.

Margaret slowly pulled herself up. She brushed back her hair with a gesture so weary that Carlson thought the effort was almost too much for her to make. "The Pied Piper did say he would call around midnight?" she asked.

There was no answer to give her except the truth: "Yes, he did."

CLINT KNEW THEY WERE NEARING La Cantina Restaurant and was worried about overshooting it. With narrowed eyes he anxiously scanned the right side of the parkway. He had dropped back to make sure the state trooper didn't get the idea he was following Lucas. Now Lucas was out of sight.

Angie was sitting beside him, rocking the sick kid in her arms. She'd been singing the same "Two Little Girls in Blue" song over and over and over again. *"But . . . we . . . have . . . drifted . . . apart,"* she crooned now, drawing out the last line.

"Angie, I wish you'd quit that damn singing," Clint snapped.

"Kathy likes me to sing," Angie retorted, her voice steely.

Clint glanced nervously at her. There was something strange about Angie tonight. She was in one of her crazy moods. When they'd gone into the bedroom to get the kids, he had seen that one of them was sleeping with a sock tied around her mouth. When he started to take it off, Angie had grabbed his hand. Then in the car she insisted that he put that kid on the floor of the backseat and cover her with an open newspaper.

His protest that she might suffocate had set Angie off. "She's not going to suffocate, and if by any chance we hit some kind of road-block, we don't need the cops looking at identical twins."

The other kid, the one Angie was holding, was whimpering. It was a good thing that she'd be back with the parents soon. You didn't have to be a doctor to see that she was pretty sick.

That building had to be the restaurant, Clint decided as he edged the car into the right lane. He could feel perspiration begin to drip from all over his body. He drove past the restaurant and turned right into the driveway beside it, then made another right into the parking lot behind. He could see that Lucas had stopped close to the building, so he pulled up directly behind him.

"They were sisters . . ." Angie sang, her voice really loud.

Kathy began to cry. "Shut up, Angie!" Clint pleaded. "If Lucas opens the door and hears you making noise, there's no telling what he'll do to you."

"I'm not afraid of him. Here, hold her." With a swift movement she thrust Kathy into his arms, opened the door, ran up to the driver's door of the stolen car, and rapped on the window.

As Clint watched, Lucas rolled down the window, and Angie leaned inside the car. An instant later a loud bang that could only be caused by a gunshot echoed through the deserted parking lot.

Angie ran back to the van, grabbed Kelly, deposited her in the backseat of the stolen car, and got in the front seat on the passenger side. When she came back, she was holding both of Lucas's cell phones and a ring of keys. "When the Pied Piper calls, we have to be able to answer," she told him, her voice warm and bubbly.

"You killed Lucas!" Clint said, his arms still around Kathy, whose crying had dissolved into a coughing fit.

Angie took Kathy from him. "He left a note. It's typed on the same typewriter as the ransom note. It says that he didn't mean to kill Kathy. She was crying so much he put his hand over her mouth, and when he realized she was dead, he put her in a box and flew out over the ocean and dumped it. Wasn't that a good idea? I had to make it look like he committed suicide. Now we have the whole million dollars, and I have my baby. Come on. Let's get out of here."

Panicked, Clint turned on the engine and floored the gas.

"Slow up, you stupid jerk," Angie snapped. "Just drive your family home, nice and easy."

As he turned back onto the highway, Angie began to sing sotto voce: *"They were sisters . . . but they have drifted apart."*

THE lights had been burning all night in the executive offices of the C.F.G.&Y. building on Park Avenue. Some of the members of the board of directors had kept the vigil, wanting to be part of the triumphant return of the Frawley twins to the arms of their parents.

Everyone was keenly aware that the Pied Piper had promised that once the cash ransom had been paid, he would make contact around midnight. As the hours after midnight wore on, the anticipation of generous press coverage and a huge public relations boost for the firm changed to worry and doubt.

At five a.m. Robinson Geisler rehearsed aloud the victory speech he would give to the media. "Paying ransom may seem to some to be cooperating with criminals. Talk to any FBI agent and they will tell you that their first concern is always to get the victims back. Only then can they relentlessly pursue the criminals. The example these criminals will set is not that they received ransom money, but that they never got a chance to spend it."

Let Gregg Stanford top *that,* he thought with a thin smile.

"The first thing we've gotta do is get rid of his car," Angie said matter-of-factly as they drove into Danbury. "First we get his share of the money out of the trunk of his car; then you drive it back and park in front of his apartment. I'll be right behind you."

"We're not going to get away with this, Angie. You can't hide the kid forever."

"Yes, I can."

"Somebody might connect Lucas to us. Once they take his fingerprints, they'll figure out that the real Lucas Wohl's been dead for twenty years, and this guy's real name was Jimmy Nelson, and he was in prison. And I was his cellmate."

"So? Your real name isn't Clint Downes. But who else knows that? The only time you and Lucas met was for a job. The only times he came to the house were these past few nights."

"He came yesterday afternoon when he picked up all that stuff."

"In his old brown Ford that looks like every other old brown Ford on the road? It might be different if he came in the limo. We know he never called you on the special phone, and now I've got it."

"I *still* think—"

"I still think we've got a million bucks, and I've got the baby I want, and that creep who treated us like dirt is out of the way, with his head on the steering wheel, so shut up."

At five after five Lucas's special phone began to ring. Clint looked at it. They had just pulled into the driveway at the cottage. "What are you going to tell him?"

"We're not going to answer," Angie said with a smirk. "Let him think we're still on the highway and maybe talking to a cop." She tossed him a set of keys. "These are his. Let's get rid of his car."

At five twenty Clint parked Lucas's car in front of the hardware store. On the second floor a faint glow showed through the shaded window. Lucas had left a light on for himself.

Clint got out of Lucas's car and scrambled back to the van. His cherubic face dripping with perspiration, he got behind the wheel. The special phone rang again. "He must be scared stiff," Angie chortled. "Okay, let's go home. My baby is waking up again."

Kathy was stirring and reaching out her hand.

"She's trying to touch her twin," Angie said. "Isn't that cute?" She tried to entwine her own fingers with Kathy's.

Kathy pulled away. "Kelly, I want Kelly," she said, her voice hoarse. "I don't want Mona."

As he turned the ignition key, Clint looked nervously at Angie. She didn't like rejection, in fact, couldn't tolerate it. He knew she'd be sick of the kid before the week was up. What then? he wondered. She was off the deep end now. He had seen her vicious streak tonight. I've got to get out of here, he thought, out of this town, out of Connecticut.

The street was quiet. Trying not to show how panicked he was becoming, he drove with the headlights off until they reached Route 7. It wasn't until they had gone through the service gate of the country club that he was able to draw a deep breath.

Kathy was crying again: "Kelly . . . Kelly . . ."

Clint stopped at the front door of the cottage and hurried to open it. Kathy in her arms, Angie went inside, walked straight to the bedroom, and dropped the little girl in the crib. "Get over it, baby doll," she said as she turned and walked back to the living room.

The special phone rang again. This time Angie picked it up. "Hello, Mr. Pied Piper," she said, then listened. "We know Lucas hasn't been answering his cell phone. There was an accident on the parkway, and it was teeming with cops. There's a law against talking on a cell phone when you're driving, you know. Everything went fine. Lucas had a hunch the Feds might decide to talk with him again, and he didn't want to be carrying this around. . . . Yeah.

Yeah. Everything went real smooth. Tell somebody where to pick up the two little girls in blue. I hope we never talk to you again. Good luck to you."

AT FIVE forty-five on Thursday morning the answering service for St. Mary's Catholic Church in Ridgefield received a phone call. "I'm desperate. I need to talk to a priest," a husky voice said.

Rita Schless, the telephone operator who took the call, was suspicious. She was sure that whoever it was was trying to disguise his voice. "Are you injured or sick?" she asked crisply.

"Put me through to a priest immediately. This is a matter of life and death."

"Hold on, sir," Rita said. I don't believe him for one minute, she thought, but I can't take a chance. Reluctantly she rang seventy-five-year-old Monsignor Romney, who had told her to direct all middle-of-the night calls to him. "I'm an insomniac, Rita," he had explained. "Try me first."

"I don't think this guy's on the level," Rita explained now. "I swear he's trying to disguise his voice."

"We'll find out soon enough," the Reverend Monsignor Joseph Romney said wryly as he sat up and swung his legs over the bed. As he reached for his glasses, he heard the click of the call being transferred. "Monsignor Romney," he said. "How can I help you?"

"Monsignor, you heard about the twins who were kidnapped?"

"Yes, of course. The Frawleys are new members of our parish." Rita is right, he acknowledged. Whoever this is, he's trying to disguise his voice.

"Kathy and Kelly are safe. They can be found in a locked car behind the old La Cantina Restaurant on the Saw Mill Parkway near Elmsford."

Joseph Romney felt his heart begin to pound. "Is this a joke?"

"It is not a joke, Monsignor. I am the Pied Piper, and I have chosen you to bring a message of joy to the Frawleys. The old La Cantina Restaurant. Have you got that straight?"

"Yes. Yes."

"Then I suggest you notify the authorities. It is an inclement night."

AT DAWN, unable any longer to watch the deepening misery on the faces of Margaret and Steve Frawley, Agent Walter Carlson sat at the dining-room table beside the phone. When it rang at five minutes to six, he grabbed the receiver.

It was Marty Martinson calling from the police station. "Walt, Monsignor Romney of St. Mary's got a call from someone claiming to be the Pied Piper. He said the twins are in a locked car at an old restaurant on the Saw Mill River Parkway. The state police will be there in five minutes."

Carlson heard the Frawleys and Dr. Harris as they rushed into the dining room. They had heard the phone ring. He turned and looked up at them. "Hold on, Marty," he told Captain Martinson. There was nothing he could offer the parents and Dr. Harris other than the simple truth. "We will know in a few minutes if a call Monsignor Romney received at the rectory is a hoax," he told them quietly.

"Was it from the Pied Piper?" Margaret gasped.

"Did he say where they are?" Steve demanded.

Carlson did not answer. "Marty," he said, speaking into the phone, "if it's for real, our guys need to do the forensics on the car."

"The troopers know that. They're calling your Westchester office."

Carlson hung up the phone. "If the call is real, the twins have been left, unharmed, in a locked car just off the Saw Mill River Parkway near Elmsford," he told the Frawleys. "The state troopers are on the way there."

"The Pied Piper kept his word," Margaret cried. She threw her arms around Steve. "Steve, my babies are coming home!"

"Margaret, it may be a hoax," Dr. Harris cautioned.

"God wouldn't do that to us," Margaret said, as Steve, unable to speak, buried his face in her hair.

When fifteen minutes went by without another call, Carlson was sure something was wrong. Then, when the doorbell rang, he knew it had to be bad news.

Steve and Margaret and Dr. Harris followed him to the foyer. Carlson opened the door. Monsignor Romney and Marty Martinson were standing on the porch.

The priest went to Margaret and Steve and, in a voice trembling with compassion, said, "God has sent you back one of your little girls. Kelly is safe. Kathy has been taken to Him."

THE news that one of the twins was dead triggered an avalanche of national sympathy. The few pictures the media were able to get of Kelly as her parents carried her from the hospital in Elmsford, where she had been taken to be examined, were distinct enough to show the difference from her birthday picture of only a week earlier. Her eyes were wide and frightened, and there seemed to be a bruise on her face. Her one arm was around her mother's neck, while the other was stretched out, as though to grasp another hand.

The state trooper who was first to arrive at La Cantina Restaurant described the scene: "The car was locked. I could see the man slumped over the wheel. There was only one little girl there. She was curled up on the floor of the backseat. The car was cold. She was wearing only pajamas, and she was shivering. She had a gag on so tight, it's a wonder she didn't choke. When I untied it, she started whimpering like a hurt puppy. I took my coat off and wrapped it around her, then carried her back to the squad car to warm her up. Right after that the other troopers and the FBI arrived and found the suicide note on the front seat."

The Frawleys had declined to be interviewed. Their statement was read to the press by Monsignor Romney: "Margaret and Steve wish to express their gratitude for all the messages of compassion they have received. At this time they need privacy to comfort Kelly, who misses her twin, and to deal with their own grief in the loss of Kathy."

Walter Carlson went on-camera with a message. "The man known as Lucas Wohl is dead, but his associate or associates are alive. We will hunt them down, and we will find them. They will be brought to justice."

At C.F.G.&Y, Robinson Geisler expressed his tremendous sorrow at the loss of one of the twins but said the cooperation of his firm had led to the safe return of the other one.

In a separate interview, board member Gregg Stanford broke ranks. "The vote to pay the ransom," he said, "was fiercely fought by a minority faction. I firmly believe that if the ransom demand had been rejected out of hand, the kidnappers would have had a decision to make. If they harmed the children, they would only add to their terrible culpability. The death sentence is still on the books in Connecticut. On the other hand, if they released Kathy and Kelly, they could expect leniency if they were caught. As a member of the board of directors, I want to assure anyone who might believe that our firm will ever deal with criminals again—listen very carefully: *It is not going to happen.*"

"Mr. Pied Piper, Lucas is dead. Maybe he killed himself. Maybe he didn't. What difference is it to you? In fact, you should be grateful. He knew who you are. We don't. Just for the record, he was taping you on his phone. He had the cassettes in the glove compartment of his Ford, probably to put the arm on you for more money."

"Is the other twin dead?"

"She is not dead. She's sleeping," Angie said. "As a matter of fact, I'm holding her right now. Don't call again. You'll wake her up." She put down the phone and kissed Kathy's cheek. "Wouldn't you think that seven million would satisfy him?" she asked Clint.

It was eleven o'clock. Clint was watching television. Every station was carrying stories about the end of the Frawley kidnapping. It had been confirmed that Lucas Wohl had flown his plane out of Danbury Airport on Wednesday afternoon, carrying a heavy box. "That box is believed to have held the body of little Kathy Frawley," the announcer speculated. "According to the suicide note, Lucas Wohl buried Kathy at sea."

"What are we going to do with her?" Clint asked. The exhaustion of the sleepless night and the shock of watching Angie shoot Lucas were taking their toll. His heavy body was slumped in the chair. His red-rimmed eyes were slits in his full face.

"We're going to take her to Florida and buy a boat and sail through the Caribbean, that's what we're going to do. But for now, she's having trouble breathing again."

"Angie, she's sick. She needs to see a doctor. If she dies on us, and we get caught—"

"She's not going to die, and stop worrying that anyone will connect us with Lucas. We did everything right. Now I want you to take her into the bathroom and let the shower run till it gets all steamed up."

Clint knew better than to try to reason with her. This kid's face has been on the front page of every newspaper in the country, he thought. She no more looks like me or Angie than I look like Elvis Presley. The minute we're in public, somebody will spot us. By now the cops must have figured out that Lucas is really Jimmy Nelson and that he did a stretch in Attica. Next they'll come up with Ralphie Hudson as his pal there, and sooner or later they'll trace him to this door. After that nobody will call me Clint anymore.

I was crazy to take Angie back after she did that stretch in the psycho hospital, he thought as he carried Kathy to the bathroom and turned on the shower.

He put the lid of the toilet seat down and sat on it. With clumsy fingers he opened the top button of her polo shirt. He turned her body so that she would breathe in the steam that was rapidly filling the small room. The kid was starting to babble. Nothing she was saying was making sense. Was that the twin talk stuff? he wondered. "I'm the only one listening, kid," he told her. "So if you have anything to say, say it straight."

DR. SYLVIA Harris knew that confronting the awful grief of losing Kathy was to some extent being postponed by Margaret and Steve. For now, their attention was riveted on Kelly. She had not spoken a single word since they had been reunited with her in the hospital. The physical exam showed that she had not been molested, but the tight gag had left bruises on her face, and black-and-blue marks on her arms suggested she had been viciously pinched.

When she first saw her parents come into the hospital room, Kelly stared at them and turned away. "She's angry with you now," Dr. Harris gently explained. "By tomorrow she won't let you out of her sight."

They got home at eleven o'clock, rushing into the house as photographers scrambled to get pictures. Margaret carried Kelly upstairs to the twins' bedroom and changed her into her Cinderella pajamas. Troubled by Kelly's absolute lack of reaction, Dr. Harris gave her a mild sedative. "She needs to sleep," she told Steve and Margaret.

Steve laid her in bed, put her teddy bear on her chest, and placed the other one on the empty pillow next to her. Kelly's eyes flew open. In a spontaneous gesture she reached out, grabbed Kathy's teddy bear, and rocking back and forth, began to hug both of them. Only then, sitting on either side of her bed, did Steve and Margaret begin to weep, silent tears that broke Sylvia's heart.

She went downstairs to find that Agent Carlson was preparing to leave. Seeing how drawn and weary he looked, she said, "I hope you're going to get some rest now."

"Yes. I'm going to go home and crash for about eight hours. Otherwise, I won't be any use to anyone."

"May I make an observation?"

"Of course."

"In my volunteer work I sometimes see abused children. Pinching is a woman's trick, not a man's."

"I would agree with you. It would make sense that a woman was involved in taking care of the twins."

"Was Lucas Wohl the Pied Piper?"

"Somehow I doubt it." Carlson did not add that, pending the autopsy report, there was a serious question about the angle of the bullet that had killed Lucas. "Dr. Harris, how long will you be staying here?"

"For at least a few days. Kelly is very fragile emotionally. I think I can help by being around for her, and Steve and Margaret."

"What about the Frawleys' families?"

"Margaret's mother and aunt are coming up next week. Margaret asked them to wait. Her mother is crying so much she can hardly speak. Steve's mother can't travel, and his father can't leave her."

Carlson nodded. "Doctor, from what I understand, Kelly is a very bright three-year-old. If she starts to speak, will you jot down anything she says that might relate to her experiences?"

"Of course."

They both turned as they heard footsteps hurrying down the stairs. It was Steve. "Kelly began to talk in her sleep," he told them. "She said 'Mona' and 'Harry.' Do you think she was referring to the kidnappers?"

"Yes, I do. Is that all Kelly said?" Carlson demanded.

Steve's eyes welled with tears. "She's lapsed into twin talk. She's trying to talk to Kathy."

"YOU'D never know it was the same kid. She looks like a little boy," Angie said cheerfully as she surveyed the effects of her makeover on Kathy. The little girl's dark blond hair was now charcoal brown, the same shade as Angie's. And it was no longer shoulder length; it barely covered her ears. "We're gonna call her Stephen. After her father, get it? Do you like your new name, Stevie? Huh?"

"Angie, this is crazy," Clint said. "We've got to pack up and get out of here."

"No, we don't. That would be the worst thing we could do. You have to write a letter to the manager of the club and say you've been offered a job in Florida and that you're giving notice."

"Angie, I *know* how the Feds work. Right now they're trying to find anyone who ever had contact with Lucas. Maybe this number is in his address book."

"Don't give me that. You never talked unless you were both on prepaid cell phones."

"Angie, if either one of us left just one fingerprint in that car, it could come up in the Feds' database."

"You wore gloves when you stole that car, gloves when you drove Lucas's car to his place. Anyhow, you've been Clint Downes for a good fifteen years. So stop, stop, stop!"

Kathy had been almost asleep. As Angie's voice rose, she slid down from Angie's lap and stood looking up at both of them. In an abrupt change of mood, Angie said, "I swear Stevie is getting to look just like me, Clint. You must have done a pretty good job with the steam. She doesn't seem so choked up."

"Angie, she needs real medicine."

"I can take care of that if I have to." Angie did not tell Clint that she had rummaged in the bathroom cabinet and found penicillin tablets and cough medicine. I'll open the pills and dilute them, she thought. Penicillin cures just about everything.

"And why did you have to go and say that I'd meet Gus tonight? I'm half dead. I don't want to go out."

"You have to go. This way you get rid of him. You can tell him you're going to take another job. Just don't have a couple of beers and start crying for your pal Lucas."

Kathy turned and was walking toward the bedroom. Angie got up to follow her and watched as Kathy pulled the blanket from the crib, wrapped herself in it, and lay down on the floor.

"Listen, baby, you have a crib to crash in," Angie snapped. She picked up the child. "Does Stevie love Mommy, hmmmm?"

Kathy closed her eyes and turned her head away. Angie shook her. "I'm getting sick and tired of the way you treat me, and don't you dare start that double-talk again."

The sudden piercing sound of the doorbell made Angie go rigid. Maybe Clint was right. Maybe the Feds did trace him through Lucas, she thought, paralyzed with fear. She heard Clint move with slow, heavy steps.

"Hello, Clint, old buddy. Thought I'd save you the trouble of driving. You can tell Angie I promise it'll be a two-beer night." It was the booming voice of Gus the plumber.

He suspects something is fishy, Angie thought angrily. He *did* hear the two kids crying, and now he's checking us out. She tucked the blanket around Kathy, allowing only the back of her head to show, and stepped into the living room. "Hi, Gus," she said.

"Angie, hi. Is this the kid you're minding?"

"Yeah. This is Stevie, the one you heard crying last night. His folks are at a family funeral in Wisconsin. I love the little guy, but I'm ready to get some sleep." With a firm hand under the blanket, she kept Kathy from turning her head.

"See you later, Angie," Clint said, edging Gus to the door.

Angie could see that Gus's pickup was in front of the cottage. Which means he came through the back gate, using the code. Which means that anytime he has an idea to drop in, he'll do it. "Bye, have a good time," she said as the door closed behind them.

She watched from the window until the truck disappeared down the lane. Then she smoothed Kathy's hair. "Baby doll, you and me and our money are making tracks right now," she said. "For once, Daddy Clint was right. It isn't safe to hang around here any longer."

7

NORMAN Bond was not surprised when two FBI agents arrived at his office on Friday morning. He knew they had been told that he had bypassed three well-qualified C.F.G.&Y. employees to hire Steve Frawley. He also assumed they had figured out that it took someone with sophisticated financial know-how to realize that some overseas banks will, for a fee, collect and instantly pass on large sums of money.

The first agent, Angus Sommers, he had met on Wednesday. The second, a slender woman of about thirty, was introduced by Sommers as Agent Ruthanne Scaturro. He knew that other agents were swarming through the building, asking questions.

Bond, dressed in a crisp white shirt, blue tie, and conservative Paul Stuart suit, acknowledged his visitors with a nod of his head. As a courtesy, he made a slight gesture of rising, but quickly settled back, his face impassive.

"Mr. Bond," Sommers began, "that was a pretty strong statement your chief financial officer, Gregg Stanford, made to the media yesterday. Did you agree with it?"

Bond raised one eyebrow. "I never agree with Gregg Stanford's position. Or let me put it another way: He is chief financial officer because his wife's family owns ten percent of the voting stock. He knows that we all consider him a lightweight. He has the ridiculous notion that by taking the opposite viewpoint from Robinson Geisler, he will attract a following. He covets our chairman's seat, and he has seized the opportunity to be a post-tragedy sage."

"Do you covet the chairman's seat, Mr. Bond?" Scaturro asked.

"In due course, I would hope to be considered for it."

"Why did you hire Steve Frawley?" Angus Sommers asked.

"It seems to me that we went over that subject two days ago, Mr. Sommers," Bond said, a note of annoyance creeping into his voice.

"Let's talk about it again. There are three rather bitter men who felt you had neither the need nor the right."

"Let me explain something about corporate politics, Mr. Sommers. The three men want *my* job. I'm a pretty good judge of people, and Steve Frawley is smart, very smart. A combination of an MBA and a law degree goes a long way. We had a long talk about this company, and I liked what I heard. Norman Bond leaned back in his chair and pressed his hands together, the fingers pointing upward. "And now, if you'll forgive me, I must get to a meeting upstairs."

"Just a few more questions, Mr. Bond," Sommers said. "You didn't tell us the other day that you lived in Ridgefield at one time."

"I have lived in many places. Ridgefield was over twenty years ago, when I was married."

"Did your wife give birth to twin boys who died at birth?"

"Yes, she did." Bond's eyes became expressionless.

"You were very much in love with your wife, but she left you shortly after that, didn't she?"

"She moved to California. She wanted to start all over. Grief separates as many people as it brings closer."

"After she left, you had something of a breakdown, didn't you, Mr. Bond?"

"Grief also causes depression, Mr. Sommers. I knew I needed help, so I checked into a facility. Today bereavement groups are common. Twenty years ago they were not."

"Did you keep in touch with your former wife?"

"She remarried fairly quickly. It was better for both of us to close that chapter in our lives."

"But unfortunately her chapter isn't closed, is it? She disappeared several years after she remarried. Were you questioned about that?"

"I was asked if I had any knowledge of where she might have gone. Of course, I did not. In fact, I contributed to the reward offered for information leading to her return."

"That reward has never been collected, has it, Mr. Bond?"

"No, it has not."

"Mr. Bond, when you met Steve Frawley, did you see something of yourself in him: a young, smart, and ambitious man with an attractive, smart wife and beautiful children?"

"Mr. Sommers, this questioning has become irrational. Are you suggesting that I might have had something to do with my late wife's disappearance, as well as the Frawley twins' kidnapping? How dare you insult me like that. Get out of my office."

"Your *late* wife, Mr. Bond? How do you know she's dead?"

I'VE always been a just-in-case person, baby doll," Angie said more to herself than to Kathy, who was lying on the bed in the motel, propped on pillows and covered with a blanket. "I think ahead all the time. That's the difference between me and Clint."

It was ten o'clock on Friday morning, and Angie was feeling pleased with herself. An hour after Clint and Gus had left for the tavern, she had the van packed and was on the road with Kathy. She had put the ransom money into suitcases, then thrown together some hastily packed clothes and the prepaid cell phones the Pied Piper had sent to Lucas and Clint. In her final trip from the house, she remembered to grab Lucas's tapes and a driver's license she had stolen from a woman whose kid she had minded last year.

Then, as an afterthought, she'd scribbled a note for Clint: "Don't worry. I'll call you in the morning."

She drove for three and a half hours straight to Cape Cod and the Hyannis motel where she had stayed years ago when she and some guy came up for a weekend. She'd liked the Cape so much that she got a summer job at the Seagull Marina in Harwich.

"I always had an escape plan in mind, just in case Clint got caught on one of the jobs he did with Lucas," she told Kathy with a chuckle. But then, seeing that Kathy was falling back asleep, she frowned and tapped the little girl's shoulder. "Listen to me when I'm talking. You might learn something."

Kathy's eyes remained closed.

"Maybe I gave you too much of that cough medicine," Angie speculated. "If it made Clint sleepy when he used to take it last year, I guess it could really knock you out."

She went to the counter where a little of the coffee she'd made earlier still remained in the pot. I'm hungry, she thought. I could use a decent breakfast, but I can't be lugging the kid around half-asleep and with no coat on her back. Maybe I'll just lock her in the room and get something for myself, then go pick up some clothes for her. I'll leave the suitcases under the bed and put a DO NOT DISTURB sign on the door. Maybe I'll give her a little more of the cough medicine—then she'll *really* sleep.

At least I was sharp enough to bring that driver's license, so I'll be officially known around here as Linda Hagen. We both have thin faces and brown hair, and if I ever get stopped, I'll put on dark glasses. Someone would really have to study the picture to know it was a phony. Anyhow, except for the Feds tracing the van if they catch up with Clint, I'm okay for a while.

After I make sure there's no heat on Clint, maybe I'll tell him where I am so he can join me. And maybe I won't. But I did tell him I'd call him this morning, so I'd better do that.

She picked up one of the prepaid cell phones and dialed. Clint answered on the first ring. "Where are you?" he demanded.

"Clint, baby, it was better I got out fast. I've got the money, don't worry. If by any chance the Feds do look you up, what if the kid was there and the money? Now listen: Get rid of the crib! Did you tell Gus you were giving notice at the club?"

"Yeah, yeah. I told him I was offered a job in Orlando."

"Good. Give your notice today. If nosy Gussy comes around again, tell him the mother of the kid I was minding asked me to take him to Wisconsin. Tell him I'm going to meet you in Florida."

"Don't mess with me, Angie."

"I'm not messing with you. I told Gus you were looking for a new car in Yonkers. Tell him you sold the van, then go rent a car for now."

"You didn't leave me a dime of the money," he said bitterly. "Not even the five hundred bucks I left on the dresser."

"Run up the credit card. In another two weeks we're gonna disappear from the earth. I gotta go. Good-bye."

Angie snapped closed the cover of the cell phone and looked down at Kathy. Was she asleep or just pretending to be asleep? she wondered. She's getting to be as nasty as the other one. No matter how nice I am, she ignores me.

The cough medicine was by the bed. She poured out a spoonful, forced apart Kathy's lips, and tipped the liquid into her mouth. "Now swallow it," she ordered.

In a sleepy, reflexive action Kathy swallowed most of the cough syrup. A few drops went into her windpipe, and she began to cough and cry. Angie pushed her back on the pillow. "Oh, for God's sake, shut up," she said through gritted teeth.

Kathy closed her eyes and pulled the blanket over her face as she turned away, trying not to cry. In her mind she could see Kelly. She didn't dare talk out loud but did move her lips silently as she felt Angie begin to tie her to the bed.

IN THE front row of St. Mary's Church, Margaret and Steve held on to Kelly's hands as they knelt on Friday morning at a private Mass of the Angels. Beside them, Dr. Sylvia Harris was blinking back tears as she listened to Monsignor Romney's opening prayer:

Lord God, from whom human sadness is never hidden
You know the burden of grief
That we feel at the loss of this child
As we mourn her passing from this life
Comfort us with the knowledge
That Kathryn Ann lives now in your loving embrace.

Kelly tugged at Margaret's hand. "Mommy," she said, her voice loud and clear for the first time since she had been returned to them. "Kathy is very scared of that lady. She's crying. She wants you to bring her home, too. Right now!"

SPECIAL Agent Chris Smith, head of the Bureau's North Carolina office, had phoned to request a meeting with the parents of Steve Frawley in Winston-Salem.

Frawley's father, Tom, a retired and highly decorated captain of the New York City Fire Department, had not been pleased. "One of our two grandchildren is dead. My wife had knee replacements three weeks ago and is still in terrible pain. Why do you want to see us?"

"We need to talk to you about Mrs. Frawley's older son, your stepson, Richie Mason," Smith had said.

"Oh, for God's sake, I might have known. Come over around eleven o'clock."

Smith, a fifty-two-year-old African American, brought along Carla Rogers, a twenty-six-year-old agent recently assigned to his staff.

At eleven Tom Frawley answered the door and invited the agents in. The first sight that greeted Smith was a collage of pictures of the twins on the wall opposite the door. Beautiful kids, he thought. What a damn shame we couldn't get both of them back.

At Frawley's invitation they followed him into the family room. Grace Frawley was seated in a leather chair with her feet on an ottoman. Smith went over to her. "Mrs. Frawley, I am terribly sorry to intrude. I won't take much of your time. Our office in Connecticut sent us to ask you and Mr. Frawley some questions about your son, Richard Mason."

"Sit down, please." Tom Frawley pointed them to the couch, then pulled up a chair for himself next to his wife. "What kind of trouble is Richie in now?" he demanded.

"Mr. Frawley, I didn't say Richie was in trouble. I don't know that he is. We wanted to talk to him, but he did not report for work at Newark Airport Wednesday evening and has not been seen around his condominium since last week."

"He told us he was going back to work," Grace Frawley said nervously. "Richie came down to visit last weekend. Could anything have happened to him? He might have been in an accident on the way home."

"Grace, be real," Tom gently insisted. "Richie hated that job. He said he was too smart to be shoving baggage around. I wouldn't be surprised if he just made up his mind to drive to Vegas or some-place like it. He's done that sort of thing before. He's okay, dear. You've got enough on your plate without worrying about *him*."

Chris Smith caught the note of irritation under Tom Frawley's words. From the record he'd read on Richie Mason, it looked as if he had been a lifelong heartache. School dropout, sealed juvenile record, five years in the slammer for a scam that had cost a dozen investors a fortune.

Grace Frawley had the drawn, exhausted look of someone in pain. She was about sixty years old, Smith judged, an attractive woman with gray hair and a slight build. Tom Frawley was a big, broad-shouldered guy, maybe a few years older than she.

"Mrs. Frawley, you had surgery three weeks ago. Why did Richie wait so long to visit you?" Smith asked.

"I was in a rehab center until last Thursday."

"When did Richie get down here and when did he leave?"

"He arrived around three o'clock Saturday morning. He got off from work at the airport at three o'clock in the afternoon, and we'd expected him by midnight," Tom Frawley answered. "But then he called to say there was a lot of traffic. I'm a light sleeper, so I heard him come in. He left about ten Tuesday morning, right after we all watched Steve and Margaret on television."

"Did he get or receive many phone calls?" Smith asked.

"Not on our phone. He had his cell, though. He used it some. I don't know how much."

"Was Richie in the habit of visiting you, Mrs. Frawley?" Carla Rogers asked.

"He stopped in when we visited Steve and Margaret right after they moved to Ridgefield. Before that, we hadn't seen him for almost a year," Grace Frawley said, her voice tired and sad. "I call him regularly. He almost never answers, but I leave a message just saying we're thinking of him and we love him. Underneath he's really a good boy. Richie's father died when he was only two. I married Tom three years later, and no human being could have been a better father than Tom has been to Richie. But when he was a teenager, he got in with the wrong crowd and never got back on track again."

"What is his relationship with Steve?"

"Not the best," Tom Frawley admitted. "He's always been jealous of Steve. Richie could have gone to college. In fact, he started attending SUNY. He's smart, really smart, but he dropped out in his freshman year and took off for Las Vegas. That's how he got in with gamblers and phonies. As you must know, he served time for a scam he got involved in."

"Richie must be financially sophisticated to deceive so many people," Smith said, his face impassive. "Mr. Frawley, if you hear from him, please tell him that we need to be in touch with him. I'll give you my card." With a nod and thanks to Grace Frawley, he turned and left the condo with Agent Rogers.

In the car, Smith put the key in the ignition and said to Carla, "Richie didn't get here until early Saturday morning, which meant he could have had time to take part in the kidnapping. He was in the Ridgefield house a couple of months ago, so he knew the layout. He may have been setting up an alibi for himself by visiting his mother. He could have been one of the two men who picked up the ransom money."

"If he was one of the kidnappers, he would have to have been wearing a mask. Even if the twins barely knew him, they might have been able to identify him."

"Suppose one of them did? And suppose for that reason she couldn't be allowed to go home? And suppose Lucas Wohl's death wasn't a suicide?"

Carla Rogers stared at her superior officer. "I didn't know the guys in New York and Connecticut were thinking that way."

"The guys in New York and Connecticut are thinking every way they can."

AFTER her outburst in church, Kelly lapsed into silence. When they arrived back home, she went upstairs and brought down the two teddy bears clasped in her arms.

Rena Chapman, their kind neighbor, was waiting for them to get home. "You have simply *got* to eat," she told them. She had set the round table in the breakfast alcove of the kitchen, and it was there that they settled, Margaret holding Kelly on her lap, Steve and Dr. Harris across from them. Rena placed the platters on the table and refused to stay. "You don't need me around now," she told them firmly.

Piping-hot scrambled eggs, thin sliced ham on toast points, and strong, hot coffee warmed all of them. While they were having their second cup, Kelly slid off Margaret's lap. "Read me my book, Mommy?" she asked.

"I will, sweetheart," Steve said. "You bring it down to me."

Margaret waited until Kelly was out of the kitchen before speaking. She knew the reaction she would receive, but she had to tell them what she felt. "Kathy is alive. She and Kelly are in touch with each other."

"Margaret, Kelly is still trying to communicate with Kathy, and she's also beginning to tell you about her own experience. She was afraid of that woman who was minding them," Dr. Harris said gently.

"She was talking to Kathy," Margaret said. "I know she was."

"Oh, honey," Steve protested. "Don't break your heart by holding to even a whisper of hope that Kathy is alive."

Kelly came back with the Dr. Seuss book they had been reading before the kidnapping. Steve pushed back his chair and picked her up. "We'll go inside to my big chair in the study, okay?"

"Kathy likes this book, too," Kelly said.

"Well, we'll pretend I'm reading to both of you." Steve managed to get the words out even as his eyes filled with tears.

"Oh, Daddy, that's silly. Kathy's asleep now, and that lady tied her to the bed."

"You mean the lady tied *you* to the bed, don't you, Kelly?" Steve asked quickly.

"No. Mona made us stay in the big crib, and we couldn't climb out of it. Kathy's in the bed now," Kelly insisted, then patted Steve's cheek. "Daddy, why are you crying?"

"MARGARET, the sooner Kelly gets back to a normal routine, the easier it will be for her to become used to not being with Kathy," Dr. Harris said later, as she prepared to leave. "I think Steve is right. Taking her to nursery school was the best thing for her."

"As long as Steve doesn't let her out of his sight," Margaret said fearfully.

"Absolutely." Sylvia Harris put her arms around Margaret and gave her a brief hug. "I have to check on some patients, but I'll be back tonight, that is if you still feel I'm any help to you."

"Remember when Kathy had pneumonia and that young nurse was about to give her penicillin? If you hadn't been there, God knows what might have happened," Margaret said. "You go down and check on your sick kids and then come back. We need you."

"We certainly found out the first time that she must never have it again," Dr. Harris said in agreement. She then added, "Margaret, grieve for her, but don't read hope into what Kelly may say. Believe me, she is reliving her own experience."

Don't try to convince her! Margaret warned herself. She doesn't believe you. Steve doesn't believe you. I've got to talk to Agent Carlson, she decided. I've got to talk to him right away.

With a final squeeze of Margaret's hand, Sylvia Harris left.

Alone in the house for the first time in a week, Margaret closed her eyes, drew in a deep breath, and hurried to the phone to dial Walter Carlson's number.

He answered on the first ring. "Margaret, what can I do?"

"Kathy is alive," she told him. Then, before he could speak, she rushed on, "I know you won't believe me, but she is. Kelly is communicating with her. An hour ago Kathy was asleep and tied to a bed. Kelly told me that."

"Margaret—"

"Don't try to placate me. *Trust* me. You have only the word of a dead man that Kathy is gone. You don't have her body. You know Lucas Wohl got into his plane carrying a big box, and you're assuming Kathy's body was in it. Stop assuming that and find her. Do you hear me? *Find her!*"

Before he could respond, Margaret slammed down the phone, then collapsed into a chair and held her head in both hands. There's something I have to remember, and it has to do with the birthday dresses, she thought. I'll go up to their closet and try to remember.

AGENTS Angus Sommers and Ruthanne Scaturro went directly from their interview with Norman Bond at the Park Avenue office of C.F.G.&Y. to a meeting with Gregg Stanford. After a full half-hour wait they were finally admitted to his office, which obviously had been furnished to reflect his own rather grand taste.

Instead of a typical desk, he had an antique writing table. Sommers, something of a furniture buff himself, recognized it as being early eighteenth century and probably worth a small fortune. Instead of bookshelves, an eighteenth-century *bureau-cabinet* on the left wall reflected sunlight that was filtering through a window that overlooked Park Avenue. A portrait of a beautiful woman in an evening gown dominated the right wall. Sommers was sure its haughty, unsmiling subject had to be Stanford's current wife, Millicent.

What a phony, Sommers thought. Did he rig this office up on his own, or was the wife in on it? She's on a couple of museum boards, so she probably knows her stuff.

Stanford remained seated, his hands clasped in front of him, until the agents sat down without being invited. "Have you made any progress in your search for the Pied Piper?" he asked abruptly.

"Yes, we have," Sommers said. "In fact, we're closing in on him fast. More than that, I'm not at liberty to tell. Mr. Stanford, we have come across some information we need to discuss with you."

"I cannot imagine what you have to discuss with me," Stanford said. "My position on the ransom payment is obviously my only area of interest to you."

"Not quite," Sommers said. "When you learned that Lucas Wohl was one of the kidnappers, it must have been quite a shock to you."

"What *are* you talking about?"

"You must have seen his picture in the newspapers?"

"I saw his picture, of course."

"Then you must have recognized that he was your chauffeur for several years."

"I don't know what you're talking about."

"I think you *do,* Mr. Stanford. Your second wife, Tina Olsen, was very active with a charity that helped ex-convicts get jobs. Through her, you met Jimmy Nelson, who at some time took on the name of his deceased cousin, Lucas Wohl. Tina Olsen had a longtime private chauffeur, but Jimmy—or Lucas or whatever you called him— drove you frequently during your marriage to her. Yesterday Tina Olsen called your first wife, Amy Lindcroft, and told her that she believes Lucas continued to drive you long after the breakup of the marriage. Is that true, Mr. Stanford?"

Stanford stared first at one agent and then the other. "If there is anything worse than one woman scorned, it is two women scorned," he said. "During my marriage to Tina, I used a car service. Quite frankly, I never established, nor did I want to establish, any kind of relationship with the various drivers who worked for that service. If you tell me that one of the kidnappers was one of them, I accept it, although, of course, I am shocked. The idea that I should have recognized him in the newspaper is ludicrous."

"Then you don't deny you know him?" Sommers asked.

"You could tell me that *any* person drove me from time to time, years ago, and I would not be able to either confirm or deny it."

"We'll be going over the records Lucas kept; they go back quite a few years," Sommers said as he stood up. "I think he was your driver far more frequently than you have cared to admit, which leads me to wonder what else you have to conceal. We will find out what it is, Mr. Stanford. I can promise you *that*."

MARGARET sat on the edge of the bed in the twins' bedroom, the blue velvet dresses draped across her lap. She tried to push aside the memory of a week ago, when she'd dressed the twins for their party. Steve had come home from work early, and the twins had been so excited that he finally had to hold Kelly on his lap while Margaret fastened the buttons on Kathy's dress.

They were giggling and talking twin talk, she remembered, and she was convinced they could read each other's minds. *That's* why I know Kathy is alive. Where can I look for her? she anguished. Where can I begin? What is it about the dresses? What is it? She ran her hands over the velvet fabric, remembering how they'd cost more than she wanted to pay. The salesgirl told me how much they'd cost at Bergdorf's. Then she said it was funny I was there because she'd just waited on another woman shopping for twins.

Margaret gasped. *That's* what I've been trying to remember! It's the clerk. She told me that she'd just sold clothes for three-year-old twins to a woman who didn't seem to know anything about what size to buy for them.

Margaret stood up and let the dresses slide to the floor. I'll know the clerk when I see her, she thought. It's probably just a crazy coincidence. But, on the other hand, it would be obvious to the kidnappers that the twins would be in pajamas when they took them and would need a change of clothes. I have to talk to that clerk.

When Margaret went downstairs, Steve was just returning with Kelly from the nursery school. "All her friends were so happy to see our little girl," he said, his voice heavy with false cheer. "Isn't that right, sweetheart?"

Without answering, Kelly let go of his hand and took off her jacket. Then she started to whisper under her breath.

Margaret looked at Steve. "She's talking to Kathy."

"She's *trying* to talk to Kathy," he corrected.

Margaret reached out her hand. "Steve, give me the car keys."

"Margaret—"

"Steve, I know what I'm doing. You stay with Kelly. Don't leave her for a minute. And make note of whatever she says, please."

"Where are you going?"

"Not far. Just to the store on Route 7 where I bought their party dresses. I have to talk to the clerk who waited on me."

"Why don't you call her?"

Margaret forced herself to draw a long breath. "Steve, just give me the keys. I'm all right. I won't be long."

"There's still a media van at the end of the street. They'll follow you."

"They won't get a chance. I'll be gone before they realize it's me."

In a sudden gesture Kelly spun around and threw her arms around Steve's leg. "I'm sorry!" she wailed. "I'm sorry!"

Steve picked her up and rocked her in his arms. "Kelly, it's okay. It's okay."

She was clutching her arm. Margaret pushed up her shirtsleeve and watched as the arm began to turn red in the same spot over the faint black-and-blue mark they had noticed when she returned home. Margaret felt her mouth go dry. "That woman just pinched Kathy," she whispered. "I know she did. Oh, God, Steve, don't you get it? Give me the keys!"

He reluctantly pulled the car keys from his pocket, and she yanked them out of his hand and ran for the door. Fifteen minutes later she entered Abby's Discount. There were about a dozen people in the store, all of them women. Margaret walked up and down the aisles, looking for the clerk, but she did not see her. Finally she approached the cashier, who directed her to the manager.

"Oh, you mean Lila Jackson," the manager said. "It's her day off. Any one of our clerks will be happy to help—"

"Does Lila have a cell phone?" Margaret interrupted.

"Yes, but I really can't give her number to you." The manager, a woman of about sixty with frosted blond hair, suddenly became less cordial. "If you have a complaint, you can speak directly to me. I'm Joan Howell, and I'm in charge here."

"It's not a complaint. It's just about when I was here last week."

Howell shook her head. "She'll be in at ten o'clock tomorrow morning. You can come back then."

Margaret caught her by the arm. "You don't understand," she pleaded, her voice rising. "My little girl is missing. I've got to find her before it's too late."

She had drawn the attention of other shoppers. Don't make a scene, she warned herself. They'll think you're crazy. "I'm sorry," she stammered as she released Howell's sleeve.

Joan Howell's expression was sympathetic. "You're Mrs. Frawley, aren't you? Lila told me that you bought the birthday dresses for your twins here. I'm so sorry about Kathy. And I'm sorry I didn't recognize you. I'll give you Lila's number. Please, come into the office."

Margaret could hear the shoppers whispering: "That's Margaret Frawley. She's the one whose twins . . ."

In a rush of grief Margaret turned and ran outside. In the car, she turned on the ignition key and floored the gas pedal. Not knowing where she was going, she began to drive. Later she remembered going on I-95 north as far as Providence, Rhode Island. There, at the first sign for Cape Cod, she stopped for gas and only then realized how far she had gone. She turned onto I-95 south and drove until she saw the sign for Route 7, then followed it, sensing that she needed to find Danbury Airport. Reaching it finally, she parked near the entrance.

He carried her body in a box, she thought. That was her casket. He took her on the plane and flew over the ocean; then he opened the door or the window and dropped the body of my beautiful little girl. It would have been a long fall. Did the box break? Did Kathy tumble out into the water? The water is so cold now.

If we go out on a boat and drop some flowers, maybe then it will feel as though I can say good-bye . . ."

A light suddenly shone in the driver's window, and Margaret looked up.

"Mrs. Frawley." The state trooper's voice was gentle. "We'd like to help you get home, ma'am. Your husband is worried."

"Yes. I just ran an errand."

"Ma'am, it's eleven o'clock at night. You left the store at four o'clock."

"Did I? I guess that's because I stopped hoping."

"Yes, ma'am. Now let me drive you home."

8

"NOW get this straight," Angie told Kathy at nine o'clock on Saturday morning. "Between the crying and the coughing, you kept me awake half the night, and I'm sick of it. I can't stay cooped up in this room all day, and I can't shut you up by taping your mouth, because with that cold you might not be able to breathe, so I'm taking you with me. I bought some clothes for you yesterday when I went out, but the shoes are too small. So we're going to go back to Sears, and I'll go in and switch the shoes for the next size. And *you* are going to stay on the floor of the van and say not one word, got it?"

Kathy nodded. Angie had dressed her in a polo shirt, corduroy overalls, and a hooded jacket. Her short brown hair lay limply on her forehead, still damp from the shower Angie had given her. A full tablespoon of cough syrup was already making her sleepy. She wanted so much to talk to Kelly, but twin talk was forbidden. That was why Angie had pinched her yesterday.

"Mommy, Daddy," she whispered in her mind. "I want to come home. I want to come home." She knew she had to try not to cry anymore.

"Don't start crying," Angie warned as she opened the door and pulled Kathy to the parking lot. It was raining hard, and Angie put down the big suitcase she was carrying and yanked the hood of the jacket over Kathy's head. "You don't need a worse cold," she said. "You're sick enough as it is."

Angie put the suitcase in the car, then made Kathy lie down on the pillow on the floor and covered her with a blanket. "That's something else. I have to get a car seat for you." She sighed. "You're more trouble than you're worth."

Kathy curled up on the floor and put her thumb in her mouth.

As Angie drove out of the motel parking lot, she said, "Just in case you're interested, you're in Cape Cod, baby doll. This street leads to the docks where the boats go over to Martha's Vineyard. I went to Martha's Vineyard once, with the guy who brought me up here. I kind of liked him. Boy, I wish I could tell *him* that I'm driving around with a million bucks in a suitcase. Wouldn't that be something?"

Kathy felt the car turn. They drove for a little while more. Angie began to sing a song about Cape Cod. She didn't know many of the words, so she'd hum and then sort of yell, *"In old Cape Cod."* She sang those words over and over. Then, after a while, the car stopped. Angie leaned over the seat, a mean expression on her face. "Okay, we're here," she said. "Now listen, don't you dare get up. I'm going to pull the blanket over your head. If I come out and find you moved one *inch,* you know what will happen, don't you?"

Kathy's eyes welled with tears, and she nodded.

"Okay. We understand each other. I'll be back fast; then we'll go to McDonald's. You and me together. Mommy and Stevie."

Kathy felt the blanket being pulled over her head. She managed not to cough until Angie had closed and locked the door. Then she let herself cry and talk to Kelly. "I don't want to be in old Cape Cod. *I want to come home.*"

"THERE he is," Agent Sean Walsh whispered to his partner, Damon Philburn. It was nine thirty on Saturday morning. He was pointing to the lanky figure of a man in a hooded sweatshirt now walking to the front door of a condominium in Clifton, New Jersey. In a swift, simultaneous movement the agents were out of their car and on either side of him before he could turn the key in the door.

Steve Frawley's half brother, Richard Mason, did not seem surprised to see them. "Come on in," he said. "But you're wasting your time. I had nothing to do with my brother's kids being kidnapped. The way you guys work, you probably had my phone bugged after you first came looking for me."

Neither agent bothered to reply as Mason turned on the foyer light and walked into the living room. To Walsh it had the look of a motel unit—a couch upholstered in a brown tweed pattern, two striped brown chairs, two end tables with matching lamps, a coffee table, beige carpeting. Mason had been there for the past ten months, but the built-in bookshelves did not hold a single book. There were no family pictures or personal items. Mason sat in one of the chairs, took out a pack of cigarettes, lit one, and looked annoyed. "Threw out the ashtrays so that I wouldn't be tempted to smoke." Shrugging, he got up, disappeared into the kitchen, came back holding a saucer, and resettled in the chair.

He's trying to show us how cool he is, Walsh thought. We can all play that game. He exchanged a quick glance with Philburn and let the silence grow.

"Listen, I've done a lot of driving these past few days and need to get to bed. What do you want?" Mason asked.

"When did you resume smoking, Mr. Mason?" Walsh asked.

"A week ago, when I heard my brother's twins were missing."

"It wasn't when you decided to kidnap them, was it?" Agent Philburn asked matter-of-factly.

"You've got to be crazy! My brother's kids?"

A deep flush colored Mason's face. Walsh noticed the strong physical resemblance to his half brother. He's trying to con us now, Walsh thought. Playing the part of the outraged uncle.

"You visited your brother and his wife in Ridgefield shortly after they moved in," he said. "You've never been very close to your brother, have you?"

"A lot of brothers aren't close. Even more half brothers aren't close," Mason replied evenly.

"You almost got away with pulling off a scam that would have made millions for you. Since Steve was hired in a job that's a straight path to the top, has it occurred to you he's bested you?"

"It never crossed my mind."

"Mr. Mason, a baggage handler has a pretty exhausting job. Somehow it doesn't seem to be the kind of occupation you'd choose."

"It's an interim position," Richard Mason said calmly.

"Aren't you afraid of losing it? You didn't show up for work all week."

"I phoned in to say I wasn't well and needed the week off."

"Funny, we weren't told that," Philburn commented.

"Then somebody messed up. I assure you, I made the call."

"Where did you go?"

"I drove to Vegas. I was feeling lucky."

"It didn't occur to you to be with your brother while his children were missing?"

"He wouldn't have wanted me. I'm an embarrassment to him. Can't you just picture the hovering ex-con brother with the media around?"

"You are sophisticated about wire transfers and banks that will forward funds and destroy records, aren't you?"

Mason stood up. "Get out. Arrest me or get out."

Neither agent made a move. "Is it a coincidence that you visited your mother in North Carolina the weekend your brother's children were kidnapped? Maybe you were trying to establish an alibi."

"Get out."

Walsh took out his notebook. "Where did you stay in Vegas?"

"I'm not answering any questions until I talk to a lawyer."

Walsh and Philburn got up. "We'll be back," Walsh said.

They left the condo but stopped at Mason's car, parked nearby.

Walsh took out a flashlight and played it on the dashboard. "Fifty thousand six hundred and forty-six miles."

"He's watching us." Philburn jotted down the figure.

"I want him to watch us. He knows what I'm doing."

"How many miles did the mother say was on the odometer?"

"In that wire-tapped phone call she made to him after he left, she reminded him that the stepfather had noticed that his car was coming up to fifty thousand miles, and his warranty would be expiring."

"Mason's some six hundred miles over fifty thousand on this car. It's about six hundred miles from Winston-Salem. He never drove this car to Vegas for sure. So where do you think he was?"

"In the tristate area, babysitting," Philburn replied.

"I KNOW why Mrs. Frawley wanted to talk to me," Lila Jackson said quietly on Saturday morning. "If it would help Mrs. Frawley to talk to me, I'd really like to talk to her."

"She didn't leave her number. I'd say, let it go." Joan Howell glanced at her watch, a clear indication that as of ten a.m. Lila was paid to sell Abby's Discount Clothes.

Lila remembered the name of the customer who hadn't known the size of the three-year-old twins. It's Downes, she thought as she headed for a sales rack. She signed the slip as Mrs. Clint Downes, but when I talked to Jim Gilbert about her, he told me her name is Angie, that she's not married to Downes, and that he's the caretaker at the Danbury Country Club and they live in a cottage on the grounds of the club.

Aware that Joan Howell's eyes were on her, she turned to a woman who had several pantsuits over her arm. "May I put these aside for you?" she asked. At the customer's grateful nod, she took the garments, and, as she waited, thought about how the police had been begging for any report that might help.

The shopper found two more suits. "There's an empty dressing room over here," Lila told her. I could talk to the police now, she thought, but they might just dismiss it the way Jim did. I've got a better idea. The country club is only ten minutes from here. On my lunch hour I'll drive over and say that I realized the polo shirts were defective and I wanted to replace them. Then, if I still feel funny about anything, I will call the police.

At one o'clock Lila tossed two size 4 polo shirts in a bag. She ran across the parking lot to her car. It had begun to rain again, and in her haste she had not bothered to take her umbrella. Twelve minutes later she was at the gate to the country club. To her dismay, it was padlocked. Driving around slowly, she found a service road with a bar across it and a code box. In the distance, behind the clubhouse, she could see a small building, which she guessed might be the caretaker's cottage.

The rain was getting heavier. I've come this far, Lila decided, I'm going ahead. At least I was smart enough to wear a raincoat. She got out of the car, ducked under the security arm, and began to jog toward the cottage, with the polo shirts under her jacket. She passed a garage that was empty, but as she got close to the cottage, she could see a light on in the front room. Here goes nothing, she thought as she went up to the porch and rang the bell.

ON FRIDAY evening Clint had gone out with Gus again, got home late, slept until noon, and now was hungover and nervous. At the bar, Gus had said that when he'd phoned the other night, he'd have sworn he heard two kids crying in the background.

I tried to make a joke of it, Clint thought. I told him he must have been drunk to think there were two kids in this chicken coop. I told him if Angie ever showed up with two kids, I'd tell her to hit the road. I think he bought it, but I don't know. He's got a big mouth. Besides that, he told me about seeing Angie buying the vaporizer and aspirin. For all I know, he could have told somebody else.

Why did Angie keep one of the kids? Why did she kill Lucas? If both kids had been returned, no one would be the wiser. Now the whole country is on the warpath because they think one is dead.

Angie will get sick of minding her. Then she'll dump her somewhere. I know she will. I just hope she doesn't . . . Clint didn't finish the thought, but the image of Angie shooting Lucas was never far from his mind.

He was hunched over the kitchen table, wearing a sweatshirt, jeans, and a two-day growth of beard, when the doorbell rang.

The cops! It would be the cops, he was sure of it. Perspiration began to pour from him. No, maybe it's Gus, he thought, grasping at straws. He had to open the door. If it was the cops, they'd have seen that the light was on.

He yanked the door open.

Lila gasped. "Is Mrs. Downes, I mean, is Angie home?" she asked.

He forced something like a smile to cross his face. "No. She's away on a babysitting job. I'm Clint. Why do you want her?"

"I'm Lila Jackson. I work at Abby's Discount. My boss sent me over to give Angie something. Do you mind if I step in?"

"Sure, come in." Clint stood aside, and Lila brushed past him, glancing at the living room, kitchen area, and open bedroom door. She handed him the polo shirts. "When Angie was in our store last week, she bought shirts for twins," she said. "We received a notice that the whole run had defects, so I came over with replacements."

"That was very nice of you," Clint said slowly, his mind scrambling to explain the purchase. "My girlfriend babysits all the time," he explained. "She drove to Wisconsin with a family to help take care of their kids for a couple of weeks. She bought that stuff because the mother called ahead to say she forgot to bring one of their suitcases."

"The mother of the three-year-old twins?" Lila asked.

"Yeah. Actually, from what Angie told me, the kids are less than a year apart. They're about the same size, though. The mother dresses them alike and calls them twins. Why don't you just leave the shirts here? I'm sending a package to Angie. I'll put them in it."

Lila handed the bag to Clint.

"I'll be on my way," she said. "Please apologize to Angie."

"Sure, glad to. No problem."

The phone rang. "Well anyhow, good-bye," Clint said as he

picked up the receiver. "Hi," he said, his eyes fixed on Lila, who was opening the door.

"Why haven't you been answering my phone?" a voice barked.

It was the Pied Piper. Clint tried to sound casual. "Not tonight, Gus," he said. "I really want to take it easy."

"Who's there with you?" the Pied Piper demanded.

Clint waited until he saw Lila outside, passing the window and hurrying back to her car. Then he said, "Angie took off with the kid. She didn't think it was safe to hang around anymore. She has the cell phones you gave us. She charged clothes for the kids to my credit card. Some woman was here from the store, replacing shirts that were no good. I don't know whether she's on the level." He knew his voice was rising as he said, "I've got to figure out what to do. I don't even know where Angie is."

"Take it easy, Clint. Do you think Angie will call again?"

"I think so. She trusts me. I think she knows she needs me."

"But you don't need *her*. What would happen if you told her a cop had come around looking for her?"

"She'd panic."

"Then tell her that. Arrange to meet her wherever she is. And remember—what she did to Lucas, she could do to you."

"Don't think I'm not thinking about that."

"And remember the child could identify you, too."

"EVERYONE has a breaking point, Margaret," Dr. Harris said gently early Saturday afternoon. It was one o'clock, and she and Kelly had just woken Margaret.

Now Margaret was sitting up in bed, Kelly snuggled beside her. She tried to smile. "Whatever did you give me to knock me out like that? Do you realize I've been sleeping for twelve hours?"

"Do you realize how much sleep you've lost in the past week?" Dr. Harris's tone was light, but her eyes were watchful. Margaret's so thin, she thought, and so terribly pale. "I hated to wake you up, but Agent Carlson wants to stop by and asked me to wake you up."

"The FBI is probably trying to decide what I was up to last night.

I wonder if they think I'm crazy. Right after you left yesterday, I called Agent Carlson. I screamed at him that Kathy was still alive and he had to find her." Margaret pulled Kelly into her arms. "Then I went to the place where I bought the dresses and practically attacked the manager. I just lost it, I guess."

"Do you have any idea of where you went after you left the store?" Dr. Harris asked. "Last night you said it was a total blank."

"I don't remember anything until a sign for Cape Cod woke me up, and I turned around. I feel so guilty. Poor Steve has had enough stress without *me* going off the deep end." Margaret brushed her finger over Kelly's cheek. "Hey, somebody's really quiet. How are we doing, Kel?"

Kelly looked up at her solemnly.

"Our little girl really has been pretty quiet all morning," Dr. Harris observed. "I slept in with you last night, didn't I, Kelly?"

Kelly nodded silently.

"Did she sleep well?" Margaret asked.

"She was having a little reaction to everything, I think. She was crying in her sleep and doing quite a bit of coughing. That's why I thought it best to stay with her."

Margaret bit her lip. "She's probably getting her sister's cold." She kissed the top of Kelly's head. "We'll take very good care of that, won't we, Dr. Harris?"

"Indeed we will, but I can assure you that her chest is absolutely clear." In fact, Dr. Harris thought, there is no reason for all that coughing. She doesn't have a cold. She stood up. "Margaret, why don't we give you a chance to shower and dress? We'll go pick out whatever story Kelly wants me to read to her."

"I think that's a wonderful idea," Margaret said.

Kelly slid off the bed and reached for Sylvia Harris's hand. They went downstairs to the study. There, Kelly selected a book and climbed onto the doctor's lap. Tucking an afghan around Kelly, Sylvia began to open the book but then pushed up Kelly's sleeve to see what Steve had said that so upset Margaret last night.

The purple bruise on her forearm was in almost the same spot as the one that was fading. It looks as though someone pinched her hard, Sylvia thought. Steve thinks she hit her arm against a table, but is it possible Margaret is right that Kelly was actually feeling Kathy's pain?

"Kelly," she asked, "can you sometimes feel what Kathy feels?"

Kelly shook her head, her eyes frightened. "Ssshhh," she whispered, then rolled into a ball, put her thumb in her mouth, and pulled the afghan over her head.

NORMAN Bond lived on the fortieth floor of an apartment building bordering the East River at Seventy-second Street in Manhattan. His panoramic, three-hundred-and-sixty-degree view enriched his solitary personal life. In the morning he often got up to watch the sunrise. At night he took particular pleasure in observing the brilliance of the lights on the bridges that spanned the river.

On Saturday morning, after the dreary weather of the past week, the day dawned crisp and clear, but even the bright sunrise did not lift his spirits. For hours he sat on his living-room couch.

How could I be so stupid, he asked himself. How could I have slipped and referred to Theresa as "my late wife"?

The FBI agents had pounced on that. Long ago they had given up questioning him about Theresa's disappearance. Now it would start all over again. But when someone has been missing for seven years and declared legally dead, isn't it natural to refer to that person as if she *were* dead? Theresa has been missing seventeen years.

It was all right to wear the wedding ring he had given Theresa, he thought, the one she left for him on the dresser. But was it safe to continue wearing her other ring, the one her second husband gave her? He unfastened the chain from around his neck and held both rings in his hand, studying them intensely. LOVE IS ETERNAL was inscribed in tiny letters on the inside of both bands.

The one he gave her is all diamonds, Norman thought enviously. I gave her a plain silver ring. It was all I could afford at that time.

"My *late* wife," he said aloud. Now, after all this time, the kidnapping of two little girls had brought him to the attention of the

FBI again. It would be dangerous to resign from C.F.G.&Y. and move abroad.

Theresa had cried and cried when the twins were born prematurely and didn't survive, and shortly after that, she left him. When they were married, he had told Theresa that someday he was going to be the chairman and CEO of C.F.G.&Y.

Now he knew, of course, that was never going to happen, but somehow it didn't matter anymore. He didn't need the grief of the job, and now he didn't need the money, either. But I can't stop wearing the rings, he thought as he clasped the chain around his neck again. They're what give me strength.

Norman smiled, remembering the terrified look on Theresa's face that night when she turned around and saw him hiding in the backseat of her car.

"THESE shoes are too big," Angie said, "but I'm not going to worry about it." She had parked outside McDonald's, near the mall where she'd bought the shoes, and now was fastening them on Kathy's feet. "Remember to keep your mouth shut, but if anyone asks your name, say it's Stevie. Got it? Say it for me now."

"Stevie," Kathy whispered.

"You got it. Now come on."

Kathy's feet kept sliding and started to come out of the shoes. Angie was pulling her along too fast. Suddenly Kathy felt her foot come out of one of the shoes.

Outside McDonald's, Angie stopped to buy a newspaper at a vending machine. Then they went inside and got on line. When she got their food, they sat at a table where Angie could see the van.

Kathy didn't want her egg sandwich and orange juice. She wasn't hungry and really just wanted to sleep.

"I think from here we go back to the motel, then look up some places to buy a used car," Angie said. "Trouble is, having piles of fifty- and twenty-dollar bills is going to attract attention."

Kathy watched as Angie opened the newspaper and said something under her breath. Then she reached over and pulled the hood back over Kathy's head. "God Almighty, your face is all over this paper," she said. "Except for the hair, any dope would recognize you. Let's get out of here."

Kathy didn't want Angie to be mad at her again. She slid off the chair and reached for Angie's hand.

"Where's your other shoe, little boy?" asked a lady who was cleaning the next table.

"Her other shoe?" Angie asked, then looked down. "Oh, hell," she said. "Did you untie that again in the car?"

"No," Kathy whispered. "It fell off. It's too big."

"Your other one's too big, too," said the lady. "What's your name, little boy?"

Kathy couldn't remember what Angie had told her to say.

"Tell me your name," the lady said.

"Kathy," she whispered, but then Angie squeezed her hand hard, and suddenly she remembered the name. "Stevie," she said. "My name is Stevie."

"Oh, I bet you have a pretend friend named Kathy," the woman said. "My granddaughter has a pretend friend, too."

"Yeah," Angie agreed hurriedly. "Well, we got to be on our way."

Kathy glanced back and saw the woman picking up a newspaper on the table she was cleaning. On it Kathy could see her photograph, and Kelly's, too. She couldn't help it. She began to talk twin talk to Kelly, then felt Angie squeeze her hand very, very hard.

"Come on," Angie said, yanking her.

The other shoe was still on the sidewalk. Angie grabbed it, then opened the back door of the van. "Get in," she said angrily, tossing the shoe inside.

Kathy scrambled to get in and lay down on the pillow and reached for the blanket. Then she heard a man ask, "Where is the safety seat for your child, ma'am?"

It was a policeman. "We're on our way to buy one," Angie said. "I didn't lock the van at a motel last night, and it was stolen."

"Where did you stay?"

"At the Soundview."

"Did you report the theft?"

"No," Angie said. "It was an old seat, not worth the effort."

"We want to know if there's theft going on in Hyannis. May I see your driver's license and registration, please?"

"Sure. Right here." Angie pulled the papers out of her wallet.

"Ms. Hagen, whose van is this?" the policeman asked.

"My boyfriend's."

"I see. Well, I'm going to give you a break. I want you to walk over to the mall and buy a new car seat. I will not allow you to drive without one."

"Thank you, officer. I'll do that. Come on, Stevie."

Angie leaned down and picked up Kathy, pressing her face against her jacket. She closed the door of the van and began to walk back to the mall.

"That cop is watching us," she hissed. "He looked at Linda Hagen's license kind of funny. God, this is a mess."

As soon as they were inside the mall, she put Kathy down. "Here, let me put that other shoe on. I can't carry you all over Cape Cod."

It seemed to Kathy they walked forever. When they did find a store that sold car seats, Kathy didn't want to tell Angie the shoe had come off again. Then, on the way back to the car, someone stopped Angie. "Your little boy has lost one of his shoes," she said.

Angie picked Kathy up. "The stupid clerk sold her the wrong size," she explained. "I mean *him*. I'll buy him another pair." She walked very quickly away. "Oh, no, that cop is still around. Don't *dare* answer if he talks to you." She got to the car and put Kathy down on the front seat, then attached the car seat in the back and lifted Kathy around to sit in it. "Turn your head," she whispered. "Turn it now. Don't look at him."

Kathy was so scared of Angie that she began to cry.

"Shut up!" Angie whispered. "That cop is watching us."

She slammed the back door and got in the driver's seat. Finally they drove off. On the way back to the motel, she screamed at Kathy, "You said your name! You were doing that twin talk stuff! I told you to shut up! The next time you open your mouth, I'll slap you silly."

Kathy could tell that Kelly was trying to talk to her, but she knew she must not talk back to her anymore, or Angie would hurt her.

When they got back to the room, Angie dropped Kathy on the bed and said, "Here, have some cough medicine and aspirin. You feel hot again."

ON SATURDAY morning a wildly restless Gregg Stanford went to his club for a game of squash, then returned to the Greenwich estate that was his wife's main residence. He showered, dressed, and ordered lunch served to him in the study. With its paneled walls, antique tapestries, and sweeping views of Long Island Sound, it was his favorite room in the mansion.

But even the perfectly cooked salmon served with a bottle of Château Cheval Blanc neither relaxed nor comforted him. The seventh anniversary of his marriage to Millicent was next Wednesday. Their prenuptial agreement read that if they were either separated or divorced before that anniversary, he would receive nothing from her. If their marriage lasted past the seventh anniversary, he would irrevocably receive twenty million dollars even if they were to break up anytime after that.

Millicent's first husband had died. Her second marriage lasted only a few years. She had divorce papers served on her third husband only a few days before the seventh anniversary. I have four more days to go, he thought. Even in the beautiful room, he started to sweat at the idea.

Gregg was sure Millicent was playing a cat-and-mouse game with him. She had been traveling in Europe visiting friends for the past three weeks, but she had phoned from Monaco on Tuesday and approved the stand he took about paying the ransom. "It's a miracle twenty other children of our employees haven't been kidnapped already," she'd said. "You showed good sense."

And when we're out together, she seems to enjoy being with me, Gregg thought in an effort to reassure himself.

The terrible possibility was that Millicent had somehow learned about one of his affairs. I've been discreet, he thought, but if she found out about any of them, it would be the end of me.

He was pouring his third glass of wine when the phone rang. It was Millicent. "Gregg, I haven't been very fair to you."

He felt his mouth go dry. "I don't know what you mean, dear," he said, hoping the tone of his voice sounded amused.

"I'll be honest. I thought you might be cheating on me, and I simply could not tolerate that. But you've been given a clean bill of health, so"—here Millicent laughed—"when I get back, how about celebrating our seventh anniversary and toasting the next seven?"

This time Gregg Stanford did not need to fake the emotion in his voice. "Oh, my dear!"

"I'll be back on Monday. I . . . I'm really quite fond of you, Gregg. Good-bye."

He hung up the phone slowly. As he suspected, she had been having him watched. It was a stroke of luck that instinct had made him stop seeing any woman these past few months.

Gregg Stanford looked around the room, at the paneling and the tapestries, at the Persian carpet and the Hepplewhite furniture. "I'll do anything not to lose all this," he said aloud.

WALTER Carlson arrived at the Frawleys' house with Agent Tony Realto and Captain Jed Gunther of the Connecticut state police. With Dr. Harris following, Margaret and Steve brought the investigators into the dining room—our command post, she thought. How many times in this past week have we sat around this table waiting for a phone call, praying that we'd get the twins back?

In the next room Kelly was setting up the play table and chairs for a tea party. She had brought down the matching baby dolls and teddy bears that were the twins' favorite toys.

"How are you feeling, Margaret?" Agent Carlson asked as they sat at the table.

"I'm okay, I guess. I'm sure you heard that I went to the dress shop where I bought the birthday dresses and asked to speak to the clerk who waited on me."

"She wasn't there, we understand," Agent Realto said. "Can you tell us your purpose in seeking to speak to her?"

"Only that she said she had just waited on a woman who was buying clothes for twins and that it seemed peculiar that the woman didn't know their sizes. I just had the crazy thought that maybe someone was anticipating kidnapping my children and . . . and"— she swallowed—"the clerk wasn't there, and I realized I was making a scene, so I ran out. Then I guess I just kept driving."

Steve drew his chair closer to hers and put an arm around her shoulder. She reached up and linked her fingers with his.

"Steve," Agent Realto said, "has Kelly said anything else that might be helpful in identifying the people who were holding her?"

"She said something about a crib, but that's all."

"Margaret, you called me yesterday and told me you believe that Kathy is still alive," Carlson said. "*Why* do you believe that?"

"Because Kelly told me she is. Because at Mass yesterday morning she said Kathy wants to come home, too, right now. Then at breakfast, when Steve said that he would read a book to her and pretend he was reading to Kathy, too, Kelly said something like, 'Oh, Daddy, that's silly. Kathy is tied up on the bed. She can't hear you.' And a few times Kelly has tried to talk twin talk to Kathy."

"Twin talk?" Gunther asked.

"They have their own special language." Margaret glanced into the living room. Then, before any of them could speak, she raised her finger to her lips and pointed. They all turned. Kelly had placed the teddy bears on chairs at the table. The doll that had been Kathy's was lying on a blanket on the floor, a sock tied around its mouth. Sitting with her own doll in her arms, Kelly was stroking the cheek of Kathy's doll and whispering. As if she sensed they were watching, she looked up and said, "She's not allowed to talk to me anymore."

AFTER the visit of Agents Walsh and Philburn, Richie Mason made coffee and coldly considered his options. The FBI was watching him. The irony of how it had all gotten out of control hit him in waves, provoking him to fury. Everything had been clicking along so smoothly, and then the one weak link in the chain, the one he always knew was a problem, had indeed become the problem.

Now the Feds were closing in. The fact that they still didn't know how close they were to learning the truth was a miracle.

I am *not* going back to prison, he told himself. The image of the tiny, crowded cell made him shiver. For the tenth time in two days he looked at the passport he had stolen from the dresser that day he'd been in Ridgefield. He looked enough like Steve to pass without anyone asking questions. All I need to do is have a nice warm smile like baby brother when they check it, he thought.

Bahrain had no extradition agreement with the United States. Should he be satisfied with what he had, or should he go for the rest of the pot of gold?

Why not? It was always better to tie up loose ends.

"Mrs. Frawley," Tony Realto said slowly, "I cannot act on your belief that Kelly is in touch with her sister. However, the only indicators that Kathy is dead are the suicide note and the fact that Lucas Wohl was seen carrying a heavy box onto the aircraft. I'm going to be absolutely honest with you. We are not completely satisfied that Lucas either typed that note or that he shot himself."

"What are you *talking* about?" Steve snapped.

"What I am saying is that if Lucas was shot by one of his cohorts, that note might be a phony and may have been left there to give the impression that Kathy is dead."

"Are you finally starting to believe she's alive?" Margaret asked.

"We are starting to believe there may be a slight possibility," Tony Realto said. "Frankly, I do not have faith in twin telepathy, but I do believe that Kelly may be able to help us. We need to question her. She might let another name slip or give us some indication where they were kept."

They watched as Kelly picked up a doll's washcloth and went into the kitchen. They heard her pull a chair over to the sink. When she came back, she put the wet washcloth on the forehead of Kathy's baby doll. They all got up from the table and moved closer.

Kelly looked up at them. "She's really coughing. Mona made her take medicine, but she spit it up."

Tony Realto and Jed Gunther exchanged glances, disbelief in their eyes. Margaret and Steve were clinging to each other, both of them now weeping.

"Dr. Harris," Carlson said quietly, "will you talk to Kelly?"

Sylvia nodded and sat on the floor next to Kelly. "You're taking good care of Kathy," she said. "Does she still feel sick?"

Kelly nodded. "She can't talk anymore. She told her name to some lady, and Mona got mad. She has to say her name is Stevie. Her head is *sooo* hot."

"Does Kathy have something tied around her mouth?"

"She started to get sick, so Mona pulled it off. Kathy's asleep now." Kelly untied the sock, then covered the dolls with the blanket, making sure their fingers were touching.

WHEN the manager of the motel rapped on Angie's door, he introduced himself as David Toomey, then asked, "What's this about your car seat being stolen last night? Officer Tyron stopped by to find out if any other cars had been broken into."

Angie tried to think fast. "It's not a big deal," she said. She glanced at the bed. Kathy was facing the wall. "My little guy has a bad cold, and I was just concerned about getting him inside."

She watched as Toomey's eyes darted around the room. She could read his mind. He didn't believe her. He sensed that something was peculiar. Maybe he could hear Kathy wheezing.

He *had* heard her. "Maybe you should take your son to the emergency room at Cape Cod Hospital," he suggested. "My wife always gets asthma after bronchitis, and he sounds as though he's building up to an asthma attack."

"That's what I was thinking," Angie said. "Can you give me directions to the hospital?"

"It's ten minutes from here. I'd be happy to drive you."

"No. No. My mother will be here around one o'clock. She'll go with us. Thanks a lot. And don't worry, the car seat was old. You know what I mean."

"I know what you mean, Ms. Hagen. There was no theft. But I gather from Officer Tyron that you do have a car seat now." Toomey closed the door behind him.

Angie immediately double-locked the door. He's gonna be watching me, she thought. He knows I didn't have a car seat, and he's mad because it makes his place look bad if there's a complaint about a theft. That cop, he's suspicious, too. I've got to get out of here, but I can't pull out with all my stuff—he'll know I'm taking off. Now I have to look as though I'm waiting for my mother. Maybe if I just wait a while, then sneak out while he's busy.

Facing left, from the window she could see the driveway in front of the office. She waited there forty minutes, as Kathy's breathing became heavier and the wheeze became stronger. I've got to get rid of her, she thought. But I don't want her to die on my hands. She got out the bottle of penicillin capsules, broke one open, diluted it with a little water in a glass from the bathroom, and grabbed a plastic spoon from the coffee machine. She shook Kathy, who stirred, opened her eyes, and immediately began to cry.

"Geez, you're burning up," Angie snapped. "Here, drink this."

Kathy shook her head, and as the first taste of the liquid touched her tongue, she pressed her lips shut. "I said, *drink* it!" Angie shouted. She managed to force some liquid into Kathy's mouth, but Kathy gagged and began to wail and cough. Angie grabbed a towel and tied it around her mouth to quiet the sound, then realized that Kathy might suffocate and pulled it off. "Keep quiet," she hissed. "You hear me good. Don't make another sound or I'll kill you. All this is your fault. Every *bit* of it."

She looked out the window and saw that several cars were now parked in front of the office. This is my chance, she thought. She picked up Kathy, ran outside, opened the door of the van, and strapped her in the car seat. Then, in a quick movement, she ran back inside the motel, grabbed the suitcase with the money and her shoulder bag, and tossed them in beside Kathy. Thirty seconds later she was backing out of the parking space.

Where do I go? she wondered. Should I get off the Cape right away? That cop might start looking for me. He has my license plate number. So does the motel. I've got to tell Clint to come up here in a rental car or something. It isn't safe for me to be driving this thing any longer.

The weather had continued to clear, and the afternoon sun was bright. At the base of Main Street the traffic became one-way, and she was forced to turn right. I need to get out of Hyannis, in case that cop is really suspicious and sends out an alarm. I don't want to get caught at one of the bridges. I'll take Route 28, she thought.

She glanced back at Kathy. The girl's eyes were closed, and her head was on her chest, but Angie could see that she was breathing in gasps through her mouth and that her cheeks were flushed. I've got to find another motel, she thought. Then I'll call Clint.

Forty minutes later, shortly after she passed the sign for Chatham, she spotted the kind of motel she was looking for. It had a flashing VACANCY sign and was next to a diner. "The Shell and Dune," she said, reading the name aloud. "It'll do." She pulled into a parking spot near the office.

The sallow-faced clerk at the desk was on the phone with his girlfriend and barely glanced up as he handed her a registration form. Still, remembering the Hyannis cop, she reluctantly pulled out her own license. She made up a plate number and scrawled it on the slip. He took the cash for an overnight stay and tossed her a key. Feeling somewhat more secure, Angie got back in the van, drove around to the back of the motel, and went into the room.

"Better than the last place," she said aloud as she hid the suitcase under the bed. She went back outside for Kathy, who did not wake up as she was taken from the car seat. Boy, that fever is getting worse, Angie thought. I'll make her take baby aspirin. But first I'd better call Clint.

He answered on the first ring. "Where the hell are you?" he barked. "Why didn't you call back sooner? I've been sweating here, wondering if you were in jail."

"The manager of the motel I was in was too nosy. I got out of there fast."

"Where are you?"

"I'm on Cape Cod."

"What?"

"It seemed like a good place to hide. And I know my way around here. Clint, the kid is really sick, and there was this cop who made me buy a car seat, he has the license number of the van. He smells something fishy. I know he does. I was afraid I'd be stopped at the bridge if I tried to leave the Cape. I'm in a different motel now. It's on Route 28, in Chatham. You came up here when you were a kid. You probably know where it is."

"I know where it is. Look, you stay there. I'll fly up to Boston and rent a car. It's three thirty now. I should make it there by nine or nine thirty."

"Did you get rid of the crib?"

"I took it apart and put it in the garage. I don't have the van to move it. You know what you've pulled on me, don't you? I couldn't leave, because this is the only phone where you could reach me. I don't have more than eighty bucks and my credit card. Now you've attracted the cops up there, and that sales clerk where you bought the kids' clothes was nosing around here."

"Why would she come to the house?" Angie's voice was fearful.

"She claimed she wanted to replace the shirts, but as far as I'm concerned, she came to snoop. That's why I've got to get out of here—and why you have to stay put until I get up there. Got it?"

Clint thought, I'm sitting here packed, waiting all this time, scared I'm gonna find out some cop has grabbed you and the kid, not to mention the suitcase full of money. She screwed this up good. I can't *wait* to get my hands on her.

"Yeah. Clint, I'm sorry I shot Lucas. I mean I know he was your friend."

"Forget about Lucas. What's the name of the motel?"

"The Shell and Dune. Isn't that corny? I love you, Clint-man."

"Okay, okay. How's the kid?"

"She's really, *really* sick. She's got a big fever. Clint, I don't want to be stuck with her anymore. I can't stand her."

"We'll leave her in the van when we sink it somewhere. In case you haven't noticed, there's a lot of water around there."

"Okay. Okay. I don't know what I'd do without you. You're smart, Clint. Lucas thought he was smarter than you, but he wasn't. I can't wait for you to get here."

"I know. You and me. That's the way it's gotta be." Clint hung up the phone. "And if you believe that, you're even dumber than I thought," he said aloud.

"MRS. Frawley," Agent Tony Realto said as he left the family home with Captain Gunther, "from this point in the investigation we are going to proceed, not on the *likelihood,* but on the *premise* that Kathy is alive. However, I don't want this to be known. Our one advantage is that whoever has her believes that we think she is dead."

After they were gone, Kelly began to fall asleep in the living room, next to the dolls. Steve slipped a pillow under her head and covered her; then he and Margaret sat cross-legged beside her.

"Sometimes she and Kathy talk in their sleep," Dr. Harris explained to Walter Carlson.

Harris and Carlson were still at the table in the dining room. "Dr. Harris," Carlson said slowly, "I am a skeptic, but that doesn't mean that Kelly's behavior hasn't shaken all of us. Isn't it possible that Kelly has been acting out her own recollection of what happened during the days she was away?"

"Kelly had a bruise on her arm when she was taken to the hospital after she was found," Sylvia Harris said flatly. "When I saw it, I said that it was the result of a vicious pinch, the sort of punishment that is usually inflicted by a woman. Yesterday afternoon Kelly began to scream. Steve thought she had hit her arm against the table in the hall. Margaret recognized that she was reacting to Kathy's pain. Mr. Carlson, Kelly has another nasty bruise, a *new* one that I would swear is the result of a pinch Kathy received yesterday. Take it or leave it."

Through his Swedish ancestors and his FBI training, Walter Carlson had learned to keep his emotions from showing. "If you are right . . ." he began.

"I *am* right, Mr. Carlson."

". . . then Kathy may be with an abusive woman."

"I'm glad you recognize that. But equally serious, she is *very* ill."

"Dr. Sylvia . . ."

They looked up as Margaret came back into the dining room.

"Did Kelly say anything?" Dr. Harris asked anxiously.

"No, but I want you to sit next to her with Steve. Agent Carlson, will you drive me back to the shop where I bought the girls' birthday dresses? I've been thinking and thinking. I *have* to talk to that clerk. I still think she felt something was wrong about the woman who bought clothes for twins almost at the same time I was there."

Carlson stood up. He recognized the expression on Margaret Frawley's face. It was that of a zealot, convinced of her mission.

"Let's go," he said. "I don't care where that clerk is. We'll find her."

FIFTEEN minutes after Angie phoned, the Pied Piper tried Clint again. "Have you heard from her again?" he asked.

"Finally. She's on Cape Cod," Clint said. "I'm going to fly up to Boston and rent a car to drive there."

"Where is she?"

"Hiding in a motel in Chatham called the Shell and Dune. She already had a run-in with a cop."

"What are you going to do when you get there?"

"Just what you think. Listen, the cab driver is blowing the horn. He can't get past the gate."

"Then this is it for us. Good luck, Clint." The Pied Piper broke the connection, waited, then dialed the number of a private plane service. "I need a plane to leave in one hour from Teterboro, to land at the airport nearest to Chatham on Cape Cod," he ordered.

SIXTY-FOUR-YEAR-OLD Elsie Stone didn't get a chance to look at a newspaper all day. Her job at McDonald's, near the Cape Cod Mall, didn't allow for reading, and this Saturday she had rushed to her daughter's house in Yarmouth to pick up her six-year-old granddaughter, Debby. She willingly babysat at any time.

Elsie had followed the Frawley kidnapping with rapt attention. The thought of someone kidnapping Debby, then killing her, was just too horrible. At least the Frawleys got *one* back, she thought, but oh, dear God, how awful for them.

Today she and Debby went back to her house in Hyannis and baked cookies. "How's your pretend friend doing?" she asked as Debby spooned the batter filled with chocolate morsels onto the baking pan.

"Oh, Nana, you forgot. I don't have a pretend friend anymore. I had her when I was little." Debby shook her head emphatically.

"Oh, that's right. I guess I was thinking of your pretend friend because there was a little boy in my restaurant today. His name was Stevie, and he has a pretend friend named Kathy."

"I'm going to make this a really big cookie," Debby announced.

So much for pretend friends, Elsie thought. After they put the baking pan in the oven, she said, "All right, Debs, while we're waiting, Nana's going to read the paper for a few minutes. You start coloring the next page in your Barbie doll book."

Elsie settled in her La-Z-Boy recliner. A follow-up story on the Frawley twins was on the front page: MASSIVE FBI SEARCH FOR KIDNAPPERS. The FBI had confirmed that the suicide note left by the man known as Lucas Wohl had contained his confession to unintentionally killing Kathy. Wohl's fingerprints identified him as Jimmy Nelson, a convicted felon who had served six years in Attica prison for a series of burglaries.

Shaking her head, Elsie closed the paper. Her eyes strayed to the front-page picture of the twins. "Kathy and Kelly on their third birthday" was the caption. What is it? she wondered, staring at the photograph, trying to figure out why something about it seemed so familiar.

Just then the oven timer went off. Debby dropped her crayon and ran to the kitchen. "Nana, the cookies are finished," she called.

Letting the newspaper slide to the floor, Elsie followed her.

ALAN Hart, the evening manager of the Soundview Motel, came on duty at seven o'clock. The first thing David Toomey, the motel manager, did was to brief him on the theft of the car seat that Linda Hagen, the woman in A-49, had reported to Officer Tyron. "I'm sure she was lying," Toomey said. "I'd bet the rest of my life she never had a car seat. Al, did you get a look at her van when she checked in last night?"

"Yeah, I did," Hart told him. "That stringy brunette checked in sometime after midnight. I could see her van plainly, and I didn't even know she had a kid. It must have been asleep in the backseat, but it sure wasn't in a car seat."

"I talked to her after Sam Tyron left. She's got a little boy, not more than three or four years old. I told her to take him to the hospital. He had one heck of an asthmatic wheeze."

"Did she do it?"

"I don't know. She claimed she was waiting for her mother to go with them."

"She's booked until tomorrow morning. She paid in cash with a wad of twenties. Has she come back with the kid?" Hart asked.

"I don't think so. Maybe I'll just knock on the door and inquire about him. If she's not there, I'll keep on going. But I will stop at the police station and let them know that we did not have a theft here last night."

With a wave of his hand Toomey went outside, turned right, and walked to ground-floor unit A-49. There was no light behind the drawn shade. He knocked, waited, then after only a brief hesitation, took out his master key, unlocked the door, and turned on the light.

There was an open suitcase on the floor with women's clothing inside it. There was a child's jacket on the bed. A quick look into the bathroom showed makeup and toiletries on the sink. She plans to come back, he thought. Maybe they kept the child at the hospital. I hope so. As he started to walk back through the room, something on the floor caught his eye. It was a twenty-dollar bill.

The bed's faded orange-and-brown dust ruffle behind the bill was hiked up. As Toomey knelt down to straighten it, his eyes widened. There were at least a dozen twenty-dollar bills under the bed. That woman is some dingbat, he thought. She must have kept her money in a bag under the bed and never even realized she was missing some of it.

ANGIE placed Kathy on a pillow on the floor of the bathroom, then plugged up the tub and turned on the shower full blast. She had managed to get Kathy to chew two more baby aspirin.

"Don't you dare die," she told Kathy. "That's just what I need, another nosy motel guy banging on the door and you not breathing. I wish I could get more penicillin in you."

On the other hand, she was beginning to wonder if maybe Kathy had been allergic to the penicillin she had swallowed. There were red spots showing up on her arms and chest, lots of them.

"Geez, is that what's happening to you?" Angie asked Kathy. "It was a lousy idea to come to Cape Cod. I forgot that if I hit any trouble, there are only two bridges I can use to get away, and now they could be watching for me. Forget old Cape Cod."

Kathy did not open her eyes. Even though she wasn't allowed to talk to Kelly, she moved her lips and whispered, "Cape Cod."

KELLY had awakened but did not get up from the living-room floor. Sylvia Harris brought in a tray with milk and cookies, but Kelly ignored it.

Steve broke the silence. "Sylvia, do you remember when they were born—Margaret had to have a C-section, and there was a tiny piece of membrane that had to be cut off between Kelly's right thumb and Kathy's left thumb?"

"Yes, I do, Steve. In that real sense of the word, they were not only identical, but conjoined twins."

"Sylvia, I don't want to let myself believe . . ." He paused. "You know what I mean. But, my God, if we only knew where Kathy is, where to look for her. Do you think it's possible that Kelly knows?"

Kelly looked up. "I know."

Sylvia Harris raised her hand as a warning to Steve. "Where is she, Kelly?" she asked quietly.

"Kathy's in Cape Cod. She just told me."

"When Margaret was in bed with Kelly this morning, she was talking about driving last night and told me that when she saw the sign for Cape Cod, she knew she had to turn around," Sylvia whispered to Steve. "That's where she heard about Cape Cod."

Kelly went into a spasm of coughing. "I want to go home," she sobbed. "I want Mommy."

AGENT Carlson rang the bell at Lila Jackson's modest house in Danbury. "She's *got* to be home," Margaret said as they heard footsteps approaching the door. "Oh, God, please let her be able to tell us something."

Lila's mother answered the door. Her welcoming smile disappeared as she saw the two strangers on the porch.

Before the woman could speak, Carlson had his FBI identification in his hand. "I am Agent Walter Carlson," he said briskly. "This is Margaret Frawley, the mother of the twins who were kidnapped. Your daughter Lila sold her their birthday dresses. We have just left Abby's Discount. Ms. Howell told us that Lila left work early. We must speak with her."

"Come in. Please come in," Lila's mother said. "Lila's caught a chill. She's on the couch in the den. Come in."

Lila was bundled up in a fleece-lined bathrobe and a blanket, and was sipping hot tea. She looked up and recognized Margaret immediately. "Mrs. Frawley!" She put the cup on the coffee table.

"Please, don't get up," Margaret said. "I'm sorry to burst in like this, but I have to talk to you. It's about something you said when I was buying the birthday dresses for my twins."

"Lila talked about that," Mrs. Jackson exclaimed. "In fact, she wanted to go to the police about it."

"Ms. Jackson, what did you want to tell the police?" Walter Carlson demanded.

Lila looked at him. "As I told Mrs. Frawley that night, I had just sold some outfits to a woman who wanted them for her three-year-old twins but didn't know what size to buy. After the kidnapping, I looked up her name, but then Jim Gilbert, a retired detective here in Danbury, didn't think it was worth reporting." She looked at Margaret. "This morning, when I heard you had come looking for me, I decided I would go talk to that woman on my lunch hour."

"You know where she is?" Margaret asked.

"Her name is Angie. She lives with the caretaker of the country club in a cottage on the grounds. I made up a story—I said that two of the shirts I sold her were damaged. But the caretaker told me what happened. Angie babysits and was hired to drive to Wisconsin with a mother and her two children. He told me they're not really twins, just close in age. The mother was on her way to pick up Angie when she realized she had forgotten one of the suitcases and phoned ahead to have Angie run out and buy some of the things they'd need. That's why she wasn't that sure of the size, you see."

Her knees suddenly weak, Margaret sank down onto the chair opposite the couch. A dead end, she thought. Our only chance. She closed her eyes.

"Was there any indication that children had been staying in that house, Ms. Jackson?" Walter Carlson asked.

Lila shook her head. "It's a really small place: living room, dining area, kitchen. The door to the bedroom was open. I'm sure that Clint guy was alone there."

"Did Clint seem nervous to you in any way?" Carlson asked.

"No, I wouldn't say he was nervous. I mean, he was sweating a lot, but I assumed that kind of heavyset guy naturally sweats." An expression of distaste came over her face. "He stank like a locker room."

Margaret stared at her. "What did you say?"

Lila looked uncomfortable. "Mrs. Frawley, I don't mean to sound flippant. I only wish to God I could have helped you."

"You did!" Margaret cried. "You did!" She turned to Carlson and knew he had recognized the importance of Lila's offhand remark.

The only impression Trish Logan, the babysitter, had of the man who had grabbed her was that he stank of perspiration.

10

EVEN though he was frantic to get to Cape Cod, the Pied Piper had taken the time to dig out a hooded sweater to wear under his jacket, as well as an old pair of dark glasses. He drove his car to the airport, parked, and went inside a small terminal, where he found the pilot waiting for him. Their exchange was brief. He was told that the plane was waiting on the tarmac. As he had requested, a car with a map of the area would be ready for him at the Chatham Airport. The pilot would fly him back later tonight.

Just over an hour later the Pied Piper was getting off the plane. It was seven o'clock. The car was exactly the kind he wanted, a black midsize sedan, a look-alike for half the vehicles on the road. A study of the map showed him that he could not be very far from the Shell and Dune Motel on Route 28.

I've got at least an hour to kill, he thought. Clint might have made the Delta Shuttle at five thirty. Otherwise he'd be on the US Air flight at six. Right now he's probably in Boston, renting a car.

Even though Lucas had somewhat derisively described Clint and Angie to him, he had never met them. Was he taking an unnecessary risk by coming up and not just letting Clint finish Angie and the kid off? So what if he got to keep the million dollars? But if all of them are dead, I can sleep at night, he thought. Lucas knew who I am. They don't. But how do I know that he didn't tell Clint? I don't need to have him looking me up after he's run through his share of the ransom.

The traffic on Route 28 was heavier than he had expected. He saw the large Shell and Dune Motel sign with the flashing VACANCY light beneath it. The exterior was white clapboard with green shutters. He saw that after the entrance sign, the driveway split, and he followed the lane that avoided the office. Looking for the van, he drove around to the back of the motel, slowing to a crawl as he studied the vehicles he was passing in the parking lot.

Finally he spotted the one that almost certainly was hers, a dark brown van, at least ten or twelve years old, with Connecticut plates. There was an empty space about five cars away in the next row. The Pied Piper parked there, got out of the sedan, and walked over. The light was sufficient to see the car seat in the back.

He checked his watch. He had plenty of time, and he was hungry. He could see the diner next door. Why not? he asked himself. He slipped on the dark glasses and began to walk across the parking lot. When he got to the diner, he saw that it was crowded. All to the good, he thought. The only seat at the counter was next to the takeout section. He sat down, and as he reached for the menu, the woman standing next to him began placing her order for a hamburger, black coffee, and a dish of orange sherbet to go.

The Pied Piper turned his head abruptly, but even before he saw the thin woman with the stringy brown hair, he recognized her harsh, aggressive voice.

He buried his face in the menu. He knew he was not mistaken. It was Angie.

ON SATURDAY evening, dressed in casual clothes, seeking to blend in with the dozens of other passengers, Agents Sean Walsh and Damon Philburn stood in the Galaxy Airlines baggage collection area at the international arrivals terminal of Newark Airport.

They both wore the exasperated expressions of travelers who, after a long flight, can't wait to see their bags tumble onto the carousel. In actual fact, they were watching a thin-faced middle-aged man who was there waiting for his luggage. When he reached down and plucked out a nondescript black suitcase, they were immediately on either side of him.

"FBI," Walsh told him. "Do you want to come quietly or make a scene?"

Without answering, the man nodded and fell into step with them. They herded him to an office in a private area of the terminal where other agents were guarding Danny Hamilton, a frightened twenty-year-old who was wearing the uniform of a baggage handler.

When the man accompanied by Walsh and Philburn saw Hamilton in handcuffs, he turned ashen and blurted, "I'm not saying anything. I want a lawyer."

Walsh laid the black suitcase on a table and snapped open the locks. He put the neat piles of folded underwear, shirts, and slacks on a chair, then took out a pocketknife and slit the edges of the false bottom of the suitcase. When he ripped it off, the hidden contents of the bag were revealed—large packages of white powder.

Walsh smiled at the courier. "You're going to need a lawyer."

Walsh and Philburn could not believe the turn of events. They had come here to speak to Richie Mason's coworkers to see if they could learn any information that might connect him to the kidnapping. They started to talk to Hamilton and had immediately sensed that he was unduly nervous.

When they pressed him, he adamantly denied any knowledge of the kidnapping, but then broke down and admitted that he knew Richie Mason was getting cocaine shipments at the airport. He said Richie had given him five hundred dollars on four occasions to keep quiet about it. He'd told them that late this afternoon Richie had called to tell him a shipment was coming in but he couldn't be there to meet it. Richie had told Hamilton to meet the courier at the carousel. From Richie's description he would recognize him, because he had seen him at the airport with Richie before. He had instructed Hamilton to give the code words "Home Free," and the courier would then know that it was safe to give the suitcase containing the cocaine to him. Hamilton said that Richie had told him to hide the bag at his apartment and that he would contact him in the next few days and would retrieve the bag.

Sean Walsh's cell phone rang. He opened it and listened, then turned to Philburn. "Mason's not at his Clifton apartment. I think he's taken off."

"MARGARET, this may be another blind alley," Agent Carlson warned as they drove from Lila Jackson's home to the caretaker cottage where Clint Downes lived.

"It's not another blind alley," Margaret insisted. "I knew, I just knew, that if I spoke to that sales clerk, she would be able to tell me something. Why didn't I do it sooner?"

"Our office is having a check run on Downes," Carlson said as he headed through downtown Danbury. "I'm having a squad car from the Danbury police meet us there, but you've got to realize that if he's not home, we have no grounds for breaking in."

It was after five o'clock, and darkness was setting in. Lila had told them they would have to park at the service road gate. Carlson ordered Margaret to wait in the car. "If this guy is connected to the kidnapping, he could be dangerous."

"Walter," Margaret said, "unless you're planning to restrain me physically, I am going to talk to him."

A squad car pulled up beside them, and two cops got out, one with sergeant's chevrons on his jacket. They listened to Carlson's brief rundown and tried to persuade Margaret to wait in the car. When she would not be dissuaded, they told her she would have to stand back until they were sure there would not be any resistance from Clint Downes.

As they approached the cottage, it was obvious to all of them that their precautions were unnecessary. The building was in darkness. The open door of the garage showed them that there was no vehicle inside. Bitterly disappointed, Margaret watched as the police went from window to window of the cottage, shining lights inside.

410 | Mary Higgins Clark

He was here around one o'clock, she thought. Did Lila frighten him off? Where would he have gone? Where did that woman Angie go?

She walked over to the garage and flipped on the light. Inside, to the right, she saw the crib that Clint had taken apart and stacked against the wall. The mattress was nearly twice the size of the mattress of a standard crib. Margaret put her face against it. The faint odor of Vicks VapoRub filled her nostrils.

She spun around and screamed at the law enforcement officers, "They were here! This is where they kept them! Where did they go? You've got to find out where they took Kathy!"

At Logan Airport, Clint went directly to the area where the car rental agencies were located. Crushingly aware that if Angie had maxed out the card, he might not be able to rent a car, he carefully studied the rates before he selected the cheapest service and the cheapest car.

A million dollars in cash, he thought, and if the credit card for the rental doesn't go through, I'll have to steal a car to get to the Cape.

But it did go through.

"You got a map for Maine?" he asked.

"Right over there." An indifferent clerk pointed to a rack.

Clint walked over and, carefully blocking his choice from observation, grabbed a map of Cape Cod and shoved it in his jacket. Twenty minutes later he was squeezing his body into the driver's seat of a budget compact. He turned on the overhead light and studied the map, then started the car.

Angie remembered me telling her I'd been on the Cape before. She forgets nothing, he thought. What I didn't tell her was that I was on a job with Lucas. We hit a house in Osterville.

Clint drove out of the airport. The map indicated he should turn left into the Ted Williams Tunnel and then watch for signs to Cape Cod. If I got it straight, Route 3 takes me to the Sagamore Bridge, he thought. Should I stop somewhere and phone Angie? he wondered. Let her know that he'd definitely be there by nine thirty?

Once again he cursed her for taking the cell phones with her.

A few minutes after the tunnel he spotted the Cape Cod sign. Maybe it's good I don't have a phone, he thought. In her own crazy way Angie is a smart babe. She just might start to figure out that it's just as easy for her to get rid of the kid on her own, and then take off again with the money, as it is to wait for me.

The thought made him slam his foot down on the gas pedal.

ON WEEKENDS when he could get away, Geoffrey Sussex Banks would race down from Bel-Air to his home in Palm Springs, California. Having stayed in Los Angeles this Saturday, however, he returned from a round of golf in late afternoon to learn that an FBI agent was waiting for him. "He gave me his card, sir. Here it is," his housekeeper said. "I'm sorry."

"Thank you, Conchita."

He had hired Conchita and Manuel years ago, when he and Theresa were first married. The couple had adored her, and when they got news that she was expecting twins, they had been thrilled. When Theresa disappeared shortly thereafter, they kept alive the hope that one day a key would turn in the door and she would be there. "And maybe she had the babies and just forgot her past and then all of a sudden remembered and came home and your little boys were with her." That was Conchita's prayer. But now Conchita knew that if the FBI was here, it was only to confirm after all these years that her remains had been found.

Geoff braced himself for the news as he walked down the hall to his library.

Dominick Telesco was from the Los Angeles FBI headquarters. He had read stories in the business section of the *L.A. Times* about Geoffrey Sussex Banks, international banker and handsome socialite, whose young wife had disappeared on her way to her baby shower seventeen years ago.

Banks was thirty-two when his wife disappeared, my age, Telesco thought as he looked out the window that faced the golf course. Wonder why he never remarried? Women must be falling all over him.

"Mr. Telesco?"

The agent turned quickly. "Mr. Banks, I apologize. I just watched someone hit a fabulous shot, and I didn't hear you come in."

"I bet I know who it might be," Banks said with a hint of a smile. "Most of our members find the sixteenth hole a problem. Only one or two have mastered it. Please sit down."

For an instant the two men studied each other. Telesco, thirty-two, had dark brown hair and eyes, a rangy build, and was wearing a business suit and tie. Banks, fifty, was wearing a golf shirt and shorts. His patrician features were slightly sunburned. His hair, more silvery than dark blond, showed signs of thinning. It was obvious that, at least at first impression, reports that Banks possessed that rare combination of authority and courtesy were justified.

"Is it about my wife?" Banks asked.

"Yes, sir. It is," Telesco said. "You may have read about the Frawley kidnapping in Connecticut?"

"Of course. I understand one twin was returned."

"Yes. Mr. Banks, are you aware that Norman Bond, your wife's first husband, is on the board of C.F.G. and Y. and that the board voted to pay the ransom money for the Frawley twins?"

"I know that Norman Bond is on the board of C.F.G. and Y."

"Mr. Banks, Norman Bond hired Steve Frawley for a job under rather unusual circumstances. Three mid-level executives at the company were the leading candidates for the position. Note that Steve Frawley is the father of identical twins and he lives in Ridgefield, Connecticut. Bond and Theresa were living in Ridgefield when she gave birth to identical twins."

Color drained from Banks's face. "Are you suggesting Bond had something to do with the Frawley kidnapping?"

"In light of the suspicions you have voiced about your wife's disappearance, do you think Norman Bond capable of planning and executing a kidnapping?"

"Norman Bond is evil," Banks said. "I am absolutely certain he was responsible for my wife's disappearance. It is a matter of record that he was wildly jealous when he learned that she was pregnant again with twins. When she disappeared, I put my life on hold, and it will remain on hold until I know what happened to her."

"Sir, there isn't a shred of evidence to tie Bond to your wife's disappearance. Witnesses saw him in New York that night."

"Witnesses *thought* they saw him, or maybe he hired someone to do the job for him. I said it then, and I say it now, he was responsible for whatever happened to Theresa."

"Last week Bond referred to your wife as his 'late wife.' We wondered if that was a slip of the tongue."

"His *late* wife!" Geoffrey Banks exclaimed. "Look through your notes. All these years that man told everybody that he believed Theresa was still alive and wanted to get away from me. You will never once hear of him referring to her as if she were dead. Are you asking me if he is capable of kidnapping the children of someone living the life he wanted? You bet he is."

"LILA Jackson told us the garage was empty," Agent Carlson said to the Danbury police officers. "She also told us that Clint Downes received a phone call from someone named Gus while she was in the cottage. Maybe this Gus picked Downes up here."

Margaret could not keep her eyes off the dismantled crib. That's where they kept my babies, she thought. Those sides are so high—it's like a cage! The morning Monsignor said Mass for Kathy, Kelly described it, talking about the big crib. I've got to go home. She's the only one who can tell us where Kathy is now.

THE Pied Piper put the menu down and slipped off the seat. As the curious eyes of the counterman caught his gaze, he pulled his cell phone from his pocket, flipped it open, and made a gesture of answering it as he walked outside.

He was standing in the shadow of the diner when Angie came out, a bag of food in her hand. Looking neither left nor right, she darted through the diner parking lot and over the curb that separated it from the motel property. As he followed her, she opened the door to a ground-floor unit.

The shade on the window was fully drawn. Hood pulled up, dark glasses on, the Pied Piper walked slowly past, hesitating only as long as it took to catch the repetitive, hiccupping wail of a child who clearly had been crying for a long time.

Everything was going according to plan.

GUS Svenson was sitting at his usual perch in the Danbury Pub when two men appeared on either side of him. "FBI," one of the men told him. "Get up."

Gus was on his third beer. "Who you kidding?"

"We're not." Tony Realto looked at the bartender. "Run a tab for him."

Five minutes later Gus was in the Danbury police station. "What's going on?" he demanded.

"Where did Clint Downes go?" Realto snapped.

"How do I know?"

"You called him at about quarter after one this afternoon."

"You're nuts. At quarter past one I was fixing the mayor's plumbing. Call him if you don't believe me. He was there."

Realto and Carlson exchanged glances. "Why would Clint act as if he's talking to you?" Carlson asked.

"Ask *him*. Maybe he didn't want his girlfriend to know another dame phoned him."

"His girlfriend, Angie?" Realto asked.

"Yeah, that nutcase."

"When was the last time you saw Clint?"

"Let me see. Today's Saturday. We had dinner last night."

"Did Angie go with you?"

"Nah. She was away on a babysitting job."

"When was the last time you saw her?"

"Clint and I went out on Thursday night, too. Angie was in the house minding a kid when I picked him up."

"You saw a child?"

"Yeah. Not much of a look. He was wrapped in a blanket. I saw the back of his head."

"Could you see what color hair he had?"

"Dark brown. Short. His name was Stevie."

Suddenly sober, Gus willingly poured out anything he remembered. "I hadn't been out to dinner with Clint for months. Then I ran into Angie at the drugstore, buying stuff for a kid who was sick. And I called Clint Wednesday night, but he was out. Angie was babysitting, and the kids were crying, so we didn't talk long."

"The *kids* were crying?" Realto snapped.

"Oh, wrong. I thought I heard two of them, but apparently it was just one."

"Let's get this straight. The last time you saw Angie was Thursday night, and the last time you saw Clint was last night?"

"Yeah. I picked him up—he had no way to get around. Angie was in Wisconsin babysitting, and he'd sold the van."

"Okay. Gus, by any chance did Clint have a lot of cash when you went out?"

"Nah. He let me pick up the check both nights."

"Do you know anyone else who might have given him a ride somewhere today?"

"No."

The sergeant from the Danbury police who had been at the cottage had been making his own inquiries. He walked into the office in time to hear Realto's last question. "Clint Downes was driven by Danbury Taxi to the Continental Airlines drop-off at LaGuardia," he said. "He got there about five thirty."

Only two hours ago, Carlson thought. We're tightening the net, but will we be fast enough to close it before it's too late for Kathy?

AT THE police station in Hyannis, the desk sergeant, Ari Schwartz, listened patiently to David Toomey's irate protest that there had been no theft in the parking lot of his motel. "I've worked at the Soundview for thirty-two years," Toomey declared, "and I'm not going to let that conniver, who doesn't even have the brains to take care of a sick kid, lie to Sam Tyron about a car seat that she never owned."

The sergeant liked Toomey. "Dave, take it easy," he said soothingly. "I'll talk to Sam. We'll correct the record."

Toomey hesitated. "I really worry about that little boy. He was one sick kid. Would you mind phoning over to the hospital and see if he was treated? His name is Steve. The mother is Linda Hagen. They'll pay a lot more attention if the call comes from you."

Schwartz made the call. No pediatric patient by that name had been admitted to the hospital.

"There's something that bothers me about her," Toomey said as much to himself as to the sergeant. "If that was my grandson, my daughter would be frantic with worry." He shrugged. "I'd better mind my own business. Thanks, Sarge."

FOUR miles away Elsie Stone was turning the key in the door of her white frame house. She had taken Debby home but turned down the offer to stay for dinner. "I'm feeling my age," she said cheerfully. "I'll go on home, heat up some of my vegetable soup, and enjoy it while I'm watching the news."

Not that the news is something you want to see, she thought as she hung up her coat. But much as that kidnapping makes me heartsick, I do want to see if they're any closer to catching those terrible people. She went straight into the den to turn on the television. The anchorman on the six-thirty news was saying, "An unnamed source has revealed that the FBI are now operating under the assumption that Kathy Frawley may still be alive."

"Lord, let them find that poor little lamb," Elsie said aloud.

She went into the kitchen, and as she poured her homemade soup into a bowl and put it in the microwave, she realized that the name "Kathy" was running through her mind.

"Kathy . . . Kathy . . . Kathy . . ." What was it? she wondered.

"SHE was there," Margaret cried as Steve held her tightly. "I saw the crib. The mattress smelled of Vicks, just as Kelly's pajamas did when we got her back. All those days, they were so near, Steve, so near. That woman who bought the clothes is the one who has Kathy now. And Kathy is sick. *She is sick!*"

Ken Lynch, a rookie cop from the Danbury police force, had driven Margaret home. Seeing the block thick with media trucks, he had rushed her into the house, past Steve, who was holding the door open for them. Now, feeling helpless, he stepped through the archway and entered the living room.

"Mommy, Mommy."

Lynch watched as Kelly threw herself into her mother's arms. Her face anguished, Margaret hugged her daughter.

Margaret put Kelly down and knelt beside her, her hands on Kelly's shoulders. "Kelly," she said softly, "have you been talking to Kathy?"

Kelly nodded. "She wants to come home."

"I know, darling. Do you know where she is? Did she tell you?"

"Yes, Mommy. I told Daddy. Kathy is in Cape Cod."

Margaret shook her head. "Oh, sweetheart, don't you remember, this morning I was the one who talked about Cape Cod. Maybe Kathy told you some other place. Can you ask her now?"

"Kathy is very sleepy now." With an injured look, Kelly turned and walked past Officer Lynch. She sat down on the living-room floor by her dolls. "You *are so* on Cape Cod," she said. Then, though Lynch strained to hear, he could not make sense of the gibberish she was whispering.

THE various law enforcement agencies had established a command post in the FBI's Danbury office. Agents Tony Realto and Walter Carlson, along with Captain Jed Gunther and the Danbury police chief were in a conference room.

"We're now certain that Clint Downes and Lucas Wohl were cell-mates in Attica," Realto said. "They both broke parole as soon as they were released from prison, assumed new identities, and somehow have managed to stay under the radar for all these years. According to Gus Svenson, Angie has been living with Downes for seven or eight years. Unfortunately there isn't a single picture of either of them anywhere in the cottage. You can bet the old mug shot of Downes doesn't look like him anymore. The best we can do is give the media an artist's sketch and description of both of them."

"Someone's been leaking to the press," Carlson said. "The rumor is already out that Kathy is alive. Are we going to verify it?"

"Not yet. As long as Clint and Angie think we believe Lucas killed her, they might very well try to travel as a family."

"Margaret Frawley swears that the twins are communicating," Carlson said. "I was hoping I'd hear from her. If Kelly had said anything significant, I know she would have called me. Is the officer who drove her home still around?"

"That would be Ken Lynch," the police chief said. He picked up the conference-room phone. "Radio Lynch to get over here."

Fifteen minutes later Lynch walked in. "I swear Kelly is in touch with her sister," he told them flatly. "I was right there, and she insisted that Kathy is on Cape Cod."

11

THE traffic was light on the Sagamore Bridge. As he crossed the Cape Cod Canal, Clint drove with increasing impatience, constantly glancing at the speedometer. He knew he had narrowly escaped being stopped by a cop on Route 3, when he'd been doing seventy in a fifty-five-mile-an-hour zone.

He looked at his watch. It was exactly eight o'clock. It's at least another forty minutes more before I get there, he thought. He turned on the radio just in time to hear the excited newscaster say, "Authorities have just released the names of two suspects in the Frawley twins' kidnapping."

Clint felt perspiration begin to pour from his body.

"An all-points bulletin has been issued for the arrest of an exconvict named Ralph Hudson, using the alias of Clint Downes, and his live-in girlfriend, Angie Ames. Downes was last seen at LaGuardia Airport sometime after five p.m. Angie Ames has not been seen since Thursday evening. She is believed to be traveling in a twelve-year-old brown Chevy van with Connecticut plate number . . ."

It won't take them anytime to trace me to the shuttle, Clint thought frantically. Next thing, they'll trace me to the rental agency and get the description of this car. I have to dump it fast. He drove off the bridge onto the Mid-Cape Highway. At least I was smart enough to ask for a map of Maine. That may buy me a little time. I've got to think. What should I do?

His eyes darted over the highway, searching for police cars as he passed the exits. It seemed an interminable time before he finally got to exit 11, Harwich/Brewster, and turned onto Route 137. I'm almost at Chatham, he thought, trying to reassure himself. Then he spotted what he was looking for, a movie complex with a crowded parking lot.

Ten minutes later, parked two rows back, he watched as a pair of teenagers left an economy sedan and walked into the lobby of the theater. He followed them into the lobby, standing in a corner as he watched them get on line. He saw the usher tear their tickets; then he went back outside.

They didn't even bother to lock the door, he thought as he tried the handle of the car. Don't make it too easy for me. He got in the car, then waited until he was sure no one was nearby. He bent down under the dashboard and with deft, practiced movements attached wires together. The sound of the engine turning over gave him his first feeling of relief since he had heard the broadcast.

"Why is Kelly so quiet, Sylvia?" Margaret asked, fear in her voice. Kelly was sitting on Steve's lap, her eyes closed.

"It's all reaction, Margaret." Sylvia Harris tried to sound convincing. "Besides, she's having an allergic response to something." She reached over and pulled up the sleeve of Kelly's shirt.

Margaret stared at the sprinkling of red marks on Kelly's arm, then glanced back and forth between Dr. Harris and Steve. "Kelly doesn't get allergies," she said. "It's one of the few ways she and Kathy are different."

"Marg, Sylvia and I have talked about it," Steve said. "It's possible Kathy may be having a reaction to some medication."

"You don't mean—not *penicillin?* Sylvia, remember when you said that might kill her."

"Margaret, we simply don't know." Sylvia Harris tried to keep her own fearful anxiety out of her voice. "Even too much aspirin can cause a reaction." Margaret was at the breaking point—or beyond it—she thought. And now a new worry, one too frightening to even consider, was pulsing through her mind. Kelly was becoming so listless. Was it possible that Kathy's and Kelly's vital functions were so entwined that if anything happened to Kathy, Kelly's reaction would be to follow her?

Sylvia had already shared that awful possibility with Steve. Now she could see it occurring to Margaret as well. Margaret was seated beside Steve on the couch in the living room. She reached over and took Kelly from him. "Sweetheart," she implored, "talk to Kathy. Ask her where she is. Tell her Mommy and Daddy love her."

Kelly opened her eyes. "She can't hear me," she said drowsily.

"Why, Kelly? Why can't she hear you?" Steve asked.

"She can't wake up anymore," Kelly said with a sigh as she curled into Margaret's arms and went back to sleep.

SLOUCHED down in the car, the Pied Piper listened to the radio. The breaking news, being repeated every few minutes, was that two suspects were being sought in the kidnapping, an ex-convict going by the name of Clint Downes and his girlfriend, Angie Ames.

After the first moment of panic passed, the Pied Piper weighed his options. He could drive to the airport and get back on the plane, which was probably the smartest thing to do. But there was always that chance that Lucas had revealed his identity to Clint Downes. If the Feds arrest Clint, he'll give me up for a lighter sentence, he thought. I can't take that chance.

With any luck I'll see Clint before he gets too near Angie's room. I've got to talk to him first.

An hour later his patience was rewarded. A sedan drove slowly around the parking lot, up one row and down the other, then pulled into the vacant spot near Angie's brown van. A heavyset figure climbed out. In an instant the Pied Piper was out of his car and positioned by Clint's side. Clint spun around, his hand reaching for his jacket pocket.

"Don't bother to pull out a gun," the Pied Piper said. "I'm here to help you."

He watched as Clint's startled look was replaced by one of cunning understanding. "You're the Pied Piper."

"Yes."

"With all the risks I took, it's about time I met you. Who are you?"

He didn't have a clue, the Pied Piper realized, and now it's too late. I have to see it through. "She's in there," he said, pointing to Angie's room. "You have to tell her that I came up here to help you get away. What car are you driving?"

"I helped myself to it. I'm safe for a couple of hours."

"Then get her and the child in that car and get out of here. Make arrangements for them as you see necessary. I'll follow you and then take you to my plane. I'll drop you off in Canada."

Clint nodded. "She's the one who ruined it all."

"Not yet, she hasn't. But get her out of here before it's too late."

"WE'VE got to try to keep her awake," Sylvia Harris said. "Put her down, Margaret. Hold her hand. You, too, Steve. Make her walk with you."

Her lips white with fear, Margaret obeyed. "Come on, Kelly," she urged. "You and Daddy and Kathy and I love to take a walk together. Come on, darling."

"I can't. . . . I don't . . ." Kelly's voice was fretful and sleepy.

"Kelly, tell Kathy she has to wake up, too," Dr. Harris urged.

Kelly's head was drooping on her chest, but she began to shake it in protest. "No . . . no more. Go away, Mona."

"Kelly, what is it?" Help me, God, Margaret thought. Let me break through to Kathy. That woman, Angie, must be the one Kelly called Mona. "Kelly, what is Mona doing to Kathy?"

Stumbling between Margaret and Steve, half carried by them, Kelly whispered, "Mona's singing." Her voice trembling, off-key, she sang, *"No . . . more . . . old Cape Cod."*

"I'M AFRAID they're going to think I'm just one of those people who want to get their names in the paper," Elsie Stone confided to her daughter. She was holding the telephone in one hand and the *Cape Cod Times* in the other. "The woman told me the child was a boy, but I'm convinced she's a girl. And Suzie, I swear that child was Kathy Frawley. I mean, she had a hood on, and it just showed some dark brown hair, but looking back, I knew there was something phony about the hair. Like a bad dye job. And when I asked her name, she said it was Kathy, but then I could see the scowl that woman gave her, and she looked real scared and said it was Stevie."

"Mom," Suzie broke in, "are you sure you're not getting carried away?"

"I don't want to make a fool of myself, but just suppose . . ."

"Mom, I'm going to tell you what to do. Call the Barnstable police, tell them *exactly* what you told me, then leave it in their hands. I love you, Mom. Debby had a wonderful time today, and the cookies she brought home are heaven."

"WALTER, this is Steve Frawley. Kathy is on Cape Cod. You've got to start looking there."

"Steve, I was about to phone you," Carlson said. "We just found out Downes took the shuttle to Boston, but when he rented a car, he asked for a map of Maine."

"Forget Maine. Kelly has been trying to tell us for hours that Kathy is on Cape Cod. She was even trying to sing that song, 'Old Cape Cod.' That woman the twins call Mona is singing it to Kathy."

"Steve, take it easy. We'll put out a special bulletin to the Cape, but I have to tell you, we're learning more about the girlfriend,

Angie. She was brought up in Maine. We think she may be hiding out there with friends."

"No. The Cape! Kathy is on the Cape!"

"Hold on, there's a call I've got to take." Carlson put Steve on hold, answered the other call, then got back on. "Steve, you may be right. We have an eyewitness who claims to have seen Kathy this morning in a McDonald's in Hyannis. An FBI plane is picking up Realto and me in fifteen minutes."

"We're coming, too."

"You're here in old Cape Cod," Angie sang, throwing her arms around Clint's neck. "Boy have I missed you, Big Man."

"You have, huh?" Clint was about to push her away from him, but then remembered that he could not let her become suspicious. Instead, he hugged her back. "And guess who missed you, little songbird?"

"Clint, I know you have to be mad at me for taking off with the money, but I started to worry that if anyone connected you to Lucas, it would be better if I was out of the way."

"It's okay. But we've gotta get out of here. Have you been listening to the radio?"

"No. I've been watching *Everybody Loves Raymond.* I gave the kid more cough medicine, and she finally fell asleep again."

Clint's glance darted to Kathy, who was lying on the bed, one shoe on, her damp hair clinging to her face. "If we did it the way we were supposed to, that kid would be home right now. And we'd be on our way to Florida with half a million and not have the whole country looking for us."

"What makes you think the whole country is looking for us?"

"Switch channels. You're big news, baby. Like it or not."

With a deliberate click of the remote, Angie turned off the television. "So what do you think we should do?"

"I've got a safe car. We get out of here and dump the kid where she won't be found. Then you and I get off the Cape."

"But we'd planned to get rid of the kid *and* the van."

"We leave the van here."

I'm registered here under my own name, Angie thought. If they really are looking for us, they'll be here soon enough. But Clint doesn't have to know that. I can tell he's lying to me. He's sore, and when dopey Clint gets sore, he gets nasty.

He wants to get rid of me.

"Clint, honey," she said. "That cop in Hyannis has the license plate of the van. By now every cop on the Cape knows I was in Hyannis this afternoon. If they think I'm still around, they'll be looking for this van. If they find it in this parking lot, they'll know we can't have gone far. I know a marina not five minutes from here that's closed this time of year. I can drive the van onto the pier with the kid in it, then jump out of it while it's still moving and let it keep going. The water's plenty deep enough to cover it. They won't find it for months. Come on, honey, we're wasting time."

She watched as Clint looked uncertainly at the window. With a chill she realized someone else was out there.

"Clint, you know I can read you like a book," she said cajolingly. "You're mad at me for getting rid of Lucas and taking off. Maybe you're right. Tell me something. Is the Pied Piper up here?"

She could tell from the expression on his face that she was right. "Do you know who he is?"

"No, but he looks familiar, like someone I've seen before. I can't place him, though. I've got to figure it out."

"So you'd be able to identify him?"

"Yeah."

"Do you really think, now that you've seen him, he's going to let you stay alive? I'll tell you something—he won't! I bet he told you to get rid of me and the kid, and you two would be pals. It don't work that way. Believe me, it don't. You're better off trusting me. We get out of this place—and we will—and then we start reminding him that we deserve a bigger share."

She could see the anger draining out of Clint's face. I could always twist him around my little finger, she thought. He's so dumb. But once he figures out who this guy is, we're set for life. "Honey," she said. "You take the suitcase. Put it in the car you're driving. But hold on a minute—is it rented in your name?"

"No. I switched cars at the movies."

"Good for you. Okay. I'll take the kid. You take the money. Let's get out of here. Is the Pied Piper gonna follow us?"

"Yeah. He thinks that I'll drive with him to where he has a plane waiting."

"And instead of that," Angie said, "when we dump the van, you and I take off in your car. You don't think he's going to chase us and risk having the cops stop him, do you? Then we get off the Cape. We change cars again and drive to Canada, get a plane out of there, and disappear."

Clint nodded. "All right. Get the kid." When Angie picked up Kathy, he noticed that the one shoe she was wearing fell off. So what, he thought. She won't need it anymore.

Three minutes later, at nine thirty-five, with Kathy wrapped in a blanket and lying on the floor, Angie drove the van out of the parking lot of the Shell and Dune Motel. Clint followed in his stolen car. Directly behind, unaware that Angie and Clint had teamed up again, the Pied Piper followed. Why is she in that van? he asked himself. But he's carrying a suitcase, and the money has to be in it. "It's all or nothing now," he said aloud as he took his place at the rear of the deadly procession.

OFFICER Sam Tyron arrived at the Soundview Motel twelve minutes after receiving a terse phone call from the Barnstable Police Department. On the way there he angrily berated himself for not following his instinct to investigate further the woman he had stopped because of the lack of a car seat in her van.

He arrived to find the motel swarming with police. The realization that the second Frawley twin was not only still alive but had been spotted in Hyannis had brought out all the brass. They were clustered in the motel room registered to Linda Hagen. The twenty-dollar bills scattered under the bed were a strong indication that this was, indeed, where the kidnapper had stayed.

An excited David Toomey had responded to a call from the night manager and returned to the motel. "That child is very, very sick," he warned. "She should have been taken to the emergency room. You'd better find her soon, or it'll be too late."

OTHER than their efforts to keep Kelly awake, everyone on the FBI plane remained silent. Kelly, her eyes closed, was in Margaret's arms. Totally lethargic, her head resting against Margaret's heart, she was becoming less and less responsive.

Agents Carlson and Realto were in the plane with them. They had been in touch with FBI headquarters in Boston. Their counterparts there would be at the Cape to take over the investigation. An FBI car would meet them at the airport and take them to police headquarters in Hyannis.

Seated beside Carlson, Realto was analyzing what he would do if he were in Clint and Angie's position. I'd get rid of the van and the rental car, and I'd also get rid of the child, he decided. Kathy's too much of a liability. If only they have the decency to leave her where she can be found quickly. But that would give us the exact location from which to begin tracking them, he concluded grimly. Something tells me these people are too desperate and too evil to have any decency in them.

EVERY cop on the Cape is on the lookout for this van, Angie thought, biting her lip as she drove nervously along Route 28 from Chatham. But the marina is only a little past the town line into Harwich, and once we dump this wreck, we'll be okay.

With her nerves on edge because any minute she expected to hear a siren, Angie reluctantly began to slow up. The turn is right along here, she thought. Yeah, not this one, the next one. A moment later, heaving a sigh of relief, she turned left off Route 28 and drove along the winding road toward Nantucket Sound. Most of the houses along the road were hidden behind high shrubbery. The ones she could see were in darkness, probably closed for the winter. It's a good spot, she thought. I hope Clint realizes that.

She went around a final bend with Clint right behind her. The Pied Piper wouldn't have the nerve to get too close, she figured. *I guess by now he knows I'm no dope.* The pier was directly ahead, and she was just about to drive onto it when she heard the faint, brief tap of a horn.

Stupid, stupid Clint. What the heck was he blowing a horn for? She stopped the van and, livid with anger, watched as he got out of his stolen car and rushed up to her. She opened the door. "You wanna kiss the brat good-bye?" she snapped.

The odor of acrid perspiration was the last thing she remembered as Clint's fist flew through the space between them and pummeled her into unconsciousness. As she slumped over the wheel, Clint put the car in gear and placed her foot on the accelerator. He closed the door just as the van began to move along the pier. He watched as it reached the end, then dropped out of sight.

PHIL King, the clerk at the Shell and Dune Motel, kept his eye on the clock. He went off duty at ten and was anxious to be on his way. He had spent all his spare time that day patching up a fight he'd had with his girlfriend, and she had finally agreed to meet him for a quiet drink at the Impudent Oyster. Only ten minutes to go.

There was a small television behind the desk, company for whoever was working the late-night shift. Remembering that the Celtics were playing the Nets in Boston, Phil flipped on the set, hoping to catch the score.

Instead he caught a breaking news story. Police had confirmed that Kathy Frawley had been seen on the Cape that morning. Her abductor, Angie Ames, was driving a twelve-year-old brown Chevy van. The announcer gave the Connecticut plate number.

Phil did not hear it. He was staring openmouthed at the television. Angie Ames, he thought. *Angie Ames!* His hand trembling, he grabbed the phone and dialed 911.

When the operator answered, he shouted, "Angie Ames is staying here! I saw her van drive out of our lot not ten minutes ago."

CLINT WATCHED THE VAN disappear. Then, with grim satisfaction, he got back in his stolen car and made a sharp U-turn. In the beams of his headlights he caught the startled look on the face of the Pied Piper, who was walking toward him. Just like I expected, he's got a gun, he thought. Sure, he was going to share with me. Real sure. I could run him over, but it would be more fun to play with him.

He drove straight at him, then watched with glee as the Pied Piper dropped the pistol he was holding and jumped out of the car's path. Now I get off the Cape, Clint thought. But first I gotta ditch this car. Those kids will be coming out of the movie in less than an hour, and then the police will be looking for this car.

He raced back to Route 28. He figured the Pied Piper might try to chase him, but he knew he had too great a lead. He'll think I'm heading for the bridge, he decided, but what could he do—that was the best way to go. He turned left. The Mid-Cape Highway would be faster, but he decided to stay on Route 28. By now they probably know that I flew to Boston and rented a car, he thought.

He turned on the radio to hear that Kathy Frawley had been sighted in Hyannis with her abductor, Angie Ames, who also used the name Linda Hagen. Roadblocks were being set up.

Clint gripped the wheel. I've got to get out of here fast, he thought. The suitcase with the money was on the floor of the backseat. The thought of what he could do with one million dollars kept Clint from dissolving into panic as he drove through the outskirts of Hyannis. Twenty more minutes and I'm at the bridge, he thought.

The sound of a police siren made him cringe. Can't be me. I'm not going too fast, he thought, then watched aghast as one police car swerved ahead and cut him off while another pulled up behind.

"Get out of the car with your hands up." The command came from a loudspeaker in the squad car behind him.

Clint felt rivulets of perspiration run down his cheeks as he slowly opened the car door and stepped out, his thick arms high over his head.

Two policemen, guns drawn, approached him. "You're out of

luck," one said. "The kids didn't like the movie and left in the middle. You are under arrest for possession of a stolen motor vehicle."

The other cop shone his flashlight in Clint's face, then did a double take. "You're Clint Downes," he said, then angrily demanded, "Where is that little girl, you bum? Where's Kathy Frawley?"

MARGARET, Steve, Dr. Harris, and Kelly were in the Hyannis police chief's office when the word came that Angie Ames had registered under her own name in a motel in Chatham and that the clerk had seen the van pull out only ten minutes ago.

"Was Kathy in it?" Margaret whispered.

"He doesn't know. But there was a child's shoe on the bed in the room Ames was staying in, and there was an indentation on the pillow. It seems probable that Kathy had been there."

Dr. Harris was holding Kelly. Suddenly she began to shake her. "Kelly, wake up. Kelly, you must wake up." She looked at the police chief. "Get a respirator. Now!"

12

THE Pied Piper had watched as the squad cars cut off Clint's stolen vehicle. He doesn't know my name, he thought, but as soon as he describes me, the FBI will be on my doorstep.

He forced back the burst of anger that made his hands tremble so much he could hardly grasp the wheel. I've got seven million dollars waiting for me in Switzerland, he thought. The passport is in my pocket. I've got to get on an overseas flight right away. I'll have the plane fly me to Canada. Clint may not give me up right away, since he can use me as a bargaining chip. I'm his ace in the hole.

His mouth dry, the Pied Piper turned off Route 28 north. Even before a handcuffed Clint was led to a police car, the Pied Piper was on Route 28 south, heading for Chatham Airport.

"WE KNOW YOUR GIRLFRIEND left the Shell and Dune twenty minutes ago. Was Kathy Frawley with her?"

"I don't know what you're talking about," Clint said.

"You know what we're talking about," FBI Agent Frank Reeves of the Boston office snapped. He, Realto, Carlson, and the Barnstable police chief were in the interview room of the Barnstable police station. "Is Kathy in that van?"

"You just read me my rights. I want a lawyer."

"Clint, listen," Carlson urged. "Kathy Frawley is very sick. If she dies, you've got two murder raps going. We know your pal Lucas didn't commit suicide."

"Lucas?"

"Clint, the twins' DNA must be all over that cottage in Danbury. A Barnstable policeman saw Angie this morning with Kathy. So did a waitress at McDonald's. Your only chance for any kind of leniency is to come clean now."

A scuffling outside the door caused them all to turn abruptly. Then they heard the voice of the sergeant at the desk. "Mrs. Frawley, I'm sorry, you can't go in there."

"I have to. You have the man who kidnapped my children."

Reeves, Realto, and Carlson exchanged glances. "Let her in," Reeves shouted.

The door burst open, and Margaret rushed in, her blue eyes now coal black, her face deathly pale. She went directly to Clint and dropped on her knees. "Kathy is sick," she said, her voice quivering. "If she dies, I don't know whether Kelly will live. I can forgive you everything if only you will let me have Kathy back now. I will plead for you at your sentencing. I promise. I promise. Please."

Clint tried to look away but found himself compelled to look into Margaret's blazing eyes. They have me cold, he reasoned. I won't give up the Pied Piper yet, but maybe there's another way to avoid a murder charge. "I didn't want the kid," he said. "That was Angie's doing. She shot Lucas and left that phony note. Then she took off with the money and phoned me to meet her up here. I told her we'd ditch the van and get off the Cape, but it didn't work out."

"What happened?" Realto asked.

"Angie knew a marina not far from that motel where we could drive the van over the pier. I was following her, but something went wrong. She didn't get out in time."

"The van went off the pier with her in it?"

"Yeah."

"Was Kathy in the van?"

"Yeah. Angie didn't mean to hurt her. We were gonna take her with us. We wanted to be a family."

"A family! A family!" The door to the interview room was still open. Margaret's heartrending cry echoed through the corridor.

Steve was already on his way to be with her. In the interrogation room, he saw Margaret lying at the feet of the pudgy man who had to be the kidnapper. He picked her up in his arms and looked at Clint Downes. "If I could get my hands on a gun, I would kill you right now," he said.

The police chief grabbed the phone after Downes described the location. "The Seagull Marina. Get diving equipment," he ordered. "Get a boat." He looked at Margaret and Steve. "There's a loading dock under that pier. In the winter the dock is supposed to have a chain across it. Maybe, maybe there will be a miracle and the chain stopped the van from going completely into the water. But the tide is coming in fast."

WE'VE got all the airports covered, Walter Carlson thought as he rode with Reeves, Realto, and the Barnstable police chief down Route 28 toward Harwich. Downes claims he's not the Pied Piper but says he can give him to us as a bargaining chip in case anyone tries to slap him with the death penalty. I believe him. He's not smart enough to have engineered the whole kidnapping. Once the Pied Piper knows we have Downes, he'll realize it's only a matter of time until Downes gives him up. He has seven million dollars stashed somewhere. The only thing he can do now is to get out of the country before it's too late.

Kelly had been rushed with Dr. Harris to Cape Cod Hospital, but

Margaret and Steve had insisted on getting in a squad car and driving to the marina. I wish they hadn't come, Carlson thought. They should not have to watch Kathy being removed from a car dragged up from Nantucket Sound.

The traffic scrambled out of the way of the caravan of police cars. In only nine minutes' time they were racing down the road to the marina. The Massachusetts state police were already there. Through the murky fog, spotlights were shining on the pier. In the distance a boat was racing through the heavy waves.

With a squeal of brakes the squad car stopped halfway down the pier. The men tumbled out, their feet pounding the wooden planks. At the end of the pier, they looked down. The back of the van was sticking out of the water, the wheels caught by the heavy linked chain. The front wheels, however, were already in the water, and waves were smashing over the hood. Carlson saw that the weight of the grappling equipment was causing the loading dock to tip forward. As they watched, one of the van's rear wheels rolled over the chain and the van sagged farther into the water.

Carlson felt himself being pushed aside, and an instant later Steve Frawley ripped off his jacket and dove into the water. He came up by the side of the van.

"Get the spotlight inside the car," Reeves barked.

The other back wheel was being lifted by the tide. It's too late, Carlson thought. There's too much pressure from the water. He can't open that door.

Margaret Frawley had run up as well and was standing at the edge of the pier.

Steve was looking inside the van. "Kathy's on the floor in the back," he shouted. "There's a woman in the driver's seat. She's not moving." Frantically he tugged at the back door. He drew his fist back and punched it against the window but could not break it. The waves were pulling him away. He grasped the door handle with one hand and again slammed his fist against the glass.

A splintering, crashing sound erupted as the glass finally gave. Heedless of his broken and bloody hand, Steve pushed the rest of the glass out of his way and thrust first his arms and then his head and shoulders inside the van.

The final wheel was now free of the chain, and the van started to lurch forward into the water.

The Coast Guard boat reached the pier, and as it pulled up beside the van, two men leaned over and grabbed Steve around the waist and legs, dragging him into the boat. His arms were wrapped around a small blanketed figure. As he fell against his rescuers, the van tipped over the edge and disappeared into churning water.

Margaret's cry, "Give her to me! Give her to me!" was drowned out by the wail of an arriving ambulance.

"MOM, I hear that there's a good chance Kathy is alive. I just want you to know, I had nothing to do with Steve's kids being kidnapped. My God, do you think I'd do anything like that to my brother? He's always been there for me."

Nervously, Richie Mason looked around the departure lounge at Kennedy Airport. He listened impatiently to his mother. "Oh, Richie, if they can save Kathy, we'll fly up for a wonderful family reunion, dear," she said.

"You bet, Mom. I've got to go. I've been offered a really great job. I'm flying out right now to the company's headquarters in Oregon. Love you, Mom. I'll stay in touch."

"We are beginning the boarding process for Continental flight 102 to Paris," the announcement began. "First-class passengers and those needing assistance . . ."

With a last, furtive glance around the lounge, Mason presented his ticket and walked on the plane to settle in seat 2B. At the last minute he had decided to skip picking up the final shipment of cocaine from Colombia. With the FBI questioning him about the missing kids, instinct warned him it was time to get out of the country. Luckily, he could count on that kid Danny Hamilton to pick up the suitcase with the cocaine and hide it for him. He still hadn't figured out which distributor he could trust to pick it up from Danny and forward his payment to him, but he'd make that decision later.

Hurry up, he wanted to yell as the plane began to fill. I'm okay, he tried to assure himself. Steve's passport worked like a charm. Thanks, Steve.

The hostess gave the departure speech. Let's go, let's go, he thought. Then his mouth went dry as he heard footsteps racing up the aisle. They stopped at his seat.

"Mr. Mason, will you please accompany us?" a voice asked.

Richie looked up. Two men were standing there. "FBI," one of them said.

"WE HAVE stabilized Kelly, but even though her lungs are clear, she is having difficulty breathing," the doctor in pediatric intensive care said gravely. "Kathy, however, is much worse. She is a very, very sick little girl. The bronchitis has developed into pneumonia, and heavy doses of adult medicine have depressed her nervous system. I wish I could be more optimistic . . ."

Steve, his arms heavily bandaged, sat with Margaret next to the hospital crib. Kathy, almost unrecognizable with her short dark hair and the oxygen mask on her face, was lying perfectly still. The alarm monitoring her respiration had already gone off twice.

Kelly's crib was down the hall in the pediatric wing. Dr. Harris was with her. "Kelly must be brought in here," Margaret ordered.

"Mrs. Frawley—"

"Right away," Margaret said. "Kathy needs her."

NORMAN Bond had stayed in his apartment all day Saturday, spending much of the time sitting on the couch, staring out over the East River and catching updates of the Frawley kidnapping on television. Why did I hire Frawley? he wondered. Was it because I wanted to pretend I could start all over again, that I could turn back time and be in Ridgefield with Theresa? Did I want to pretend that our twins had lived? They'd be twenty-one years old now.

They think I had something to do with the kidnapping. I was such a fool to refer to Theresa as "my late wife." I've always been careful to say that I believed she was alive and that she'd dumped Banks the same way she dumped me.

Ever since the FBI had questioned him, Bond hadn't been able to get Theresa out of his mind, not for a minute. Before he killed her, she had begged for the life of the twins she was expecting the way Margaret Frawley had begged for the safe return of her children.

At seven o'clock he made himself a drink. "A suspect was believed to have been spotted on Cape Cod," a news brief reported.

"Norman . . . please . . . don't . . ."

Weekends are always the hardest, he thought.

A half hour later Norman made himself another drink, then sipped it as he ran his hand over Theresa's wedding rings on the chain around his neck—the one he had given her that she'd left on the dresser and the circle of diamonds her rich, cultured second husband had given her. He remembered how he had to struggle to pull that one off her finger. Her slender fingers were swollen because of the pregnancy.

At eight thirty he decided to shower and dress and go out for dinner. Somewhat unsteady on his feet, he got up, went to the closet, and laid out a business suit, white shirt, and one of the ties the Paul Stuart salesman had assured him complemented the suit.

Forty minutes later, as he was leaving his apartment building, he happened to glance across the street. Two men were getting out of a car. One of the men was the FBI agent who had come to his office. In a sudden panic Norman Bond darted down the block, then dashed across Seventy-second Street.

The impact of the truck was an explosion that seemed to rip him apart. He felt himself lifted into the air; then the awful pain hit as his body crashed against the sidewalk. He tasted blood gushing from his mouth.

The face of the agent was swimming above him. The chain with Theresa's rings, he thought. I've got to get rid of it. But he could not move his hand. He could feel his white shirt becoming soaked with blood. His lips formed her name: Theresa.

Agent Angus Sommers was kneeling beside Norman Bond. He put his finger on Bond's neck. "He's gone," he said.

AGENTS Reeves, Carlson, and Realto entered Clint's holding cell. "They got the little girl out, but she may not make it," Carlson said angrily. "Your girlfriend is dead. They'll do an autopsy, but you know what? We think she was already gone before she hit the water. Someone punched her hard enough to kill her. I wonder who that was."

Feeling as if he'd been hit by a cement block, Clint realized that it was all over for him. He bitterly decided that he wasn't going down alone. Telling them who the Pied Piper is may or may not help me with my sentence, he thought, but I'm not going to rot in prison while he lives it up on seven million bucks.

"I don't know the Pied Piper's name," he told the agents, "but I can tell you what he looks like. He's tall. I'd guess a couple of inches over six feet. Sandy blond hair. Classy looking. Early forties. When he wanted me to dump Angie, he told me that I should follow him to Chatham Airport, where he had a plane waiting."

Clint paused. "Wait a minute!" he exclaimed. "I do know who he is. I thought I had seen him someplace before. He's the big shot from that company that paid the ransom. He was on TV saying that they shouldn't have paid it."

"Gregg Stanford!" Carlson said as Realto nodded in agreement. Reeves was instantly on his cell phone.

"If only we can grab him before his plane takes off," Carlson said. With contempt and fury in his voice he told Clint, "You better get down on your knees, you lowlife, and start praying that Kathy Frawley pulls through."

"THE Frawley twins have been rushed to Cape Cod Hospital," the announcer on Channel 5 reported. "Kathy Frawley's condition is extremely critical. The body of one of the kidnappers, Angie Ames, has been recovered from the sunken van at the Harwich marina. Her accomplice, Clint Downes, is under arrest. The man believed to be the mastermind of the kidnapping, the 'Pied Piper,' is still at large."

They don't say that I'm on the Cape, the Pied Piper thought frantically as he sat in the departure lounge of Chatham Airport and watched the breaking news on television. That means Clint hasn't described me to them yet.

I've got to get out of the country now. But the drenching rain and enveloping fog was temporarily grounding all the planes. His pilot had told him that he hoped that the delay wouldn't be much longer.

Why did I panic and come up with that crazy idea of kidnapping those kids? he asked himself. I did it because I was scared. I did it because I was afraid Millicent might discover that I was fooling around with other women. If she had decided to dump me, I'd be out of a job, and I don't have a nickel in my own name. I did it because I thought I could trust Lucas. He knew how to keep his mouth shut. In the end he still didn't give me away.

If only I hadn't come to Cape Cod. I could have been out of the country by now with all those millions waiting for me. I'll have the plane take me to the Maldives. There's no extradition there.

The door of the lounge burst open, and two men rushed in. One slipped behind him and ordered him to stand with his hands spread out. Quickly the man frisked him.

"FBI, Mr. Stanford," the other one said. "What a surprise. What brings you to the Cape this evening?"

Gregg Stanford looked directly at him. "I was visiting a friend, a young woman. A private matter, which is none of your business."

"By any chance was her name Angie?"

"What are you talking about?" Stanford demanded. "This is outrageous."

"You know exactly what we're talking about," the agent replied. "You won't be catching a plane tonight, Mr. Stanford. Or perhaps I should ask, would you prefer to be addressed as the Pied Piper?"

KELLY, still in her crib and accompanied by Dr. Harris, was wheeled into the intensive care unit. Like her sister, she was wearing an oxygen mask. Margaret stood up. "Disconnect her mask," she said. "I'm putting her in the crib with Kathy."

"Margaret, Kathy has pneumonia." The protest died on Sylvia Harris's lips.

"Do it," Margaret told the nurse. "You can hook it up again as soon as I settle her."

The nurse looked at Steve. "Go ahead," he told her.

Margaret picked up Kelly and for an instant held her head against her neck. "Kathy needs you," she whispered. "And you need her."

The nurse rolled down the side of the crib, and Margaret placed Kelly next to her twin, with Kelly's right thumb touching Kathy's left one.

It's where they were conjoined, Sylvia thought.

The nurse reattached Kelly's mask to the oxygen.

In silent prayer Margaret, Steve, and Sylvia kept a heartsick vigil by the crib all night. The twins did not stir from their deep sleep. Then, as the first light of dawn filtered into the room, Kathy stirred, moved her hand, and entwined her fingers in Kelly's.

Kelly opened her eyes and turned her head to look at her sister.

Kathy's eyes opened wide. She looked around the room, going from one person to another. Her lips began to move.

A smile lit Kelly's face, and she murmured something in Kathy's ear.

"Twin talk," Steve said softly.

"What is she telling you, Kelly?" Margaret whispered.

"She missed us very, very much. And she wants to go home."

EPILOGUE

THREE weeks later Walter Carlson sat at the dining-room table with Steve and Margaret, lingering over second cups of coffee. All through dinner he kept thinking of the first time he had seen them, the handsome young couple in evening clothes who had arrived home to learn that their children were gone. In the following days they had become shadows of their former selves, pale and gaunt, clinging to each other in despair.

Now Steve's manner was relaxed and confident. Margaret, lovely in a white sweater and dark slacks, her hair loose around her shoulders, a smile on her lips, was a different person from the half-crazed woman who had pleaded with them to believe that Kathy was alive.

Even so, Carlson noticed how, during dinner, her eyes often darted to the living room, where the twins, dressed in their pajamas, were having a tea party with their dolls and teddy bears. She needs to keep reassuring herself that they're both still there, he thought.

The Frawleys had invited him to dinner to celebrate their return to normal life, as Margaret had put it. But now, inevitably, it was natural to let them in on some of the information revealed through the confessions of Gregg Stanford and Clint Downes.

He had not intended to talk about Steve's half brother, Richard Mason, but when Steve mentioned that his mother and father had been up for a visit, he asked about them.

"You can understand how tough it is for my mother to know that Richie is in trouble again," Steve said. "Smuggling cocaine is even worse than that scam he was involved in years ago. She knows the kind of prison term he's facing, and, like all mothers, she's trying to figure what she did wrong to make him turn out like this."

"She didn't do anything wrong," Carlson said bluntly. "He's a bad apple, pure and simple."

Then, with a final sip of coffee, he said, "If there's anything good that came out of all this, it's that we know that Norman Bond killed his ex-wife, Theresa. Her wedding ring given her by her second husband was on a chain around his neck. She was wearing it the night she disappeared. At least now her second husband can get on with his life."

Carlson could not stop glancing at the twins. "They're as alike as two peas in a pod," he said.

"Aren't they?" Margaret said in agreement. "Just last week we took Kathy to the hairdresser and got rid of that terrible dye job, and then I had them cut Kelly's hair so that now they both have the same pixie cut. It's sweet on them, isn't it?"

She sighed. "I get up at least three times a night and check on them, just to be sure they're still here. We have a state-of-the-art alarm system. But even with that protection, I still can't bear to have them out of my sight."

"That will ease," Carlson assured her. "Maybe not for a while, but it will get better in time. How are the girls doing?"

"Kathy still has nightmares. In her sleep she says, 'No more Mona. No more Mona.' Then, the other day when we were out shopping, she saw a thin woman with messy long, brown hair who, I guess, reminded her of Angie. Kathy started shrieking and threw her arms around my legs. It just about broke my heart. But Dr. Sylvia has recommended a wonderful child psychiatrist, Dr. Judith Knowles. We'll be taking the twins to her every week. It will take time, but she assured us they'll be fine eventually."

"Is Stanford going to plea-bargain?" Steve asked.

"He hasn't got much to bargain with. He plotted the kidnapping because he was panicking. He was afraid his wife had found out about his philandering and was going to divorce him. If she had, he wouldn't have a penny. He was in on some of the company's financial problems last year and was still afraid of being caught. He had to have a backup fund, and, Steve, when he met you at the office and you were showing pictures of the twins, he hatched his scheme.

"Lucas Wohl and he had a strange relationship," Carlson continued. "Lucas was his trusted driver when he had his little affairs. Then one day during his second marriage, Stanford came home unexpectedly and found Lucas jimmying the safe in which his wife kept her jewels. He told him to go ahead with the robbery, but he had to cut him in on the proceeds. After that, he would sometimes tip Lucas off on houses to rob. Stanford always has lived on the edge. What I like about the way this played out is that he might have gotten away with all of it if he had trusted Lucas not to tell

Clint who he was. He was high on our list of suspects, and he'd been under surveillance, but we didn't really have anything on him. That's what's going to haunt Stanford for the rest of his life when he wakes up every morning in a prison cell."

"What about Downes?" Margaret asked. "Has he confessed?"

"He's a kidnapper and murderer. He's still trying to say Angie's death was an accident, but lots of luck with that one. The federal courts will deal with him. I'm sure he's had his last beer at the Danbury Pub. He'll never get out of prison again."

The twins had finished the tea party and scampered into the dining room. A moment later a smiling Kathy was on Margaret's lap and a giggling Kelly was being lifted up by Steve.

Walter Carlson felt a lump in his throat. If only it was always like this, he thought. If only we could bring all the kids home. If only we could rid the world of all the predators. But this time at least, we got a happy ending.

The twins were wearing blue-flowered pajamas. Two little girls in blue, he thought. Two little girls in blue . . .

The Family Secret of
Mary Higgins Clark

Vital Stats

BORN: New York City, 1929
RESIDENCES: Saddle River, NJ;
   Manhattan; Cape Cod
HUSBAND: John J. Conheeney,
   retired business executive
AWARDS: Grand Master Award
   from the Mystery Writers of
   America; Outstanding Mother
   Award from the National
   Mother's Day Council
WEBSITE:
   www.maryhigginsclark.com

MORE than one critic has remarked that publishing phenom Mary Higgins Clark is a genius at writing crime tales involving children in peril. Her first mega-bestseller, *Where Are the Children?* (1975), was about a mother's desperate attempt to protect her kids from a twisted kidnapper in Cape Cod, Massachusetts. Her latest, *Two Little Girls in Blue,* is a similar chiller about a kidnapping, a Cape Cod setting, and a young mother who just won't give up.

This family focus is no surprise to fans of the Queen of Suspense, whose twenty-five whodunits have set the gold standard for mysteries featuring ordinary people with strong family bonds.

The secret of this storyteller's immense success with family drama is not just a matter of mere application. (Clark, a notoriously hard worker, began her writing career as a single mother scribbling mornings between five and seven before getting the kids off to school.) This mother of five, grandmother of six, and step-grandmother of ten knows all about family, and she draws on her own experiences to write about family relationships with complete authority.

She also knows about families living in the shadow of hardship. In 1964 she became a young widow when her first husband, Warren, died of a heart attack, leaving her with five kids to raise. But this was not her first family tragedy. In fact, it was a mournful echo of her own childhood. Her growing-up years in New York City during the Great Depression were humble but magical. Her father, Luke Higgins, was a popular pub owner. Her mother, Nora was a stylish, generous-hearted family woman. But sadly, in 1939, Luke Higgins died suddenly in his sleep. He was fifty-four. Mary was ten.

As her daughter would do years later, Nora Higgins was forced to provide for her growing children—a daughter and two sons—with very little money in the bank. She took in lodgers, babysat, and did anything else she could to make ends meet. "My

Twin Talk

From early childhood, Mary Higgins Clark has been captivated by telepathy. Of her exciting new novel, *Two Little Girls in Blue,* she says: "I have used telepathy to a degree in some of my books. But the bond that exists between twins, particularly identical twins, is nothing short of fascinating."

To learn more about the curious topic that inspired the story of Kathy and Kelly Frawley, the author recommends these nonfiction books:

Twin Telepathy
   by Guy Lyon Playfair

Entwined Lives
   by Nancy L. Segal, PhD

Twin Tales (for ages 9–12)
   by Donna M. Jackson

mother's occupation and hobby, vocation and avocation was motherhood," Clark says. "She loved the three of us fiercely."

Fiercely devoted to her own family, Clark has co-authored three books with her daughter Carol Higgins Clark. She is currently at work on her own next novel to provide for her ever-expanding family of readers. ■

Alan Titchmarsh

Rosie

Chapter 1

"IT'S your grandmother."

"Yes?"

"She's been arrested."

This is not a conversation that many people expect to have. We know that grannies are not what they were, but even allowing for the fact that many are proficient on the Internet, lunatic behind the wheel, and capable of doing full justice to the drinks cabinet, the discovery that our own had been detained at Her Majesty's pleasure would, if we are honest, come as a bit of a shock. A shock likely to provoke either disbelief or outrage.

As the policeman at the other end of the line delivered the grave news, in the particularly self-righteous manner that only someone wearing a uniform can, Nick Robertson found himself in the former camp. "She's been what?"

"Arrested, sir. Well, detained, actually."

"But what for?"

"Disturbing the peace."

"Where?"

"In London, sir. She's at Bow Street police station. If you could come and collect her? We don't want to release her on her own and . . . Well, I'd rather not say any more over the phone. We'll fill you in when you get here."

"But why me?"

"Yours was the name and number she gave us, sir."

There were many things Nick wanted to say, the first being: "But I live on the Isle of Wight." Instead he settled for: "Right. It will take me a couple of hours to get there."

"No problem, sir. We'll keep her comfortable."

"She's all right, isn't she? I mean, she's not hurt?"

"Oh, no, sir. She's absolutely fine. Keeping my officers well entertained."

"She would. I'll be there as soon as I can."

And that was it. No more information. What had she done? And why hadn't she called his mother? She was nearer. But the answer to that was obvious: His mother would have given her mother-in-law what for. Or his father—her son? No again. Nick's dad would have been at the races—or at some meeting for his next moneymaking wheeze. Not much chance of finding him at the end of a telephone.

Which was why, on a bright May morning, when he should have been staring out of the window and moping about the end of a three-year relationship with a girl, who was now sitting on a British Airways flight to New York, Nick found himself rattling into Waterloo Station on the eleven fifteen from Southampton. Briefly, he pictured his grandmother sitting in a cell, cowed and tearful, but, if he was honest with himself, he knew that was unlikely.

He wasn't wrong: He found her at the front desk of the police station, regaling a wide-eyed trio of uniformed officers with the reasons behind her forecast for a Chelsea football victory over Manchester United. She looked round as he came in and smiled at him. "Hello, love! Come to take me home?"

He nodded.

The desk sergeant broke away from the group, looking sheepish, negotiated the narrow opening to one side of the counter with some difficulty, and beckoned Nick toward the room opposite. "Would you mind, sir?" As the door closed behind them, he heaved a sigh. "Quite a character, your granny."

"Yes."

"I should think she takes a bit of looking after."

"Well, most of the time she's fine."

"Lives on her own, I gather."

"Yes. She's not helpless," Nick said defensively.

"I can see that. But it might be worth keeping an eye on her."

"What's she done? Nothing serious, surely?"

"Well, not serious. Just silly. We're letting her off with a caution. I think the Russian embassy was surprised more than anything. It's normally students who chain themselves to their railings. And dissidents. Not that we get many of them nowadays." Then: "We don't get many grannies either."

"No. I suppose not," Nick said thoughtfully. There were so many things he could have asked, but in the event he only managed, "I mean . . . why did she do it?"

"Some sort of protest. Mind you, her equipment wasn't up to much. One of those bicycle safety chains. We just snipped it off."

"I see."

"The worry is that I think she rather enjoyed the attention, and we've enough on without coping with protesting pensioners."

"I'm sorry. I'll try to make sure she stays out of trouble."

"If you would."

"Can I take her home, then?"

"Yes, of course." He hesitated. "Can I just ask you, sir . . . what your granny was saying. I suppose it's just her funny way, isn't it? I mean . . ." He looked at Nick sideways. "She's not really related to the Russian royal family, is she?"

"What?" It was one of those defining moments: the moment when your granny, who you've always perceived as adorable and ever-so-slightly . . . individual, might have turned a corner. Nick shook his head. "No. I think you misunderstood. Her family was Russian. Gran left when there was all that bother with the Russian royal family when she was a baby. She's lived in Britain ever since."

The policeman stared at Nick for a moment. "Well, the embassy were very good about it. They had a particularly reasonable attaché on duty today. I suggested to him that your granny was just a bit—well, doolally."

Nick's eyes widened.

"So, if you could just make sure she gets home safely. And maybe keep her away from bicycle chains for a while."

"Yes. Yes, of course. It won't happen again," he said, and added, under his breath, "I hope."

SHE was standing by the door of the police station, smiling, her silver-gray hair in its familiar soft curls, sensible shoes polished, and tweed skirt pressed. Thanks to the morning's excitement, her pale blue eyes were sparkling as she pushed her hands deep into the pockets of her red, woolly jacket.

Nick's greeting came as a bit of a letdown.

"Come on, Granny." Nick's tone was impatient.

She frowned. "There's no need for that."

"All right, then—Rosie."

"Better."

He sighed. "Tea?"

"Ooh! Yes, please. Best thing anybody's said all day."

"I thought police stations were famous for their tea."

"Yes. But they don't do Earl Grey. Terrible stuff, theirs."

"There's a café across the road. Come on; they'll probably do a range of designer teas."

She stood quite still and shook her head.

"What's the matter?"

"I'm not having tea there, designer range or no."

"Where, then?"

"The Ritz. As a celebration."

"A celebration of what?"

"Mission accomplished."

"What sort of mission? You've just been arrested."

"I achieved what I set out to do."

"Which was?"

She pulled up the collar of her jacket and held it with a leather-gloved hand. "To draw attention to my life in exile."

"Oh, Rosie!"

She fixed him with flashing eyes. "I mean it." The stern expression subsided, and she grinned. "Oh, go on, take me for tea at the Ritz. You look as though you could do with a bit of fun."

He shook his head. "What are you like?"

She put her head on one side. "A duchess?"

"I DO wish you wouldn't look so smug."

Rosie sipped the Earl Grey in the china cup. "Why shouldn't I?"

"Because you should be ashamed of yourself. Wasting police time."

"Well, it was all in a good cause." She picked up a tiny cucumber sandwich and popped it into her mouth, whole, chewing it purposefully and scrutinizing her surroundings. "Look at him. Over there." She gestured toward a small, bespectacled man in a gray suit. He was looking around the room as though he was waiting for someone. "He looks suspicious. Do you think he's here to meet a lover?"

The reply was impatient. "I really don't know."

"Well, he might be. They come in the most unlikely disguises, you know."

"Who do?"

"Lovers."

"Like duchesses?"

She avoided his eye, then muttered, "What, love?"

"What were you telling that policeman?"

"Have you finished with the sandwiches? Shall we go on to the cakes?"

"Is this how it's going to be now?"

"How what's going to be?" She was examining the cake stand.

"Are you going to carry on being childish?"

She looked hurt. "That's a very mean thing to say." He saw that her eyes were glistening with tears.

"Oh, don't do that!" He searched his pockets for a handkerchief, found it, and handed it to her. "You know what I mean."

Rosie blew her nose. "Oh, yes, I know what you mean. You're eighty-seven. Why can't you just be a normal granny? The usual stuff."

"Well, what's wrong with that? Has Mum been at it again?"

She wiped the tears off her cheeks. "A bit. But it's not just her."

"But why chain yourself to the railings of the Russian embassy?"

"To scare myself." She blew her nose again. "To make myself feel as though I'm doing more than just sitting around waiting." She sniffed. "It's to prove to myself that I can still feel things."

"Since Granddad?"

She nodded.

Nick reached forward and squeezed her hand. "I know."

"I'm glad he's not in pain anymore. It wasn't much of a life at the end. But at least he minded. Once. Well . . . I think he did. About me."

"Of course he did. We all do."

"Huh! Some more than others."

"Is that why you didn't ask the police to call Mum or Dad?"

She dabbed her cheek with the handkerchief. "Not much point, was there? Your mum would have given me what for, and your dad wouldn't have been there. No, I wanted you."

"But you've got to find another way. You can't keep getting yourself arrested."

"It was the first time!"

"You know what I mean."

"If you mean will I promise I won't be any more trouble, the answer's no."

"But why should you want to be trouble?"

"Because I want to do something with myself. It's time I had a life."

"But you've had a life." As soon as he'd said it, he could have bitten out his tongue.

"So, that's it, then. Because I'm eighty-seven I shouldn't have expectations?"

"No, I didn't mean that—"

"Well, what did you mean? I've got a new hip and a new knee. It'd be a crime not to use them."

"It is a crime when you chain them to railings."

"It's just that I don't want to go quietly. To give in. I want to take risks."

"Like imprisonment?"

She bit her lip, and her eyes brimmed with tears again. "I suppose it's hard for you to understand."

"Not really. In one way, yes, but not in another." He sat back in his chair. "I just worry that—"

"That I'm getting dementia? Well, I'm not. At least, I don't think I am. But, then, I don't suppose you realize it when it's happening to you, do you?"

Nick watched her as she sipped her tea. She had looked confident in the police station, Nick thought. Now she looked crestfallen, fearful. He felt guilty: He was responsible for the change in her. He offered an olive branch. "Tell me about it, then."

She avoided his eyes. "About what?"

"This Russian thing."

"You know perfectly well what it's about." She picked up another tiny sandwich, nibbled the corner, then finished it.

"The policeman said something about the royal family."

She looked vague. "Did he?"

"Can you remember what you said to him?"

"I have perfect recall."

"Well?"

"Not telling you now. Wrong time. Wrong place. One day. When I'm ready." She eyed the cake stand and settled on an elaborate cream horn. "That'll put me right." She began to dissect it. "I know what you're thinking," she murmured through a mouthful of pastry, "but I can't be bothered what people think anymore."

"Why?"

"Because people think what the newspapers and the television tell them to think. And, anyway, it's all geared to people under forty. Thirty, even. Get to my age and they think all you want to watch is repeats of Miss Marple. I can remember all the endings, you know."

"So you do watch them?"

"Only once." She snapped the end off the cream horn. "Most of the time, people just patronize you. Last week I was standing on the pavement looking at some may blossom. It was so pretty, but before I knew it, I was halfway across the road with this man gripping me by the arm and booming in my ear. They treat you as though you're educationally subnormal. And deaf—they always shout at you. And I'm not deaf. Or daft."

"No," he said with feeling.

She was warming to her theme, and the cream horn was yielding to the pressure of a pastry fork. "The trouble is, you get used to it. You do! You begin to believe that you are past it. You start acting like a child because you're expected to, and before you know it, you've given up. Take that over-sixties club I went to. What a waste of time. Arguing over the teapot, painting Christmas cards. Being fawned over. Heavens! There's more to life than that. I was twenty years older than most of them, and I ended up running round after them—picking up their paints, passing them their coats, taking them to the toilet. It was like being back at school. No, thank you. I've still got a brain—what's left of it—and I still have opinions, but they don't seem to count anymore. Who cares what I think?"

"I do."

She looked at him suspiciously. "Do you? Do you really?"

"Yes."

"Even if it means being embarrassed?"

Nick leaned forward. "I'd prefer to avoid that bit but, on the whole, yes, even if it means being embarrassed."

Her face brightened. "So will you help me?"

"Help you with what?"

"To live a bit."

Her request took him by surprise. It seemed so innocent and plaintive. "Well, I don't know . . ."

"I won't be a burden. I don't want to take over your life or anything. I just need a bit of support. Encouragement, I suppose."

"I'll try."

She smiled weakly. "I know it must look like attention-seeking, but it's not that. It's just . . ." She sighed. "Do you know that Peggy Lee song, 'Is That All There Is'?"

He nodded.

"Well, I suppose I just want to keep dancing a bit longer. That's all."

Nick put his arm round her and squeezed her gently. She smelt faintly of Chanel No. 5. Not like a granny at all.

He eased away and looked into her shimmering eyes. "Well, no more chaining yourself to railings. Promise?"

She hesitated, then saw him raise his eyebrows in warning. "I promise."

He sat back in his chair. "And this Russian thing. You'll talk to me about it when you're ready?"

"Yes. When I'm ready. I never told your dad when he was little. I was waiting until he was older, but by then I knew there was no point. He was always a bit . . . well . . ."

"Cynical?"

"Yes. No imagination—except when he's dreaming he can make a fortune on some harebrained scheme or a horse. I told him his grandmother was Russian and that she stayed behind during the revolution when I was brought over here. I never told him any more. I've never told anyone. No one would have believed me."

"Why not?"

"Not now. I'll tell you when there's more time. And, anyway, there are other things I want to do as well."

"What sort of things?" Nick asked uneasily.

"Things that nobody else has thought of. Like Marks and Spencer."

"What?"

She hunched forward conspiratorially. "I've had this brilliant idea. If Marks and Spencer change the labels on all their clothes, marking them as a size smaller than they really are, more people would shop there."

"I'm sorry?"

She sighed impatiently. "You're so slow. Think about it. Women don't like to think they're fat. They want to be a size eight, and most of them are a size ten—or more. All M and S have to do is change the labels on their clothes, and then the size-ten women will be able to fit into a size eight." She glanced about her to make sure they were not overheard, then carried on: "Stands to reason that Mrs. Smith will keep going back there, rather than to Laura Ashley, because she feels better about herself in clothes from M and S. Come to think of it," she went on reflectively, "maybe they should mark them down two sizes. Imagine a size-sixteen woman suddenly being able to fit into a twelve. Ha! Mind you, if I write and tell them, I don't expect I shall hear anything. Next thing you know, they'll be doing it and won't pay me a penny."

Nick gaped at her.

"Shut your mouth, dear, or you'll catch a fly." She winked. "Cakes have all gone. Shall we make a move?"

As THEY walked down the street in the London borough of Richmond toward his grandmother's flat, Rosie clung tightly to Nick's arm. "Come in for a while?"

Nick looked at his watch. "Just for a few minutes. I have to catch the ferry back to the island."

"Aah! Doesn't that sound lovely? Almost like an adventure."

Nick smiled. "I suppose it does. I still like crossing the water to go home. Makes it a bit special."

"Yes. And I've always liked the Isle of Wight. Ever since that holiday when you were little."

"It's a bit quiet now."

"Oh? I'd have thought it would have been busier than it was."

"No. I mean quieter for me."

Rosie looked at him inquiringly.

"Debs has gone."

She stopped walking. "What? But you'd been together such a long time."

"Three years."

"Oh, love! I'm so sorry."

"Thanks." He tried to sound noncommittal.

"What was it? You or her?"

"A real estate agent, actually."

"Huh. Never liked real estate agents. Too smug by half. Wearing cuff links during the day." She took his arm and started walking again. "Was it a shock?"

"Well, it was a bit of a surprise. I thought we were . . . comfortable."

"I always think that's dangerous."

"What do you mean?"

"Being comfortable can mean being taken for granted." Rosie stopped at the curb, looked right and left, then steered him across the road. Only when they had mounted the opposite pavement did she continue. "Your trouble is that you always undersell yourself."

"I'm a realist."

"No, you're not. You're an apologist."

"That's a big word."

"Well, you're a big boy. Look at you—six foot what?"

"And a bit."

"Good-looking, in a crooked sort of way."

"Careful!"

"Well, no, you are—you're not George Clooney, but you've got a lovely smile and all your own hair."

Nick winced. "What is this? Are you starting up a dating agency?"

"Now, there's a thought . . ."

"Don't go there!"

"All right. Too much paperwork anyway. But you're not a bad catch, and you're only in your thirties."

"Just coming up for the final year."

"You needn't worry. People leave it much longer now before they get married. Most don't seem to bother. And if you get someone younger, you've still time to have children."

"If you've quite finished planning my life for me . . ."

She looked up at him, winked, and tugged at his arm. "Sorry. I suppose I'm just an interfering old granny." She smiled.

"You're incorrigible." He smiled back.

"Oh, I do hope I am. . . . So what now?" she asked.

"I don't know. I'm painting like a lunatic. Trying to get on."

"You need me to sort you out."

"I thought I was sorting you out."

"Bit of a joint venture, then." She let go of his arm and rummaged in her cavernous crocodile handbag for the key. "It's in here somewhere."

"Let me." He reached out for the bag, but she shot him a withering look.

"It's the light, not my sight." She fished out a pair of glasses, put them on, and continued to delve into the depths of the bag until, triumphantly, she located the key and slipped it into the lock.

It was certainly different from the house where Nick's grandparents had lived when he was a child. Until widowhood, Rosie's home had been a modest Victorian terraced house in Cheltenham. Inside, the walls were barley white and peppered with bright prints and some of Nick's early paintings. The floors were polished boards, part covered with Indian rugs, bright throws to disguise the timeworn upholstery of the sofas. Nick had always liked it.

His grandfather had been easygoing about Rosie's taste: She had been the arty one, and he had deferred to that. He had been content to spend his retirement from the insurance company with the *Daily Telegraph* and the television. Then a stroke had robbed him of movement and speech and confined him to the hospital. Rosie had visited him twice a day for four years, until he had slipped away one evening while she was at home having supper.

She had wanted to stay in the family house, but Nick's mother had insisted it was too large and Cheltenham too far away. Rosie, normally strong-willed enough to stand up for herself, had allowed herself, in the wake of her bereavement, to be moved into a flat in a small block where her daughter-in-law could keep an eye on her.

Nick watched her hang up her coat and adjust her hair in the mirror, then turn on the lamps in the sitting room and walk through to the kitchen.

"Coffee?" she asked, filling the kettle.

"Just a quick one."

The events of the day caused him to look at her more critically than usual as she made the coffee, then deftly collected cups and saucers from the dresser. Nobody would take her for eighty-seven. Sixty-seven, maybe, or seventy—but not three years short of ninety. She had always been Rosie to him, at her own insistence, never Granny. But was she finally losing her grip?

He pulled out a pine chair from the small breakfast table, sat down, and looked around. The flat was more sparsely furnished than the house had been, but there were always flowers: today a handful of dried lavender poked out of a painted jug, and scarlet tulips swallow-dived from a square glass vase on the fitted worktop.

"Will you stay here?" he asked, curiosity getting the better of him.

"No."

The answer came so quickly that it surprised him. "Why?"

"Because I hate it." She brought the cups and saucers to the table.

"But where will you go?"

"I don't know yet." She dropped two spoons into the saucers. "If I stay here, I'll just sulk and fade away. Let's be honest. I probably haven't long to go."

"Don't say that."

She leaned on the back of a chair, and the piercing eyes fixed him. "Now who's not being realistic?"

"It's just that—"

"You don't want to admit it."

"No."

"All right, then, we won't talk about it again, so long as you don't try to wrap me in cotton wool."

"I don't think I could."

HE LEFT her at six, and as he kissed her on both cheeks at the door of her flat, he noticed the photograph on a side table. It was a sepia-toned portrait of a girl with dark hair, fine features, and a clear complexion. She stood in falling snow, which powdered the front of her high-buttoned coat. A pale scarf was wrapped round her neck, and her mouth was open a little, as if she was catching her breath in the ice-cold winter air. She stood to the left of a small boy in a thick, barathea sailor suit and a bearded man in a military uniform.

"She's still here, then."

Rosie turned and picked up the photograph. "Mama? Oh, yes. She always is. Doesn't she look lovely?"

"She does."

Rosie replaced the photograph. "We'll talk about it soon."

"I'll call you. I can get back next week, if that's okay?"

"Fine." As he walked out, she called after him, "You're not too cross with me, are you?"

"You're not very easy to be cross with," he said, and left with a wave.

Chapter 2

THE northern coast of the Isle of Wight is divided into two by the Medina River. The eastern half looks toward Portsmouth and Hayling Island, and the western toward Lymington and Dorset. West of Cowes, between Gurnard and Thorness Bay, there is a craggy, crumbling stretch of coastline opposite the Beaulieu River. Cattle graze the pale green undulating meadows above the cliff, where a snaking pathway cuts its way between banks of blackthorn and quickthorn, brambles and gorse. In winter, the salt-laden winds rip through the undergrowth, and heavy rains wash swathes of the greasy gray clay into the waters of the Solent. In summer, the hedgerows are wreathed in dog roses and bryony, and clouded yellow butterflies flit over clover and vetches while the song thrush sings in the twisted trees.

For five years, Nick Robertson had lived in a clapboard cottage perched on the top of this bare patch of coastline, just about making a living from painting watercolors and selling them through a local gallery.

His grandmother had impinged rarely on his life. He called her on the phone every week or so, and she would ask how things were going with the painting and his love life—she was never backward in coming forward and always spoke her mind.

His mother, Anna, having raised her three children—Alice, now married and living in South Africa; Sophie, single and traveling in South America; and Nick, the arty one—was doing an Open University degree in medieval history and worked at her local library. "It's my time now," she had told her family, and proceeded to live an almost independent life. After the children had gone, she had told her husband she wanted out. He surprised her by saying that so did he, then upped and left. Rosie had not been pleased.

Derek Robertson was known to most people outside the family as "a bit of a lad." His ex-wife used less endearing terms to describe him. After a moderately successful spell in business, he had cashed in his chips and devoted himself to the turf—often with surprising success. The *Racing Post* was his daily paper, and when he wasn't placing bets on horses, he took a chance on anything vaguely entrepreneurial that came his way. He loved his daughters, did his best to understand his son, and enjoyed the wheeler-dealer life.

Which explained why, when Rosie was in trouble, she called on Nick, the one member of her family who she knew she could always contact and would get her out of a spot.

Nick sat in his studio gazing at the sea, today the color of pewter and merging with the sky. The north island—the locals' disparaging name for the mainland—had disappeared from view, as if it didn't exist. He liked the feeling of being cut off. As he was now—in more ways than one.

The phone rang, and he was surprised to hear his mother. "Nick?"

"Hi."

"The front page of the *Richmond and Twickenham Times* is plastered with pictures of your grandmother chained to some railings. Do you know anything about this?"

"Well . . . yes."

"And you didn't tell me? Why not, for God's sake?"

"Because I knew you'd be furious."

"I am! The Russian embassy! She's not started all that again, has she?"

"All what?"

"About her mother being wronged by the Bolsheviks. She's not fit to be on her own anymore!"

"Oh, come on, Mum. That's a bit much."

"Well, clearly she can't look after herself. I'm going round to her flat today to find out what it's all about."

"Don't do that—you'll only upset her."

"Too right. She has to know that she just can't do this sort of thing."

He could visualize Anna at the other end of the phone: the gray mane held back with a black velvet band, the finely plucked eyebrows, the pearls, the black pashmina draped round her shoulders, the Jaeger tweed skirt and the black tights.

"Just leave it to me, Mum."

"But what can you do, over there?"

"I can come over. I've already been once, as it is."

"It's May. Aren't you up to your ears in painting?"

"Well, yes, but . . ."

"I must sort this out before she embarrasses us even more. Thank God I use my maiden name on the Open University course. At least nobody will guess I'm related to her."

"That's not a very nice thing to say."

"What she did was not a very nice thing to do. I'm going to get some brochures about nursing homes."

"But she's not ill! Look, don't do anything yet. I'll talk to her."

"It won't make any difference."

"At least let me try."

After a few more placatory remarks, he put the phone down. It rang again, almost immediately, and the pompous voice at the other end made him smile.

"By my elegant little Cartier watch, it's forty-eight minutes past the hour of eleven, which means that you are now exactly eighteen minutes late. As it takes a good half hour to get to my little gallery in Seaview from your shack in the back-of-beyond, that means I shall not see you until lunchtime. Do I take it that you'll be requiring refreshments?"

HENRY Kinross Fine Art was to be found at the top of a short flight of worn stone steps by a slipway that sloped down to the sea. The gallery had once been a boathouse, but the bitumen-painted feather-edged boards were now a delicate shade of eau de nil, and scallop shells had been fixed in a double row on either side of the door. As Nick opened the door, the bell pinged loudly. The gallery owner was holding a dreary seascape and frowning at it through half-moon spectacles. "Look at this! Drive a man to drink."

Henry Kinross was not a small man. He had a sizable belly, short legs, and the sort of face that looked as if someone had sat on it. His hair was gray, his cheeks were the color of a Victoria plum, and his voice was refined by years of claret.

Nick glanced at the picture. "Mmm. Do you want me to bring mine in?"

Henry laid the painting on the white-painted table in the center of the room and took off his glasses. Then he waved at the blank wall at one end of the gallery. "It'll look pretty bare if you don't. How many have you got?"

"About a dozen." Nick propped open the door and began to carry in the framed watercolors.

"Wonderful. That should keep me going for a couple of weeks."

"Longer than that, I hope. I'm not a machine."

Henry began to line up the paintings against the wall. "No gratitude, that's your trouble. Not everyone sells like you do, you know. Look at old what's-his-face." He nodded in the direction of the gray seascape. "That'll never shift. Too depressing."

"Accurate, though," Nick told him.

"If people want accuracy, they can take a photograph."

"Maybe mine will start to get a bit more dreary now."

"Ah." Henry put down the painting he was carrying. "She's gone, then?"

Nick nodded.

"And you're feeling sorry for yourself. Well, can't say I blame you. She was a nice girl."

"I don't need reminding."

"I suppose not. But you probably need cheering up. Let's get out of here and into some food. Starving artist and all that."

"I'm not hungry."

"Well, I am, so you'll just have to watch me. Come and have a glass at least."

Henry prodded Nick across the road and into the bar of the Red Duster. He ordered a bottle of the house red and two glasses. They planted themselves, on Henry's instructions, at a table just opposite the door. "Cheers, old bean! First of the day." Henry took a gulp of wine and sighed with satisfaction. "Oh, little grape, how great thou art! Now, then . . . We'll wait to order food. Someone else is joining us."

"Oh?"

"Artist. Wants me to take her stuff. I'm interested to know what you think. Thought you'd like to meet her first, and then we'll look at her paintings."

"No fear. I'm happy to meet her, Henry, but I'm not going to sit in judgment on her stuff. One artist criticizing another?"

"That's all you lot ever do, isn't it?"

"In private, maybe, but not to each other's faces."

The uneasy silence that might have followed was preempted by an almighty clatter outside the pub. All conversation stopped, and there was a general movement toward the door. Nick and Henry were first onto the pavement, followed by the barman and a couple of local builders.

"Bloody 'ell." One of the builders had summed up the scene neatly. In front of them, where earlier Nick's Morris Minor van had sat by the pavement, was a hybrid vehicle, half Morris, half Fiat, with no visible distinction between the two.

A dark-haired young woman was sitting at the wheel of the Fiat, her head in her hands. Nick tried to open the car door, but it refused to budge. He ran round to the other side and tugged at the passenger door, which yielded. "Are you all right?"

The woman lowered her hands.

"It's okay. Don't worry. Come on, let me help you out."

She gazed at him apologetically. "It was my brakes." She began to shake.

"Best get her out," offered Henry.

"Yes, come on. Can you slide across?"

She swiveled her denim-covered legs across the passenger seat and got out onto the pavement. She was slight, about thirty. Her long dark hair had been pinned back but was now falling over her face—fine-boned and olive-skinned, but pale with shock. Nick put his arm round her to steady her. The baggy pink and white sailing shirt she wore made her appear waiflike.

"I tried to stop, but nothing happened," she said.

Nick glanced at the fused vehicles. "No."

"God, what a mess!" said Henry, and the woman burst into tears.

"Thank you, Henry. We can see that."

Nick eyed his van and realized that their long association was at an end. Then he looked at the Fiat. Not much hope there either. In the back of the car, he spotted a tangled mixture of blankets and canvas, and grasped that the woman must be the artist Henry had been so keen for him to meet.

"Come inside," he said to her. "Let's get you a drink."

By the time they had walked through the door of the pub and sat down at the table, a large Scotch had appeared courtesy of the barman. But the girl shook her head. "Just water, please. Tap." She reached into her pocket for a tissue and tried to smile. "What a way to start."

"Do you feel okay?" asked Henry. "No bones broken?"

"I don't think so. Just a bit stiff." She wiped her eyes with the tissue and thanked the barman for the water.

Henry took a gulp of his wine. "I think I'm going to need this."

"What about the cars?" asked the barman. "Shall I call the police?"

"Not unless you want to?" Nick directed his question at the woman.

"But whose is the van?" she asked.

"Mine."

"You'll want to claim on your insurance."

Nick shook his head. "Not worth losing my 'no claims.' But what about yours?"

"Same."

"Shall we just call the breakdown truck to clear them away, then?"

"Are we allowed to?"

"Don't see why not. If we're quick."

Within an hour, the only trace of the collision was a scattering of dried mud and a bucketful of broken glass on the road. Passers-by had been hurried along, and the police had failed to put in an appearance.

Henry never did get his lunch. Instead, he helped to salvage the paintings from the Fiat and carried them into the gallery.

It was a good half hour before Nick discovered the identity of the woman who had written off his dear old van. Her name was Alexandra Pollen.

SHE turned out to be nothing like as frail as he had thought. But, then, you can't make judgments about anyone's character on the basis of having pulled them out of a crumpled car.

Over tea in the back room, she explained that she'd discovered Henry's gallery the previous year on a day-trip to the island. She had thought he might like some stuff that wasn't run-of-the-mill and had told him on the phone that her oils might be just that.

Nick admired her nerve, if not her paintings. They were vivid and simplistic, not at all his style, but they did have a raw energy.

"Can you sell them, do you think?" Alex asked Henry.

"Well, there's only one way to find out." He looked across at Nick. "What do you think?"

Nick did his best not to glare at Henry for putting him in such a position. "I think they're . . . exhilarating."

Alex wasn't fooled. "Well, I can't expect everyone to like them. But I'll be happy enough if you'll give them a go, Henry."

The remaining conversation was polite. Then it was time for Alex to leave, and the question arose as to how that might be achieved.

"Well, I'd run you to the ferry, dear, except that I don't drive," said Henry. "What about you?" he asked Nick.

"I'd better hire a car . . . until I can do better."

"I'm so sorry," Alex said.

"There's no need. You probably just moved things on a bit."

A call to a friendly local garage resulted in a car being delivered to the gallery within the hour, and Nick took Alex to the ferry terminal. "Where's home?" he asked.

"Portsmouth."

"Handy."

"Very. That's why I wasn't too worried about getting home. I can walk from the ferry at the other side."

She got out of the car, walked round to the driver's window, and leaned in. "Thank you for being so good about the car. I really don't know what to say."

"Don't worry."

"Just in case you change your mind." She handed him a piece of paper on which she had written her name, address, and telephone number. "I expect we'll meet again soon. I like coming over to the island."

He motored home, deep in thought, considering an Austin A30—and Alexandra Pollen. He was not considering Rosie. Until he saw her standing in the doorway of his house.

"What the . . ." He leapt out of the car and strode up to her. "What are you doing here?"

"Getting away from your mother."

"What do you mean?"

"She came round this morning. Did you tell her?"

"I didn't tell her anything. It was in the local paper."

"Wants to put me in a home. Even had some brochures with her."

Nick looked at her, laden with a small suitcase and two shopping bags. "How have you managed?"

"I got a taxi—both ends."

Nick unloaded her. "Come on. Let's get you inside."

Rosie glanced down the path to the road. "Where's the van?"

"In a scrapyard somewhere near Bembridge."

"Oh, dear. Has it finally given up? Never mind—perhaps you can get a sports car now instead."

"Will you stop changing the subject?" He fumbled in his pocket for the key and ushered her in.

Over tea and biscuits, the story tumbled out. "She didn't even ask if I was all right."

"I don't suppose she needed to."

"Didn't care, more like."

"Oh, now, stop feeling sorry for yourself."

Rosie looked at him pleadingly. "But to put me away!"

"She doesn't want to put you away; she wants to make sure you're taken care of. That's all."

"Dreadful expression! Taken care of! Makes me sound senile. Just so that I don't get in her way."

Nick realized this particular conversation was going nowhere. "Why have you come here?"

"Because you're the only person I can trust."

He smiled. "You sound like a secret agent."

"Mmm." She paused. "That would be fun."

He shot her a look.

"I thought it might be a bit of a break," she went on. "Do me good."

"Have you booked somewhere?"

"No."

"Where will you stay, then?"

Rosie looked about her.

"Oh, Rosie! There's no space."

"There's the little bedroom."

"But it's full of painting stuff, and it's tiny."

"You'll hardly know I'm here—and it won't be for long, just till I get myself organized. I won't get in the way."

He sighed. "It's not that I don't want you here; it's just that . . ." But when he looked into her eyes, he knew he had lost: She wasn't going anywhere. And he was, as she had known he would be, a soft touch. He bent down and kissed her cheek. "I'd better clear out the little bedroom."

"Thank you, sweetheart. You're a lifesaver." She squeezed his hand and walked over to the window. "What a wonderful view." She turned back to face him. "What a lark, eh?"

MANY THINGS MIGHT HAVE happened over the next few days: She might have irritated the pants off him; she might have been demanding; she might have fussed over him and driven him mad. In the event, she did none of these.

Over the first day, she observed him at work and noted his modus operandi. By day three, he worried that he was not looking after her enough. She had breakfast just after he did, then pulled on a pair of soft boots and a windbreaker and went out. He didn't see her again until early evening when she joined him for supper and then went to bed early.

He was concerned about her walking along the cliff unaided, so he bought her a stick. She was indignant, until he explained that all proper walkers carried one like this, a modified ski pole.

By day four, he pushed her a bit. "Are you managing?"

"Yes, thanks. Are you?"

"Yes. Surprisingly."

"You see, I told you I wouldn't be much trouble. And I'm not, am I?"

"Not so far, no."

"Hmph!"

"Have you got enough clothes and things?"

"Oh, yes. I think so. I thought I might have a bit of an expedition, though. There's some nice sailing stuff in Cowes."

He grinned. "Don't tell me you're thinking of going sailing."

"Oh, yes. I've booked the course."

He nearly choked on his coffee. "What?"

"At the sailing academy." She saw the look on his face. "It's for five days."

"But you—"

"They've had older people than me doing it. The man said so." She noted his look of wide-eyed astonishment but carried on, savoring the moment. "I've always fancied getting out on the water, but your granddad never liked it, so we never did."

"No."

"Only little dinghies. Toppers, they're called. Quite fast, though."

"Yes."

"Should be all right as long as I can remember to keep my head down." His jaw dropped. "Catching flies again?" she asked.

Nick closed his mouth hastily. "You crack me up. You really do."

"What a lovely thing to say. I must remember that." As she went toward her room, he heard her chuckle to herself, then murmur, "You crack me up; you really do!"

NICK turned into the gravel path at the front of his cottage. "The Anchorage" said the small slate sign. He couldn't help thinking that, as far as Rosie was concerned, the name was appropriate.

He walked along the verandah at the front of the house, between the forest of bright green montbretia leaves, and glanced into the tiny box-room next to the front door. It was the one place where he could tuck a computer. The desk lamp was turned on, and Rosie was hunched over the keyboard.

Nick let himself in through the front door and poked his head into the little room. "What are you doing?"

Rosie almost leapt out of the chair. "You made me jump!"

He glanced at the screen, and then at his grandmother. "When did you learn how to use a computer?"

"At night school when your granddad was ill. It took my mind off things." Then she said brightly, "I've found you a car. On the Internet. It's an MG."

"But I don't want an MG. You can't get paintings into an MG."

"Yes, you can. You can have a rack on the boot lid over the spare tire. I've checked. And, anyway, the small ones would fit in the footwell at the front."

"What about when it rains?"

She looked at him through narrowed eyes. "It does have a hood, you know."

There was nothing for it but to look over her shoulder at the screen.

"You see?" she said. "Perfect. Very sporty. Bit of fun. Take you out of yourself. I'll print it off." And then, evidently fearful that she had overstepped the mark, she added, "You don't mind, do you, about me using the computer?"

Nick shook his head. "No. Not at all. I'm just surprised."

The printer whirred, and Rosie picked up the piece of paper and handed it to him. She stood up and indicated the finer points of the car. "It's British racing green with a red radiator grille—you can't tell that from the printout. And the hood is black. It says it's in its original condition and has had the same owner for the last thirty years."

Nick read out: " 'MG TC, 1949. Mechanically this car is superb. The engine, when being driven, has an excellent oil pressure and is entirely sound.' "

"And it has the original logbook, showing owners back to 1963, and all the bills and receipts for the last thirty years. It was bought in 1969 for a hundred and fifteen pounds," said Rosie. Her enthusiasm was infectious.

"How much is it now?" asked Nick, his eye drifting down to the foot of the page. "Bloody hell! Eleven thousand two hundred and fifty quid! Not a chance! I haven't got that sort of money."

Rosie's eyes lit up. "I have!"

"What?"

"I could buy it."

"Don't be silly."

"I'm not being silly. I could buy it as an investment. I've got plenty saved up and nothing else to do with it. The banks aren't paying much interest. Much more fun to have a sports car. That way, you can drive it, and I can come out for a spin occasionally. Can't I?"

"Well, yes. But no! I mean, this isn't right."

"If you're worrying about your sisters and their inheritance, don't. I've sorted all that out."

"But I want a van!"

"Don't be ridiculous. Can you hear yourself? 'I want a van'! What a feeble thing to say when you could be spinning around in that."

Nick looked at the printout. It was indeed a lovely car. "I don't know . . ."

"Do it for me?"

He folded his arms. "And if I don't?"

"I shall be unhappy."

"Where is this flash car?"

"In Portsmouth. We could be there in an hour."

IT WAS love at first sight. The rolling wave of the mudguard. The neatly spoked wheels. The crimson-reeded radiator grille. Nick ran his hand over one of the bulbous, glistening headlights, and Rosie knew he was enslaved.

They hardly needed to take her out for a test drive. Nick knew how she would feel. Strong, but nimble. Spirited, but of a certain age. Obliging, as long as she was handled sensitively. The car had a lot in common with his grandmother.

He felt embarrassed when she wrote out the check, and tried not to look like a little boy who had just been indulged by his granny.

The salesman waved as they drove away like an excitable couple of newlyweds. From her position deep in the bucketlike passenger seat, Rosie glanced at Nick as they sped toward the ferry. He was beaming from ear to ear. She had not seen him so happy for a long while. It made her smile, too.

And then she remembered how it had felt to be taken for a spin in a fast car by a good-looking young man. She had been twenty-two. Her hair streaming out behind her, she was laughing and looking sideways at the handsome doctor, who brushed her knee lightly with his hand. For a month they were barely apart. Then he was called up, and she never saw him again. Six years later, they engraved his name on the war memorial.

"Can we stop for a minute?" she asked.

Nick had been lost in his thoughts. "Sorry?"

"I just wondered if we could pull up for a minute. My eyes are watering."

He drew in to the side of the road. "Yes, of course. Are you all right?" He watched her reach into her pocket for a tissue.

"Oh, yes. Just remembering."

He leaned toward her and kissed her cheek. "Thank you." He tapped the steering wheel. "She's lovely."

"Oh, she's a she, is she?"

"Of course."

She pushed the tissue back into her pocket, pulled out a brightly patterned headscarf, and tied it under her chin. "Come on, then, or we'll miss the boat."

AT SIX thirty the following morning, he found himself leaning out of his bedroom window gazing dreamily at the car parked below.

He looked up at the sky, which was flushed with the amber glow of a clear morning. The sea was glassy calm, and there was no sound, except the distant kleep-kleep of half a dozen oystercatchers on the shore. He'd go to Sleepyhead Bay, find himself a quiet corner by some rocks, then paint the cottages and the little café. He hadn't felt like taking out his brushes for the better part of a week. Today he was anxious to get started.

"Will you be all right?" he asked later as he loaded his bag into the passenger side of the car.

She was standing by the front door. "Of course I'll be all right. Perfectly capable, now that I've got my stick." She grinned. "I shall go for a little walk. Catch a bus somewhere. Not sure."

"Well, take care. I'll be back late afternoon. We can have supper together if you want."

"That'd be nice." She waved, then went indoors as he steered the car down the track toward the village and out across the island.

WITH his board on his lap, he was sketching the scene before him—the towering cliff, the neat row of cottages tucked in beneath it, the apron of rocks, girdled by shallow pools, and the children dipping for shrimps and crabs with their bamboo-poled nets. A couple of small yachts played nip and tuck half a mile out, and the lobster fisherman was carrying his catch up the steps to the little café. Nick had picked a good day.

He did not like being watched while he painted, but out here, especially during the school holidays, it was an occupational hazard. He had just finished the sky when he became aware of a child at his side. "That's nice," she said. Her dark hair was tied into plaits, and she was leaning on her shrimping net to examine his work.

"I'm glad you like it."

"It's better than my mum can do."

"Does she paint?" he asked politely.

"Yes. She tries to sell them." The child shrugged, dismissive.

"So do I."

"I bet you sell more than she does."

"Oh, I don't know."

"I do. She hasn't sold one yet."

"Oh. I see." He laughed.

"Would you like to come and see her painting?"

"Well, I'm a bit busy at the moment." He frowned, hoping she'd leave him in peace.

"She's only over there. And she'd probably appreciate some advice."

He was amused by the child's conversation, which was older than her years. She was nine or ten and was wearing a white T-shirt and a pair of baggy yellow shorts. Her feet were bare, her skin honey-colored from the early summer sun, and her turned-up nose was dusted with freckles. She had the darkest eyes he had ever seen.

"What's your name?" she asked.

"Nick."

"Nick what?"

"Nick Robertson. What's yours?"

"Victoria."

"Victoria what?"

"I'm not going to tell you. My mum says I shouldn't—in case you're not very nice."

Nick grinned. "Quite right, too."

The child pointed her shrimping net to the other end of the cove. "She's over there. Will you come and look? Please?"

He could see that he would not get any peace until he did as she asked, so he put down his board, anchored it with a rock, and followed her as she picked her way nimbly through the sharp stones.

Around a particularly large and craggy outcrop, they came upon a woman seated on a smooth, round boulder, with a stubby easel jammed among the smaller rocks in front of her. She was dressed like the child—in T-shirt and shorts—with her dark hair pinned up at the back of her head.

"I've brought someone to look at it, Mum."

"Oh, poppet, why do you think . . . ?"

The woman looked up. It was Alexandra Pollen.

Nick laughed.

Alex scrambled to her feet. "Hello! Fancy meeting you here."

The child looked from one to the other. "Do you two know each other?"

"Well, yes," Alex said, and colored. "This is the man whose car I crashed into."

"Oh!" Victoria turned to Nick. "I expect you're pretty cross with us, then."

"No. Well, a bit. But not much."

"We've got another one." She prodded the net into the pool at her feet. "It's not very good, but it was all we could afford."

Alex brushed down her shorts. "Sorry about this. She's a bit annoyed with me for pranging the car."

"Not your fault when your brakes fail," said Nick.

"Daddy came round and she got in a bit of a state," Victoria chipped in. "She always does."

Nick felt uncomfortable. "I'd better get back to my painting."

"Fancy a coffee?" Alex pointed toward the café.

"I really should get back. The light . . ."

"Ah, yes. The light," she teased.

He saw the look in her eyes and gave in. "Just a quick one."

Alex turned to her daughter. "Shall I bring you back an ice cream?"

"No, thanks." She bent down to pick something out of her net. "I'd rather have a Diet Coke, please."

"Okay."

"She's quite a character," Nick remarked as they walked toward the café. "How old is she?"

"Ten, going on twenty-nine," she said.

"I had no idea you had children."

"It's just Victoria and me. I'm a single mum."

"Oh?"

"Most of the time anyway. He keeps coming back—or trying to. We're over here for a few days to get a break."

Nick said nothing, unsure how to respond.

Alex covered the awkward moment. "Oh, dear! This is all getting rather intense, isn't it? Too much information."

"No—please, go on. I wasn't . . . I mean . . . Would you like that coffee?"

She laughed and broke the tension. "Yes. And I'd kill for a biscuit."

He ordered two coffees and some tartan-wrapped shortbread biscuits, then sat down opposite her at a little table on a sun-bleached deck among some old fishing nets. "Shall we start again?" he asked.

"Third time lucky? Sorry. You must think I'm a complete wacko."

"Only a bit of a wacko." He tilted his head. "Have you had a difficult time at home?"

"Yes. It's better than it was, but it's still a bit iffy. We married too young and stayed together for eleven years because of Victoria. He's not a bad guy, but we're just not suited, and the rows seem to get worse."

"What now, then?"

Alex shrugged. "Who knows? He's starting a new job next week, and he's going abroad on business for a few months. I wanted to be out of the way, and I like it over here."

He looked out toward the sea. "Nobody knows about it, really."

"About the island?"

"England's best-kept secret."

"It's supposed to be for white-haired ladies and men with fawn anoraks, isn't it?"

"Well, I love it here. But, then, I'm not your typical thirty-something."

"That's a relief." Alex grinned.

"Thank you!" He sipped his coffee.

"So, what are you?" she asked.

"Almost thirty-nine."

"And never been kissed?" she asked with a wry smile.

Nick frowned. "Another disaster area, I suppose. Not much to tell. Just come out of a long relationship—well, not as long as yours, but three years. Debs went off to the States last week."

"Oh, I'm sorry." Alex stirred her coffee. "Are you in mourning?"

"Not really. A bit fed up. And hurt, I suppose."

"Are you committed to staying here?" she asked.

"For now, yes. I love painting on the island—and I love it in winter when there's nobody about."

"I think you're just a loner, really," she told him.

"Maybe. Not always though." He pushed a shortbread biscuit across the table. "Another?"

"No. I'll wait until lunchtime. Are you staying?"

"Well, I've got a painting to finish. . . ." He hesitated.

"Why don't you have some lunch with us? You can give me some advice on my painting."

"I wouldn't dream—"

"I'll settle for a bit of company, then . . . if you don't mind?"

HE WATCHED them as they pored over the menu, Victoria leaning over Alex's shoulder. They were like sisters, each advising the other on the best choice.

"You should have that," said Victoria, pointing to "freshly fried fish and salad."

"What about you?" asked her mother.

"That." Victoria darted a finger at "Pint of prawns with brown bread and butter," then slipped the straw of her Diet Coke into her mouth and sucked.

"Can you peel them?" asked Nick.

Victoria nodded without looking up.

"She's been able to peel prawns since she was little," said Alex. "We had a holiday in Spain, and she learned when she was three. She loves seafood."

"Expensive tastes," said Nick.

"Yes. She gets it from her father. I'm very low maintenance." Victoria sat back. "How long are we going to stay on the island?"

"Just for the week," Alex told her. "Then we'll go home."

"We can't see home from here, can we?"

"Not from this side of the island, but we can from the north side."

"I prefer this side," said Victoria. "There's more sea."

"Do you like the sea?" asked Nick.

"It's not that. It's just that it takes longer to get home from here."

"Well, we can come back lots if you like," her mother told her.

"Yes, please."

VICTORIA finished her prawns, leaving a neat pile of shells on her plate, while Nick and Alex were still eating. She excused herself from the table and went back to her rock pool. They watched her concentrate on fishing.

"Does she get on with her dad?" asked Nick.

"So-so. He spoils her rotten, and he's not bad-mouthed me."

"Will he still be able to see her?"

"Oh, yes. But if this new job takes off, he'll be away quite a lot."

"You get on really well with her."

"Most of the time, yes. There is the occasional tantrum."

"Well, that's growing up, isn't it?" He smiled ruefully.

"That's what I tell myself. And I'm the only one she can let off steam with."

"Grandparents?"

"No."

"That's a shame."

"Yes. I think she must get pretty pissed off with me sometimes."

"You're a bit hard on yourself."

"I deserve to be. I've made a real mess of things so far."

Nick pointed to Victoria. "Not with her."

"No," she said softly. "Bless her. I'm just determined that things will get better. That's what keeps me going."

"Is that why you're painting?"

"Partly. It's a bit selfish, too. I can escape when I'm painting. Go somewhere else. Be someone else."

Nick watched as Alex traced patterns on the table with a finger. "So you're not a career painter?" he asked.

"Oh, come on! You knew I wasn't a professional painter when you saw my canvases." She looked worried for a moment. "Do you think Henry knew?"

"Probably, but he doesn't care as long as things sell. He thinks you're worth a punt."

Her face lightened again. "Well, that's something, I suppose."

"What did you do before?"

"I was an English teacher. Then Victoria came along, and I didn't want to be a part-time mum, so I gave it up. But I can read a cracking bedtime story."

"Lucky girl."

"Oh, I hope so. I really want her to have a good life, and I don't feel I've done very well for her so far." Alex gazed at her daughter wistfully, then asked, "What about you?"

"Well, no kids. Two sisters, both abroad. And a granny."

"No mum and dad?"

"Yes. But the granny's the one who takes up most of my time." Alex laughed. "Why?"

"She's a bit of a liability. Eighty-seven. Sharp as a razor but she has her moments."

"How?"

"Oh, she's just taken it into her head that she hasn't lived enough, so she's starting now, which is very nice in one way but a real pain in another. She's staying with me at the moment."

"Here? On the island?"

"Yes. You ought to meet her. Why don't you come for supper

one evening?" Then he worried that he had pushed himself too much. "But perhaps . . ."

"It would be lovely," she said.

They sat quietly for a few minutes, then Nick got up. "I'd better get on. Painting to finish."

"Yes."

"Look . . ." He pulled a stubby pencil and a scrap of paper out of his pocket and quickly scribbled something down. "This is where I am. I've promised my grandmother supper tonight, so if you two want to come, you'll be very welcome. It would be good for her, too. And Victoria. They might be a match for each other."

She took the note, glanced at the address and the map he had sketched.

"Are you sure?" she asked. "We're a bit of a handful."

"I'm positive." He leaned forward and kissed her cheek. "And thank you." He turned and walked away across the rocks.

"My pleasure," she whispered as she slipped the note into her pocket.

"WHAT sort of company?" asked Rosie.

"Female company," said Nick.

"Ooh!"

"There's no need to say it like that."

"I didn't say it like anything."

"Well, that's all right, then."

"Do I get a clue?" Rosie asked.

Nick sighed, then said, "An artist and her daughter."

"That's nice."

Rosie put knives, forks and spoons, napkins and place mats on the pine table that stood in the bay window. She liked his little place. The outside walls were black-painted clapboard with yellow window frames, and inside, the wooden paneling was white. Nick's taste was minimalist without being cold: there were pieces of gnarled driftwood and shells on the doorstep, cream linen curtains at the windows, and white-painted furniture.

The two bedrooms were warmer: brightly colored quilts covered the mattresses, and dried flower wreaths hung over the brass bedsteads. The bathroom sported a tub on ball and claw feet. It was the perfect seaside bachelor pad.

Rosie finished the table by placing a small bowl of wildflowers in the center—dog roses, campion, grasses, and buttercups.

"Where did you find those?" Nick asked.

"On the clifftop. I nearly got blown away picking them."

"They're lovely. Thank you."

Rosie smiled at him fondly. "Now tell me about this artist."

He told her about the crash, about Alex's paintings, and about meeting her at Sleepyhead Bay. He told her about Victoria and about the child's father. About how Alex had turned from being an English teacher to being a painter and about how she was hoping to change her life. By the end, Rosie couldn't suppress a grin.

"Why are you smiling?"

"Because you're so happy to talk about her. And she has the most wonderful name."

"Alexandra?"

"Yes. Very Russian."

Nick frowned. "How come you were called Rosie?" he asked.

"To put people off the scent when I was smuggled out of Russia. My real name is Alice Marie Xenia. All family names."

He flopped into a chair. "If you're so pleased that Alex has a Russian name, why on earth did you christen Dad Derek?"

"I wanted to call him Alexander, but your granddad put his foot down. Derek was the name of a good friend of mine who was killed in the war. A doctor."

"And me? Was Nicholas your idea?"

"As luck would have it, that was your mother. All I had to do was sit quietly and smile to myself. Mind you, I was a bit worried. There was a point when she thought she might call you Torquil. Tricky for all of us, that was."

Nick winced. "It would have been even trickier for me."

Rosie laughed. "Sometimes you really crack me up," she said.

Chapter 3

"I DON'T know whether to feel guilty or relieved." Alex was looking at the MG parked outside the house.

"Oh, think of yourself as a catalyst," said Nick, a twinkle in his eyes.

"You do say the nicest things to a girl."

"It's a way I have."

"Are they all right in there, do you think?" Alex looked toward the house, where Rosie was showing Victoria Nick's treasures.

"Oh, yes. She's had lots of practice."

Rosie had slipped into great-grandmother mode while Nick and Alex drank coffee on the verandah.

"She'll be reading her a bedtime story next."

"Talking of which . . ." Alex looked at her watch.

"There's no rush," said Nick. "It's a lovely evening."

He gazed at her sitting in the cane chair, feet curled under her. Her dark hair was still pinned up, but she had changed into a pale pink shirt and jeans. He could see the candlelight reflected in her dark eyes.

"It's the most perfect spot," she said. "You're very lucky."

"I suppose I am."

"So did . . . Debs live here with you?"

"Some of the time—when she wasn't abroad."

"She traveled a lot?"

"A fair bit. Absence made her heart grow fonder . . . of somebody else."

"How was it? The ending, I mean."

"Strangely civilized. Scary, really."

"Oh, don't be scared of civility. It's better than the other option."

"I guess. But it's not very passionate, is it?"

Alex grinned mischievously. "And are you a passionate man?"

He was about to reply when he became aware of another voice: It was Rosie's, and she was getting into her stride. "And then the princess met the most wonderful man."

"How was he wonderful? Was he good-looking?" Victoria asked.

"Oh, yes. Definitely."

"And did she fancy him?"

"Well, yes, I suppose she did. . . . The princess lived in a country that was very large, and a lot of the working people didn't have much money. This meant that they didn't like the princess's family because they had too many lovely things, like Fabergé eggs and suchlike."

"What's a Fabergé egg?"

Suddenly Nick grasped the drift of their conversation and sprang up. "Rosie!"

"Yes, darling?"

"What are you talking about?"

Before she could reply, Victoria said, "A princess and a . . . What was he?"

"A pauper."

Nick endeavored to steer her away from what to him were uncharted waters and a possible source of embarrassment. "Don't you think it's a bit late for stories?"

"Yes," Alex put in. "We really must be going."

"No—I didn't mean—" He looked pleadingly at his grandmother. She beamed at him innocently. "It's only a quarter to ten—and they are on holiday."

Alex stood up and slipped on her shoes. "No. You're quite right. It's way past Victoria's bedtime."

Nick tried to retrieve the situation. "Don't go. It was just—"

"We've had a lovely time. Perhaps we'll see you again before the end of our holiday. Say good night, Victoria, and thank Rosie for a nice evening."

"Oh, do we have to? I want to hear the end of the story."

Alex shot her a look.

"Okay." Victoria sounded resigned. "Good night, Rosie, and

thanks for having me." She stretched up to give Rosie a peck on the cheek. "Good night, Nick."

"Good night, Victoria. Thank you for coming." He was embarrassed now. He turned to Alex, but she was collecting Victoria's jacket from the back of a chair and did not meet his eye.

As they walked down the verandah steps together, he tried to make amends. "I'm sorry. I mean about . . . just then . . ."

"It's fine, really. Thank you for a lovely meal." She squeezed his arm, then walked round their battered old Ford, let Victoria into the backseat, and belted her in. "Have a good rest of the week," she said.

Nick watched the scarlet taillights disappearing down the stony track. How could a perfectly pleasant evening have soured so quickly? It was only minutes since he and Alex had been sitting on the verandah. . . .

He stormed inside. "You promised!"

"Promised what?"

"Not to go on about your past."

"But I was only telling her about the princess and the pauper."

"Oh, yes? A princess who had Fabergé eggs and lived in a large country where the poor people didn't like the princess's family."

"Well, I was only embellishing it a bit with things I knew. I don't understand why you're so cross with me."

"Because I worry about you."

"But if you worried about me, you'd care, and if you cared, you'd listen, instead of treating me as though I'm stupid." Rosie shook her head, blinking back tears. "I might as well give up. Nobody really cares."

"That's not true. Look." He squeezed her hand. "Let me get you a drink. What do you want? Tea? Coffee?"

"Scotch."

"Scotch it is. And then you can tell me, if you want to."

She looked up at him. "Depends if you want to hear."

"Of course I do." He poured her a large Scotch and one for himself, then went over to where she sat and handed her the glass. "I'm all ears." He sat at her feet and tried to look sympathetic.

"I DIDN'T KNOW ANYTHING about it until I was twenty. Until then, I just thought my parents had given me away when I was a baby. They were poor, and they had five children already—one more mouth to feed would have finished them off. I was brought up by a couple in Cheltenham. They told me I was properly adopted when I was about seven. My father died when I was fifteen. It was so sad. He had a stroke, and Mum and I nursed him for months before he slipped away."

"Like Granddad?"

"Yes, but it was worse in a way. I was so young. Then, when I was twenty, Mum was taken ill. I was desperate for her to get better, but she lay in bed getting paler and thinner. Just before the end came—a couple of days before, it must have been—she said she had something important to tell me about my real family but that it might be better if I kept it to myself. All sorts of things went through my mind—that they might be criminals or something." She paused.

Nick squeezed her hand. "Go on."

"She told me I hadn't been born in Cheltenham, as I had been told, but that I was born in St. Petersburg and smuggled out of Russia as a baby to avoid a scandal. I thought she must be rambling, but she kept on. She said that back in 1917 some sort of delegation was sent to Russia from Britain—to do with King George the Fifth and the tsar. They were cousins, you know. Used to be mistaken for each other." Rosie's eyes were misty.

"And?"

"The tsar had five children. Olga and Tatiana were in their early twenties; Anastasia and Marie were in their teens; and their son, the tsarevitch Alexis, was about twelve. There was a young diplomat in the delegation. My mother didn't know his name. Apparently he'd got on a bit too well with one of the tsar's elder daughters, as a result of which . . . well . . . I was the result."

"*What?*"

"That's what she said."

"But if it's true, why were you shipped out?"

"For one of the tsar's daughters to have an illegitimate child would have been unthinkable."

"But why didn't they just . . . get rid of you?"

"Abortion? Too risky. Imagine if anything had gone wrong."

"But you're not—"

"No. No, I'm not. The empress, the tsarina, was the carrier. The tsarevitch was the only one of the tsar's children who was a hemophiliac."

"But how did they keep the pregnancy secret?"

"I suppose my mother was simply kept out of the public eye. I was born in 1917, just before the revolution, and spirited away."

"How?"

"I've no idea. By diplomatic means, I suppose."

"What does it say on your birth certificate?"

"Not much. Two fictitious names were given as my parents. I'd always thought the names must be made up, so about six months ago I went to check at the Public Records Office—the National Archive, they call it now. They have no record of any married couple called George Michaels and Matilda Kitching."

"So they were just made up."

"Yes. By the people who smuggled me out, I suppose."

"But you said your real name was Alice Marie Xenia."

"That's what it says on my birth certificate, but my adoptive mum always called me Rosie." She took a deep breath. "As for the tsar's family, they were all killed. I can remember the dates off by heart. The tsar abdicated on the fifteenth of March, 1917, and on the sixteenth of July, 1918, the whole family was assassinated."

Nick saw Rosie's fist tighten, and her knuckles turned white.

"Wasn't there something about one of them escaping? Anastasia?"

"She was an impostor. Her name was Anna Anderson. The tsar's cousin—another Grand Duchess Olga—escaped to Britain with her sister Xenia on a British warship, and she met all the impostors. She knew Anna Anderson was a fraud. No. They all died. They were herded into a basement room and shot. Even little Alexis. And my mother's dog."

"So you know which one was your mother?"

"Yes." Rosie got up and walked into her bedroom. She returned holding the framed photograph of the man in the army uniform, the boy in the sailor suit, the girl with the wonderful eyes and the clear complexion.

"That's my grandfather, the tsar; my uncle, the tsarevitch; and my mother, the Grand Duchess Tatiana."

Nick took a deep breath. "And you believe all this?"

"Oh, yes. I know it's true. I can *feel* it's true."

Nick stared at her.

"But why should anybody want to believe me? I mean, I don't look like a grand duchess, do I? It's the most ridiculous story they've ever heard. It's the most ridiculous story *I've* ever heard."

"But who told your mother—the one who adopted you?"

"I don't know."

"So if it's true, it means . . ." He was trying to make sense of it all.

"Yes, love. You're in the line of succession to the Russian imperial throne. After your dad, that is. But somehow I don't think Tsar Derek has the right ring to it. Do you?"

NICK didn't sleep much that night. There were a hundred unanswered questions in his head. Had Rosie really told no one else the full story? Was she telling the truth, or was she simply unbalanced?

Early the next morning, he got up, showered, and went out onto the verandah. A skein of mist hung over the sea, and a watery sun was doing its best to break through. He shivered in the morning chill. It was six thirty. He loaded his painting bag, board, and paper into the MG and folded down the hood. Then he released the hand brake and let her roll down the track before starting up out of Rosie's earshot.

The mist was clearing as he drove on past green fields and light woodland, then turned right on the narrow lane that led to Newtown Creek. He drew up on a rough gravel car park, took out his bag and board, and made his way along the boardwalk that crossed the narrow inlets. He found a spot for his folding chair and easel and set to work. Three small boats bobbed gently in the river, their owners still asleep belowdecks.

He worked on the painting until the light had changed too much. Then he packed away his paints and walked back to the car. He drove through sleepy Calbourne and sprawling Carisbrooke to Newport, and went into a bookshop. Under the section headed "European History," he found what he was looking for: a book on the Russian royal family.

By the time he had returned to The Anchorage, Rosie had gone out. He made some coffee and opened the book. Three hours later, he closed it and sat back in his chair. He was now acquainted with the tsar's family, but he still couldn't begin to think of it as his family. Did it matter? Whether he was related to them or not, the story was compelling, and the way in which the imperial family had met their end was shocking and inhumane.

He looked at his watch. Half past one. Alex would probably be out painting. He had her mobile phone number but was reluctant to call. Then his own phone rang.

"Hello?"

"Is Rosie with you?" It was his mother. She was not calm.

"Yes."

"Bloody typical! I arrange for her to see two lots of sheltered accommodation and she buggers off."

"Well, did you ask her if she wanted to see them?"

"I told her I'd—"

"Yes. You told her."

Most daughters-in-law would have been only too willing to relinquish a relationship with their mother-in-law on the breakdown of their marriage. Not so Anna Robertson. Rosie was a loose end, and loose ends had to be tidied up.

"She'll have to come back. I've made appointments."

"Well, unmake them. She's here for a while now. Till she feels better."

"Now, listen, Nick—"

"No, Mum. You listen. She's getting on in years, and she's a bit unreliable, but that doesn't mean you can shut her away."

"I'm not shutting her away. These are nice places, and they'll look after her."

"Well, I'm looking after her at the moment, so that's all right, isn't it? And she's having fun here. She's even booked to go on a sailing course."

"What?"

"It's okay. She says they've taught people older than her."

"Maybe, but I bet they had all their marbles."

He changed the subject, careful to ask the question offhandedly: "What do you know about her family?"

"Oh, it's quite ridiculous. She's got it into her head that her mother was somehow caught up in the Russian Revolution. She thinks she was smuggled out when she was a baby."

"Does Dad know who her parents were?"

"Well, if he does, he's never bored me with the story. Look, I haven't time to talk. I've got a lecture in five minutes. I'm relying on you, Nick, to look after her and see that she doesn't get into any more trouble."

"Mmm."

"Speak soon. Must dash. Oh, and don't let her spend any money. Apparently her bank account is overdrawn."

TROUBLES are like buses: They come in convoys. Nick had quite a collection now. His grandmother's presence, his grandmother's state of mind, his grandmother's apparent lack of funds, Alex's opinion of him.

Then two more buses turned up at The Anchorage. The pair were clad in charcoal-gray suits and wore dark glasses. They stood on the doorstep of The Anchorage looking strangely out of place. They were both sturdy men with close-shaven heads and no necks.

"Mr. Nick Robertson?" asked the shorter of the two.

"Yes."

"Are you expecting us?"

"No. Should I be?"

The taller one looked down at the smaller one, then at Nick. "Your father hasn't been in contact, then?"

"Not for a week or two."

"So you haven't got the package?"

"What package?"

The shorter hulk looked up at the taller hulk and frowned, then looked back at Nick. "Look, son, this is serious. We've come all the way here because we were told that this was where it would be."

"I'm sorry, but I really don't know what you're talking about. Is this some sort of joke?"

"No," said the big hulk.

Nick felt uneasy. "Well, I can call my father, if you like, but he keeps changing his mobile, so I'm not sure he'll still be on the same number."

At this, the larger man took a step forward, almost crushing Nick against the door frame. "We don't mess about, you know."

"Hello, I'm back," said a voice. "Had a lovely walk along the cliff path. Oh, hello—I'm Nick's granny." The two men wheeled round in time to see Rosie hold out her hand. They didn't take it. They just stared, while Rosie twittered on: "Shame it's not brighter, isn't it? I expect you needed your sunglasses when you set off, but it's a bit threatening now." She looked up at the sky.

The two men froze as though they had been anesthetized.

"Are you staying for lunch? I think we've some salad left from last night."

Nick made to stop her, but the shorter of the two men spoke first: "No, thanks, lady," he said. "We've got to be going." He turned to Nick. "We'll come back. You'll have it by then." He gestured his companion toward the path, then nodded at Rosie. "Take care, lady."

Nick and Rosie watched as the pair lumbered down the path and out of the gate. They heard a car start up and drive away. Then Rosie asked, "Did I do all right? I'm quite good at playing the harmless old lady. Did it help?"

"I'll say."

"Who were they? Are you in some sort of trouble?"

"I have absolutely no idea." And then, trying to sound casual, he said, "When did you last hear from Dad?"

"A fortnight ago. You don't think they're anything to do with him, do you?"

"No, no. I just wondered if his mobile phone number had changed again."

"Only one way to find out," she said.

"Yes." So he tried. The number was unobtainable.

THE lighthouse at St. Catherine's Point winked out over the sea as Alex and Victoria ate their picnic lunch on the clifftop.

Victoria was nibbling an apple. "Are you cross with me?"

"Why should I be?"

"Because of last night. You know. With Nick."

"What do you mean?"

"Do you fancy him?"

Alex looked at her admonishingly. "What's it got to do with you?"

The child shrugged. "Just wondered."

They sat in silence for a while longer.

"What if I do?" asked Alex evenly.

Victoria examined her apple core. "Don't you think he's a bit quiet?"

"Not at all. He's just . . . thoughtful." Alex took a bite of her sandwich.

"I think he's quite nice." Victoria put her apple core into an empty potato chip packet. "Will you see him again?"

"Who knows?"

Victoria stood up. "You can go without me, you know. I don't want to cramp your style."

"What?" Her mother looked at her hard.

"I don't mind if you want to be on your own."

Alex patted the ground next to her. "Come and sit down."

Victoria flopped onto the plaid car rug beside her mother, leaned against her, and gazed out over the sea. Alex stroked her hair. "You've never cramped my style—understand? And I don't want you thinking you have to keep out of the way. It's you and me in this, okay?"

Victoria nodded. A few moments later she said, "I liked Rosie."

"Yes. Me too."

"She's fun. And not old. Well, I mean she is old, but she doesn't seem old."

"Some people are like that. They don't fit other people's preconceptions."

"What are they?"

"Preconceptions? Oh, like prejudices. People don't always fit into boxes. Sometimes they surprise you."

"Do you think Nick might be surprising?"

"Too early to say. Maybe."

"So you will see him again?"

Alex stood up and brushed the crumbs off her jeans. "We'll see. Anyway, we've only a few days left here, so there may not be time."

"Do we really have to go back? Couldn't we just stay here?" Concern was etched on Victoria's face as she got to her feet.

Alex folded up the rug. "You've got school next week."

The child pushed her hands into her pockets. "They have schools here, too."

Alex put her arm round her. "Don't you think we're being a bit premature?"

Victoria shrugged.

"Let's just take our time, shall we?" She handed Victoria the bag that contained the remains of the picnic and set off for the car.

HENRY Kinross had had a good day. He had sold seven paintings: four of Nick's, one of the gloomy canvases and two of Alex's brightest creations, which had been snapped up by a young couple from Fulham. He felt vindicated for having given her a chance. He had a new protégé, and an attractive one at that. Perhaps he should ask

Alexandra Pollen out to lunch. But Nick seemed to have taken a shine to her. It wouldn't do to fall out over a woman.

The sound of the bell broke in on his musings. He looked up to see Nick standing in the doorway with a bright-eyed lady on his arm. "Henry, can I introduce you to Rosie?"

"Dear boy! Of course!"

Over a bottle of claret in the Red Duster, Rosie and Henry became better acquainted. After a few minutes, Henry realized that, had she been a few years younger, she would have been the woman of his dreams. She was startlingly knowledgeable about art, easy to talk to, and surprisingly coquettish for someone of her advanced years.

Nick was listening to the two of them talking and marveled at his grandmother. She could find common ground with anybody, whoever they were, raise her game, or lower it, to suit the occasion. He watched as she put away a couple of glasses of claret and a plate of steak and Guinness pie. She glanced at him occasionally, but Henry had her full attention, and she his.

By eight o'clock, Rosie was living up to her name: Her cheeks were brightly flushed. She was noticeably giggly, too. Nick saw the warning signs and decided to take her home.

"Oh! Do we have to go? I'm having such a lovely time." She didn't slur her words, but there was a slight overenunciation.

"Stay for another bottle, Rosie," Henry said. "Don't let this dauber take you home yet."

Nick looked at Henry, whose countenance almost matched the liquid in his glass, and raised an eyebrow at his grandmother. For once she took the hint.

"No. Nick's right. We'd better be going. Things to see, people to do, you know. Ha-ha." She pushed herself up and steadied herself on the table.

Henry stood up. "Well, it's been a pleasure. Perhaps we can do it again some time."

Rosie beamed. "Oh, I do hope so. Thank you for your company."

As Nick helped her on with her coat, Henry ambled over to her, bent down, and kissed her cheek. "Take great care, precious lady."

She beamed. "To hell with that! Life's for living, and I'm going sailing tomorrow." She took Nick's arm and walked out of the Red Duster, swaying gently from side to side in a decidedly regal sashay.

THE silver Mercedes with the brand-new number plate completely blocked the track to The Anchorage.

"Bloody holidaymakers! Think they can park anywhere." He maneuvered the MG onto the verge. "Can you walk from here?"

"Of course. "S'not far, is it?"

Her speech was sibilant now. He suppressed a grin. "Take my arm."

He walked her up the final curve of the track, and his heart missed a beat as the verandah came into view. Someone he had not seen in months was sitting on the step.

"Hello, Nick! How ya doin'?"

"Dad! What are you doing here?"

"Come to see you and Mum. Hello, old girl."

Rosie screwed up her eyes. "Derek! Who told you I was here?" And then, with a note of anger in her voice, "You've not come to take me away, have you?"

Derek Robertson got up. "What would I want to do that for?"

"Because of Anna. She wants me in a home."

Nick's father shrugged. "Nothing to do with me, old love. I'm happy as long as you are."

They stared at each other for a few minutes, until Derek asked, "Can we go inside, then? It's a bit nippy out here."

Nick handed his grandmother over to her son, unlocked the front door, and let them in. He put on lights, motioned Rosie and Derek to take a seat, and asked his father what he would like to drink.

"Scotch, please, old lad."

"Some things never change," said Nick wryly. He left his father and grandmother while he went into the kitchen to fix the drinks.

Derek Robertson could not have looked more different from his son. For a start he lacked height, and his manner of dress had a showy look, from the slip-on buckled loafers to the black shirt. He even had crinkly dark hair and a thin moustache. He could have been taken for an Italian with Mafia connections.

Nick watched as his father sipped his Scotch. After a few minutes, Rosie excused herself. "I'd love to sit up and talk to you, Derek, but I'm afraid I must go to bed." Rosie was doing her best to concentrate, but the alcohol had taken its toll. "I'm completely done in. Knacked, I think, is the word. Yes, I'm completely knacked." She giggled, pushed herself out of the chair, and tottered elegantly toward her son, who rose to meet her. "Good night, dear." She pecked him on the cheek and wobbled unsteadily. "Oops. Steady the buffs."

"Good night, old girl. Look after yourself."

"Oh, I don't need to. I've found somebody else to do that. I met a very nice gentleman today. In the pub. Henry. Art dealer. Very good company. Mmm. Lovely big hands." Without a backward glance, she walked carefully in the direction of her bedroom.

Derek looked at his son. "Is she behaving herself?"

"Depends what you mean."

"Always done her own thing, Rosie. Never been one to conform." He winked.

"No." Nick paused. "Dad? I had two guys here today asking for you. Something to do with a package."

"Oh, damn. I told them it wouldn't be here till tomorrow."

"What won't be here till tomorrow?"

Derek Robertson knocked back the contents of his glass and reached into a pocket. He lifted out a small padded envelope.

"What's that?" asked Nick.

"You don't need to know," replied his father. "When those guys come back, just hand it over to them, will you?"

"But why can't you give it to them?"

"Because I won't be here. I've got a plane to catch."

"Dad!"

"I know what you're thinking, but it's all aboveboard. It's just better if I'm not here, that's all. It's just safer for all concerned if you do the handover. You don't need to know what it is."

Nick folded his arms. "I'm not doing it. You can't just swan in here like some shady character, pull out a package, and expect me to hand it over to a couple of thugs without asking a few questions."

Derek sighed. "I'd like you to trust me."

"I'd like to as well, but I haven't got much to go on."

His father laid a hand on his shoulder. "Will you or won't you? Just say yes or no and I'll be out of your hair."

Nick struggled with his conscience. "You promise it's nothing illegal?"

"Good God, no. It's just . . . well . . . private. That's all. Look, son, I just need you to do this one small thing for me. Okay?" Then he played his trump card. "It's to help Rosie."

There was a silence. Nick was annoyed with himself for having been cornered. He had little choice. And his father knew it.

"Okay—but I must be mad."

"And I must be going. Those ferries are a bugger—never turn up when you want them to." He slapped Nick on the back and made for the door.

"Dad!"

His father turned.

"When will I see you again?"

Derek Robertson shrugged. "Not sure. Probably later rather than sooner."

He swung out of sight.

Nick ran after him, calling in his wake, "What do you know about Russia?"

His father stopped dead in his tracks halfway down the lane, then turned to face him. "What do you mean?"

"Rosie's past. What do you know about Russia?"

"Oh, that." He looked thoughtful. "Bloody big country, Russia. Lot of people." He got into his car and drove off into the night.

Chapter 4

HOW she had managed to be up and out of the house before him was a mystery. Why wasn't she stumbling around with a hangover? He was rattled by her apparent self-sufficiency and that he had not asked more about her sailing course. Then the absurdity of the role-reversal struck him, and he felt slightly ashamed.

He ruffled his hair, yawned, and gazed out at the sea. She had chosen a good day to start: enough wind to fill her sails but nothing strong enough to give trouble.

The ship's clock on the kitchen wall told him it was eight thirty. He went to fill the kettle and saw an envelope propped up against it. He opened it and found his birthday card. He had quite forgotten. He was thirty-nine.

But the card lifted his spirits. It was not of the "Happy Birthday to My Favorite Grandson" type; instead it bore a black-and-white thirties photograph of a man in a suit holding the hand of a delicate-featured girl who was staring, rather distractedly, off-camera. The caption above it, in purple, read: *Emily is told that "Philip's 12 inch" is, in fact, his television.*

He opened it and read the inscription: *Thought this might make you smile! Thanks for putting up with me. All my love, Rosie xxx.*

He looked at the front of the card again and laughed out loud.

NICK made himself a cup of coffee and walked over to the window again. The sun was glinting on the water. It was the perfect May day. The perfect day for a birthday.

What a joke. Here he was, with a mad granny who thought she was the empress of Russia and a package of heaven-knows-what waiting to be collected by a couple of heavies who would probably break his legs. His car was likely to be impounded at any moment by a debt collector, his father arrested for trafficking in stolen goods, and himself banged up for perverting the course of justice. Even the most optimistic soul would have to admit this was not a promising way to celebrate the end of your fourth decade.

And then he saw her walking up the lane. Alex, with a package in her hand. She saw him at the window and waved. She was alone.

"Hi! Come in." He was at the open door to welcome her.

"You look happy."

"Don't be deceived by appearances."

She balanced on her toes and kissed his cheek. "Happy birthday."

"How did you know?"

"Grannies talking to ten-year-olds."

"Ah!" He smiled apologetically.

"You're not having a good day, then?"

"Oh, just things." And then he felt guilty for not welcoming her properly. "Look, I'm sorry about the other night. I was a bit impatient with Rosie. I shouldn't have been, but . . . anyway, coffee?"

"Please."

Once inside, she turned to him and held out the packet. "We made this for you, we girls. Victoria's with her friends, or she'd have come as well."

He looked at the homemade envelope, which bulged at the seams, and at the scraps of colored paper and feathers stuck to it. "What is it?"

"You may well ask. Open it."

Carefully, he pulled at the seams of the envelope and tipped the contents onto the kitchen table.

"Oh! Treasure trove!" He gazed at the objects that had tumbled from their paper wrapping: a tiny starfish, the black purse of a dogfish egg, green and blue glass shards washed smooth by the sea, two shiny razor shells, a piece of bleached white coral, and a dozen or more shells no bigger than his thumbnail in creamy white, soft purple, and dusky pink. "They're beautiful. What a wonderful present." His eyes darted over the treasures. "Thank you so much."

Then he looked at her in her loose white shirt and calf-length jeans, the shiny dark hair held back today with a tortoiseshell clip. He stepped forward, put his arms round her, and gave her a hug. "That's the nicest thirty-ninth birthday present I've ever had."

She grinned. "I'm glad."

He bent down and kissed her forehead. "I don't suppose you fancy a birthday supper, do you? I mean . . ."

"Just the two of us?"

"Well . . . if that's all right."

She laughed. "I'd love to."

Over coffee they talked of Rosie's foray into the world of spinnakers and mainsails, and of Victoria's day on the beach with the friends she'd made in Sleepyhead Bay. Then Alex said she'd better be getting back before Victoria outstayed her welcome with her holiday chums, and he arranged to pick her up that evening. They parted with a double-cheeked kiss on the verandah.

He came back inside and went into the kitchen again. He picked up the padded envelope his father had given him the night before. It was fastened with staples. It would be a simple job to bend them back, open the end, and examine the contents. Carefully he slipped the blade of a kitchen knife under each staple, prized back the teeth, then popped back the flap and eased out the contents. The self-sealing polyethylene bag seemed to be full of cotton wool. He pulled it open and tipped the wadding onto the kitchen worktop. As he moved it apart, out fell four stones that glittered and dazzled in the light.

He had never seen such astonishingly beautiful diamonds.

He felt sick. Quickly he put them back into the wadding, careful to avoid marking them with fingerprints, then slipped the bundle back into the polyethylene bag, the bag into the padded envelope, and nipped the jaws of the staples into place. He put the envelope under a cushion in the sitting room and sat down to think. His heart was hammering, and his mind raced. Were the stones stolen? Surely not. His father had always lived on his wits but had never been on the wrong side of the law. And yet he said he was leaving the country by plane. Why, if he had nothing to hide? And why couldn't he hand over the diamonds himself? What were they worth?

A knock at the door brought him to his senses. He looked up and saw the silhouettes of the two burly men.

IT WAS six o'clock when Rosie returned, her cheeks flushed with fresh air and excitement, but her eyes betrayed her tiredness. She flopped into a chair and said, "Oh, yes, please!" when Nick offered her a gin and tonic. "What a day. I don't remember when I last enjoyed myself so much. And the instructor says I'm a natural." She took a sip from her glass, then looked up at him. "How are we celebrating your birthday?"

"Ah." A pang of guilt caught him. "Well, er, I've arranged to go out."

"Oh. Oh, I see."

He heard the disappointment in her voice.

"With Alex. You could come if you like."

She smiled. "And Granny came, too? I don't think so. You go and enjoy yourself. I'll have an early night. We sailors have to be up in good time. We're sailing at Gurnard tomorrow."

He crouched in front of her and rested his hand on her knee. "I'm very proud of you, you know. But you're not overdoing it, are you?"

"I'm pacing myself. I told you. And that reminds me. Could you nip into my bedroom and fetch the little parcel that's on my bedside table? I'd go and get it myself, only my grandson tells me I have to be careful."

He went to her room and returned with a small package that was, perhaps, three inches square. He gave it to her, and she handed it straight back to him.

"Happy birthday, my love." She took another sip of her gin.

He pulled off the wrapping to reveal a small box. For the second time that day, his heart thumped. He lifted the lid of the box. A diamond winked at him. It was the same size as those he had seen earlier in the day.

"But, Rosie, you've bought me a car, and now this and . . . I mean your bank account—"

Rosie raised an eyebrow. "Your mother's been talking to you."

"Yes."

"I wondered how long it would be before she found out."

"But how could you afford—"

"By being careful for the best part of eighty-seven years."

Nick flopped down in a chair. "I don't understand."

"I got the idea from the Queen Mother." Rosie took a restorative sip of her gin. "She gave all her assets to her grandchildren. That way you can avoid death duties, provided you live for seven years after you've handed the stuff over."

Nick looked at her with a plaintive expression. He was sure he'd read something about "gift tax" or "capital gains." His thoughts were cut short.

"Oh, I know what you're thinking," Rosie said. "I'm eighty-seven; am I likely to last until I'm ninety-four?"

"No!"

"Don't interrupt. I looked at my bank account and at how much interest had built up, and it was pathetic. So I looked at the financial pages in the papers and worked out what the best investment was. And the financial experts seemed to think it was the right time to invest in diamonds. So I emptied my bank account and bought a few. This one's yours. At the moment it's worth about twenty-five thousand. Hopefully a bit more in a few years' time. And I've taken care of your sisters. Sophie and Alice have one each as well."

"I see." Nick gazed at the stone. "It's beautiful," he said.

"Yes. I'd take it to the bank and leave it there for a while, if I were you. Until you need to cash it in."

Nick shut the lid of the box and looked at his grandmother. "We've just got to make sure you live for another seven years, then." His lips curled into a grin.

"Oh, I wouldn't worry about that. As far as the government's concerned, I've just spent my money. No need for them to know where. It's yours now."

"Rosie! Is that legal?"

"Probably not—but it's no more wicked than taxing old ladies so that they can't afford to live on their savings, is it? Anyway, hadn't you better be getting ready to go out for dinner? Don't want to keep Alex waiting."

She winked at him. As he smiled back at her, he thought that, royal or not, she was the most amazing person he knew.

THEY were given a corner table in the dusky, cream-painted restaurant, and ushered to it by a girl in her teens. Nick ordered a bottle of Rioja, and she brought it to their table rather hesitantly. Nick noticed that her black shoes were huge, almost like clogs, at the end of her sparrowlike legs.

Alex had followed the direction of his gaze. "Surprising she can lift them, isn't it?"

Nick shook his head. "I must be getting old." He lifted his glass of wine and clinked it against Alex's. "Cheers!"

"Happy birthday! And lovely to spend it with you."

Alex was wearing a loose-fitting white shirt and a pair of black trousers that hugged her slim figure. Her hair shone like ebony. Nick was entranced. As the evening wore on, he could not recall anyone, apart from his grandmother, to whom he found it so easy to talk. He watched her animated face over the glow of the candle. Her flashing eyes seemed almost jet black.

She told him of her childhood on a farm in Devon, of losing her parents when she was in her teens, of her marriage to Paul and their broken relationship, her hopes for Victoria.

"And what about you? What do you want?" he asked.

"Oh, that's a big one. Don't really have time to think about me." She looked away. "I'm a bit scared, I suppose. Don't want to rush into something that might not work out. I can't mess it up any more for Victoria."

"There she is again."

"You see? It's impossible for any man to understand my responsibilities."

"I think you might be underestimating any man."

"You think so?"

"I think so." He laid his hand on hers. "Don't sell yourself short," he said.

She wrapped her fingers round his, and he squeezed her hand.

Their eyes met. Then the silence was broken by a plaintive voice: "Was everything all right?" asked the waitress.

Nick began to speak, but Alex beat him to it. "Oh, yes. It was lovely."

HE OPENED the car door for her, then walked round to the driver's side and slid in. The engine roared into life, and he steered the MG out of the car park. They said nothing, but he could feel her sitting closer than before. He caught an occasional whiff of her perfume. Suddenly it started to rain heavily.

"Oh, God!" He swerved into the side of the lane, beneath the shelter of the overhanging sycamores. "It won't take a minute! Hang on!"

He leapt out of the car and fought with the hood. It took several minutes to fasten it in place, during which time Alex shrieked, at first from the shock of the freezing deluge, but then with hilarity as he battled with the canopy and its collection of poppers and zips that seemed to bear no relation to the fittings on the car. Eventually, she jumped out to help, and soon the car was shielded from the worst of the elements by the ancient black shroud.

"Get in! Get in!" Nick roared as he ran round to his side and stumbled into the damp interior. He was greeted by a drenched Alex, laughing until tears and raindrops were running down her cheeks in tandem.

"Look at you!" he exclaimed, and wiped the water off her cheeks. Then he leaned forward and kissed her gently with unexpected longing. Her scent filled his nostrils as he felt the softness of her lips on his. She made no move to resist, and he slid closer to her, in spite of the gear lever, finally resting his head on her shoulder as their breathing returned to normal.

Then he raised his head and looked into her eyes. "Sorry."

She shook her head. "No, no. Don't be sorry."

He stroked the back of her head, then kissed her forehead tenderly before starting up the engine and driving her home.

THE following morning, Nick was lying in bed, listening to the rain pounding on the roof. He replayed the events of the previous evening over and over again in his mind. He had not expected to be so affected by Alex and wondered if she felt the same.

He slid out from under the duvet and padded across to the window. A stiff breeze was blowing the rain in diagonal sheets across the steel-gray sea and into the cliff face. Battalions of droplets rattled against the window of the cottage and trickled down the panes. Not a good day for sailing. He pulled on a bathrobe and went into the sitting room, expecting to find Rosie in her dressing gown.

Rosie was fully clothed and pulling on a raincoat.

"What are you doing?" he asked. "You can't go out in this."

"Are you suggesting I'm a fair-weather sailor?"

"I'm suggesting you should be." He looked at her with his head on one side. "Have you seen the weather out there?"

"Yes."

"And you're still going?"

"I'll take my stick." She made the concession grudgingly.

"Well, that won't stop you being blown off the cliff. Look, give me a minute to get dressed, and I'll drive you there. At least I can make sure you arrive in one piece."

He showered quickly, threw on jeans, sweatshirt, and trainers, and met her at the front door with his hair in a damp tangle. He put his arm through hers as they walked into the windy morning.

"Car smells nice," she said as he opened the MG door for her.

"It got a bit damp last night. Caught out by the rain."

"First rain I've known that smells of Chanel Number Five."

Nick said nothing as he eased into the driver's seat and started the engine.

"Did you have a nice time?"

He pulled out into the road. "Yes, thanks."

"Nice girl. Lovely dark eyes."

They motored on in silence.

As he turned into the road that led to the sailing academy, she tapped his arm. "Here will do. I can walk the rest. Need a breath of air."

The rain had eased slightly, so he let her have her way. She got out and straightened in the stiff breeze.

"What about tonight?" Nick asked. "What time shall I pick you up?"

"Oh, don't worry. I'll get one of my friends to drop me off."

He leaned back in his seat and heaved a sigh. He hoped to God they wouldn't take her out on the water on a day like this.

THE man at the bank took the package with little ceremony and assured Nick that he could have it back whenever he wanted. It was a weight off his mind to know that the diamond was somewhere safe, even though he was not sure that converting money into diamonds was a particularly sensible course of action. From what he had read, the diamond and gold markets were more volatile than bank interest rates, not less so, as Rosie had suggested.

But what worried him even more was the possibility that his father was involving his own mother in some kind of scam. If only he would answer his bloody phone.

VICTORIA was unsure of her mother's mood, and when you're trying to persuade a parent to buy you something, you need to be certain that your strategy is going to work. She had decided that she, too, was an artist, but rather than accepting the box of poster paints her mother was prepared to buy her, she had set her heart on a watercolor outfit in a varnished wooden box. She knew that now was not the moment to admit this, and settled instead for a guidebook to the Isle of Wight so that she could get to know it better. And, hopefully, find somewhere to live.

Alex, knowing that her daughter's intransigence could be epic when she put her mind to it, bought the modestly priced guidebook without demur and resigned herself to the fact that something was clearly brewing.

"Where are we?" Victoria asked as she pored over the map in the guidebook.

Alex peered over her shoulder. "Here." She pointed to the bottom right-hand corner.

"And where is Nick?"

"Here." Alex indicated the northernmost tip.

"How far away is that?"

"Well, look at the scale. There you are—that line. Five miles is about as long as . . . your finger."

Victoria measured the map with her finger. "Fifteen miles. Is that close?"

"Fairly."

"What about you and Nick?" she asked casually as she folded up the map. "Are you close?"

"I think he's a very nice man, that's all. I've only just met him."

Victoria folded her arms. "Honestly, you're like Elinor Dashwood in *Sense and Sensibility.*"

"Don't be ridiculous. That story was written nearly two hundred years ago, and this is the twenty-first century."

Victoria gave her a quizzical look. "It's funny how some things don't change, isn't it?"

THE Red Duster was unusually busy, but Henry, having forewarned the landlord of their arrival, had secured a table in the corner of the bar, albeit with only one chair. With a pint in one fist and a piece of bentwood furniture in the other, Nick elbowed his way through a group of yachties and eased himself opposite his patron.

They had barely begun to converse when a voice cut through the crowd. "Sorry! Thank you so much. Excuse me!" And there she was, standing before them, with a gin and tonic.

Rosie smiled at Henry, who attempted unsuccessfully to stand up. He bowed over his bottle of claret and indicated the chair that Nick was putting down. "Dear lady!" he exclaimed. "What are you do-ing here? Afternoon off?"

"Oh, no. Just a lunch break. Too lumpy out on the water. They've brought us to see some special boats that they make here." She raised her head and looked at Nick, who, having given away his seat, was standing beside the bar.

"Everything okay, then?" he asked.

"Fine dear. Henry will take care of me, won't you, Henry?"

"Of course. My pleasure." Henry laid a large hand over hers. "So, what's it to be? Lamb hot pot or red snapper?"

"Oh, the snapper, I think. Sounds so much more sparky, doesn't it?"

"A bit like you," offered Henry with a roguish tilt of his head.

Nick raised his eyes heavenward and drained his glass.

ROSIE put her head through the doorway of the tiny room where Nick was finishing off a couple of picture frames and asked, "Coffee?"

He turned to answer her and saw that, although she was smiling, her eyes were filled with tears. "Hey!" He got up and enfolded her in his arms. "What's the matter?"

"Oh, nothing. It's just that . . . Oh, I'm so silly." She pulled a tissue from the pocket of the pink sailing trousers she was wearing.

Nick released her and stood back to look at her. "What do you mean?"

"It's just that I don't remember being so happy in a long time."

"That's not silly; that's lovely."

"I suppose it is."

"What do you mean, you suppose? Of course it is." He gave her a squeeze. "Is it to do with Henry?"

"Oh, no, not really. Well, maybe a bit. He's very attentive. Only he believes I'm younger than I am." Rosie looked away. "I told him I was sixty-nine."

"What?"

"Oh, I know it was silly of me but . . . He was so nice, and I didn't want him to think I was some senile old woman. Sixty-nine would make me only eleven years older than him, and it's not too much of an age gap, is it?"

Nick was surprised. "Well, no, but—"

"He's asked me out on Friday night," she interrupted. "But I can't go. It's the final evening at the sailing academy. We're all going out for a drink."

"I see." Nick was trying to keep a straight face. "Couldn't you go out for a meal afterward?"

"Well, yes, I am. But not with Henry."

Just for a moment, Nick felt like the father of a teenage daughter who was enquiring after her movements. "Who with, then?"

"There's a man at the sailing academy. He's single, too. In his sixties."

"And have you told him how old you are?"

"I said I was sixty-six," Rosie said sheepishly.

AT TEN o'clock Nick tapped on her bedroom door. "Can I come in?"

"Of course."

He opened the door and peeped in. She was tucked up under her duvet, with just her head visible. She pushed herself up a little, and Nick spotted the lace on her nightie. She was elegant even in bed.

"I'm sorry about tonight," she said. "For being a stupid old woman. Mutton done up as lamb."

"Don't be silly." He sat on the edge of her bed. "But, you know, I still don't understand you. You're supposed to be out of touch and helpless, and here you are on a sailing course with people half your age—"

"Be careful!" she admonished him.

"—but you hold your own in conversation with anyone and line up dinner dates like there's no tomorrow."

"Well, there might not be." Rosie laughed. "You are funny."

"Me?"

"Yes. You. You're thirty-nine and far more staid than I am. If I were you, I'd start to live a bit."

Nick sighed. "Am I in for an advice session, then?"

"No. Well . . . maybe just a bit of friendly advice." She looked right at him. "Get on with it. Don't hang about."

"Get on with what?"

"Your relationship with Alex."

"There is no relationship."

"Exactly. But there could be. You should be having a bit of fun. She's a lovely girl, and she should be having fun, too."

"What about Victoria?"

"Oh, don't worry about her. She's got her head screwed on. She's older than all of us."

"You think?"

"Oh, yes. Funny, isn't it? Victoria's ten but more like forty. You're thirty-nine and more like seventy, and I'm eighty-seven going on thirty! Nobody's the age they seem, are they?"

"You know, there are days when I think you'll live forever," Nick said. "Where do you get your energy?"

Rosie nodded at the empty glass beside her bed. "Out of a bottle." Then she became serious. "Oh, sometimes I have to work hard to get up. But I tell myself it's only natural at my age. You have to fight it. I just grit my teeth and get on with it. Other days I have a good cry and feel completely done in. Then the sun shines, and I feel better."

"You're a star."

"Oh, no. I'm quite scared, if I'm honest. I feel a bit funny some days. A bit disconnected. It's me and yet it isn't me." She picked up a small black book. "I always keep this by my bed. *The Book of Common Prayer.* Lovely language." She looked up at him and asked evenly, "Do you say your prayers?"

Nick nodded. "Sometimes."

"I say mine every night: 'Gentle Jesus, meek and mild, look upon a little child; pity my simplicity; give me grace to come to thee—but not yet.' I always put that bit in. Hope it makes Him smile."

He watched as she lay back on the pillow. Calm now. Peaceful.

"He knows, doesn't He?" she said. "Where I came from."

Nick nodded again.

Rosie squeezed his hand. "Try to find out for me."

He sighed. "If you want me to."

Rosie smiled contentedly. Her eyes were closing, and soon her conversation was replaced by gentle breathing. Nick turned out the light, kissed her cheek, and quietly shut the door behind him.

THE next morning, as Nick switched on the computer, he called up assorted sites with the word *Romanov* in the title and, after some sifting, found one that looked promising. He felt a frisson of excitement as he started to read:

> The Romanov Dynasty began with the ascension of Tsar Mikhail Fedorovich to the Russian throne in 1613. Though still a young dynasty, by the 18th century the succession was seriously tested, but with the accession of Peter III, the crisis ended. In 1797, at his crowning, Peter's son, the Emperor Paul, issued Succession Laws.
>
> Under the "Pauline Laws," the succession followed a certain sequence, based on seniority. The emperor as head of the family and after him his eldest son was heir, then son of the eldest son and so on. If the male line died out completely, then the throne would pass to a female closest in relation to the last reigning emperor. Also, no member could now be denied their succession rights, except those who had voluntarily relinquished them.

He slumped back in his chair and took a deep breath. If Rosie could prove she was of the female line, and should the monarchy be reinstated, Rosie could legitimately claim her position as heir to the Russian throne. For one brief moment, Nick understood what it was like to be a male Cinderella. He could be only a hair's breadth away from becoming Tsar Nicholas III, after Tsar Derek had taken over from Empress Rosie. No: Empress Alice Marie Xenia. There was no denying it had a certain ring to it.

And then he read the paragraph that followed. It ended his reverie and brought him down to earth with a welcome bump:

> The laws were further altered in 1820, and to be considered a member of the Imperial House, members of the family had to marry a person of equal rank; meaning persons from another sovereign house. Accordingly, the offspring of these marriages were considered dynastic, while children of unequal marriages were not considered members of the Imperial House.

So if Rosie had indeed been next in line to the throne, she had relinquished her claim when she had married his grandfather.

He read the rest of the article and discovered that the current heir to the Russian throne was Grand Duchess Maria Vladimorovna, who was now forty-one and living in Madrid. She had had the foresight to marry Prince Franz of Prussia, keeping the marriage dynastic, and they had a son and heir: Grand Duke George Mihailovich, "the present successor to the Russian throne."

So that was that. If Rosie had once been heir to the House of Romanov, she was heir no longer. And neither was he. But how was it that Rosie had not known this particular information? He would ask her when she came home.

But that night Rosie didn't come home: she went instead to Queen Mary's Hospital in Newport, with a broken hip.

Chapter 5

"SHE'S been sedated," said the doctor. "It was a clean break, and we've put her back together again. It wasn't the artificial hip, fortunately."

"And will she be all right?" Nick sat by the hospital bed in which Rosie was sleeping.

"Well, at her age it's difficult to say. It's likely that she'll be less mobile than she was before. That said, she's fit for her age."

Nick stroked Rosie's hand and listened to her breathing.

"We'll need to keep her in for a while, get her on her feet as soon as we can, and then I would suggest a period of convalescence in a home. There are one or two good ones on the island—unless you want her to go back to the mainland so that she can be nearer her friends?"

"I'd rather she was here, but I'll have to check with the rest of the family. My mother's on her way."

"Yes, of course. We can talk about it later. She's in good hands for now."

Nick looked back at Rosie. She was wearing a rough-textured hospital gown that was far too big for her, and her normally neatly curled hair was lopsided and unkempt. She looked like a refugee.

The sound of sensible shoes on a hard floor broke in on his thoughts. He looked up. His mother was standing over him.

THE grilling took place in the hospital waiting room. "Well, how did it happen?"

"She slipped. On a boat."

"Oh, Nick! What was she doing on a boat?"

"I told you, she was on a sailing course."

"Stupid idea." Anna Robertson's face was a picture of righteous indignation.

"I just wanted her to have a bit of fun. And so did she."

"And this is where it's led. So, what happens now?"

Nick was leaning forward with his elbows resting on his knees. "They'll have to keep her in for a while, and then they recommend a convalescent home."

"Of course. Whereabouts?"

"I suggested here, but I thought you'd probably have an opinion on that."

"It's out of the question. She'll have to come back to Richmond where I can keep an eye on her."

"Lucky her."

"Nick!"

He sat up. "Well, we want her to get better, don't we? And she'll need encouragement for that, not you barking at her all the time."

"That's not very kind." She looked hurt.

"No, but it's accurate," Nick continued stubbornly. "You know you don't get on, and it would probably be better for both of you if she stayed on the island."

Anna shrugged. "Does your father know?"

"Not yet. I've tried ringing him, but there was no reply. I think he was going abroad." He avoided meeting her eye. There was no way he would mention the package. "He's probably changed phones yet again."

"More than likely." She drummed her fingers on her handbag. "Is she likely to be asleep for long?"

"A few hours. She's only just come out of the operating room."

"I see." Anna glanced at her watch. "I've a meeting tonight, and I really can't miss it. If you think I should . . ."

"No. You get back. I can keep an eye."

"Well, if you're sure . . ." His mother got up and laid a hand on his shoulder. "We'll talk tomorrow, yes? Work out what to do."

He nodded and turned to look out of the window as the purple haze of dusk settled on the hospital car park.

A PHONE call to the hospital at nine o'clock the next morning confirmed that Rosie had had a comfortable night and was now sleeping peacefully. "Peacefully" sounded as if she'd given in, and that wasn't Rosie. He admonished himself for the thought and confirmed that he would visit her at lunchtime when she would be sitting up, they said.

He went into Rosie's bedroom. It was tidy and ordered, the photo of the tsar, and a smaller one of Granddad, on the bedside table. He could see her nightie peeping out from under her pillow. Her traveling alarm clock ticked loudly, but the house was strangely quiet without her. Life was quiet.

And then he remembered: It was Alex and Victoria's last day on the island. He wanted to tell Alex what had happened, but more than that, he wanted to see her. He punched in her mobile phone number and waited for it to ring. Her phone was switched off, so he left a message: "Hi. It's Nick. Just to say hello and . . . hope you're okay. Sorry I've not been in touch. Rosie's taken a bit of a tumble. She's okay, but she's in the hospital. I'll tell you about it when we can speak. That's all, really. Hope I'll speak to you soon. Bye."

He looked out of the window at the pale gray day. At least it was fine. He grabbed his windbreaker. He would buy some flowers to take to the hospital. Better still, he would pick some from the clifftop. She'd like that.

THE young woman on the Isle of Wight ferry looked nothing like Nick. She was short and well rounded, with close-cropped hair and a tanned complexion. The rucksack on her back gave away nothing about her travels, but her brown legs and well-worn boots showed that she had been out of doors for some time. Sophie Robertson was back from South America and had headed straight from Heathrow to the ferry at Portsmouth.

Since arriving on the island, she had walked the couple of miles to The Anchorage, only to find that her brother was out. Not to worry, she would wait. She had food and water in her rucksack and would make herself comfortable in a chair on the verandah until he returned.

She had been sitting there for an hour, reading, when a woman with a young girl walked up the drive. They seemed surprised to see her. Sophie got up and leaned over the rail. "Hi!"

"Hello. Is Nick in?"

Sophie glanced at the house. "If he was, I wouldn't be sitting on the verandah."

"I just wanted to tell him we're leaving the island today."

"Oh. Righto. I'll pass on a message, if you like."

"I tried to ring him on my mobile, but it's bust. If you could just say that Alex and Victoria called."

"Fine. I'll do that." Sophie sat down again and picked up her book.

"Yes. Right. Well, we'll be going, then."

"Okay. Good-bye, Alex and Victoria. I'll tell him you came."

ROSIE was indeed sitting up in bed when Nick arrived. His relief was unbounded as he bent to kiss her. "Hello!"

She smiled, with what seemed like an effort, and whispered, "Hello."

He sat down on the chair by her bed and lifted the flowers for her to see: red campion and buttercups, stitchwort and cow parsley. He saw her eyes glint and her mouth force itself into a smile. "Lovely," she mouthed.

"I'll find some water for them in a minute. How are you feeling?"

"Sore," she said.

"I'm not surprised. You had a bit of a tumble."

Rosie nodded and closed her eyes.

"What am I going to do with you?" he asked gently.

"Don't know." The voice was resigned, lacked energy, but that was hardly surprising. She opened her eyes and beckoned him closer. He leaned toward her. "They want to get me on my feet, but . . . there's no . . . life in me."

He held her hand and rubbed his thumb on the back. "Oh, don't you worry, there will be. You're just woozy from the anesthetic."

A nurse walked purposefully toward the bed and spoke in a loud voice: "Hello, Mrs. Robertson. We're a bit out of it at the moment, aren't we?"

"Mmm." Rosie sounded distant.

The nurse tucked in a wayward length of sheet. "We'll soon have you back on your feet, though. Would you like a drink? Cup of tea?"

Rosie shook her head and murmured, "No, thank you."

Nick was alarmed. He had prepared himself for her to be frustrated and difficult, but not compliant or world-weary.

The nurse read the concern on his face. "Still a bit under the weather, but she should pull round over the next day or so, get her bearings. We're just a bit confused, aren't we, Mrs. Robertson?"

Nick wanted to explain that, although his grandmother was of a certain age, she was neither gaga nor deaf and that she was a "you" not a "we." But he thought better of it.

"Shall I put those in water for you?"

"Please."

The nurse took the flowers. "You could probably leave it until this evening if you want, Mr. Robertson. She should be with us a bit more by then."

"I'll just sit with her for a while, if that's all right."

"Sure. No problem."

He stayed by the bed for half an hour while Rosie slept; then he reluctantly headed for home.

THE sailing to Portsmouth was uncharacteristically quiet. Victoria had her nose buried in the guidebook, occasionally writing something down in a small exercise book.

Eventually the Wight-Link ferry lowered its ramp onto the Portsmouth soil, and they got back into their car and drove off.

It was then that Victoria broke the silence. "Who do you think it was?"

"I don't know," Alex said curtly.

"Maybe she was his old girlfriend come back."

Alex had been doing her best to put that thought out of her mind. She had seen the rucksack with the airline luggage label beside the tanned stranger on Nick's verandah and had concluded that Debs had returned. "Look, can we just stop speculating and wait and see? We don't know who it was, and no amount of guessing is going to help us."

"Are you cross?"

"No, I'm just a bit tired of being asked questions."

"All right, all right. I'm sorry." Victoria folded her arms, pursed her lips, and stared out of the window at nothing in particular.

Alex felt mean. "I'm sorry, too. It's just that . . . Well, it's all very confusing, that's all." She tried to placate her daughter. "What have you been writing in your book?"

"Now who's asking questions?"

Alex sighed. "I'm only interested."

"No, you're not. You're just trying to make conversation."

Alex laughed. "Listen to us. We sound like an old married couple."

"Yeugh!"

"Exactly. So, you tell me what you were writing and I won't snap your head off if you mention Nick."

"We-ell," she hesitated. "I was writing down good places to live."

"Ah, I see. And what conclusions did you come to?"

"Shanklin and Sandown are too busy, Newport is too far from the sea, and Cowes is too full of boaty people."

"So you didn't find anywhere nice?"

"I like Sleepyhead Bay."

"But there are only about ten houses, and I don't think you'd want to live there in winter."

"I thought of that. Godshill is pretty, and it's not too far away."

"Mmm. A bit chocolate-boxy for me." Alex wondered why she had instigated this conversation. If their suspicions about Nick's visitor were accurate, the Isle of Wight was the last place she wanted to be.

"You didn't tell me you were coming home!" Nick flung his arms round his little sister.

"Didn't know I was until a couple of days ago."

Nick took a pace back and eyed her up and down. "You look so well!"

"All that walking."

"So where did you get to, and why have you come back?"

"Well, if you let me in, I'll tell you."

Nick sat and listened as Sophie talked of her six months in Costa Rica, of tropical rain forests and coffee plantations, and of transiting the Panama Canal on a banana boat.

"You haven't said why you came home."

"Dunno. Just felt I needed to for a bit."

Nick grinned. "I'm glad you did. Will you go back?"

"Not there. Chile, though, and Peru. Give myself a couple of weeks to get my breath back and then I'm off."

"What will you do for money?"

"I've got some saved. I worked quite a lot of the time. Didn't earn much, but I don't need much."

"Well, you might have a bit more than you think."

"What do you mean?"

Nick filled in his sister on the events of the past weeks—of Rosie's relocation to the Isle of Wight, her sailing course and the accident, and the diamond legacy that was also Sophie's. He did not mention the Russian royal family. It seemed unnecessary, especially now that he had discovered there was no immediate danger of the Robertsons being called upon to take the throne.

"But why's she doing all this?" asked Sophie.

"For the same reason that you came home, I suppose. It's her time."

"What does Mum think about it all?"

"She's furious that I let it all happen. I haven't told her about the diamonds. She knows Rosie's bank account is empty, but she doesn't know why. She's probably just putting her head in the sand."

"Just wants to get on with her own life, I suppose," Sophie mused. "But this diamond you say I'm getting. I suppose it will make things a bit easier. Where do you think it is?"

"In a bank somewhere, I imagine. Are you going to blow the lot on first-class travel, then?"

"Don't be stupid. Do I look like the sort who travels first class?"

"Er, no. A steerage girl if ever I saw one," Nick told her.

"I tell you what I could do with, though. A bath."

"I thought you'd never ask. I was just going to open all the windows."

"Cheeky bugger!" She lunged forward to swipe him with her hand, but he caught it, spun her round, and kissed her cheek.

"Nice to have you home," he said. "Get yourself cleaned up, and then I'll cook you some dinner before we go and see your granny."

"Now, there's an offer a girl can't refuse."

To HIS relief, Rosie was sitting up in bed, and something of her old self had come back. "Where've you been?" she asked.

"Waiting for you to come round. You were a bit out of it before."

"Huh. I'm bored stiff, stuck in here," she grumbled.

"I've brought someone to see you."

"Oh, not your mother. Tell me you've not brought her!"

"Ssssh! Keep your voice down. No, I haven't brought Mum. She came while you were asleep."

"That was good timing."

Nick beckoned to the figure hidden behind the door.

"Sophie! Oh, my love, what are you doing here? I thought you were in . . . wherever you were . . . South Africa."

"South America. Hello, Rosie." Sophie bent to kiss her grandmother.

Rosie, in a surge of affection, put her arm round Sophie's neck and hugged her. Then she spoke rapidly, through mounting emotion: "I thought I'd never see you again. This is so lovely. So lovely." She stroked the back of her granddaughter's head, ruffling the golden stubble. Then she let Sophie stand up but took her hands. "Look at you! You're brown as a berry! But your hair! There's not much left, is there?"

Sophie grinned. "It's easier if it's short out there. Insects and stuff."

Rosie frowned slightly. "Now there's only Alice, but I don't expect she'll be home for a while."

"Not if you behave," offered Nick. "And her home *is* in South Africa."

"Hey!" said Rosie. "I haven't forgotten—it's just that it's easy to muddle South Africa and South America."

Nick patted her hand. "I know."

"Now, we should be able to get some tea," said Rosie. "And you, Sophie, can tell me everything you've been doing."

Nick could not remember when he had last felt so relieved.

SOPHIE eased herself into the sleeping bag on the sofa in Nick's sitting room. "I'm knackered."

"I'm not surprised," Nick called from his room next door. Then he laughed. "What does this remind you of?"

"When we were little," his sister said.

He laughed again. "You always wanted to talk, and I always wanted to sleep."

"Well, I shan't keep you awake tonight."

"That's a relief."

"Oh," murmured Sophie as she fought to stay awake, "I almost forgot. A woman and a little girl were asking for you this afternoon when you were out. Alex and Victoria. Said she'd been trying to get hold of you but that her phone was bust or something. Does that make sense?"

HE HAD wanted to ring her the night before, but it had been too late. He called her on her home number as soon as it seemed decent to do so—at around eight thirty. Victoria answered. "Hello?"

"Victoria? It's Nick Robertson. Is your mum there?"

"No. She's out." She sounded distracted.

"Oh." Nick was flustered. "Could you just say I rang and that I'm trying to get in touch with her? Maybe she could ring me later."

"Will you be there all the time?"

"I have to go out to do a few things."

"What about lunchtime? Will you be in then?" she asked.

"No. I have to go and see Rosie."

"Isn't she with you anymore?"

"No. She's had an accident." Nick sighed.

There was silence at the other end of the line.

"Don't worry," he said. "She's okay, but she's in the hospital."

Silence again.

"Look, if you could pass on the message, and I'm sure we'll manage to speak some time today. Okay?"

"Okay." And she hung up.

"Damn," muttered Nick. He had wanted to tell Alex everything that had happened since they had last seen each other—and he'd wanted to tell her about Rosie himself.

He left The Anchorage and walked toward the cliffs, where he set up his easel. He worked all morning until half past twelve, when he packed up his brushes and drove to the hospital to meet Sophie at Rosie's bedside.

When he arrived, the two were deep in conversation.

"How are you today, Duchess? Have they started you walking?"

"Have they? I'll say. Up and down the ward like a sentry." Her eyes lit up. "That reminds me. Did you tell Sophie"—she glanced from side to side, like a spy—"about the legacy thing?"

"Well, I did mention it."

"But, Rosie, it's really not necessary," Sophie told her.

"No buts. It's all sorted out. I've given Nick his, and he's put it in the bank." She turned to him. "You have put it in the bank, haven't you?"

"Yes."

"Well, I'll give you yours, Sophie, and you can do the same. As soon as your father comes back."

Nick was horrified. "Dad?" he managed weakly.

"Yes. I gave them to him for safekeeping. I couldn't get to the bank so he said he'd take them for me."

SOPHIE knew something was wrong. All day Nick was preoccupied, and she assumed it was to do with the woman and little girl who had come to the house. She kicked herself for having forgotten to give him the message earlier.

During the afternoon, Nick called Alex several times but there was no reply. Then, at around five, the phone was picked up by Alex.

"Hi!" He felt as though someone had opened a valve in his head, so great was his relief at hearing her voice. "I'm sorry I missed you. I didn't get the message that you'd dropped by until late."

"Oh. I see." She sounded cooler than he had hoped. "What's this about Rosie? Victoria said she'd had an accident, but there was no need to worry."

"She's broken her hip, messing about in boats, but she's on the mend. She was a bit dopey at first, but she's almost back to her old self."

"Oh, good. We did worry."

"Yes. Sorry. Look, I couldn't see you again, could I? Soon."

"Oh, well . . . It's a bit tricky . . . Victoria's at school and . . ."

She seemed distant. Nick tried again. "Perhaps I can ring you tomorrow?"

"If you like."

"Is everything okay? It's just that . . . well, okay. I'll call tomorrow."

He put down the phone. Why had she gone so cool on him? He ambled out to the verandah and flopped into a chair. Bloody hell! He'd cocked it up again. But this time he had no idea why.

"MAVIS?"

"Yes?"

"It's Nick. Any news on Pa? Has he done a bunk?"

Mavis was a sixty-something, amply proportioned spinster who lived with five cats on the edge of Epping Forest. She had devoted the last twenty years of her life to Nick's father—as his secretary-cum-personal assistant—but six months ago Derek had decided that he wanted to be more independent and that Mavis was always too keen to tie him down.

"Oh, I shouldn't think so. He'll just have gone to ground until the deal's done."

"What sort of deal?"

"Now, you know better than to ask me that. There was a time when I would have known all, but your father prefers to work as a free agent nowadays."

"Agent? What sort of agent?"

"Don't be dramatic, dear. He's never done anything on the wrong side of the law, and I'm sure he's too old to start now. I'll give you a new phone number, and you can keep trying it, but other than that, I've nothing to offer."

Nick tried the number. The line was dead as a doornail. Just like his love life.

"COME on, then, what is it?" Sophie popped a piece of melon into her mouth. "You've not said more than half a dozen sentences all day."

"Oh, just girl trouble." Nick nodded in the direction of the mainland.

Sophie looked guilty. "Maybe I've frightened her off—by being here."

"Don't be silly. She's not that feeble."

"Certainly didn't look feeble. She seemed very . . . capable."

"She is." He laid his fork on the table and leaned back in his chair. "Was she okay when you saw her?"

Sophie shrugged. "Suppose so. If anything, she looked a bit disapproving. I saw her eyeing up my rucksack. Probably thought I was some sort of gypsy."

Nick sat up. "Did you tell her you were my sister?"

Sophie hesitated. "I . . . don't think so."

Nick stood up and pointed at the rucksack in the corner. "That was on the verandah, with airline labels all over it, and you didn't tell her who you were?"

"No. And what have my stickers got to do with it?"

"Alex comes here to tell me she's leaving, and she sees you sitting on the verandah. And she knows I had a girlfriend who ran off to America."

"Oh." Sophie sat quite still, and then said, "Oh, God!"

"Yes. Oh, God. She only thinks that Debs has come back."

"YOUR sister?"

"Yes."

"Oh." There was a pause, then Alex chuckled. "How silly."

"Silly of her not to say."

"And silly of me to jump to conclusions."

"Typical Sophie. She's a great sister—love her to bits—but she can be a bit short with people she doesn't know."

Alex brightened and made to brush it aside. "Yes. Well, never mind."

"No, but I do mind." There was a pause. "More than I realized."

"Oh. That's very nice."

"Look, can I see you tomorrow night?"

"Well, I . . . yes . . . I suppose so."

"Shall I come over to you? I mean, you've been over here a lot lately."

"No. No. I'll come to you. I'll just have to find a sitter, that's all. Oh, and I have a new mobile phone. Same number."

"Right. See you tomorrow, then."

Moments later, Nick's mother rang. She had been giving some thought to Rosie's convalescence and had decided, she said, that perhaps it would be best if Rosie stayed on the island. Her resigned manner spoke volumes.

He hung up. It was a defining moment. To all intents and purposes, his grandmother's future care was in his hands.

"I DON'T really want to go out," grumbled Sophie the following evening.

"I know, but you owe it to me, don't you?"

"Mmm. I suppose so." She was changing in the bathroom and talked to him through the half-open door. "I'll be back about ten."

"What?"

Sophie grinned to herself. "Only teasing. I've booked a room at the Royal London—I'm meeting up with a few old drinking mates."

Nick backpedaled: "Look, you can come back here. Nothing's going to happen. I just want to have a bit of time on my own with Alex."

"Of course. And who'd want their sister hanging around, even if she has only been home a couple of days."

"Soph!"

She came out of the bathroom wearing a T-shirt and jeans. "You're so easy to wind up." She reached up and ruffled his hair. "Better clean yourself up a bit, though. Don't want to put her off."

"I will—now I can get into the bathroom."

He met Alex at the ferry terminal, in the MG with the hood down.

"Is this wise?" she asked. "Having the hood down?"

He leaned across and kissed her cheek. "No rain forecast."

"Where are we going?"

"I thought we'd eat in. Try to do a bit better than last time."

Alex grinned. "That's nice. No need to worry about anyone else."

He looked at her meaningfully. "No."

They didn't speak much on the journey, just sat back, happy to be in each other's company.

She smiled at him as he opened the door for her to get out of the car once they had reached The Anchorage. "Here we are," he said. "Dry as a bone."

"In more ways than one."

"Oh, don't worry. The champagne is on ice."

"Champagne? Are we celebrating or something?"

"Yes," he said. "The end of a misunderstanding."

He ushered her up the steps and onto the verandah, where a small table was laid for two. Alex sat down, and Nick disappeared into the cottage. He returned with a bottle of champagne and two glasses. He poured, they drank, and looked out over the sea as the sun sank below the horizon.

"Do you ever take this view for granted?" she asked.

"No. It's never the same twice."

"A bit different from my view in Portsmouth," she said. "You're so lucky."

He smiled at her. "I know."

Over supper—lobster, bought from the fisherman at Sleepyhead Bay—he told her about Rosie's accident. Then, feeling the need to unburden himself, he explained about Rosie's preoccupation with her Russian ancestry and his researches into the royal family. It no longer sounded ridiculous. He found himself talking easily, and she was attentive, absorbed.

Finally he said, "Unbelievable, isn't it?"

Alex shook her head. "No. Unusual, but not unbelievable." And then, "Oh, my God!"

"What?" He stared at her.

"Our names."

He sighed with relief. "I know. Silly, isn't it?"

She grinned. "I think it's rather sweet. Did Rosie notice?"

"Immediately."

"I'm not surprised." Alex looked more serious. "And you still don't know for certain who her parents were?"

"No, and I don't really know where to start."

"Maybe I could do a bit of reading. Research." She hesitated, not sure if she'd overstepped the mark.

"That would be great!" Nick said enthusiastically.

"You jot down the facts and the names you know, and I'll have a dig around, if you're sure you don't mind."

"I'm pleased you want to bother—that you think it's worth it."

"Of course! It's fascinating. It'll be a bit of an adventure."

"As long as you want one."

Alex looked across the table at him, and then laid her hand on his. "Oh, I think so."

His heart was pounding. "Do you have to go back tonight?"

"Victoria's with friends—I couldn't get a sitter."

"Stay, then?"

"Yes."

Chapter 6

HE WATCHED her as she woke. The early morning light caught her dark hair and made it shine like polished jet. Nick could not remember ever feeling so calm as he did at that moment. Lying next to her in his bed. Feeling her warm body next to his.

She stirred, then opened her eyes, squinting at the rays of dawn. For a moment he thought she might not remember where she was. Might suddenly regret the impulse of the night before, jump out of his bed and throw on her clothes, but she didn't. Instead, she smiled at him and snuggled closer. "Hello, you," she murmured.

"Hello, you," he echoed.

They lay still for a few moments, silent except for their soft breathing. Alex laid her arm across his chest. "What are you thinking?" she asked.

"About you."

She raised herself up on one elbow and looked him in the eye. "You don't think I was . . . well . . . a bit fast."

He nodded. "Like lightning."

"Oh, God! I didn't mean to be. I'm not usually . . ."

"Hey!" He squeezed her shoulders. "Just kidding."

"Oh. Well, that's all right." She relaxed. "I wish I could stay."

"Can't you?" He looked at her, his eyes hopeful.

"No. The neighbors will take Victoria to school—with their little girl—but I've got to get back. There's shopping to do."

"What?" Nick sat up and looked at her incredulously. "You're lying in bed with me and all you can think of is doing the shopping?"

"It's all right for you! You have no responsibilities, but I have another mouth to feed."

Nick frowned at her. "So do I."

"Yes, but yours is being taken care of by the health service at the moment." She kissed him lightly on the forehead and slid out of bed.

HENRY sat by Rosie's bed while the nurse arranged a bunch of red roses in a vase on the bedside cabinet. "They're beautiful," said Rosie, her eyes shining. "They must have cost a fortune."

"Worth it to see your face, dear lady. I've been a bit worried about you. Glad to see you're on the mend."

"Slowly. Very slowly."

"So, what happens now?" he asked.

"Another week or so in here, and then I've got to go into a nursing home." She grimaced.

"What?" He looked horrified.

"Not permanently, just to convalesce. Nick's going to arrange it."

"Here or on the north island?" Henry still looked worried.

"Here. I don't want to go back there just yet."

"Oh, good." He reached out his hand and held hers. "I wouldn't want to think you were going away."

Rosie smiled. "You're very kind, Henry."

"Not kind at all. Just, well . . ."

"Whatever it is, I'm grateful."

Henry gazed at her, sitting there. Somehow Rosie didn't fit here. She was a doer, and doers are always up and about, not lying in bed.

"Not much fun, is it?" she asked. "Getting old, I mean."

"No," Henry agreed ruefully.

"But we're no different from the way we've always been, really."

"Except that some bits don't work as well," Henry said wistfully.

"I just wish younger people would understand."

"Understand what?"

"That you never stop being you. That you still have feelings just as much as you did when you were younger." Rosie sighed. "I mean, I'm every bit as passionate and interested, it's just that somehow it all gets . . . blunted."

"Is that how you feel now?" he asked gently.

"When I'm a bit down, yes. I just wish I could feel the joy in life that I felt when I was younger." She looked distant, distracted.

"I think you should try to get some sleep." Henry patted her hand, worried that her fighting spirit had been dented. It must be the medication. "It's only natural," he said. "Probably something to do with the anesthetic. It's still wearing off. We've got to get you back on your feet as soon as we can and out of this place. Then, perhaps, you'll let me take you out to dinner."

Rosie looked anxious. "Henry, there's something you should know. You remember when we were talking in the pub?"

"Mmm?"

"I was less than honest with you. I didn't want you to think that I was a feeble old lady so . . ."

Henry cleared his throat. "If you're about to say something about your age, then I should mention something before you do. I lied to you. I'm not really fifty-eight. I'm actually sixty-three."

For a moment Rosie's face bore a look of surprise.

"Will you forgive me?"

She looked at him with mock admonishment, then melted. "Of course I will."

"You're very kind. Very generous."

Rosie squeezed his hand. "You know what that means, don't you?"

Henry raised an eyebrow.

"It means that you're only six years younger than me."

It WAS eight thirty that evening before Nick had a moment to phone Alex. After the mundanities of life—doing his own shopping, taking the car for an oil change, repairing a window at The Anchorage—and visiting Rosie in the hospital, he dialed the number.

"Hello?"

"Shopping successful?" he asked sarcastically.

"Yes, thank you!" She was stifling a laugh. "And thank you for last night. It was very . . . special."

"Yes." He paused. "Yes, it was. I'm glad you stayed."

"Me too."

"And how's Victoria? You weren't in trouble?" he enquired.

"Not exactly. I got a few what you might call 'old-fashioned' looks. You know—about staying out all night."

"It's going to be tricky, isn't it?"

"I suppose so," she said. "But don't worry—I'll handle it. It's my problem. Just give me a couple of days to sort myself out."

They said good-bye fondly, but he felt uneasy. He told himself to give her time. To give them both time. This was something not to be rushed.

He got up and walked outside onto the verandah. Dusk was falling. In the far distance, through the rising mist, the green light of a container ship floated across the water. Another day, another night. He was alone with his thoughts—of Rosie, his father, wherever he was, and Alex.

WHATEVER else Nick expected to happen the following morning, it was not Henry's arrival on his doorstep.

"Are you feeling all right?" Nick asked. "Normally you never venture this far without your passport and immunization."

"There's no need for that. I'm on an errand of mercy."

"That sounds ominous. Do you want some coffee?"

"I went to see Rosie yesterday."

"That was kind of you." Nick was busy with the kettle and didn't look up.

"She was talking about what will happen when she comes out of the hospital."

"It won't be for a couple of weeks yet."

"Three days, actually."

"What?"

"I asked the nurse. The consultant had just done his rounds. They can get her a physiotherapist in her rest home, and they reckon she'll be fit to go there by the end of the week."

Nick put down the kettle. "They didn't tell me that. I haven't sorted anything out yet. It will be difficult to find somewhere at such short notice." He could hear the panic in his voice.

"I'd thought of that. I might be able to help." Henry fished into his inside pocket. "My card."

Nick took the small rectangular business card. It was a little crumpled at the edges. "Henry J. Kinross, MCSP, SRP" it said in minute copperplate.

"Henry, why do I need this? I know where you live."

Henry pointed to the letters after his name. "MCSP stands for Member of the Chartered Society of Physiotherapists. And SRP means State Registered Physiotherapist."

Nick stared at him. "You're a physiotherapist?"

"Correct."

"But you're an art dealer."

"The two are not mutually exclusive. And I wasn't always an art dealer."

"But . . . how long is it since you practiced?"

"Ooh, about half an hour."

"What?"

"I have a few private patients. It keeps the old skill going, and it takes my mind off temperamental artists. I spoke to the consultant at the hospital, and he agreed that Rosie could stay with me. I have a niece on the mainland who can come over and keep an eye on the gallery, and Rosie will recover more quickly than she would in some impersonal nursing home."

Nick was stunned. The kettle whistled, and he took it off the hob. "You never said anything."

"Dear boy, if there is one thing in life that I've learned, it's that it doesn't do for people to know everything about you until they need to."

Nick handed him a mug of coffee. "You know" he said with a twinkle in his eye, "I'm not sure I should trust you with my grandmother."

"Dear boy, I never mix business with pleasure."

"Good." Nick laughed.

"But in the case of your grandmother, I'm prepared to make an exception."

ALEX HAD JUST GOTTEN HOME from a trip to the library, where she'd done some research into Rosie's past, when there was a knock at her door. Whoever else she had expected to find when she opened it, it was not her husband.

She looked at him, standing there with his hands in the pockets of his well-cut suit. He was six feet three, darkly good-looking, and immaculately dressed. His self-assurance had once attracted her, but now she found it repellent. They had grown to realize they were fundamentally different in outlook, always had been, but they had put it to one side and allowed the physical attraction to carry them along.

"What are you doing here? I thought you'd gone."

"Not till tomorrow. I was delayed. I came to say good-bye to Vicks."

"She's at school. She'll be home any minute."

"Can I come in and wait?"

"No. No, you can't. Look, we've been through all this. You know it will only upset her. Last time you saw her, it was supposed to be for the last time. She had nightmares for days afterward, Paul."

"Don't exaggerate."

"I'm not. It's not that she doesn't love you, it's just that . . . She's frightened of you."

"But that's ridiculous. I've never touched her."

Alex tried to sound sympathetic. "I know that, but she needs stability. She can't cope with this whirlwind who descends on the house, fights with her mother, then takes off again." She shook her head. "No, I'm sorry, you'll have to go. Right now she just needs to get her mind round the fact that her mother and father don't live together anymore."

Paul leaned against the wall. "So that's that, then?"

"Yes. That was that three months ago—three years ago."

"Oh, don't bring all that up again. She's not coming with me."

"Only because someone else is."

Paul looked away.

"Go on. Go to America. You can see Victoria when you come back."

He walked toward the door, then turned to face her. "It didn't have to be like this, you know."

Alex sighed. "Oh, it did."

ROSIE was sitting up in bed as a manicurist varnished her nails.

"I thought this was a hospital, not a beauty clinic," Nick said as he arrived beside her.

Rosie looked up at him and beamed. "Hello, love! I'm just having my nails done. They come once a week. Useful, isn't it?" She nodded toward the young woman in the pink overall who was bent over her right hand. "This is Clare. She's come to get me ready for my trip."

"Trip?"

"To Henry's."

"Ah, yes." He smiled at Clare, who, evidently aware that a family heart-to-heart was about to ensue, packed away her varnishes and bustled off.

Nick sat down by the bed. "Are you sure about moving in with Henry?"

"Oh, I'm not moving in with him like that! We're not—what do they call it? Co-something."

"Cohabiting."

"Yes. I'm not doing that."

"Well, you'll be under the same roof."

"Not in the same bed, though."

Nick spluttered. "I should hope not."

Rosie looked at him with a serious expression on her face. "Would it be so terrible if we were?"

"Rosie!"

She shook her head. "People your age are all the same. Always imagining that sex is something for the under-fifties."

Nick glanced around apprehensively. "Will you keep your voice down?"

Rosie grinned. "You don't stop suddenly, you know, when you've had your children."

Nick leaned back in his chair. "Are you trying to shock me?"

She looked him in the eye. "Maybe."

"Well, thanks for being honest, at least."

Rosie leaned back on the pillow and closed her eyes. "I'm tired."

"I'm not surprised."

She opened them again. "But I'm happier. I've got something to look forward to now."

Nick paused, more serious now. "Look, don't you think you'd be better off where they can look after you properly?"

"Henry can look after me properly," Rosie insisted.

"But he has a gallery to run." Nick took her hand. "All I'm saying is that I don't think Henry knows what he's letting himself in for."

Rosie squeezed his hand. "Shall I tell you something? I know he doesn't."

"You're a wicked old lady!"

"I know. But it's more fun that way!" She grinned.

Nick laughed, relieved that her old spirit was back.

"I'm going to stay with Henry," Rosie continued. "He likes the prospect of looking after me, but I expect it will wear off. I'm ready for it, though, so I'll take the chance."

"Do you take more chances now?"

"Heavens, yes." She saw his face and smiled. "I know I'm odd, and your granddad found it wearing—he was happy to do the same things every day, bless him. But I can't. Too many things I've not done, and not much time left to do them." Then she said, pointedly, "It's in my blood." Then came the expected question: "Have you found anything out?" she asked. "About my parents?"

"A tiny bit," he said, "but nothing very helpful."

Rosie pushed herself up in the bed a little. "Well?"

Nick explained about marriages with members of sovereign houses and told Rosie about the true heir to the Russian throne.

"So we're not in line, then?" she asked evenly.

"No." He paused. "But you knew that, didn't you?"

Rosie was silent for a moment. "Yes. But I wanted you to find out for yourself. I wanted you to be curious about your family history."

Nick said nothing, just looked at her lying back on her pillow, eyes a clear forget-me-not blue, skin soft and smooth, lips perfectly made up. She was, he had to admit, the eighth wonder of the world.

"And what about you?" she asked. "Alex. Is it going well?"

"I think so."

"Don't want to rush it? Is that why you're not seeing more of each other?"

He nodded, looking preoccupied. "She's still married—separated, but not divorced—and there's Victoria to think about."

"Oh, those things will sort themselves out." Rosie was dismissive.

"You seem very sure."

"Stands to reason. If she wants you as much as you want her, then the first one needn't be a problem, and Victoria—well, I think she knows a good man when she sees one. Take things a day at a time. Just chill out."

"What?"

"Chill out."

Nick laughed.

Rosie looked concerned. "What's so funny?"

"You are."

"Why?" She was indignant now.

"Nothing. It's nothing."

"Some days I worry about you," Rosie told him.

"Yes," he replied. "And some days I worry about you. Though for the life of me I can't imagine why."

He sat with her for another hour, and when he left, he felt strangely confident. He knew it wouldn't last, but for the moment he would enjoy it. Outside, the rain that had been threatening all day was now falling, that fine rain that soaks you to the skin. He had already put up the hood on the MG and drove home with the inefficient wipers doing their best to clear the windscreen.

He made a dash for the verandah, and as he slipped his key into the lock, he heard the telephone. It took him a moment to recognize the voice at the other end of the line, who was gasping out seemingly disconnected phrases between the sobs: "Paul . . . good-bye . . . Victoria . . . school . . . missing."

WHEN he could finally make sense of what Alex had said, the seriousness of it sank in. Paul had been to see her. He had asked if he could say good-bye to Victoria. She had refused. Victoria had not come home from school. Alex thought it likely that he had taken the child with him. She'd rung him, but there had been no answer.

"Have you told the police?"

"No. Not yet."

"Well, I think you should."

"Oh, God!"

Nick could hear the rising panic in her voice.

"Has she taken anything with her?" he asked, not knowing why that should be important but clutching at straws. "Clothes, washbag, that sort of thing."

"No. Only the clothes she was wearing. And her school bag."

"And she didn't say anything this morning?"

"No." Her desperation was audible.

"Was she okay?"

"She's been a bit distant lately. Her mind's been elsewhere. She always has her head buried in that Isle of Wight guidebook she made me buy her . . . Oh, Nick . . . You don't think she's gone to the island, do you?"

"It's possible. She didn't say anything about coming here?"

"Nothing."

"I think she's most likely to be with Paul, if you want my honest opinion, but I'll go and look in all the places she knew. Sleepyhead Bay and the place where you stayed. I'll ask Sophie to wait here in case she shows up."

"But how will I get in touch with you?" Alex asked.

"Ring The Anchorage and let Sophie know if anything happens. I'll give her both your numbers so that she can call you."

After a few more placatory phrases, he put down the phone and went to the yacht club to find Sophie.

"SHE'S what?"

"Gone missing."

"Oh, hell! Any clues?"

"Well, her father, Paul, came round just before Victoria was expected home from school, and Alex wouldn't let him stay to see her."

"Was that wise?"

"Victoria's always in a state when her father's been. I think Alex was just trying to keep her on an even keel. Anyway, she thinks Paul might have taken her, and it does seem likely. The only other thing is that she was welded to an Isle of Wight guidebook. I think she's fallen for the place."

"Oh, poor Alex." Then the organizer in Sophie came to the fore. "I'll get back to the house. Have you rung the ferry company to see if she was spotted coming over? No? Then I'll do that. You go and look wherever you think she might be. Now, take this." She handed him a mobile phone. "It's new. I've stuck the number on it so I don't forget. I'll ring Alex and give her the number; then she can ring you—or ring me at The Anchorage—if she hears anything. Now get off and look." Sophie strode off up the lane in the direction of The Anchorage.

"Thanks!" he yelled after her.

The sun was sinking below the horizon as he walked down the steps to Sleepyhead Bay. The rain had stopped, but the rough wooden planks were wet and slippery, as were the rocks in the cove. He hopped from one to another, looking for a small girl he hoped might be fishing for shrimps.

He knocked on the doors of the small cottages, but with no luck. Nobody had seen a small girl on her own. He tried the hotel where Alex and Victoria had stayed. They remembered mother and daughter but had seen neither of them since. On he drove, to places where he knew Alex had taken Victoria, but his inquiries yielded nothing, and it was getting dark.

At half past eight, he rang Sophie. "Have you heard anything?" he asked.

"No. But they had a school party on board the last ferry. They said it's possible she could have slipped on without them seeing."

"Damn." He tried to think straight. "Oh, Soph, what do I do now?"

"Ring Alex and tell her you've no news—bad or good."

He did as Sophie suggested and told Alex where he had searched.

"Is there still no sign of Paul?"

"No. The police have alerted the airports and the ferry terminals, and they're talking to the Newport station."

"Look, I'm not giving up. We'll find her. You mustn't think the worst."

"I'm so glad you're there," whispered Alex. "I don't know what I'd do without you."

As he set off again on his search, patchy cloud gave way to small expanses of sky studded with stars, and the moon ducked in and out. Victoria was out there somewhere. But where? Where would a child go if she was disturbed by her parents splitting up and was looking for some kind of escape? She'd look for somewhere comforting. Somewhere she felt at home . . .

His reverie was broken by the shrill ring of the mobile phone in his pocket. He pulled over and answered the call.

"Nick?"

"Soph?"

"I think I've seen her. I was making some tea about five minutes ago, and I glanced up at the window, and I'm sure I saw a face. I ran out as fast as I could, but I couldn't see anyone. I'm sure I didn't imagine it, though."

"And you think it was Victoria?"

"Well, I only met her once, and I wasn't taking that much notice, but I'm as sure as I can be that it was her. Do you want to phone Alex?"

"Not until we're certain."

He slipped the phone back into his pocket and leaned against the car, gazing up at the moon in the hope that it would offer inspiration.

But the moon wasn't playing. It slid tantalizingly behind a cloud.

The phone in his pocket rang again. This time it was Alex.

"The police say they can't do anything until morning now. Have you found anything?"

He was unable to keep from her the glimmer of hope. "Sophie thinks she saw a face at the window of the cottage and that it was Victoria's."

"Oh, God!"

"Now, stay calm. When Sophie ran outside, there was no sign of anyone. But I reckon if she's here on the island, she's probably sheltering from the rain and there's no way we're going to find her till morning."

"No," she said flatly, trying to hold on to her emotions.

"Why don't you try to get some sleep?" Nick said gently.

"I can't." She let out a sob, and the phone clicked off.

He wished he could be with her. He could only imagine what she was going through. He replaced the phone in his pocket, drove round for a while longer, and then returned to The Anchorage. He found Sophie dozing in an armchair. She started up when he walked in. "Any news?"

Nick flopped onto the sofa. "Nothing. Nothing at all. I'm beginning to wonder if it was your imagination. Maybe it was just rain on the window."

Sophie shook her head. "No, it wasn't. Unless rain wears a woolly hat." She held up a lavender-blue knitted hat. "Found it in the rosebush by the window."

"Why didn't you ring me?" he asked angrily.

"I did. You had no signal."

"Bloody mobile phones! I'm going to phone Alex. I don't think she'll be asleep." He walked over to the phone and dialed the number.

Alex answered almost immediately. "Hello."

"Alex, it's me. Does Victoria have a blue woolly hat?"

"Yes. She always wears it to school, even when it's sunny. In case it rains."

"Thank heavens! We've found it outside the house. On a rose-bush. She must be over here."

WITHIN the hour, the police had turned up at The Anchorage and searched the house and garden. They sat down with Nick and Sophie and questioned them in detail about their knowledge of and relationship with Victoria. When they finally departed, dawn was breaking.

Sophie pushed herself out of the chair. "Better have a shower. No. Come to think of it, you look terrible. You have one."

"No. I can't. I need to start looking again."

With the bossiness reserved for sisters, she ushered him to the bathroom, then cooked him breakfast.

"How do you feel now?" she asked as he slumped down at the table.

"Better than I should," he replied, rubbing his face.

"Nervous energy." Sophie put her hand on his. "Victoria will be fine. You'll see. She'll be cold, fed up, and hungry by now. When you're cold and hungry, two things become irresistible."

Nick looked at her questioningly. "Warmth and food?"

"Exactly." Sophie came to the table and sat down opposite him. "What's Victoria like? Do you get on?"

"I think so, but it must be a bit hard, seeing your dad and mum break up, then having your mum find a new friend so soon."

"I guess so."

"But it just sort of happened. I don't think either of us was look-ing to start a relationship. It just . . . crept up on us."

"Love on the rebound?"

"No. I don't think so. She's fun, good company. No. It's more than that."

"Hey! There's no need to defend yourself. You know what I think?"

Nick shook his head.

"I think you're in love. You're a changed man—you're cheerful, fun to be with. Not like you were with Debs."

Nick raised an eyebrow.

"Sorry, but it's true. She did put a bit of a damper on you."

He nodded. Seeing it clearly for the first time.

"Are you sure you can take on a ready-made family, though?"

"I think that depends on whether or not she's prepared to take on me . . . But it was Victoria who introduced me to her mum."

"She was quite bold, then?"

"Yes. It's since then that she's gotten more thoughtful. She came round one evening with Alex. She was talking to Rosie. They seemed to be getting on really well; then Rosie started talking about the Russian royal family thing."

"What?"

Nick realized he'd put his foot in it. "I forgot to tell you—well, I didn't, actually. I was waiting for the right moment."

"For what?"

"This isn't the right moment either, but, in a nutshell, you know Rosie was born in Russia?"

"Ye-es?"

"And she never knew who her real parents were?"

"Ye-es."

"Well, she's got this bee in her bonnet that she's related to the tsar."

"What?"

"Exactly." Nick got up from the table. "I haven't really got the time to tell you now—I need to get out and start looking again—but the long and the short of it is that Rosie thinks her mother was Grand Duchess Tatiana who was assassinated with the rest of the Russian royal family in 1918, but she doesn't know who her father was."

Sophie cleared her throat. "This is a dream. I'm hallucinating."

"No, you're not." Nick was pulling on his coat and making for the door. "You're just part of a family with some colorful history." He opened the door. "Wish me luck."

Chapter 7

HE DROVE to Carisbrooke. Maybe the castle ruins had captured her imagination. Victoria loved Jane Austen, Alex had said, and Jane Austen had loved the Isle of Wight. Maybe there was a connection.

Leaving the car outside the towering walls, he circumnavigated the castle. It was so large, so impregnable; the vast hill on which it stood must have been capable of withstanding the most determined army. And yet he felt that there was no threat in the air. The castle was protective, benign. Its bloody history was behind it now, and it sat, like some battle-scarred leviathan, on its hill, ready to offer shelter to all who needed it. Perhaps he had become an incurable romantic, but he wanted to believe that the islanders were good people who, on seeing a lost ten-year-old, would take her in, find out where she was from, and get her safely home to her mother.

Then he remembered what Rosie had said during their tea at the Ritz. "People think what the newspapers and the television tell them to think."

Of course there were more good people in the world than bad. It was just that you never heard about them.

Rosie. He had put her out of his mind—there had barely been room for her during the events of the night. She had got on so well with Victoria and would be desperate when she heard the news. Unless . . . He slipped back into the car and drove to the hospital.

He walked down the long corridor, then turned the corner that led into Rosie's ward. She lay in her bed, sipping her morning tea. "Hello, love!" she said. "Guess who's come to visit me?"

At first he could see nobody. But then, as he approached the bed, he saw, at Rosie's shoulder, a small figure sitting on a chair. She was bedraggled and tired, and her face bore a worried frown. "Have you been looking for me?" she asked.

THE PHONE CALLS WERE THE first thing. Alex burst into tears at the news, said, "Thank you, thank you . . . oh, thank you," then hung up to rush for the ferry. He called the police, and then Sophie, who agreed to meet Alex at the ferry terminal. Then he sat down in the hospital waiting room and talked to Victoria, trying to understand.

"I just wanted to see if Rosie was all right," she said.

"I thought you knew she was?"

"I wanted to see for myself." She looked up at him now, suddenly shy. "And I wanted to see you."

Nick felt stunned. "Why?"

"To try to understand what was going on."

Nick put his arm round her. "Is it very confusing?"

Victoria looked at the floor and nodded.

"It's just that . . . well . . . Things happen sometimes, and you don't have much control over them," he said.

She looked up. "Like you and Mum?"

"Yes."

"I just wanted to know if you love her as much as she loves you?"

Her candor took his breath away. "Do you think she loves me?"

Victoria nodded. "Oh, yes. I just think she's a bit scared."

Nick cleared his throat. "I think we're all a bit scared. What do you think?"

She managed a weak smile. "That you're very nice."

Nick gave her a hug. "I think you're nice, too. But why did you run away?"

"Because of Dad. When I was going home from school, I saw him going to the house. I didn't want to see him, so I walked into town and got onto the ferry. I didn't want to make Mum worry. I was going to go back when I'd seen Rosie and you. But it took longer to get to your house than I thought. Then I looked through your window and that lady was there, the one we saw when you were out."

"My sister?"

"I think so. She saw me, so I hid under the verandah, in case she stopped me finding Rosie. When she'd gone, and I knew you weren't there, I walked into Newport. Was Mum cross?"

"She was very worried."

"What about Dad?" She looked frightened now. "Is he coming?"

"No. He's gone. We thought you might have gone with him."

She shook her head violently.

Nick wondered whether he should ask the question but found it impossible not to. "You don't seem to get on with your dad."

Victoria shook her head again.

Nick sat and waited. He didn't like to probe.

Eventually she said, "He's all right with me, but he's not nice to Mum." She looked up at him. "You make her happy." She had a quizzical look on her face. "Are you a good man?"

Nick was taken aback. "Well . . . I try to be."

"Because I think she deserves a good man."

The power of speech temporarily deserted him—such old-fashioned, adult conversation from a ten-year-old! "So do I," he stammered eventually.

"I hope you're not wasting her time."

There was no possible answer to this, so Nick said, "We'd better get you cleaned up. Do you want to come back to the cottage and wait for your mum?"

"If it's not too much trouble."

"Oh, it's no trouble. No trouble at all."

"THIS place is beginning to seem like a seaside hotel."

They were sitting round the small table at The Anchorage—Alex and Victoria, Nick and Sophie.

"Not for long. I'm off next week," said Sophie.

"It wasn't a hint," said Nick, "just an observation."

Alex had been waiting for Nick and Victoria on their return from the hospital. Nick had left them to talk while he and Sophie had gone food shopping.

When they returned, they found mother and daughter curled up together on the sofa, Victoria lying against Alex, who was stroking her hair. They got up when Nick and Sophie came in, and then they had all set about preparing lunch. Nothing more had been said about Victoria's adventure. Until now.

"I'm sorry for all this," said Alex, "but I think we've cleared it up now." She stood up, clearly wanting to change the subject. "How's Rosie?" she asked.

"She comes out of the hospital in a couple of days." Nick told them about the plan for Rosie to stay with Henry.

"Henry? A physiotherapist?" asked Alex.

"I've tried to tell him that he'll have bitten off more than he can chew," Nick said, "but he's insistent. As soon as the doctor gives the nod, Rosie's going back to chez Henry for rest and recuperation."

"He's mad!" opined Sophie. "She'll drive him bonkers."

"No, she won't," Victoria chipped in. "She has lots of good stories."

"Well, I just hope he's appreciative," said Sophie.

Alex asked softly, "Is this wise?"

"Probably not," said Nick. "But if you can stand in the way of those two when they've set their minds on something, you're a lot braver than I am."

"You talk about them as if they were a couple."

"Well, they seem to be, in a funny sort of way. Rosie's old enough to be his mother, but they've taken a shine to each other."

Victoria, who was eating ice cream, said, "I don't think age matters. It's whether or not people are suited that matters."

Without thinking, Sophie said, "And you're an expert on this, are you?"

Victoria nodded. "A bit. Mummy and Daddy were the same age, and they didn't get on. But Nick is much older than Mummy and they do."

"Excuse me!" protested Nick. "I'm only—"

"Ahem." Alex coughed.

"—slightly older," he murmured.

"So, what happens now?" asked Sophie, and began to clear away the plates.

"I think we'll head home," said Alex, looking at her watch.

"Can't we stay here?" asked Victoria, turning her attention fully to her mother and putting down her spoon.

"No, sweetheart. We ought to get back to normal."

"But you can come back soon," offered Nick.

"How soon?"

"We'll see," said Alex. "We'll see."

THROUGH the open bedroom door, Nick and Sophie held their nightly conversation.

"Are you as knackered as I am?" she asked.

"No. I'm more knackered. Stop talking and go to sleep."

"Victoria's wonderfully old-fashioned, isn't she?" she said thoughtfully.

"Comes of reading too much Jane Austen."

Sophie heard a rustle of bedclothes, and then he was standing in the open doorway.

"Do you think she's just old-fashioned or a bit scary?"

She sat up in bed. "She's not scary, just scared."

"Scared of her mum getting it wrong again?"

"Yes."

Nick sat on the edge of Sophie's bed. "With me?"

"Oh, no. Quite the reverse. I think she's worried her mum will let you go."

Nick looked stunned. "Are you sure?"

"Yes. And Victoria's pretty astute, too. She's got a great mum in Alex, but it's not enough. She needs a dad, too. Look at me, I should know."

Nick looked bewildered. "You didn't say anything . . ."

"Of course I didn't. I wasn't going to admit it. But Dad was just never there."

"But you . . ."

"Oh, I always jollied myself along. No point in getting depressed about it. But I got out as soon as I could. That's what makes me keep on traveling. Stupid, really. One day I'll have to stop and face up to it. Life. Relationships. Someone like you, that's what I want. Someone pleasant and malleable."

Nick pushed her shoulder so she fell back against the pillow. "Pleasant and malleable? Is that how you see me?"

"It was meant as a compliment," she said seriously.

"I'll take it as one." He laughed. Then he became serious. "It's a big step, isn't it?"

She sat up again and looked him in the eye.

"Oh, yes. Just make up your mind whether you're ready to become a dad as well as a lover. That kid is not the sort to watch her mum having loads of boyfriends. She wants to believe that all relationships turn out well in the end, like in her Jane Austen novels—that's why she's hooked on them. They're her escape into a world she'd like to live in. I know it's all happened so suddenly, but if you're not serious about Alex—and about Victoria—then get out of this thing right now. Or I'll never forgive you. And I'm your sister."

NICK took his keys from the table and closed the door quietly behind him. Sophie was still asleep. For a moment he stood on the verandah, leaned on the rail, and breathed in the fresh morning air. The sea was unusually calm, like a polished pewter plate.

His thoughts were interrupted by the postman. "You look as if you've lost a shilling and found sixpence."

Nick came to with a start. "Mmm? Sorry?"

"It can't be that bad."

"No, it's not. Morning!"

"I'm glad I caught you. I've got a special for you."

Nick looked down at the package. It was addressed in his father's writing.

HE PULLED up on a small, rough track that looked out over the bay. He had not wanted to open the package in the house, where Sophie might have appeared and been curious.

He ripped off the tape and slid out the contents. A small white linen bag landed in his hand. He loosened the knot and tipped out the contents. In his palm lay four large diamonds. From memory they were not the ones he had handed over to the heavies at his father's request, but they were of a similar size and clarity.

He tipped them back into the bag and drew the string tight. Then he fished inside the envelope and pulled out a folded sheet of hotel writing paper. There was no date.

Dear Nick,

Sorry I had to ask you to do that bit of business for me, but it all seems to have turned out okay. I'd have done the job myself but I had rather pressing business here in Moscow.

The enclosed were given to me by Rosie to take care of. Well, their friends were. I'm sending them back now in the safest way I know. It would be a good idea if you put them in the bank.

Don't worry, old lad. It's all quite aboveboard.

Yours ever,
Dad

The note was, in his father's usual style, short and sweet. And what did he mean by "well, their friends were"? If these were not Rosie's diamonds, had his father substituted fakes? He must get them valued as soon as possible, but for now he had to put them somewhere safe.

Nick folded the note and slipped it back into the padded envelope with the linen bag. Then he drove straight to the bank and deposited the contents. By the time he arrived at the hospital, his head was swimming, but Rosie was on cracking form.

"I think I've sorted them out."

"Sorted who out?"

"The nurses here. One of them has boyfriend trouble, and the other one's husband has just run off."

"Oh."

"In a bit of a state, both of them."

"So you sorted them out." There was irony in his tone.

"Are you going to be unpleasant?" Rosie asked, her brow furrowed.

Nick felt suitably chastened. "Sorry. It's been a bit of a morning, that's all."

She was sitting up in bed, fresh as a daisy, her hair coiffed, her lipstick freshly applied, and her cheeks rouged. She looked like a duchess about to receive visitors at a morning audience. How appropriate, he thought, and smiled.

"Victoria's all right now?" she asked.

"Yes, thank God."

"And Alex?"

"As far as I know." He looked distracted.

"Oh. That sounds ominous." He didn't reply, so she took his hand. "Sorry. I expect Sophie gave you the female point of view?"

"Yes," he admitted.

"She's good at that." Rosie chuckled. "Headstrong we used to call it. It sounds old-fashioned now, what with all this feminism stuff."

"Are you not a feminist, then?"

"Oh, yes. A different kind, though. Wily."

"In what way?"

"Well, I look at all these women moaning on about men. Using a sledgehammer to crack a nut. You don't have to do that. You can get where you want to go much more quickly if you gentle them along—flatter them, flutter your eyelashes, instead of all this bra-burning business."

"But wasn't that liberating?"

"Only for breasts. Damned uncomfortable for everything else." She was warming to her subject now, eyes glowing. It was good to see her back on form, bright as a button, trying to shock.

"And another thing. Breast enlargements. Why do they make them so big?"

"Keep your voice down!"

"What sort of man is going to want to go out with a woman with a pair of footballs fastened to her chest?"

"Stop it!"

"I mean, she only has to turn round sharpish and she'll knock you over."

She paused. Nick was squeezing in the sides of his mouth to stifle the laughter. "Stop, stop!" he said.

Rosie lay back on her pillow. "Better now?"

He nodded. "Much better." And then, with feeling, "Thank you."

"Don't mention it, love. And you just keep your end up."

"Rosie!"

"Oh, I know. It's a difficult time, and lots of people's emotions are involved, but don't underestimate your own. Just remember that your feelings are as important as anybody else's. You're a good man, and Alex'll see that."

"Victoria asked me if I was a good man."

Rosie shook her head. "Funny child. Astute."

"And scared? Sophie thinks she's scared."

"Oh, yes. But all children of that age are. They just have different ways of dealing with it. Some lash out. Those like Victoria go into their imagination."

"So how do you solve the problem, apart from just giving it time?"

"If I knew that, love, I'd be sitting in the House of Lords." She smiled.

"Now, there's a thought. You'd look good in ermine."

"And I might have been, mightn't I, if things had turned out differently?" He watched her expression change. "We will find out, won't we?" she asked. "About my mother?"

"Of course." He stroked her hand.

"Only I would like to know before . . . well, soon."

HE PHONED Alex from the hospital. They had not spoken for thirty-six hours. He did not know how she was feeling or what she was doing. He wanted to ask if she and Victoria would like to come over and stay for the weekend, though he was fearful of putting the question; afraid of being turned down.

"I'm not sure," she said. She sounded preoccupied, hesitant. It was as if the passion and conviction they had shared only a few days ago had evaporated.

"Do you want to meet first? To talk?" he asked.

"Yes. Yes, that might be best."

"Shall I come to you?" He knew at once what the answer would be. She seemed anxious to keep him out of her world.

"No. I'll come to you. I'll get the seven o'clock ferry."

"Fine. I'll pick you up."

And she was gone, with no talk of love, just a brief good-bye.

WHEN he got back to The Anchorage, Sophie was packing her bag.

"I thought you weren't going until the weekend?"

"Given you enough grief. Thought I'd better move out."

"Don't be stupid!"

"No, it's all right. You need your space. Especially now."

"But you can stay. I don't mind."

Sophie stopped folding a shirt. "What I said last night. Sorry if I got carried away. Too much wine."

"Don't worry—you were quite right. I was talking to Rosie today, and she was telling me her side of the story."

"Poor Nick. You're getting it from all sides, aren't you?"

"Oh, I can cope. I'm made of tough stuff."

Sophie zipped up her bag and picked up her jacket. She put her head on one side. "Do you know? I think you are!"

HE WAS waiting for her in the MG at half past six, in case the ferry was early. They never were, but tonight he wanted to be sure.

Eventually the ferry shimmied up to the slipway, and the ramp descended. Cars flooded off, and to either side of them came foot passengers: teenagers with rucksacks, parents with children, old men and women, some with sticks. There were a couple of dogs and half a dozen cyclists, but no sign of Alex.

Perhaps she was waiting until all the traffic had disembarked. Yes, that must be it. But after ten minutes, when the last car and pedestrian had walked up the slipway, and the cars for the return crossing were being driven down to the water's edge and up the ramp of the ferry, he realized she had not come.

He got out of the car, ran across to the booking office, bought a ticket, then drove onto the ferry. He had her address. If she wouldn't come to him, he'd go to her.

The ferry seemed to take an age, waltzing around the Solent as though it were on a dance floor. He looked at his watch. A quarter to eight. With any luck he'd be there within fifteen minutes. Thirty at the outside.

HE FOUND it difficult to talk in front of Victoria, and so did Alex. "Why don't you pop up to your room, sweetheart?" she said.

Victoria looked from one to the other. "Do I have to?"

"Yes," Alex told her.

"Okay." She paused in the kitchen doorway and said, "Good-bye, Nick."

He raised a hand, then turned back to Alex, who was filling the kettle. "Why did you say you would come?"

"Because I didn't want to disappoint you." She looked agonized. "I'm sorry, I really am." She motioned him to sit at the kitchen table.

"What is it?" he asked. "It seemed to be going so well. Even when Victoria went missing, we found her together."

"I know. It's just that . . ." She seemed reluctant to meet his eye. She looked embarrassed, ashamed. "I just think we'd better stop seeing each other."

"But why?"

"Because I don't want to upset Victoria any more. She's been through a lot lately, what with her dad leaving, and then going missing . . ."

"But she only went missing because she wanted to see Rosie."

"No. She went missing because she was upset, unsettled, and frightened."

"Is that what she said? She told me it was because she wanted to see Rosie." He hesitated. "And me."

Alex studied him carefully, then came and sat down. "I can't risk anything going wrong between her and me. I just can't. She's all I've got."

Nick sat back. "She's not. You've got me; you know you have."

Alex shook her head. "No, I don't. I know we've had a good time, but I don't really know you. And you don't really know me. It might be fun for a few more weeks, months even, but what if it all ended then? Where would that leave Victoria?"

Nick bridled. "How can you say that? How can you say that we simply 'had a good time'? You know it was more than that."

She spoke quickly now. "You just can't see why I have to do this, can you?"

"No, I can't."

"But then you've never had a child."

He was stung and hesitated a moment before he spoke. "It doesn't mean I can't see how important Victoria is and why it's important that she's happy. But you can't simply live your life for her."

"Why not? I brought her into the world. She's my responsibility. I can't mess up."

He was exasperated now. "Why this obsession with 'messing up'? It can't be right to shut yourself away and not have any relationships of your own."

"The point is that Victoria's life—"

"Victoria, Victoria, always Victoria! What about Alex?" Nick stood up. "You have a bright child up there"—he pointed in the direction of Victoria's room—"and she'll know it makes no sense for her mother to be alone."

"She's only ten—"

"Yes, and she's sharper than many fifteen-year-olds. But she's not emotionally equipped yet, and treating her like some china doll isn't going to help her."

"And neither is a string of boyfriends."

"Oh, I see." He was angry now. "You reckon I'm first in a long line, do you?"

"No. But that's what might happen."

"It might. But that's not my intention. I came here because I love you, and I want to be with you. And I've thought about Victoria, too. I know how important she is to you, and she'll become important to me, if you give me a chance. But if you just shut yourself away because of what might happen, then you'll never know joy. The sort of joy that we knew the other night. Or am I the one who's fooling myself?"

"No," she said quietly. "You're not. But you can't promise that it will turn out all right."

"No, I can't. But I can promise you I'll try—with every fiber in my body. If it doesn't work out in the end, I'll have done everything I possibly can to make it work, and that must count for something."

The kettle's shrill whistle brought a halt to the conversation. Alex got up and turned off the gas. "I'm sorry. It's just that with Paul coming back and Victoria going off the rails . . ."

"She didn't go off the rails." He spoke softly now, his tone conciliatory. "She just got a bit . . . lost inside herself."

"And I wasn't there."

"You were. It's just that Paul was there, too, and that threw her."

Alex turned to face him. "I'm sorry." She lowered her head, and he could see tears flowing down her cheeks. He walked across to comfort her, but she turned away from him and stared out of the window. Then she wiped her face with the back of her hand. "You'd better go now. It'll be for the best. Sorry."

He stood for a moment, one hand outstretched as if it was frozen. He lowered it. "What a lot of sorries," he said. And then, quietly, "Good-bye."

As he left, he did not turn back. If he had, he would have seen the face of a small girl framed in the upstairs window.

Chapter 8

HENRY was beside Rosie's bed as soon as the hospital doors opened. "You're amazing!" he said.

"Why's that?" she asked.

"Look at you! It's barely eight thirty, and you're all done up and ready to go!"

"Well, they wake us up so early, and I've never been one to hang around. Not that I've got much choice on that front."

"How's the walking coming along?"

"Slowly. And it's a bit painful. Anyway, I've been thinking."

"That sounds dangerous."

"Be serious, Henry. If I do come and stay with you . . . Well, there are one or two things I want to sort out."

"Yes?"

She was clearly trying to measure her words. "Well . . . I will have my own bedroom, won't I?"

Henry roared with laughter. "Of course you will! Good heavens! The very idea! I'd be struck off."

Rosie brightened. "Well, I knew I would, really. It's just that we've never talked about . . . arrangements, and I thought we should."

"Quite so." Henry tried to suppress a smile, not altogether successfully.

"And then there's the problem of getting dressed. I'm very self-sufficient—but at the moment it's a bit difficult to . . ."

Henry patted her hand. "I've thought of all that. The niece who's coming over to help me in the gallery is a sweet girl, and she can do all the bits you wouldn't want me doing."

"I see." She looked thoughtful. "Why are you going to all this trouble? I'm no catch, you know."

Henry laughed again. "On that subject, madam, I beg to differ." He smiled at her, his eyes twinkling. "Do you really want to know? Honestly?"

Rosie nodded. "Yes. Honestly."

"There are two reasons." Henry pushed his hands into his pockets. "One is because when my mother grew older, I saw what an amazing lady she was. I was too late to help her at the end, and I never managed to tell her that."

"I see. So you're salving your conscience by looking after me?"

"A bit," he admitted. "The second reason is that I don't think I've ever met anyone like you in my life."

"Oh, Henry!" She smiled, then looked down coyly.

"It's true! You make me laugh, and you make me glad to be alive."

"Well . . ." Rosie glanced away. "I don't know what to say."

Through the dampness in his own eyes, he saw the tears in Rosie's. "Don't say anything, then." He cleared his throat. "Don't they serve coffee here?"

"Not until nine o'clock, but if you turn on the charm with that nurse over there, I'm sure she'll oblige. In a manner of speaking."

ALEX threw back the covers, got out of bed, stretched, then caught sight of herself in the mirror, standing there with her dark hair tumbling over her shoulders, her body encased in a baggy white T-shirt. God, she looked old. Wearily she crossed the landing.

She tapped on Victoria's door, then opened it. The child was sitting up in bed with a book. "Don't you ever stop reading?" asked Alex teasingly.

Victoria shook her head, still concentrating.

"What is it today?" She pushed back her hair.

Victoria held up *Sense and Sensibility*.

"Again?"

Victoria shrugged. "I like the stories."

"Do you know how many other ten-year-olds read those books?"

"No."

"Very few."

"It's not wrong, is it?" Victoria asked anxiously.

"Of course not." Her mother ruffled her hair.

"Read a bit to me?"

"Oh, love, I don't think I can focus at this hour."

"Please!" There was insistence in her voice, but not of the sort that says "if you don't, I'll make your life hell for the rest of the day." Just a positive note that made Alex sit on the edge of the bed and take up the book.

"From there," instructed Victoria, pointing to a passage in the book.

"Budge up, then." Alex slipped into bed beside her daughter, who rested her head on her shoulder as she read.

" 'Marianne Dashwood was born to an extraordinary fate. She was born to discover the falsehood of her own opinions, and to counteract, by her conduct, her most favorite maxims. She was born to overcome an affection formed so late in life as at seventeen, and with no sentiment superior to strong esteem and lively friendship, voluntarily to give her hand to another!' " Alex stopped.

"Go on! Go on!"

Alex spoke softly. " 'And that other, a man who had suffered no less than herself under the event of a former attachment . . .' "

She closed the book. "Oh," she murmured.

It was midway through the afternoon when the hospital called. Nick was cleaning a wooden garden bench with wire wool. It was a mindless task, but the only thing he could settle to. When the phone rang, he dropped what he was doing and ran inside, hoping it might be Alex. When he discovered it was a nurse, his heart sank.

"Mr. Robertson? It's Sister Bettany from the hospital. It's Mrs. Robertson. She's a little under the weather, and we wondered if you could come in."

"Of course. I'll be there as soon as I can. Is she . . . ?"

"She's comfortable at the moment, but she'd like to see you."

"Yes, of course."

His mind raced as he made the short drive to the hospital. As he walked down the corridor to the ward, Sister Bettany put her head out of her office and beckoned him in.

"Is it serious?" he asked.

"It's difficult to say," she said. "She has a urinary infection. She was fine earlier, but she's declined over the day."

"But will she recover?"

"Oh, we hope so. She's strong for an old lady, but we must take account of her age."

Nick was more worried than ever now. Nobody took account of Rosie's age, because she took no account of it herself. He walked along to her bed. Her eyes were closed. He sat down and took her hand. He squeezed it gently, and she opened her eyes. She smiled. "Hello, my love. How are you?" she whispered.

He was appalled to see her so weak.

"I'm fine, but what about you?"

She tried to say something, failed, and drifted off again.

He sat with her for an hour as she slept fitfully. Then he walked down to the office and waited for Sister Bettany to return from her rounds.

"We'll keep a close eye on her for the next day or so," she said. "Pop in whenever you want."

"Thank you." It was all so sudden. Things seemed to have been going so well. He asked the obvious question. "Does this mean she won't be coming out quite so quickly?"

"Yes, I'm afraid so. We'll just have to play it by ear now."

"Yes, of course." He hesitated. "How serious is it?"

"Serious but not critical," she said. She smiled kindly.

HENRY was incredulous. "But I was with her first thing this morning, and she was in fine fettle."

"I know. Apparently it happened quite suddenly."

Henry plonked himself down on a wooden captain's chair, which creaked under his weight. "Well, I'll be . . . she was so . . ."

Nick nodded. "I know."

"So I suppose I can stand my niece down."

"Yes. I'm afraid they don't know when she'll be coming out now."

Henry looked at him. "And are you all right?"

"Yes. Yes, I'm fine," he said distractedly.

"Well, you don't look it. You look exhausted. Let me make you some coffee with something stronger in it." Henry pushed himself out of the chair.

"Thanks." Nick wandered through to the back room in the wake of his burly patron.

Henry switched on the kettle. "And that's not all, is it?"

"Mmm?" Nick was distant. Preoccupied.

"There's something else, isn't there?" And then, seeing he was not getting through, "Woman trouble, is it?"

"What?" Nick came to. "What do you mean?"

"Look, dear boy, I've not asked any questions—I've been very circumspect, and after all, it's none of my business, but if two of my protégés are at a tricky stage in their relationship, I'd just like to know."

Nick hesitated, then tried to speak but settled instead for a sigh.

Henry busied himself with cups, sugar, and coffee, and spoke over his shoulder. His tone was gentle, his language considered. "Look. It was never going to be easy, was it? There's a lot of history there."

Nick was staring at the floor. "It's all so confusing," he murmured.

"Oh. Right. Well, if we're going there, you'll need quite a large tot." He tipped a generous measure of Famous Grouse into the coffee and handed the cup to Nick. "She did talk to me, you know," Henry went on. "Alex."

Nick took a sip of the brew and gasped at its strength.

"Nothing intimate. Not about you," Henry assured him, "but about . . . what was his name? Paul."

Nick said nothing.

Henry continued. "He wasn't the most faithful of husbands, you see. He was a serial adulterer, by the sound of it. Traveled a lot, woman in every port—that sort of thing. She never found out until about three years ago, when he started living a double life, half in the States and half over here."

Nick was shocked. "She didn't tell me about the women."

"No? Well, it's not something to boast about. Eventually she told him she'd had enough. He agreed to go—there was yet another woman. Now she just wants to give her daughter a fresh start."

"I know. That's the trouble." Nick paused. "She doesn't seem to set much store by her own happiness. She'd rather stay on her own so that Victoria has a stable upbringing."

"Shame," said Henry.

"That's what I think." Nick drained his cup. "I'd better be off."

"What are you going to do now?"

"Who knows? I'll go back and see Rosie this evening. Nothing else to do except"—he pointed to the walls of the gallery—"fill these, I suppose. But I can't get into the mood."

"Look," said Henry, "there's no pressure. I have enough to keep me going for a week or so. You'll need time to sort Rosie out, and yourself. Concentrate on the important things for now." As Nick closed the door, he shouted after him, "Both of them."

BY EVENING, Rosie seemed to have rallied a little. Nick sat with her, holding her hand, for the better part of two hours. Sometimes she drifted off to sleep, sometimes she woke and lay with her eyes open but said nothing. Then her eyes would close again.

He worried about her long-term prospects. She couldn't die! She was never ill! He needed her to get better and listen to him. Then he was ashamed of his selfishness.

Someone touched his shoulder, and he looked up.

Alex was standing over him. "Hello," she said.

He slipped his hand out of Rosie's and got up. "Hello," he said uncertainly.

They looked at each other; then Alex put her arms round him and laid her head on his chest. "I'm sorry."

At first he thought she was talking about Rosie. "They think she'll be all right, but they can't be certain yet," he said stiffly.

Alex nodded. "I do hope so." She stepped away from him.

"Thank you for coming," he said, hoping that she'd leave soon and not prolong the agony.

"I had to come. Too many things to say."

Nick looked at her quizzically.

"I was a bit hasty," she went on. "Like you said, if I shut myself away in case of what might happen, I'll never know joy. . . ." There was a catch in her voice. "And I'd quite like to know joy. So, if it's all right with you . . ."

Nick held out his arms and said, "Come here."

Alex saw the tears welling up and wrapped her arms round him again.

"I'm so glad you're back," he whispered. "So glad."

LATER that evening, he took her to the ferry, kissed her tenderly, then watched the lights of the vessel recede into the distance. She had gone again, but this time he knew she would return.

Tomorrow was Sunday, and she had said she would bring Victoria over for the day. His pleasure at the prospect was tempered by concern for Rosie. He looked up at the star-filled sky and hoped with all his heart that both of the women he loved would make tomorrow a day to remember.

"I HAVE a surprise for you," said Alex.

They were sitting in a café at Seaview, breakfasting outdoors in the early morning sun before they drove to Newport to see Rosie.

"Mummy's been researching," Victoria told him.

"That sounds very official."

"Well, I promised you I'd do some digging around to see if I could discover anything about Rosie's parents," Alex said. "And I've been at the library in Portsmouth." Alex dug into her rucksack. "You know you said that Rosie's mother's name—I mean her real mother—was given as Matilda Kitching?"

Nick dipped a piece of croissant into his coffee and popped it into his mouth. "Well?"

"And her father's name"—Alex flipped through her shorthand pad until she found the page she wanted—"was George Michaels?"

"Yes." Nick nodded as he chewed.

"Well, as Rosie said, there was no mention of either in the National Archive at Kew. Not with the right dates, anyway."

"No joy, then?"

"Not until I started to look at the names of other people involved, who might have been around at the time."

"And?" Nick took a sip of coffee.

"George Michaels was supposed to be part of a British delegation, wasn't he? I tracked down that particular visit. It struck me that I'd often seen pictures of the two of them—George the Fifth and the tsar—in naval uniform. I found a naval archive in Portsmouth library that dealt with diplomatic relations between the British and Russian navies during the late nineteenth and early twentieth centuries. In 1917, the British sent a secret delegation to Russia. It was during the First World War, remember, so it must have been difficult."

"They didn't give the names of all the people involved, did they?" asked Nick excitedly.

Alex paused, the better to build the tension. "Oh, yes, they did. The junior naval attaché at the Admiralty was called . . . George Carmichael."

"You clever thing!" Nick made to take the pad from Alex's hand.

"Not so fast. I've not finished yet."

Victoria beamed. "She's very clever, isn't she?"

"Brilliant!" he agreed.

"That was too much of a coincidence to pass over. But what it didn't do, of course, was give me any information about the mother. It also failed to show any meeting between the grand duchesses and the delegation. In fact, they had been in two different places—the delegation was sent to Murmansk, right up north on the Barents Sea. Murmansk had only been linked to St. Petersburg by rail in 1916 and was just about to become an important port because it remained ice-free all the year round. Anyway, when the delegation was in Murmansk, most of the royal family were in St. Petersburg, more than five hundred miles away, and there is no record of the delegation going there. They sailed from Portsmouth, up round the Norwegian coast and the North Cape, direct to Murmansk, where they met the tsar. They did not go via the Baltic to St. Petersburg and take the train north."

"Which knocks Rosie's theory on the head," said Nick.

"Well, it does seem to rule out the grand duchesses."

"I feel a but coming on," said Nick.

"And there is one. Before he was married, the tsar had a mistress. Now, I can only guess at this, and I may be wrong, and there are a lot of ifs."

"Go on."

"If the tsar had not relinquished his mistress, and they still had liaisons, and one happened to be in Murmansk during the occasion of the naval delegation . . . and if the mistress did not confine her attentions to the tsar . . ."

"You're right—there are a lot of ifs."

"It would hardly stand up in court. Pure conjecture, that's all."

"But what was the mistress's name?"

Alex spun the book round and showed him. "Mathilde Kschessinska."

He was stunned. "Matilda Kitching?" he wondered aloud.

"It's possible." She smiled tentatively.

"What happened to her?"

"She eventually married one of the tsar's cousins, Grand Duke Andrei, in Cannes in 1921."

"They escaped the revolution, then?"

"Yes, although Mathilde's mansion was ransacked. She eventually ran a ballet studio in Paris—even taught Margot Fonteyn."

"But she's dead now?"

"Oh, yes."

"So I don't suppose we'll ever know for certain?"

Alex shook her head. "It seems unlikely."

Nick squeezed her hand. "Thank you for going to all the trouble."

THE three of them walked down the long corridor toward Rosie's bed, Victoria in the middle, holding Nick and Alex's hands.

As they rounded the corner, they saw Rosie propped up on a mountain of pillows. She raised both hands in greeting, and Victoria rushed across to plant a kiss on her cheek.

"Hello, sweetheart!" Rosie murmured. "How lovely to see you."

Nick and Alex bent down and kissed her, too, and Nick asked, "How are you?"

"Oh, you know. A bit feak and weeble," she said to Victoria, who grinned at the little joke.

"Mummy's been finding things out," volunteered Victoria. "About your mummy and daddy."

Rosie's face brightened. "Has she?"

Nick cut in: "She's been working very hard, but I think we should tell you later when you can take it all in."

Rosie did not demur. She half closed her eyes. "Weary. Sorry."

Nick glanced at Alex, who read his mind. "Come on, Victoria. We'll let Rosie rest for a while," she said. "We'll come back later." And then, softly, to Nick, "We'll wait for you by the car."

He nodded in agreement, and they left with a wave. Then he sat on a chair and leaned close to Rosie's head.

"Sorry," she whispered. "It was lovely to see them both."

"Yes."

"Lucky boy." She opened her eyes and nodded in the direction Alex and Victoria had gone. "Special. Very special."

"I know." He stroked her cheek lightly. "You sleep now," he said. "We all need you better."

She smiled weakly and closed her eyes again.

"WOULD you come with me to the jeweller's to have them valued?" he asked Alex quietly.

"But isn't it a bit personal? I mean, do you really want me to know?"

They were sitting on the verandah at The Anchorage, sipping coffee after an early dinner. Victoria was sitting in Nick's dinghy, pulled out from beneath the verandah and beached on the rough grass in front of the house. Her head was buried in a book.

"I don't want to have any secrets from you. Not even financial ones." Nick was adamant. "Could you come over again tomorrow?"

Alex smiled resignedly. "I'm turning into a commuter. But I'll have to be back for Victoria coming out of school. If I catch the nine o'clock ferry over, I could take the two o'clock back. Would that be okay?"

"Fine. I shall miss you, though, when you go. I always miss you." Nick stood up, lifted her off her chair, and sat down with her on his lap.

"Hey!" she said. "I'm far too heavy for this. You'll regret it."

"Never." He put his arms round her waist, and they watched Victoria in the boat until the sun sank behind the Dorset hills.

NICK was nervous. He had the entire contents of the bank safety-deposit box in the inside pocket of his jacket. Before they made their way to the jeweller's, he opened the bag in the car to show Alex.

"Oh, my God, they're huge!" she said. "Are you sure they're real?"

"Well, no, I'm not—apart from the one Rosie gave me."

Alex pushed at them with her finger. "I've never seen anything like them. And you don't know where they came from?"

"Not exactly. Rosie said she converted her savings into diamonds—bought in London presumably—then handed them to Dad for safekeeping. She kept mine back to give me on my birthday. That's this one." He indicated the smallest of the five stones.

"And you think the other four came from Russia?"

"That's what the hotel writing paper said." Nick had already explained about the visits from his father and the two heavies.

"And the note said nothing about where they were from?"

"Here it is." Nick handed the note to Alex.

Alex read it. Then she repeated, " 'The enclosed were given to me by Rosie to take care of. Well, their friends were.' Then these aren't the diamonds Rosie gave him?"

"No. But are they better ones or fakes?" He tipped the stones back into the bag. "There's only one way to find out, isn't there?"

ELLIOTT Williams, the jeweller, reached under the counter and took out a roll of dark blue velvet, which he smoothed out across the glass surface. Nick handed him the small linen bag and watched as he undid the top and tipped the stones out onto the fabric.

At first the jeweller said nothing. He put the magnifying loupe into his eye and held up each stone to it for what seemed an age. As he lowered the last of the five stones, he removed the glass from his eye and cleared his throat. "Yes, well . . . We have here three different grades of diamond." He gently pushed the one Rosie had given Nick toward the front of the cloth with his little finger. "This one is pretty good. Not flawless, but very fine nevertheless. Value? Around the twenty to twenty-five thousand mark."

"That's what I thought," said Nick involuntarily. Elliott Williams shot him a look. "Oh, that's the only one I was given a value for," Nick added.

"Right. These three here"—the jeweller pushed a matching trio forward—"are internally flawless and worth probably around seventy-five thousand apiece."

"Gosh!" Nick tried to hide his surprise.

"And this one—" Elliott Williams pushed forward a diamond the size of his fingernail—"is flawless. Quite beautiful and very well cut. It will be worth between seven hundred and seven hundred and fifty thousand pounds."

Alex gasped. Nick said, "Good God!" and Elliott Williams said, "You're a very lucky man."

"Yes. I suppose I am." And then, "Are you sure I don't owe you anything for the valuation?"

"Absolutely not. It was my pleasure to see them. And if you need them set—in a ring or a pendant—I'll be happy to do the job for you."

"Thank you. Yes. Thank you very much."

The jeweller scooped up the diamonds, tipped them back into the bag, pulled the drawstring tight, and handed it back over the counter. "I'd get to the bank as soon as you can, sir," he said.

"Yes. Thank you. We will. And thank you again."

ONCE Alex was safely on the ferry to Portsmouth, Nick drove to the hospital and was delighted to find Rosie sitting up in bed, hair and makeup in apple-pie order.

"Look at you!" he said.

"I did. In the mirror. Much better," she retorted.

"Are you back to your old self?" he asked.

"Getting there. Oh, I did feel ropy, but I'm on the mend, I think."

He bent to kiss her and was relieved to smell Chanel No. 5 once more. "You really had us worried," he said, patting the back of her hand.

"Oh, I'm a tough old bird," Rosie replied, but he noticed that her voice did not hold its usual conviction. "What have you been up to?" she asked.

"I found a girl, and she found me." He sat down and tried not to sound too pleased.

"Anyone I know?" she asked.

"Oh, yes." He beamed.

"Two girls, then? That's nice."

"Are you sure you're okay?" he asked. Something about her seemed not quite right.

"Yes, of course," she said. "Anyway, I'm glad about you." She smoothed the blanket. "You said yesterday that you had some news for me, didn't you, about my mother? Or was I dreaming?"

Nick hesitated. "Yes. But only when you're ready."

"I'm ready. Go on. Tell me."

The prospect of disappointing her filled him with dread, but he told her of Alex's researches, the delegation and George Carmichael. Then he mentioned Mathilde Kschessinska. "MK, the same initials."

"Well I never. So instead of using my real mother's name, Tatiana, they used one belonging to the tsar's previous mistress to avoid suspicion?"

Nick found it impossible to contradict her: She thought the naval attaché had had an affair with Grand Duchess Tatiana and that the tsar's former mistress had been brought in as a smoke screen.

He shrugged. "That's as much as we've been able to find out," he said.

Rosie's eyes were shining now. "So they did exist. This man, George Carmichael, did go there. And it's true."

Nick could only smile, he hoped not deceitfully.

"Oh, what a relief." Rosie put out her hand and took his. "I knew you'd come through for me."

"Not me. Alex."

Rosie nodded. "Good girl. I knew she would, too." She looked at him pleadingly. "Do something for me?"

"Of course."

"When you next hear from your dad . . ." She beckoned him closer. "Thank him for sorting out the diamonds."

"What?" He was astonished.

Rosie pointed to her bedside cabinet. "There's a letter from him in there."

Nick opened the door, and among the cotton wool and tissues, he found a letter on identical stationery to the one he had received from his father.

"How did he know where you were?" he asked.

"Oh, your father seems to know everything. Open it."

Nick did so, and unfolded the letter.

Dear Rosie,

I hope this finds you well. I took care of the stones as you asked, but I had an opportunity to make them grow a bit. Don't ask how. There was nothing underhand about the deal (I know you worry about that!), but I've been doing a bit of business over here—Russian capitalists are grateful for all the help they can get from wide-boy Westerners like me and have interesting ways of showing their gratitude.

I've sent the stones back to Nick—the slightly better versions of them—and told him to put them in a bank for safekeeping. I'll leave you to tell him what they're all for.

See you soon. And don't worry.

Your boy Derek xxx

"So, does Dad keep in touch with you, then, when nobody else knows where he is?"

"Sometimes. When he feels like it."

"But the diamonds . . ."

"Mmm?"

"I had them valued today."

"Did you? Well, don't tell me," said Rosie. "I don't want to know."

"As well as the one you gave to me, there are four, one large one and three smaller ones."

"That's right. Now, can you make sure that, of the three smaller ones, one each goes to Sophie and Alice—wherever they happen to be. I know Sophie's gone off on the toot again because she came and told me. And Alice is in South . . . well, you know."

"I'll make sure they get them," he assured her.

"And you've got yours, haven't you? But it was a bit smaller than the ones your dad sent back, or so he said."

"Oh, that doesn't matter," Nick said dismissively.

"Well, hopefully it doesn't. You see, the third one is for Alex."

At first he thought he had misheard her. "What do you mean?"

"Well, I could see that you two were made for each other. And it wasn't just that you were called Nicholas and Alexandra. I'm not that stupid."

"You can't—"

"Oh, I can. Old lady's prerogative. You can't stop me."

"I suppose not."

"And the last one . . . the last one is to be sold and the proceeds are to be put into a trust fund. I don't know what it will amount to, but it should make sure that the brightest little girl I've ever encountered gets a decent education." She looked hard at Nick. "I take it you're managing to keep up?"

"Victoria?" he asked.

Rosie nodded. "Yes. Something tells me she's going to be very special."

"But this is so sudden! How do you know—"

"How do I know that you'll stick together?"

Nick nodded.

"I don't. I just have a feeling. And it's such a strong feeling that I see no reason to question it. Sometimes you have to rely on your instincts. You're a good man, and she's a good woman. You're also crazy about each other, and the child. Anyone can see that. You've got your heads screwed on. You'll manage."

Nick's face bore the expression of someone with a concussion.

Rosie leaned back on her pillow mountain and smiled. "Go on," she said. "Say it for me."

"Say what?"

"Oh, I think you know."

For a moment he looked bewildered, and then he smiled. And as he smiled, so the tears welled up in his eyes. "You know," he said, "you really crack me up."

Just three days later, Rosie Robertson died peacefully in her sleep. Nick was with her, holding her hand. There were no last words, just a sigh, and a great calm. He eased his hand out of hers and kissed her forehead. Unable to stop the tears cascading down his face, he sat with his head in his hands for a while and wept, remembering nothing but the good times.

Victoria, too, took it hard. It was her first experience of death.

Alex was a rock to them both, and a comforting shoulder to cry on. There were lots of tears, but Rosie had left many happy memories—and quite a lot of money. It was some time before Alex could come to terms with her bequest and her daughter's legacy. "For now," she said, "do you mind if I just leave it in the bank?"

The day of the funeral was warm and sunny. There were few people at the Newport crematorium. Henry spent most of his time blowing his nose into a large red and white spotted handkerchief, and blaming the pollen from the flowers. Rosie would have liked that.

There were no hymns, just prayers of thanksgiving, and Rosie had asked that Nick read something for her. It took all his willpower to get through it, but get through it he did. With clarity and with great feeling, he spoke the words of a poem that Rosie had loved:

Do not stand at my grave and weep;
I am not there. I do not sleep.
I am a thousand winds that blow.
I am the diamond glints on snow.
I am the sunlight on ripened grain.
I am the gentle autumn rain.
When you awaken in the morning's hush
I am the swift uplifting rush
Of quiet birds in circled flight.
I am the soft stars that shine at night.
Do not stand at my grave and cry:
I am not there. I did not die.

And then came the only piece of music in the short ceremony, which generated both smiles and tears as it rang out from the speakers at the front of the chapel. Rosie's coffin disappeared to the strains of "Lara's Theme" from *Dr. Zhivago.* Whether or not she had come into the world as a Russian princess, she certainly went out as one.

It was only as they emerged into the sunlight that Nick noticed the solitary figure laying a wreath of lilies under the card that bore Rosie's name, where the family flowers had been placed.

Nick walked over and introduced himself. "Hello. I'm Nick Robertson. Thank you for coming."

"My pleasure," said the old man, with a neat bow. He wore a dark coat and was tall, with iron-gray hair. He had a thick accent.

"I'm afraid I don't know who you are," Nick confessed.

The man bowed once more. "I am sorry. I should have introduced myself. I am Oleg Vassilievsky."

"Ah." Nick hesitated. "You must have known my grandmother."

"Not exactly. But I was aware of her. Your grandmother was from Russia. She was a Romanov."

"Ah, yes. Well, she thought she might have been, but we've discovered that it was very unlikely."

The old man shook his head. "She was a Romanov. Not a legitimate one, but a Romanov nevertheless."

Nick was incredulous. "How do you know?"

The man smiled kindly. "We know all the members of the family. We try to keep track of them."

"That sounds a bit sinister."

Oleg Vassilievsky shrugged. "It is not intended to be. We like to think of it as loyal support."

"I don't understand . . ." Nick looked over his shoulder at Alex and Victoria, who were deep in conversation with Sophie.

"We had rather lost track of Mrs. Robertson until our attention was drawn to her." He nodded at Alex.

Nick began to feel as though he were having a bad dream. "So who were her parents?"

"Her father was an English naval officer."

"We'd worked that out. But what about her mother? It wasn't really Grand Duchess Tatiana, was it?"

"No, it was not."

"Thank God for that."

"It was her sister, Grand Duchess Olga."

Nick looked for something on which to steady himself. He found nothing. After several seconds, he managed to speak. "How can you be sure?"

"We are sure," he said firmly.

"But . . . what does this mean?"

Oleg shook his head. "Very little now. Your grandmother is dead. We came to say good-bye. That is all."

He offered his hand. Nick shook it and asked, "Who is 'we'?"

"You will not have heard of us. We are a small group of people loyal to the Russian royal family. We do not think that they should be forgotten. Please accept our condolences. Good day to you." He turned and walked toward a black car, whose engine was already running, and got into the rear seat. The car moved off and disappeared from view.

"YOU'RE NOT saying much."

"Sorry?" He jumped, startled.

"You're very quiet," said Alex as they sat at the table in the Red Duster.

"No. Just thinking." He smiled, giving her his full attention.

"Well, it's been quite a day. I think she'd have been happy with her send-off."

"I hope so."

Casually she asked, "Who was that man you were talking to?"

"Just an old acquaintance of Rosie's," Nick said.

One day he would tell her about the man. And about Rosie. But not now. For now he just wanted to take Alex and Victoria home and try to start a new life. A normal life. A life as a husband, and as a father. There was nobody with whom he would rather spend the rest of his life.

His thoughts drifted off once more. To Rosie. "Good-bye, my love," he murmured. "And thanks for everything." And as he did so, all he could hear was the music from *Dr. Zhivago*.

The Many Interests of
Alan Titchmarsh

"I HAVE to garden and I have to write," says Alan Titchmarsh. "They are the two most fulfilling addictions I know." And these combined addictions have led the author of *Rosie* to a rewarding career as one of the most familiar figures in England.

Born and brought up on the edge of the moorlands in the northern part of the country, Titchmarsh started growing things at the age of ten in his parents' back garden. He was less successful at formal schooling. "I was your classic late developer," he says. "My brain seemed fuddled, filled with fog. My old French teacher stopped me a couple of years ago and said, 'We never thought you'd amount to much.'"

But Titchmarsh confounded his teacher's estimation of his abilities in every way. He trained

Vital Stats

BORN: Ilkley, North Yorkshire, England, May 2, 1949
RESIDENCE: Hampshire, England
TITLE OF HIS MEMOIR: *Trowel and Error* (2002)
FAVORITE BRITISH AUTHOR: P. G. Wodehouse
FAVORITE BRITISH MEAL: Steak and kidney pie
WEBSITE: www.alantitchmarsh.com

England's Best-Kept Secret?

That's what lead character Nick Robertson calls the Isle of Wight in *Rosie,* a sentiment no doubt shared by author Alan Titchmarsh, who

maintains a second home on the island. Yet it is only two hours from London and easily accessible, with up to 350 ferry crossings a day. What exactly is this secret place?

Nestled snugly near the center of southern Britain in the English Channel, the Isle of Wight measures 23 by 13 miles and is home to a mix of ancient churches and manor houses, leafy lanes and meadows, forests and beaches. And farmland. Thanks to its moderate climate, cereal and vegetable crops are grown extensively, including some of the finest garlic and sweet corn in Britain, and the island is self-sufficient in milk and vegetables.

As www.islandbreaks.co.uk, the island's official tourism website, proclaims: "Wherever you go on the Isle of Wight, you will see evidence of a fascinating past, going back to the time of the dinosaurs. Roman villas, medieval castles, historic houses, and exhibitions reflect life in a bygone age." If you decide to visit, you will be in good company. Some guests of the past have included Charles Darwin, who is thought to have begun planning *The Origin of Species* there, and Charles Dickens, who is said to have written *David Copperfield* during a stay on the island. Even Karl Marx dropped by for a visit.

And there have been famous residents of the place, those who came to stay or at least set up a second household. Alfred Lord Tennyson is believed to have written "The Charge of the Light Brigade" at his house on the island. Queen Victoria's beloved retreat, Osborne House, is now open to the public. And in his early years, actor David Niven brought a touch of Hollywood when he took up residence at Rose Cottage. If you need any more inducement to visit this illustrious island, a life-sized bronze

statue of legendary guitarist Jimi Hendrix has been installed close to the site of the pop festival where he gave one of his last performances in 1970.

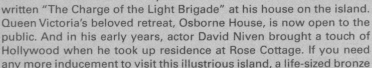

and worked at the Royal Botanic Gardens and eventually took an editorial job in the gardening department of a major publisher. This led Titchmarsh into broadcasting, and he has gone on to become one of the best-loved faces on British television, presenting various gardening shows on the air for over a decade.

Titchmarsh's broadcasting career has included stints as host of shows such as *The 20th Century Roadshow*—the BBC version of *Antiques Roadshow*—and *The Natural History of the British Isles.* "It's not just about the pretty things that flower or feed; it's about how the land was formed," Titchmarsh says. "I was a bit daunted at first. But to get such an opportunity to explore the British Isles has been wonderful." He is also the voice of a cartoon character known as Gordon the Garden Gnome.

In the meantime, Titchmarsh never abandoned his second addiction. He has written for newspapers and magazines and has dozens of gardening books to his credit, many of which were bestsellers. But somewhere along the line, another kind of writing came along. "By the mid-1990s I had written more than thirty gardening books, but there was a niggle at the back of my mind. Why couldn't I write stories? I wanted to exercise that part of the imagination which most grown-ups have to keep locked away. It is the supreme luxury—discovering characters, dreaming up a story."

His first novel, *Only Dad,* was published in 2001; *Rosie* is his fifth foray into fiction. "All authors are asked, 'Where do you get your ideas from?' " he says. "My reply is always the same: I have no idea. This may sound odd. Aren't you supposed to plan the sort of book you write? Maybe you are. . . . I have a basic idea for the plot, which I try to arrive at when I'm mowing the grass or weeding in borders. It's a rough structure. Rosamunde Pilcher describes it as a washing line on which ideas and events can be hung.

"When I finish one novel I have not the faintest idea what the next one will be. And success genuinely surprises me. Where fiction is concerned, I still have the feeling that I've been allowed to play with the grown-ups."

Titchmarsh's honors are as far-ranging as his interests, including the Royal Horticultural Society's Victoria Medal of Honour for outstanding services to horticulture. He has even been immortalized in Madame Tussaud's Wax Museum! ∎

ACKNOWLEDGMENTS

Page 173: Sigrid Estrada. Page 174: nyc-architecture.com. Page 294: Sears. Page 295: iStockphoto.com. Page 442: Bernard Vidal. Page 443: Photos.com. Page 573: Frank Noon. Page 574: Isle of Wight Tourism.

The original editions of the books in this volume are published and copyrighted as follows:

THE HARD WAY, published at $25.00 by Delacorte Press, an imprint of The Bantam Dell Publishing Group, a division of Random House, Inc.
© 2006 by Lee Child

WHERE MERCY FLOWS, published at $12.95 by Center Street, an imprint of Warner Books, Inc., a subsidiary of Hachette Book Group USA
© 2006 by Karen Harter

TWO LITTLE GIRLS IN BLUE, published at $25.95 by Simon & Schuster, Inc.
© 2006 by Mary Higgins Clark

ROSIE, published at $27.50 by Simon & Schuster UK, Ltd.
© 2004 by Alan Titchmarsh

The volumes in this series are issued every two to three months.
The typical volume contains four outstanding books in condensed form.
None of the selections in any volume has appeared in *Reader's Digest* itself.
Any reader may receive this service by writing
The Reader's Digest Association, Inc., Pleasantville, NY 10570
or by calling 1-800-481-1454.
In Canada write to:
The Reader's Digest Association (Canada) Ltd.,
1125 Stanley Street, Montreal, Quebec H3B 5H5
or call 1-800-465-0780.

Some of the titles in this volume are also available in a large-print format.
For information about Select Editions Large Type call 1-800-877-5293.

Visit us on the Web at:
www.rd.com (in the U.S.)
www.readersdigest.ca (in Canada)